GW00983146

SECOND SIGHT

SECOND TALE OF THE LIFESONG

by GREG HAMERTON

Second Sight
First published June 2010

Other titles by the same author

Paragliding
Beyond The Invisible
The Journey
The Fresh Air Site Guide

Fantasy
The Riddler's Gift
The Riddler's Gift Audiobook

Publishers
ETERNITY PRESS
info@eternitypress.com
www.eternitypress.com
London | Cape Town | Worldwide

Printed by Thomson Press

BIC: FM

ISBN 978-0-9585118-8-9

FIRST THINGS FIRST?

You can enjoy this book on its own, even though it is part of a series. Here's what they said about the First Tale of the Lifesong:

"Utterly compelling...with a blistering climax."
Terry Grimwood, Author: The Exaggerated Man

"I felt quite immersed in his creation."
Nerine Dorman: Cape Times, South Africa

"A highly recommended fantasy novel—enormous fun to read and extremely easy to lose yourself within." *FantasyBookReview (UK)*

"When you reach the end of The Riddler's Gift, you're left wanting more. Highly, highly recommended." *FantasyBookCritic (USA)*

ABOUT THE AUTHOR

Greg Hamerton is fascinated by magic and is a disciple of transforming paper into gold, one word at a time. Originally from Cape Town, he lives near London with his wife and a small stone dragon.

He is an adventure enthusiast, extreme-sports writer and film maker, but mostly enjoys soaring over mountains on his paraglider and writing imaginative fiction.

Second Sight is his second novel in the Lifesong cycle.

THE FIRST MOVEMENT

FROM EYRI

A song in heart, borne through the veins,
to live in simple silence;
the knowledge that the song remains,
to die in perfect peace.

1. A QUIVER IП THE STRIПGS

"How can you understand the language of music,
if you will not be an instrument?"—Zarost

*There was a time when the winds of change blew across Oldenworld,
scattering the dry leaves of autumn like manic heralds through the
avenues. The winds might have been recognised, had there been
anyone wise enough to interpret the subtle signs. Filaments shook
free from the cotton plants in western Orenland, only to be caught
again in the thorn trees further east, where they flapped like tattered
pennants in clusters of three. Fretful fires began in the forests of
Koraman, brief blazes that suffocated upon their own smoke as the
wild wind passed. High over Moral kingdom, threads of lightning
crossed a bruised and purple sky as whirlwinds stalked beneath the
clouds. The harbinger swept onward over the Winterblades, twisting
and tumbling through the grasslands until it reached the smooth
sands of the southern deserts and there, at last, found its peace.*

The people of the Three Kingdoms had been warned, but they had
become too learnéd to pay heed to omens. They feared no one in those
years. Order ruled their culture; order built upon the advancing lore of
magic. Into that time did the Destroyer choose to plant his seed.

Celebrations were held to mark the end of another plentiful summer.
In the town of Fairway, three days north-east from the capital city of
Kingsmeet, the bells pealed long and loud. A night had come that could
not be missed: the festival of Summerset Eve. It brought troupes of
entertainers from far and wide to Fairway's tiered Rank-hall. Actors,
jesters and musicians filled the pits. There was something for every
class of citizen, from cock-fights and cheap ale for the grovellers in
the basements to fine food and song for the trading families. In the
uppermost chambers, the high nobility attended an elegant exclusive
ball. The servants scuttled among these levels bearing all manner of
wines, delicacies, and other pleasures more discreetly offered.

Of these pleasures, none was as popular as the saccharine dust
called Joy. It was said that from the greatest refinement came the
sweetest sugar, and Joy was the taste of that elegance. The wizards had
originally devised it to bring happiness to those prone to melancholy,

but strangely enough it was most sought after by the nobility, who surely did not suffer at all. Yet, it was accepted that one should have some of the wizard's white powder to cap the celebrations at the stroke of midnight.

The Baroness Elam-Rye had enjoyed the ball. As the recently widowed wife of a minor baron, Katrine Elam-Rye had inherited a small estate, but also the first rung on the ladder of nobility, and she was determined to climb higher. She noted the men who turned their eyes toward her that night, even some whom were married, and she offered them thimbles of the sweet dust at the turn of the celebration. She consumed much herself.

And so the strictures of ceremony dissolved with the Joy in her veins.

Summerset Eve surrounded her with wild delight. The gilded ballroom swirled to become a dance of coloured lights and liquid passions, captivating in its intensity. The Baroness lost track of whom she danced with, and whether they promised to court her. The effect of the Joy dust should have begun to fade, but Katrine found herself falling further and further into abandonment. Perspiring beneath her long gown, she tore it off above the knees. She sang, almost in tune with the musicians. The dancing and drumming grew wilder and wilder. She found herself in the lower levels of the Rank-hall, lower than her class afforded her, and yet she was excited and entranced and bewildered by it all.

Wine that bubbled, fingers that dipped into cream, cherries that filled her mouth with juice as their ripe skins split upon her teeth— men, strong men, young men, laughing with her, kissing her, wanting her.

Faster and faster the world turned. The room grew dim. The sounds encircled her, like a chanting crowd then like rabid dogs, barking and snarling and closing on her as her knees ground into the floor. She rode the rhythms of her body's climax in a dark corner somewhere in the lowest level of the Rank-hall. She couldn't see, couldn't feel. She couldn't understand what was happening to her. But she knew enough to be scared.

Then an ancient face that filled the darkness with its fire rose before her. A sonorous voice spoke in a language of echoing tones, unintelligible yet filled with a hunger that rushed through her, carrying an awful heat, an awesome power. The shimmering silver patterns upon his deep eyes made her weak. His presence dominated her, even though she understood that He was not of this world; that He was separated by a gulf. She experienced only a sliver of what He could be. He watched her a moment longer then reached into His face to tear the left eye from its place. He thrust it toward Katrine, thrust it into her, and she cried out.

She was burning, burning, burning.

Katrine came to shaking uncontrollably, pressed to the floor on her knees in a curtained alcove beside a rough wooden stage. The effect of the Joy dust had worn off. Stealing a cowled actor's robe to cover her shamefully torn dress, Katrine ran from the vile basement.

But she could not run from the sin she had committed that Summerset Eve, and from the sin that had been committed upon her.

She threw up in the morning, into the waters of her bathing pool. She told herself it was because of bad cherries, but the heat of the nightmare still clung to her, and soon she could not bear to wear any clothes at all. After a month of terrible pains and sweating, Katrine called a great wizard to her chambers, and he confirmed what she dreaded. She was with child. At once she demanded of the wizard that he provide her with a foetal poison to end her pregnancy, and this he did, for a large fee, but after another month the foetus still clung to her womb like a terrible cancer. The wizard suggested using a needle of cold steel, but as soon as it entered her it burned the wizard's hand to the bone. The wizard staggered away, clutching at his ruined hand, while tearing the air with threads of light as he tried to heal himself. He did not approach Katrine Elam-Rye again, demanding that she tell him the full story of the night of conception. Afterward, he hurried away to consult his lore.

When he returned, he said he knew what was within her, and that there was nothing to worry about, but he spoke too loudly, and beads of sweat ran from his bald head. He told the baroness he would use his magic to kill what was in her womb. For a long time he turned the scattering pages of his collected notes, spoke slow words of power and covered himself with magical wards. Then, at last, he touched his hand to her swollen belly and called out a spell. He didn't finish the words. Suddenly rigid, the wizard dropped to the floor—dead.

Katrine Elam-Rye was terrified of the child she carried, but after the wizard, she could do nothing but count herself ever closer to the dreaded month of delivery. She cried at the injustice of her condition. Some of the men who had enjoyed her Summersend advances came to seek her out. One was even an Earl. She could not receive him.

Katrine hid in shame and nakedness, her body red and bloated. No one answered further visitors at all, because she dismissed the servants for fear they would speak of her condition. Among the nobility it would be whispered that the Baroness Elam-Rye had squandered her meagre wealth, and that she was likely to slip below even the humble class of her own parents, who had been *traders*.

The callers stopped coming. They did not wish to court a peasant.

No one guessed what was really happening to her.

It was high summer in Oldenworld, and the month of her great heaviness ended when her waters broke. She staggered to the forest, where there would be no witnesses. She took a butcher's knife with her, pretending she would use it to cut the umbilical cord, but in secret a darker thought turned over and over in her mind. She could kill the abomination that had brought her such shame, ending its terror forever.

But she fainted from the pain of trying to pass the enormous child. When she awoke there was a great amount of blood, too great to stop. A small fire burnt among the leaves, throwing smoke and heat against her face.

Something had latched onto her breast, something bulbous, deformed, devil-marked. She gave a small cry, and the thing upon her lifted its head. She looked into its eye, and screamed…

A single eye set in a pallid, crushed face. So close, the eye too focused, the dark iris marked with shimmering, spiralled silver patterns. The babe looked at her as if it knew what she had done to it, what she had tried to do.

There was too much blood, too much to stop.

She died looking into that single eye, the last of her life having soaked into the leaves beneath her.

Ametheus: deformed from the magical poison fed to him, scarred from the spell which had sought out his mind and divided it in three, abandoned by a mother who left only one offering of milk to him before her breasts went cold beneath his bloodless lips.

He would be persecuted; he would be blamed and cursed and feared all of his life.

Ay, he had reason to hate magic and all those who wielded it.

2. TROUBLED CLEFF

"In the middle of power is the little word owe;
the duty you have to use what you know." —Zarost

Magic was a treacherous craft, Tabitha Serannon decided, because it gave one a sense of power yet made one so terribly weak. She hadn't slept at all for two days, she was tired and hungry and her throat was sore. Yet her art demanded more of her. Because she could heal people, she had to. They came, in their hundreds, to her hall in Levin, to be touched by the Wizard. She could not escape from her duty. She could not escape from her magic.

Echoes of the Lifesong quivered through her veins. The more she worked with the song, the more she understood how it was drawn from the sounds of the world around her, and how the sounds themselves defined the shape and form of what was real. She was wrapped in a melody; the kingdom of Eyri was a melody.

Dawn over Eyri had been spectacular and the sky had been filled with that subtle music she heard ever more within her soul, the call of the many voices combining to form the day. When the mist had burnt away from the great central Amberlake, the softer, whiter sounds among the chorus had been lost, the song becoming clearer. The warm hum of the Amberlake grew richer and deeper as the waters became visible. That sound was divided by the high tone of the long and narrow black causeway stretching away from Levin to the distant glittering settlement of Stormhaven upon the King's Isle. Tabitha's gaze was drawn to the glistening white peak of Fynn's Tooth, which stood sentinel on the western horizon, its ice and bare rock jingling in her ears. Below the Tooth grew a rumpled skirt of forests, and below that, the distant green hills of Meadowmoor County rang with their verdant health.

So much music blended she could hardly discern the melodies. The sun playing against her hands was the coloured symphony of full daylight, the air against her face, the soft dampness of the dew on the grass, the arching blue sky... All cast a music toward her. All resonated to form a harmonious and ever-changing theme. So many things touched her with their sound, and she was connected to them all. She realised then how little she used to see, before she had become a wizard. Eyri was more beautiful than she had ever known. It pulsed with the golden sounds of living creatures, of people, of dancing lights and silent shadows, and the ever-shifting patterns of the elements. All that was real, was song.

Yet now, as the afternoon drew on, *her* song was failing. Although the music sustained her spirit, she sensed the other theme below it— the deep fatigue gnawing at her bones.

She sank to the floor then gazed about her domain. The hall was full—fuller than full. Wherever a blanket could be laid upon the straw there were two. She had asked them to bring bunches of flowers to sweeten the air, but nothing could hide the ripe smell of blood and sweat. The petals had been trampled and scattered upon the floor. The same could be said for many of the injured men.

They had seen her sit, so they expected her to perform again. Those who could rise began to converge on her, stumbling between the makeshift beds. Some dragged their blankets with them, some were clothed, and some crawled closer through the dirty straw.

The world closed in upon her, a gathering crush of needy humanity; the men who had been caught in the horror of the battle upon the Kingsbridge. Only the circle of her wardens kept Tabitha from being overrun. She had to ignore the many pleas for healing, because she had already chosen her sufferer when she had sat beside him. She could serve no more than one at a time.

His lips were parched and cracked, his face pale. A bloody crust stained his chest where an arrowhead protruded through his breastplate. A second shaft had been broken close to the fabric of his trousers, where the wound wept angry colours into the threads. The true danger lay deeper, though, an infection near his heart. Tabitha could see the approach of death in his eyes.

"Help me. Heal me," the man pleaded.

She bowed her head, but gripped the man's hand, to let him know she would try. To heal him, she had to deny someone else a chance at healing. That was difficult to bear, but there was no other way—she was too tired to heal them all. Some of them would have to die.

The wounded man pulled weakly on her hand. "Please," he said.

Tabitha raised her lyre. She had sung her first stanza of the Lifesong so many times that it came to her without any effort. It had once been an inspiration, to release such wonderful power, but with every iteration, the Lifesong became more of a burden, a responsibility.

When she plucked the first note from the lyre, the crowd thickened even more. Some of the patients had missed her preparations, and they wailed and ran to get as close to the source of her magic as possible, to be near the Wizard, who could save them from their misery.

Hands reached out to touch her. Fingers brushed against her hair. Someone touched her lyre briefly. A child tugged at her dress. It was as if they believed she was a charm that needed to be rubbed for the magical effect to be passed on. Tabitha hunched over to avoid the crowd's pressing need. She reached inward, to that place of solitude, wherein the Lifesong rang clear and true.

Heads pushed in past the wardens' defensive circle. Soon the crowd would crush the man she was trying to heal. It always happened, no matter how many times she tried to explain the truth to them: only the place that she held in mind would be touched by the magic of the Lifesong. The people believed her mere presence brought healing, and if they could touch Tabitha or one she had healed, they would draw some of that healing power onto themselves.

Too many hands touched her. Hands crept all over her body. People pressed too close.

Tabitha didn't scream, or move, or fight against the crowd. She had learnt it was futile, for if she shouted, her words touched more of them, and so more were drawn. There was only one answer to their need.

She sat quite still, and waited.

A sighing, mournful whisper spread through the crowd. Those closest to her knew what to do. They knew the spell had been stopped; the Wizard was not singing. They tried to push back against the press of the crowd, but it was fifty deep, and most of the people were still trying to move inward, to get as close to the Wizard as possible, to be touched by her healing aura as she worked her magic. Tabitha waited for the jostling and shoving and whispered arguments to spread. At last the people fell back, but only slightly, just enough for her wardens to re-establish their circle. At least the people weren't touching the lyre any more.

She began again. Her ring warmed, and her eyesight sharpened. Clear essence danced through the air all around her. Despite her use of it, there always seemed to be more clear essence, as if it was intrinsic to everything. The clear essence shimmered as she sang. Swirls of rainbow colours hinted at where her voice touched.

She considered the wounded man. The two arrows had brought

infection along the length of their shafts. They would complicate the healing.

"Bastion!" she called out, keeping the melody of the Lifesong thrumming through her lyre. "Bastion! I need the arrows removed, both of them."

The tallest of her wardens came to her side. His loden cloak hung almost to the floor, the cowl hiding his face completely. He would not emerge from that cowl in public. The crowds had to believe he was a warden, one of many healed men who strived to repay the wizard through devoted service.

Bastion squatted down. He set the stump of his left wrist against the dying man's chest, and gripped the arrow shaft in his right.

"Ready?" he asked.

Tabitha gathered the clear essence, and nodded. As Bastion tore the shaft from the man's chest, she guided her essence into the fresh wound. Thankfully, the arrow had a slender, armour-piercing head, not the broad-heads some of the men had taken, which opened them terribly. A bloom of blood spilled across his breastplate nonetheless, and the man gaped with the pain. He croaked as Bastion pulled the second arrow free.

Tabitha had to be quick. She had learnt it was crucial to be focused with the first stanza. One stray thought and the clear essence would turn into whatever she fantasised about. She had to imagine all the flesh that would be replacing the injury; she had to envisage all the organs in their perfect state. There were so many delicate complexities in the human body.

As she visualised the healing, she sang with all her heart.

Five small birds arrived, as many had of late, to frolic in the air above her head. They added to the Lifesong with their short trills and warbles, as if they were part of the performance. Tabitha welcomed their joyous calls, but did not let them distract her from the task.

There were splinters in both wounds. She envisaged flesh sealing the splinters, harder flesh, to protect the rest from damage. She saw the dark poisoned areas within the man, and saw them as healed. She visualised the man as whole and complete in the place where he had been wounded. The power of the Lifesong flooded through her. She touched the place of silent thunder, where a hundred voices joined in song, beyond the clamour of the crowd. She became a channel for the return of life to a place that was dead.

Then the song was done.

An awed murmur passed through the crowd. The small birds swirled one last time over Tabitha then flitted through the hall's open doors. The man on the floor sank back against her knees and breathed a shuddering sigh. His blue eyes were clear of pain. She stroked his forehead.

"Thank you, your Holiness," he said. "Thank you."

Holiness? She shook her head. *I've been called Seraph, Saviour, Glory and Enchantress, but never yet Holiness.*

"Rest a while," she answered. "You need to recover, so eat at our kitchens tonight—eat well. By the morning you should be strong enough to leave, but I urge you to stay and help, if you can. I need strong wardens and I would be honoured to have you helping."

The man grinned and nodded.

A slim youth reached through one of the warden's legs, and laid his hand on the healed man's foot, before he was pulled away. The needy palms turned to Tabitha again. Poor folk of Levin, scared folk of Stormhaven, wounded Swords, people of all age and condition. They pressed close; the pleas for favour soon became a clamour, then a roar.

"My head, my head, touch my head, wizard," urged a man close to the front of the press. He had dirty bandage wrapped under his chin and over the crown of his head. She recognised him. He came regularly, in various guises, just to be touched.

"Sing to me, sing to me," cried a woman as she pushed the bandaged man aside. "I am dying from the sickness, wizard. Look!" she cried, and shamelessly lifted her shift to reveal her scabrous skin and swollen breasts. "Heal me."

The woman would not die. Tabitha had to conserve her strength for the serious ailments. She tried to turn away from the pleading masses, but they were all around her.

"Touch me!"

"Heal me!"

"Save me!"

"Make me beautiful."

"Riches! Wizard, I offer you gold! Make me young again!"

Tabitha covered her ears with her hands.

"Bastion, get me out of here!"

He dropped to one knee before her and turned so that she could mount his shoulders. He took her weight, and rose. She was lifted above the sea of heads and palms.

"Make way!" he commanded. "Make way! Wardens, an escort!"

The wardens fought through the press of humanity. The people didn't part easily. Hands reached up to touch Tabitha's legs, her boots and her robe. She clutched onto her lyre, so it would not be pulled from her. The crowd followed them, like a school of hungry fish feeding on a lump of raw meat.

They took too much, always too much.

She could sing no more.

ᏨᏍᎣᏟᏍᎣ

Tabitha collapsed onto the bed.

The door was closed, bolted and barred against the flood of followers outside. Their room was cool and almost quiet. Bastion sat beside her and just held her for a time. She hoped it wasn't his desire to touch the magic of the wizard that made him do it. Then she recognised her own callousness born of fatigue and she returned Bastion's embrace. He was strong and he smelled of healing oils and wool.

She must not forget who he was.

It was better that the crowds did not know the truth about him. Garyll Glavenor had wanted to leave Levin altogether, because some regarded him a traitor. His word had led them into the false battlefront. His command had opened the gates to the Shadowcasters. Such critics ignored that it was his blade that had slain the Darkmaster and without him there might have been no survivors at all. Still, he had made a deal that troubled Tabitha. How could he have traded the defence of Stormhaven just to keep her safe?

He was no longer respected, as he had once been. He had set the title of Swordmaster aside. He stayed in Levin because she needed him, to keep her safe among so many people.

"Will they ever leave me be?" she asked.

"If you stop performing for them, perhaps."

Tabitha reached for Garyll's cowl. He stayed her hands, an automatic reaction, but then he accepted her gentle touch. Tabitha looked into his eyes—so dark, so deep, those complex currents which hid the hurt.

"How can I stop, when they are in such need?"

"Aye, I understand that you cannot stop. But rest, regain your strength. You wither before my eyes."

"People are dying while I sleep, Garyll. People are suffering and crying."

"You cannot change all the world, my love. You have done more than anyone to bring life to Eyri. Rest now. You really need to sleep." Garyll kissed her gently on the forehead then rose and went to the hearth.

Tabitha smiled. Her skin tingled where he had kissed her. There was a warm place in her heart, and the warmth softened her body's brittleness. Garyll had his own kind of magic, though he was not aware of it. She wished he had kissed her lips.

He began to lay a fire. It was not really cold, but Tabitha understood his habit. It would be a companion, to hold back the night. He didn't like it being completely dark, anymore. Garyll struck a spark off his flint and blew on the kindling.

Their cottage was small, by Levin standards, but it was perfect. Tabitha hadn't intended to stay for long, but the healing work demanded that she be near the hall. It was still difficult to accept the way the occupants of the cottage had so suddenly offered her the place to stay, for as long as she wished, for free. Her fame had strange consequences, honours and noble preferences that rested uncomfortably on her shoulders. But, sometimes, such privileges could be useful. They had the cottage to themselves.

"That'll catch ablaze in a moment," said Garyll, straightening from his task. "I'll leave you, then, your Grace."

"Garyll! Please don't call me that again. It might serve Bastion in the hall, but I'm Tabitha when we're here together, not Grace or Eminence or anything like that."

"You are too humble of your abilities."

"What I do should not come between us."

"How can it not? You gift life! I have only ever captured, punished, or killed. Sometimes I feel very small, beside you." He made for the door to the next room.

Small? Tabitha thought. Garyll Glavenor was a towering icon of justice in Eyri. Or so he had been. The Darkmaster had taken much from him.

"Garyll, wait," she said. "Don't go."

He paused. "It would be best for you to get some rest now," he said gruffly.

"Stay with me tonight."

He turned slowly, but shook his head. "And repeat that night in Stormhaven?" He didn't need to explain. The heartache she had caused by trying to seduce him was still fresh in her memory.

"Will you ever forgive me?" she asked.

"You? It was never you who needed forgiveness."

"Garyll, I—"

But he was gone, in a swirl of his green cloak. Silence, as he stood waiting, or thinking. Then the bed creaked in the room next door, and his boots thumped to the floor, one after the other.

I forgive you, damn it! Tabitha thought, but she had told him that before, and telling him had changed nothing. The only way for Garyll to find peace was for him to forgive himself. The more she came to know his discipline, the more unlikely that seemed. She wished he wasn't so severe with himself.

But then he wouldn't be Garyll. He set his standards so high, that he was made taller just by reaching for them. Any other man would have given up trying to be Garyll Glavenor long ago. She wanted to be close to him so badly, but there was a chasm between them—a divide scribed in darkness.

She considered demanding he return and lie beside her; compelling him. Then she knuckled her eyes. She was too tired to think straight. It was a stupid idea—she didn't want to use her power to manipulate. That was how the trouble had begun in the first place, in his quarters in the Swordhouse in Stormhaven.

Tabitha's thoughts turned over and over; despite her exhaustion, she couldn't sleep. She stared at the flames as they rose higher through the wood Garyll had left in the hearth. There had to be a way to heal the man she loved.

A small sound came from the kitchen. Tabitha couldn't see past the reed screen. The glow of the fire was suddenly too dull. Her hearing sharpened as her need activated the Ring and brought a rush of clarity.

Breathing. There was somebody in the kitchen, someone who shouldn't be there.

Something skittered on the kitchen floor, and the intruder cursed under his breath. Tabitha backed to the fireplace. Her hands found the fire-iron.

Garyll came through his door in a blur. There was a surprised yelp from the kitchen, scuffling then angry whispers. Tabitha tiptoed to the edge of the screen.

Garyll held a waif by the back of his collar. "Please, Bastion-sir," he croaked, "I just wanted a see the wizard, I not be stealing anything, please mister-warden-sir." The boy's face was pale in the moonlight and he shivered with fright.

"Garyll, it's alright," Tabitha assured him. "I—"

"No," he hissed. "Treat with this urchin now, and tomorrow there'll be another fifty trying to get in this window if he tells of his success. I'll not have it! He's not even injured. Out you go, rubbish!" Garyll lips were firmly set.

"You're not Bastion, you're the Swordmaster!" crowed the boy.

In his haste, Garyll had forgotten to raise his cowl. It was dark in the kitchen, but evidently not dark enough to hide his characteristic square jaw and sleek black hair from the urchin's sharp eyes, and she had named him Garyll.

"Out!"

"No, Master Glavenor, no, I must see the wizard, I must, I'm dying, I'm sick, very very sick." The urchin coughed, and clutched at his chest. "All I want is a healing, a touch from the wizard."

Suddenly there was another figure in the window, and a third person muttered urgently from outside.

"No, out!" commanded Garyll, and head-butted the urchin hard, releasing him to stagger back toward the window. The muscles in Glavenor's neck were corded; his jaw caught the light from the lamps like a hard fist.

"Garyll!" Tabitha called out in fright.

A mug fell from the intruder's pocket and shattered upon the tiles.

"Stealing as well?" Garyll gripped the boy again.

The boy began to cry. "It's a thing what the wizard used, it's a blessed thing, it's a holy thing—anything what is near the wizard is." He squirmed in Garyll's grip, trying to reach the nearest piece of the broken mug, but Garyll jerked him upright and lifted him clear of the floor.

"You'll take nothing with you—you're hoping to sell it, this talisman. Begone! The wizard deserves peace!" He thrust the boy roughly through the open window, flailing legs and all.

"And don't you come back, or I'll break your bones, all of you!" he shouted into the night after the sound of hastening footsteps. He closed the shutters and bolted them before closing the windows again. "There's always a hole the wardens can't close," he muttered as he crossed the kitchen to where Tabitha still hid. "You alright?"

"He was just a boy, Garyll. Just a boy."

He didn't meet Tabitha's eyes. "He was making bad choices."

Garyll left. There was a long moment before his bed creaked in his room.

ⵏⵙⵟⵞⵙⵟ

Later, when the fire had burnt so low the coals only peeped from their covering of ash like rubies in old snow, Tabitha reached for her lyre. Garyll slept at last. She could hear the steady rhythm of his breathing in the next room. She drew her nightgown close, and tiptoed through the silent cottage.

He was stretched upon his bed, still fully clothed except for his boots.

Oh Garyll, the battle is over, she thought. *We have won.* His foe was still with him.

His brow was furrowed. His cheeks were still hollow, though he had regained some of the weight that the tortures at Ravenscroft had stolen from him. His scarred eyelids flickered as his eyes danced in the clutch of a vivid dream.

Suddenly he arched his back then reached out his hand as if to grasp something in the air. "No!" he cried out. "You said their lives would be spared!" He curled inward upon the bed. "What girl?" he cried. "Cabal! She must not come here!"

Tabitha recognised the nightmare. In the depth of his tortures, so he had told her, he had made a pact with the Darkmaster, to save Tabitha from harm. But the Darkmaster had compelled him thereafter, to return to Stormhaven and betray the city's defence. He saw it as the moment when he had become a traitor.

"So dark, so cold," Garyll murmured. He gripped the fabric at his throat. She knew he held an imaginary Darkstone in his clenched fist. She had released his orb, but in his dreams he remembered what it had been. For a terrible time, he had been a Shadowcaster, bonded to Cabal's will.

"Forgive yourself, Garyll, the darkness within you has gone," she whispered.

Garyll kicked out at the air and writhed on his blankets. A new scene was playing its torture across his mind, another betrayal from which he would find no release. "I shall hold the Gate!" he cried. "I shall hold it. I shall hold it." Garyll rocked from side to side.

Tabitha brushed the lyre with her fingertips, just a tracing of music, like a breath of air through a willow tree. Garyll's fists slowly unclenched. Tabitha had to resist the urge to reach out and touch him where he lay. If he awoke she would lose her chance, for he would not accept healing from her when he knew how fatigued she was. Her legs shook they were so weak.

She hummed the familiar melody of the Lifesong but didn't sing, for there was little wrong with Garyll's body. She had healed the battle injuries long ago, and he would not allow her to work on his severed hand. She needed something else besides her first stanza. The second was too deadly to even consider. She closed her eyes. There was more to the Lifesong than the words. By opening herself to the power as she hummed, she could reach an awareness beyond language. She followed the delicate currents of sound with her mind to their source. Somewhere, beyond the seen world, was the Goddess Ethea—that presence she had touched before, that potent soul who sang with many voices, who filled her with inspiration. Tabitha suspected that if she could reach out to the Goddess, she might receive an answer to her need, if she was sincere. Maybe she could learn a song that would bring strength to Garyll's wounded spirit. She sharpened her senses to hear beyond the lyre's accompaniment. She spread her feeling as she moved along the thread of the Lifesong, upward, tracing the vein of power back to the heart, through faint patterns and symbols, through music, through vastness...

Quite suddenly she was wrenched away, pulled downward by an overwhelming force. A wailing cry grew in her ears as she spiralled down and down. Tabitha was scared, but she held onto her purpose, because she could feel the Goddess drawing close. She tried to reason her fear away. She told herself the sensations of falling and danger came from her unfamiliarity with the dimension she was in, but her heart beat faster and faster. There *was* something pulling at her, something awful that had interfered, something that gripped her and the delicate threads of the Lifesong with steel talons. She fell down and down, into a mounting pressure. The wailing cry grew intense. Blaring horns crashed against her. The Goddess was there, in the midst of the chaos. In an instant she saw a great feathered form, iridescent wings splayed wide against a grey stone wall, a high-cheeked beautiful face raised towards her, lips parted in that cry. Tabitha was flattened by a wave of anguish. Ethea, trapped in that place of heaviness and heat.

Tabitha called out. The vision exploded in a bright flash that stung her eyes.

The room lay before her; dark, silent, real. She felt numb.

Garyll turned toward her sound in his sleep.

She covered her mouth with her hands.

What she had seen could not be true. She sank onto the floor.

Sweet Goddess! Who had enough power to hold her, who would wield power in that way?

Tabitha felt weak, helpless and violated. Tears spilled down her cheeks. The vision played over and over in her mind. Something terrible had happened. The sound of Ethea's lament...it was so wrong, it rebelled against Tabitha's senses. That voice should have been singing the Lifesong, it should have been triumphant, liberating, free. Instead, Ethea was trapped.

Tabitha sat on the floor, in the dark corner of Garyll's room. She sat there for a long time.

She wanted to be close to Garyll, she needed him, but she couldn't offer what he needed in return. She could not lift Garyll's spirit by singing, any more than she could lift her own.

"I grow weak, my love," Tabitha whispered. She feared what might happen in the morning, when her duty to her people compelled her to call upon the Lifesong again.

Garyll's chest rose and fell. He did not wake.

3. THREE OF A KIND

"Chance gives you one fool, a bad deal yields two,
but three and the Chaos is coming for you."—Zarost

Twardy Zarost was in the Gyre Sanctuary, down in the cool gloomy library. He had recently completed his Restitution and so returned to a renewed body, and yet he was not at all relieved. Trouble hung in the air like a lingering scent of wildfire.

He stared at the ragged stubs of what had been a precious ancient text. By the curséd toad, whole pages had been torn out! The Book of Is had been violated in its most sacred section, near the beginning, where the accounts of The Witness laid out the primeval pantheon in all its fascination and ferocity. Zarost knew it held detailed invocations and even an instruction on the ancient language, but he remembered little of it, for the knowledge had never served his purposes.

The Gods wouldn't listen to *his* kind.

But there had been rare folk who *had* transcended their humanity in the past, and that worried him. It was possible. Who wanted to speak to the Gods now, and which God had they chosen? Some Gods were best left undisturbed. To have stolen the pages right out of the Book meant the thief had been very hurried and had wanted to work in secret. This suggested the thief would be calling upon one of those best-left-undisturbed Gods, not the kind who caused fair winds and sunny skies. Trouble was afoot. A company of phantom soldiers began to march in his head, with a *stomp stomp stomp* that echoed in his thoughts; a new fate marching him toward his doom.

Zarost set the Book carefully on a reading stand, and waved over the slender spritebulb. The light was a relic of the old Moral kingdom, the metal upright crossed with a fine copper weave that glinted as the essence began to glow within the glass sphere. Overhead, two spiders scuttled hurriedly away into the surrounding gloom of the low-roofed basement—spiders, despite the wardings around the Gyre's Sanctuary. They got in everywhere, the little devils, even here, in the middle of the great southern desert of Oldenworld.

The Book of Is didn't lie flat, and when he turned to the appendix, Zarost found more page stubs. The formulae were gone, the complicated mathematical works explaining the forces and dimensions governing the Gods, and the theorems proving the growing separation of the Present from the Eternal. Zarost had never truly understood them. They had been penned by a genius beyond his reach, and he'd allowed the formulae to slip from his memory to make space for more important lores, such as causing barking dogs to fall silent, or keeping your hat on your head.

Zarost bent until his bristled chin scratched the paper. He sniffed— nothing, not even the delicate sting of magic that could have been used to cover a trace. Whoever had ripped the knowledge from the Book had left no clues. The very fact that the pages were gone was a clue in itself. Either there was a thief within the Gyre's eight, or someone not of the Gyre had visited the Sanctuary. Either possibility made his scalp crawl. The Gyre had gone to great lengths to keep the Sanctuary hidden from the Sorcerer Ametheus, for it would spell disaster with a great exploding 'D' if *he* located their refuge. If a stranger had entered the building, its location was no longer secret. That was no good at all.

Alternatively, another one of the octad had turned against the flow of the Gyre. But who?

Something fluttered near the stairs. Zarost looked quickly over his shoulder, but it was just the wind tumbling a loose page. No, there couldn't be a traitor within the Gyre he didn't know about. To steal knowledge from a library every Wizard had access to made less sense than nonsense. Besides, they had risked their lives together; they had proved their alliance too many times over for too many centuries to fail now.

Ametheus's last spell had almost broken them. They had dispersed the wild chaos of the Writhe near the border of Eyri. Most of his colleagues were still healing their wounds by remaining comatose in the nurturing vagueness of Infinity. They had faced down their first eighth-level spell, and Zarost knew that if the Sorcerer's power grew any further, their lives would all be forfeit. There had never been a worse time for a division in the Gyre. They needed to be united, to able to lift the One high enough to end the Sorcerer for good. No, there couldn't be a traitor hidden among the other seven.

But the Book of Is was torn.

Knowledge had been stolen from within the Gyre's sacred Loreward—arcane knowledge only a wizard could have sought out. Zarost felt along the damaged binding, a jagged signature that spelled out 'Chaos' clearer than a stroke of wildfire. Uncertainty gnawed at his stomach. It had to be an outsider who had stolen the lore, but he didn't know of any wizards still alive beyond the octad, except for Tabitha Serannon. She was the most unlikely candidate for a thief among all of them—he would suspect the Gods themselves before Tabitha. She hadn't even emerged yet—she was still in Eyri, and there she would have to stay until he introduced the trigger event.

He retrieved the single loose page lying beside the stairs. The margin was torn, ruining a carefully rendered diagram of an altar used for the invocation of Zorzese, detailed down to the placing of the runestones, the preparation of the sweet nectars and the precise position that the elements needed to be in.

Zorzese wasn't the one he was worried about—a gentle west wind would pose no threat—but if someone beat upon fiery Baalbashãn's door, or that of warring Rgnøtheris, there was a chance, however small, that they would be answered with celestial wrath. Someone as mad as Ametheus might even attempt to reach the upper hierarchy, to attempt a dialogue with the Destroyer himself, and that would spell disaster.

As soon as he framed that thought, a chill ran up his spine. Ametheus would do such a thing, oh yes indeed! The omens of Chaos were upon this event, they stood out like goblins among gold.

Whoever had stolen the lore for the Sorcerer wanted to prevent the Gyre members from using the same lore. The Book had once been a popular religious text in the days before Order, before the Three Kingdoms had united. Zarost knew of a place where a copy might have been preserved. He folded the loose page neatly in half and thrust it into a pocket—it would be useful to match against a copy to verify its authenticity.

He needed that missing lore! To understand the reason for the theft and to know what they faced, they would need to study it, and if Zarost remembered correctly, the Book of Is had contained rituals to end a dialogue with the Gods, a way to restore the Veil of Uncertainty that protected fragile human minds from the immensity and intensity of the Gods. The Gyre might have great need of such a ritual, to sever any dialogue that had been set up and restore the natural rift between the dimensions.

The Destroyer had a fire-dappled skin, and a terrible stare that struck all who saw Him speechless. Zarost remembered that much from his reading of the Book. Zarost calmed the sprites in their bulb, and lifted the tome from the reading stand. Should he announce his findings to the other wizards when they recovered? Who should he tell, until he was certain the Gyre numbered eight, and not seven and one traitor?

No, he should keep his discovery a secret, and begin his investigation alone, because he had his own special plans for the Gyre—ones which relied on the element of surprise. He couldn't afford to be surprised himself. Not with so much at stake.

He slipped the damaged Book of Is carefully back into its place. It had fallen from the shelf when he had entered the library, probably a result of the thief's hasty exit. But had it been a wizard from within, or one from without—a hole in the circle, or a circled hole? Solving such riddles had earned him his seat in the Gyre. Zarost was determined to find the truth.

Ametheus was more than enough on his own. They did not need a wrathful God to fight as well.

಄ಬಿ಄

Prince Bevn stared at the hated door. They said the Serannon girl stayed there now, the singer, with one of her wardens. Bevn sneered. He knew what that really meant, he wasn't a child anymore. She took that warden to her bed. She probably took a different one every night, whichever of her wardens she chose.

He wanted to get close to the window. Maybe he could sneak a look through the curtains, and catch them at it.

"Come away," hissed the woman behind him. "That place is too well guarded. See the men in the alley beside it? Don't be a fool. We must move! Come away."

Bevn wouldn't listen to the woman, because she was a woman, so he waited for her to brush angrily past him and continue along the street. But she was right—they had a greater purpose. He spat at the distant door then followed Gabrielle. They passed through Levin, keeping to the shadows.

Black Saladon had promised them great things. A skilled wizard, much more powerful than anyone Eyri had ever seen! Black Saladon had said he was only a *servant* of the great Chaos-wielder. The excitement of that night returned to Bevn.

They had been in Ravenscroft. He and a few Shadowcasters had fled there after the disastrous end to the battle in Stormhaven. There they were, stuck in the tunnels below the Keep. Bevn felt like one of those stupid flies that always came over to see what their friends were doing in the sticky pot, among the gum and syrup. Eventually his father would send the Swords into the vale to clean out the last survivors, and he would be found, but he'd learnt that people did silly things when they were scared. He'd stolen the crown, and he didn't know where else to hide. He couldn't identify himself to anyone, so he had become a Nobody. And Nobodies, he had discovered, ended up hungry and cold. At least there was food and shelter in Ravenscroft. It was the farthest away from Stormhaven that he could go, so he stayed there, with the others. He hated it, because it was such a stupid place to hide.

He'd often saved those flies in the sticky-pot then pulled one of their wings off, to watch them fly in tight circles. Would his father would punish him? His father was a soft-hearted fool. He never struck Bevn for anything. He would forgive him after a few days of pretending to be angry, if Bevn said he was sorry. Bevn could say he'd been made mad by the Darkmaster, and he hadn't known what he was doing. Maybe he should return to the palace before he was caught. *That* would be smarter than being a fly.

Smarter, but still pointless. He knew what kind of life he'd return to: a cosseted life, where he was treated like a showpiece, a young thing not old enough to matter. He was thirteen, for pity's sake, he was practically a man! Yet he wasn't allowed to be one. He'd never been in a fight at home. Even the butcher's boys whom he always taunted hadn't faced him down because they knew his father would have their necks if they laid a hand on him. He had all that protection, but he had no importance of his own, it was always "Yes Master Bevn, but I'll have to see what your father the King says", and "Have you asked your father the king if he thinks it's wise?" He had royal blood in his veins, but he was not allowed to wield that power. Nothing changed, no matter how many years passed. Of course not! His father didn't want him to have power. He wanted to keep all the power for himself. That was why Bevn had taken the crown, in that moment of confusion when the Morgloth had dived upon Stormhaven, and he was going to keep it.

So he stayed in Ravenscroft.

He was playing with the Darkstones, arranging them over the headboard of the late Darkmaster's bed, when a Shadowcaster sneaked up on him unnoticed. The Shadowcaster gripped his ears from behind and pulled him away.

"You leave the stones alone, or I'll tear these little flaps off your head, piglet." The woman's voice was deep and self-assured.

"I'll call the Swords!" he squeaked at once. It was his standard threat. It left his lips before he could consider his words. The blood was rushing to his face, pounding in his ears.

"If that were likely, you wouldn't be hiding here. You have no power to call upon," the Shadowcaster said, her tone full of mocking laughter. "Promise to leave the stones alone." His ears were burning with pain as she twisted his ears harder and harder. Shameful tears were getting ready to betray him.

The bitch. He *did* have power. He would show her.

But he didn't.

"Promise?"

He nodded, but suddenly he felt her hot breath on his ear, and her teeth as she nipped him. Then she let him go and he spun around to face her. There was an exciting twinge in his groin.

"Hey! What was that for?"

She didn't answer him, only raised one eyebrow and smiled. "You're younger than I thought. What are you doing here?"

He didn't answer her at once—he recognised her, he had seen her around Ravenscroft. Her name was Gabrielle. He'd heard the whispers between the Shadowcasters during the time he'd been held 'captive'—men who wanted her, women who wanted to be like her. He'd never spoken to someone who had actually been *with* her, except maybe the Darkmaster, but he'd had all of the women. Gabrielle was reputed to be the best seductress in the Croft, and seeing her now, up close, he had little doubt that the rumours were true. The light from the smoking cresset danced over her strong face, the full lips, the deep dark eyes, and the glistening hair cascading over her shoulders. The furs she wore didn't hide the swell of her body and her tight waist; the cut of the clothes emphasised those curves. He was so confused. A growing need thumped through his loins, but she had twisted his ears and mocked him.

"I-I was looking for a way to get my rock off," he stammered, pretending to pull at his chain.

Her lip twitched. "Why are you in Ravenscroft? You belong with your daddy."

"I can go wherever I want to!"

"You were just the master's pet when he was alive. You are not a Shadowcaster. Go home, copper top."

She had a way of looking at him that was both condescending and enticing, as if she wanted him to challenge her, as if she was looking for a fight.

"I don't want to be a *Shadowcaster*. You're just cheats and criminals. Without your master, you're nothing. None of you are important! But I'm going to be King!"

Her expression darkened. "Keep flapping your lips and you're not going to live long enough."

"I can say what I want. You can't stop me! Tart!"

Gabrielle swung an open hand at his head. She was quick, but he'd been expecting it. Bevn ducked, and kicked for her groin. The Darkmaster had taught him a bit about fighting, and he'd said you always should start a fight with a groin kick—that way your opponent would taste the first fear, because he knew you'd fight dirty. Gabrielle didn't have the same equipment down there as a man did, but she folded over nicely nonetheless.

He had won the fight! "Don't get too big for your boots, pussy," he added. It was something the Darkmaster had loved to say—he'd always laughed and Bevn had too, though he'd never really caught the joke.

Gabrielle slowly raised her head. There was no sign of pain on her face, no hint of defeat, but she did remind him of a cat—a mean and angry cat. He really, really shouldn't have kicked her. He began to back away.

"My father will send the Swords in! They'll clean you out!"

Gabrielle stalked towards him, her eyes never leaving him, her hands loose and low.

"This place isn't going to last a week!" he blurted out. "Then you'll need *my* mercy."

She had backed him into a corner. He was suddenly very scared of what she might do. He panicked, and he tried to dive aside as she drew close, but she hooked his chin and threw him back against the wall. If he hadn't been wearing his knapsack his head would have struck the rock hard. He dived the other way, but she blocked him with her leg and placed her foot on the wall, trapping him with her body. She reached quickly into the darkness then struck with gathered fingers into his shoulders, and his arms became numb and useless.

Dark essence! She must have used Dark essence on him! He'd thought it was all used up, he'd bet on it. If she had use of motes, even a few, she could do terrible things to him.

Gabrielle paused, watching his face impassively; then she slowly raised her right hand and slapped him across his ear, hard. Pain jammed his mind. Bevn almost wet himself. It wasn't anything close to pleasure, like they said it could be. It was horrible. He lost his balance, but Gabrielle's leg stopped him from falling.

Her open hand waited, high above him.

"What am I?" she asked. A flicker of a smile curled her parted lips. She was enjoying this! Be damned, he wouldn't let her win. She was just a commoner! She was just a woman.

"A tart!"

Wham.

Pain. Worse than the first time, it ran all through him. He was sure something had broken in his head. What if he couldn't think any more, what if she turned him into an idiot? He couldn't see straight enough to read her expression, but she was waiting for him.

"What am I?" she whispered, her breath warm against his cheek once more. She had a scent like brandy pudding, sweet and heady.

Bevn wouldn't answer. She wouldn't make him cry. She wouldn't. Hot tears stung his cheek.

"I can do this all day, little boy, until you wish you hadn't been born." She smacked his wet cheek with the back of her hand, over and over, and it stung like fire.

"I'm sorry, I'm sorry, I didn't mean it!" he heard himself say. "You're not a tart, you're a lady, a lady, you're a lady!"

Gabrielle gripped him by his hair and looked into his eyes.

"So, you do have a brain beneath this mop."

He nodded. Just don't hit me again. Please don't hit me again.

"You're wrong about the Swords," she said. "You'd be surprised how much we can hide from prying eyes. The Swords will think they've been through every tunnel, and not have explored half of Ravenscroft."

She cocked her head. She shouldn't be able to look so pretty when she was being so ugly to him. He wanted to touch her face.

"You didn't come all this way to play with stones. What are you doing here?"

He couldn't get his feet under his body—she was holding him by his hair in an awkward position.

"Hiding," he answered. He didn't want to tell her about the crown. She might want to steal it from him, or worse.

"What have you done? You're hiding from your father, aren't

you?"

"Can you let me go now? Please?"

"Will you answer my questions without trying to be clever?"

"Yes. Yes! Anything you ask. Just let me go."

"You have less spunk than I thought. Very well." She let him slip to the floor. "Just remember, it'll be far worse if you don't behave now." She gestured over him, and a shadow seemed to leave his shoulders and return to her hands.

Then Bevn caught a movement behind her, at the entrance to the chamber where the arched walls tapered to frame the heavy door, although it wasn't quite a movement, rather a *change*. Something took form in the gloom, it took form *from* the gloom, and as it became, he felt the arrival of its presence pressing on his heart.

Gabrielle turned, she'd felt it too.

A man with wide shoulders and a mantle bore a great hook-bladed battleaxe, taller than his head. Bevn couldn't make out anymore, for the guttering torch on the bedpost didn't cast enough light.

The newcomer stamped the shaft of his axe down, and the floor heaved. The rats in the corners of the room squeaked and ran. The rocks began to glow with red light, and the air was filled with sudden warmth. Everything was plain to see.

He was a seriously *heavy* man. Bronze fabric glinted on his chest. His skin was dark. He had a single plait of hair that fell backward like a tail from the crown of his shaven head. Two smaller plaits framed his unsmiling lips. He watched them from smouldering eyes.

Bevn was immediately impressed with him. He looked strong, he looked fearsome. Bevn didn't think he was a Shadowcaster. He'd never seen them doing that trick with the light in the rocks. Even the Darkmaster hadn't been able to keep the caverns of Ravenscroft warm. Heat and light was something the Lightgifters wielded, but Bevn was certain the newcomer wasn't a Lightgifter either. He was something else.

"Do you understand what you've done?" the man asked. The voice made him jump, and it drove into his head.

"I-I… yes," Bevn answered, without any idea of what the stranger meant. He wanted to appear certain of himself before the mighty newcomer.

"Who are you to be here in the secrecy of Ravenscroft?" Gabrielle challenged.

"This is called Ravenscroft? What a smelly smoky dung-hole! You don't have to *live* in darkness to be able to use darkness. You live with rats!" The newcomer flicked his hand so that his index finger cracked like a whip. The sudden chorus of high squeaks ended in awful silence.

"And what do you know about darkness, stranger?" Gabrielle demanded.

"A great many things more than you, if that simple essence in your hand is all you have learnt to use. Did you capture the boy?"

"No! I came here myself!" Bevn insisted before Gabrielle could answer. *And I'm not a boy!* he thought, but he wasn't going to push the newcomer that far. He'd just learnt that picking a fight could be risky, and the newcomer was a whole lot scarier than the Shadowcaster. "I go wherever I want to!" he added. "The King is my father."

"Yet you have his crown, and that marks you as a royal scoundrel," the newcomer said.

Gabrielle whirled to face Bevn. "Is that why you're here? You've stolen the crown?" She looked into his eyes. "You have!"

So the truth was out, without him wanting it to be. The man with the battleaxe had known, somehow. Bevn moved away from Gabrielle, skipping sideways with his precious knapsack to the wall, but the newcomer pressed his finger and thumb together, and Bevn was suddenly rooted to the spot.

"Who are you?" Bevn cried.

"You can call me Black Saladon. Stop running away. We have much to discuss."

"What are you?" asked Gabrielle.

"A man, as you are a woman. I was a wizard once, but I am learning to transcend that limitation."

"A wizard, as they have named the Serannon girl?" Gabrielle asked scornfully. "Do you know her?"

"I know of her. She is a newling. She will not last a month! She comes too late. She will be crushed, just as they all shall be. We have our own special plan for the singer. No, I am a wizard as they have named those who studied in the great College in Kingsmeet, those defenders of Oldenworld who mastered the three axes of magic, those learnéd fools who founded Eyri."

Bevn remembered the legend of the founding of Eyri from his endless history tutorials. Those wizards had been very strong, yet Black Saladon had called them fools.

"You are from *beyond* Eyri?" Gabrielle asked.

"Most of the *world* is beyond Eyri, Miss Leather-and-Whips," Saladon answered.

"My name is Gabrielle. Gabrielle Aramonde."

The wizard strode closer. He halted near Gabrielle, and looked her over slowly. "You should venture from these caverns more often."

"But there is nothing else than Eyri! Where is there a road that leads out of this kingdom?"

"Woman, you were born in confinement! Again we see the flaw of learning only from knowledge—if the knowledge is kept from you, you can be so easily controlled. You'll have to do better than believing only what you're told if you want to escape. You have not found the way that leads out of this kingdom because you believe you need a road to follow. Maybe you still do. The weakest point is a gap north by north-west, known as the Penitent's Pass. For the one who bears the Kingsrim shall the way be open." He had a funny way of phrasing things, thought Bevn, an *old* way. His penetrating gaze was resting on Bevn.

"How did you know about the crown?" Bevn asked. It was still hidden in his knapsack.

"I can sense it, princeling, even though it is by nature difficult to trace. The warping in the shield of Eyri points to this place, to this room, to you."

"But if you're from beyond Eyri, then how do you know what goes on here? How do you know about the crown?"

"I helped to forge it."

Bevn knew the crown had been passed down from generation to generation within his family. It was impossible, but Black Saladon wasn't joking. He wasn't that kind of man, not at all. How old *was* he? What was he capable of? He was still watching Bevn, his tall fighting-stave motionless in his left hand. The hooked and hollowed blade was grim. Shivers! Saladon didn't even need the blade, he could probably split Bevn down the middle just by clapping his hands or gesturing. Suddenly Bevn knew: he had come for the crown!

Bevn still couldn't move; the wizard's spell bound his feet. *I really am the fly in the sticky-pot,* he thought. "Are you going to take it from me?" he asked in a small voice. He'd so wished to keep it, to find some way to use it. It had special powers, he knew.

Black Saladon laughed then, but it wasn't the kind of laughter that made Bevn feel welcome to join in. "No, princeling, I hope I have not misjudged you that badly. You have done well to take the crown.

You have already served to disrupt the order, maybe without meaning to. You might yet keep the crown. I have an offer for you, an offer of power, on behalf of my…superior. First I must ask what you wish to do with the Kingsrim?"

A hard knot of excitement formed in Bevn's belly. An offer of power? Nothing could be better in all the world than power. Once you had power, you could get anything you wanted, anything at all.

"I want the throne of Eyri," he answered. "I want to be king."

Gabrielle snorted, but Saladon didn't, and that was what mattered to Bevn. He looked into the wizard's eyes wherein the red light of the room was reflected, and he saw a new future in them, a future where he dared to deal with wizards, where he became mighty, fearless, and feared. The vision rushed into him, like a hallucination, as if he'd just bitten into a jurrum leaf and swallowed its delicious poison. All the colours and feelings of his grand premonition filled his head.

Black Saladon was speaking. "Then you have a great journey ahead of you, you cannot be king from where you stand. Turmodin in Oldenworld, that's where you should be, there you'll get the guidance you need. The great Sorcerer will find you and your crown very interesting. He rewards service. I can vouch for it."

"But how am I to find Ter-Termalin? I've never been out…there."

"Turmodin," Black Saladon corrected. "Think of it as a trial. Are you man enough to face a trial? You'll have to be, if you really want power. You are ready? Good. Listen closely. After you've left Eyri, you will travel through Oldenworld, through the woven six-sided land of the Lûk, to Koom, at its heart, then north to the terraced border fortress of Slipper, down to Gredy and then farther north on the remains of the great slipway to the old glass-blown city of Wrynn at the coast, where the ships can sail west around the worst of the Lowlands to reach Rundirrian Run. From there you can walk to Turmodin. Don't say where you're going to in the end, even when you've taken passage on the ships, or you'll lose your head on some vengeful blade. You'll be looked at strangely enough for whom you are, and for wanting to go north. The same goes for speaking about the Sorcerer—you might discover that his name is Ametheus. Do not use that name anywhere in Oldenworld, especially if you stand before the legend himself. Do not speak his name out loud."

Bevn had never heard of Oldenworld, or Slipper, or the land of the Lûk. But most of all, he'd never heard of the Sorcerer Ametheus. What did a sorcerer do that made him more than a wizard? Would the rewards that Black Saladon promised include learning magic? Bevn guessed it might. He wet his lips.

"How powerful is Ametheus?"

Black Saladon cuffed him on the ear, without moving a muscle, he just *looked* the strike at Bevn.

"Did you not hear me? Do not speak his name. Now you know of it, keep it secret. Hah! You want to know how powerful he is? He is the wrecker of Oldenworld, the rage against Order, the inventor of the silvered wildfire, the innovator, the arch-mage, the answer. He is the reason that Eyri has a Shield. He is the greatest wielder of magic, and its most feared enemy. He is contradiction, change. He is Chaos. Even the Gyre of Wizards can not meet the level of his spells anymore. He is the future. If we don't side with the Sorcerer, we shall die, it has become that simple."

The conviction in Black Saladon's voice made Bevn's skin crawl. Maybe it wasn't a good idea to seek out the Sorcerer. Maybe they would find more trouble than they could manage, outside.

"What if we just stay in Eyri? He hasn't been able to reach in here, has he?"

Saladon laughed, that same private laugh. "Wait until you witness his power. Wait until you are outside your little playpen. It is time for you to grow up! Eyri has been safe only because the Sorcerer has been distracted from it all these years. Now he is aware of it. He will demonstrate his—contempt—to the Gyre, by changing it in a particular way. Everyone who stands in the way of that change will wish they hadn't." He looked meaningfully towards Bevn.

"I don't get it!" Gabrielle objected. "If the Sorcerer is so powerful, why does he need this little snot to work for him? I could take the crown to Turmodin. I would have a much better chance of surviving. All this boy knows is pretty clothes and simpering servants. He knows nothing of survival, or stealth. I am a Shadowcaster. Let me take the crown to Turmodin and claim the reward!"

Bevn's face grew hot. "It's mine," he said. Gabrielle laughed.

"Aah. There is something you do not understand, Miss Gabrielle Aramonde. You cannot use your simple power beyond the borders of Eyri, or you will die. There is a network that reacts to any kind of magic. Remember that. You will be eliminated if you use Dark essence, because that marks you as a threat in the Sorcerer's eyes. And the prince is right—the crown is his. Only someone of royal blood can bear the crown without going mad, for that is the way it was forged. It is the mainstay upon which Order is fastened in this realm. It is the mainstay upon which Chaos can feed."

"I cannot *believe* you would leave such an important task in *his* hands."

"That is why I shall not," replied Saladon. "You look like a— capable—woman. You shall escort the prince to Turmodin."

Anger crimped the corner of her eyes, but Gabrielle's voice was warm. "What do I get in return?"

"What do you want?"

There was a long moment as Gabrielle and the mighty mage considered each other.

"The journey sounds perilous, and the task of great significance. I want a fair price: my weight in gold." She licked her lips. She must have guessed she was pushing her luck, but she had asked nonetheless.

"Gold? Gold! Ah, you shall have it, Miss Gabrielle. That is too easy for words, even I can pay you *that*. You really do still *think* on the first axis of magic, but that is good, you shall attract less attention in Oldenworld. I need you to keep the prince close to you. See that he survives, see that he keeps going. In Turmodin you shall get your reward, and more."

"And you, Saladon?" Gabrielle asked, in a gentle way Bevn thought odd. "Where will you go? Can you not join us?"

The wizard looked distracted. He ran his hand up the shaft of his battleaxe and gripped it near the head. "I shall attempt to, from time to time, but I travel in a different way to you. You must protect the Kingsrim—although it will help you, for it resists the touch of magic in many ways. I cannot get a grip upon it with any spell. That is why you must use your own feet. I shall meet you once you're beyond Eyri. For now, I must be brief. There are eyes that look for me and the farther I am from you both, the better. Prince Bevn, do you wish to please the Sorcerer and earn the power to rule?"

Black Saladon held his eye, and Bevn felt suddenly important. When the wizard winked, he felt as if they shared a secret, something only between them, the men: the power to rule. The Sorcerer would show him magic, real magic, not the dark trickery of the Shadowcasters, but things such as Saladon knew—how to appear out of nowhere, to fill the room with power, to own a demanding presence. You didn't argue with someone like Black Saladon. He commanded respect. That was the kind of king he wanted to be.

"Yes!" Bevn cried.

"Then go! Don't piddle about! I shall wait for you in Koom. I shall see you there as well, Miss Gabrielle Aramonde."

Black Saladon vanished, and the warmth and light left the room.

"The bastard! What makes him think I will do as he says?" Gabrielle said.

They wasted no time leaving Ravenscroft, however. There was no doubt that their visitor had been serious.

As they sneaked through the night-time calm of Levin, the excitement of their quest still squirreled in Bevn's belly. They were going to leave Eyri altogether! He would keep the crown! He was going to learn real power!

The wizard Saladon had seemed so very powerful, and he'd just been the messenger. Bevn couldn't wait to meet the Sorcerer. Black Saladon had called him Ametheus—a secret name, a feared name, not to be spoken aloud.

"Ametheus," he whispered in the dark. "Ametheus, Ametheus, Ametheus!"

০৪৪৪০৫৪৪০

The world was pale; the daylight was dreary despite the fullness of the sun. Ravens circled languidly over the burial site. No Morrigán those, they were hungry birds with sharp beaks.

Kirjath Arkell was dead.

His body had been thrown in a pit among the Darkswords. His slack corpse tumbled down; his wasted limbs broke upon the heap. He watched from above, feeling nothing.

They tossed his head down afterwards.

No ceremony for him. No kind words.

He had expected none.

A man who raised the Morgloth and set them upon the people would never be remembered kindly.

Kirjath didn't care what they thought. The three gravediggers stood on the lip of the deep grave, carelessly close to the edge. The drudgers didn't even seem to understand that he was there at all.

He looked down at himself. He was a glistening disturbance, like a robe of dirty spider webs, nothing more. His limbs were so flimsy they would surely pass right through living flesh. His impotence made him so angry he could kill.

The gravediggers were surveying their handiwork. "To the earth, keep the bastards down!" commanded the eldest gravedigger, a wiry cretin wearing a dirty orange neckerchief. He could be a failed fishmonger. He could be the father of a Fendwarren whore. Yet he thought to lord over Kirjath's corpse.

The men fetched their shovels, and began to strike them into the great mound of fresh soil bordering the grave. The younger men bent their backs to the task, shovelling over their shoulders, not wanting to look to where their loads fell, but the veteran carried his shovel to the brink, and watched the soil fall as he cast it from the very edge.

Schrink! the soil left his blade, dropped away.

Fdoff! it fell upon the dead, splattering grit into their open mouths and staring eyes.

The veteran laughed down at the corpses. "You shouldn't have dabbled in the dark!"

"Come on, Dirk!" complained the youngest digger, a slack-lipped lout with nervous eyes. "Don't mess with the spirits! We must be done by nightfall!"

"Spirits be damned, boy! The only thing'll rise from these rotters is their stench!"

Kirjath clenched his fist; it formed a barely visible lump in the air. It would not be solid enough to hurt the gravedigger Dirk, not in the way he deserved to be hurt. The old gravedigger went to the heap again, struck a load with his shovel, and returned to the brink of the grave, his chalky lips stretched in a sardonic grin.

"This one's for you, demon-rider!" He turned slightly to address the others. "You heard about the demon-rider, eh? He was a bad piece of work. Good bloody riddance, I says!"

Kirjath swooped down on the gravedigger from behind. The man turned casually back to the pit, heaved his shovel.

Schrink! The soil arced away.

Kirjath slammed into the back of Dirk's head, arm outstretched. He lost his left hand.

Fdoff. The soil cascaded over the abandoned bodies below.

The veteran spun. "Who was that?" he demanded.

"What?" asked the youngest digger.

"You be careful where you swing your load," the veteran warned. "One of you clipped me then."

"Can't be, Dirk. We're throwing the other way."

"Well, I felt the wind of it over here, I'm telling you!"

"Hey, what's that above you?" asked the young digger.

Dirk searched the air, but he was looking toward the sun, and couldn't see. Kirjath tried to fade by spreading himself outward and it seemed to work.

"Where?"

The younger digger looked uncertain. "Nothing. Thought I saw something, is all."

"Don't mess around, boys! Don't screw with me." Dirk the gravedigger glared at the other two until they resumed their work. Dirk's heels were barely a foot from the crumbling edge. Kirjath pulled himself together upon his malice, and his glistening form returned. Below, Dirk bent to shift his grip lower on the shaft of his shovel. Kirjath came at him, fast. He tried to scream as he swooped, but he could make no sound.

The veteran straightened, and as he did so he looked up. His eyes widened. He raised his shovel to defend his face and took one, doomed step backward. Kirjath swept at him with all the force of his rage.

"B-bullshit!" the man cried, stumbling and fending awkwardly with the shovel, but the flailing strike carried his weight further over the edge. The ground gave way. Kirjath advanced, careful to avoid the living man's flesh this time. The veteran cried out desperately as he wheeled his arms to regain his balance, but he'd already lost it, and Kirjath was too close, right there, in his face.

"Dirk! Dirk!" the youngest digger shouted as he ran, but the veteran had already toppled into the pit. Kirjath smiled as the man fell away, turned slowly and landed hard on his head among the corpses. His shovel followed him, and smacked into the back of his skull with a resounding clang.

The old gravedigger lay still. Kirjath sank down and spread out beside him, amid the soiled corpses.

"Dirk! Shit! Dirk!" The youngster stared down into the crowded grave.

The second gravedigger clipped him on the back of the head for the curse. "Get up, you wagwit!" he called down. "Stop messing with us. That's enough, Dirk!"

Kirjath could see the awkward angle of Dirk's spine. The back of his neck was folded over. The scornful expression drained from the second digger's face.

"D-did he jump?" the youngster asked. "Did you see why he fell in?"

"He's not going to get up. He's dead, oh sweet Ethea, he's dead, man!"

"Why'd he fall in?" The youngster's voice was shrill. "What happened? Barrok! What just happened?"

Kirjath rose, and this time they saw him rippling toward them, his ghostly lips drawn back in a snarl, his fury written in his eyes. He wished he could tear them apart, let them feel his spirit invading them, infecting them, ruining them. It was maddening to see them so alive and vital, when he was so...wasted.

The youth cried out, fleeing from the lip of the grave. The other gravedigger fell on his butt. He scrabbled at the ground as Kirjath rose overhead then he found his feet and fled.

Kirjath chased them. He knew that once the wedge of fear had found a crack, one should keep driving it in but there was little he could do. The gravediggers ran from what had risen from the dead. Maybe they could be encouraged to find misfortune on the windy rocky trail—a stumble at the wrong moment to run headlong into a spiked branch, a swerve to avoid him at a steep corner. The nearest gravedigger threw a glance over his shoulder and saw Kirjath right behind him. He ran fast enough to overtake his comrade, but then the younger man ran even harder.

Kirjath chased, but he allowed a gap to grow between them. It would cost him too much if he touched them by accident. He'd lost his left hand when he'd hit the veteran. His arm was still missing, up to the elbow.

Essence, I'm made of essence, a few shades greyer than clear, a cloud of spirit held together by—what? Maybe I only exist until my essence has dispersed. Maybe that was how one finally ceased to be. Every time his essence was brushed aside by the denseness of living flesh, his spirit-body was damaged. Maybe his awareness would fade as well, until he truly did not exist at all. His body had died with a sudden dagger in his back, but his spirit would die a slow whimpering death, dissolving bit by bit until he was a part of everyone else, until his essence simply dispersed upon the wind.

He would be gone, in the end.

He refused to accept that. No! He was dead, but he was not ended.

He would keep a grasp on life as long as possible, even if it was only a half-life. He allowed the gravediggers to flee into the choked ravine ahead. They were not worth the risk. He would conserve his energy. By the blood of a needle-scoured babe! He would find a way to live again. He needed time to think it over.

He was somewhere near Slurryrig, he guessed, in the Broken Lands of Rockroute County. That was where they always buried peasants, paupers and criminals. Kirjath floated downhill, leaving the trail to travel westward, towards the Amberlake, Levin and the distant King's Isle. Moving took no effort at all. He could glide as fast as he could keep up with his mind.

Behind him in the ravine, the crows would feast in the uncovered grave. The veteran would rot among the others, sharing the worms and liquids of decomposition. The crows would eat his eyes, as they would eat Kirjath's own. He didn't care. He didn't need that body any more.

He needed another one. He needed someone who was alive, alive but tired. What if they were asleep? Yes. They said that when you slept, your spirit drifted away from your body, attached only by the thinnest of cords. If he came upon someone who was asleep, he might snip that cord and steal into the body himself.

It needed more thought, for sure. That host would need to be weakened or troubled, so that their spirits wouldn't put up much of a fight. Who bore the greatest burden? He wouldn't take the first tormented fool he encountered. He should choose carefully. He wanted to be…someone of influence.

He looked forward to nightfall. He was going to go hunting.

4. GODDESS

"How do you choose between two lives,
when you can only save one?"—Zarost

This man is going to die, thought Tabitha.

He was a small man, with an unkempt scattering of beard upon his chin. He had the delicate hands of a clerk; he shouldn't have been a soldier. He had been run through with a sword during the taking of the Kingsbridge, and he had staggered away from the battle. He had been found many days later beside a stream on the way to Kironkiln. His open wound was an angry blight of infected flesh, his belly bloated. His eyes flickered. Tabitha didn't know what kept him going. Maybe it was the desperate strength of his wife, who stood beside the raised stretcher and clasped onto those delicate hands while crying.

Tabitha stood with her lyre in hand, but she couldn't begin her song. She turned her face away, to hide what she was feeling. Today, at least, she had space. She could not risk being down among the crowds anymore, so she had asked the wardens to create a separate area at the front of the Hall, where patients would be brought on stretchers, one by one. Those who simply wished to see her could do so, but from a distance.

The result was grander than Tabitha had intended. A great high-backed chair commanded a stage. Bowls of floating petals bordered the stairs. Flowers had been woven around two tall cressets. Red blossoms had been scattered upon the stage. Golden drapes formed wings, and a beautiful painting had been hung on the back wall, a great canvas depicting Tabitha singing, her arms spread wide. She couldn't refuse it—the poor artist had pawned his boots and his silverware to buy the cloth and paints, and the artist had done good work, but Tabitha couldn't help feeling self-conscious about it. In the painting, she was huge, and surrounded only by light, which wasn't really the truth of how it had been that day in Stormhaven. Hundreds of Morgloth crossed the sky beneath boiling clouds, and an endless dark army marched towards her. Behind her, in the shelter of her light, people rejoiced. The King was among them, standing proud and tall, but due to the perspective he seemed shorter than Tabitha.

Garyll Glavenor was nowhere to be seen in the painting.

Despite her misgivings about the grandness of it all, the new arrangement seemed to work. The wardens could control the crowd to the edge of the stage, and the people seemed pacified by Tabitha's regal status—she was higher than them, and therefore untouchable, and so some order was imposed upon the chaos.

There were more people in the hall than ever. Tabitha had expected the numbers of the sick and ailing to diminish with time, but the multitude was swelling as the news of her work spread. The crowd extended into the marketplace, she knew, interfering with the trading, as well as congesting the traffic there.

Tabitha closed her eyes. They weren't going to stop coming, they'd keep on and on until she couldn't sing another note, until her voice failed and her lyre broke. She was a phenomenon. She was the Wizard of Eyri, and they waited now, with hushed voices, for the first miracle of the day.

She feared what might happen when she began her song. She couldn't forget what she had seen when she'd last reached toward Ethea for inspiration.

A hand touched her arm. It was the soldier's wife. "Please, your Holiness. Please. He's dying."

She could not deny him the chance to live. She had to try.

She wished she wasn't a wizard, but she had picked up the ring, and chosen to keep it.

The only way to hide the shaking of her hands was to play the lyre.

The music began the shift. Her ring warmed on her finger, the world became suddenly noisy then whispered and distant as she gathered her senses and focused her attention deeper within the dying man. Her wizard's attention allowed her to see the inner flesh around the wounds, the troubled areas within the body; the course of the disease.

She drew a sharp breath. Every cell in his body was tainted by the poisonous infection. Every organ was soaked in the acids of decay. He was ruined.

"Don't let him die! Don't let him die!" whispered the wife.

"The Wizard will heal him!" one of the nearby wardens promised. "Just you watch."

"She's changing him already," a second warden reassured. "Look! His lips are growing redder."

Tabitha had done nothing; she hadn't yet begun to sing.

She threw a glance to Garyll where he stood at the end of the stretcher, but his face was hidden in his cowl. The crowd grew restless behind her. She had never failed them. Yet to heal the soldier, she would have to draw deeply on her power, deeper than ever before. She needed to visualise every detail of his ravaged body in its healed form, perfected, created anew. She needed the Goddess to work through her.

Her hands played on and the rhythm of the Lifesong took her.

She sang. Clear essence came to her, a shimmering cloud of clarity. Her mind spiralled upward, beyond the vaulted roof of the hall, following the thread of music back to the source: further, deeper, into realms of pure music, back to living sound, back to the Goddess Ethea. She opened her soul, and reached out for the power to bring life into the world.

She touched vastness; currents of vaporous symbols passed her, releasing faint themes and trailing patterns. Soft voices sang in many layers of harmony. Then, suddenly, a silvery light spiralled beneath her. The voices became discordant, their harmony ruptured, their melody disturbing. She tried to veer away, but something pulled her down, down, as if a hidden beast grasped at her ankles. The air was becoming bright, opaque, changing and growing warm. A warped sound grew in her ears, like a single voice stretched out in time, calling.

It came again, louder, and the pressure mounted around Tabitha. "Hhhe...llp."

Then the call was all around her. "Help. Help."

The air cleared. Blaring horns crashed against her. Heat pressed upon her skin. Tabitha lost her sense of balance. The world tipped. A grey stone slab was beneath her, designs scored in its surface. A heavy sky the colour of blood hung overhead, cluttered with wheeling birds: pigeons, doves, swallows, larks and finches—every size and colour—winging about in a spiralled current. Many fires burned around her, on the top of tall stakes, throwing thick smoke through the swirling birds. Before her stood a great and beautiful creature, almost a woman in form, many times taller, her body covered with shimmering feathers, her iridescent wings splayed up to where her hands were shackled to the hard rock. Her face was turned to the sky, to the birds.

Tabitha was stunned. It was Ethea, as she had been portrayed in the myths, as Tabitha knew she should be. Chained! Surely the Goddess couldn't be trapped? She wasn't of the Earth, she existed in the worlds beyond! But Tabitha had seen this before, and knew it was true.

"Help," Ethea called out, softly, as if she guessed no one could really hear her.

The air felt almost solid. It smelled of salt and smoke.

Where is this place? Could *she* escape?

The trumpets were upsetting; they seemed to be blown deliberately out of time. Large metal cymbals clashed, all discordant. She looked up to the top of the high bluff, and saw the people who were making the noise. Strange men clutched great tapered tubes in their arms, others rippled sheets of metal between them. More figures squatted casually on the rim as if waiting for something interesting to happen.

No one reacted to her presence. She looked down at herself. Nothing. She wasn't really there at all, and yet her attention was bound to that place. She could not be anywhere else.

"Goddess, can I—can I *talk* to you?" Tabitha tried. "Can you hear me?"

Ethea turned her face from the sky: a beautiful face, with high cheeks and a noble nose. Her skin was wet with tears. Her eyes, so full of anguish, narrowed as she focused on Tabitha far below.

"A singer?" Her voice was so musical it danced in Tabitha's ears like crystal chimes, despite the clamour created by the noisemakers above.

"I am Tabitha, I have learnt some of your song," Tabitha answered. "Goddess! What has happened to you?"

"You have come, you will come, you came?"

Tabitha didn't know how to answer the question. "Goddess, where are we?"

Ethea tilted her head to one side. "The angry brothers would know. So much is wrong. It is here, it is not everywhere. *Ay-oh-la-ray-oh.*" Her answer ended in a snatch of mournful song.

"Are we in Eyri?" Tabitha asked.

"I do not know the names you call your places. We are here, where the angry brothers are, in the noise. Beyond the hill I saw—buildings growing upon buildings, into the air. *Ay-oh-la-rah.* You came?"

Tabitha turned around, but she couldn't see what Ethea saw from her higher vantage. The ground sloped upward, carved from a dirty green rock in shallow curved steps. Randomly spaced channels came down toward Tabitha, as if great claws had raked through the rock.

The circling birds swooped low over the steps, some landing briefly before taking fright and beating into the churning air again, turning and turning in frantic circles.

It's like a whirlpool, with the Goddess at the centre.

"When are you here?" Ethea asked from behind her.

Tabitha turned. Again, Ethea's question made no sense. "When? Now. Oh, Goddess, what do you mean?"

"Time is—strange—here. Time is not complete, as it should be. Time has sides, or a direction, a before, and after. *Why-oh-ai-oh-ai.* Time should be a loop, it should be renewed. How can *this* be?" She slipped to one side as if she had lost her balance, but the shackles held her wrists tight. The pain was evident on her face.

"Ethea! Can I help? What can I do?"

Ethea watched her sadly for a moment then shook her head. "Help is strange to think upon. I have never needed aid. Aid is what I offer, as a Goddess. I can sense that you are somewhere else than I am. I do not know how to reach to you from where I find myself. Different— places—make no sense. I am trapped in this—body. *Ah-nahno-nay-me.* They turned me into this flesh, the three of them together. I must escape this form that binds my voice to this pool. Who shall sing through the stars? *Oh-way-na-no.* This should not be."

"What if I came to you, what if I found you, wherever you are. Could I do anything to help?"

Ethea cocked her head again, as if she was thinking. A flurry of birds passed across her face, each bird racing to lead the others. The horns blared louder suddenly, and the crashing sound of rippling metal became intense. "Perhaps I need your song, upon this skin," Ethea shouted. "Perhaps." She stiffened against her shackles. "Oh! *Oh-way-oh-woe!* They have caught another one!"

The avalanche of discords pressed against her so strongly, that for a moment Tabitha couldn't turn. She felt trapped, by sound. "What is it?" Tabitha cried. "What do you see?"

"Another innocent. Look! Oh look!"

Tabitha managed to turn, at last. A bare-chested man clothed only in patterned orange trousers and a pale red helmet was pulling a struggling dove from a net. His helmet had two large eyeholes and a slit for his nose. His tanned body was slick with sweat.

"What is he doing?" Tabitha asked. "Why has he caught the bird?"

"Oh my songbirds, my little ones! They carry my voice, in their own way, they sing, they sing! Oh don't die here, songbird, don't die, not here, not here!"

The bare-chested man pinned the struggling dove to the step with one splayed hand. With the other hand, he reached for his belt. The dove kicked and flapped frantically.

"They want me to call to one of the others!" Ethea cried. "To grant him life here, but I cannot, he does not belong here, he belongs where I belong. He belongs beyond the stars! We should exist through all time, everywhere. I cannot do what they demand. I cannot. No, no, no."

The man held the dove in one of the downward-sloping channels, which Tabitha noticed was stained in many places with something like oil. A dark puddle had built up on the edge of the inscribed grey slab upon which they stood at the bottom of the amphitheatre. A horrible realisation swept through her. The bird was to be a sacrifice.

"No!" she cried out. "No!"

The man didn't hear her . She had no power in this strange place of smoke and pressure. The clash and clamour rose to a crescendo, the man punched a wicked spike down.

Ethea screamed. It was a terrible, forlorn sound, as if the beautiful crystal chimes in her voice had been shattered. The world exploded around Tabitha. She felt as if she had been stabbed in her heart.

The pressure was gone. The heat faded. There was silence, or near silence. Only the sound of crying continued, on and on, a quiet sobbing. Tabitha was still and numb. She didn't know where she was for a moment.

She looked down to where her hand lay upon someone's chest.

The soldier...the soldier in her healing hall in Levin. He had died.

Her knees buckled. She fell forward and slipped to the floor.

5. THIEVES IN THE NIGHT

"When you are paid by a thief,
it is always with someone else's money."—Zarost

The sun passed behind the clouds on the western horizon and for a moment the light became pearly. The spire of Fynn's Tooth glistened like a crystal, the forests grew still and the peaks seemed to stand higher, black ridges forming the rim of a crown held up to the sky. The breeze was soft upon the grasses, a mere whisper through the trees. A hare tested the air with its nose and watched without comprehension as three pieces of wool drifted by to be caught in the lower branches of a silken tree. The breeze searched deeper into the forest, where a few shy deer turned in surprise yet saw nothing. Three leaves dropped from a strangle-oak, twisting lazily as they fell. Then the air began to purple as the day cooled and the night came softly upon Eyri. One by one, the stars glittered into place, defining the astronomer's map of the ages. The constellation of The Angel waited; The Hunter chased The Serpent in an eternal dance. An owl hooted in anticipation; once, twice, then once more, and in the village of Llury, the prince followed the Shadowcaster.

Bevn looked for Gabrielle and noticed her ducking out of an open doorway farther up the street. She tucked something into her shoulder bag. She looked his way then beckoned sharply to him before stalking away without waiting to see if he would follow.

Bevn knew she was right—they should leave Llury before they were noticed, but he would not be ordered around by her, no matter how she could sway her hips when she walked.

One day I'll have enough gold to buy *you.*

Gold was her weakness; he had watched her as she had almost begged for it from Black Saladon. His father had uncountable riches and he would inherit it all when he was made king, and she would come to him, begging to serve him. When he'd reached Ametheus, he'd get powers. He would make her do all kinds of things. She would have to undress before him, yes, and she wouldn't be able to refuse, because she'd want the gold. Bevn grinned, raised his hood, and followed her before she was lost to the darkness.

Bevn slowed as he passed the light of the last inn. There'd be food in there, and warmth, and…something else, a choice, a possibility that nagged at him, but it was too vague and shadowy, too unformed to matter. Nonetheless, he felt he'd lost something when he turned and entered the darkness beyond. He caught up to Gabrielle, where she waited for him at a fork in the trail.

"Tiresome brat! I don't want to wait for you again." Gabrielle's eyes flashed darkly in the moonlight.

Good, he had got under her skin. "But you *have to* wait for me," he said. "You are *my* escort. The wizard said I shouldn't come to any harm." He imagined he could feel the heat of Gabrielle's anger as he neared her. Bevn grinned. "You want to impress *him*, don't you?"

Gabrielle turned swiftly away.

Oh, he was going to have fun with her. She wasn't as important as she thought.

She strode off on the forest trail. Bevn decided to keep his witty comments to himself for a while. He needed her abilities as a Shadowcaster to find the path in the dark. They both wanted to find the pass Wizard Saladon had told them about as soon as possible. Swords might block them at any moment, but outside Eyri—well, nobody knew how to *get* outside, except Bevn and Gabrielle. He didn't even know *what* was out there, but Black Saladon had said he'd meet them. Once they were outside, he could go to see the great Sorcerer Ametheus. Then the Swords wouldn't matter at all.

Gabrielle was far ahead already. He trotted to catch her, following her vague outline as he scrambled over roots, across banks of springy moss and between the looming trees that blocked out even the wan starlight. Minute by minute she pulled ahead of him.

"Hey!" he called out to her. "Hey, wait!"

She didn't hear him.

*Tart! She's trying to make me scared again, that's what she's doing. I won't be scared, I can be alone in a forest like this, there's only wolves and bears and foxes out, and holes to fall into, and snakes, and…*he stopped suddenly. *What if she can summon Morgloths, like Arkell?*

He ran through the next clearing, but the trees drew closer, oaks with tangled boughs, roots like grasping hands.

"Gabrielle?"

A gust of wind swirled through the leaves.

"Gabrielle!"

A tree creaked.

He forced himself to walk on. He would show her. It became darker and darker. Not even his months in the gloomy depths of Ravenscroft helped him anymore. He couldn't see. He had lost Gabrielle. He was lost, himself. He thought he saw her off to the right, and he scampered after her as fast as he dared, but when his groping hands reached for her he found the rough bark of an old tree stump. The forest crept closer, pressing against him from all sides. Creatures swelled out of the ground but faded when he looked at them. Another tree creaked. Something ran light-footed over a carpet of leaves.

He promised himself he would be calm. Cold sweat beaded on his forehead.

She must have headed for the high ground. He tried to walk slowly, but he was soon running again. An owl hooted in the dark. He crashed over a rotten log. The vegetation beyond it gripped his legs. Vicious little thorns bit into his skin as he tried to pull free. He was trapped. Anything that came at him from out of the darkness would find easy prey in the brambles. He thought of wicked little eyes watching him from the darkness.

"Hey!" His voice sounded small in his ears. Shadows shifted through the cold air, coming closer, coming fast. "Gabrielle! Don't leave me. Please don't leave me here! Come back!"

"I'm here," she answered coolly, so close he jumped at the sound. She was leaning against the tree beside him as if she had been there all the time.

"You're not playing fair. You led me into these briars on purpose!" He refused to let her know how relieved he was to see her.

"Let me explain something to you," she answered. "I'm with you because of the gold and because Black Saladon asked me to escort you. I'm not here to play nursemaid to a spoilt little boy. The Penitent's Pass is no place for games. I've never heard of anyone succeeding in escaping from Eyri, or at least if they did, they never returned. You are not even a man. If I am to lead us through it, then you must obey me, without any arguments. Do we understand each other?"

"I am a man! You'll see!"

"Do. We. Understand?"

Bevn glowered at her. The trollop! She had forgotten that *he* was the reason Black Saladon had come to Ravenscroft in the first place. "What do you know of the pass, anyway?"

She just looked at him. "I'm waiting."

He really didn't want her to leave him, not here, not in the forest. He'd pretend to obey her, just for the night. Maybe for the following day.

"I promise to follow you." He looked somewhere into the leaves.

She stretched like a cat then extended her hand to help him from the brambles.

"Good, then we might have a chance when we reach the Penitent's Pass," Gabrielle said. She stalked easily away through the dark, and Bevn followed at her heels.

"Why are you so scared of the pass?"

"We had a pass behind Ravenscroft. There was something that the Master liked to do before awarding rank to anyone, his private little joke: he would send us to retrieve a rock from the head of the pass as a test. Nobody could do it. Nobody ever did it. Something within the pass repelled every attempt. Those who tried were crushed with bitter cold. Some tried too hard and they died. Others cheated, but he always knew. Cabal! He used to tell us it was the bond of our Darkstones that prevented our passage, and that we should always remember how we had learnt our limit against him, that we could never escape his grasp. We believed many things, while he lived."

"That was the shield of Eyri, in the Gap?"

"What do you know of it?"

"Only what everyone *royal* knows. It encloses all of Eyri. It's funny…I never before wondered what was outside Eyri. I suppose I never thought about it."

"I expect we'll find the shield on this Penitent's Pass then."

"What's it like, when you get close?"

Gabrielle was silent for so long Bevn thought that she wasn't going to answer. She picked her way over a fallen tree, led Bevn onward along a small game trail.

"Expect a lot of pain," she said at last.

He couldn't be sure in the gloom, but for a moment she had almost appeared to smile.

જાજીભ્છ

They walked and walked for what seemed like all night, but at last Gabrielle called a halt. They were high in the forest and the wind sighed constantly through the trees. Clouds whipped above the swaying boughs and obscured the stars.

Bevn's feet ached, his face and hands were scratched and he had a pounding headache from trying to see in the darkness. He wished Black Saladon had never allowed Gabrielle to accompany him on his quest.

He sank to the ground. "About bloody time," he muttered, just loud enough for her to hear.

Gabrielle didn't react. She produced a flattened object from her pocket, tore it roughly in half and passed him his share.

"What's this?" It smelled of meat and spices, but it looked like a wet turd caught in pastry. Cold liquid oozed over his fingers.

"Supper. Eat up. It'll be the last good food we'll find for a while, I'll bet."

"Where does this come from?" But he knew. He had seen her ducking out of a doorway in Llury.

"Never pass up an opportunity to steal something," Gabrielle replied. She licked her fingers, and munched her pie, watching him all the while. Bevn clutched his knapsack tighter. The crown of Eyri! She knew about it. He vowed to keep it closer than his underwear.

When Gabrielle wrapped herself in her cloak and settled at last in a leaf-filled hollow, Bevn sat watching her from beneath his cowl. Maybe he should just leave her and go it alone. Maybe she was too dangerous to trust on the strength of promised gold alone.

The dark night crept closer through the trees. Bevn shivered. No, he would be better off with Gabrielle near. She had knives belted to her hip, and she knew how to use them. He would rather have those knives between him and the dangers than at his back. He shifted as close to her as he dared.

The ground was hard. The points of the stolen crown within his makeshift pillow were harder still.

Did his father sleep without his crown?

His father had always kept it near, even at night. He'd told Bevn once that the crown bound his thoughts together like glue, that it gave him the strength to rule and that the ancient patterns of magic in the Kingsrim helped the Eyrian people to believe in their king. Bevn remembered sitting on his lap, watching the way his father had looked at the crown, turning it over and over in his hands. He remembered the smell of rum on his father's breath and the ticklish prod of his beard in his ear. His father had said that power came at a price, that when a king retired and passed his crown on to his son, the strength he had enjoyed during his rule deserted his mind, 'like a chair pulled out from under your bum when you need it most'. Every old king in their royal family had gone as mad as the moon after giving the crown up at the customary age of sixty. After his father had taken over from his grandfather, Ol'king Mellar had become a gibbering idiot within a year, and by the time he died he did not even know his own name. He had died not knowing he had ever been a king.

Bevn's father had slapped his hand on the table then, and Bevn had jumped from his knee in fright. There was a strange look in his father's eye. "You'll be very old before I hand this on," his father had growled. "You took my queen's life with your coming, and I'll not have you taking mine. I've given you everything else, but I'll keep my wits, yes, I'll not be turned mad."

Later, his father had laughed and tossed his son in the air, and told Bevn not to worry about a thing he'd said, that it was just his silly father thinking idle thoughts. *Well, father, I remember that story, even though you thought I was too young to understand what you'd said. You told me it would be yours forever when you put this crown back on your head.*

6. KING OF THE CASTLE

"The greater the castle, the longer its shadow."—Zarost

Kirjath Arkell burned with cold anger as he swept through the halls of the palace; the King's palace in Stormhaven, the royal house of wealth and waste. Every detail of the opulence made him clench himself tighter, every lavish carpet, rare tapestry and painted urn made him shake. Here the King had lived in luxury, while Kirjath had struggled in poverty. Here the King had bathed in gilded bathtubs, while Kirjath had ground his hands to the bone in the lowest and most dust-choked shafts of the mines at Respite, during his fatherless youth. Why should the King have such a fine life and decree that Kirjath Arkell should endure such misery? Mellar had done nothing but fall from the womb of a royal broodmare. There was nothing special about him. He had too much wealth for one man, yet he hadn't shared it, not with Kirjath Arkell. All Kirjath had received thanks to this king was his own father's boots.

He suddenly wanted to hit someone, anyone, but the passage was empty except for a row of mocking statues which stood beneath a single lamp—busts of the past rulers of Eyri—all the Mellars in a line. One whole curséd family, an unbroken monopoly of privilege.

For a moment he considered finding a sledgehammer.

He knew he shouldn't be looking for Mellar, not in his current state. When he saw the man, his anger would become rage. He should find another place to haunt. The man would be too strong—he should be looking for a weak and troubled courtier to use as a potential host, not the king, but his hatred ran too deep, his anger too old. Anger. Maybe that was why he had survived still. His anger kept him from slipping away. He did not want to let go. He was not yet done with the living. There was unfinished business, a debt was unpaid.

Father swings upon a rope,
Face has gone as white as soap,
Father swings upon a rope,
in the village square!

They had sung it over and over, the brats in Rhyme, even the ones who'd pretended to be friends before. They'd spat upon him where he'd stood, while his tears were running.

"'ere we go, lad, 'e won't be needing 'is boots no more," said the gallowsman.

The brats had howled and hooted and begun their special little jeer again.

Billyboy and Norma Lin, Robson and Wolley, each of them with wide eyes, their faces framed in blood... But that justice had only come later, much later. In the end, only one debt had not been settled. So quick was he to judge, that young king, so despising of a man he'd never met. *Kirjath* knew the little girls were liars. *Kirjath* knew Father wouldn't have done those things to them, but nobody would listen to a poor boy. He knew they were liars, they couldn't be right. He *knew*.

So what if Father had liked little girls? *They* were still alive; his father wasn't.

Oh how he had wanted that young king dead, how he had cursed his name. King Mellar the Fourteenth.

Kirjath rounded a corner in the palace. Ahead, two dozing guards stood on either side of a heavy-looking gold-wrought door. That was it! Kirjath surged forward, and spread his presence out. The guards stared off into the middle distance, gripping their pikes. He slid under the door like a wisp of smoke. If only he could have done this before, as a Shadowcaster! Mellar would have blown red bubbles in his sleep!

He lost nothing of himself, sliding over the wood. He slid under a second door and just like that, he was inside.

He drew himself up. The room looked cosy, but he couldn't feel the warmth. The walls were washed with a deep red and a fire glowed in a low hearth, beyond a grand rumpled bed, where two figures lay on the shaggy carpet—a fat woman on her side, with her back to Kirjath. Her blonde curls spilled over her shoulders, her figure plain beneath the pale nightdress. The man had copper-coloured hair, and he rested on the woman's stomach, his hairy arm thrown lazily over her rump. The woman idled her fingers through the man's hair. Kirjath had to get closer. He passed over their heads, his ethereal body not even casting a shadow on the gloomy roof.

Mellar. It was him.

The king raised a half-glass of rum to his lips with a shaking hand. His face was lined, the flesh below his troubled eyes dark. A crystal decanter balanced on the carpet, what was left of its contents a mere puddle in the base.

"He won't hide forever," said the woman in a soft, motherly voice. "Surely Bevn will miss his life here too much?"

"No, Maybelle, I don't believe my boy is hiding, not from me, he wouldn't do that. Someone must have captured him again, kept him against his will, but why don't they announce themselves, for the love of the sun and the moon, just ask me for a ransom? You know what I'd be willing to pay! Anything to get the crown back."

"And Bevn."

"Yes of course, Bevn, my son."

"He must have been shocked by his ordeal."

"He did not know what he did!" the king exclaimed.

The fat lady smoothed the king's creased brow. "I know, I know. And the Swords? Any news from Ravenscroft?"

"They searched there, and here, and Fendwarrow, and Levin, even Chink and Southwind! No one has seen him, nor heard of his passing. *Aie!*"

The king sat up quickly, and pressed his hands to his temples.

"The headache again?"

"Worse than ever," he answered.

"Oh my love, is there no remedy for this cruelty?"

The king spun to face her with a snarl. "You know there isn't! You have read the histories! Not one of my ancestors has beaten this curse. Not one!" He turned away from her again, and stared into the fire. "Sorry for that," he muttered. "I become more and more what I fear to be."

The fat lady reached for him. "I know who you really are," she said.

He rocked backward and forward, watching the flames.

"I see the shapes and faces more now, faces in the air, faces in the fire. They move as my head moves. They are there when I close my eyes. Why does my father watch me, Ol'king Mellar, why?"

He jerked out of the fat lady's hands and lurched to his feet.

"No, leave me be!"

He staggered back a step and knocked the crystal decanter over. Before the fat lady could stop it, a dark stain had spread into the carpet, as dark as blood. The fat lady covered her mouth with her hands.

King Mellar strode away from the fire and he struck the air as if slicing it with a sword. "I will not succumb to this! I will not!" he shouted. "Go and plague my son, if you would plague a Mellar! You gather round me like beggars, I will not give anything to you, my sleep and my life are my own!"

The king steadied himself on a bedpost. He was weak, Kirjath thought, tired, weak and troubled, but he was angry, and that might give him the strength to resist what Kirjath wanted to do to him.

He shouldn't have hesitated when he had first entered. His initial rage was fading, and his strength with it.

The fat lady cried softly beneath Kirjath, at the fire. He contemplated using her. She must be influential, for she was not just a royal harlot. A harlot would have been dismissed as soon as the king had satisfied himself upon her. This woman was still in his chambers, offering comfort in a private affair. A relative then or a lady whom he was courting. Yes, she would have influence indeed, but Kirjath looked at her full rump. To take her, to use her as a host, Kirjath would have to be more than just inside her flesh. He would have to be part of her, as she would be a part of him. She was a woman, full of whimsy, weakening fluids and scents which had to be applied to mask the odours beneath. No, he could not bring himself to be a woman. She would not do at all.

"Go away, you badgers, get away from me!" exclaimed the king. "I'll hang you! I'll hang you all!"

The king's words detonated his anger like a spark in a barrel of pitch. He was clenched so tightly in rage that the outline of his presence glistened with reflected light, as if he was solid. Kirjath rushed across the room. Anger pounded in him, as vital as a heartbeat. Those little singsong voices returned, from the village so long ago.

Father swings upon a rope.

He was going to take Mellar. He was going to reclaim his life from the king. He would not just fade away.

Face has gone as white as soap.

Kirjath leapt like a spring-spider upon its prey. His glistening form might be shattered by the king's flesh, but he would live inside his mind as a Morgloth lived in its master. Ultimately, the demon could rule—he knew that better than anyone alive.

Father swings upon a rope.

The king clawed against his invented tormentors and turned his face to the roof, as if looking beyond it for mercy from the gods. His eyes went wide.

Here's your mercy! Kirjath drove himself into Mellar's eyes.

There would be no return to the outside. Living flesh absorbed his essence.

"*In the village square!*" cried the king. "In the village square!"

Then he fell.

CʒꙄꙄꙄ

The stairs to Stormhaven's old dungeons were moist. The dank air was almost thick enough to smother the fitful light of his lamp. Ashley Logán steadied himself against the mossy wall at the base of the stairs.

Someone was babbling away in the darkness, but his tune changed as Ashley approached the cells.

"Bring the light! Bring the light! Bring it to me!"

A figure fluttered into the pool of light on the far side of the bars—tufts of hair protruding from his head in dirty clumps, his yellow robe soiled. The man knelt against the bars looking up at Ashley with tearful eyes.

"Bring it closer. Bring it, bring it, please good gifter, bring the light. Ah, the light, the light!"

A hand shot out between the bars. Ashley wasn't quick enough to dance clear of the grasp; his leg was caught in a shaking grip, but the prisoner was weak, and Ashley twisted free, dancing away from the man's reach.

"The light! The light! I want the light back!" Lethin Tarrok cried.

"I'll blow the lamp out and leave again, if you misbehave," Ashley threatened. He lifted the lid of the lamp threateningly.

"No! No! No, don't take it, don't leave me blind, I'll be still, I'll be quiet. Keep the light. Keep it here!"

Ashley set the lamp on a barrel, and approached the cell again. Tarrok had his face pressed against the bars now, as if to be as close to the dancing flame as possible. He didn't seem to notice Ashley at all.

Tarrok should have been executed by now, but Ashley could understand that the king was reluctant to kill his nephew—there had been too much killing recently. True, the court official had betrayed too much trust. Nonetheless, Ashley felt some pity for the miserable wretch—he thought execution was a severe penalty for burning some boats, but it wasn't for him to judge; he was only the one who had testified to the arson he had witnessed the man commit in the Stormhaven harbour. Tarrok's fate was sealed, and Ashley had sealed that fate. He shouldn't feel guilty about it, but he did.

For the corrupt Rector Shamgar, deeper within the cell, Ashley had less sympathy. Ashley could sense the Rector's presence—he seethed in the darkness, his thoughts a boiling knot of resentment. The Rector would be watching him with a disdainful twist to his lips. To read his mind Ashley had to be nearer. There was a lack of hard evidence against the man, even though Ashley suspected the Rector was at the heart of the corruption in Eyri. He stood as close to the bars as he could while still avoiding Tarrok.

The Rector challenged him from the shadows at the back of the cell. "So, boy, you are here to gloat, what?" A lash of unsavoury thoughts struck Ashley and he used it to dart up the mental cord to its source. The Rector was arrogant; he had to unsettle him, to open up more cracks in his conceit.

"No, Shamgar, I am only here to ask questions. I want to understand."

"Shamgar? Rector, to you. You mean you wish to trick me into admitting something incriminating, not so? You probably have some deceitful witness lurking in the darkness behind you."

"You'll get nothing from me!" he shouted to the dim stairs. Then he dropped his voice. "You are a little boy, with a little wit. Do not try to better your betters."

Ashley felt his own anger rising. The Rector was a villain—he had betrayed the trust of his followers and abused his power. He was falsely pious, a hypocrite. He deserved to be fed to the fish at the bottom of the Amberlake. Ashley drew himself up. "I may be young, but I stand on this side of the bars."

"You forget yourself, Logán. You will regret your words when I am released, what. You shall have to serve me, you know, you are just a Lightgifter, you shall always be a Lightfgifter."

"You have no sprites to compel me by my Vow," Ashley retorted. "I would never serve you by choice."

"Oh, you are so righteous, and such a fool, Logán. I do not need your consent to be able to influence you. Have you learnt nothing from your experience with the ways of the Dark?"

"Why did you betray us?" Ashley demanded. "Why did you sell the essence to the Darkmaster?"

"Ah-ah, not so easy! You'll not compel false admissions from me. You have no proof of your scandalous assumption, except for the Serannon girl's wild tales about me. We both know she has claimed all the power for herself, but you and I, we are left to struggle on without any essence. Consider that. Consider who has ended the gift of the Light."

The flame guttered for a while then burned bright. The Rector was revealed where he sat on the raised stone bed, arrayed upon a cushion with a thick blanket covering the bed. Beside him lay three unfinished plates of food.

The Rector was being well cared for. Ashley guessed he had already found a way to convince the jailors that it would be wise to look after him. He was planning on being released, that much was clear—he had not abandoned himself to his fate, as Tarrok had. Ashley could not believe anyone would think Shamgar was innocent. Yet to convict him, Ashley needed evidence, and the Rector was wording his answers carefully. He was thinking carefully too. Ashley guessed he would have to provoke Shamgar more openly to get any results.

"You'll never see the light of day, you two-faced porker!" Ashley declared. He turned half away from the cell, pretending to be readying himself to leave, but at the same time he listened very, very carefully. The private thoughts were there, barely discernible under a hot layer of fury.

The boy is desperate to believe I'm wrong, but he's uncertain. Maybe I can use him yet.

"Come, come, Logán. I will pretend I didn't hear that insult, and I'll humour you a while to show you my good faith. What proof do you think you have against me?"

Ashley didn't turn. He considered his answer carefully. "You were working with the Darkmaster. You sent us to Ravenscroft, into his trap."

"Yet this was in response to a Sword's message that proclaimed the vale conquered!" Shamgar insisted. *And Sword Harrisson was paid well for his talented tongue*, the Rector thought.

"You handed Tabitha Serannon over to a Shadowcaster," Ashley accused.

"Did you see that, halfknot? Did anyone see that?"

"No."

That's a relief, thought the Rector.

"I fear she has concocted a wild story to cover the fact that she traded for that Darkstone with all of her gold. She yearned for power." *I should have silenced that girl when I had the chance. I shall have to see that an accident happens to her. She could still expose me if she decides to search the Dovecote for her belongings. She has an unnerving way of uncovering secrets.*

Ashley turned to face the bars again. "But she told me that her gold had been stolen."

"And you can surely see how that is just another fabrication to cover her true actions." *That gold will still be there when I am released, the gold and all the rest.*

"What about that day in the Dovecote, when we came to defend the Source. You let the Shadowcasters into the Hall."

"Oh my avowed apprentice, so little do you know! I was trying to convert them to serve our holy Light! Their Turning spell was too weak to change the mighty Source. I was deceiving them. They would have been turned to Lightgifters had their spell matured. I was trying to fight back, for the Light. Instead, the traitorous Serannon girl destroyed the holiest artefact in the realm. She desecrated our most high temple. She has taken your power, Logán! She is the villain, not I."

Ashley wouldn't give up. "You sold our essence to the Shadowcasters."

"Oh bosh, boy! The only essence to leave the Dovecote went on missions of mercy with trusted Gifters." *Straight to Fendwarrow. What a good middleman Mukwallis proved to be. He still owes me money, too, a lot of it.*

Shamgar rose from his shadowed bed, and came slowly closer. He dropped his voice low as he neared Ashley. "Do you long for the essence, boy? Do you wish you could be a Lightgifter again, feel the sprites in your hand?"

"What are you saying?" Ashley stammered, backing a few steps away. The Rector's thoughts were loud and clear now, as if their minds were joined by a wide open corridor; he was suddenly worried that Shamgar would reach into *his* mind. "There is no Light essence any more. The Source is shattered."

"I can make one anew," the Rector whispered. *There's a damn mountain of crystal at the end of the third lode in Respite. Those miners are also paid well to keep it hidden.*

"Why have you kept that a secret?"

"I have always found demand increases the price for a commodity. A little more time to allow the Gifters and Shadowcasters to feel the bind of being powerless can only serve to increase the price of essence. No doubt someone will see the value of freeing me, given the time." The Rector waited long enough for the words to sink in.

"Not so, apprentice?"

Ashley felt strange. The Rector had drawn him in, offered him this in confidence. He was being bribed with an offer of unlimited Light essence. It should not affect him; he would not be corrupted by the man on the other side of the bars. The problem was he missed the magic, desperately. Without sprites, he had no special talent. The Rector knew how to prepare the mined crystal. He could re-establish the Lightgifters' power.

Shamgar smiled. "I can offer your power back. You could be a full Gifter, at my side. You could lead the return of the Light to Eyri. Now that we are free of the threat of the Shadowcasters, we could do great work." Behind the veil of his bright eyes, the Rector turned another thought over in his mind. *The Shadowcasters will pay even more for the chance to turn that essence. The price will be higher than ever.*

"Without you dictating to me?" asked Ashley. "I would be free to do as I pleased?"

"Yes, you could be free," the Rector said.

You won't know the difference. You don't realise your Lightstone is a shackle that keeps you tame, and I have the Keystone. They have been taught so well to believe they need the source I control, and they'll never be free of their stones, because the seal is made by their hunger for magic, and we all know, nobody ever is ready to give it up, once they've tasted the smallest bit of it.

"Freedom," said Ashley. "What else?"

"A three-score of gold, in exchange for your testimony of my innocence."

"And to save your friend here?"

"Tarrok? He is no friend of mine," answered the Rector. Tarrok didn't react—he gripped the bars and stared at the flickering flame. "He will die, and why should I save his neck?" *Such a useful spy, lost to us now.* "Tell me Logán, how did you know to follow him? You must be commended for bringing such a criminal in. How did you find out what he was up to?"

"I could hear what he was thinking. I knew his thoughts..."

Nonsense!

"... just as I know yours."

Rector Shamgar looked at him without moving. *The kid's bluffing,* Rector Shamgar thought.

"I'm not bluffing, and you'd be wrong to think I'm a kid," Ashley replied.

No, it's impossible! Nobody has such a skill! I would have known if Logán was gifted. He must be bluffing.

"I've always wondered if the Lightstone was a shackle to keep me tamc. Now I know."

By the balls of Krakus, it can't be! What have I been thinking while he was here?

"You've been thinking about a great many things," Ashley replied. Truth be told, he had more than enough to go on now, enough to convict the Rector for good. He left the cell and turned to lift the lamp from the barrel.

"No! Oh! Oh! Keep the light! Keep the light, I'll tell you things to keep the light!" Tarrok blurted. Ashley ignored him—he doubted the wretch had anything new to offer. He had used up all his revelations in the first day of captivity, trying in vain to earn his release.

"Sword Harrison, Mukwallis and the third lode in Respite," Ashley called out to the Rector. "It has been great talking to you." He still hadn't found out where the Rector's secret trove of stolen goods was—it was worth a try. "The things you try the hardest to hide are the easiest to sense," he called out as he paced slowly away towards the stairs. "You think about them all the time. Like your special little vault."

The bloody treasury in the north wall of the chapel! thought Rector Shamgar. *If he finds out about that, he'll have all the evidence he needs.*

"Like his brothel of little boys in Levin's Mallard Street!" Lethin Tarrok called out. "Funded by the Rector. I know about that! Ask them! Bring the light back. I'll tell—"

"Shut up, you stupid bastard! Shut up!"

There was a frantic scuffling, and a few muffled thumps. Ashley walked away. You couldn't save a man from his own stupidity.

"Bring the light! The light! bring back—"

"You little wanker!"

The iron bars rang like a gong then there was silence.

Ashley climbed the stairs.

7. THE EDGE OF REASON

"A hat is there to steer the rain,
it keeps the water off the brain;
A crown has a royal reason—
a target for all acts of treason."—Zarost

"Well, what did you expect?" said Gabrielle. "Why did you ever think you were going to breach the pass? You, of all people?"

Bevn pouted. She was such a witch—she always assumed that young meant foolish instead of brave. "Black Saladon said so, and he wasn't the only one. There's a prophecy too, I've read it! For the one who bears the crown of Eyri, shall the way to power be open."

"A prophecy?" Gabrielle laughed. "And I suppose you are the Chosen One?"

"You wouldn't know about the Revelations," Bevn retorted. "It's only shown to members of the *royal* family."

Gabrielle gave him an empty smile. "Things are not working as the prophecy foretold."

"It's because *you're* with me," he retorted. "If I was by myself, I'd be through by now!"

She didn't respond; she didn't need to. He had crawled away from the pass first. A hint of amusement crossed her lips. "Maybe the way is not open because you don't bear the crown as your right. You stole it."

"I didn't steal it! I claimed it! My father surrendered his crown to Cabal, and Cabal was killed. So it passes to me, by royal suss-sess-succession. It *is* mine!"

"If you are the rightful owner, then why don't you wear it, bring it out for the world to see?"

"That's stupid. The Swords will recognise me at once."

"There's nobody up here but you and me."

"I-I must wait until I'm ready," he said.

"Hah! Stripling! I thought as much. You know you're too young to be a king. So why do you pretend this sorcerer can make you into one?"

"That's not true!" Bevn shouted. "I'll be fourteen in four months' time! And the first king of Eyri was my age!" He wished he had the courage to strike her for her cheek. "The Kingsrim has a special power. My father told me that the people are sworn to serve the bearer of the crown, they can't refuse the bond—it's an even stronger spell than the old Master had with the Darkstones. If I wear it, everyone must obey me!"

She would have to obey him as well.

"I can wear it any time I want to!" he warned.

She ignored him. She stretched back against the slanted edge of the ancient cairn of rocks she was standing beside and closed her eyes. "I can't believe Black Saladon needs you in his plans. You're such a stupid little prick." She knuckled her forehead.

Bitch! Her eyes were still closed, so he watched the rise and fall of her covered breasts with sullen fascination. She had come too close to the truth. He *was* afraid to wear the crown, but not because he was too young. What if the strange magic of the Kingsrim rejected him? He knew all about that terrible death which came upon false kings. His father had told him the tales. If Cabal had actually worn the crown for any length of time, wouldn't he have gone mad too? Had his father really surrendered the crown, or had it been a clever trick to sabotage the invaders? Glavenor hadn't needed to skewer the Darkmaster—the crown would have done it to his mind.

Bevn wondered about that as he clutched his bag close to his chest. The treasure was still there, jagged and circular, his inheritance, his prize. The weight of the whole kingdom pressed upon your head when you wore the crown, his father had told him, but that was just nonsense. It was because his father tried to be fair all the time that the crown had been a burden for him. He was King, for Fynn's sake, he could do anything. Why be fair if it meant it would cost you? When *he* wore the crown, it would be light; it would make him feel strong.

But the more he contemplated the crown, the more intimidated he became.

It was this place, he decided. This lonely, windy passage between the high rocks and bittergrass. It had a depressing mood that made him feel small, but he knew he couldn't really blame the scenery. They had failed.

The Shield of Eyri had beaten them. He hated it. He had so badly wanted to be through the Penitent's pass, into the legendary lands beyond, on his way to finding the great Sorcerer Ametheus. There was no future for him if he turned back but they had already tried the pass ahead and the pain hadn't faded yet. Neither had the shame. The Shield was daunting, up close.

They had entered the Penitent's pass as the last shreds of morning mist blew down to meet them beneath a pallid sun. The slopes on either side met in a shallow defile choked with talus and smothered with green moss. The pass had an eerie feel to it, even the biting wind sounded hollow. When they passed the crumbled cairn Bevn noticed a weathered skull in the bittergrass, its empty sockets looking through him. He felt a twinge between his shoulder blades and a weight upon his head but said nothing about it. When they reached the last lonely pine, Bevn began to feel a horrible ache in his bones. The lone pine seemed to feel it too, for it had grown gnarled and hunched over, as if yearning to be farther downslope.

Gabrielle led him on and Bevn couldn't let her know of his mounting panic for she wasn't showing any signs of suffering under the eerie burden that crushed him. Bevn's breath began to catch in his throat—his chest was too tight. Then his knees felt as if they would burst and buckle. His skin felt as heavy as lead. He was terrified that his blood was boiling, and it felt as if beetles crawled everywhere under his flesh. His headache was crushing, and his traitorous eyes streamed with tears.

Gabrielle moved on. He couldn't call her back. She would know he was a weakling.

At the place where the scraggly moss finally gave way to bare rock, Gabrielle stopped. She nodded, as if recognising a familiarity to the atmosphere.

"You might be feeling the first hint of discomfort here," she said over her shoulder. "From here on it will double for every step you take. If this pass is anything like the Icerind Gap above Ravenscroft, then you'll make a little headway, but eventually you will go blind from pain. You will still be able to hear and feel. Don't go past where you lose feeling, because only hearing remains and that shall be the only means to find your way back to safety. Listen to the sound of the wind over your ears, so that you may crawl away from it, downslope.

"If you go farther than that, you will hear an endless ringing—there is only madness to be found there, madness and death."

She turned then to see if Bevn had understood her warnings.

He was cowering at her feet. He tried to tell her that he couldn't go on, but his words came out as a horrible pleading whine. He knew he was crying. He didn't look up. The pain trampled him like a hundred angry bears. How much worse could it get? He crawled away from her feet, downhill, like a beaten dog.

She went on, farther into that wall of pain, and he suspected that it was only to prove to him that she could. He waited for her far down the slope, beyond the pine tree, in the shelter of the cairn, where the pressure was so faint it was bearable. He dried his tears, but the bitter taste of shame remained. She was a woman! She shouldn't be able to make such a fool of him.

He had been relieved to see her return. Her drawn expression had told him everything. She had failed to breach the pass as well. How much pain had she taken on before she had reached her limit?

Bevn brought his mind back to the present. He was tired of watching her covered breasts as she rested against the boulder. He was tired of being afraid of the treasure he carried. He was tired of being prevented from following his ambition.

Now, while her eyes were closed, he should try the Kingsrim on. If it rejected him, then at least that would be his secret alone. He fumbled with his bag's straps. His fingers were cold, he told himself. That was why they were shaking.

He slipped the crown from the bag. The Kingsrim glinted when he held it up. It was a beauty, the spidery inscriptions so fine, the gold so pure, the jewels placed in perfect symmetry within the curling patterns of the bands of rare metals. He turned the crown until the uneven border of the crest matched the rim of Eyri. There was the distant profile of the Zunskar, Fynn's Tooth to his right and the gap of River's End to the left. That was how his father always wore it, with the single misty ruby facing forward.

Terrible death came upon false kings, terrible death.

He held his breath. He lowered the crown, but sank to his knees at the same time so the crown came no closer to his head. He screwed his eyes closed, but then he could escape the moment no longer. He pulled the crown down. Cool metal pressed against his temples. His breath came in, went out. The wind continued to blow past overhead. Beyond that, a great silence had descended on the world.

He opened one eye. Gabrielle was still there, languishing in the sun, regaining her strength.

He stood.

It was staying on his head!

The crown rested firmly in place. The gentle grip on his skull made him want to stand even straighter. The court, the nobles, the villagers and vassals, all would be his to command. His thoughts came together. He would travel the realm in his royal carriage, and the best Swords would be his escort. Wherever he went, they would bow and kneel before him, grant him favours, obey his wishes. He could tax them as he pleased, trade with whoever he liked, terrify everyone else.

King!

He stood there for a long time, with the sun in his eyes, feeling tall. The crown of Eyri had accepted him! He *could* be King Bevn, he who had dared to be brave and claim his rulership at such a young age. He *would* be King Bevn. He would rule for years and years.

His father had been wrong about the weight of the crown. Bevn felt elated, glorious, mighty. King!

With a start he realised why it was so quiet. The grinding presence of the Shield was gone, or at least, he couldn't feel it. His heart leapt again—maybe Black Saladon had been right, after all. For the bearer of the Kingsrim shall the pass be open. His mistake had been to carry it in his bag, instead of to wear it.

"Open your eyes, and behold your king!" he called out. He liked that tone of royal command, very much.

Her dark eyes flew open. She appeared surprised for a moment, as if she wanted to say something, but then didn't.

"I am King Bevn, fifteenth Mellar of Eyri, and by my crown I prove my royal right to rule."

"So, you are not entirely without balls," she said. "The crown seems to suit you well."

He took encouragement from the lack of mockery in her voice. She actually meant it.

"Then kneel and pay homage to me," he commanded. "I am the King of Eyri."

She seemed puzzled and approached him slowly, and her eyes became downcast.

Bevn was amazed and delighted.

Gabrielle drew one leg back in a manly bow. He wasn't surprised—a woman like Gabrielle would not curtsy, but she looked up suddenly, with a glare that warned him something was coming. Her boot found his groin quicker than he could defend against it.

He hunched over clutching his gonads. There was no pain yet, only numbness, but he knew it was coming, like a charging bull.

"I've owed you that for some time now," said Gabrielle. "Don't you dare try to lord over me. I wouldn't care if you were the king, I won't be made a slave by anyone again. I am my own!"

He couldn't answer her. The sickening tide hit him. He dropped to the ground.

"—greater opinion of himself than the Darkmaster," Gabrielle muttered as she stalked away. "Little bugger."

Bevn squirmed on his back. He didn't understand. How could she rebel against her king like that? Maybe the magic of the Kingsrim hadn't worked upon either of them for long enough. He kicked his heels against the ground, which they said helped to ease the pain, but his heels got sore and his nuts still felt like they wanted to come out of his throat. No one had ever done that to him before. No one.

He retched upon the bittergrass.

She wouldn't have been so angry if the Kingsrim hadn't affected her. She would have just cuffed him, or laughed. Yes, it did *something* to her. He felt shaky, but he staggered to his feet. He would show her; there was something he'd discovered about the crown she didn't know about.

He retrieved his bag, closed it roughly, and shouldered the weight. She was sitting on a rock a short way off, watching him. He ignored her, and set off up the trail. He passed the lone sentinel pine, and quickened his pace. His groin still burned, but that was all—the pressure of the Shield was gone altogether. The magic dispersed ahead of his crown like smoke before the wind.

He glanced over his shoulder, and saw that Gabrielle had left her rock and was loping behind him. Good. She thought he was trying to prove how tough he was. Let her taste the limits of her endurance and beyond—he doubted his crown afforded her any protection, unless she was very close. She would buckle under the growing torture of the shield. Let her go blind with pain. Then he would talk to her. She had told him that hearing was the last sense to go. He had many things he wished to say to her, once she was down.

She wasn't stupid—she was trying to catch up to him. Bevn ran.

The way ahead was clear, the ground rose to a saddle, beyond which a watery light beckoned. The incline was steeper than it looked, and he was puffing by the time he neared the crest, but all the way he was free from pain, apart from the fire in his groin. The air shimmered ahead of him, in a great wall which arched upward and inward, high overhead. He paused there, not wanting to go on alone, but not wanting to help the woman either.

It took some time for Gabrielle to reach him. She came hunched over, using her knees for support. Her breath rasped as if she had been fighting for her life all day. Her face was red and bloated. Some blood ran from her nose! She hung on his arm as if she was drowning, and she made strange little sounds in her throat.

Bevn was disappointed that she had caught him so soon. He shook himself free.

"Don't you feel anything here?" he asked her. "Don't you still feel some pain and pressure?"

When she had regained some of her breath, she looked his way

"Now, when I'm near you, the pain is less." Oh, and how she hated that, he could see. "I felt it when you passed me," she added. "It's that crown, isn't it? Catching up to you was—taxing. Don't do that again."

Bevn smiled at her. She really did look haggard. "Say please."

Her expression darkened—she was recovering her temper quicker than her strength. "Piss off."

She needed to be reminded.

Bevn jumped away and she tried to grab him but he weaved sideways and ran out of her range.

Gabrielle screamed as the sudden return of pressure hit her, falling to her knees on the bare rocks. She screwed her face up against the pain and shook. Bevn backed away as she crawled towards him. She raised her hand.

"Please!" she cried. "Please come back, damn you!"

Bevn rejoiced. "Walk beside your King, if you must," he offered.

He sauntered over to her. She didn't meet his gaze this time.

"Come," he said, and led the way towards the pass's crest.

The air ahead shimmered like a mirror with an imperfect image held upon its surface, but when Bevn pushed against it, the Shield seemed to have no substance at all. He walked through the swirling air, with Gabrielle holding onto his arm.

A strange sensation passed over him, as if the air had been taken away and replaced again in the same instant. The Shield was behind them. They had entered the lands beyond Eyri.

8. GOOD GRACIOUS ME

"Some pasts are a present,
but some presents belong to the past."—Zarost

Tabitha fell ill after the death of the soldier. The fever burned in her chest and made her limbs tremble. She couldn't forget that horrible vision—the Goddess Ethea in that place of noise and heat and blood, and the birds, circling, so frantic and forlorn. Her heartbeat stabbed in her heart, reminding her that every moment she lay in her bed was another moment Ethea could not afford. But what could she do? She was weak from the fever, she was scared of what she had seen, and she didn't know where to begin. She tossed and turned among the heavy sheets.

A place where buildings grew upon buildings, into the air, where it was so hot men walked bare-chested, where the air smelled of salt and fire. She had never seen such a place. It was not in Eyri; nothing about the people had been familiar, the carved pit and the red sky above it were strange. And yet, where *could* it be if it was not in Eyri?

The three brothers...Ethea had spoken of the three brothers, but never named them.

Oh, Ethea, who would torture you so?

Fear consumed Tabitha. If the Goddess lost the struggle against her tormentors, Tabitha was sure the Lifesong would be lost. She had sensed that Ethea was the source of the power beyond the music, the essence of beauty, the essence of song. Without that power, Tabitha's talents were useless. She would be an empty voice singing only a lament. She supposed everyone would lose their spirit—their vital sound. She couldn't guess if the World would die, but now that she knew the song was *in* everything, she couldn't imagine a world without it. Yet that would come to pass, if she did nothing.

She shivered at night. Garyll lay beside her and warmed her in his arms. She loved him for that, for his silence. When she cried, he held her. When she hungered, he fed her soup and barley cakes. She wished she was well enough to enjoy the intimacy. The nights crawled by.

The dawns brought no relief, but Tabitha knew an avalanche of duty awaited her outside.

She had allowed a man to die. More died while she lay in bed.

She tried to rise, but Garyll would not allow her to. Tabitha could not fight him in her weakened state. She did not want to fight him—he took her responsibility away, if only for a precious few hours, which meant there was no need for guilt, because she could not answer the call to duty. Her own bed held her prisoner

She fell back into sleep at last; heavy, heart-sore. Strange things grew in scorched earth, shapes formed of dust and cruel fantasy. Dreams became darkness, and time passed slowly by.

A beating of drums. Discordant horns, blown out of time.

Or were they? They sounded again, in tune, a clear call, like the trumpets of Stormhaven.

Tabitha awoke. The sunlight on the bedroom wall told her that it was morning again. Many hours has passed. It was probably the following day, for her body ached, and she was hungry and weak. A whole day had been lost!

Garyll lay beside her, a protective arm looped around her waist. He was snoring softly into his pillow, face down. She slipped herself carefully out of her keeper's grasp and went in search of food.

Before she had reached the kitchen, someone knocked on the front door. Two men argued outside.

"Give the wizard time to respond. Hold, Swords!"

"It's high morning! We're being denied!"

"You didn't knock loudly enough!"

"I said hold!"

Tabitha rushed to the door, and looked through the peephole. Two wardens stood close outside, and down in the street more wardens were clustered around a group of uniformed soldiers. Swords!

"What is it?" she asked.

"Oi! Stop your rumpus!" the nearest warden shouted to the others. "The wizard speaks!" He turned his face to the door. "Royal messenger, your grace."

"Messenger? Can't he just leave the message with you?"

"Uhh, it's an envoy, your grace, here in person, with an escort."

An envoy of the king? What did the king want from her?

"Give me a minute!" she said. "Give me a minute!"

She hurried to her wardrobe, and pulled on a simple skirt and boots. There was no time to be fussy with her appearance. She fumbled with the buttons of her flared blouse. Silly goose! She was still so weak.

The king isn't here as well, is he?

She splashed some water on her face and quickly bound her hair with a cord, certain she appeared a right mess.

"Where are you off to?" asked Garyll in a sleepy voice. a sleepy voice challenged her.

"There's an envoy outside."

She heard his feet hit the floor, but she got to the door before him. He wouldn't forestall her, not for this. How could she deny a royal envoy? Her wardens shouldn't be blocking their approach either. Tabitha opened the door and tottered outside.

As she emerged upon her terrace the trumpets pealed. Tabitha clapped her hands to her ears. They might be in tune, but by the blazing sun! They were too close to be played with such zeal. The sun was bright. The Swords stood to attention in formation. Their chainmail gleamed. The blue standard with the King's crossed circle flapped calmly at the head of the formation, over a stately man in elegant robes. Tabitha's loyal wardens had stopped the procession at the edge of the circle where they held back the crowds. Hundreds of people crammed the streets, standing in flowerbeds or on carts, hanging from windows. Some urchins were even up on the roofs. When they saw Tabitha at her door, the mass cheered.

What was she to do? She didn't deserve this reverence. She raised her hand uncertainly, to silence the commotion, but the crowds cheered louder and waved back.

The great Wizard of Eyri. Magnificence. Grace. Holiness. How did it ever come to this? "Let the escort come through, please," she called out in the loudest voice she could manage.

She shouldn't have to issue such an order. Her wardens' role was to control the crowd in her healing hall. They were volunteers in her service. They did not outrank a royal envoy, and should never defy uniformed Swords. What had they been thinking? Her wardens parted reluctantly then flanked the procession itself as it approached Tabitha, as if the newcomers might pose a threat to the Wizard, a threat they would counter. They went too far in their devotion.

The envoy assembled at the bottom of her stairs, and the stately man spoke up. "Good morning, Wizard Serannon. I am Kingsman Rood, King Mellar's new advisor. I wish to deliver a letter from the king to you, if I may."

"Please, come up, Kingsman Rood." She was not going to lord

over them from the small terrace above, but her legs were still too unsteady to trust going down the stairs. The elderly statesman came up, and bowed politely when he reached her level. He bore himself proudly, in his azure robes and starched white clothing. She made a point of bowing lower than him.

"I am sorry you were stopped," she said at once, loud enough to carry. "You are on the king's business, and should be allowed everywhere. I am subject to the king's rule, as are we all."

The envoy nodded. He had a kind smile. "You wear your power lightly, your grace. As kingsman, I have been entrusted to bring you this and see it delivered in person." He offered a scroll to her.

How could she reprimand him without seeming impolite? If Kingsman Rood thought it was appropriate to call her grace, it was not for her to correct him.

It was a fresh parchment, and the delicate traceries inscribed on it appeared to be drawn in gold—real gold. She pressed down on the wax at the edge of the scroll, and the crossed circle split under her fingernail.

May it please the most honourable and serene Wizard Serannon to receive this missive from the imperial majesty King Mellar, fourteenth ruler of Eyri and monarch of Stormhaven. The King hereby invites the benevolent Wizard Serannon to an interlocution concerning affairs of the crown at her earliest convenience, and further wishes to honour the Wizard for her services to Eyri and his person. It would therefore greatly please his Highness King Mellar this evening if the Wizard Serannon were to join him at Repast in her honour, notwithstanding her current engagements.

There were some flowery squiggles at the bottom of the page, some important looking seals, and another design of gold. The scroll was more valuably embellished than a ceremonial certificate of wedding.

Tabitha read it again.

"An interlo-cution?" she asked Kingsman Rood.

"It is an audience, your eminence."

An audience? Concerning matters of the crown? Why did the king need *her* advice?

"Repast?"

"A banquet."

"Oh, Kingsman Rood, this day finds me in no shape for enjoying such pleasures." Seeing his obvious disappointment she quickly added, "But I cannot refuse the king's command, can I? I must go."

"Not exactly, your grace. The King has *invited* you, he stressed that it was important for this to be your choice, but you should know his need for you is urgent."

A banquet, in her honour.

"We are to await your decision, and escort you to Stormhaven should you wish."

Should I wish? It is the King's wish, not mine. How can I refuse an invitation written in royal gold? How can the kingsman be obliged to await my response, and so be bound upon my whim? Being a wizard was affecting the world in strange ways.

Shouts went up from the people in the street. The wardens to her right had linked arms to restrain the crowd but were losing ground toward her. Tabitha considered her answer. If she accepted the king's invitation, she would be abandoning her people to their suffering. Nobody could do what she was doing for them. But if she refused the invitation, she would be declaring her time to be more important than that of the king. She realised that as she grew in stature, so did the consequences of her decisions and the meaning people would read into everything she did. Maybe the king could advise her on how to deal with such fame. He had lived with the reins of power in his hands for years. She would go to Stormhaven.

"I shall be pleased to accept the invitation," she said to Rood. "Please allow me an hour to prepare for the journey."

Rood looked much relieved. "Certainly, your grace. The king will be most pleased to receive you in his palace tonight."

CREÐCRÐ

When Tabitha had packed for Stormhaven, someone knocked sharply on her door. A dozen of her wardens stood outside in a huddle, as if braced for something.

"Your holiness, we must warn you that everything is not as it seems!" the senior warden announced. He was a round-faced man with clear eyes and a scent of tobacco. He pulled on his short beard, and looked around at his fellows. "There's a stone in the pie and a lump in the custard, they say, and we can't ever judge men by the faces they wear."

"What are you talking about?"

"Me an' these eleven, we wish to ride with you as honour guard."

"I don't think I'll need guarding now," Tabitha replied. "The king's Swords will escort me!"

"There's still the danger, your eminence."

"Who would threaten me?" Tabitha asked. "The king? You know how foolish that sounds!"

The warden looked at his feet, and shifted about. Some of the other men glanced from time to time into the cottage behind her. She still couldn't understand why they thought she needed guarding. "The king is a kind man."

"Not the king, your eminence, not him."

Who then, she wondered. The crowds? "I am not in danger from my own people!" she said. "And I'll not be healing among the crowds in Stormhaven. The Swords shall be enough. Besides, I shall take Bastion at my side."

The warden drew himself up. "With respect, your holiness, he is the problem. We all know who he is. He hides in your protection. We came to warn you, and to insist you take a guard against the old Swordmaster."

Tabitha was stunned.

She had expected that some of the men would know Bastion was Garyll, but then they knew also what he had done to save lives after the Darkmaster's hold on his mind had been broken. Their attitude toward him was outrageous. "Don't you dare suspect him! I would choose him to protect me over anyone."

The senior warden seemed desperately embarrassed. The others looked as if they expected Garyll to burst from the depths of the cottage behind Tabitha at any moment, but there was a grim determination upon their faces. They must have talked it over before coming to Tabitha, and decided that the risk of a fight was one worth taking.

"How can you be sure his allegiance will not turn?" muttered the senior warden.

Tabitha wanted to shake the warden until some sense entered his empty head.

Garyll had endured so much. He didn't deserve suspicion and should be allowed to find peace. Strangely enough, Garyll did not emerge from within the cottage, though he'd been near enough when she had answered the door. He must be close enough to hear what was being said.

She faced the warden. "Would you have fared better in his position? There isn't a man alive who is as true as Garyll Glavenor."

"Then why does he hide, your eminence? A true man doesn't need to hide."

"He does not wish for a confrontation. He does not want another battle, with words or weapons."

"If he isn't going to confront anyone, then what use is he at your side? You have need of protection, your holiness."

She glared at him. "The day I need protection from Garyll is the day that is not worth living."

The senior warden held her eye bravely then he bowed his head. "As you wish, yor'mnence."

"My honour is my own to guard," Tabitha declared. "Go and keep the crowds at bay, if you wish to be useful. Go! All of you. Go!"

When she emerged from the cottage with Garyll to join Kingsman Rood and his escort, the crowds surged inward. A wail arose from all around. People were calling, crying, pleading, for the news that she was leaving had spread like a spark in dry leaves. Her wardens strained to hold them back, but lost ground.

"Most esteemed wizard! I have a dying son!"

"My wife suffers! Her pulse is weak—"

"I am blind! I am blind! Heal me before you go!"

Garyll kept Tabitha close, and she used his strong arm for support. They walked down to the two great horses and the pale coach. The trumpeters sounded their alarum once more, and the flanking Swords stood to stiff attention.

Tabitha paused on the running board of the coach and held up her hand. The people cheered, cried and called all together. She had hoped to address them, to tell them to abandon their devotion and to get on with their lives, but there was no chance to speak over the clamour. She gave a final wave and slipped inside.

The coach had elegant curves of light woods, oval windows, dark brown seats. Kingsman Rood and a retainer travelled with them.

"They fear you will be offered a grander life in Stormhaven, where they cannot follow," Rood said. "One man even offered me a great portion of his wealth if I would let you stay in Levin, where he can come to your hall each day."

Tabitha shook her head, and Rood looked at her in a way that told her he understood. The world was becoming strange; change was upon them all. The coach gathered speed and the crowd fell away.

"You shall be fairly treated, Sir Glavenor. You have no need to hide."

Garyll threw back his hood. His dark brows were troubled, and his strong jaw held a shadow of stubble. "Forgive my disguise, kingsman, but my name works against me these days."

"The wardens came to warn me before we left," Rood explained. "I told them we would be doubly honoured by your presence, and that they were fools to consider you a threat. I trust that my judgement shall prove correct?"

"They have bitter memories," Garyll answered. "They need a target for their anger, but the Darkmaster is dead. I remain the only focus for their blame."

Tabitha noticed how he reached for where his sword ought to be on his left hip, but checked himself almost at once.

He looked out of the window. "Maybe that is right."

Tabitha caught his hand. "If you do not forgive yourself, the people will not be able to believe you are to be trusted. You only add fuel to the rumours by doubting."

Garyll was silent for a moment, his troubled eyes dancing upon her face. "Aye, I heard them speak at our door," he said at last. "I understand that I have done little to dispel the suspicions, but I do not wish to pretend to be a hero either."

"There is no need to pretend anything!" Tabitha declared.

"Ah Tabitha, how do you emerge from every challenge with your innocence intact? I know you want to believe the best of me. I agreed to stay to protect you, and yet it is you who protects me from others who wish to take my place."

"No, Garyll, you are my strength."

"What you see and what I see are different. I suspect that I drain your strength and you do not realise it."

"No, Garyll, that is unfair."

"You change the world," he said gently. "I am glad for it, but I belong to the simpler life, the one without magic." He turned aside abruptly and gazed out of the window again, reminding Tabitha that they were speaking before strangers. She squeezed Garyll's hand, to let him know she loved him. A man like Garyll needed a purpose, something definite, like a steel blade. Maybe the king could give him that.

Despite the horses' steady pace, they were accompanied by a crowd all the way to the Kingsbridge. People who had been awaiting healing ran to keep pace with the coach as if their ailments had disappeared on the breeze of the Wizard's passage. The swiftest runners ranged ahead to claim the honour of being the last to see her escort pass.

Tabitha could offer the crowds no more attention. She turned her mind toward Stormhaven.

"Kingsman, do you know the reason for the urgency?"

"A…private matter, your grace. I don't understand questions of magic. Best for the likes of you and the king to discuss such things… ahem…best for you and the king."

ೞఙఞೞ

As silent as a snake he was, the child who watched the hunters from the darkness. His one eye struggled to follow their movements, for the image of the forest was disturbed by other images, vivid scenes of flame and fire and terrible wrath; things that came before, things that came after.

He had survived the years of starvation. He had endured those terrible first months of abandonment, once because of the stubborn attentions of a goat. She had dragged him wailing from his mother's corpse and into the depths of the forest. He had suckled the bitter milk from her hairy nipples, but had needed ever more. When he was strong enough to cling to the fur of her belly, she had wandered with him, farther west, away from the smells of the industry of Moral kingdom.

Years had passed, and he had survived unsheltered storms, and thirst, and disease, yet this hunting of him in the dark forest was the worst peril he had faced, for they knew of him now, and they would not stop seeking him out. Him, not the dear goat he had known as Nå, whom the callous children had slain in the wild orchards in Orenland. Him, not the outcast goatherd Gadd, who had protected him for five years, only to be condemned. Gadd had been set upon by the wizards until he screamed out the name the child had come to know as his own, calling to him over and over to come and save him from the pain. The child had not gone to him. He could not, for Gadd had named him three times, and each name belonged to him in a different way—Amyar, the scar-faced dissident who saw only into the past; Ethan, witnessing the present with his single dreaded eye; and Seus, the seer. Amyar, Ethan and Seus, and when they were spoken together, he heard all three, as Am-eth-eus. It was not his name, it was all of his names fighting together to be heard. Gadd had known that. Gadd had saved him by keeping him paralysed, and they had killed the good shepherd for his kindness and charity, while the child had watched.

Ametheus, the child that was too ugly to be loved, the one misshapen, the one touched by evil, the one who should be feared and who should be killed before he grew. They hunted him now, with dogs, weapons and bands of rude men. He had learnt to change, not because he wanted to but because he didn't want to die. He *stepped* backward and appeared in the place he had been before. If they reached him there, he *stepped* forward, to the place he would come to be in. They could never move as fast as he could move through his thoughts, passing himself from brother to brother.

He had learnt quickly because he had three minds to learn with and they shared their learning in that time, before they began to argue and fight for precious supremacy, and yet all learning was clouded by the rage, for the poisons and the magic inflicted upon him as a foetus had cursed him to a life of division. He was split ever more from his brothers as they developed their own desires. He was cursed to live a life of anger, of conflict—of Chaos. So he would make it his own.

The dark forest had been his home for a year; he knew every briar-choked stream, deep-boughed tree and covered tunnel. The hunters were learning of each hideaway too and they would not leave until they had found their quarry. He could not convince them to go away for he was not yet strong enough to fight. He could only hide. Ametheus watched the hunters from the darkness and wondered if he should run.

Then the hunters began to call out that terrible name, his name, and he was bonded to the present, paralysed by his own complexity. All he could do was remain still and hope they would miss him.

Subtle threads of light came off some of the men, filaments of charge which they commanded, searching with tentacles through the trees. Wizards! Ametheus shrank down among the roots of a giant oak. Feet crunched through the dry undergrowth. Someone called out. The hounds bayed in response to the excitement. Torches began to converge on the giant oak where he cowered. The dreaded men of magic gathered their power; he could see it collect about them like pools of liquid clarity.

That clarity brought tears to his eyes. He didn't want to use the ability he had been cursed with; he didn't want to touch that power. It was magic, it was what *they* used. He hated magic yet they forced him to use it. The hunters loosed their hounds; they rushed toward him in a race for his blood, paws tearing at the dirt, jagged jaws agape. A marksman aimed his lightning-rod. Three wizards raised their hands, but they had forgotten to continue chanting his name.

Ametheus focused his awareness in the brother who could see what would come to be—he became brother Seus. He reached into a time beyond that dark forest, centuries ahead, when he would have the abilities he had yet to learn. It was a shortcut to power, and in pushing his brother to reach so far into the future, he worsened the rift in his mind.

He called out a single word. The dogs whipped back as if tied to a cord. Disturbed leaves slapped down into their original places. The men retraced the steps they had already taken, moving backward in a mad rush. Sounds altered in the forest, the barking reversed into the calls and cries of the men, a sudden babble of confusion, tumbling away from him. The gathered essence that surrounded the wizards became white-hot, then ignited.

Time flowed forward again.

Flames leapt upon the wizards. The dogs ran at Ametheus, rushing toward him in a race for his blood, paws tearing at the dirt, jagged jaws agape, but the fire swept across the forest floor and caught them from behind, washing over them even as they leapt for the child, searing them with intense heat, so their bodies became ash, and only their blackened skulls fell out of the flames to land at the infant's feet.

He stepped backward, into the brother who knew of what had been before. Amyar remembered, he always remembered. He found himself a fair distance away. Somehow, the fire roared behind him, eating through old trees and undergrowth alike, so fierce it even drew the air inward to feed its hot yellow breath.

He waded into the first stream and followed its cold course away into the night. He cried, for had not wanted to burn down so much of his forest. The fire would kill the small things too—he knew that—it had happened before. Stoats and weasels, squirrels and hares, and hogs and deer, many of them would be trapped. They were the only friends he knew.

He added their deaths to the debt the wizards of Oldenworld owed him.

ଔଓଓଔଓ

Stormhaven was bustling with excitement. Trumpeters heralded their arrival from the battlements as they swept through the grand city gates. Despite the crowds in the streets welcoming the Wizard, the coach moved quickly, for ranks of bright-armoured Swords joined the procession and kept the way clear.

At Kingsman Rood's suggestion, Tabitha opened her door and waved to the people. She was met with a surge of applause and shouting. A rain of petals and grass seeds showered upon her from the high windows. Men and women threw colourful flowers over the heads of the Swords. Roses, goldenbell and even daisies soon littered the cobbles. How many poor flowerbeds had been raided for the welcome?

The coach climbed through the Merchant's Quarter, through the houses and greens of the Upper District toward the forecourt in front of the great King's Palace. The crowds followed the coach, but their applause became more restrained. Here the Darkmaster had forced the King to surrender his crown; here the Morgloth had swept down upon the defenceless people. The blood had been washed away but the stones held its memory.

The coach halted. The trumpets pealed again. Kingsman Rood stepped out then offered his hand to her. A deep blue carpet lay upon the cobbles, leading through the gold-tipped spears of the palace gates.

Garyll was right, the world had changed around her. When she had first come to Stormhaven, they had almost refused her entrance to the city.

Now the King laid a carpet out for *her*.

So many eyes watched how she walked, so many faces turned to follow her movement. Tabitha was positioned near the head of the escort. Garyll walked beside her in his long green hooded cloak. The crowds cheered and clapped, but were prevented from following beyond the perimeter of the palace grounds, where they stood with faces pressed to the grill bars, watching.

Tabitha ascended the grand stairway and passed through the arched pillars into the cool privacy of the palace beyond. A dozen nobles waited in the first reception hall, the lords with medallion-chains, the ladies with fine circlets in their hair. They rose at once from their places and joined the procession, behind her.

At last they arrived at the King's dining hall. The doors were thrown wide upon their approach. Two pageboys bowed like a mirror-image, one on either side of the doors. A gong sounded and the hammered note reverberated through the silence. They entered the hall.

"King Mellar!" Rood called proudly, "might I present—Tabitha Serannon, our Wizard of Eyri!"

Tabitha bowed. She was relieved to see that the king remained seated at the head of the long table. It would have been difficult to accept the king offering obeisance to her, and by not even standing to receive her he reinforced his authority in the hall. A large woman in a mauve dress stood at his side—Maybelle Westerbrook, the Lady of Ceremony. Maybelle smiled at Tabitha then looked quickly down at the king.

King Mellar faced Tabitha but his focus was upon the air between them. His hands were clenched into fists upon the marble tabletop. Tabitha grew alarmed. Had she offended him in some way? Kingsman Rood seemed for a moment unsure of what to do as well—he waited for the king's response, as did they all.

May slipped her hand gently onto the king's shoulder.

"Welcome, Miss Serannon," said King Mellar in a tight voice.

Then, as if his anger suddenly abandoned him, his scowl was replaced with a determined smile that made his copper beard jut out toward her. "Yes, indeed, you are welcome in my hall! Come, have a seat beside me, and let us call out your name in the first toast of the banquet. We have all waited anxiously for your arrival, especially Lord Bolingar, whose belly I am sure has long since marked the passing of noon!"

Relieved laughter spread among the nobles. Lord Bolingar was probably the large man who laughed the loudest. The king's expression was warm and welcoming. She went to the offered seat beside him and bowed again in his presence.

"Your highness, thank you for the invitation, I am most honoured by all you have done for me."

"Contrary, contrary! It is you who have done so much for us all."

"Hear-hear!" came a chorus from among the nobles. Tabitha blushed. She didn't know what to say.

"Come, my Rood, introduce all of our noble friends to the table so that they can be seated."

Kingsman Rood named all the lords and ladies present, ending with the green-cloaked figure beside Tabitha. "And Glavenor, of course." Garyll pushed his cowl back. He should have lifted his cowl at the door, to be proper. His face was unreadable. He bowed deeply.

"Glavenor, yes, it is good that you are here as well, my old Swordmaster. We must not forget Garyll Glavenor, or what he did for us."

The words echoed with tension, despite King Mellar's smile.

Tabitha told herself it was nothing. Her ears collected too much detail sometimes. Nonetheless, a knot of uncertainty formed in her stomach. Did the king distrust Garyll? Surely not. Garyll had proven his allegiance by slaying the Darkmaster and by fighting off the Morgloth, but had Garyll truly redeemed himself in Mellar's eyes?

"Let it be said that I was saddened by the need to replace you. You served us well for so many years."

"And in exchange for that service, I am grateful to have my life, your highness."

The two men maintained eye contact. Tabitha realised with a start that Garyll was making an appeal. She had never considered that he might be punished for his actions. It must have seemed a real possibility to Garyll, for him to be watching the king so intently.

"That you have, and few know how precious life really is," the king answered.

"Precious." Garyll looked aside and mumbled, "But the way we lead it can make it worthless."

The king's expression grew hard. Tabitha caught a fleeting sense of violent thoughts that turned like a phantom in the space between the two men. "You would know more about that than I!" declared King Mellar.

Garyll said nothing.

"Do not try to cast your shadows and guilt upon me! I will not have them!" Mellar hammered upon the table with a clenched fist.

Garyll threw a surprised glance at Tabitha.

"Have we all forgotten our toast?" Lady Westerbrook asked quickly, touching the king's shoulder again. "We should take our glasses, so that the banquet might begin in honour."

King Mellar tensed but then looked at May and smiled—a broad smile which lit up his face. When he turned to Tabitha, she felt welcomed, loved and reassured. Had she imagined his anger?

"Yes, the Wizard Serannon, who blesses us all with her presence. I forget myself. Draw near with the wine, my servants. I must wet my tongue to find sweeter words for the praise she deserves."

A small man offered her a tray of drinks, and Tabitha gathered a glass of what looked to be honeydew. The criss-crossed light from the high windows danced in the fluid like a golden haze of sprites.

"Our honoured Tabitha Serannon!" the king began. "She hid her talents in the quiet of Meadowmoor. If that fearsome Shadowcaster had not roused her from her humble life, to flee to us and then to fight for us, we might be living in dark times indeed." He turned his head quickly to one side. "No! We owe nothing to that Shadowcaster." He lifted his chin proudly. "Tabitha alone conquered her challenges and gathered her power. The tale of her tragedies and triumphs I shall leave to the bards, who have a more adequate language to describe such monumental events. Nonetheless, we have all witnessed the miracles she has shared with so many. We owe this woman our lives! We drink with you, to your health, Wizard Serannon."

The king lifted his glass toward her and the nobles followed his example. Tabitha had never been toasted. She suspected that they waited for her to drink and raised her glass, taking a nervous sip. The wine was sweet but delicate; the refined flavour of blossoms was present like the taste of a summer's breeze. It was infinitely better than the vintages she had served in First Light. The wine's lightness rose through her like sunshine and she relaxed as the guests sipped and smiled at her. Lord Bolingar tilted his head back and drained his entire glass.

"So, let us enjoy the meal at your side, dear wizard. Be seated, all of you. I am sure Miss Serannon has much to tell us, and we all have much to ask. Take your time, and please, be at ease."

Three harpers played gently in an alcove, following an inconspicuous melody that filtered softly through the air. Servants hurried flagons of wine to the table. Baskets of warm breads and cheeses nestled among the fruit and cream already there. A small plate was placed before Tabitha beside her silverware. A sprinkle of herbs rested upon a rich, savoury paste piled upon strips of crisp pastry. It was extraordinary—the spices punctuated the smooth textures with mouth-watering delight.

As more food arrived upon the table, the conversation began. Higgenhed, Lord of Ways, asked her about her healing work in Levin, and the other nobles nearby kept up a lively competition for her attention after that. The king continued to smile, and Maybelle Westerbrook offered friendly comments from time to time. Despite the warm atmosphere and wonderful food on array, Tabitha found it impossible to eat, for everyone wanted to talk to her. Her mother had always insisted that a woman who spoke through her food deserved to be stabled with the pigs and horses. She took the occasional nibble from her plate, but the many courses came and were whisked away from her before she could sample much of any one. She resigned herself to enjoying the wonderful scents which drifted off the table.

It was a sensual torture. Her fever and the hurried departure of the morning had left her weak and ravenous, but she couldn't let it show in front of such noble company.

The worst were the lords and ladies seated at the far end of the table, because they seemed overeager to assert their right to converse with the Wizard, as if by their placing they might be considered less worthy than their peers. They hung on Tabitha's every word then asked new questions which showed no consideration of her answers at all. She found herself making weak jests all the time; it was the easiest way to answer questions without answering them, to skim past the issue. No one seemed to care; they just wanted her to talk, or rather, to be seen to be talking with them.

At last the king clinked a knife against his glass, and Tabitha had brief respite from the attention. The king stood to make his announcement. "We pondered for a long time on how best to honour our wizard, for I know that with her gracious nature she takes little pleasure from lavish awards. Those of you who have tried to bestow great gifts upon her at her healing hall in Levin might know how soon those gifts were converted to items for charity." This raised a few knowing chuckles. "But she has served us all by deeds too great and selfless to ignore, and for that service to Eyri I would award her something fair."

Tabitha considered her plate as her mind churned. An award? She didn't need an award for anything. She wished only to be able to pop one of the steaming gravy-soaked potatoes into her mouth.

"No person has ever fought so hard against a threat to Eyri's peace. No one has ever dedicated so much to bring healing and hope to our land as Tabitha Serannon."

The nobles applauded loudly.

Tabitha had fought for her own life; she had healed the people because it was her responsibility. She had been showered with gifts already—she didn't need any further awards. But she couldn't refuse the king's decree. He was looking directly at her, and Maybelle Westerbrook stood beside the king, holding something which glinted in her hands.

"Tabitha Serannon! I hereby pronounce you Lady Tabitha, and award you a life retainer, and the title to your ancestral farm of Phantom Acres. The lands have been repurchased from Lord Winterborn. They belong to you now."

Tabitha felt suddenly heavy in her chair. She couldn't have heard him correctly. She had been made a Lady? A noble? Was that allowed? The air felt thin, as if everyone had drawn breath at once and not left enough over for her to breathe. They waited for her.

"Come forward, Lady Tabitha, and receive your new title."

Garyll squeezed her hand under the table then pushed her away. She stood on unsteady legs. The nobles all thundered with applause, some clanking the bases of silver goblets upon the table as well, adding to the joyous clamour. She was only a few steps away from the king, but those steps seemed to take forever. The king offered her his best bristly smile, but suddenly some anger boiled in his eyes. Tabitha couldn't understand him. He seemed so changeable, so full of conflicting moods. She couldn't think why he would be cross with her. He said something but she couldn't distinguish the words from the applause, so she curtsied hurriedly, whereupon he jerked his head, stepped closer and said, "I owe you more," in a voice that would not have been heard by anyone else.

King Mellar glared at her over his smile, and she began to kneel, thinking she had not offered adequate respect, but he exclaimed "No!" and caught her hands, guiding her up. She had misread him again. Maybe the anger wasn't meant for her, after all. Maybe it was anger at himself, for something she had no part of. He turned her to face the Lady of Ceremony.

Maybelle held up a delicate tiara, a beautiful work of intricate silverwork with suspended indigo stones. "You were always a lady, Tabitha. This merely announces it to all." She lowered the symbolic circlet of nobility over Tabitha's head. The tiara pressed so lightly upon her hair, it seemed to weigh nothing at all.

King Mellar handed her two gilded scroll-cases: the retainer and the title deeds to her land. Her land! Her parents had been tenants on Phantom Acres all of their lives. She owned a piece of Eyri.

"So you will always have something to return to," explained King Mellar.

"Thank you," she said, but Mellar waved her thanks aside.

"This is our moment to thank you!" he announced loudly. "Lords and ladies, we now welcome among our ranks our wizard of Eyri, Lady Serannon!"

She looked down the length of the table, and they greeted her with continued applause. The lords and ladies seemed pleased with themselves, as if they had acquired a great prize. Not knowing quite what to do, Tabitha returned to her place beside Garyll. His expression was worth more than a hundred noble titles, his eyes holding a spark she had not seen in weeks. If only for that moment, he was happy, and immensely proud. He grinned foolishly and hugged her to his chest. She thought her heart would burst.

Lady Westerbrook was the first to speak into the silence of the fading applause. "You may have escaped your speech, but would you honour us with a song instead, Lady Serannon?" The request brought an instant hush through the dining hall.

Tabitha grew cold. The Lifesong...they wanted the Lifesong. The joy of receiving royal favour suddenly became an empty thing, a folly of words and titles that meant nothing. The vision she had tried to ignore all day rushed at her and her heart ached. She was dragged down and down, into that pit where the Goddess was chained, into the agony of Ethea's condition. Tabitha's present fame and fortune was founded upon the Lifesong, she was the Wizard only because she had been able to tune her voice to Ethea's call. Now, with the Goddess in such a plight, with the source of her power failing, she had no heart to sing. She had no right to receive these honours, when the Goddess Ethea was the real source of her inspiration, and Ethea was suffering! Oh how she had cried out when the bird had been slain!

Tabitha caught onto Garyll's shirt as the sudden weakness threatened to suck her under.

Maybelle was distraught. "Forgive me, Lady Tabitha, I was not thinking! You must be very tired from your work in Levin. Forget I asked. We should give you a rest from your troubles, a respite from all the terrible burdens you have borne. Oh forgive me, my dear Tabitha, I thought it might be a happy thing for you to do—"

Tabitha pulled herself back from the edge of despair. She didn't want to alarm the gentle Lady of Ceremony. May was such a caring soul. She didn't know of the world Tabitha had seen, she didn't know of the cries that echoed in Tabitha's ears, the place of heat and sweat, where buildings grew upon buildings, up into the air. Tabitha vowed she would ask Maybelle if she knew of such a place, but only when they were alone, so her tears wouldn't matter.

"It's all right, May, really, it's all right. I am just very tired, but if you would like to give me a gift tonight, let it be that I don't have to sing. I need peace, more than anything."

"Of course, let us speak no more of it now! Servants! Bring the sweets, and let us find the good taste of the meal again." The harpers began a lively jig without needing to be prompted, and the nobles took to their seats with casual, friendly glances her way. Tabitha sank gratefully into her seat. She felt quivery in her bones. A bowl of sumptuous delights was placed before her, and she sank her spoon into the treacle-smothered cake before she could be stopped. If her mouth was always full, she decided, they'd have to wait until she was finished her dessert before asking questions. She closed her lips upon the spoon, and the sweet indulgence drowned her senses.

"Peace! Peace never lasts! Those days are gone!" she heard King Mellar say, but he did not expand on his bitter words. He merely gripped his glass and looked into the depths of his red wine. The nobles looked as disturbed by his pronouncement as Tabitha felt, but after a pause they resumed their eating and conversations, none being bold enough to challenge the king in his present mood. Tabitha took a few more spoonfuls before risking a glance King Mellar's way. In that moment he looked suddenly poorly, like an old man who was dismayed by his own mean reflection. Why wasn't he wearing his crown? Something troubled the king deeply, but who could guess what it was?

She decided to wait. The king had summoned her to an audience as well as to the banquet. He would speak his mind when he was ready, no doubt. She signalled to the serving-man for more dessert. It would do no harm to be fortified with sweetness when the time came to meet the king in private.

9. A SHADE OF ANGER

*"It is a delicate dance of deception
to fight your own shadow."*—Zarost

Kirjath Arkell drove the king's attention down into the blood-coloured wine. It was much like trying to stuff a man's head into a rain-barrel—you could get him to the barrel easily enough, but to get his head all the way down took a long time. If only he could get the king to drink some more.

Drink! Drown your misery, you worthless shred of a man. Raise your bloody hand!

But the king sat motionless in his chair.

He had had a grip on Mellar that first night when he was soggy with rum, but when the king had sobered he had become tough again and Kirjath had been driven to the back of his mind. Curse him! Kirjath had found other ways to move through the king's thoughts. There was a mind beneath the Mind, a realm of desires and forces over which Mellar had no control. When Kirjath concentrated his anger in one area, he could aggravate the hidden mind until those deep things erupted through the higher levels of thought. So he had clawed back brief moments of power for himself, but it was not enough! For the most part, the king was still too determined to rule, too lucid, and Kirjath was like the fluid in the glass: the king held him in his clutch, confined, contained.

He watched the king's reflected face. It rocked hypnotically in the dark surface. Thin, fat, thin, fat again.

Curséd miserable meddling king! Of all the men to be trapped inside! I should kill this man, and yet he is my life.

What made Kirjath's rage worse was that he had known it would begin like this. A Morgloth began in the strict vessel of the demonlord's command. He had known of the trap, yet he could do nothing to avoid it. Now he understood the fury that drove the Morgloth. He felt the same wrath at being denied freedom. He wanted to dominate the body he was in.

Ever since he had entered Mellar's body, he had suffered from a hollow dread. He was in a body, but it wasn't *him*, he couldn't *feel* any of it. He was only *aware*, that was all, he had neither the shroud of essence nor the body which had absorbed the essence—he was merely *there*. He'd used Orangecap mushrooms when he was young—those acidic visions that stole your identity away for a terrifying few days. The deprivation of being in Mellar was many times worse. Everything was ruled by a persistent panic that he would come to nothing. Just a sudden impulse from Mellar, and he would be gone, dispersed forever. Ended.

No, that would not be! He would not fail! He would possess the king entirely. He would taste the fine foods the king chewed on, he would speak his own thoughts to the nobles and he would command them all to his own will. He would feel the weight in his arms and the pressure in his own head. Strange, he realised, the things he wanted most were such ordinary things he had never even noticed that he had possessed them, in life. He would feel his own breath filling his chest. Yes, he would breathe, then he would know that he was alive. He writhed within the king's skull like bad blood held in a wound, but he would get out. He would seep into every vein.

Old king, I'm going to tear you up inside like a butchered lamb. You cannot refuse me. Drink the wine!

The king was weakening. The glass shook in his hand. He squeezed harder and harder, and with a sudden crunch, the glass shattered in his fist.

Kirjath felt the jagged cut. He felt it! The blood flowed quickly from his fist, amid the shards and wine. He rushed up through the king's thoughts, borne upon the eruption of pain.

The king was looking straight at the girl-wizard now. No! He would not have her interfering. He would not let the king ask for her healing. The little bitch! He should have defiled her when he'd had the chance. She wouldn't be so high and noble now. She would know her place and not pretend to be a lady. The people worshipped her, even the nobles, just because the strumpet could sing.

Kirjath watched her face, through Mellar's eyes. Her cheeks were pale, but her skin was healthy, young and unblemished. Her nose was delicate, her big brown eyes were flecked with gold—so innocent, so sweet. Kirjath grinned.

She jumped to her feet, her hands to her mouth.

Kirjath-and-the-King stood, his chair scraping backward. He opened his fist, and threw the remaining shards down with his blood upon the table.

"Meet me in my high chambers when you are done pleasing yourself," he said. "We have dire things to discuss."

ᚲ℘℘ᚲ℘℘

Kingsman Rood led them up and up, toward the king's high chamber.

Tabitha was glad Garyll was with her. The look the king had given her before departing had terrified her. He had seemed possessed by such deep rage. Garyll had noticed it too. He walked quickly, with his hands free, scanning everything around him. Tabitha recognised his martial awareness. His hand strayed to the sword that wasn't there.

The stairway was narrow, the roof low. They passed a few deep window-slits, where the gloom was punctured with thin rays of cold afternoon light. As they rose, the roof seemed to get closer, until they were right up underneath the heavy stonewood. The walls were bare, except for an old mounted battleaxe they passed on the third landing. The limp pennant upon its shaft showed signs of losing its blue-and-gold threads to the moths.

When at last they reached the squat, studded door at the head of the final flight of stairs, Rood knocked and ushered Tabitha and Garyll in.

They bowed at the threshold. The room was simply furnished with a reading table, chairs, some bookshelves and a few great tapestries. A rank of gold-rimmed windows looked down over the city of Stormhaven and allowed the sunlight to filter in. Stacked clouds balanced upon the peaks of the eastern horizon.

King Mellar sat in a window chair, looking outward.

They stood silently, not daring to say a word lest the king was still in his foul mood.

A white dove fluttered past the window then glided, angel-winged, away over the city. All was quiet.

"So peaceful it seems," said the king. "From up here, you never would suspect how fragile the web of Order is." He rose and turned toward them. His gaze was hooded and intense, but his face was calm. He had a clumsy wrapping of linen upon his right hand.

"See? I have bandaged the wound myself, I have stemmed the bleeding. I am in no danger."

He approached. "At last, I have you to myself. Pardon the need for all those stairs, but this is the one chamber I can be sure has no place for spies—no sounds can carry through these thick walls. I can take no chances at all." He suddenly bowed low before Tabitha. "Most noble wizard, you grace all of Stormhaven with your wondrous presence!" He took her hand and kissed it. Tabitha felt a rush of blood to her head. He shouldn't be so reverential before her. He was the king!

"Th thank you, your highness, I enjoyed the banquet."

King Mellar smiled. "Did you enjoy travelling in the royal coach, your holiness?"

"Please, my king, please don't use such titles. I am not holy, or wondrous, or magnificent."

"And you never think of how it is to be called King? Magnificence! I'd not thought of that one! But you surely are! You destroyed the Morgloth. You turned the Darkmaster's tide! You cannot deny that you have changed everything. Your disappearance and reappearance are now matters of legend. We must acknowledge that your power is prodigal, oh divine wizard."

"Please, your highness, I feel so wrong when your words elevate me. You are my king."

"Does that make *me* highness? The people of Eyri need a figurehead to place their dreams upon. Glavenor here didn't hold a steady sword, but you! You fought the challengers, you broke the dark spell. You triumphed! If I elevate you, the people are made proud, they follow my lead, and we have a kingdom at peace."

Tabitha had never thought of it that way.

"I did my best to correct my mistakes," Garyll said gruffly.

The king looked hard at Garyll. "You left Stormhaven before I could speak to you." Mellar held up his bandaged hand to forestall any explanations. "I know—you were reeling from the battle. Those who bear the Darkstones have revealed what it was like to feel the horror at awakening to their own deeds. I know a taste of the spell that plagued you. I understand. The Darkmaster was the foe, not you, but you were wise to leave your sword in Stormhaven. A broken oath cannot be mended."

That was too unfair to be left unanswered. "Without Garyll we would not have triumphed!" Tabitha objected. "The Morgloth would have taken me."

"True, true, and so he proved his worth to you, but a king needs a Swordmaster who stands at his own side against all threats to the crown."

"You said yourself that the Darkmaster was the foe, not Garyll. He should be pardoned!"

"No, my love," Garyll interrupted. "Our king is right. I know he can never forget what might have been. You know what could have happened if you hadn't laid your own sweet neck in the way of my blade. You saved both our lives in that moment, so I expect no pardon. I can give none myself, that is why I set my sword and title aside. You, however, are deserving of all the praise heaped upon you."

"But I'm just Tabitha, underneath the titles. I'm just me!"

"And what did you think I felt when I was first called highness?" the king asked. "I am just a man, under all these robes, Borace Montgomery Mellar. It is just the same. You cannot deny that you have power now, Lady Serannon. You must learn to wear it."

It still seemed unfair to her, that Garyll was scorned as she was praised. They were two parts of the union which had saved Eyri, but she could not argue with the king. She had already defied him far beyond her station. "Your *highness*, there is surely more to our being here than the conferring of titles."

King Mellar nodded before motioning them toward seats beside the window. "Indeed," he said. "Indeed."

Before sitting, he glanced to the door where Rood stood. "Kingsman."

"On my way, highness," the statesman said. He slipped out of the door and closed it gently. This was a very private matter, Tabitha realised. Rood had seemed a very trustworthy man to her. Mellar looked from Tabitha to Garyll, then back again. He seemed uncertain of how to begin, or maybe he was considering whether he was going to extend his trust to Garyll. Tabitha firmed her resolve to demand that he remain. The king probably guessed she would confide in Garyll anyway, so there would be no point in excluding him. Mellar edged closer on his chair. "I need your help." He clenched his bandaged fist, but didn't wince at the pain it must have caused him. "My crown has been stolen."

The room was perfectly still. Tabitha immediately looked to where the crown should have rested. The king's copper hair kinked outward from his temples, so accustomed had it been to the pressure of the metal rim upon it. The shine had gone from his hair. It was dull, and lifeless.

"When was it stolen, my lord?" Garyll asked.

"During the battle on the forecourt, when the Morgloth came. I only had a moment to think about it then. I saw the boy but did not realise I was looking at a thief. Then we were all running."

"Who stole it?"

"Oh, he stood among the scattering crowd with my crown as if he was waking from his nightmare, as if he was considering how shameful his behaviour had been. Oh my Bevn, my son! I was so wrong. Bevn has not returned. He has gone. He tempts forces he does not understand. He casts a bitter fate upon his father."

"The Sword should be alerted, they should search for him in force," Garyll declared.

"I have despatched a few teams, but they've not found hide nor hair of him. I fear he has learnt some of the Shadowcasters' tricks. I cannot send too many Swords on such a mission. Word will get out that the crown has been lost. I cannot afford that, not now." His suddenly hard eyes bored into Tabitha then Garyll. "I demand absolute secrecy in this matter!"

"Do you intend to let him go?" Garyll demanded.

"Do you?" King Mellar replied. The challenge was plain. "You sought my pardon, Glavenor. Here is your chance to prove your honesty and your worth. Find the Kingsrim, bring it to me, and you shall receive your royal pardon, in public."

"And what would you have me do?" Tabitha asked.

"Lady Tabitha, with your skills you might find a clue where others have found nothing. I cannot leave Stormhaven, but I can supply you with whatever you need to accomplish the task. The Kingsrim must be retrieved."

"Can't it—can't it be replicated?" Tabitha asked. "Couldn't a jeweller forge one anew?"

"No!" The king gripped the arms of his chair. "No. There is more to the Kingsrim than just the metal. It must be retrieved, and soon! A month from now will be too late! It must come back upon my head. The peace of the whole kingdom is at stake."

"But why, your highness? You remain the king, regardless of where your crown has been secreted away. Surely the peace of the kingdom continues with your governance? Prince Bevn cannot succeed you until he is much older, when you retire. Eventually he must come out from hiding and lose what he has stolen."

King Mellar gave her a haunted look. "I have no time to wait. Oh, I suppose you should know all of it. The Kingsrim has old magic, from the time of the Gyre of Wizards, from the time of the Forming. It is this same magic which keeps the order of Eyri together. Without it, so much will be lost. The Kingsrim is the axis upon which the wheel of Eyri's order turns. It must be upon my head, upon this Isle, or the wheel shall fall off its axle. The pressure of disorder is too great. Do you know how much work is required to keep Order intact, to keep the rules in place? There are so many details to pay attention to, so many fine disputes which must be continually resolved to keep control. I must keep all of it in mind, every day. If I ignore any detail, it only becomes worse upon the next day, more urgent, then worse, and more urgent still. I must have the Kingsrim back."

The king turned aside to stare out of the windows. People scurried through the streets far below, like ants before the rain, each with their own task. From here, he directed their endeavours, she realised, not just Stormhaven's people, but all through Eyri. He guided their behaviour with the administering of justice. He discouraged certain endeavours with laws or taxes, encouraged others with trade agreements, stimulated activity with building roads, bridges and waterways through the farmlands, collected surplus grain in good harvests and distributed food in times of hardship. He ensured that funding went to the healers and scribes and all the many learned folk who worked in the Houses of Rule around the forecourt, every one of whom were vital to maintain the systems of Eyrian public service. It all came through Stormhaven in the end. Every thread was held tightly in his fist.

"I shall lose my grip. I shall lose my grip on it all," he whispered to the windows.

Suddenly Tabitha understood. The Kingsrim was something like the ring she wore, the Wizard's Ring. It was magically fortified. It allowed the bearer to rule the realm with clarity. Her ring, however, could be removed if she wished. She had developed her talent sufficiently and did not need the catalyst anymore.

"Can you truly not do without it?" she asked gently.

"No. No!" He hid his face in his hands. "Without it, I lose my strength as king. I begin—"

Just then there was a loud knocking. King Mellar jerked around to glare at the door. "What!" he shouted. "We are in private audience, Kingsman!"

"Sire, I am not Rood. I am your Swordmaster!"

Mellar stiffened. "Do you have news, Vance? Come in if you have news! Come in at once!"

The door swung inward and a lean-faced soldier entered. He seemed surprised at first to see Garyll and Tabitha in the chamber, but that expression was soon replaced with a hungry smile as he approached. Tabitha wondered if moustaches always made men look slightly mean, or if it was just an unfortunate consequence of this man's weedy growth. Although his light armour was burnished and his boots polished to a shine, he wasn't completely neat. He saluted the king with his right fist brought hard against his breastplate.

"Your highness, do you wish me to deliver my report now?" He had earned a recent scar upon his cheek, a deep slash which had left a seam of hard pink skin from eye to chin. He was deliberately ignoring them, waiting for the king to decide if they were to be privy to his news.

"Yes, Swordmaster Vance, the Lady Serannon and Fullerman Glavenor are a part of this matter now. Speak freely. Have you found him?"

The King had used the title of fullerman for Garyll—that of a retired soldier—as would be used upon any Sword, even the lowest ranked guard who ended his service. She supposed there wasn't a special title for a retired Swordmaster. They didn't retire. Mostly they died, in the Fifth Challenge, upon the sword of their successor.

"The prince was sighted at Penitent's pass!" Vance declared.

"And so, Swordmaster? Have they been caught? Have you the crown?"

Vance's moustache twitched nervously. "No, sire, the wretches on that Llury patrol failed their duty. A mere boy, and they let him get away! They say they couldn't follow, that a great force pressed down upon them in that pass. They admit to terrible weaknesses, your highness, of falling upon their knees and coughing up blood. One claims to have burst his eardrums. I don't believe a word of it. I think the men were trying to cover their failure. Some old enemies lurk about. Not all the Shadowcasters have been accounted for. The prince travels with a woman we think was known as Gabrielle, and I believe that's what happened. She threw her magic upon the Swords, and they were overcome. I shall marshal a force of city Swords, strong Swords, and take them over the pass. They can't have gone far from there, and we have men stationed throughout the upper forests, waiting for them to come back down."

"It is the Shield, your highness," Garyll interjected. "I have been up there, above Llury, to the cairn of the fallen. No one can climb beyond the cairn without taking on pain. There is nowhere for Prince Bevn to go. No one can endure the torture for long."

"Pah!" exclaimed Vance.

"You've never been up to the Shield, have you?"

"The Shield is a myth! There is nothing but high peaks and hunger up there. We will drive Prince Bevn out."

"Was he wearing the crown?" King Mellar demanded suddenly. "Was he wearing the crown!"

Vance looked confused. "I don't know, I suppose, yes, they said the boy had the crown with him, so they must have seen it …"

The blood drained from King Mellar's face. "He's gone beyond the Shield. Oh, ancestors forgive me, he's gone outside!" he whispered.

"Beyond—beyond Eyri, your highness?" Tabitha asked. Her heartbeat quickened. "Is such a thing possible?"

"Oh fire and chaos and death upon us all! Oh, we are done for."

"My lord?" Garyll asked.

The King rose and went to the farthest window, where he turned his back to them and stared at the northern horizon. Past his sagging shoulders Tabitha could see the distant twinkling mists of River's End, and the gentle peaks to its west through which the braided afternoon shadows crept. Where the grey rock thrust through the upper reaches of the forest, somewhere around Llury, Prince Bevn had gone over the mountains.

Tabitha couldn't contain herself. "Could there be a way through the mountains?" Her ring was burning on her finger. Visions of strange lands flooded her mind, places inhabited by the fierce warriors of the legends of the Forming. "Your highness, what is there beyond the edge of Eyri?"

The king wouldn't answer her. He clutched at the window frame with shaking hands.

"What does it matter?" asked Vance. "We know where the prince has gone, and I shall see him found. The Sword shall ride in the morning."

Garyll rose abruptly, to face Vance. "The Shield is real, man! The men shall be taken down."

"Who are you to question me, fullerman?" Vance made a face like a growling dog. "I am the Swordmaster now."

Tabitha slipped out of her chair, to get out from between the men. The air between them crackled with tension.

"How were you chosen for your position, Vance?" Garyll asked, his words soft but deliberate.

Vance's eyes glinted coldly. "I bested my opponents in each of the challenges."

"You did not face the Fifth," Garyll stated flatly.

"Fullerman, you were absent, and unfit to challenge my claim! The men agreed that there was no need for the Fifth, for the man who had been the Swordmaster was already dead."

Felltang, the deadly Swordmaster's blade, glistened at Vance's side, strangely unsheathed on its baldric. Garyll's eyes lingered on the naked steel. "Someone should have held it against you."

"Who are you to judge! I am the law and the justice now. I will not be bound by every petty tradition. We need to do things differently if we are to avoid the failures of the past."

Tabitha went quickly to King Mellar and tugged on his shoulder, but he continued to ignore them all.

"You must uphold tradition," Garyll challenged Vance. "You are not above the law."

"Oh, and yet you think of yourself differently? You live in sin, don't you? Living with an unmarried woman, in her house."

A burst of heat came from Garyll, and Tabitha tensed.

"Follow that course of insults and I shall crack your skull!" Garyll shouted.

Vance seemed to take the threat too easily. There was still a hint of the lingering laughter in his voice. "You know, you really shouldn't try to threaten me. I am the Swordmaster. I can put you in the dungeons for weeks if I wish. And if you touch me, you shall be in greater trouble than you can wheedle your way out of. I don't care what happened during your time. Justice will be served under my hand."

"Vance," Garyll warned. "Enough. My lord king, can this matter be ended?"

King Mellar was shaking, but he wouldn't turn to face the room. He seemed to be crying.

"Leave the king alone!" demanded Vance. "He is troubled. He doesn't hear us now. I have seen his fits before!"

"Then go about your business, Vance, and we shall go about ours," Garyll said.

"You will address me by my title!" Vance shouted. "You will acknowledge my command, Darksword!"

"It is over!" Garyll quivered. "Don't you ever call me that again!"

"And you will address me as Swordmaster, or I'll arrest you, right now!" Vance roared.

Garyll said nothing. The pulse in his temples counted out the seconds.

Vance drew Felltang swiftly, but not so well that Garyll could not have blocked his advance.

Garyll staggered against the window as Vance's blade touched his throat. "My lord, command your soldier, this is madness!" he called out, but the king still did not intervene. He had slid down against the wall, and he was staring blankly at the floor, mouthing words she couldn't hear. What had happened to him?

"Taste the edge of your old sword!" Vance shouted. "Am I the Swordmaster? Say it!"

Tabitha hesitated before reaching for her power, frightened by what she might have to do. She could not believe what was happening. *He brandishes that blade as if it is a toy!* Felltang was deadly, as sharp as a razor along its entire length. It should not be drawn unless it was meant to kill.

"You are not going anywhere except the dungeons," Vance threatened Garyll. He whispered in Garyll's face, but he underestimated her hearing. "Please, try to fight me, give me the excuse to end you, you forked-tongue traitor!" Then he raised his voice as he pulled his head back. "I would have beaten you in the test, spilled your blood in the Swordhouse, but you slight me by questioning my triumph in the Fifth Challenge, as if I am not worthy! I bled on the Kingsbridge because of your treachery, you bastard! Men half your age died there. You don't deserve life for your failures. You deserve no pardon at all!"

"Your duty is to exercise the king's justice, not to seek your own revenge," Garyll declared. "My lord, this should not be!"

"Don't you talk to me of duty!" Vance screamed in his face. "You swore to protect Eyri against peril, but you brought it upon us all!"

To protect me. How many times must we repeat this challenge? Oh, why doesn't anybody see what I see?

"On your knees, traitor," Vance ordered. "I want to hear your dark heart beg for mercy from me!"

It was horrible to see Garyll so degraded. He seemed determined not to fight, but Vance didn't care.

"Stop it, stop it. Stop!" she cried. She reached for Vance's arm, to pull the sword away from Garyll's throat.

Vance swapped his grip on Felltang and pushed her away, a sudden shove which caught her in the chest. She would have kept her balance had it not been for the chair behind her. Her knees were knocked to one side, and in her weakness from the fever she tumbled onto the floor. The impact made her nauseous. She couldn't get up for a moment.

A chair splintered. A sword whined through the air. Someone fell to the ground; there was the clang of metal upon metal, then three solid thumps in rapid succession. A sword clattered on the stone. She sat up to find Garyll standing upon Felltang and Vance clutching his arm to his chest, his face blood red with frustration. Garyll could have picked up the deadly blade, but he didn't, he just stood there, poised, ready. His left sleeve hung in tatters, but she couldn't see any blood. Yet.

"What is going on?" the king demanded, suddenly at her side.

"He attacked me!" Vance cried out. "He insulted me and attacked me!"

"Don't ever touch the Lady Serannon," Garyll said.

"Glavenor, give him back his sword!" the king exclaimed. Tabitha noticed how much his visage had changed. No longer was he staring defeated into the middle distance. That terrible anger of before had returned, his face seemed stretched, his lips curled into something between a snarl and a sneer.

Garyll considered the advancing king for a moment then kicked Felltang across the floor. "As you wish, my lord."

In his hurry to pick up the blade, Vance dropped it again, cursed then lifted it from the floor. He didn't look at Glavenor or the king, but his gaze dragged over Tabitha like a ragged comb. His ears looked as if they were burning they were so red. Then he dashed out of the chamber and thundered down the stairs.

"What did you do?" King Mellar demanded.

"He is not fit for his position, your highness."

"In your opinion! In *your* opinion! You are in no position to judge him, none at all. You will go and apologise to Vance."

Garyll was visibly shocked. He raised his hand then dropped it at his side again. "I will let him cool for a while, your highness. He is—"

"You will go now!" the king roared. "I will not have you defying my new Swordmaster!"

"My lord, did you not hear—"

"Go now! Go now! Go now! I do not care the reason. I care that you know I am your king, and that you follow my command! Begone!"

Did the king support Vance's arguments? Surely not!

Garyll looked at Tabitha. He didn't want to leave her alone.

"Are you all right? I shall stay if you need me."

"The wizard's wishes do not supersede mine! I am the king! This is my chamber! Do you defy me as well, Glavenor? Begone! I do not wish to see your face. I shall have counsel with the wizard in private!"

Garyll walked reluctantly to the door. There was nothing else he could do. The king had given him a direct order and he couldn't refuse. He didn't turn to bow as he left, as he should have. He merely strode out.

"And don't lurk on the stairs, either!" King Mellar shouted after him. "Find Swordmaster Vance and apologise." Garyll's heavy tread as he descended the stairs sounded like the slow beating of an ominous drum.

The king crossed the room and closed the door himself.

Tabitha was scared but she didn't know what to do. She rose shakily and found a chair. She pretended to take an interest in the outline of the Zunskar mountains, but all she could see were jagged teeth. Her heartbeat pounded in her ears.

"Nice up here, isn't it?" the king said from close behind her. He rested his left hand on her shoulder. His fingers were quite chill.

"Your highness, is something wrong?"

"You pretend to be so innocent, but you know how the world works, don't you, pretty?"

She kept her eyes upon the horizon. "How so, your highness?" she asked slowly.

"The king has a weakness. The king has needs. The king must be served."

She went cold. Was he suggesting what she suspected?

He spoke over her head. "With the power you wield, you challenge my authority. I cannot have that. I must see that you are willing, willing to submit to my authority. Because of who you are, you must be made to be more of an example, not less. Yes?"

What was wrong with him?

"Your highness, I am only healing people. I don't challenge you."

"Maybe I don't want healing, any kind of healing!" he declared, bringing his cheek down beside hers, so that the corner of his beard scratched her face.

"I can—" she began then thought better of suggesting that she could help him. She wasn't sure if she *could* use the Lifesong. She couldn't look up to him; she couldn't look into those angry eyes. How could she distract him? How could she redirect the thrust of the conversation?

"You do want me to find the crown?" she asked.

"No! I don't care! It will come too late to make any difference."

"But you said—"

"I don't care what you thought I said! It is useless to fight the ruin now. The end will come upon us all. It will come! And I shall have my fun. Yes, I shall not die without my pleasures! Why of course!"

Suddenly he left her chair and strode across the room.

Tabitha let out a shaky breath, half turning, to watch him. If he left the room she was going to make a run for it. He seemed terribly unstable. Was this the effect of the missing crown? Was it so bad already?

King Mellar opened the door, where he called out in a strong voice, "Kingsman!"

A distant reply came from within the bowels of the stairways.

"Come up!" ordered the king. When Rood appeared, he was short of breath.

"Yes, my lord?"

"Jurrum! The purple leaf. Get me some jurrum!" Mellar boomed.

"Ahm… jurrum, sire? What is it for?"

"I am the king! If I want jurrum, I shall have jurrum! It calms distress and eases headaches, of which I have both in too great a measure. Go! Find it! I know there are places in this city where it passes hands."

Kingsman Rood gave Tabitha a horrified look then looked back to the king. He bowed low, but lingered in the doorway. King Mellar slammed the door in his face. He returned to Tabitha with a resolute gaze. "So, my pretty little singer, do you wish to please your King?"

Tabitha jumped to her feet and began to sidle away. "Your highness, I am weak and tired. Might I come to another audience tomorrow? Maybe after sleeping I could devise a way to find the crown quickly enough to make a difference." She was grabbing at straws.

His gaze was unmoving, not resolute. He watched her and never stopped watching her. "It is too late. The prophecy foretold this, and the coming doom! There is no escape from our fate!"

Tabitha tried to angle towards the door, but King Mellar blocked her path with widespread hands. The blood had soaked through the linen on his right hand. Slow drops splashed upon the pale carpet.

"What prophecy, m-my lord? What fate?" She had to keep him talking, keep his mind active.

"The fat-arsed historian knows! Ask her, not me!"

"You mean M-may?" She put her hands to her mouth. How could he call her that? Her back met with the corner pillar beside the last window. Mellar approached her with that leeching gaze. "Yes! You shall sing for me, and you shall stay in this chamber, and keep the body I use alive forever. Yes! That shall be our secret, our sweet little secret. You shall sing to me!"

He reached for her.

"King Mellar, no! You are not yourself!" She windmilled her hands to fend him off. "Think of Eyri's future! Think of the people!"

He laughed. "Eyri does not matter to me any more! Only I matter."

Behind him, the door burst open. Maybelle Westerbrook entered, followed by Garyll Glavenor, and Rood.

"Borace!" Maybelle cried out. "My love, resist their call, be strong, be strong!"

For a moment King Mellar paused, uncertain. A terrible anguish pulled at his face, as if rage and horror chased each other for control of his features. Tabitha thought he was going to strike Maybelle when she reached for him, but he just quivered where he stood.

"My love, listen to my voice. Remember me." Maybelle came between them, trapping Tabitha against the wall and shielding her from the king. Maybelle held Mellar's head between her palms and brought her face close to his, as if by staring into his eyes she would see inside his mind. "Come back to me, my love, come back."

"Leave me alone!" Mellar shouted. "It is better this way!"

"My love, remember yourself. You are king. You are my Borace."

King Mellar groaned heavily, and pulled Lady Westerbrook close.

"I am here, my love," he whispered. He looked at Tabitha over May's shoulder with a dazed and sickly expression. "You are in great danger, Lady Serannon. Do not come near me. Do not return to me without the crown."

He pushed himself away from Maybelle's embrace. "Take me out of here, Glavenor, take me from these women. Take me where I can do no harm. Rood, be at my side as well, do not let me fight." He staggered away a few paces and Garyll caught him firmly around the waist. Rood took his bloodied hand carefully, and they led him from the chamber.

He tried to shake Rood's hand off at the door, but then he cried out, "Begone, ancestors! I will not hear your dead voices. No! I shall not be mad! No, no, no!" They stumbled out, and down the stairs. "Find the crown, my wizard! Find the crown! Find the crown!" Mellar's voice echoed as he was led away.

Then they were gone.

10. THE WRY PROPHET

"When you solve a riddle, do you find the riddler,
Or does the riddler find you?"—Zarost

May was rosy-cheeked from climbing the stairs. She said nothing,
she just smothered Tabitha in a warm embrace. Tabitha sagged against
the Lady of Ceremony and breathed in her soft sweet perfume.

"He wasn't himself, May. He was so angry, and so...strange."

May held her until Tabitha was steady on her feet.

"He has told you of the crown?" May asked.

"Yes."

"Its absence affects him worse than he'll admit. He isn't well,
Tabitha. He's been suffering. He sees the strong walls of his own mind
crumbling. I think he's mostly scared, the poor man, but he hides that
with the anger. Oh, it's a cruel thing that is happening to him. I don't
think Prince Bevn realises what he is doing to his father."

Tabitha looked away from May, resting her eyes upon the stairwell's
empty mouth beyond the open door. "It was more than anger. For a
while he seemed like another man altogether."

"I know what you mean," May said. "He spoke to me of the faces
he can see, his dead forefathers. They all went mad, did you know
that? Every one of them. It is the cost of wearing the Kingsrim. I
hadn't realised it until he told me, and then I looked carefully through
the histories. The royals always tried to conceal the painful truth from
the people, but there are accounts if you know what to look for." Her
voice softened. "He had a seizure last night, in his bedroom. Since
then it's been worse than ever. This is the first time he's lost command
of his mind during the day. Maybe it was the wine during the banquet.
I don't know. Rood says he was calling for jurrum. Jurrum!" May's
eyebrows peaked in alarm.

"Thank you for coming, May," Tabitha said softly.

"Thank your good man Glavenor for coming to warn me. I assumed
he would be by your side. When he told me he'd been banished from
the audience, I knew—" May faltered. "Oh, Tabitha! I must know. Do
you think you can heal him?"

Tabitha tried to fight off the rising panic that question brought with it. Healing meant singing, singing meant the Lifesong, and the Lifesong meant reaching for Ethea. Ethea!

"He—he didn't ask me to."

"He didn't?" May looked more worried than ever. "He promised he would. It... I..." She paused. "Could it be done while he is asleep?"

Tabitha had to tell her. She could trust May.

"I cannot sing, May. I cannot heal anyone. The last man I tried to heal, he didn't... Ah, he died." Tears stung her eyes. The memory was too painful. The shivers of her fever grew deep within her again. "I dare not sing. The Goddess Ethea... she is my source. When I sing, I am drawn to her."

"It must be special, to hear her song."

"She has been captured."

May's mouth hung open. "Ethea? The Goddess Ethea is captured?

"It is too painful to witness her torture. I must find a way to help her first."

"But she is eternal, immortal. How can this be?"

"I don't understand it myself, May. But I have seen it. I know it to be true."

"You had a vision of it?"

Tabitha nodded. "A place I've never seen before, a land where the air is hot and humid and salty, where the men are bronzed by the sun, where the sky is red... A place of clamorous noise, where the three brothers rule." *They have her shackled to the rock among the blood of sacrifices.* She couldn't bear to say it out loud.

"But that doesn't sound like anywhere in Eyri!" May exclaimed. "And if it is beyond Eyri, then the only place to find such a land is in the myths. Oh, poor Tabitha. How can you help the Goddess if she is in a land which doesn't exist anymore? Your vision must have been of another time."

"What if we *can* go through the Shield, May? What if those lands still exist beyond the rim of Eyri?"

"Three brothers, three brothers," May muttered to herself. "I've read that somewhere." She looked at Tabitha in a puzzled way. "How would you get through the Shield? It is the edge of Eyri. No one has ever passed it since the Forming."

"The king fears Bevn has. The new Swordmaster said Bevn was sighted at a pass above Llury. The Swords could not follow where he went. That was when the king grew weak and his behaviour became strange. He spoke of chaos and death coming upon Eyri, and later of the fate foretold by a prophecy."

"He spoke of the prophecy? Oh, Borace! You waste too much of your thought upon the Revelations."

"The Revelations?" Tabitha asked.

"It is a suspicious old text, a strange and disturbing work to dwell upon. I showed it to him after the great battle, hoping we might find clues to Bevn's whereabouts in its verses, for it is littered with references to the Kingsrim. Now I wish I hadn't shown it to him. He seems to have dwelled upon it too heavily. But oh! That is where I read it. The Revelations mention three brothers. They are at the centre of the chaos which is supposed to wreak havoc in the mythical world beyond Eyri. 'Three brothers, 'midst fire and smoke and blight, all of Oldenworld scoured by their dreadful sight.' Maybe you saw something of the world the prophet saw! Maybe it really *is* there. I don't know, Tabitha, the writings are mostly a muddle, but the king seems to have taken some of their warnings to heart. I think you should see the writings—you might see something which we have missed."

"Where is it kept?" Tabitha asked.

"We can go there now, if you'd like."

She was glad to leave that high desolate chamber, with its shattered chair and lingering atmosphere of disorder. She followed Maybelle down the stairs, taking care not to hurry the lady's ponderous steps. Drops of blood stained the stairs.

"Who was the prophet who wrote these Revelations?" she asked May.

"A man known as Wry Tad Zastor," May answered over her shoulder. "He suffered a great many visions and omens regarding Eyri."

Wry Tad Zastor.

She turned the words over and over in her mind.

"What kind of a name is that?"

"Wry Tad? He had a caustic tongue, I suppose." May paused on a landing, and turned to face Tabitha. "Prophets are prone to being rather...eccentric, to use the polite term. You know Mad Zac, up in the caves near Respite. No? He's a crusty one, he is. He must have predicted the end of Eyri on five different occasions. It's best for prophets to predict events a little beyond their lifespan, so they don't have to live through their failures. Yet sometimes even that hermit has been oddly prescient. The great fire of Levin in four-sixteen? He predicted that two years before it came to pass. Then again, many said he laid that fire, just to fulfil his prophecy. Either way, he proved that sometimes he was worth listening to."

They continued down the stairs.

"What of Wry Tad Zastor?" Tabitha asked, after a while. "Have any of his prophecies come true?"

"Oh yes, a great many," said May. "I would say he's the best we've ever had, but none of his verses have ever been unravelled in time to prevent what he has foreseen. I suppose he took delight in protecting his own genius. If we had warning of something bad, we would try to change it, and so the event would not come to pass."

"What good is a prophecy if it can only be understood after the event?" Tabitha exclaimed. "What use is that? Why write it down at all?"

May spread her hands. "Ask Wry Tad. Well, you can't, he must have been dead three hundred years. Nonetheless, come and read what he wrote. You might recognise his skill even better than I."

May took her to a scrollroom within the palace, a cool chamber guarded by a locked door one of the guardsmen opened for them. The air inside was still and stale, but the floors reflected the gleam of the torches they lit. The works appeared far more valuable than those Tabitha had seen in the Stormhaven Library. Here gilt-edged charts of the night sky lay casually upon a reading table, and those manuscripts she could see were illuminated with bright inks and fine silver outlines. May led her to a heavy reader of some sort, where a great scroll was wrapped around two axles. Finely penned verses were exposed on the paper stretched across the space between the cartridges.

"The Revelations of Wry Tad Zastor," May announced. She rolled the stacks by running her palms on the wheels at either end until she came to a verse that had been marked with a short thread stitched once through the thin paper.

"Here," said May. "This is one which recently caught my eye."
Tabitha read the words of the ancient prophet.

an argent smear upon the fair lake
left in the month when the winter did break
the year twenty-three crows and fourteen doves chased
shall follow the path of the morning sun's haste

the walls cannot hold the night and mist
for those who shelter from the tempest
shall feel the cruel bite of the disturbéd air
spawned from the opened gate, elsewhere

A strange feeling came upon her as she stared at the prophecy, like a wind in her mind. There was more to the verses than the words themselves, as if there were ideas hiding in the ink. An argent smear upon the fair lake.

"Argent is silver, isn't it?" Tabitha asked.

"Yes," May replied. "I believe that was a reference to the starburst we had just over a month ago. That was the sign., the first in the month of Wintersbreach, the month when winter is broken. Mellar has been ruling for twenty-three years since his father passed away. He is the fourteenth to take the Kingsrim. See there in the third line how the numbers are hidden? I should have seen this, I've known of the Revelations for a while, but it all appeared to be nonsense. Most of it still is. The future is no clearer than before, but Zastor mocks us with a past foreseen."

"Forgive me, May, but you've had longer to consider this than I have. I don't see what he's trying to say."

"Look," said May, stabbing at the scroll with her finger. "'Shall follow the path of the morning sun'. The sun comes from the east, thus the threat of Ravenscroft was identified. This Zastor was no fool. He even marked where the conflict would end, in Stormhaven. The morning sun ends at noon, overhead, in the centre of the realm, and then near the end, he mentions shelter from the tempest. That's storm-haven. It was all there, everything. But only if you choose to read it in that way."

"There are more crows than doves, more Shadowcasters than Lightgifters," noted Tabitha, beginning to understand the eccentric style of the prophet. "And the cruel bite of disturbed air is the Morgloth, winged beasts striking from the sky. Sweet Ethea!" The prophet's words seemed to darken as Tabitha concentrated on the page. Each word was a window to many possible associations. The verses were finely inked, and the writing ran off the visible roll at both the top and the bottom.

"How many verses did he write?"

"Thousands," May replied. "Yet we understood none of them in time."

Tabitha was awestruck. "How could he foresee such a thing as the rise of the Shadowcasters, and give the King no real warning?"

"Oh, he did, in his way," May replied. "Remember he's writing over three centuries ago. Maybe he couldn't see things as clearly as we can, looking back. Maybe the verses are as precise as he could make them. Maybe he receives these visions in poetic terms, not as exact definitions. We've been poring over these Revelations but all we've achieved is to mark some quatrains as likely predictions of historic events."

Tabitha's eye was drawn back to the scroll.

the straightest blade shall bend upon the hilt
master of an armoured heart, so pierced with guilt
many lives shall save, many lives shall shed
until day and night balance upon a metal thread

She didn't read it aloud. The first line was about Garyll. He was surely the blade who had been bent upon itself. The straightest Sword had been the Swordmaster. His fall had cost many lives, but had ultimately left him in a position to claim victory back from the Darkmaster. The master of a cold heart could be interpreted in various ways: the Darkmaster, or the Swordmaster. The balance of power had been critical, resting on Garyll's final moment of defiance, balanced upon a thread.

Or upon the string of her lyre, a 'metal thread'. That lent a whole different slant to the quatrain. Maybe she had been the one to cost many lives, because Garyll had made his sacrifice to protect her. She had toiled in Levin to heal those hurt in the conflict, and so had fulfilled the condition 'many lives shall forfeit, more shall save'.

The ambiguities made the interpretation complex, but she understood enough to know there was truth in the prediction—an uncanny kind of truth. It would have been impossible to anticipate the events from what had been written, but in hindsight, the verse described the two events of Garyll's ordeal and her balancing of the essence with eerie accuracy. There was a riddle, hiding in that verse. Tabitha was beginning to suspect that Wry Tad Zastor was more than just a gifted visionary.

She ran her finger across the yellowed verse of prophecy. The paper was smooth, age-worn.

"You said it mentioned the Kingsrim?"

"Those verses are closer to the end." May rolled the wheels carefully, and as she did so, the many quatrains of the prophet blurred by and were wound around the growing upper cartridge.

"This is the first." May pointed to another thread-tagged verse. "This is the one that eats at Mellar so."

if the rulers' horizon can't be seen from the isle
the cracks shall soon cross over that central tile
the shelter shall crumble under three moons falling
the order shall drown in fire and chaos appalling

Tabitha considered the words for some time.

"Rulers' horizon meaning the crown, the Kingsrim?" she guessed. One had to think laterally with Zastor's riddles, that was for sure.

"Yes," May replied. "That is the way Mellar has interpreted it, but I suggested it could also mean the outline of the mountains, and thus speaks of a day of mist when you can't see the horizon."

Tabitha struggled to define her feelings. May's interpretation didn't satisfy her truth-sense. She preferred the king's, but if the king's version was correct, they would soon see 'order drown in fire and chaos appalling'.

"The isle must be Stormhaven," May offered.

"Yet you thought it might be a misty day, in another time."

"Can you see why I said you should read it?" May asked. "Does Wry Tad Zastor really warn of doom for Eyri should the Kingsrim leave the realm, or is the king reading too much into these riddles?"

As Tabitha gazed at the verse before her, the words blurred and she found a quiet place of perspective. Two thoughts came together—the idea that what she was looking at were riddles, and the name of the prophet.

Wry Tad Zastor. Scramble the letters slightly and you had one devious scoundrel of a man.

Tabitha would have laughed if the mood of the prophecies had been less ominous. Wry Tad was surely Twardy, Zastor was Zarost— he had twisted his name. If Twardy Zarost had penned these words, nothing would be false, for the Riddler never lied. His truth could be more crooked than a stunted vine, but for someone who knew how to interpret his wisdom, there would be truth ripe for the picking.

She imagined Zarost grinning at her from within the scroll, bobbing his bristly beard from side to side with glee, his furry hat askew atop his head. He had looked different when he'd been masquerading as Tsoraz, but when she thought of him, he always had his bristly beard and hat, and he was always grinning. Zarost! He had never come back after their strange parting amid the stars, when he had returned her to Eyri to find Garyll. Where was he now? She needed him more than ever.

And yet here he was before her.

"Oh, the tricky rascal. When did you say this was written, May?"

"The Year 110, in the reign of Mellar the Fourth. It is dated at the beginning."

Tabitha whistled softly. She had a lot to ask the Riddler when she saw him next, especially about not growing old. "Wouldn't this event be far in the future, if the sequencing is right? The verse is so far after the ones about the battle against the Darkmaster."

"It should be so," Maybelle agreed, "but the king must fear it has begun already, that Bevn has forced it to begin…"

"Because he has stolen the crown, and taken it off the isle," Tabitha finished. The condition was satisfied, and so this verse of the prophecy had begun. Three falling moons might mean three months, the time it would take for the shelter to crumble. The end of the Shield of Eyri?

"What do you know of the Shield?" Tabitha asked. "It is real, isn't it?"

"The Shield? Yes, it is real enough, though nobody can claim to understand how it works. From what I can gather in the early histories, the Gyre of Wizards left the Shield to protect Eyri from the scourge of chaos which was ruining the mythical realm of Oldenworld. It is a magical construction. Maybe you can understand it better than I, Tabitha. However, it prevents our passage beyond Eyri, and prevents anything else getting in."

"So if Bevn finds a way to bypass the Shield, he will find great peril beyond it?" Tabitha asked.

Not only that, Tabitha realised, but he would also allow it in. In leaving, he displayed his ignorance of Zastor's prophecy, that the crown had to remain in Stormhaven for the shield to remain intact. What would come upon Eyri from the lands beyond the rim? The vicious fighting Lûk, the marauding Hunters, the massive savages, all of them were mentioned in the legends Tabitha had read, with hideous and fearsome creatures that would frighten grown men to death just to look upon them. But what then of the Morgloth? She had seen them. She knew they were real enough, so what part of the legends could she discard? All of the ancient foes could still exist. The chaos could be real.

"And the other verses that deal with the Kingsrim?"

May spun the Revelations on a few rolls.

where the trail that ends with painful knees
above young shadows of Zunskar in the trees
there lies the weakest seal, and so where swords fell down
shall pass the one who bears the ragged crown

"Oh, I understand this one now," said May. "Swordmaster Vance mentioned they'd lost Bevn at a pass above Llury? There are no real passes, but there is the Penitent's pass, a trail that pains the knees. It is to the west, where the young shadows of the Zunskar are in the trees. Botheration! I should have solved this one. We might have caught the Prince in time."

"But the Zunskar mountains are to the east, aren't they?"

"Yes, but their *young* shadows would be at dawn, and that would be cast across the realm, onto the western peaks above Llury and First Light. So this verse tells us the shield is weakest at dawn, upon the Penitent's pass."

"Why is it called the Penitent's pass?"

"Penitent means kneeling. That pass is an ancient memorial. The First Swordmaster Stevenson drove the last of the savages there for their final stand. The legend has it that they were gripped by an overwhelming fear and knelt before him, but when he advanced to retrieve their surrendered weapons, Stevenson and his men felt the strange burden too, a weight of enchantment which grew heavier with every passing moment. The savages were crushed to the ground, and yet still they tried to fight. Stevenson's men faced them on their knees. When the fighting was done at last, they crawled from that high place, even though they were victorious. Stevenson built a cairn to commemorate those fallen in battle, and to warn wayfarers of the peril in the pass. The memorial marks the end of the trail now. If it is a pass, it has never been used in our time."

Shall pass the one who bears the ragged crown. Wry Tad did not call him the king, merely the bearer of the crown, so he had foreseen something? He had known the crown would be stolen. Did he have a part to play in the prince's escape from Eyri? Was this a riddle he was laying for his apprentice to follow?

Tabitha didn't know, but the answers would surely be somewhere in the text. She wanted to roll it right to the beginning, and pore over every verse. The prophecy was a wonderwork. She would never be able to read it all. Such a study would take years. The last verse confirmed that Bevn had gone beyond Eyri. Every day he would be getting farther away. She had no time to waste.

But if she was going to follow the Prince, she needed to know what to expect. She needed to know about the world beyond Eyri, who inhabited it, who ruled it. She began combing the Revelations for facts. Hours passed, and night descended upon the palace. A servant brought a platter of finger-pies, but most of them were ignored. The oil burned low in the lamps, and a guardsman replenished it. The air grew stale and thin, and the chill came out of the bones of the palace to carpet the floor in silence. The sounds of the last activity in the palace faded away.

"You still awake, Tabitha?"

"*Mm.*"

"You stopped turning the rollers long ago."

The taste of dry pastry filled her mouth. She needed sleep, she had been up for too long, with Maybelle at her side. They had to stop.

Tabitha knuckled her eyes. She couldn't think clearly anymore. That was a sure sign. If she used her skills as a wizard and drew clarity from her ring, she might see everything and understand the patterns in the words. If only she could lay the Revelations out on the floor, and see all of the prophecy at once. Every time she wanted to cross-reference a verse, she had to roll the first one away, and it became consumed in the gyrating cartridge. She had memorised some of the important verses, but it felt as if her brain was overflowing. The words made whispers in her mind, echoes which competed with one another, all in the Riddler's jocular voice.

"I feel like a village square after market day, too trampled by the feet."

"Maybe it's time for bed," May said. She had wrapped herself in blankets, and was leaning heavily on the arm of her chair. Her voice was weak and her eyelids heavy, but she had not abandoned her task as historian. She knew how important Tabitha's research was.

Tabitha couldn't leave until she had filled the gaps in her knowledge, but the meaning of the verses seemed to be elusive. They teased her mind with possibilities. Just when she thought she had isolated the truth, a new interpretation of the words came to mind, and she was sent off on another diversion through the lore. This was the Riddler at his best, and just like Twardy Zarost, the words were disturbing, challenging, shifty. She felt no closer to understanding the world beyond Eyri, though to be fair she had learnt of many names and places, like Moral kingdom, and Kaskanzr, the Winterblade mountains, Highbough and Kinsfall, and the downs of Koom. But they were meaningless without a map, and it wasn't what she needed to know. She wanted to understand the Shield, and how to pass through it. She wanted to prepare herself for what she might face in the land called Oldenworld, the 'wildfire' which seemed to wind through so many of the verses like a malignant vine. And above all, she needed to find something to guide her to the place of heat and salt and sweat, where the buildings grew upon one another into the air and the horns blared upon the Goddess.

"One last try. Can you remember where it mentioned the three brothers?"

Under May's guidance, the Revelations spun, blurred, spun, blurred and stopped. Tabitha tried to focus, but she was too tired, and the words seemed to swim across the paper. She put her hand on the page to hold the words still, and looked through the page.

> *three brothers, 'midst fire and smoke and blight,*
> *all of Oldenworld scoured by their dreadful sight*
> *the sky bleeds with wildfire seeds and beasts unholy roar*
> *until the Pillar in the lowlands claims life evermore*

Then a strange thing happened. The prophet's vision rushed at her as if it had leapt from the page, a sudden assault of light and sound. In an altered instant, she saw a red and bleeding sky. Wind threw her hair awry. The roar of beasts, horns and clashing metal filled her ears. The air was thick with smoke, and it was wet, and hot. Tight balls of lightning seared the low clouds, and where the charge struck ground it bloomed silver and rippled like boiling liquid. The wind pulled a shroud of dirty rain aside, and before her was a tower, a lopsided veined megalith that pointed at the sky like a rude and broken finger straining against the ropes of its cancerous tendons. So haphazard was its construction that it should have fallen upon its own weight. It was almost organic; it seemed to move and shift like a nightmare of melting wax forced to remain upright. The best stonemasons in

Eyri could not have made such a pillar, no matter what mortar they used. It should have been a pile of rubble, and yet it stood, huge and grey-streaked, encrusted with windows and defying every principle of balance and order. Tabitha clenched her stomach against the nausea of its hypnotic attraction. It was more than just a building. It housed a presence. Someone waited there within that awesome shape. Someone watched.

She jumped back in fright.

The instant of vision shut like a slamming door, and it was silent again.

Tabitha took a slow, shuddering breath.

The words had encapsulated the vision, she realised. The sights and sounds were held within the writing in the same way a familiar smell could contain a memory. The words sparked the vision. They took one closer to seeing the truth. It was wrong to only interpret the verses of the Revelations literally. They were supposed to be experienced.

May touched her gently. "You all right?"

She knew where she had been. Ethea was in that place, close by, chained and helpless. The Pillar. In the lowlands.

"Stay with me, May. I need you now more than ever."

She slid her hand down the page, feeling the rippled texture pass under her fingers.

across Oldenworld shall his Wildfire spread
massing Chaos upon every caster's thread
ending the work of the wise and the ordered
'til Eyri alone stands protected, shield-bordered.

hold still your tongue when you translate –
each founding letter of these verses eight
uncovers the provoking name of that capricious-headed
Sorcerer of the silver fire, thrice-dreaded.

After reading the words, she tried to see through them again, as she had before.

Nothing happened. The words were silent. They kept their secret.

She willed herself into the page, through the network of inked letters, striving for the vision behind them, but she was denied, as if it was a closed iron gate and there was a key she had yet to find. She shook her head to clear her thoughts then pored over the writing more carefully.

Sorcerer—it was a new word for her, although she guessed that a sorcerer would be a great magic-user. She wondered what the difference was between a sorcerer and a wizard. She had the dreadful suspicion that of the two, the sorcerer wielded more power. And why was he thrice dreaded? She read the verses again, and lingered on the last few lines. "Each founding letter of these verses eight." It was a clue to a riddle.

Tabitha scanned the left margin of the verses, to find the name, the name she should not speak, the name of the Sorcerer.

Ametheus.

As soon as she saw the word, the vision came at her, hard, fast and furious.

She was in the Pillar in the lowlands, this she knew, for beyond the strange misshapen windows was that same blood-red sky which spat knots of silver charge through sheets of windblown rain, but the ground, before so close, was now far below. The clouds' ragged bottoms dragged by the windows, and through the gaps between them she could make out a great expanse of water: restless, green and foam flecked. Through another stretched window she could see rumpled land, tilted at an awkward angle.

The roof hunched low over her head, a knuckled surface of glass, as if many globes of random size and colour had been glued together above her, a glistening collection of gelatinous eggs. Suddenly a face filled the closest globe, a distorted face with wide-set eyes and bulbous nose, and she instinctively cowered away from its intrusive stare, but it swirled upon itself and became a pile of leaves then a stretch of desert sands. All the globes held scenes within them, she realised: shifting faces, crowds, beasts, villages, landscapes and starscapes, and some that only showed a soup of sullied colours.

The wide chamber smelled potent, not a truly bad smell, but not good either, like a brewing-house, or a tannery, a mix of growth and decay where neither reigned supreme. The continuous disturbance in the air left a spicy metallic tang in her mouth. Magic, she realised, like the taste of her ring, only...hotter. She drew a sharp breath as she realised she was not alone.

At a central window, his back toward her, stood a large figure in a divided robe. Tabitha had a horrible sense of falling inward toward that figure, as if the floor she stood upon heaved beneath her feet, and yet at the same time her eyes slid away from the man, even as she was drawn to concentrate on him. The conflict of rejection and attraction disturbed her mind worse than it did her body. Reality itself seemed to be shifting around the large figure.

He bunched his wide shoulders as if readying himself for something. His face was obscured by his headpiece, a crown with flared metal wings that came down to his collar, a glinting red metal, like that used in the helmet she had seen upon the bare-chested man who had killed the dove in the sacrificial pit. The back of his head was covered with a loose fold of black silk with spiralled silver patterns upon it. He spread his hands like a bird taking flight, and the knots of silver fire wriggling through the sky turned and streaked outward, away from the humid tension of the Pillar, away from the Sorcerer.

"Ametheus," she whispered to herself.

He turned his head slightly toward her, as if she had spoken louder than she'd meant to. His eyes searched the room, as if he could not quite make out who was there. His face, bracketed by the engraved strips of red metal, was smooth and youthful, dark browed and intense.

"I see the future, not you!" he shouted, and lunged toward her with an outstretched hand.

She fell back, struck in her chest by the Sorcerer's repulsion, as if he had gathered the bonds of gravity itself and hurled them against her.

The instant of prophecy snapped shut. She windmilled her arms in a vain attempt to regain her balance, and sat hard in her chair.

Sorcerer of the silver fire, thrice-dreaded.

Had Ametheus reached for her, or for the prophet in his act of committing the verse to the page? The Sorcerer's touch lingered upon her skin like the sting that came as one warmed after too long in the snow. She rubbed her arms.

"Tabitha?" May was close beside her. Tabitha nodded to show May she was all right.

"What was that? There was a strange gust of wind that blew in your hair and passed me like a dervish."

"That came from the Sorcerer."

"How can he...?" May fell silent. Some things were beyond understanding.

"I saw him, but I don't think he saw me. There is a lot more to the Riddler's work than there seems to be."

"The Riddler. You mean Twardy Zarost? What does he have to do with this?"

"He is Wry Tad, May. This is his work."

"Oh." May counted slowly on her fingers. "Zastor and Zarost, Twardy and Wry Tad. It's the Riddler again? He is a perplexing man." She gave a tired smile. "That reminds me, there's one verse right at the very end which refers to the crown. Shall I?"

Tabitha stared at the heavy rolls of the Revelations. She didn't want to meet the Sorcerer again, there might even be worse things than Ametheus in there. In fact, she was sure there were. How far would she have to go? The prophecy was like a never-ending river. At the end of every verse there was always another to be drawn toward. It might even be possible that when she had read all the verses, she would begin all over again, seeing them in a new way.

She would be lost for days in its study. It wouldn't let her sleep.

"Last one," Tabitha said. "The absolute last one."

Maybelle spun the wheel, on and on, and Tabitha sensed time advancing as paper whispered onto the lower stack, until they came to the tail of the Revelations, where the trimmed end of the fine paper was bound to the lower roller with crisscrossed golden ribbons.

if the Riddler has gone when you first reach this sign
if the Crown has slipped from the right royal line
if the Ring has been claimed but your power's run dry
then Time has been bent and the Ending is nigh

a slim thread of chance might twist through your doom
but this Gyre-sheltered realm is more likely a tomb
so be quick, be so quick! and seek out the others
to mould a new world and deny the three brothers

And there, below the final words, a symbol had been drawn, like two tangled open-ended eights, or fish with interlocking tails. She recognised it from her apprenticeship; the heart rune, the mark of wizardry. The writing was intended for her. She was supposed to have read it. It was some kind of preparation, or an education. Or a warning.

The Riddler was gone. The Crown had slipped away, and her power was in jeopardy.

Tabitha jumped to her feet. She was dizzy with tiredness, but she knew that it didn't matter.

The stakes were higher than she'd ever believed.

"I must find Garyll. We must go, we must go at once."

11. THINKING OF GREATNESS

"People can be measured by two important things:
Unspoken thoughts, and humble beginnings."—Zarost

Ashley Logán ambled along the street in the dark. Ahead, the imposing outline of a mural tower and its flanking ridge of battlements rose against the pale stars. The tower looked outward over the Stormhaven harbour, and inward over both the commercial half of the upper district and the Merchants Quarter below. There would be Swords up there, patrolling the wall.

He kicked a pebble across the paving stones. Maybe he could become a Sword. That would be a secure profession. Once he was a Sword, he would be paid monthly wages from the king's coffers, and eat meals in the Swordhouses, and he would have that job until he retired. Even then, as a fullerman, he'd get a small retainer to see him through his fading years. Yes, he could see himself being a Sword. He liked the idea that criminals met with justice, and honest folk were protected. There was honour in maintaining the law, and so many men had been lost in the recent battle the Sword captains were recruiting hard. He might even get a preferential placement, because he had brought both the traitor Tarrok and the Rector Shamgar to the dungeons. The Swords would know of that. He had brought warning of Ravenscroft to Stormhaven as well, so the King might even put in a good word for him! He could become an Officer-of-the-Watch, or a Second-Sword, or even serve in a Captain's Crossbelt.

But he'd be a Sword, with a grim face and a deadly blade, only called upon when there was trouble.

When he'd left home, he'd so wanted to be a Lightgifter: a man who brought healing and happiness, warmth and well-being, a man who would fill the air with his joyful sprites, a master of the magic art. The day when he had been selected as an apprentice in the Dovecote had seemed like the beginning of his life, he had been so elated. He had worked hard, despite the difficulties and politics within the Cote. He had earned the Gifters' white robe that he wore, and probably more than earned the right to tie a full knot in his rope, but it would remain a half-knot for the present, because the Rector was in the dungeons, and Ashley had put him there.

The offer the Rector had made still turned over and over in his mind, despite his firm resolution to refuse the bribery. A new Source could be carved from the Rector's secret crystal lode. The Lightgifters could sing, and spark new sprites into being. They could regain their power. No, he had refused the Rector's offer. It was wrong, a trap which led to worse things.

Would it be possible to make a rogue Source, without involving the Rector?

The sad truth was that without the sprites, being a Lightgifter didn't mean anything. With so little Light essence remaining after the battle and so much of it used to heal the survivors, there was nothing to be a Gifter with. Even his orb had gone pale at his throat, a milky translucence where once had dwelt a continuous glow. Even in the dark it barely showed up. The Order of Lightgifters was in disarray. Father Keegan was dead. Father Angelos was dead. Too many of the others had been irrevocably changed by their tortures in Ravenscroft. All their stones held the dark taint like a stain of disgrace upon the virginal white. Only Sister Grace could be considered as a candidate for the new Rector, but she had refused the title, preferring to be the guardian, which she insisted was a temporary position, until a new Rector could be selected. That was assuming a future for the Order of Lightgifters existed at all.

Ashley watched the stars as he walked beneath them. He wished there was some way of using those specks of light to navigate through the seas of a young man's life. It had seemed so easy when the goal of becoming a Lightgifter had lain before him. He'd had a purpose and he could progress toward it as if rowing for an island, but suddenly the isle had been washed away, leaving only the rude rock and the tangled dead roots of the truth. To be a Gifter under Shamgar was to be an accomplice in fraud. Ashley's faith in the holiness of the senior Gifters had been shattered; his dream of becoming one himself seemed empty and worthless. Now he was adrift under that silent scattering of stars which hid the secret of his destiny in its complex pattern. If only he could see what he was meant to be, what he could become, then he could walk that path with conviction. But the stars were so very far away, and the dark towers swallowed them all the more.

Tabitha Serannon had the power to change their fate. She could make sprites. He had witnessed the miracle in the palace forecourt, as had most of the others. Tonight's prolonged meeting in the Gifters-hall had been aflutter with speculation and suspicion, but in the end the resolution had been good. They would all seek to become apprenticed to the Wizard, to serve her, and to learn her ways. When he had voiced his support for the movement, he had been applauded, and appointed as the spokesman. He would be the one to approach the Wizard, because he knew her; he was her friend. He hoped that was still true. At least, he had thought that they were friends for a time in the Dovecote. But she was different now. She was a wizard.

He didn't know if he had the right to assume their friendship would continue.

How would he approach her? She was so famous she was always surrounded by a crowd, twenty deep. When she had arrived in Stormhaven, she had been whisked past him in her coach and gone directly into the palace, and Ashley couldn't guess when she would appear in public again. It was rumoured that the king was courting her for a queen. It was rumoured that only the nobles would be allowed to enjoy her counsel, but then it was also rumoured that she kept the old Swordmaster Glavenor at her side as her slave, and Ashley knew that was untrue.

Some people crossed ahead of him, in the deep shadows at the base of the city wall, two figures, cloaked and bearing packs. The one was tall and broad-shouldered, the other shorter and light-footed. For a desperate moment Ashley thought they were Shadowcasters, but they passed on as if trying to avoid looking at him in the street. They were no threat to him; he was a threat to them. What mischief was afoot? He sent his mind questing outward with the gentlest of threads, even though he knew he shouldn't. He had a talent, and it demanded to be used.

He recognised them at once. Garyll Glavenor and Tabitha! He froze in the street.

She had a burning quest in mind, a need to leave Stormhaven and reach a pass as soon as possible, somewhere leading to the outside—a trail beyond Eyri. She was fearful and uncertain but deep down she had a greater fear, something about a great figure with feathered arms and a forlorn face. And birds, many birds, flying in tight circles.

She looked suddenly back at him as his thoughts touched hers, and he snapped the questing tendril back with embarrassment. Light almighty! The Wizard! He hadn't meant to snoop in *her* head.

"Ashley? Is that you?"

She had stopped, and she spoke quietly, as if not wanting to alert anyone beyond them to their presence.

His chance had come sooner than he'd expected. "A most humble Gifter requests the pleasure of a few precious moments with you, your grace." He bowed low in the street.

"Ashley! Stop that! It's wonderful to see you!" she exclaimed in a loud whisper, coming closer.

"Sorry to stop you, I'm sure you're in a hurry, but it's so difficult to get close enough to you to be noticed these days, peace-bringer."

She had a fresh fragrance of cherry blossoms that lingered in the air between them. He tingled with excitement at being so close to her—Tabitha the Singer of the Lifesong, Tabitha the Wizard. He controlled himself as he realised that Glavenor had stopped in the shadows as well, where he stood tall and ominous, like a mirror of the great mural tower above him.

Tabitha smiled in the dark, he could feel it. "Peace seems further from my reach every day. Funny that, I thought I would bring peace by ending the Darkmaster's advance, but it was peace for the people, and not for me. I'm caught up in this commotion."

"You are the commotion," Ashley noted.

"What are you doing out here this late?" Tabitha asked.

"I, er, I'm trying to make sense of being a Lightgifter. We had a meeting tonight, in the Gifters-hall. I was asked to find you." He dropped to one knee right before her. "Your worship, on behalf of the Lightgifters, I wish to ask that we might become your disciples."

"Ashley, no, not you as well!" she exclaimed, in a taught whisper. "I don't want you to worship me. Get up. I'm just Tabitha, just like I always was."

"As you wish, your...wizard...Tabitha," he stammered, and stood again. His cheeks burned. "How would you it please you that I ask it, your eminence? We wish to learn your magic, and to help with your healing in Levin."

Tabitha reached out and shook his arm. "Ashley, you're still doing it! Stop using the silly titles! I've had my fill of them. It's me, for goodness sake! You know who I am. I need friends, not worshippers."

Ashley nodded nervously, and rubbed his arm where she had touched him, where his skin danced with crazy feelings.

"Ashley? You can see through all the nonsense, can't you?"

Glavenor stepped up to her side then, and Ashley hesitated to say anything.

"Logán. It's been a while."

Ashley dipped his head. "Swordm...ah, Glavenor, sir. Pleased to meet you again."

"Garyll will do."

Those three words told a story. Ashley regarded Glavenor anew. The man was humble. He had lost his armoured aura of authority. The iron note of command was absent from his words. Ashley felt humbled himself for the Swordmaster had borne a far greater burden during the battle for freedom. Doubtless he had more troublesome questions about his future to consider than Ashley's own.

"I am sorry that—" Ashley began.

"No, you earned my respect for what you did! I shall call you Logán until I have earned yours."

Ashley supposed he was referring to his duplicity when possessed by the Darkmaster's spells. Some of the old Swordmaster's scars hadn't healed.

"Then you must call me Ashley," he offered.

"You are too quick to trust, young Logán," Garyll said. "There are many deceptions in the world." Glavenor came close, and his cloak parted suddenly. Ashley was relieved to find a hand thrust toward him, not a weapon. "I am no judge!" Garyll declared. "I'll take your hand in friendship, if that is how it is offered."

Ashley extended his hand. Garyll's grip was like iron. Some things about the man hadn't changed.

Garyll pulled away. "Forgive me, master Logán, but we cannot be delayed. My love, we must go. The king—"

He left his sentence unfinished, but a moment of understanding passed between the two.

"I'm sorry, Ashley, but Garyll is right, we have to go."

Ashley could see they were packed for a journey, and he knew that if he let Tabitha get away now, he probably wouldn't see her for some days. He didn't want to spend more time adrift beneath the stars, hunting for clues in a future to which he had no map. He needed her answers. "Can I talk while you walk?" he asked. "Please, Tabitha, I must have a few more words with you."

"All right, come quickly. We're on our way to the harbour."

"Be quiet about it," Garyll added. "We don't want the crowd to form. We can't afford attention tonight."

They turned as one, and moved through the empty street. As they passed the tower, they reached the divide, and padded down the many stairs leading to the lower district of the Merchant's Quarter. The Gatehouse loomed over the neatly tiled roofs ahead.

"So *can* you see through all the nonsense, Ashley?"

"You can't deny that you are a wizard," he said. "You can teach us in your way, and we can spread your good work."

"I hardly know what I'm doing. I don't have the right to teach what I haven't mastered."

"But we have nothing else to do, your—" He caught himself just in time. "Tabitha. No sprites have been sparked since...you shattered the Source. We have no Light to gift, so how can we be Lightgifters? I have thought long and hard since the battle. There is nothing for me if I cannot work with the essence. I have been trained for healing. I need sprites to cast my spells, but you seem to do without, your magic works despite the lack of essence."

"It's the clear essence I use, Ashley."

"But the clear has no power!"

"That is why it isn't something which I could teach. I call upon something beyond the Light and Dark."

"Could you try, at least?"

"Who should I teach, Ashley?"

"Well, the Gifters. There's myself, and Sister Grace, and—"

"And very few others who were not turned by the Darkmaster," Tabitha finished for him.

"I've spoken to them. They want to be Gifters again, now that the Darkmaster is dead. His hold on their stones has faded."

"So I should teach them as well, do you think?"

Like Glavenor, they had been unfairly tainted by the Darkmaster's possession. They should be given a chance to redeem themselves. "Yes," Ashley answered.

"What of the surviving Shadowcasters, Ashley? They have lost their magic too, and their master."

Ashley was uncertain.

"I-I don't think they have the right, not after what they brought upon the people of Eyri."

"I would have to teach them, Ashley. I would be obliged to. You see, it was only because I could use both Light and Dark that I succeeded. I think that is part of what I do now. Part of it is the singing. Part of it is because I have both of these." She lifted two orbs out of her collar, once white and obsidian, now both as clear as glass. "I can command both the motes and the sprites, and therefore can work the clear essence. It is the balance point between Light and Dark. It is the fusion of the two. So to learn how to manipulate the clear essence, you would need to allow Shadowcasters to learn at your side. You would need to learn from them, as well as with them."

That was a lot to think about. They were almost within earshot of the Gatehouse sentry before he said, "I can do that."

"Then what of the people here? Those not already orbed as Gifters or Casters. Should they be excluded, because the Rector or the Darkmaster never chose them for service? The fishermen, the merchants, the mothers, the bureaucrats. Everyone. They have no less right to learn than anyone else. If I am to offer power, then I must offer it to everyone, to be fair, to avoid an imbalance. Can you imagine what the school would be like?"

Ashley began to understand the impossibility of Tabitha sharing her magic.

"Can you imagine the chaos, if everyone could manipulate the world around them?" Tabitha asked. "How am I to select the rightful candidates?"

Ashley brightened. "Well, you should choose only those who you know are ready for the power."

"Who would those be? Those who can develop the skill themselves?"

"Yes!" A troublesome insight settled upon him. "Oh. I see what you mean, now." His hopes were coming to nothing. He wanted to ask Tabitha if she would make an exception in his case, but they had come to the Gatehouse and he had to hold his tongue.

"Halt! Who's there?" A sword *schralped* from its sheath.

"Put your steel away, Sword," Garyll ordered. "Dunbar, isn't it? I am Glavenor, this is the Lady Serannon with me, and Gifter Logán."

"Evenin', sire, lady-your-grace, evenin' Gifter. Gate's closed, sire."

"We are on the king's business, Sword Dunbar, we have to go now, and discreetly. Don't make a fuss."

"Sorry sire, I've been told not to let you out sire—"

"Really? Does that apply to everyone, or just to me?"

"Sorry sire, it's a specific order, I can't let you out!"

"A specific order from whom?" Glavenor demanded.

"Swordmaster Vance, sire." The sentry dropped his troubled eyes to the ground.

A knuckle popped in someone's hand.

"And who do you think has more authority, Sword Dunbar? The Swordmaster, or the king?"

Sword Dunbar didn't answer. He cast miserably around as if looking for support from other sentries, but there were none. Glavenor didn't miss the movement.

"What are you doing on night watch without your second?"

"I...er, don't have one, sire. New orders."

"Bad orders. Who's in charge of your unit?"

"Captain Malick, sire."

"Malick! He's newly promoted. Has he told you not to salute your seniors as well?"

"No, sire! Sorry, sire."

Garyll returned the belated salute, fist to chest.

"And your bow? Where is your bow?"

The Sword mumbled something.

"You are not a fletched archer, and yet you are stationed on the gate? Why is this?"

The poor Sword didn't attempt to answer. He just watched his own feet. Even in the dark, Ashley could see beads of sweat forming on his upper lip. Ashley understood what Glavenor was trying to do—make the Sword so uncomfortable he'd rather let them pass than face the barrage of questions from the old Swordmaster. It intrigued Ashley to know how effectively Glavenor's tactic was working. He reached for Sword Dunbar's thoughts, and found a pounding nervous confusion.

"Do you have no one to patrol the block? What of when the cresset burns low, who replaces it? And why is your helm tarnished? Will you explain to the king tomorrow why you chose to follow Vance's orders over his own?"

"No, sire. I mean yes, sire. I... Ah... Sire?"

Ashley imagined what it would be like if he could plant a thought amid Dunbar's confusion, like dropping a snake among barefooted wrestlers. Logic, reason and orders would run for high ground, leaving panic to fend for itself. What if the Sword were to think that Glavenor was about to attack him, and he desperately needed backup?

"Go to the Swordhouse, and tell Captain Malick I want to see him at once!" Garyll demanded. "We shall settle this matter about prohibitions on the gate right now."

"Sire, what about my post? I can't—"

The old Swordmaster has an unsheathed blade hidden in his

cloak.

"Now do you understand why you always stand guard in twos?" Garyll asked in a cold hard voice. He leant toward the sentry. "I shall keep your post! Go, I haven't all night to correct your mistakes!"

Sword Dunbar ran away.

"I can't believe how eager he was to leave," Tabitha said in a hushed voice. With her cowl raised it was difficult to tell, but Ashley thought she was watching him, not Garyll.

"It was easier than I expected." Garyll shrugged. "Old habits die hard. He's used to obeying orders. Come, we must be quick. If there's any hope for him as a Sword, he'll realise his mistake long before reaching his captain."

They passed into the mouth of the Gatehouse, and walked briskly down the wide corridor that formed the entrance to Stormhaven City. It always reminded Ashley of a ribcage. It was framed with slitted walls and roof, where defenders could fire arrows and throw pitch upon passing attackers from within the safety of the secondary corridors. Little use that had been when the Shadowcasters had come upon Stormhaven. Defenders who couldn't see in the Dark or who fled in terror weren't very effective at stringing bows. Nonetheless, Ashley looked nervously through the arrow loops, but the only movement came from the dancing of the flames in the occasional oil lamps. They hurried to the end, where the mighty drawbridge lay across the moat, as wide as the road beyond it. Ashley was surprised it lay down at night. He'd thought it was always raised at sunset.

"The cable from Chink is taking longer to weave than it should," Glavenor commented.

Their footfalls were absorbed by the thick bridge as if it were solid rock. They hurried away from the gates with more than one glance back toward the open arch.

The harbour was almost empty of boats. Only a tall-masted ketch was at anchor, and a skiff was tied to the wharf. Some men were offloading crates and stacking them against the wall of a wide-roofed warehouse nearby. Most of the harbour was blackened by the fire. Many of the buildings close to the water's edge had been burnt to the ground, and a dark spike protruding from the water showed where a sunken boat still lay. There had been many more boats at anchor that night when Ashley had witnessed Tarrok lighting his blaze. Divers must have been working hard to clear the wreckage. Already, a new wharf was under construction, and a tall building, half-clad in new timbers, grew at its head. A pile of planks lay beside it, awaiting the break of day.

Tabitha led them directly to the skiff. A thickset man stood in the bowels of the boat lifting crates to the wharf.

"Mulrano?" Tabitha asked.

The man grunted.

"Kingsman Rood told us you'd be here. It's Tabitha, Tabitha Serannon. You brought me here."

The man stopped in his work, and looked up to the three of them. He had bluff features and bushy brows. He cocked his head as he looked at the cowled figure of Glavenor.

"Hu he?" he asked.

His speech was tortured, as if he was speaking around a mouthful of twigs. Then Ashley remembered. Tabitha had told him of the poor fisherman from Southwind who'd had his tongue cut out by the Shadowcasters to prevent him testifying against them. Ashley supposed Mulrano was working so late at night because so many of the boats in Stormhaven had been burnt out. Someone had to deliver the perishable essentials to Stormhaven. He probably earned better money at it than by trying to string fish out of the lake.

"It's just Garyll," Tabitha reassured Mulrano. Glavenor lifted his cowl.

But if anything, the fisherman looked more wary than ever. He pointed to Garyll then gestured at his own neck.

"You can be at ease, goodman Mulrano," Garyll said. "I'll not be threatening you in any way. I'm not the Swordmaster any more, and I've come to learn the truth about you. I believe you are an honest man, from what Tabitha has told me."

"Mulrano, we need passage to Southwind," Tabitha explained. "Quick passage."

Mulrano was silent. Ashley couldn't make out if he was glowering, or grinning.

He hadn't even tried to probe the fisherman's mind, when a gruff voice sounded within his head.

"The last time he helped you it cost him dearly," Ashley recited. "All of his boats holed but one, and a sunken canoe, but he shall hear you and help you, because you are friends with the Riddler. He is actually very impressed with Garyll, because he killed the Darkmaster."

Mulrano stared at Ashley. Then he shook his fist at him, and clambered out of the boat onto the wharf.

Ashley backed away. "Sorry," he mumbled. "I... You said it so clearly. Ahh—"

What had he been thinking! He shouldn't have spoken those thoughts out loud!

Luckily Tabitha laid a restraining hand on the fisherman's arm, and Mulrano seemed content not to chase Ashley. "We don't mean to alarm you," Tabitha said. "We need to leave for Southwind at once. We had to give the guards the slip."

Mulrano glared one last time at Ashley then nodded at Tabitha, as if he understood how these things went.

"Thank you, Mulrano," said Tabitha. "I'll pay for my passage this time."

He shook his hands in the air, plainly refusing her offer. He made a gruff noise in his throat, and beckoned Garyll closer to shake his hand. They looked one another in the eye for a long moment. When Mulrano released Garyll's hand he tilted his head Ashley's way, and shrugged meaningfully.

"He's Ashley Logán, he's a Lightgifter," said Garyll. "He's not coming with us, but he is to be trusted."

They couldn't leave without him! He had to talk to Tabitha. He hadn't finished what he'd begun. Ashley stepped closer to the others. "When shall I see you again, Tabitha? I have to speak to you."

Tabitha shook her head as if she couldn't guess how long she would be gone. "If you want to talk, Ashley, come with the boat to Southwind. He'll be coming back tomorrow morning, won't you, Mulrano?

Mulrano grunted in acknowledgement, but then he pointed an accusatory finger at the young Gifter, pointed at his own head, and stirred the air.

"I meant no disrespect when I spoke, sir," Ashley said hastily. "It's just...you strained to get the words out, they were plain to me. Sometimes I-I can't help finding people's thoughts in my own head. I wanted to help."

Mulrano considered this for a moment then extended his broad hand. Ashley was relieved to be let off the hook, but he had to rub his fingers after the firm introduction. Light! The man had a stronger grip than Glavenor.

Mulrano jumped down into his boat again, and began hauling crates up to the wharf at a feverish pace. Garyll slid them away into a cluster and, in less than a minute, the last of the skiff's load was clear. An old man whom Ashley hadn't noticed before approached from the darkness of the warehouse, and a heavy bag of coins was passed down to Mulrano. Then the three of them boarded the skiff, Mulrano cast off, and they were away.

The wind tugged at the sail and drove the boat forward to scatter a wave of pearls from the bow.

ᚙᚘᚙᚘ

Tabitha breathed Garyll in. He smelled good. She sat in the curl of his arms, where the warmth of his body protected her from the stiff breeze driving the boat. The mouth of the harbour diminished in their wake.

A stray curl of hair touched her forehead, and she brushed it aside.

Things had become strange on Stormhaven. She had come to the isle in great honour, but had to flee from it in secret. In truth, it was a relief to escape from the city. She felt she was leaving her fame behind. She would be with Garyll now, they would travel quickly to the Penitent's pass and face whatever came upon them, together. Their future was like an arrow shot into the dark. After the crown they would go, beyond the Shield, into what remained of the legendary Oldenworld. When they had found the prince, Tabitha would drive onward and not rest until she had found Ethea.

There was a problem. If she kept the Kingsrim as she sought out Ethea, she would be taking it farther from Eyri, which would cause the kingdom ever greater danger. The crown had to be returned to the king, and soon. Stormhaven, with its mighty stonewood walls, did nothing to keep the order of the realm intact. Mellar did. Without his crown, it seemed the king would crumble.

The granite headland of the isle's western heights obscured the city; only a dispersed glow escaped. The stray curl of hair touched her forehead again, and she left it to wander in the breeze this time. It would just get loose again.

Maybe Garyll could bring the crown back while she went on, but with only two of them, she would be alone in Oldenworld, alone against the unknown threats—alone against Ametheus. A cold doubt turned in her stomach, but the danger could not be helped. No one else could be expected to take the risks she would to, to save the Goddess. She didn't even have the first idea of how she would save

Ethea, only that she had to find the Goddess, in that place beneath the Pillar, in the lowlands, where the sky was red and hot. She tried not to think of that powerful figure in the split robe, looking out of that unbalanced megalith, hunching under his glass-eyed roof, throwing his Chaos like knots of ruin across the lands.

She steadied her breathing. For now, the night air was clean on her face; the stars were clear and bright above. She savoured the simplicity.

Ashley was watching her. He seemed eager to speak. She supposed that she was being rude by not engaging him, for he had come out of his way to discuss his concerns. Helping him with his problem might keep her mind off her own. She owed him a hearing, at least. She liked him, he was a gentle-natured young man, sensitive yet energetic and quite brave as well. His blond hair streamed back with the wind like silk, and his fine features gave him a pure innocence that was charming to behold. Maidens across the realm would chase him for a husband, if they weren't chasing him already.

He turned his gaze down and away from her, as if embarrassed by something, and in that instant the touch of her loose hair upon her forehead was gone. Loose hair? Maybe he was not as innocent as his face led people to believe. She vowed to think as quietly as possible around Ashley in future.

"What did you want to say, Ashley?"

"I'd like to help, Tabitha. I'd like to come with you on your quest."

Tabitha held his eye. "What do you know about the journey?"

"Well I…that is, it is…you're going a long way?"

"What do you know?"

"More than I should," he admitted, looking desperately embarrassed. "I understand there's much danger. I'd like to help, your gr-Tabitha."

Tabitha frowned at the swallowed word. "Only if you're coming as a friend, and not a disciple."

He smiled. "I promise."

"He'll need a pack," said Garyll. "And a weapon of sorts."

He had a useful talent, so long as it was turned away from them, not toward them. "We can equip him in Southwind, can't we Garyll? We need to find horses there as well, don't we?"

"You need to get some rest before you climb on a horse, my love."

"I'll sleep when I know we cannot be stopped," she said, but she was very tired, and she knew it showed. "We have to get away."

"If I had some sprites I could help you," Ashley offered.

She knew what he was asking. "I can't make Light essence for you, Ashley. Not at the moment."

He looked disappointed. "Do you think I'll ever be able to learn to use the clear essence?" he asked.

Tabitha looked at him critically. She was sure she'd caught a glimpse of disturbance around him when he'd reached for her thoughts. "I think you already do, Ashley. The way you hear other people's thoughts, I don't understand it, but I can see your ability when I look for it. The essence spreads around you in tendrils. I felt your touch, just now. I'll know it now if you try again."

He mumbled an apology, looking again like an honest boy caught stealing sweets from a jar.

"I know you don't mean any harm, but be careful how you use your talent. Sometimes things are thought that are never meant to be said. A woman likes to have her secrets."

"So does a man," added Garyll from behind her. "So does a man."

The conversation died away after that, and Tabitha dozed against Garyll's warm chest. The night became colder, and very quiet. Somewhere on the water a bird hooted. A fish flopped into the Amberlake. The moon was out, a great pale eye on the horizon. It seemed they had only just settled into the journey when Mulrano aimed higher upwind to meet the approaching western shore of Southwind. The jumbled buildings of the lakeside village rose out of the darkness. The boat eased up to a jetty where many vessels lay tethered, the lake lapping against their hulls. Mulrano untied the mainsheet and the sail flapped loose, a sudden whip-crack in the night. He cursed and furled it against the mast. He glared into the night, but there was nothing to see.

A huge yawn crept up on Tabitha. She was stiff and too tired to care. All she wanted was somewhere to lie down.

"Kum," said Mulrano, as soon as they were on the jetty. He gathered their packs before they could shoulder them, and strode away along the planks. Tabitha staggered as the jetty tilted beneath her feet, but Garyll steadied her. Mulrano's boatshed was dark, as was the house crouched over and behind it. Then a light was struck within the house, and they saw the stairs ahead of them leading up to an open door.

"I think he means to offer us a bed," Garyll suggested. "I was going to hammer on the inn's door."

"He is a good man," Ashley added, in a whisper. "He is dead tired himself. He's been running supplies to Stormhaven all week. He was going to sleep in the harbour at Stormhaven, but he brought us here anyway."

Mulrano seated them in his lounge. He had lit a tall lamp and set a kettle upon the stove. The roof was low, thick-beamed, the walls planked with a warm-coloured oak. The carpet was soft beneath her feet, the chair deep and safe. As the solidity of the room embraced Tabitha's senses, she remembered another night when she had welcomed its refuge. She had sat in this room with the Riddler, so long ago, after their day-long flight from the Shadowcaster—another night Mulrano had been kept from his bed—a good man, indeed.

Mulrano hung his heavy coat upon a hook then came to stand before her.

"Whe you gong?" Mulrano asked.

"Sorry Mulrano, but it's a secret," Tabitha replied. "Somewhere we don't want anyone to follow us to."

"Ah wong tawk," he said.

"Already you talk more than I expected," said Garyll. "It is good to see you defy your tortures."

Mulrano turned away quickly. He collected four mugs from a shelf.

"Peppahmingk? Cbahk? Mehihah," he asked then grunted, his brow furrowing. "Mememah!"

He thumped his fist against the counter. "Meheehok!"

"Mellilot," Ashley said. "He wants to know if anyone would like some of the herb in their drink. It gives a really good sleep, especially if it's to be a short deep one." Mulrano glared at Ashley, and Ashley looked immediately alarmed, but a smile grew beneath the fisherman's frown, then he burst into laughter. He wagged a firm finger in the Lightgifter's direction.

Tabitha knew the herb. "Thanks, I'll have some, Mulrano. Just don't make it too strong. We need to be gone by first light. We might have some Swords following us."

"Kay. Ah wake hu up," Mulrano said, including them all in his gesture. "Hu dingk?

"Peppermint for me," said Ashley.

"Good for me too," Garyll said.

While Mulrano prepared their mugs, Tabitha's eyes strayed around the room. A great chart hung on the wall. It had many lines drawn on it over the Amberlake, linking trees and buildings inked near the shore with features on the rim like Fynn's Tooth, Riversend and the edge of the Zunskar mountains. Where the lines intersected each other, symbols and numbers cluttered the chart. Tabitha supposed it had something to do with positioning his boats on the Amberlake to find the best fish. But one inscription at the edge of the map caught her eye. She rose and approached the chart, and stood to one side to allow the light of the lamp to fall fully upon the parchment. High up in the forest above Llury, one of Mulrano's reference points was unmistakable.

"Do you know anything about the Penitent's pass?" she asked over her shoulder.

Mulrano brought her steaming mug with him, and passed it to her when he reached her side. He tapped against the chart with a thick finger.

He exhaled then waved his hand at her. "Uh-uh, uh-uh. Hu go up heah?"

Tabitha delayed her answer by taking a sip from the mug. He had mixed some honey in with the mellilot. It was soothing, and warm. It was no use denying that they were going to the Pass.

"Yes," she answered. "We might have to leave Eyri."

"Cahngk. No way ouk!" he said. "Nok foo Pengikank pahff."

"Why? What's there?"

Mulrano screwed up his face, but although it was obvious he wanted to say something, he only chewed on the words. At last he turned to Ashley, and tapped his forehead with his forefinger.

"He had some friends when he was young. They used to dare each other to do stupid things, like jumping from galloping horses or... What is that? Oh, standing on hot coals! You really did that?" Ashley raised his eyebrows. "They went up to the pass, ignoring the warnings of the folk of Llury, or probably because of them. But there is a good reason why the old pass is avoided. His two friends fell down from the crushing magic there. He crawled in to fetch them, and dragged them away, but they were dead."

"Oh dear. Dear oh dear oh dear. I'm so sorry, Mulrano."

Mulrano waved his hand dismissively, as if it was too long in the past to worry him now.

"Did you get through the pass?" Ashley asked. "Is there anything beyond it?"

Mulrano shook his head. "Ing ang back. Nok ouk." He screwed up his face again, obviously distressed.

"What's wrong?" Tabitha asked.

"It's sore to try and speak," said Ashley. "What's left of his tongue strains against his scars. That's why he's usually silent."

"Oh, forgive me, Mulrano. I didn't mean to be such a nuisance. We shouldn't be keeping you up, anyway. You've been so good to us."

He nodded to show it was all right then he pointed to them and rested his head on his clasped hands. He stomped to a big chest, pulled three thick blankets from it, and laid them on the floor beside the windows. He meant for them to sleep on the floor. The carpet was dense and soft—it would do fine. Mulrano's simple hospitality was refreshing. He showed no danger of revering or worshipping the Wizard of Eyri, and that frankness made Tabitha trust him all the more. He had offered them a place on the floor, not his own bed.

Mulrano looked at Ashley before he left, and shook his head, chuckling to himself as he left. When Mulrano had left the room, they sat close to the lamp and finished off their drinks. When they had taken their blankets and Garyll had snuffed out the lamp, Tabitha lay in the dark listening to the lapping of the lake and the sudden wind that gusted at the windows.

"I hope the Shield has weakened since he tried the pass," she whispered to Garyll.

Garyll grunted in acknowledgement. "He was turned away, and he's as solid as an oak."

"I wonder what it's like…outside."

12. WITNESS OF RUIN

"The prophet has spoken, but so have the others;
the madmen, the mockers and all their brothers."—Zarost

When Twardy Zarost encountered the first drops of blood, he began to run.

His boots made the only sound in the vaulted hallways of the Temple of the Word as he raced along wide corridors and between towering stone columns and tall staring faces. As if to mock the spattered trail, the floor was gaily patterned with the intricate designs of the monks and monikers of the Word, clerics who should have been thronging past him with their serene faces, turning their time-wheels, ringing their allotted note of the day, touching their foreheads after every word they spoke. No tattooed initiates, no braid-headed exclamants. Not even one reciter in any of the high boxes.

It was unnatural. With no one repeating the holy words and names, it seemed that the Gods themselves had died. Zarost knew what he would find, yet he had to find it. The awful silence of the Temple of the Word could only mean one thing.

The time for praying was over. Or maybe it had just begun, for everyone outside the temple.

Zarost had left the Gyre's library as soon as he had discovered the ruined Book of Is, those torn page stubs so ragged and so wrong. He had set his mind on reaching the temple in Qirrh, to find copies of the book. But his spell of Transference had failed to bring him to the temple. Instead of Qirrh, he had found himself farther east in Azique, where the disrupted gravity caused the perpetual mist of gravel and where the restless scorpion-scrub had conquered the once-fertile citrus and mulberry groves, leaving only wizened stalks behind. The hungry creatures of the wastelands galloped in straggling herds, their terrible ancestry forgotten. Zarost had left there in a hurry, but no matter how many times he cast the Transference he could not eliminate the uncertainty variable in the destination—Qirrh slipped from his grasp like a greasy melon seed. Wildfire threads grew thickly in the sky over Qirrh; something terrible was at work. He tried to approach the temple from the west instead, but the closest he could get to the settlement was the savannah of the Unclaimed Plains, and from there it had taken three days on foot to reach the great swing bridge spanning the chasm on the dry western border of Azique. From the first step upon the bridge he had sensed the wrongness in the air, the touch of Chaos ahead. Qirrh had been spared for centuries. The rest of the land of Azique had fallen, but the temple and its people had been spared; Ametheus had feared to induce the wrath of the Gods.

Evidently, Ametheus feared no more.

Zarost ran up a shallow flight of stairs. The spattered trail underfoot became a long red smear leading toward the Witness Chamber where the clerics kept their religious texts. For centuries the Clerics of the Word had held onto their faith—that eventually one of the Gods would answer their call, and their spiritual power would be restored. They would be the revered intermediaries once again, interpreting the word of the Gods for the people of the world, presenting prayers and requests on the people's behalf.

For the Clerics of the Word to stop calling would be to acknowledge the failure of their religion and the end of their hope. They would never abandon hope. They were that kind of people. And so they called, using the words and ceremonies detailed in the Book of Is, teaching the exacting lists of rules and procedures to their young acolytes, burning the holy glyphs onto their shaven scalps just as they impressed their promises of lifelong service onto their minds, before allowing the hair to grow and be braided into the ever-lengthening strands of their years at the temple. From monk to monk, from monniker to monniker, father to son and mother to daughter, a ladder of disciplic succession led back quite a few generations.

It had been going on for two millennia now.

Astonishing faith or stubbornness, their belief was a part of their restricted family tree. To deny it would be to deny that they carried the blood of their ancestors; to abandon the Word would be to call every relative a fool. Even mockery had no effect on their beliefs. There were no outsiders in the faith, for the monks of the Word were only permitted to enter the Chamber of Eternal Love with a monniker, and one only became a monk or monniker by being born in the Temple. Every new child became a child of the Word, and was considered to be the offspring of everyone in the temple, and was cared for and loved as such. The whole of Qirrh lived in service to the Temple and the Word, every member of the whole inbred family devoted to one purpose—to call out the Words and to await the return of the Gods.

It was sad that no one outside the temple remembered the Gods, for that was what they really needed. They didn't need Gods, they needed people.

When the empire of Azique fell under the Sorcerer's wrath, the temple lost many of the pilgrims and parishioners who came to listen to the Word and offer tokens of respect to the temple. Without that income, the inhabitants of Qirrh were forced to scrape out ever more from the soils around their settlement, but the land was left dry by what Ametheus had done to it, and so the monks and monnikers of the Word became thinner and thinner, their monastic life ever more ascetic and gruelling.

The Temple at Qirrh had not always been the only one. Many copies of the Book of Is had been penned before the years of Order and lesser temples had sprung up all over the lands, each proclaiming to offer a truer faith. Then the combined lores of magic and technology wove the web of Order across Oldenworld. Order was an irresistable path to wealth, and so the faith in the Gods was abandoned. A few monasteries had endured, but in the end those temples had been shot through with wildfire, the disciples had become undisciplined. As far as Zarost knew, only the Temple at Qirrh remained true to their ancient convictions.

The saddest part of their tale was that even Zarost knew their faith was misplaced. The Gods would not be returning to the earthly plane. That early age had passed, and for good reason. The Parting of Disbelief had been introduced to protect humankind. The separation ensured that the dialogue between humans and Gods was one-sided. Most people didn't think deeply enough to be able to hold a dialogue with the Gods. People prayed for superficial things they forgot soon thereafter. They found a way to achieve the really important matters themselves, if left to their own devices, or they began to dream. If the Gods answered every request, there would be no need for dreams to form, and without dreams, humankind would be a dull species indeed—duller than a jumble of jackasses, Zarost thought.

And people were also very predictable. Sooner or later they would launch into the other kind of prayer. Everyone wanted to live forever. The ones who were the most outspoken in their right to eternal life were those least worthy of it—people who didn't know what to do with their time on a rainy Sunday afternoon and yet demanded a millennium or more to complete the important tasks they had yet to do. Those most worthy of immortality were the ones who never asked for it. They went humbly about their diminishing days, giving of their precious time to serve others, grateful for what they had received.

Zarost often wondered if he gave enough of what had been gifted to him. For the moment his service seemed to be adequate. He knew this because he was still alive, but he would not be the Riddler forever; he was only a Riddler while there was a need for a Riddler. Then again, he wasn't beyond ensuring that the need remained.

Even he didn't try to understand the Gods. Most Gods didn't *think* simply enough to be able to hold a dialogue with humans. They were complex, complicated, eternal beings whose thoughts spanned aeons. They had a language too powerful for humans to utter. Each syllable would burn flesh and bone to cinders. The words of the Gods held the essence of many concepts; each word was able to affect fundamentals across the universe. Most of them had little compassion for the souls trapped in the present and bonded in flesh. They could not understand what it was like, for they saw the eternal. They knew people in terms of the movement of generations, and when viewed over time, humanity repeated the same actions, over and over. No wonder the Gods considered humankind to be barely intelligent. No wonder they had become ruthless with their manipulations to improve the variety of colours in the threads of lineage, wiping out peoples with floods, pestilence and war. The Parting of Disbelief was as much a protection for humans as it was a curtain of privacy for the Gods. Gods and men could not live shoulder to shoulder. That truth would never change, and yet the Clerics of the Word had prayed for the chance every day.

Zarost had come to the high arched door of the Witness Chamber, where the clerics observed their daily ceremonies. The trail of blood led under the door. Zarost dreaded what he was going to find. He reached for the gilded handle, the door burst outward and dark fluid washed against his legs. The chamber was filled with humped shapes. The stench hit him in his stomach and doubled him over. He gagged. Flies rushed past him in a swarm of little eyes and dirty mouths. The sticky air was full of their villainous buzz. The current against his knees was thick with hidden textures, and something dragged by his right leg, touching him with a dead caress. He jerked his foot up. Weed clung to his trousers.

Weed. That was odd. He straightened against his nausea.

The humped objects were as randomly shaped as fallen trees. They weren't human forms at all. The floor of the Witness Chamber was grey, pink and green around dark liquid pools, uneven and mottled like the speckled flesh of soft mushrooms, like a membrane of organic debris floating on vitriol. The books of lore were gone, the narrow benches, the dais and its nectar cups, the dishes for the traditional flowers, sweets and incense had all vanished. And so had the people, those monks and monikers who should have been clustered around the dais, their faces turned to the sky in hope, their little chimes jangling on their wrists as they spun their time-wheels in the hope of returning to the age when they would be heard.

No trace of them remained.

On the far side of the chamber, a tangle of vines explored an empty temple torch, but even as Zarost looked at them, the vines dropped off the glass sconce and began to search up a nearby pillar. Elsewhere, the speckled surface puckered into a mouth, issued a low moan, then shivered and was gone. Ripples passed outward like the twitching of a horse's hide. A ripe gust pushed against Zarost's face.

Everywhere, the flies skittered about, flying from moist slit to weeping carbuncle, crawling into pinched crevasses, feasting on the oozing fluids of the unnatural landscape. It was as if the entire floor of the chamber had been replaced with a restless rotten bog. Yes, that *was* the answer to this riddle, Zarost realised. This was no illusion, it was a discontinuity. He was facing another part of the world, a sliver of space from somewhere like the Growing Lands on the coast north of Turmodin.

He stepped back at once, out of the weakening flow of the liquid which poured from the doorway. He put a shaking hand upon the cool stone wall. Fool! That had been too close. He had to be more alert. If he had gone any farther into the chamber, he would have fallen into the discontinuity; he would have crossed into it and found himself in the ruined coast, in the lowlands, far away. Once there, so close to Turmodin and the source of Chaos, his own magic could have become lethal to him. Wildfire would react to his presence before his Transference spell could engage. He would have been annihilated.

The trap of the mottled bog lurked beyond the door, a place that shouldn't be there. Zarost had seen this kind of spell before, where the Sorcerer had swapped pieces of the world as if they were parts of a jigsaw puzzle. He paid no heed to the Grand Pattern; he mocked the symmetry and order of the Universe. It was sorcery at its worst. Rearranging parts of the world at will caused untold repercussions. One part of the universal matrix held the pattern of the whole, just as the whole held the pattern of each single matrix. Changes of this magnitude ruptured the concurrency of the matrices, and caused chaos in the Universe.

Chaos, the only element that never changed.

Ametheus had used discontinuity spells before, adding foreign parts to his almost-sentient coastline as one would feed scraps of meat to a pet. But the trail of blood through the Temple told Zarost that this was not idle foraging. Someone had been here, there had been a struggle, and someone had ensured that all the clerics had been taken to the Witness Chamber. Ametheus had worked on the temple for a reason, and he had someone to help him.

But why take the Clerics of the Word somewhere in the stinking morass of the Growing Lands? They would surely die in that mire. Why now, after all these years, did he decide to end the last temple?

Zarost couldn't guess, but he knew finding a copy of the Book of Is was even more urgent than before. No trace of the book remained here. The clerics had been the only ones who knew the lore inside out, and they had been silenced.

If Ametheus did find a way to begin an audience with a God, there would be nobody who knew how to engage the Parting of Disbelief to terminate it. The Sorcerer, holding an audience with a God, now that was a terrifying thought. If Ametheus succeeded in awakening a Prime God like the Destroyer, and the Gyre had no mechanism to sever that dialogue, then the end would truly come upon them all. It was an unlikely scenario, but then the Sorcerer delighted in the art of the unlikely.

The sky bleeds with wildfire seeds and beasts unholy roar
until the Pillar in the lowlands claims life evermore

Could that fate come upon them so soon? He refused to believe it. Prophecy was as unreliable as juggling frogs—all those possible futures dancing in one's hands. He needed something definite to settle his unease. He needed the Book of Is, but it was gone. If fate was bearing down upon them like a knotted ball of wildfire, then there had to be a way for the Gyre to prepare itself. There had to be, or everything he understood about the geometry of Chance was wrong. There was always a path to follow to re-establish the balance; Chaos could not triumph without a chance having been present for Order to triumph as well. It might be a well-hidden chance, but a chance there would be.

Zarost scratched in his beard. There was only one place where such a text could be, and it was highly unlikely. There had been a man in the Temple who had turned his back on his faith, one cynical monk who had been a misfit among his simple brethren. He had walked a long way to find his peace. Something of that monk's legacy might linger still in the Passover trading post. Perhaps a copy of the sacred book he had taken with him might have been kept for its antique value. An obscure chance, Zarost knew, but the more he considered it the more he liked it. Such an out-of-the-way place, such an obscure solution—precisely the kind of path where well-hidden chances lurked, precisely the kind of path he was so practiced at finding.

Yes, he would find the Book in Passover. That was where the slim chance lay for the Gyre to oppose the momentum of the Sorcerer. Zarost turned on his heel. He would have to return to the Unclaimed Plains before attempting the Transference spell, the wildfire web above Qirrh was too thickly corded to trust. He left the violated Witness Chamber of the Temple of the Word behind him and hurried away.

"This place will never be the same again," he muttered to himself.

It couldn't be. It was now part of the coastline of old Orenland.

The fear of corruption chased his thoughts ahead of him. He tried his best to keep up.

13. FRIENDS FOR LIFE

"The measure of a friend's faith
is weighed on scales of sacrifice."—Zarost

Mulrano presented them with four horses just after dawn. He had even found some riding clothes for Tabitha. He was packed; he was going to the pass with them, come downpours or demons. Ashley guessed Tabitha just gave in to his stubbornness in the end because she couldn't afford to argue any longer with a man who couldn't speak, and the horses were a real boon. She was in a hurry to be off, but whatever weighed on her mind was held too deeply for Ashley to see. Not that he tried, of course.

He had a good-natured grey mare called Sugarlump, who twisted her ears to listen to his voice as he rode. After the easy climb up the stone-bordered trail from Southwind they slowed around Westmill, where the trail was rutted from heavy use by the flour wagons and grain carts. They rode the horses carefully to avoid twisting a hoof. After Westmill, the trail improved again, until the washouts where they climbed from the border farms of Meadowmoor County into the lowest fringe of the Great Forest. A work crew was busy repairing the road, stacking pebbles and earth against staked planks, and they waved cheerful hellos as the four riders picked their way past them. Once they reached the ramshackle village of Brimstone, they watered the horses and bought some bread and cheese, not even pausing long enough for the sweat to cool on the horses' coats. They let the horses stretch their legs on the log-scoured High Way running north from Brimstone. They steered clear of the village of Llury altogether, with its busy timber yards, rough-humoured loggers and carved-trinket peddlers, leaving the main road in the late afternoon, hidden by a ridge and the thick forest. Tabitha wanted to avoid the crowds, and Ashley didn't blame her. He had seen the spectacle in Stormhaven. It would be better if nobody knew. They were well beyond Llury when they came upon a greensward amid the trees and struck camp for the night.

They picketed the horses on a piece of turf after watering them at the rivulet nearby. Mulrano rigged a basic shelter for the night, using lightweight sailcloth and a few long branches. He even collected a great bank of dry leaves and grasses for them to lie upon—he was trying to give them every comfort before tomorrow's task. The anticipation of danger weighed upon them all.

But the danger came upon Ashley sooner than he'd expected, because Garyll decided that he needed some weapons' training, and no sooner had he suggested it than he advanced upon Ashley, as if to prove his point.

Garyll's baton scythed through the air toward him.

Ashley ducked, the weapon passing so close it brushed his hair. Garyll struck fast, driving Ashley back, alarmingly intent. The sun had faded from the trees, and it was difficult making out the swordmaster's movements in the half-light.

Ashley caught the next blow on his staff quite by accident as he thrust it down to balance himself. The impact sent a jarring vibration through his arm. Garyll spun and struck from the other side. Ashley just met it in time with the lower end of his staff.

Smack! That would have been his knee.

Garyll wouldn't really hurt me, would he?

He stumbled backward, allowing the staff to rotate with the momentum of the strike, but it pulled his arms aside and there was a moment when his ribs were exposed to an attack. Garyll was suddenly too close, his baton raised in a fatal position above his head. Ashley hurriedly brought the staff up, but too slowly. The baton stung his scalp.

It was a light rap, no more. Garyll's control was incredible. He steadied Ashley a moment later.

"You let me get inside you," Garyll chided. "Stop retreating in a straight line. Step aside, move around me and keep yourself out of range. Your staff is longer than my baton. Use that to your advantage. Keep me where you can hit me but where I can't hit *you*."

Ashley smiled weakly and nodded. So begun a spirited half hour. Being worked over by the Swordmaster was as intense as being in a real fight. Not the Swordmaster any more, Ashley reminded himself, although he couldn't really believe it. He knew he was ill-prepared, if any of the prophecies Tabitha had told him about were true. He was certain that if he faced someone half as good as Garyll Glavenor in combat, he had a good plan. He would run.

Glavenor had only the baton, a slender tapered club with a wire-bound hilt. It was a harmless-looking weapon when compared to the formidable blade he used to wield, but Ashley soon learnt the baton was not at all harmless. It may not kill an opponent, but it would certainly discourage anyone once they learnt of Garyll's skill. Ashley's staff, which had felt so light when Mulrano had given it to him that morning, grew heavy all on its own. Garyll corrected his weak grip, so that he held the staff with one palm up and the other down, shoulder width apart, balanced in the centre. It gave him two ends to use, though he wasn't any good with either of them. Ashley concentrated on keeping hold of the shaft. If he lost it, he was sure he would earn a new bruise. Garyll had a hard sense of humour.

Tabitha was watching from beside the fire. Garyll came at him again, and this time Ashley jumped to the side. The baton caught him against the ribs.

"*Oof.*"

"Other side," said Garyll. "I've got more reach on the beginning of the stroke." He swung the baton again. "See?" Ashley skittered away to Garyll's left. The baton missed, which felt much better.

Garyll's mind was closed. Ashley had sensed him change as soon as they had squared up. It was as if Garyll watched all of him, and from a great height. Ashley tried to avoid being hit, but after a long series of failures, he tried to copy what Garyll did. As his attention rose to watch his body from above, his reactions improved. He began to parry and move without thinking. He even forced Garyll to block, once. He just hoped he wouldn't have to take too many bruises before Glavenor called an end to the session.

His improvements didn't go unnoticed, and he spent the next few minutes running away as Garyll piled on the pressure. Ashley's tunic was soaked with sweat when they finally joined Tabitha at the campfire. He flopped down onto the grass beside her.

"Your man is a big bully," he stated, out of breath. "Please make him stop hitting me."

Tabitha laughed softly. Garyll came up close to her.

"Come down here, big bully," she scolded, taking his hand into her own.

Garyll reclined beside Tabitha and the flames, and she threaded her arms around his neck. Ashley wondered what it would feel like to be held by her like that. Tabitha was beautiful with the firelight on her face. Flecks of gold danced in her brown eyes, and the warm flame light was caught in her loose dark curls. The ruddy colour of her brushed-leather coat just made her skin look cleaner. Ashley's eyes wandered. Beneath the bunched collar of her jersey was a gentle swelling where her two crystals lay hidden, her mystery of clear essence. What would it be like to touch them? Would they be cool, or warm, where they lay? Her throat was very smooth.

Garyll turned and looked at him, his level gaze measuring him as if they were still sparring. "Sit closer to the fire, Ashley. Keep warm while you dry or you'll be as stiff as an old crone tomorrow."

Ashley laughed nervously. "I'm stiffer than that already, thanks." A day in the saddle hadn't helped. "I'll make you regret training me. You'll taste the end of that staff yet."

"I look forward to the day," said Garyll with a faint smile. The collar of his tunic wasn't even damp.

Don't be crazy. You meant that as a joke, didn't you? What were you thinking of doing? Challenging Glavenor for his girl?

He rolled closer to the fire and kept his eyes studiously on the dancing flames. The heat slowly evaporated the sweat from his clothes. He could feel a bruise between his ribs that was going to be a shiner in the morning. He wished he had some Light essence. A quick Heal-all spell would erase everything in an instant.

Night crept upon them from the western horizon, slipping down between the two knuckled peaks poking from the green-tinged saddle above them. A sense of foreboding settled on Ashley's shoulders as he remembered where they would be, come morning: the Penitent's pass, no more than an hour away.

Tabitha had said that dawn was the weakest time for the Shield, but the way Mulrano had coughed and looked away into the distance when she'd said that had told him it wouldn't make much of a difference.

Mulrano returned from the forest with another armful of logs.

Once the fire had produced a good bed of coals, Mulrano produced a fat fish wrapped in dark leaves. It lost its head to his big-bladed axe. He cleaned and salted it, and it hissed, steamed and smoked as it cooked upon the coals. Mulrano shared it in steaming portions. Garyll added some crusty panbread to make their supper.

Later, before turning to his blanket, Ashley joined Mulrano against a log near the fire. He wondered what to say to make friends with the bluff fisherman. Garyll and Tabitha nestled down in the shelter, although Ashley sensed Glavenor wasn't really asleep. The night thickened around them, filled with the gentle calls of forest creatures. The fire burnt lower. Mulrano tossed another branch into the coals and a shower of sparks soared upward.

"It must be terrible to be dumb," Ashley said. Too late he realised how that had sounded.

Mulrano's hand shot out and grabbed his tunic, anger in his eye and a snarl upon his lips. With his free hand he grabbed the big-bladed axe and adjusted his grip on it, ready to swing. Its edge was wickedly sharp. Ashley scrambled for the fisherman's thoughts.

A chop through his scrawny neck will keep the suffering greenfly quiet! Just there, above his collar!

Ashley panicked and tried to pull away but he couldn't break Mulrano's powerful grip. He raised his arms and wriggled out of his tunic instead, scrabbling frantically on the ground to get away. He tripped and fell down on his backside beside the fire.

Garyll was beside him, having launched from his bed like a hunting cat, but he stopped just as suddenly. He stooped to help Ashley up. He began to chuckle.

"What's going on?" asked Tabitha sleepily.

Ashley turned toward Mulrano and saw his wolfish grin. Mulrano laughed with deep, booming laughter.

"Young Ashley here yanked the wrong chain," Glavenor answered.

Ashley retrieved his crumpled tunic from Mulrano, feeling foolish. "I really believed you were going to chop my head off like the fish. You thought it so clearly." Mulrano laughed again and tapped the side of his forehead with a finger, then threw an open hand of air at Ashley. Ashley caught the thought. "I'm not as bloody clever as I think I am, and I'd best be careful whom I pinch my thoughts from."

Mulrano clapped his hands together in delight. He tapped his forehead again, inviting Ashley to take another thought.

"It is good for you to hear your thoughts spoken aloud again, even if by a dumb Lightgifter," Ashley recited.

Mulrano roared with laughter and gripped Ashley in a comradely embrace. Ashley was overwhelmed by the fisherman's gruff humour.

"Right, now play quietly, boys," Garyll admonished, before settling down with Tabitha once more.

As Ashley relaxed beside Mulrano he began to laugh at himself as well. He really had been caught, good and proper. He wished he'd talked more with the fisherman during their journey instead of finding excuses to ride beside Tabitha.

"Will you come with us through the pass, Mulrano?"

Mulrano nodded. "I owe ik koo her."

Ashley waved his hand. "Let me pick your thoughts."

Mulrano held his eye. "Ngo buggahee?"

"No buggery?" He smiled. "Promise."

Mulrano relaxed, and his thoughts came up clearly like rocks through a retreating tide. "Young Tabitha stood against that blue-mouthed half-bred bastard who called himself the Darkmaster, she stopped him. I owe her my life for that, we all do. My grandfather was Golan the Great. Who am I? What have I done? I am just a fisherman, but here is my chance to do something greater. And, besides, I promised a friend I would help Tabitha no matter what, and I'll bloody well not break that promise."

Ashley nodded. "Who is the friend who you made the promise to?"

Mulrano's thoughts moved like a pool of rippled sunlight. "Ah, the Riddler, the old pipe twiddler. He is an elusive fellow. Have you met the Riddler?"

Ashley wasn't sure. "I...think so, the bard who helped Tabitha in First Light. Tsoraz. She said there was more to him than meets the eye, though she wouldn't explain."

"Hah, and that's the truth of it!" thought Mulrano. "If he told you his name was Tsoraz, then he was playing a trick on you. His name's Twardy Zarost. He's a strange fellow, make no mistake, but he saved my life."

"Tsoraz. I've got it...backward. Zarost!"

As Mulrano tapped his forehead again, Ashley extended his mind further. The thoughts were so clear he could feel the words as if they lay carved before him. Beyond the words were images, and beyond these were the vague hot-and-cold of Mulrano's feelings. Ashley entered another world through the gateway of Mulrano's eyes, a world beyond the surface of the man, a place where his memory and experience lived in a fury of light, sound and colour.

Ashley was suddenly nervous; he was deeper into his mind than the fisherman realised. Bright images surrounded Ashley, and beyond them darker memories lingered. He guided himself backward, out of the intimate depths, back to the surface of Mulrano's mind where he felt more comfortable. A clear sequence of thoughts took form before him in stark relief, a vision narrated in Mulrano's gruff voice. Ashley supposed that everyone *thought* with their own voice, in their own manner.

"Haven't seen the Riddler much until recently," thought Mulrano. "I knew him long ago. There was a day, back when I had no more than the boat my old man had left me to my name, when I was out on the water, a calm day with a lazy sun. I was dozing against the rail with a line over the back, trolling for the greenfin. A stupid slackwit I, with even a cleat in the mainsheet. I heard the gust approaching across the water, whipping spray, but I didn't move quick enough to avoid the boom. Empty-headed ass! It clipped me on my bloody crown, and the Riddler says I was hit clear out of the boat, but I'd lost my thinking and remembering by then. I'd have drowned, I would have, but he pulled me from the lake. He never did tell me how he came so far out on the water to save me. Funny that, but when I came around I was coughing out the foul taste of my own death and breathing again, and he was sitting there grinning at me. And the day was fine, hardly a breath of wind on the water, it was the strangest thing. My boat was still out there, drifting on a slack sail.

"I offered him a meal, and the Riddler stayed on. We spent months fishing together, though he was looking for something deeper than the greenfins or even soles. He'd never bait his hook, only send it to the bottom with the sinkers, and stare into the depths as if he could see where he stirred it about in the mud. I thought he was a bloody nutter at times. There was a day he seemed excited. He washed his hook off as if there was something on it, but it was clean. He pretended to pocket something, said he'd found the path again. He's full of strange comments like that. He left. I seldom saw him after that day, but our friendship won't be weakened by the years. He's a good man, he is, even if he is the strangest fellow I know. He can tie a man's head in knots with his riddles."

"And where is he now?"

"Oh, he can be scarce when he wants to be. I think he could have hidden on the Darkmaster's door and they wouldn't have known it. Miss Tabitha might know more than I of his whereabouts; he took a great interest in her. Who wouldn't, eh? She's a rare jewel, that one."

"And yet she seems to draw trouble upon herself," Ashley commented.

He clapped Ashley on the back. "That's what we are here for," he seemed to think, but the link was clouded for a moment, and Ashley couldn't be sure.

"It has been good talking with you this strange way in my head, fella, but you're beginning to addle my brain, and I think you'd best get a good night's sleep if you're to have any hope in the pass."

Ashley turned to Mulrano. "How bad is the pass, really?"

"Gheep, young fe'ow. You gohng'k wong koo know."

It was strange to hear Mulrano's tortured speech again. Ashley realised that he might not have spoken at all during the discussion with Mulrano, he'd only thought of the words. He was developing his ability to *send* his thoughts.

"I don't want to know?" he asked out loud. Mulrano nodded.

Ashley rose, wincing against stiff muscles. "What about you? When do you want to be relieved of the night watch?"

Mulrano shook his head. "I've beeng up koo va paff befoh. I wong'k gheep."

Ashley walked slowly to his blanket, and eased in behind Tabitha and Garyll. His ribs ached, but in a way he wished that the training with Garyll had been longer. It had taken his mind off worrying about the pass.

Tomorrow their strength would be tested.

଼ଓଓଊଊ

They ascended toward the rim of Eyri early the next morning— four riders under the pale pre-dawn sky. Tabitha opened her senses to the sounds of the elements. The air had a cold delicate music to it, the rivulet chuckled and the earth pulsed with a soft undertone. But the sounds faded as they climbed. The tall trees of the forest gave way to shorter relatives: wizened, crouching on either side of the wash like cowed slaves chained to the place Fate had assigned their roots. Then the foliage was altogether defeated. Only a green moss clung belligerently to the rocks, and a mist came searching toward them from the west, through the bald saddle high above that was the Penitent's pass.

Tabitha reined in. Something had passed her, on the limit of her hearing, but it was gone again. Garyll looked back at her. She flicked the reins to urge her mount on. Her ring warmed as she drew on it for clarity, but there was nothing immediate to sense. Just an unsettling impression of space closing in, something she couldn't see, taste or touch, but she knew it was there—the Shield of Eyri, the limit to the realm, ahead of them among the peaks.

They encountered a lone weathered cairn. Among the rough stones was a plaque, so eroded by the years only a sliver of script remained on the smoothened slab—'Our Eyr...' and '...nevermore.' Tabitha paused. So many years had passed since the legendary final battle against the invaders, and yet a sense of violence lingered in the air, as if the Swords still fought to rid Eyri of those savage men in this oppressive channel.

And they were hoping to push beyond the pass. Garyll sat silently on his roan horse beside her, watching.

"Not a restful place for the fallen men of Stevenson's company," she whispered.

He nodded, but said nothing.

The sense of conflict became worse as they rode higher in the valley, as if the narrowing cliffs pressed in on them from either side. Something hummed beneath the sounds of the wind and the gentle movements of the horses, something deep and ominous, filling the air with a strange potency. Tabitha's breath caught in her throat; the air became thicker and awkward to inhale. The weight of it began to press upon her.

They came across three boulders huddled together like a natural windbreak. As Mulrano began to lead the way past them, his horse balked. He spurred it on with a vigorous heel, but the black stallion tossed its head then reared and whinnied loudly.

"Wait, Mulrano!" shouted Ashley, dismounting and approaching the distressed horse. "Your stallion thinks there's something ahead. He's just put his nose into something."

"Paing," Mulrano declared, nodding his head as if he'd expected it.

Ashley pushed past the boulders, then yelped and jumped back.

"What is it?" shouted Garyll, dropping from his own horse, his baton drawn.

Ashley's face was pale. "I don't know, it's like...being hit with a hundred arrows."

Garyll strode past Ashley at once, wielding his baton ahead of him like a sword. He slowed, grunted softly, and bowed his head then he waded on for a few paces with his shoulders squared. Tabitha could see it was an effort for him.

Mulrano didn't bother to dismount. "We cahnk go ong," he declared in his laboured way, pointing past Garyll. "More ang more paing, heavy, heavy paing. If hu go fah ong..." He clapped his hands to his temples, pretending to crush his head. "Cum back!" he called out to Garyll. "Ik mek hu weak!"

Tabitha asked Ashley to take her horse's reins, but Mulrano reached out of his saddle and stopped her when she dismounted. His concern was plainly written on his weathered face. "Heavy paing."

"I must understand it," Tabitha told him. If they were going to get through the pass, she had to overcome the magic the Gyre had cast to seal Eyri in. She had to experience the repulsion of the Shield, if that was what Garyll laboured against.

She followed him beyond the boulders. The power assaulted her, a force like a solid sound that hammered against her suddenly clammy skin. Her knees threatened to give in, but she refused to step away. The barrage was like a massive drumbeat against her sensitive ears, loud yet low, the tone so deep it went below the lowest musical scale she knew, as if it wasn't sound but rather a rarefied form of pure volume. The surges threatened to crumple her skull.

To escape she took her awareness forward and away, and as she did so her pain became displaced; the agony was left behind in her aching body. She ranged ahead quickly, trying to perceive the source of the resonance before her strength gave in. Clear essence shimmered in a corded web before her, a web that became denser in successive layers the higher up the pass she searched. The patterns within the essence were complex, the clarity intense, yet despite the order of the weave, there were places where it was disturbed, as if a wind had swirled through the finely threaded pattern and twisted it awry, leaving caverns of stillness within the malignant thrumming web. Tabitha tried to understand the pattern of the spell, but the many layers of the coiled network prevented her from sensing a signature in the essence. Perhaps at the terminal face of the Shield it would be clearer to perceive.

The deepsound was everywhere ahead. The resonance sought to crush her into an extremely dense, unified, fused being. She turned her gaze away from the power. It was too much; she couldn't bear it any more. She choked and coughed, and staggered away, back toward the boulders, but as she did so she noticed pale marks upon the rocks, a ghostly imprint of feet which veered away from her own trail. She spun around. The pale trace of the footprints stretched onward, beside Garyll's tracks, past him and toward the mists.

She couldn't breathe for the pressure on her chest. She retreated to the rocks, where the sudden release from the spell left her heaving for air.

Garyll returned a moment later. He'd been farther in than Tabitha.

He rested on his knees while he stared at the ground and coughed quietly. Tabitha rested her hand on his shoulder. "Someone's come through here recently," she said, when he had recovered. She pointed to the separate trail, which she could see held two pairs of feet. Both prints were mid-sized. It had to be Bevn and the Shadowcaster.

Garyll shook his head. "I don't see a thing."

She walked downhill to where an imprint lay faintly in a depressed patch of moss. "Here," she said to the others. "Those aren't my prints, and they're too small to belong to any of you."

"You have sharp eyes," said Garyll. "I saw nothing there, but I think you are right. One set."

"Two," she corrected, pointing to the ghostly image upon undisturbed soil. "I see a second pair."

Garyll squinted his eyes and then shook his head, but Tabitha knew that he believed her.

"The prince and another?" he asked.

"Could be."

"So we have no choice. We must go on."

"Ngo!" objected Mulrano. "Ik gek werff! Hu've beeng owngyee ing egg! Werff vang a hoff kikker ing yo heg. Fuk!" He punched the air in frustration at his words.

"I could help," offered Ashley. "He meant to say—"

Tabitha held up her hand. "It's all right, Ashley, we got the gist of it. Mulrano, I have to try it to be sure, "but it doesn't look as harsh all the way through. There are pockets where I think we might shelter. Maybe Bevn disturbed the spell by passing through it."

Garyll was at once attentive. "How far in?"

"Twice as far as you went and off to the left a bit. That's the first one."

"The horses won't like it," Ashley noted.

Tabitha hadn't considered the horses. Ashley was right, they'd hate it. She wondered if they might have to leave the beasts behind, but knew at once that they couldn't. The horses were loaded with provisions, including the food for the riders. If they had to carry all those packs themselves, they'd never catch up to the prince and the Kingsrim. Besides, with the prince on foot, they'd soon be able to ride him down. They needed the horses more than ever.

"I might be able to do something," Ashley said suddenly. He rubbed the nose of his grey mare tenderly, gazing into her eyes. The mare tossed her head and snorted, but only the once, then she seemed to become calm. Ashley grinned, pleased with himself. He backed beyond the boulders, and the mare followed, but although he seemed to have comforted the horse, he couldn't pretend that he didn't feel the awful pressure himself. He grimaced, and his hands began to shake.

"What about the others?" Tabitha shouted. "Do you want us to ride them alongside you, or in file?"

"Just keep them close. I'll do what I can." He grimaced again as he mounted. "Hurry, lead us in. Let's try it."

Mulrano went second. There was a mix of excitement and dread on his face. He loosened his great axe from its baldric, and held it like a staff ahead of himself. He grunted as he entered the affected area, and when he led his stallion forward, it resisted, but Tabitha saw the concentration deepen on Ashley's face, and the horse stepped up. Mulrano mounted then gestured to Ashley.

"Mulrano thinks it is weaker than normal," Ashley exclaimed. "Weaker? Just how bad?" His voice trailed off as he conferred in silence with Mulrano. "He says that in this place it was once much stronger."

"How far in did he go?" Tabitha wondered aloud.

"Beyond where the moss ends, into the shale band," Ashley called out. "He was young and stubborn. He almost killed himself. Ai! Come, Tabitha, come! It's bad for me already."

She moved, and the pain came upon her. Both her horse and Garyll's behind her reared against the wall of magic, and both times Ashley appeared to take more of a load before they calmed. He began to look greyer than his mare. "I don't know how long I can do this and resist the pressure," Ashley pleaded hoarsely as she passed him. "I'm going to lose one of them. I get all their pain, all of it!"

"Then ride!" she answered, jumping to her saddle and spurring her horse into a gallop to take the lead. They charged against the deadly threaded matrix of the Shield.

The deepsound threatened every part of her body; she fled by projecting her awareness again, but the sanctuary eluded her, for the projection only allowed her to sense the whole valley thrumming with that one fusing note. The awesome volume rose against her with every stride her horse took. The sky descended upon her shoulders. She was pressed hard into the ground. The air stamped against her head, her streaming eyes felt ready to burst and the air was like cold treacle in her lungs. What if she was wrong? What if they reached that space in the spell ahead and found nothing changed, or found the pressure to be worse? Her horse neighed suddenly, and wrenched at the reins. It bucked her from the saddle, and she caught at its neck as she fell, able to steady herself as her feet reached the ground. She couldn't ride it any more, but she had to go on, and she would not abandon her horse where it was. She gathered the reins and strained forward in a faltering run. Ashley must have helped her, for the horse followed her and did not fight.

Before long she could hardly walk. She dragged the horse after her, pleaded with it, coaxing it until there was just one last step. And there, just as the mist wrapped around them in a thin veil, silent and sinuous, Tabitha reached the first haven.

The pressure was off. The filtered sun cast an eerie light upon the green moss. She sank down beside her horse. The others were almost there; they'd make it for sure. Relief washed over her and she cried softly as the pain eased from her limbs. That had been bad—far worse than she'd expected.

Mulrano came in fast behind her, leading his stallion, but Garyll laboured with Ashley at the edge of the mists. The Lightgifter clung to Garyll's belt, his feet dragging across the rocks and moss. Garyll hauled the two horses behind him as well, using the crook of his elbow to hold their reins, and they weren't calm. Tabitha winced as Garyll's roan stallion reared and landed heavily with its hooves either side of Ashley.

She wanted to get up and run to help him, but her body refused— her legs wouldn't respond. She knew she had taken too much pain in the crossing and she could not bear any more. She had reached her limit. No, she had pushed beyond it, and now she was paying for it. She watched helplessly as Garyll crumpled to his knees, then rose again, then fell. He was spending too long in the pressure. He was being crushed because he was held back by Ashley and the horses.

Mercy! It was even worse for Ashley, she realised. He'd taken on the pain of all the horses, as well as his own. Tabitha cried out as she realised how much agony she had caused them all with her impatience to be through the Shield. It was all her fault.

Without a word, Mulrano surged to his feet and charged into the barrage again. When he reached Garyll, he took Ashley from him, scooping him up in his corded arms as if he weighed no more than a child. They shouldered their way toward Tabitha, and at last, they broke through.

The men tumbled to the ground. Garyll coughed against his knees.

Mulrano pressed his head against the stones, and clutched at the moss with clenched fists. Ashley curled into a ball and gulped at the air, quivering where he lay.

Tabitha watched them through her tears. She knew that the farther they went, the deeper the sound would become, deeper and more penetrating. The turf soon became bare rock ahead, stripped of all green by the harsh atmosphere. The spell was horrible—it coursed through everything. It vibrated in her bones even within the queer shelter of the green-aired refuge. And the clear essence became a tight, almost seamless web ahead, disturbed only in a narrow swathe where the trail of footprints lay. There was not enough space for all of them and the horses. Even if she went alone...

Someone retched behind her. She turned. Ashley's lips were blue. He arched suddenly, and retched again on the rocks. Then he cried softly, quivering against his pain.

Mulrano was watching her.

"Ngo," he said fiercely. "Ngo more fo him."

She met Mulrano's eye, and nodded. They couldn't go on, not like this.

She had to face what she was trying to avoid: she had to use her power, reach for the Lifesong, to summon it, regardless of the dread she felt. Reaching for the Lifesong meant reaching for Ethea, but she had no choice. She forced her legs to bear her weight, and fetched her lyre from the pack. Its familiar music would help her find her voice. The deep note of fusion dominated everything. It threatened to bind, to crush, to seal them together. Tabitha tried to block it out of her mind as she sat beside Ashley and considered what she would do. Her body heat was drawn away in the whispering wind; if she waited in this place, it would turn her to stone in the end. At last, she strummed the taut strings of her lyre.

The Lifesong came to her slowly, as if the ancient lore was frustrated by the pounding presence of the Shield. She sang the first stanza once, then again, and the music slowly filled her senses. She set the lyre aside, laid her hands gently on Ashley's body and continued to sing. His quivering eased, but the pale cast to his face and lips did not. His eyes were unseeing and he looked somewhere beyond her. She couldn't reach enough of her power to restore him.

No. It wasn't that she couldn't reach the power, she was afraid to. She was only pretending to reach for the Lifesong. She had to do more. She sang with a full voice and let herself go, pouring her healing through her hands into Ashley, linking herself to him.

The dimension of the Lifesong opened to her. She raced along threads of shimmering music. Vital cords thrummed with audible colours against the limitless backcloth of eternity. More and more voices joined hers, echoes which reached her ahead of her own voice, drawing her onward to the source. She was drawn away, outward across the stars.

She reached for the power, but just then, as she had feared, she fell, into that spiral of awful power which she had known was coming, the pit of swirling smoke and noise and chaos. As the Lifesong grew stronger in her veins, she was drawn close to the Goddess Ethea, and she saw.

The Goddess was trapped in agony.

Ethea was still upright, shackled to the bare stone, but she no longer stood. She no longer looked to the sky in appeal. Rude iron hasps held her up by her wrists. Her head hung over and her tears dropped like slow pearls to the water covering her slender feet and filling the base of the pit. Rain sheeted upon her from the ruddy clouds, rain that bonded the slack folds of her green garments to her body, driving the iridescence from the plumage of her outstretched wings, leaving the feathers dull and lifeless. Smoke still came from somewhere over the crest of the cliff, acrid and fierce, pouring down into the cavernous pit and swirling with the gusts, driving a scattered mass of feathers across the bloody water. The remains of the little birds, Tabitha realised, those poor creatures that had been sacrificed in Ethea's presence and left to drain their blood upon the tilted stones forming the semicircle before her.

"Goddess?"

Ethea did not seem to hear Tabitha. She looked down the straight spine of her nose, her beautiful eyes plagued by deep shadows. Despite her immense size, she seemed frail and vulnerable: her long legs not able to bear her own weight and her slender arms bowed under the burden of her sodden feathers. Tabitha dared not disturb her, this great deity, this mystery of divinity, and yet she seemed so helpless.

"Goddess?"

Ethea moved her head and looked at Tabitha through the wet green jewels of her giant eyes.

"Lifesinger."

Ethea's expression was so anguished. Tabitha wanted to rush to the

Goddess and enfold her in her arms, but the impossible dynamics of the projection kept her where she was, standing upon the bedrock of the amphitheatre, waist-deep in the corrupted water. She was so small compared with Ethea, and her own body was only an outline, a faint form of shimmering clear essence, strangely doubled as if there were two of her. She could sense everything around her. She could feel the liquid against her legs and the rain on her face, but she guessed she probably couldn't affect anything because she wasn't wholly there. The mighty figure of Ethea towered over her.

"I am coming, my Goddess, I will search for you."

"Why have you not come already?" Ethea asked forlornly, her shaky tearfulness expressing a depth of abandonment. Tabitha felt guilty at once. She had promised to come before, during her previous vision, and yet she had avoided reaching for Ethea because of the horror of the place she was now witnessing. Here, it seemed, she could do nothing about it. So she had set her mind to finding Ethea, and she had begun her quest as soon as she was able to. It had taken four days and she was at the edge of Eyri. She suspected it was going to take much longer than four days before she found the lowlands of Oldenworld, and even longer to locate the Pillar where Ametheus ruled. Didn't Ethea understand it would take a long time for Tabitha to reach her side?

Ethea was a Goddess, accustomed to an eternal existence. Maybe she did not appreciate the limitations of time and place as Tabitha understood them. "I—my body is elsewhere, Goddess. I must travel far to reach you, it will take much time."

"But travel is being in another place, is this not so?" Ethea asked slowly. Her face shimmered as she spoke, and sound came off her in little waves of pressure, like ripples in reality. Her skin was alive with a green and growing power. "You do not need time to travel, I know this. I have seen this, there are some of your kind who move within everything. I thought you were one of those."

Tabitha remembered the strange spell which Twardy Zarost had cast upon her to save her from death in Stormhaven. He had taken her to the stars and brought her back. Maybe that was what Ethea referred to—the movement through infinity. She had no idea how to do what he had done.

"A wizard? I, well, I am new at it. I haven't learnt to move in that way."

"And yet you are here." It was an observation, not an accusation, but Tabitha could see Ethea still did not understand.

"I can see...into...this place where you are. I am not here. My body is where I am."

"You mean you are trapped, as I am, yet somewhere else? *Oh-ay-a-way.*" She gave a sonorous sad trill, and her skin rippled with power that sparkled greenly in the rain drops before turning them to mist. A thrill of music passed through Tabitha, but the rain returned.

"No, Goddess, I am not trapped. I am free to move but it will take time for my body to find your body." Why was it so hard to explain? The Goddess seemed to have difficulty with the concept of separation. Yet she had breathed life into every living thing. Tabitha had expected that she would know everything about their condition, but this was clearly not so.

"Aah." Ethea blinked slowly, the great lids coming down and rising again like a door to another world. "You are like only one note taken out of the song. You have not sunk into the song yet. You have not yet heard that you are all of it."

"All of it?"

"Music is unbroken, little one, from high to low, from soft to loud. All of the notes are available to be sung. You can be any part of the song you wish to sing, because it must all be there, if *you* are there."

Now it was Tabitha's turn to be puzzled. Ethea's terms of reference were so different to her own.

The sound of frantic flapping came from behind Tabitha. She turned and saw that a white swan had been brought to the edge of the slippery rock slope, held by its feet by a man with a red helmet. He wore a glistening sealskin coat, open at the chest. Whether it was the same man who had performed the previous sacrifice that Tabitha had witnessed she couldn't tell, but he had the same sharply-pointed dirk, and the same murderous purpose.

The blade rose. It fell.

The swan's blood ran freely onto the sloped stones, washing with the rain to swirl through the polluted water around Ethea's ankles. "No, no, no," moaned Ethea, her great eyes glistening with tears once more. "How can you use lives like that?" she cried, glaring down at Tabitha. "How can you people kill creatures for the effect killing will have on others?" Tabitha felt Ethea's horror and revulsion. She couldn't bear to watch to see what the man would do with the bloodstained body of the swan.

"I don't do such things, Goddess," she whispered. "I wouldn't do this!"

"But you live here, in this world! You must understand what it is they do?"

"We are all different, Goddess. I don't understand these wicked men. I don't know why they torture you. We are not the same kind of people. We are not even of the same kingdom."

"You are not linked? Of course you are linked! My song runs through everything and you live together. You are the part that has taken flesh. Oh my swan, my swan!"

"No. It is not so, Goddess! We are individuals! We are isolated within ourselves. Very few hear the song as I hear it. Most people would not believe it is there."

Ethea looked down at her for a long time. The water rose slowly up her shins, lapping desecration against the holy giver of life. "That isolation you speak of must be what I feel. I can not hear my sisters and brothers, I can not feel our bond. Is this what it means to be alive? Oh, it is horrible. How do you live with that? We Godkind are all unified. We are all part of One. We live in each other. Oh, oh, oh, I am so alone."

"What can I do to help you?" Tabitha asked. There had to be something she could do.

"They say they shall fill this with blood and water until I have no air to breathe. If I do not sing the song they want, they will keep me shackled here and leave me to die. I do not understand how to die. I have taken the force of life from creatures before and moved it to new beings, but always I remained, I must remain, or there cannot be life. I am the channel. I cannot be gone! I am at the beginning and the end. But I am here, in this terrible place, instead of…everywhere. What happens if I am still here when the water comes to my head? This form they have forced upon me does not work in that element. It needs air to breathe. This is so wrong. This form will fail. It will fail! What will happen to me? *Oh-me-oh-my*."

She will die. She is trapped in the Present and they will kill her if she doesn't do what they require of her. Tabitha had to reach her quicker than ever.

But first she had to cross the Shield of Eyri.

"I need your strength," Tabitha explained. "I must sing to be free from where I am held. How can I reach more of the Lifesong's power?"

Ethea looked forlorn. "I have no song here. I can not reach any power. They do not understand this. They have forced me into a form I cannot be in; they expect something of me I cannot do. In the days when I had an audience, those who spoke the Word always released me again so I could answer their prayers from within the plane of my power. But the three brothers do not release me, they have bonded me to this earthly plane, they have cast their foul silver upon me, and I have been trapped in this weak flesh. I cannot help you. Only you can find the highest levels, Lifesinger. Only you can save me. Oh! Look at what they have done to my little messengers. I cannot sing! I cannot sing!" She cried as she uttered the words, as if her heart had been torn from her breast. Tabitha followed Ethea's gaze to where a small white dove lay on its back in the pooling water, flapping hopelessly against the dragging force of the water. It twitched, opened its beak, then it lay still, floating in a spreading bloom of blood. The rain drove it deeper into the water.

Fear and horror grasped at Tabitha's throat and the vision darkened. That was how Ethea would end if Tabitha didn't find her in time— butchered by a madman's greed. She came back to herself, through layers of sound, along cords of elusive music within a deep groaning darkness, rising until a familiar pressure pounded in her ears. She came through the blackness of eternity into two blue pools, which shifted, then blinked.

She was staring into blue eyes. She was on her knees on the cold stones of the Penitent's pass.

Ashley!

He smiled up at her weakly. His fair face was calm, but he looked immensely sad.

"I feel better, thank you, but I understand now why we have to go. She will not last long there."

"You saw?" Tabitha asked incredulously. She struggled to adjust to the sudden change. She had been in one world, now she was in another.

Ashley nodded. He had been with her.

He squeezed her hand, looking deeply into her eyes.

"Only you can find the highest levels, Lifesinger. She cannot sing. You must do it."

He had been with her.

"I think you know what to do, but you are too afraid to. You have become like a child wanting to hide behind your weakness, when in fact you have more power than any of us."

Her ears stung.

How dare he say that?

"You don't understand!"

"You told me you command the clear essence because you combine your talents. Well, I think a Shadowcaster would fight. A Shadowcaster would use every way to win, no matter the cost."

"How can I fight this? It's too big, Ashley! I'm too small!"

"You have a stanza for destruction. I shouldn't know it, but I do, now."

"You've been in my head again! You've been in my head!"

"You must use it. You must break the Shield."

"You had no right!"

"What does it matter, when you have Ethea to save?"

She glowered at him. "I can't use my power. If I draw on the Lifesong I will weaken Ethea."

"That's a lie! You're thinking that if you use the Lifesong you will use the last bit of it up and you will lose your power. You're thinking about yourself, not the Goddess!"

"How dare you!" she cried out. "I'm not lying!" But she was, and she was angry that he knew it. "You don't know how hard it is!"

He rose on unsteady legs and dusted himself off. "Everything you do separates you more from ordinary people, from...us." He understood, which made his criticism all the more enraging. He should know she was afraid. "I thought you were a wizard," he said. "You're just being a weakling."

Tabitha filled with cold rage. "Oh yes? And what are *you* doing to get us out of Eyri?"

"Using what power I have to get the reaction we need," he said, looking down on her.

She jumped to her feet. "You're *trying* to anger me? Hang you! Hang you!" Her anger at Ashley pounded in her head. Knowing he was playing her just made her angrier.

"I can't fight—*this*," he said, indicating the daunting wall of magic ahead of them, "but I can fight your despair. Look around you. This place is going to kill us if you don't do something now!"

Garyll was standing beside the horses, watching Ashley with a hard stare. The green-tinged mist whipped past them, the horses stamped nervously upon the patchy moss, and all around them the Shield crushed life to the bare ground. Ashley was right, the pressure had begun to hammer against them again even in their little haven.

The seven wizards had woven the spell. What hope was there of her unravelling it? She didn't even know how they had cast it.

Tabitha tried to ignore her rising panic. Even if they decided to abandon the attempt, they would have to endure the ordeal of pain on the way out. They might not even make it back. It was so unfair. She had to save Ethea, but the wizards had penned her with this deadly ward of clear essence that enclosed the entire realm. She found her hand upon one of the two orbs at her throat, and under her fingers it grew cold again as she explored the strength it offered, the fury. The power was welcome. Darkness escaped through her fingers. She did not have to accept this denial of her freedom. The violence could be returned. She would break its hold, tear it away, destroy it! All of it.

Garyll backed away from her when she turned, but she didn't stop to think what that might mean.

The edge of their little haven in the mists rippled. She faced the ordered threads of liquid energy which bound them in their prison of pain—clear essence. If she could destroy the binding pattern she could exploit it to form her own creations. She should break the pattern and impose her own.

She sang the Lifesong. Her voice rang out with the defiance she felt—her magic, her song—and yet the effort weakened her at the same time. She had to reach *farther away* to find the flow of the Lifesong, and in doing so she felt ever more stretched. The effect of the first stanza pushed against the mist, billowing outward from her spreading hands, searching through the pattern as she extended her will and claimed the right to command the world before her. She sang on into the second stanza of the Lifesong, careful to keep her focus tightly on the Shield and nothing else. If she slipped just slightly in her attention, one of them would die, blown away in a violent gust of unbinding energy.

She experienced the spell-pattern of the Shield as a sound—it was that deep binding guttural pulse, the impossibly low chant of an ancient mantra. The antithesis of that grinding thrum was...the Shiver, as perfect and as high a note as she had ever sung. She lifted her voice up, up and up, and drew on the Lifesong to carry her intent.

Something small and fundamental turned in the pattern, like a key turning in a lock that was repeated thousands of times through a crystalline structure of thought. The first layer of clear essence was hers to command. She had to do something with it at once or the influence of the spell she was fighting would recreate the inner layer of her prison.

Trees, she would create an avenue of trees out of the essence, she decided, silken trees, the ones in which sprites danced. She threw her vision against the tide of essence. The mists were blown ahead of her wrath, and the trees formed in a moment of rainbow brilliance, silken trees, bending away from her as if years of great winds had sculpted their growth. She sang harder, and another layer of the Shield broke; she demanded more power and another layer cracked. For each layer her trees changed in nature—the first of them showed a pale timber, but as her spell progressed outward through the layers of the Shield the trunks changed; darker and darker they became as her fury found its focus, until the last of the trees were as black as pitch, gnarled and tough, with branches gathered like claws against the unnatural wall, their dry leaves rattling.

Tabitha hit the final limit. The seventh membrane of the Shield denied her; the spell bound the essence too tightly. The wizards had trapped her; it made her mad. She reached into the depths of her fury. The sky grew dark and the wind howled. It was unfair! There had been seven wizards. The power of seven wills, against her one. They had made Eyri into a prison, and the thief Bevn had been able to pass through with the Kingsrim, yet she was being denied that right to freedom!

It was unacceptable. The Shield was old and some part of its power must have faded during the four hundred years since the Forming. It was supposed to weaken if the Kingsrim left the realm. It had to break! She realised what the howling sound was. She was screaming.

The black trees thrashed, leaves were torn from the closer boughs then broken limbs flew in the gale. Stones struck her body. Somewhere, horses squealed and men shouted. She took her anger to the sky. She raised her scream, up and up beyond the notes of the Lifesong again to the Shiver note, the polar opposite of the booming of the Shield. Then, she *pushed* with her sound, into the space between one binding pulse and the next.

She felt the Shield flex outward. It contracted again at once, pressing her down with more force than ever, but it had moved. She knew what she could do now. She delivered the Shiver note in short burst, and felt the shield bend away from her, then come back to crush her down with terrible might.

She pushed back, faster and faster, singing her Shiver in a staccato pace until she had matched the Shield pulse for pulse, every push outward finding less resistance, every nadir pressing back against her worse than before, and all the while the Shield wobbled like a great sheet of glass being flexed by an insistent finger, the warping growing wilder and wilder. She drew her rhythm toward perfection. Her spirit expanded, reaching outward, seeking freedom from bondage. She drove her intent against the Shield.

It gave way.

A bright explosion lit the sky above the crest of the pass, and a rainbow flashed away in a circle. Then the sound came to her, a random music which danced across the entire scale, released as her note rippled across the fabric of the Shield.

The mighty spell broke with a great sundering crack; a giant jagged separation ran upward through the bonded essence, arching over Tabitha's avenue of trees, ripping and crashing, high into the sky overhead. From there it splintered in a thousand directions, like the lines in a shattered bowl of glass.

Tabitha shuddered with the after-effects of wielding so much power. The black rage faded slowly from her mind. She walked unsteadily to her horse. It rolled its eyes at her and danced sideways, but after a while it accepted her presence. Garyll gave her a leg-up and she sat quite still, hholding the pommel of her saddle, looking up the avenue to the crest of the pass. Only then did she appreciate the terrible danger of what she had done. She had broken the Shield of Eyri, and she didn't know how to repair the damage.

Chaos could strike into her homeland now. There was no protection for anyone.

With a final roll like distant thunder, it was over.

The breeze pulled at her hair.

"Come," said Tabitha. "We must go now, before there is nothing left."

THE SECOND MOVEMENT

into OLDENWORLD

She'd never seen a dance so fair—
Life's melody of light and air.

—On the Goddess Ethea,
Revenant Ruellen, Book of Is.

14. BROTHERHOOD

"Bad blood between brothers
is a potent poison."—Zarost

The misshapen youth sang in an off-key voice as he stomped along the shoreline.
"He had two brothers and they went *with him,*
he had two brothers and they went *with him,*
he had two brothers and they went *with him,*
every wherever that he went.*"*
The others sang along too.

There was no getting away from them. They were his brothers, they were his beginning and his end. They were his left and his right, and he was facing backward, staring with his single eye through the clumps of white hair at his broad retreating footprints.

It was so unfair, to be at the back. Brother Amyar should have been born at the rear, not him. Amyar was the one who looked ever into the past. The word Amyar meant 'the one who was loved'. It was so ironic he almost laughed. Amyar, the scar-faced grunt, all he was good for was dwelling on the pain, remembering all that had been done to them and seething in hatred. Ethan couldn't get him to think about where the next meal would be coming from, or ask him for any practical solutions to their problems. Amyar was useless. Just blame blame blame all the time.

Talk about a chip on his shoulder. Ethan had a whole lifetime.

Brother Seus was even less help, always gazing off into the distance, seeing so far into the future, entranced by the great power they would one day inherit. What did it matter? Plans for tomorrow didn't put food in their belly now. Dreams didn't spare them from discomfort. "Reach into the future," his noble-faced brother would say, "reach with me, and you can have everything you need; you can change the world." But Ethan refused the swelling seductive awareness of his brother Seus, just as he refused his vision, because he knew that a life in Seus would be short-lived. Seus would neglect their body. Seus would steal his mind. But most of all, Seus was a magic-user.

Ethan hated magic.

Magic was a foul, terrible thing, a perversion, an ugly trick that had already scarred them for life. The *wizards* used it. *They* forced nature into false and rigid patterns. *They* restricted things which would grow free. *They* demanded that the world behaved according to their decrees. They hid things from people—under the temptations of technology there were bitter laws—but Ethan knew what was going on. Ethan could see through all the deception because he was outside the system, forced to be an outcast, forced to watch from the shadows.

As the years had passed he had grown stronger, and his awareness of the present extended ever more into the time that his brothers saw. As he claimed more of Seus, so he understood the things his brother would come to understand. Ethan had begun to bleed further backward into Amyar's mind as well. He supposed that in a way, all three of them looked out of his single eye at the present and witnessed the corruption of Oldenworld. What they saw was magic, rigid lines of cruel structure, laced through every enterprise, a spreading network of compulsion that was taking control of the world.

There was an evil idea beneath the growing system. It was wrongness that they called Order. Men and women placed themselves *above* other men and women, in levels and levels, from slaves to servants to artisans to supervisors to managers to directors to clerks to mayors to lords to regents until at the very top were the kings and queens. And the people didn't see what was really happening! The true power was in the wizards' hands. They manipulated the system they had helped to develop, tilting their crossed sceptres in their hands, while the puppets danced beneath them.

People began to believe that they had the right to condemn, deprive and kill others because they had been told to do so by someone higher up in the hierarchy of Order. Few people questioned what they did, because they were being rewarded with comforts and wealth, all the way through the system. Even the slaves were given better meals, clothes and shelter than they could find as outcasts, and they were consoled to help forget their hankering after freedom. The system was designed to rob the populace of power. When anyone was given a difficult decision to make, it would always be easier to pass on the decision to someone higher up, but they never seemed to realise they passed on their power as well, and all that power flowed upward, through the ranks, until it reached the wizards.

Soon no one would question the order that was being imposed

across every inch of land between the tipped mountains to the east of Koraman to the soulful seas west of Orenland, everywhere in the fertile plains north of the great range known as the Winterblades. Once the order was complete in the Three Kingdoms, they would spread south beyond the mountains. Ethan couldn't guess what was there, for he'd never been over the glistening barrier. He wanted to go one day, and as he considered it a hope flickered in his heart. Maybe the lands there were still untainted, natural—wild! But he suspected that nature herself would not be strong enough; the mountains would not stop the wizards. They wanted everything… they wanted all life to dance according to their pleasure.

And so, he had fled from their fanaticism.

Only here, in the misty northern seas, on the Isle of Bonk, had he found a place where their order hadn't reached yet, where he could live unchallenged, where he wasn't hunted. It was his island. He had even named it with that silly name when he'd first reached it because it was such a silly place, just a grassy plot with a bluff, a creek and a few clumps of wild olive trees. He'd dug himself a hovel out of the crumbling east-facing cliffs, which he'd extended and extended until the whole cliff face was held together by a lacework of luck. At any moment it might all slip into the sea. He liked it that way. It made his life more daring, and part of him didn't care that he might be hastening his own death. He had fish, seaweed and swallows' eggs, and lots of those stringy samphire plants growing thickly on the shore—food was almost easy to find, but nourishment was not.

He had nothing to do except stomp up and down the shoreline or watch the pounding surf. It was the most peaceful place he'd ever been in; he had spent the most miserable years of his life there. There wasn't a single soul on the island besides him. He idly wished for his early years again.

He had lived well among the outcasts of Rundirrian Run. He had thought he had some friends among them, until old Geffery had sold the secret of their hideaway to the wizards for a handful of gold. Mullie, Crust and little Fellowan—all of them dead. He told himself it was the wizards' fault, though the power had come from his own hands—horrible power, uncontrollable power. Sheets of silver fire that ran backward on the threads of the wizards' spells and burnt them to cinders and destroyed the outcasts who'd been clustered before them to receive their punishment. The oversized shack had been filled with writhing forms and hideous screams.

No, he would not go back. Never.

"But what if we find a way to control the power?" Seus asked from in front. "What if we could make it do what we wanted it to do?"

No. Control was what the wizards did with their Order. If he had to control himself, he would be bowing down to their false God.

"Why don't we just use the power instead of pretending we don't have it?" Seus insisted.

"We should burn more of those scurvy-tongued wizards to ashes," Amyar joined in, his gruff voice, irritating Ethan more than ever. "Yellow-livered cowards! How could they ever stop us?"

No! Ethan thought. If he went back he would be hunted. He would have to use magic to hide who he was, and magic was what the wizards used. He would *never* be a wizard. They were mean, they enforced Order, they were wicked, they'd made him burn down his forest, they were evil, they'd killed Gedd the shepherd, and the dear goat Nå. They had placed the scars upon him, crippled him before he was even out of his mother's womb. Brother Amyar remembered that, and he wouldn't let Ethan ever forget it. The wizards should not be allowed to live. They should not be free to do as they pleased, when they denied others that same right. They should pay in blood for what they were doing. Someone should stop them.

He felt the familiar rage swelling within him and realised, almost too late, that brother Amyar was doing the thinking. He had been talking to himself as well. He should have realised the others were aroused. Ethan resisted, clawing back his command, reclaiming the lifeblood. *He* would do the thinking. *He* was the best and the strongest of the three. *He* was the special one, the one who had drank of mother's milk, just the once. Despite his pale puckered face and the terrifying eye, *he* was the sane one, the one living in the present.

Ethan, because he was strong. Ethan, because he was the leader of his own life.

"Then why are you stuck on a little plot in the ocean?" asked Seus. "You won't stay here, you know."

"Then why haven't you made the wizards pay for all they've done yet?" asked Amyar.

"Ethan, Ethan, Ethan!" he cried out loud, using the sound of his own name to bring him back to himself, but the others were too strong for him when they worked together, and he could feel the blood leaving his mind, flowing to the other lobes, forcing him to lose his train of thought, forcing him to… sleep.

The other brothers stomped along the beach, arguing as they always did, and Ethan dreamed.

Warm darkness swirled around him, and he sank into a dizzying depth. He tried to flail his arms but he couldn't use them because his brothers had taken his body away from him. *Vapour.* He fell, and as darkness whipped past him, a great face formed. *Illusion.* He fell toward it, but it was so vast that he came no closer to the cracked and red-fired skin. *It shall end.* The world tipped, and the face rose over him, and yet it still felt as if he was falling, falling. Gravity made no sense. Time slipped away, and he ached, oh how he ached, all over, inside and out.

The face filled his vision. One dark eye watched him. The other socket was terribly hollow.

He knew who it was. He wanted to refuse, but his own pale lips betrayed him in the dream, beginning the mantra that would only strengthen their bond. "The world is a vapour, an illusion in my mind. We shall be wrenched from our folly to join the emptiness behind. We shall be broken by your will, life will burst and bend, for this world never was; what has begun shall end. What has begun shall end."

How long have you been standing there in the corner of my mind, watching my every move, not saying a word, laughing now at how I will come to you in the end, how I resist, how I fight with all I have, and when that is not enough I must justify my failure with the words you have taught me?

"Father, you have the most power," he said, completing the mantra, knowing it to be true. "Father, I cannot resist because nothing can resist you."

The answer, in the sonorous awesome volume of the ancient language, shook him through and through.

"*Søøŋ çæss ÿ.*"

Although the language his father used was always strange, the meaning of the words infused the sounds and resonated in his bones. *I see you, my son.* Ethan trembled before the timeless face. He could feel the fragility of his own existence; he knew how impermanent he was. Everything would be ended, everything *had* been ended in the moment it had begun, and he was alive only within the illusion. A tide of worthlessness flooded over him, as if he was drowning in black oil. It was always like this. He always made Ethan feel so very, very small. Ethan knew that defiance was the only stance to take; if he surrendered he would fall to pieces and go mad.

"I don't want to be here," he said.

"I understand." That great voice was like an audible form of rock and fire and thunder; it swept him away. "I see what you see, I know what you know. You are ready to follow my will."

"Why me?" Ethan asked, knowing he had no choice, but wanting to demand something, at least.

The great black eye watched him through slit lids, its silver patterns quivering. The hollow socket seemed to watch him even more intently. Ethan felt his own single eye trembling in his head. "My power would break anyone else. Do my bidding and you will survive until the very end. Now leave your island. I do not want peace!"

Other people were too weak to be used by his Father, Ethan realised, and so He left them untested. They believed it must be because they were strong that they were able to resist his call. They had to believe that, because the truth would be so terrible to accept, that they were worthless to Him and so they had been left, for His power would break them in an instant. They were not worthy of His attention, but Ethan was.

"I have not seen all that there is to see about this time. You will travel, through the length and breadth of Oldenworld you will travel. You do not need to understand the magic to destroy it, but we must find the nodes of Chaos if we are to collect your power."

"They will hunt me, Father, they always hunt me."

"You will cloak yourself in the way of your far-sighted brother. They will not know until it is too late. You will walk alone, and you will carry my eye through the world."

He would hide in plain view, using magic.

"No!" Ethan cried. "Magic is what *they* use. I will never use magic!"

But the Destroyer had just boomed with laughter, and Ethan had been swept forward on a great avalanche. He had felt what it was to be destroyed, to be truly ended, with no memory and no significance, to have no time and no place, to be erased—the dismay of death in emptiness. He came back gasping for life. He saw his footprints leaving the island, and his brothers had carried him into the horror of the next chapter of his life.

15. OLDENWORLD

"Imagination can build the most wonderful palaces
for reality to tear down."—Zarost

A vast and blinding desert of silver sand stretched away before
them. Oldenworld was not at all what Prince Bevn had expected.

Nothing moved. For a long time Bevn couldn't comprehend what
he was seeing on that morning when they escaped Eyri. He had
passed through the last of the Shield with great eagerness. The thrill
of the newly donned Kingsrim had added confidence to his steps.
His advantage over Gabrielle had made him feel like a man. He had
believed he was prepared for anything.

He stood in shock. A glinting wasteland, total ruin, extended
almost to the horizon but for a hopelessly distant dark line. Nothing
lived out here! It seemed to Bevn that Black Saladon had told them a
terrible joke. There was no Oldenworld left.

Bevn had expected to see a great vista of wonders all laid out
before him like a tapestry of jewels. According to the wizard, there
was supposed to be a well-populated land, with woven places, and
terraced border fortresses, great roads, old kingdoms and glass-blown
cities. Instead, there was just a scoured, pockmarked dead landscape,
vast and empty beneath the huge curved sky.

It made him feel small. It made him feel lost.

Maybe I should turn back. Maybe we've gone out the wrong pass!

His gaze lingered on the blue sky overhead. There was something
wrong with the air, it had cracks in it, and slightly different shades
of blue, as though it was a jigsaw puzzle made of immense pieces
which hadn't been put together correctly. Slanted clouds occupied the
middle distance, but they ran across three sections of sky and stopped
abruptly at the border to the fourth, as if cut by a knife at the edge. ,
as if a crazy artist had sketched irregular lines in the air then coloured
the sky in at slightly different times.

The sun beat down from on high, searing a hole through one tilted
patch of sky. It was a blinding orb with a crisp outline—no hint of
the swirling corona he was accustomed to which made the sun soft
around the edges. It was also too bright. Bevn dropped his gaze but

the light coming off the desert was harsh as well—the silver sands reflected too much. He blinked away his tears. The land farther out was crossed with streaks of grey, but close by it was as sparkly, as if splinters of steel had been piled on the ground, all the way up to the edge of the bare weathered rocks on which they stood. He turned. The shimmering wall of the Shield behind them hid Eyri altogether. It reflected the view ahead, out across the desert.

Everything had become a silvery blue.

Oldenworld... Where was Oldenworld? Maybe it began beyond the wasteland, but how was he supposed to travel through *this*? He reached up nervously to run his hand through his hair but knocked the crown off instead. He caught it hastily and set it back upon his head. He looked to Gabrielle, to see if she'd noticed, but she was just scowling at the scene before them as if it would turn into something else if she concentrated hard enough. He guessed she was also trying to recover from the pain of pushing through the Shield, of trying to catch up to the protection of the Kingsrim.

He was her king now, he reminded himself. And kings didn't look for guidance—they *knew* what to do. Bevn lifted his head as his father often did, and tried to *believe* himself confident.

Ridges and ridges, silver and grey, miles and miles of sand.

He couldn't fool himself. The Kingsrim might be a great defence against magic, but it wasn't going to help them cross the endless desert. What would they do for water? The terrain ahead looked horribly dry. They only had two water skins each and they'd already drunk some since the last stream. Hell, he didn't even know which way to go across the wasteland. He wished he'd concentrated harder on what Black Saladon had said.

North, he'd said north, through a woven land, or was it the Low Land first? Either way it was north, but which way *was* that? Somewhere away from the high sun, possibly to the right of where he was facing, out where the ridges of silver and grey formed lines as if they had been rippled beneath the desert wind.

He squinted against the glare.

Something moved in the wasteland. He caught his breath. Shreds of bright colour danced over each other, up and down like playful birds, yet they were far away and too large to be birds. Their movement was hypnotic, rhythmical, and... they were gone. Was he seeing things that weren't there? Another movement caught his eye, closer this time. The colours rode the air again, weaving up and down, coming toward him. Either it was a different set of a similar thing, or it had moved *very* fast. Bevn rubbed his eyes. Something else moved beneath the three coloured shapes, a cluster of solid objects that chased the dancing shadows of the flying colours across the sands. Their course was steady; they cut across the desert like arrows fired toward Bevn and Gabrielle.

Bevn stood transfixed. Even when he could discern the details, he wasn't sure what he was seeing. Some kind of craft—there were three of them and the biggest one was leading. It looked like a giant spider, but he could see it was a construction of some sort. Figures moved within its raised and elongated body. The craft moved on runners bound on the ends of its four innermost legs. The long outer legs also held runners across their tips, but these were clear of the sand, as if they were placed as stays to prevent the craft from rolling completely over if it tipped to one side or the other. The two smaller vessels scudded along in a wide 'V' formation, each one with a single rider straddling a central seat, which formed the apex of four splayed legs that again ended in runners. The smaller ones looked like sleds, although Bevn still couldn't work out how they were powered. The coloured shapes still danced above the crafts, and Bevn was certain now that they weren't birds. They didn't move right and didn't flap at all. But what were they?

The closer they came, the more apprehensive he grew. The vessels were running straight for them. At least five figures stood in the spider-sled, burly-looking figures with bright red hoods and flapping clothing. They were clustered at their high rail. One gestured and shouted to the outriders, and they began to converge on Bevn.

He wanted to run, but where could he run to? Out into the desert? He wouldn't stand a chance against such speed. Back into Eyri? That wouldn't prove a thing. It wouldn't get him to Turmodin and the Sorcerer.

King... I'm the King, he reminded himself. Kings didn't get scared.

"Maybe we can get a ride with them," Gabrielle said. She seemed calm, but he noticed that she loosened her knives in their sheaths.

The vessels came swooping up the final stretch. They made a scraping *schhhrit* as their runners cut the silver sand. A figure in the bow heaved on a wheel of sorts. The other four passed poles between themselves, and then took spaced positions on the rail. Bevn realised what they held: spears—long straight spears. The tips were wickedly sharp, like reeds sliced at an acute angle. The men threw their free arms up suddenly as if to shield themselves from something, and the spider-sled tilted to one side and ran with the aid of its outrigger. It kept on coming at Bevn and Gabrielle until the last moment, when it slewed to one side, threw a feather of sand away from its runners, and came to a halt with the edge of the outrigger almost touching Bevn's knees.

Four spears pointed at him. Their polished shafts were covered with spiralled script. The nearest man's skin was grey and rough. His muscled forearm had been tattooed up to the elbow, where a long-tailed ribbon bound his coarse shirt sleeve tight. The face watching him over the spear was hard and craggy, with a nose like an axe-blade and a chin that jutted out like a handle. His face reminded Bevn of a sculpture, all covered with fretwork. He'd never seen such grey stony skin on anyone before. A dark stripe ran above the man's eyes, swept up and away to his temples. On his head was a soft red fabric cap, covered in the same swirling patterns, looking like a kerchief weighted down with knots.

Hard eyes watched him. The men looked the same—all had the grey patterned skin, all wore the weighted red head-scarves. They didn't speak, and they didn't move their spears. The spider-ship seemed to be poised on its long legs, ready to leap away. Some kind of skin stretched between the eight legs, just above the ground. A latticework of braided cane strengthened the inner legs from runnerboard to the basket. High above, one coloured wing waited, hovering like a kite on the breeze. It was made of fabric, scooped like a sickle. They must be like sails, Bevn thought, sails that danced in the wind and pulled them wherever they wanted to go.

"*Ya chienny carom?*" the rear-most spear-wielder demanded. His bristled white beard made his chin look even rougher than the others. He pushed out his hand at them as if trying to push them away.

"*Yal morente cochinta!*" added one of his companions, the one with the stripe over his eyes.

The bow-man, the only one who didn't brandish a spear, hit him on the shoulder.

"*Yal morente? Scollip!* The old tongue of the Kingdoms, did he say."

"Kingdoms three?"

"*Du.*"

The bowman peered down at Bevn and Gabrielle again. "Show for us your palms!" His words were spiced with an unusual accent.

Bevn couldn't see any benefit to being defiant. He may be a king, but *they* had spears. He spread his hands. The spider-ship creaked as the men above leant further over their rail to inspect the two Eyrians.

"Look good for me," the stripe-eyed man said, aside, "they look as hunters, clean as ugly."

"I can't see if they devildusters are, or not," argued the bearded fellow. "They must first talk!"

"Bevinn? Gabreel?" asked the bow-man.

How did he know their names? Bevn wondered.

"He is Bevn, I am Gabrielle," answered the Shadowcaster.

"King Bevn!" Bevn corrected hastily. "I can speak for myself!"

Gabrielle snorted beside him.

"Rook!" the bow-man ordered. His men lifted the spears up and away, and stowed them alongside their basket. "Come onto," the bow-man offered, extending his hand and waving them up.

"Don't on the silversand stand!" a voice shouted from above. "Use the board outer and the ropes!"

Bevn stopped where he had been about to walk around the outrigger to reach the ladder of lattice-worked cane which he had presumed was the easiest way aboard. He had almost set his foot down into the metallic grit of the desert.

"Why not?" he demanded.

"Because it is dorra! Malaka! Magic!" shouted the bow-man. The others clustered at the rail again, as if something was about to happen.

"Where?" Bevn looked suspiciously at the ground.

"In the sand. Silver is the potentest, it waits for living flesh. Stand away!"

The silver was magic? He saw the desert sands anew. From horizon to horizon, the landscape had been ravaged. Maybe there had been trees, people and even cities on those barren plains, before the silver magic had turned it to sand. A thrill passed through him. He had to ask.

"Whose magic is it? Where does it come from?"

"Who else?" answered the bow-man with a scowl. "It is of the one whose name should not spoken be."

The Sorcerer Ametheus. He had wielded great power here. He had laid waste to an entire land. Someone must have upset him, but the

Sorcerer obviously had an immense store of magic, and he wasn't afraid to use it.

This was the Sorcerer they were trying to find; the one who ruled Oldenworld with his awesome might.

Bevn breathed out slowly.

He followed Gabrielle's lead and stepped onto the outer running-board then used the thin rope to reach the ladder. The rope was unfamiliar, it was translucent and it gripped his skin lightly when he held it. Everything about the spider-craft was strange: its slanted, curving geometry, its delicate appearance, the pale woven material of the long basket, the coloured designs painted upon its sides. As Bevn climbed up the wide-spaced ladder he noticed there were streaks of black and grey upon its legs, just above the running-boards, as if fire had licked at it. He scooted up the rungs, away from the glinting malice of the dry naked earth.

The bow-man introduced himself as Jek. He looked more weathered and sterner than the others, if that were possible. But he extended a rough hand nonetheless, and welcomed them on board his *cutter*. So he called the craft.

"A messenger to us came, he had said that he for another man worked, one who wished a secret to remain," the captain explained. "But his word is as good like his gems. South-west from Eastmark by five leagues did he say, and south-west by five did we you find. We shall you to Rôgspar ride, the first corner of our land of sides six, wherefrom you to Koom the woven roads can take. There you shall find further aid from the man who said you would know him by the meeting in a cavern. Makes this sense for you?"

A cavern... They were talking about the wizard. Black Saladon had sent the men with their sandcraft to collect them. The mention of the six-sided land reminded Bevn of something else the wizard had said about the peoples of Oldenworld.

"You are all Lûk?"

Jek nodded, and then grinned wryly. "Some Lûkfolk would disagree, they'd say we are only half Lûk, and half madness. We are windrunners, are we not, comrades?"

"Full with the wind!"

"We laugh in danger's face!"

"Zigana krom jak jin jeer!"

The last comment by the bearded man must have been in Lûkish, because it produced a round of laughter from the other Lûk men.

"Few of our kin would choose to live like this," Jek continued, "but we—we find it harder to live in any suffocating *down*. You'll see few of any kind out on the wastes; fewer still come out this far. Know you that we two days from the forest are, even with good winds?" He looked to where Bevn and Gabrielle had come from with a puzzled expression, but seemed to catch himself. "We were told your journey urgent is, and so we shall ride the sands while the winds hold. Meet the crew of my cutter."

The others had short names. Käl, Lowki, Ska—his black stripe set askew by laconic eyebrows—and Mûs, the wire-bearded fellow who manned the trailing oar. All the Lûk men were short, no taller than Bevn, but they outweighed him by far—their hunched shoulders, broad chests and bowed legs displaying all the muscular thickness of smiths or loggers. They seemed tough and impressive, intelligent for savages, for that was what they must be, thought Bevn. They all smelled of smoke and spices—pungent—a healthy smell but one that gave a strange sting to Bevn's nostrils.

The outriders, who waited farther out in the desert on their *skuds* with the sails raised, were named Eitan and Hack. As soon as the brief introductions were made, Jek resumed his place at the bow and gripped the curved bar that was set upon a swivelled steering column. He hauled to the left, and the shimmering yellow sail dived from its tethered position in the sky. The bow of the great spidery craft whipped around and they scudded away across the sands.

The wind whistled in Bevn's ears. After a juddering start, the sand-cutter settled into a smooth motion, as straight as an arrow and whispering-fast. It seemed to glide over the sand, hardly touching it at all, the running-boards only churning in the sand when they crossed an uneven ridge or gully. Bevn wondered if the thin skin stretched taut and low between the cutter's legs had something to do with it—maybe it made something like a cushion of air upon which they rode.

As they descended from the higher ground, the wind became warmer. Jek told them it had changed direction, coming more from the south, but Bevn knew the savage was just confused, because the wind was still blowing in his face from the bow of the cutter, which had to be from the north. He didn't question the windrunner captain. The stony-faced savage probably couldn't recognise the direction of his own farts in a bathtub. Besides, he looked as if he was concentrating hard enough just to guide the sail to catch the wind and to scan the ground ahead. Now and again he shouted terse commands back to bearded Mûs, who altered their course with his oar to follow the darkest streaks in the soil.

The sun followed them erratically, tracking through the tilted panels of the sky like a light behind fractured glass. As the day passed, it wandered from its proper arc, and the light often seemed to come down at the wrong angle given its position, though Bevn knew that that illusion might be partly due to the changing course of the cutter and his growing disorientation. He couldn't get his head around what he was seeing. The ground wasn't steady, either. The cutter sometimes felt as if it was crossing crests and troughs when the ground appeared level. He could swear that out of the corner of his eye he had seen one long ridge move, and a large area of boulders become standing stones once they had passed. Soon Bevn couldn't tell which way they were headed at all, except that Jek drove the cutter forward across an endless sea of silver, ahead of the dry winds. The desert gave off a burnt scent, savoury-sweet, like cinnamon upon overcooked meat.

He could not believe how big it was. The distant dark line on the horizon had come no closer. The Lûk cutter almost flew across the desert and yet had gone nowhere.

Rock rock rock rock rock.

Sand sand sand sand sand.

He began to wonder if the silver grit really was dangerous to walk on. The Lûk were convinced it held the raw power of the Sorcerer, but maybe that was just a story to make them get onto the cutter, to force them to pay some reward for taking them across the desert. The savages were going to ask them for something, like gold or his crown, Bevn just knew it. And they were sailing in circles, just to make Bevn and Gabrielle think they had performed a great service for them. They must be sailing in circles, or they would have reached the edge of the wasteland. Bevn was sure he could have walked on the silver stuff. It couldn't be that bad, it was just like ash.

Maybe one of the tailriders would crash, and he'd get to see if there was any truth to the danger.

He could always hope.

"Po jis fon! Bajar!"

The woven deck tilted beneath Bevn's feet as Captain Jek swung the flying sail hard across their bow, forcing them to double back on their track. The cutter rolled sickeningly outward in the turn and tested the full strength of the outrigger. Bevn was tipped against the rail and could see deep mounds of silver grit whipping by below him, sand which burned the nose of the foremost outrigger. A strong hand gripped him and pulled him away from the rail. He sat heavily on the central bench as the cutter flopped back onto a level course.

The lanky one called Lowki had pulled him back. He was looking behind the cutter now, gesturing wildly with the others, to the two riders who trailed them. *Right, right,* his gestures said. The tail-riders barely needed to be warned; they read the cutter's movement instinctively and changed their course with graceful sliding turns.

They were approaching something dangerous.

"What is it?" Bevn asked excitedly, tugging on Lowki's sleeve.

"Bajar! A time-spaw!" Lowki shouted. His speech slowed as he considered the right words to use. "If we enter might we a day lose, or worse, is it a slow-spaw. Might a quick-spaw be, but you can never sure be from the outside, even with the way the stones they are."

The sunlight wasn't as harsh as it had been at noon, but it still set the mottled desert sands a-shimmer. Bevn looked hard into the shallow depression they skirted. Dark patches lay in the silver sand, but they were hardly remarkable—he'd seen such streaks before. The ground in the hollow was smooth except for the scattering of loose stones littering its surface, and a semicircle of white pebbles.

"What's a time-spaw?"

"That is."

"How can you tell?"

"They spit always those white pebbles out. And the shadows fall on the wrong side of the stones. Look."

They scudded past the area Lowki had indicated. Bevn looked and looked but he couldn't see what they were talking about. The tail-riders were giving the hollow an even wider berth than the cutter. Bevn wondered if the savages had spent too long in the desert under the blinding sun.

Only as he looked away from the affected area, did he begin to see the difference. The stones everywhere else squatted upon afternoon shadows lurking under their north-eastern sides. Within the hollow those shadows were absent or hidden on the far side so they couldn't be seen. How had Jek noticed such a small detail in time to avoid it? What else did their captain watch out for in the desert ahead?

"How can it...do that to the shadows?" Bevn asked.

"When wildfire too many changes in one place forces, it can

through the pattern that the elements have been stitched upon eat and the ordered passage of hours beneath unravel. It's like a run in a loom when a stitch is dropped—the rest of the tapestry remains unaffected for a while, but the line what through one place runs is upset and follows not the pattern of those on either side. Inside a slowspaw, time slips back. It won't a slowspaw stay, it cycles backward and forward, gains it time, loses it time. Some of them fade away. Some of them stay unbalanced for years. There's a horrible one near Rôgspar, the worst quickspaw I've ever seen. Kal and Eitan run it on their bugboards in high summer, when the days long enough are a jump to span."

"They run it?"

"You've got it to see, just it see!" Lowki exclaimed.

"Right through the core and out in a heartbeat!" Kal admitted, a sparkle in his eye. "That's four leagues and it takes me a quarter-day to back come. But the speed! Nothing like it!"

"One day it's going to flip, the quickspaw will flip, and they'll still in there be when the snows to Koom come," Jek grumbled over his shoulder.

"Jek-ai, you can by the colour of the crystal tell." Kal turned to Bevn. "You throw a clear rock in, and if it still speeding is then flashes it red, if it's blue it's cold gone."

"Scollip!" cursed Jek. "That's not an exact art, and you know it! The surface isn't smooth, you might a fold on the edge just hit."

Kal grinned at his captain's back. "If there not some danger was who'd it want to do?"

Behind Kal, out in the desert, Bevn caught a sudden movement. One of the tailriders had cut in hard across their trail, heading for the timespaw.

"Look, it's Hak! Hak's going it to sketch!" cried Lowki.

Jek cursed in Lûkish behind Bevn, but the other Lûk men turned as one to watch the mad rush of the tailrider.

"He's the line read!" shouted Mûs.

"He's got grey to use!" Lowki added.

"What's he going to do?" asked Bevn, not understanding why the tailrider had chosen to ride into the timespaw. "Didn't you say it was dangerous to go in?"

"Right. We can't in go with the sickle-sails. The lines are so long they'll outside the spaw be while you're in. You'll a sickle that way lose and a strike in the dorra have."

"So what's he doing?"

Lowki held up a finger. "Watch."

The tailrider called Hak was standing astride his *skud*, racing across the sand at breakneck speed. Bevn lost sight of him as he crossed behind the rear of the cutter. His gold-streaked sail blurred by. Bevn clambered over the central bench and saw Hak again just as the tailrider threw his body to the near side of his *skud* and turned hard at the very edge of the hollowed area in the desert. Dirty sand sprayed away from his outside rail in a wide rooster tail of silver-grey as he skidded precariously behind his whipping sail. Then he turned his sail upward and came shooting out of the turn like a bolt from a crossbow. He lifted one hand and punched the air as he howled like a wolf.

Mûs at the rear-oar lifted a hollowed reed to his lips and blew a piercing note on the horn. The others yelped, barked and yodelled in a chorus of clamorous sounds.

They were all completely mad, Bevn decided. Strange, savage, smelly and insane.

Back at the edge of the timespaw, a long arc of sand still hung in the air, a perfect curling wave of frozen grey. The timespaw had caught the tailrider's wake as it passed, and the moment had not ended yet.

"Probably a slowspaw then," Lowki said, nodding his head. "That side at least."

Bevn watched the curve of suspended sand, but it still did not fall, at least not as fast as it should have. Eventually it began to settle at the far end, rolling toward them like a snake slowly laying itself on its belly.

"Rock-head! It's so dangerous!" cursed Jek from the bow.

But when Bevn turned to look at the captain he could see his shoulders shook with laughter. Bevn didn't understand how the captain could let his men disobey his wishes and not care. "Why are you laughing? Aren't you going to flog him, or something? In my land we always flog a disobedient underling."

"We do not have...underlings...in Lûk. You must live in a sad place, Bevynn."

The dumb grey-skin was still pronouncing his name wrong, giving it a comical ring to the last syllable.

"Eyri is so much better than this stupid sandy desert you madmen ride on! So much better!"

Jek ignored his outburst. "You don't understand. If Hak didn't do that sort of thing, he wouldn't be a windrunner, now would he?" Jek watched Bevn for a while then shook his head.

They ate on the cutter—flattened dried fruit of some kind with some spiced papery meat rolled into soft uncooked dough. It was awful. A long tube of water was passed around, a stoppered pipe of polished wood which gave the water a bitter taste. Bevn preferred the water in his own waterskin, and he drank the one dry. The food didn't improve with the second tasting. The look Lowki gave him when he asked if there was anything different to eat warned him to keep his distaste to himself. He guessed the savages were feeding them badly because Black Saladon wasn't there. Bevn wished the mighty wizard would come to them. He'd put these uncultured pockmarked peasants in their place.

They stopped before sunset because the wind died away. The sun was an orange orb sinking through the last lines of distant haze above the stark landscape. To the right of the sun, along the entire northern horizon, the desert ended at the dark green line Bevn had seen earlier in the day. At last the edge of the wasteland was visibly closer. Jek told him the cutter had slipped a bit west of their true course that day, but they had more than made up for it with speed. They would reach the forest by midday, given good winds, and tack across to the trailhead for Rôgspar by late afternoon. Jek guided them up a saddle and onto a wide plateau of dark sand, where the silver blight had long since lost its potency. The grey sand would be safe, Jek told them, so long as the surface was good and you didn't dig under the crust.

Two of the crew came up beside Jek and spun the windlasses which wound in the lines that held the great sail in the sky. The windlass axles were set against reinforced columns on either side of the main swivelstay and, while the crewmen wound, Jek continued to guide the sail overhead on the last of the failing breeze. It fluttered down upon their heads, threatening to swamp the entire basket. Bevn noticed that the yellow-washed fabric was translucent, and it had been sewn into many parallel pockets to catch the wind. It was an impressive piece of sewing—such a flimsy thing, and yet it could pull the cutter and all of them in it. At the last moment the crew members reached up and caught hold of the tips of the sail, and with a great *whoosh* it fell to their feet and slipped across the basket in an uneven pile of silky colour. It was lighter than paper, yet it seemed stronger than canvas. Bevn tried, surreptitiously, but he couldn't push his finger through it. The men disconnected the lines off the tips, rolled it up and stowed it within the central bench.

When Bevn joined Gabrielle on the sand below, the ground rolled unsteadily beneath his feet. The Lûk laughed among themselves as he staggered away to relieve himself off the edge of the plateau.

When he returned, the Lûk had laid out items for a makeshift camp and were lashing the tips of four tall spears together, probably for some kind of tent, Bevn guessed. They had marked the perimeter of the camp with a great double circle scribed in the sand, with various symbols scribbled in the rim.

Jek was sitting beside Gabrielle talking, as if he had nothing better to do. Gabrielle didn't even notice Bevn's return, she was holding the captain's left arm and tracing the lines of his tattoos as Jek explained their significance. Bevn grew jealous. Gabrielle was *his* woman, not theirs. They had no rights to her.

"What about supper?" Bevn demanded.

Jek looked up mildly. "Food? We have eaten today."

"I need more than those mingy scraps you gave us during the ride," Bevn declared.

"With your little body? I think not." His jibe had a sinister undertone, as if the Lûk captain might lose his patience.

"But I must have supper. I always have supper!"

Jek just turned away and looked out over the desert. "How much food do you see out there?"

"Don't you eat more than once a day?" Bevn cried out, refusing to let them get away with their bad treatment of him. He couldn't believe the big men weren't hungry. Jek had food, he knew it. The Lûk were just hiding it from him and Gabrielle.

Jek rose and regarded Bevn with a hard stare. "It seems that we do not have the luxuries you are accustomed to, Bevynn of Eyri. Whatever the Black paid us, it was not for keeping you in the manner of a spoiled *bogadin*. When you travel with us, you live like we do. If you don't like it, you can go and walk upon the wildfire."

The man was hard, the muscles stood out in his arms like tree roots. The Kingsrim did not seem to affect him at all, but then Bevn supposed he had no Eyrian blood—none at all. He was truly a savage.

Bevn clamped his jaw shut and ground his teeth, but said nothing more. He whirled and strode away.

Two crew-members were strolling away from the camp with some tools, two shield-like boards, some short spears and a big pale sack. Bevn trotted after them.

"Where are you going?" he asked, when he'd caught up.

The two Lûk carried on walking. When he asked again, the nearest one, Kal, answered reluctantly. "To our fortune find. Big lode of jeweldust at the edge of the grey, as we in came."

Digging for treasure! Now *that* was something worth doing.

"Can I watch? Please can I watch?"

Kal shot a glance to the second one. "Eitan?" The man just shrugged.

"All right, but don't in our way get," Kal warned. "This is delicate work. What we find belongs to the cutter."

"I'll come with you as well," said Gabrielle, suddenly there at his side. "If the men don't mind."

She had come after him! She preferred him to the captain, but when he glanced her way he wasn't so sure it was devotion that caused her eyes to glint. She looked as dangerous as ever. Maybe Jek had sent her, to keep him out of trouble. "I'll be fine," he said curtly.

"So you think, but you never know when you need to be careful." She smiled disarmingly, and Bevn decided she must have meant it in a nice way. He contented himself with having a shapely rump to watch. Besides, Gabrielle wore a tight leather halter-top. The Lûk men didn't seem to notice her body the way Bevn did. They probably preferred women to be craggy, grey and all covered with tattoos, the ignorant idiots. They just strode on with an even pace, their eyes on the feathered edge of the plateau where the grey ended.

"What do you look for?" Bevn asked.

"Depends," answered Kal. He pointed to a section where the lip had collapsed and spilled chunks of rock onto the soft angled skirt of silver sand. "When wildfire on certain minerals ignites it forces them new forms to take. Clusters like that can blasting oil within them have. Blackballs on the surface means there's cracklesalt nearby, which is many a hair in our land worth, and even more if trade to the Hunters open is. Then there's *krong*, spring-rock, the red ore, which the miners by Clankorin so much like, but it's a long way such a heavy harvest to take and it's hardly worth taking it anymore, with the great shaft of it what opened was when the Writhe through the Winterblades came. Maybe we bluemitre find, which our wine-makers in Sess will be happy about. The Lakelanders want singing beads to have, they want always singing beads. Who knows what they with them do. Right now hoping I to a lode of purple *mishkr* find. You just do not get a sealant better than purple *mishkr*, because it is light-shedding as well as like glue sticking. There is a great need for it in Rek and Jho while they on rebuilding the woven road work."

Bevn didn't understood much of what Kal said, but he could work out the basic tools they carried. The shield-like boards still puzzled him. They were glittery green and polished, and they looked hard and too narrow and long to be useful shields.

"What are the green things for?"

"What, these? *Jojotin*. Bugboards. We can walk out on the wildfire a short way if we need to. Now hold your tongue and let us our work to do."

Bevn dropped back a few steps from the rude Lûk. What were the boards made of, that they were resistant to the wildfire? Probably the same shiny green substance that was used on the running-boards of the cutter.

They walked quite a way, and the ridge of grey soil rose until they were on a narrow crusty finger pointing out over the silver desert below. Kal told Bevn and Gabrielle to wait where they stood because it looked too unstable ahead. Gabrielle sat obediently, and told Bevn to do the same, but he just pretended he hadn't heard her. The two Lûk men edged forward, using their spears to balance upon as they leant over the rim of the ridge.

"Mishkr!" shouted Eitan, beckoning to his companion. "You were right, it is a good one."

Kal went cautiously to where Eitan kneeled. He gripped Eitan's ankles, which allowed the bigger man to lie on his stomach and reach over the lip. Eitan pulled the pale sack close then scooped something into it. He reached down again and scooped another load into the sack, but Bevn couldn't see what it was. He'd never heard of mishkr before.

He moved to take a closer look. Gabrielle lunged to catch his ankles, but he'd expected her to do that. He jumped and she missed. He ran up to the Lûk men and set his foot close to the rim to see around Eitan's back.

Kal turned around. "No! Get back!" he cried.

There was a sharp crack, and the ground gave way under Bevn's feet. He kicked back and scrabbled to get away from the collapsing bank. A cloud of gritty dust billowed past his knees. Slabs of grey crust tumbled onto the slope below, throwing silver sand outward as they thumped down. A whole section of the ridge gave way.

"*Boh, Eitan, boh!*" cried Kal. He was lying on his stomach at the edge of a hollow little cliff, his arms outstretched. But his hands were empty.

Amidst the jumbled scree, the fallen Lûk man fought, a writhing fury of grey arms and patterned trouser legs and a bright red headscarf. He was too deep in the silver sand, deep in the wildfire, and he fought with himself.

Bevn watched, horrified but fascinated, as the magic fed upon the living man's flesh. Chaos.

The Lûk tried to beat at his back with his hands, and he screamed. The sand shifted around him as if it consisted of motes and he was a Shadowcaster summoning power to himself. The silver essence swarmed toward him, collecting upon his chest, and his hands became like glistening mercury balls as he tried to slap the advancing wildfire away. His fingers smoked and his palms turned white then erupted with rampant growth, swelling, changing—growing fat and pincer-like. His head bulged under the red headscarf, the whitening skin spread outward in a ring from his temples, making his head flat and wide, and beastly. His eyes were stretched into slits under the deepening forehead. His screams were cut off as his chin sank into his chest. He leant forward as his back became elongated, curving and curving until his awful pincered hands pushed into the sand. The headscarf fell off, revealing a scalp that was hard, shiny-white and hairless. His knees burst through his trousers—sharp, barbed knees.

He shrieked, a horribly alien sound that sent a chill up Bevn's spine, then the Lûk-that-was-not-a-Lûk crouched down on all fours as if readying himself to spring. His mouth was lipless and full of small serrated teeth.

Kal held his spear high as if intending to kill the creature, but he seemed incapable of loosing the deadly weapon. He shook all over, and his face was the colour of ruddy clay. A horn blew back at the camp. They must have seen the rising dust and heard the screams. They would be coming.

The creature watched Kal. It rocked backward and forward on all fours, uncertain. The tatters of patterned trousers still hung from its waist. The inked symbols of the Lûk still showed in some places on its hardened skin, but it would never be a man again—it was a truly fearsome beast. The transformation was incredible.

"Did you see that?" Bevn whispered to Gabrielle. "The freak grew crab arms! The wildfire is awesome!"

The creature moved. The spear flew from Kal's hand.

But he had not thrown it at the monster. The tipped shaft whistled through the air, spinning directly at Bevn's chest. His legs went weak and wouldn't respond. The leading point was like a sword, the edges of the oval circle as sharp as a blade. He could see down the throat of the hollow spear, the throat that would drink his blood.

Oh father I'm going to die!

Gabrielle slammed into his shoulder, knocking him aside, but the spear was faster. It pierced his shirt, and sliced his arm, throwing him to his left and pinning his shirt to ground where he fell. He was aware of the Lûk man approaching, fast.

"That was my brother!" Kal screamed as he leapt for Bevn's throat.

Gabrielle moved in a blur.

Then the spear shivered, once. Pain ripped through his arm. A gurgling sound came from above him, and something warm rained upon his cheek. Bevn turned his head. The world began to swirl. A booted foot was hooked around the shaft of the spear, just above his arm. At the far end of the spear, the Lûk man hung, his thick arms slack, his head forced back. His neck gushed blood. He had been impaled on the other end of the twin-tipped spear. Gabrielle stepped up to the Lûk quickly, gripped his head and shoulder, and pushed him off the spear. The pain in Bevn's arm flared as the spear moved against his wound, and he cried out.

Gabrielle ignored him as she set the Lûk gently down onto the dirt. Blood pumped all over him.

"Shit-oh-shit-oh-shit!" Gabrielle cursed. "He's dead. We don't need this now. We don't need this!"

She spun on Bevn, gripped the spear and heaved it out of his arm. Bevn screamed.

"Get up!" she shouted at him. "We have to run!"

Bevn didn't understand what she was saying. He was just filled with a sickening bright fire of agony. She had pulled the spear out! Was there a hole in his arm? Had it gone right through? He rolled his eyes at the wound beside his face, and saw the blood spreading through his torn shirt.

"Get up!" Gabrielle screamed. "They won't understand this! Get up!"

Bevn shook. He couldn't move. He was bleeding!

Gabrielle grasped his shirt by the collar, and hauled him to his feet.

"Now run!" she ordered, and sprang away with the spear.

Bevn reeled. There was blood on his arm—his own blood, his precious royal blood—and it was leaking out of his body. Dizziness rushed through him. He staggered back, one step then two. He remembered the collapsed ground, and took a last quick step to regain his balance. But there wasn't another step of ridge-top to take.

He toppled off the edge. A little cry escaped from his lips.

As he hit the slope, he managed to grasp onto his crown. *I won't be changed by the wildfire, the Kingsrim will save me, please let its magic save me, please don't let me die!* He clutched with dumb terror to his crown as he rolled toes-over-nose down the slope. All he could think about was that horrible creature waiting for him somewhere down on the sand, and the way the silverness had rushed toward the Lûk man, searching out his lifeblood, dancing on his body until there was nothing left of what he had been before the change.

Sand rammed its way down his shirt, into his boots, into his clenched teeth.

Bevn rolled out of the soft slope and onto the hard-packed desert floor. He came to a sudden stop against something hard, face down. His heart thundered in his ears. For a while he didn't even feel the pain in his left arm, he just waited, breathless, for something to happen. He could feel the metallic roughness of the silver sand against his lips. Something hissed beside his wounded arm.

Slowly he righted himself.

The air shimmered with disturbed grit, but it was a brownish golden colour, not the silver he'd expected. He spat out the sand that had crept into his mouth—dull gold mud. A horn sounded off to the left, drawing near. There were shouted words and commands, unintelligible foreign words. The Lûk were coming.

Gabrielle was standing alone on the crest of the ridge, gripping the long spear, staring down at him.

Bevn stood and brushed himself clean. The dust and grit fell off his clothes, fading into the soft-coloured sand at his feet. The wildfire upon which he stood had been transformed, as if he was the centre of a small place of calm, a few paces wide. He took a step, and the circle moved with him. The Kingsrim did something to the chaos magic in the soil! It altered the silver essence, but only close by. A golden haze surrounded him, as if the sun shone on his crown and reflected light into a mist. Points of gold winked out of sight at the edge of his halo where they touched the last of the airborne silver grit. Then the haze cleared and the disturbance around him faded away.

He could stand in the wildfire! He didn't need the Lûk and their stupid spider-ship. He could run away across the desert, and they couldn't follow him now, not without wind.

Gabrielle was still on the ridge above. The Lûk burst into sight over the ridge top. They were almost upon her, and they would kill her for what she had done. So what? It wasn't his problem. The Lûk had spears and he knew they could throw them hard. He didn't have time to wait for the woman. He had to get out of range himself. He didn't need her. Besides, she was a Shadowcaster, she knew how to fight. But he knew he was lying to himself. She hadn't drawn any Dark essence to her hands—he didn't think there was any Dark essence out here in the desert. And, although she could fight, her style of fighting relied on stealth. There she was, in plain view, one woman against five angry men, strong angry Lûk men with grey skin like tough stony hide. The leading Lûk howled with rage—Jek, the captain. He had seen the body at her feet, and the blood splashed across her chest.

Bevn paused. He would be leaving her to her death.

Well, *he* hadn't asked her to come. *He* couldn't help it that she wasn't a king and didn't have a magical crown. A while ago she'd said she was only with him because she'd been promised gold by the wizard. She was a greedy trollop, that's all she was.

Then why did he feel so wrong when he wanted to abandon her? He couldn't understand his feelings. She shouldn't matter. He ignored the uneasiness in his thoughts and began to run away, into the desert, but he just had to see what was going to happen.

Gabrielle dropped her spear and bent down beside the dead Lûk. She fretted with something at her feet. Why wasn't she standing ready to fight? Bevn slowed to a trot, trying to keep an eye on both the ground ahead and Gabrielle behind. Just as the Lûk threw the first of their spears, Gabrielle jumped over the edge of the cliff. She had two green plates upon her feet. The bugboards! Bevn had forgotten about the sand-shoes the Lûk scouts had carried. Gabrielle landed hard on the slope, but kept her balance. The boards were shiny and curved underneath, and the silver sand sprayed out to each side as she slid down the slope. She stumbled at the base of the slope and careened on the hardpacked silver on one foot for a while, then regained her balance as she slewed to a stop. She looked over her shoulder and began to scamper toward him, moving the boards awkwardly like oversized snowshoes.

A spear thudded into the ground beside her. The Lûk had gathered in a cluster on the ridge. Gabrielle turned and dodged from side to side, reading the trajectory of each spear before it reached her. The Lûk were throwing from too far away to be effective. As soon as the barrage stopped, Gabrielle turned to Bevn again.

"Now wait for me, you little bastard! I can throw my knives from this distance."

She plucked the last spear from the ground and used it to punt herself forward across the sand. She glanced nervously over her shoulder as she moved, but the Lûk had used the few spears they had brought with them, and nothing came down upon her.

Gabrielle reached the perimeter of the Kingsrim's protection, where the silver sand was altered. She slid right up to him before daring to test the sand with her leather boot. Her sole rested on the surface, so she transferred more weight onto the sand. The boot held firm, it didn't smoke or go white or do anything strange. Gabrielle slipped her other foot out of the strap on the top of the board, and stood wholly on the golden sand.

"Move out of my range, and the knife will be in the back of your head before the wildfire burns me."

Her face quivered, and her nostrils flared with every breath. She was spitting mad and Bevn was worried she might reach for the knives at any moment and kill him. Gabrielle had a few reasons to be angry with him; Bevn decided not to test her mercy. After trying to find a way to carry the boards, she dropped them, probably deciding that they were too heavy. They ran together into the desert.

"Eyrians!" came a distant shout from the ridge-top. "I will find you!" It was Jek. "The wastelands are not big enough you from me to hide! You will for Eitan pay! You will for Kal pay!"

That was when Bevn got really scared. He didn't doubt Jek would follow them. He didn't want to think about how he was going to escape from the Lûk cutter when the wind began to blow again. They left clear tracks in the sand whenever they crossed the soft patches. For now all they could do was run.

He suddenly remembered the crab-like creature; he hadn't seen it for some time. All he could see was the huge open expanses of mottled sands, and the ridge they had come from. The Lûk were running for their sand-crafts, back toward their camp. Bevn couldn't tell if there was a breeze or not; he didn't think so. He kept aiming for where he had seen the distant forest, keeping the setting sun on his left. Captain Jek had said it was only half a day away on the cutter, so if they ran all night and into the morning, they might get close. That was all he could hope for.

It was the longest night of his life.

Gabrielle kept pace with him. Soon she was running ahead of him with her hand on his shirt. Then she was dragging him on, forcing him to run. She wouldn't let him stop for water, she wouldn't let him rest. The light faded from the sky, and the moon came up, only adding to the silver of the sands with its pale illumination. It was no problem to find their way at night on the wastes. In some ways it was easier than during the day, because they didn't have to squint against the glare. Every now and again, as they crested a hillock or rise, they would catch a clearer glimpse of the darkness in the distance that was the forest. The golden sphere of the Kingsrim's influence ghosted with them over the ground, vanishing when they crossed dead grey earth, returning when they struck out over silver. But the crown was made a stupid size, just too large to wedge tightly on his head. As he jogged along, it slipped down to rest on top of his ears, and he had to keep on pushing it back up. It rubbed a raw patch on his forehead, then it really began to hurt.

Bevn's feet burned in his boots. He could feel blisters grinding away into his soft skin.

Gabrielle just slapped him when he began to whimper. He tried to ignore the sting of his tears.

After what seemed like hours, Gabrielle let him stop for a watering break. She told him to have only a few sips, but when she turned aside he gulped down all of his drinking-bladder. She said nothing, but took one of her blades out of its sheath. They went on. His stomach soon cramped from running on so much water. He felt a prick against his neck and hobbled on. He felt the prick again. He ran.

She had a steady lope which ate up the leagues with apparent ease. He tried to copy her motion, but the long strides put more pressure on his blistered toes, and he soon developed cramps in his calves as well. He supposed she had learnt to run so well from living in Ravenscroft all those years, moving up and down the long pass from Fendwarrow to the Shadowcasters' secret keep. She was a terribly good runner, but he was a royal prince, and he had always travelled in a coach. His father had insisted on filling his days with studies of stupid laws or complicated systems of commerce, not sword-fighting or tumbling or steal-and-run that the other boys his age got to play. Then for the last few months he'd been in Ravenscroft, staying close to the Darkmaster. His body just wasn't ready for this torture, it wasn't built for *loping*, not so fast, not for so long. He just wanted to fall over and lie still. He began to stumble on every hundredth step, then every fiftieth, then every tenth.

"But I can't any more, Gabrielle, I can't!" he cried.

"You will."

"But my arm is still bleeding! I'm getting faint! I'm going to die!" It wasn't bleeding, the wound had formed a crust, but in the dark she wouldn't be able to see the difference. The sleeve of his shirt was well-stained.

"You'll run until your feet bleed as well," Gabrielle hissed. "You got us into this mess. You will not expose my life again."

The night itself seemed to grow hard around Bevn. The moon cut a scar in the polished marble of the night sky, the pinpricks of the stars were frozen in their place, and the darkness on the horizon that was the forest waited but didn't move any closer. Only the ground passed by, it bashed up at his feet, hammering at him like the implacable face of a mallet wielded by Ravenscroft's best, bludgeoning upon his poor delicate soles until it felt as if all the flesh had been bruised to a pulp, one mass of liquid blisters, and he was running on the naked bones. He began to whimper despite the slaps, and soon Gabrielle stopped hitting him and just drove him on from behind with her blade. He fled like a pitiful wretch before her fury. He was too tired to feel angry, too tired to feel shame. He wished he would die so the nightmare would stop, but he didn't, and it carried on and on.

Later they encountered a field of boulders, strange misshapen lumps of rock which crouched beneath the moonlight like mute robbers waiting for their prey. They had been formed into almost lifelike shapes by the wind of ages. As Bevn ran by the first of them he thought of the monster the Lûk had become, and he wondered how rocklike the rocks really were. Some were as white and polished as the Lûk-creature had been, while some were larger and more fearsome. But Gabrielle threaded a path through them, and after a while he was too frightened to care. Things skittered around the walls of his imagination, and the night became a phantasmagoria of fear.

16. THE BEAST AND BEAUTY

"Ah, sorrow; ah, regret!
The seeds we sow shape the harvest we get."—Zarost

Upon a time in the Three Kingdoms, when the spring buds were bursting with eager dreams, and the bright sun drove flocks of clouds across the unspoilt canvas of breathless blue, Ametheus came to Kingsmeet, alone, but not unbidden.

It was considered a beautiful place in those days, the jewel on the crest of a sceptre, the gilded pinnacle of the many peaks of Moralese endeavour. It was the capital of the ordered realms, and as such was not given to the throb and stain of commerce seen in Maddock and Chagrim. Kingsmeet was reserved for governance, for the rulers of the spreading state. Highest among these rulers were the wizards, men who made the rules others enforced, although the common folk believed it was the king's will they obeyed. Those who thought in this way had not paid close enough attention to the written histories of Oldenworld, for there it could be seen that kings were replaced at will, as were queens, lords and ladies. Barons were as dispensable as frosted glass goblets.

Wizards, on the other hand, were never replaced. They perfected their art of control from within the hallowed halls of the college, in the heart of pristine Kingsmeet, in the district known as Northing Torr. Around here their influence was tangible. Order could be seen in the regular geometry of the tall clustered columns. It could be seen in the latticed veins of gold in the walls, and in the braided bronze and copper worked into the stalks of the spritelights lining the sweeping stitchstone roads. Order could be seen in the great shining road, the slipway, which caught the northern edge of the city like a loop stitch, joining Kingsmeet to Wrynn, to Thren Fernigan, even to Ygris, in the cold northernmost peninsula of Koraman.

Ametheus had avoided the slipway. He distrusted the slick patterns woven through the thickened air above it, the way they pushed things ahead in the relentlessly swift current. He could guess why it had been built. It was a lure. When people used such a wonder, they came to love it, to rely on it, to need it, and then they were bound to support the system which maintained it; they were bound to support the state. It was just another one of the many seductions of Order: the sweets the wizards offered to draw attention away from the freedoms they stole. People didn't care to notice how the power flowed into that college at the end of the street; into, not out of.

He was scared, more scared than he'd ever been before, because he was facing a test of faith and there had been little in his life to make him have faith. Perhaps that was why he was prepared to try, just this once.

He had to enter that sinister building, to find the one hidden inside. He had to enter the Wizard's College.

The curves upon the building looked to have been measured to within a hair's breadth to ensure that a precise geometric progression was represented in their grand lines. The wide stairs leading upward from the clean forecourt were perfectly spaced; the great arched doorway was an exact replica of the curved outline of the building above. Even Ametheus had to admit it was beautiful.

But to Ametheus, the beauty had a sharp edge. For he was ugly, a monster, an atrocity, and every example of perfection cut him like a knife. He would never be as beautiful as the men who walked the streets, their fair faces shining with health, their young eyes holding the clearness of the spring sky. He would never be as refined and as delicate as the women, who glided by as gracefully as swans on the tranquil glistening surfaces that made up the walkways, across lawns like pools of green glass, pathways of polished stone, trees that grew in perfect symmetrical forms.

He knew that he did not belong in Kingsmeet. It was plain to see—almost every trace of Chaos had been eliminated from the city—hunted, eradicated. And he was born to Chaos, he was born of Chaos. There could not be a worse place for him to come to, and yet here he was, drawn by a message that had been sent to him alone.

His heart beat wildly in his chest.

He paced slowly toward the keen-edged steps leading up to the hollow door of the college, being careful to avoid the people passing him in the street. He wore his cloak of omnium brother Seus had devised, a blend of pure conflict that collected all the visible colours into one fabric, so that it was not white, but every colour at once, a tearfully intense distortion from which all eyes would turn, a colour most minds would not recognise and would therefore discard from their image of reality, choosing the known over the unknown, the sane over the inexplicable.

Selective disbelief, brother Seus called it. People didn't see what they weren't ready to see. It had proved to be effective, but it still made Ethan nervous to be so close to the citizens of Kingsmeet with nothing but a cloak to protect him from their stares. Even more worrying was the prospect of facing the wizards he'd find within the college. They worked with essence, they might sense the disturbance of his cloak, and they might realise he was there even though they might not be able to see him.

He'd worried about that a hundred times already and had already decided to take the risk. All he had to do was place one foot in front of the other and let his body take him there.

Only he and Seus were awake. Brother Amyar was asleep, kept unconscious by their mutual agreement. Their raging sibling could not be allowed to become aware of where they were, he would not understand. Amyar harboured too much hatred at the past, for all that the wizards had done. They would not be able to control him, and the slim chance of the secret meeting would be lost. For this to work they must set aside the hatred to make place for hope.

Hope. It was such a sweet and unfamiliar emotion that he couldn't think clearly around it.

Somebody in Oldenworld actually cared about him. He knew that because she'd said so, and she had closed her message with a bloodseal. Nobody would do that unless their word was true.

Annah. She was different to all the others, just like him, and yet she was a wizard.

Ethan watched the stairs pass by under his heels, and suddenly couldn't bear to be at the back. He knew Seus would take care, but he was too excited to see where they were going. For a time their attention became shared as he gathered vitality from his brother, and as he did so he saw the hand reaching out for his head. He ducked and slipped underneath the junior wizard's probing grasp. He almost lost his balance because of his heavy deformity, but he caught himself and lurched into the open doorway. With his backward-seeing eye he saw the puzzled wizard turn to a uniformed guard beside the door.

"Did you see that?"

"What? Nothing. I didn't see nothing!"

"There was something *there*, I'm telling you, sirrah!"

"Where, guv'nor?"

"It came past…it went…somewhere…" The wizard indicated

vaguely after the fleeing brothers. The doorman at his side stared but saw nothing. The wizard raised his hands to probe with magic, but his gaze slipped aside, diverted by the omnium cloak, and his aim went wide.

Ametheus ran, thankful that the plush purple carpet absorbed the sound of his hurrying feet. He followed the directions Annah had given him, deeper into the forbidding majesty of the college—off the first corridor, down a narrow flight of stairs, past an open-sided room containing shelves and shelves of books, down another flight of stairs and through an iron archway into a quiet and bare passage with a rune-scribed floor. Spritebulbs glowed on the walls. There was nobody around, which seemed strange. He had expected all levels of the college to be filled with eager acolytes.

Despite the lack of people or pursuit, Ethan felt more and more apprehensive. There was too much Order here. It pressed upon him like the sides of a narrowing trap. There was Order blended into the Energy-figure that warmed the floor, there was Order in the subtle Matter-spell which moved air through the corridor with an even flow. There was no way to avoid his mounting fear except to turn around and flee, but he could not do that, not until he had met with her, not until he knew.

He came to a wide doorway set across the corner of a bend, heavily adorned with incised designs. The thick door was ajar, and above a heavy steel bolt was a triangular golden plate, adorned with a single red jewel, and with a dark sigil upon it. ANG. Her name, her sign, he recognised it from the message—Annah Nerine Good.

He looked around suspiciously, but nobody was lurking in the passageways.

He reached out his hand to push the door further inward, but hesitated. What if someone else was with her? He strained to hear if there were voices within. She had specified the time he should come, but he had no way of knowing if he was standing in that exact moment or not. He didn't measure his days the way the wizards did, he could not. There was no exactness to his life, no 'now'. Ethan spanned the area between the latest past that Amyar saw and the earliest future of Seus. The 'now' was a space centred on Ethan's slowly expanding influence over his brothers, an awareness, not a moment. How could he tell which sliver of his own awareness was the one Annah had wanted to meet him in? His brain throbbed with confusion. He could feel a headache coming on.

Waiting would bring no more certainty. He didn't need certainty. He needed what Annah had offered. If it was true: hope and friendship.

He pushed against the heavy door, as gently as his clumsy strength would allow. It eased back soundlessly. He stood poised, ready to flee, but nothing threatened him. Just a bluish metal wall, rivet-studded, curving gradually inward so that it obscured any view of the room itself. The bluish metal puzzled him. He wondered if it was a magical alloy, like rippled steel. He didn't like the new metals they forged in Moral Kingdom. They were too highly refined and difficult to change, too ordered and resistant to be natural.

A small sound drew his attention forward—the soft scrape of a file, a puff of breath, as if someone had blown upon something to clear it, then the file again, rasping. She was working on something.

She was in there: Annah. He tiptoed forward, and entered her chamber.

She was as strangely beautiful as he'd expected her to be: painfully slender, but sprung like a willow sapling, with a pert nose and windblown auburn hair that was shot with grey, despite her youth. She had a dark full-length garment made of strips of fabric plaited tightly around the contours of her body. Her shoulders were bare but her arms were covered.

Annah hadn't looked up from her work at the small forge or indicated that she had noticed his entrance, so he moved closer, keeping the cloak of omnium gripped tightly around him.

Something silvery, like magnesia, was brushed on the skin above her eyes. Light metal hoops dangled from her ears and a bright stud glinted on the side of her nose. The pierced adornment was strange for a woman of Kingsmeet, but the more he looked at her the more he realised how different she was to the others. Her expression was melancholic and vulnerable, so unlike the aloof crispness of most of the women he'd seen in the capital, but then he'd not seen many women in their chambers. Maybe they all looked sad and pensive when they were there.

She must like metal, Ethan decided, for she wore a wide studded bluish collar and similar bands on her wrists—a similar alloy to the one in the walls, he realised. Annah was working on a chalice, twisting a band of silver around a band of gold to adorn the rim then drawing absently on a pool of essence and casting brief bursts of flame into the pattern. A flame caught on the edge of her dress, and she slapped it out. That mistake alone told Ametheus that she wasn't a true Order-wizard. Order didn't tolerate random fires and imprecision. She rasped at the rough edges of the chalice with a small file.

Annah looked how he felt: lonely.

She had said that they might be friends.

He looked again at what Annah was making again. Silver and gold—chaos and order twisted together. The hope swelled in his chest, driving his doubts and suspicions away. She was delightful. It was worth being there just to feel the hope, that blessed feeling of space inside his cramped heart.

She set the half-finished chalice aside, and went to her desk, where she began to work on a manuscript. Unfinished projects lay scattered upon her desk. He watched her for some time, just watching her write, watching the hand that had set those beautiful words upon the face of the sun, just for him. The messenger-spell had passed upward on one ray and came back down on another. It had a chaotic pulse he'd never expected to feel from any spell, other than his own. It had travelled too fast to be a constricted Order-spell, and its aim was too tangled in the riotous fire of the sun to have survived as an Energy or Matter manipulation. It was too inaccurate to satisfy the rules of the Order-wizards. Its pattern was pure innovation, its message was pure risk, its presence pure Chaos.

It presented the information packed into a gap between two instants. Thoughts, words and images, all delivered in a flicker. When Ametheus had blinked against the sun, it had gone, but the memory of the message had never faded.

Take this message as a sign of my trust, that I know where to find you and yet keep it a secret between us.

I am Annah and I am dying. I want to give you something I have learnt before I go. I am like you, I am flawed in the eyes of our time, but I understand Order, I have been forced to learn its many ways, and I think I can show you a way to end the persecution it delivers upon you. Come to me. Come in secret, for the wizards here will not understand. I am watched, I am in a cage. I cannot come to you. There will be great risk, but I know you have a way of shrouding yourself. You passed me in Culcarägh one day, and I sensed your movement but could not gain your sight. You probably don't remember me, but I have thought of you ever since that day, and I have studied what you have done and what has been done unto you. Nobody can repair what has been broken in the name of Order, but I can see to it that you are made stronger.

I can offer my friendship, until I am gone.

After that had followed the directions to her chamber, and when he should come, but the words of promise had lingered the most clearly. *I can offer my friendship, until I am gone.* A brief taste of her life had punctuated the end of the message like a sip of truth—a seal of blood. A friend, she had said. A friend.

"Are you going to inspect me all day or can I have the pleasure of seeing you too?" Her voice was soft, warm, with a hint of tiredness or sadness beneath the surface. "There's no one but me down here to see you."

She was speaking to him! She knew he was there! He held his breath. He hadn't ever planned to reveal himself. No, she couldn't see him. She wouldn't find it a pleasure. She would be horrified. Everyone was horrified, the first time—forever after, with most of them.

"It's all right. I know about your brothers, and I know which one you are, Ethan. The body is just a vessel for the soul, and it is your soul I care for, your soul I wish to speak to. Appearances can be changed, or have you not thought to turn your power upon your own deformity yet?"

He had thought of it, but he knew he didn't have the fine control he'd need to work on something as complicated as his own body. Fine control required the patterns of Order, and those he would never touch.

"Have it your way then. I am comfortable speaking to the air. I do it all the time." There was no bitterness to her comment, rather a kind of gentle humour. She pointed to the chalice on her workbench. "See? I am trying to make a new metal, an alloy. They don't like it when I smelt the gold and silver together to make electrum, but they'd be more than unhappy if they learnt my real work on this. I'm trying to weave a mix of Order and Chaos spells so they unify inside the alloy. It will be the first time the world has seen mend-metal. You'll be able to dent it or scratch it or even break it and the inner index will always return it to be like the original. The pulse fluctuates from Order to Chaos and back again. The Chaos releases material from the Order structure, the Order binds the elements into their pattern. Instead of needing a spell to be cast upon it every time it is damaged, my spell is a continuum, it lives in the metal itself. It works because it maintains the balance around the origin. Well, almost. I haven't got it right yet, but I'm close."

Magic, she was working on magic. Ametheus hated magic. He stared at her, not seeing her for a while, wishing she would be otherwise so she could be his friend. What had he expected? She was a wizard, she was in the college in Kingsmeet. Of course she would be working on magic.

"I've written a book about you, did you know that? I called it *Thricety*, it's got all the facts I've been able to find, without the horror-stories and old-wives' tales. I wanted to show the others how unique and special you really are, and the benefits of allowing you to be free, but they condemned the book and took it away! They won't let anyone read it. Now what's the use of that, I ask you? All those years of work, and nobody but me to gain from it. Knowledge should be spread out again once it has been collected, like honey on bread. Yes, I like that, like honey on bread." She bent over her manuscript again, and scribbled furiously in the margin.

Ametheus glanced around the room. All the walls, the floor and the low roof were that steel-blue metal. A bed, a chest of drawers, other furniture laid out haphazardly, clothes draped upon them—a closed-off area in the corner. She had a fire burning in the little forge. He liked fires. He could watch fires for hours on end. The flames danced with unpredictable beauty, those ever-changing forms within the fire.

"This is all that I am allowed, in here, all that I own. Not much for the daughter of an earl-palatine, wouldn't you say? He's forgotten he had a daughter; I'm such a disgrace to the good name. So now I'm in this prison with the door that I can't close, where everyone can come in, but I can never leave. The blue metal is gallium—lattice-bonded gallium. It's the only thing they could find that I couldn't tear down with my forbidden Chaos flux. It's too fluid, it becomes liquid just after water would boil; it just becomes a mess. If you have to use your power, keep it away from the walls. Come, Ethan, we don't have much time. I have nothing to hide in here. Please don't hide from me. I can't look at you with your strange cloaking spell. It brings tears to my eyes. Let me speak to a face, at least."

If she was a prisoner of the wizards, then she couldn't be a threat to him. Ethan scrunched up his face as he tried to think. Logic wasn't one of his strong points. He definitely had a headache now, a real pounder. Annah must be a good person, because she kept a fire burning, he decided. He wanted her to like him. He wanted to have a friend.

Ethan opened the hood of the cloak just a little bit, so that Seus could peep out from the front. It wasn't his true face, but then Seus was the best-looking of the three, and that was all she should see. Best-looking? Well, that was like saying that a frog was prettier than a toad, he supposed. He knew how ugly he was. Seus had a somewhat noble, handsome face, and so long as he kept a firm grip on his cloak, she didn't need to see anything else. The only problem was that Seus's eyes wouldn't follow her properly and he was prone to dropping comments which often made no sense in the present at all.

Her eyes brightened at once. "Oh, there you are! And I was looking way off to the left! I am glad you came to me, I feel so privileged to have you here. Please, have a chair."

Who was she, this woman who smiled at him, this woman that didn't fear him? A privilege to have him near? Almost everybody he'd ever met considered him a curse.

"I-I'd r-r-rather sss-sss-stand. I b-b-break th-things." He always stuttered when he spoke through one of his brothers, but it seemed worse than ever.

She smiled. "Yes, but of course! What is the good of having Order spells, if there's nothing broken to fix? Go ahead, I have nothing here I don't mind breaking myself."

Ametheus pulled out the widest-looking chair, and eased down upon it. It sagged under his weight, but held, for the moment. He kept his feet wide in case it yielded to the Chaos of his omnium cloak and disintegrated.

"I l-liked y-your m-m-message. It w-was p-pretty."

"The sun-glower pattern? I hoped it would work. It was the only way I could send a message without them knowing. They take me out to see the sunshine once a week. I had the spell prepared, and it was gone before they could stop me. They didn't know what I'd done, or where I'd sent the essence, but they suspected something, because I haven't been allowed out since."

How long had it been since he'd received the message? Two weeks? Three? He couldn't tell. He just knew that he'd walked most of the way, because he wouldn't use magic unless he really had to, and time-jumping messed up his mind.

"Am-m I l-late?

"Only by ten days. Don't worry, I'm still alive, so it's not too late."

"I-I d-didn't kn-n-now wh-when to ss-ssay h-h-hullo. Ji-Annah, Annah! A d-day is-ss too p-p-precise for m-me."

"Oh. I hadn't thought of that. Yes, it would be, wouldn't it? I'm sorry. I really must find out more about you. I know so little."

They talked for some time, just about what he'd done and where he'd been, what he liked and didn't—simple talk, the kind of talking that was strange and joyous to Ametheus. As they talked, his nervousness faded, although his stutter remained. Then she began to explain why she'd called to him, what his presence meant to her. He didn't follow a lot of what she talked about. It was complicated and to do with magic, but he didn't let on how the explanation was passing him by—he preferred to watch the way her delicate hands danced in the air as she outlined her ideas on Chaos and Order and the balance which should exist between them. When she looked at him he nodded with his brother's head. Whenever she smiled at him, his thoughts would spin.

She wanted to try a spell called Wholefood; one they would perform together, right there in the blue room. She was excited about it, and he became excited for her. He tried to warn her how unruly his power was, but she just insisted that they try, at least once. "I'll protect the walls from inside. I've done it before, but I need your strength to fill a fractal that is powerful enough. I can't make the flux and contain it. I can't do it alone."

Flux. That was what she called his silver essence. He hadn't known that it had a special name. The Order essence, that terrifying golden vapour, she called *flax*. She would weave it around his burst of power, very tightly, so that the Chaos was contained, and the result would be a harmony of the two opposing natures.

"Wh-what will it b-be?"

"Something wonderful," she answered. "A food that will never diminish. Nobody need ever go hungry again."

Ametheus knew about hunger. He'd spent years and years being hungry. It would be a good thing, he decided. She was so excited. She collected flax in her palm and drew him out into a space on the floor by his hand. He realised that his cloak must have slipped open.

"Why? Why did you betray me?!" asked Seus suddenly, in a clear voice.

Ethan reeled. He hadn't meant to allow Seus to speak of his own accord, but in his eagerness to pay attention to Annah he'd let his grip on his brother's mind slip. He fought to regain control. The cynical brother was interfering in their fun, blurting out things that had nothing to do with them.

Annah looked confused. "Ethan? I...I never did. Nobody knows you're here, only me. What do you mean?" She looked hurt, scared. All his hopes of friendship seemed to be crumbling to dust.

"N-no! J-just ig-ig-ignore him! I-I didn't m-mean to s-s-say that!"

She looked at him askance, and then understanding dawned on her face. "That's not Ethan I'm seeing, is it? You're still hiding somewhere in the cloak! That's one of your brothers, isn't it?"

Stupid stupid stupid brother Seus. Now she knew he was ugly. He thought of putting Seus to sleep with a hard knock to the head, but he couldn't do that. He needed Seus, he needed him now, to use the magic that he would one day know.

"I-I'm ready to c-c-cast the s-spell n-n-now," he said, holding up his hand and wrenching the horrid silver flux from the liquid clarity of the air just as Seus had shown him.

Annah didn't hesitate to bring her golden essence to him, and to weave it quickly into her desired design.

Their hands met, and Ametheus released his hold on the flux. The gold and silver flared brightly on contact, Annah's design spun wildly, then a rainbow formed in its place, a glistening, solid rainbow, taking the form of an apple.

"Oh!" she exclaimed, "I didn't know the colours would come out like that! It's beautiful. Don't you think it's beautiful?"

The apple looked solid and shiny. It was just the right size. Annah held it up to him on a flat hand. "Here, you have the first bite. You deserve it, for being so brave and coming here. Oh, I'm so happy, I was right, I was right! Take it. It's a token of our friendship. I'm sure it tastes very nice. I worked on the flavour index for months."

The rainbow colours shifted slowly across the skin. He reached for it, but didn't get to take it. For as he reached up he felt sudden probing fingers of essence rush past, around and over him. Someone had entered the room behind him; someone was searching through the room! He whipped his cloak closed across his face and dived to the side. Annah just froze where she was, standing with the raised apple, a shocked look on her face.

The searching fingers came again, and Ametheus stumbled against the chair and kicked it aside as he ran. There was nowhere to hide in this room! He knew those searching fingers; he had felt that kind of power before, in a forest in Orenland, in a shack in Rundirrian Run, any number of times across Oldenworld. Wizards! More than one.

They were massed around the exit, five of them, a terrible web of shimmering power growing between their hands, searching the room, seeking him out. One ginger-haired wizard ran forward and snatched at Annah's arm, and began to drag her away with a snarl on his lips, dragging her toward the door. She lashed out with a burst of red-hot flame, and he howled and fell away from her.

"How can you do this!" Annah cried. "He trusted me. He trusted me!"

"Just as we trusted that you would find a way to meet, before the end!" shouted an old white-haired wizard, casting a swirl of liquid gold which wrapped around Annah and seemed to prevent her from casting a counter-spell.

Two younger wizards leapt for her, a bitter-faced woman and a burly, balding man. They caught her by her feet. They began to drag her toward the door again.

"No, I won't let you take me out! You'll kill him if I'm out! They'll kill you, Ethan!" She kicked and thrashed and tripped the burly man up by his legs. She jumped to her feet and slapped the woman across her face with her metal wristband. Annah was so slender, so light, and yet she became a sudden slashing, kicking and striking fury, leaping from one wizard to the next. The wizards backed away from her.

"Then stay in here!" the white-haired wizard shouted, signalling to the others.

"Ametheus!" they said, and he was paralysed.

"Ethan!" Annah shouted. "Ethan, no! Don't listen to them." She understood his dilemma. When he heard that name, all three were called. All three would strive to take control—his own name that drove him mad. She'd probably written about it in her book. She was wrong about her wasted work. Someone else had read her notes.

"Ametheus!" they shouted, and brother Amyar woke to the call.

"Ethan!" she cried, looking around for him but not seeing him.

"Ametheus!" they cried, then the door slammed and a bolt thudded home.

"No!" Annah wailed. "No! How can you do this?"

They were trapped in the blue room. The rage that was Amyar flooded into him like a hot poison. Only then did Ethan realise how stupid it had been to come here with his angry brother asleep. He could not use his normal technique for escaping from trouble, he could not 'step back' into the past that Amyar had seen, because it was too long ago since Amyar had been conscious. There was a limit on how far Ethan could reach into his brother's mind, and he only spanned a few hours at most. Amyar had been put to sleep long before they had come near Kingsmeet, long before he would suspect something to do with the wizards was being planned. And now Amyar was right there with him, in the same moment. There was no recent past to step into, no way out of the blue room through his angry brother.

Something tightened around them, something had changed. "Oh Gods no," said Annah. It was growing warmer. Ethan desperately tried to think. He could still escape, but he could only step forward, into Seus, and he could only do that alone, for she did not exist in his future yet. He could not save Annah.

She crumpled to the floor with a keening animal wail.

He ran to her, lifted her in his arms.

"*No!*" she cried. "These shackles bind me to this room. The metal is in my blood. I cannot leave with you. The room is my prison. I will die beyond it, without their antidotes! I will die in it! Leave me here! Go!"

He held onto her, wanting to say goodbye, wanting to ask her to forgive him, but he could not. He held her to one side and turned his head so that he could see her with his true eye. She didn't even flinch when she saw his pasty face. "Goodbye," she whispered.

He couldn't let go.

"In your m-message, you s-said you were d-d-dying. What w-were you dying of?" he asked.

She looked up into his eye. "Hatred. I am dying of hatred. They forced me to be something I am not. I refuse to eat while they keep me in bondage, and they refuse to set me free."

An oppressive heat pierced the room. The walls became yellow.

"Let me go! Save yourself, Ethan! Save yourself! I will be free at last. Go, my friend, go!"

She slipped from his awkward arms, slapped his grasping hands aside, backing away from him on the floor. Tears were streaming down her face.

Then brother Seus saw, and brought the vision unto Ethan, and then he knew, that she would be sealed in this tomb of gallium, that the wizards would melt the walls, roof and floor an instant forward of where he was standing in time, and that in only one future could he live. He must flee into Seus or be entombed himself.

Seus gripped his stunned awareness with brutish force, for he had Amyar to assist him. Ethan was wrenched forward, into the future Seus witnessed, to the foremost limit of the 'now' which intersected with Ethan's mind. He experienced the blinding flash and painful jolt that always came with moving faster than the laws of space and time allowed. Chaos broke him and rebuilt him in the same instant, but it was another instant, taken from a life that was not yet his own.

He lurched to his knees on a purple carpet—the upper corridor. He drew a shuddering breath and scrambled to his feet, running for the exit. He was alone, but she was still trapped in that room in the basement. A solid *whump!* shook the building underfoot. Annah!

He ran, with his awkward lumbering gait, not caring about how the omnium cloak flapped open and whipped behind his shoulders, not caring how the few apprentice wizards and the doorman gaped, crying out as he fled by, not hearing the shouts behind him. He jumped into Seus again and again, cutting out hours of his life at a time, and each time the pain was deeper, but he ran and ran until he could bear to run no longer and he could only hunch down upon his agony.

Kingsmeet would soon be named Kinsfall.

His wrath would be great.

Ah, those wizards of the college in Kingsmeet, they did not see that so much Order-use had left a legacy in the balance of essence, so that Ametheus could spark tons of flux from the origin, in that time, and also long after the Three Kingdoms had fallen.

The Chaos that came to ruin the world was because of the Order that ruled before it.

17. FOLLOW THE LEADER

"If you see the dragon fly,
best you drink the flagon dry."—Zarost

Bevn couldn't remember how long they'd run through the silver sands of his nightmare, or how long he had walked on rigid, cramped legs, or how long Gabrielle had just dragged him, but he came around with her slapping his face, over and over.

He was lying beneath a tall, twisted tree. It seemed to be formed from thickened roots, or cords of green rope which had been tied, stretched and tangled into one painful knotted and angry mass. In his half-conscious state he understood what it would be like to be that tree. Every muscle in his body felt that way.

Daylight played through the bright-edged leaves far above, and trails of old silk ran between them, fluttering translucently. A warm wind pushed the burnt-meat-and-cinnamon scent of the desert sands into Bevn's nose. The high boughs shook, and a single red leaf broke free with a snap. It tumbled down toward him, falling faster than it should. It seemed heavy, and hard. It flipped over and veered away, picking up speed.

Thud! The leaf pierced the ground as if it was a sword. Bevn sat up sharply, and moaned against the instant pain through his muscles. This was no ordinary place. He was in Oldenworld. Gabrielle gripped his chin and turned his face to look at her. She spilled some water into his parched mouth, and he spluttered, coughed then gulped at the bladder's nozzle. Water! He was so thirsty! She pulled it away from him before he was done. He groaned and lay back again. There hadn't been much more water left anyway.

"Get up!" Gabrielle ordered. "I can't drag you anymore. Get up!" She kicked him and he yelped. "We must hide deeper in the forest. The windrunners are coming."

He turned to look to where she pointed. The tree he was seated underneath wasn't very deep into the forest; the bright sands were close at hand. The spinney of trees formed a wedge around them that searched into the desert like a finger, or was it the wastes that had pushed into the forest on either side? The gnarled trunks were so tall they would tower over the battlements of Stormhaven. Out on the desert, a diving shred of colour wound backward and forward in the air, and at first Bevn couldn't remember what it meant.

Then it returned to him, with a sudden rush of memory and fear. The collapsing ridge, the Lûk corrupted in the wildfire, the warm blood on Bevn's face and the spears raining down after Gabrielle. Two of the Lûk were dead. The windrunners would be seeking revenge upon him, and they would be able to follow footprints to the edge of the forest.

Another gust rushed through the trees above, and Bevn scurried to his feet, despite the agony. He looked up nervously, but nothing broke free to fall upon them this time. Gabrielle led the way into the forest, her raven-black plait swinging like an angry tail across her bared lower back. She had cleaned herself of blood and grime, but she hadn't bothered with him—he was filthy. Then he noticed the bandage tied around his wounded left arm, a bandage that had been cut from the lower hem of his shirt. Maybe she did care about him, after all. He followed on at an agonisingly slow pace. He couldn't get his legs to bend. He felt like a cripple fleeing a charge of mounted Swords. The Lûk would be able to run after them. They would be fresh and uninjured. Panic rose in his throat as he stumbled after Gabrielle.

"Wait!" he cried. "Don't leave me!"

She didn't need the protection of the Kingsrim here, he realised. They were running on solid ground. She was getting farther and farther ahead, making for the safety of the shadows and tangled growth. He couldn't go faster. He dared not look back any more, he couldn't bear to see.

The ground was littered with brown bark chips and bubbles of earth, green scalloped fungi, and desiccated pale roots. Deeper in the sheltering gloom, things burped from within the piles of heavy leaves. Strange birds called from high up among the sharp-fringed boughs, some with gibbering little songs, others with grating cries. Everywhere, there were trees, impossibly big trees, little trees, trees that grew from the arms of other trees and strange hanging vines which looped through them all. The vines were the worst. They tried to reach out and grab his ankles; they seemed to slither through the undergrowth when he wasn't looking. Nothing grew straight; every trunk was covered in knurrs and knots, as if they suffered much in the course of their growth. Now and again a large leaf thudded into the ground with deadly force. Bevn began to understand how a piglet felt when it tried to escape a butcher's knife. He ran and he ran, but he never knew which step was going to be his last.

After a while they came to another break. The dappled shade gave way abruptly to bright silver sand, where the desert had cut deep into the forest, forcing a channel of wildfire across their path. Huge fallen trees littered the ground at the perimeter, as white as skeletons, leaving a swath of open sky beyond.

Gabrielle waited for him there, but as he slowed, she grabbed him and pulled him on.

"We should keep to the trees!" he shouted to her. "We should go around!"

She shook her head. "Come, princeling, follow me! We can lose them here—they wouldn't have carried their boards. Come, don't make me hurt you."

Bevn followed her like a puppy. No, not a puppy, he told himself, he just chose to accept her guidance because he couldn't stand any more pain. Besides, she was good at this; she had been escaping from people all her life. That she was still alive was testimony to her ability—she always survived. He just had to stay with her and he'd be all right.

Gabrielle kept him close as they moved across the sand. The jumbled debris was easy to negotiate. It crushed to dust underfoot, staining their boots and leaving dirty clouds swirling in the air. He was thankful for the Kingsrim once again. The dust turned golden as it neared him, and remained so until he had passed, when it turned back to silver again in his wake, drifting idly to the ground.

Bevn felt very exposed in the clearing. Their pursuers would spot them easily, and if not they'd still see the clear tracks in the sand. He tried to run faster. When Gabrielle came to an abrupt halt, he couldn't stop himself from cannoning into her.

He caught hold of her with both hands to avoid tumbling to the ground.

"Why have you stopped?" he gasped.

"It is too late to run," said Gabrielle.

"Why? What is it?" he asked, pushing himself upright.

"There. Look where we are running to."

Furtive figures moved between the trees. They wore dappled clothing that blended in with the forest background. Bevn couldn't be sure how many were hidden from his eyes. Only when they moved, could he see anything at all, and even then it was only the flash and blur of a head, or hand, or a weapon. They weren't Lûk though, they were something else and they were armed with wicked recurved bows. Ten figures, at least. Would they use their arrows? Sharp tips pointed down from the lowest boughs of the trees, all of them aimed on the point where he and Gabrielle would exit from the wildfire.

"Let's run back!" Bevn said. "Come on! We can escape before the Lûk arrive."

Gabrielle shook his hand free.

"No," she said. "I have an idea. We can't just keep on running. you move too slowly."

That much was true. The Lûk were surely closing the gap behind them, and this time they would be ready for a fight, ready to kill.

"Listen. These strangers don't know us. They don't know what we've done. We can use that to our advantage."

Bevn stared dumbly at her. He couldn't see how people who were pointing arrows at him could ever be manipulated. He tried to come up with a better solution. The forest folk wouldn't come out onto the wildfire, he observed. They kept to the trees. They were afraid of the silver essence, just like the Lûk.

"Why don't we wait in the middle?"

"And do what?" she asked archly. "Sit out here until we starve? No, we must bargain with these foresters. We must bargain for our lives. Come, we haven't much time."

"Be ready to retreat, if we need to," she added.

His feet became as heavy as lead as they neared the forest. More archers were drawn out by their approach; they stepped into the spaces between the trees with arrows nocked. Twenty figures blocked the way. Gabrielle halted just short of bow-range, and raised her hands.

"People! We bring you no harm!"

A man called out harshly, and in an instant the archers were gone, hidden among the trees again. Bevn imagined he could hear the creak of many drawn bows, which made him feel itchy behind the ears. Sweat trickled down his back and into the crack of his bum.

"Be ready," warned Gabrielle.

"Tetaris?" someone called out. "Whattayee?"

"Na!" a man replied. "Na! Theyarenee fierspawner, ah kin seether whole. Bestill yor arrow."

A tall man stepped out from behind the closest tree. He had wild white hair, and wore a mottled leather breastplate and a cloak of russet leaf-patterns. A narrowly trimmed beard striped the centre of his chin. Bevn took him to be the commander.

"Whyaree na firespawner?" he shouted. "Howcanee standerinnin wither firewyld?"

The man's lilting accent was incomprehensible.

"We are travellers," Gabrielle announced. "We are no threat to you."

"Silliver chaosdusts!" shouted the forester. "Burnbane? Howaree innit, wither na chainge?"

"In it? What, this blasted soil?" Gabrielle asked, stamping her foot. "We carry a special ward!"

That was true. It was the crown that kept them from harm. If it weren't for the Kingsrim, they would have been dead long ago, just like that Lûk scout. Bevn felt suddenly itchy between his toes. He wanted to be anywhere but in the blasted circle. Don't be a fool, he told himself. The crown had protected him across the wastelands; there was no reason for it to fail him now.

The men came from behind the trees again, their lethal bows held steady. They wore leathers and the same leaf-patterned cloaks, and most had narrow beards like their leader.

"We seek your help, we don't want to fight," Gabrielle shouted. "Can we come closer?"

"Werearee coming, thatta walk onna firewyld?"

Gabrielle paused, deciphering his words. "Eyri, we are from the kingdom of Eyri," she answered loudly, and gestured away across the wastes. "In the mountains, south of here." Gabrielle seemed to have a better ear for the strange dialect than Bevn did—he was still making little sense of it.

"Ayryee? Owe long thessertoo walkaway?"

"We have run for a day, and we were on a windrunner with the Lûk for another."

"Lûk!" the commander exclaimed. The archers tensed. One of the archers made a sharp comment to the commander, and a short disagreement followed, which Bevn understood nothing of. They talked too fast between themselves, their language like wind thrashing in the trees.

"Can we approach you without threat?" Gabrielle called out. "I am tired of shouting."

"Ther Lûk," the commander challenged. "Why yee wither Lûk?"

"We were coming to you, but they captured us," Gabrielle lied smoothly. "They stole our food, they hurt us. They tried to kill the boy, but we fought them off, and killed two of theirs. They hunt us now."

Bevn tried to conceal his amazement. Gabrielle had lied for him, to cover the shameful truth. She had said just the right thing too, for the commander seemed impressed.

"You anner boy is as toughtimbered asser ironwood, ther Lûk na softly inna fight. Why are yee coming to huntersland?"

Gabrielle paused for a moment. "We have an offer of trade for the leader of your people. Eyri has great things to offer, and we brought the first sample for your leader, but the Lûk stole our gifts."

It was a flagrant lie, but it was a lie that might keep them alive.

"Ah, ye be freetraders. The Lûk stole ther treasury for our Hidesman Raherro?"

"Yes, that's right, it was for Raherro. We still wish to speak with him. We have much to offer—our secret ward, for one." The commander considered this, then nodded to the men on either side and they lowered their bows slightly.

"Come, this is where we must keep our wits," Gabrielle whispered over her shoulder. She paced confidently toward the forest people, into the range of the bows. Bevn couldn't afford to look frightened. Though his heart pounded, he followed.

"Be ye easy!" said the leader when they were before him. "Ther Lûk have na rights here. This is Hunters land. If yee would trade, thenner ye be welcome." He extended his palm toward them, fingers pointing to the sky. "I be Tetaris of er Bradach Hide."

"I am known as Gabrielle Aramonde," she said. "And this is Bevn Mellar, of Eyri."

Bevn didn't know quite what was expected of him, but he raised his hand as Gabrielle did, in a similar fashion to the Hunters. After an awkward pause, the commander stepped forward to press his hand against theirs.

"Ye nanarow our custom? Ye nounce the eldertongs astrange, I kin see ye are na Lûk, but ye make a lie to us here." Tetaris the commander knew they were lying. Bevn's mouth grew dry. "Ye na cross ther whiterlands!" Tetaris exclaimed. "Two days southward is desert, silversand then brown, na Ayree, na living thing but wind errockery. Ye come wander on from Korin, ya, beyonder ther six landerside of Lûk?"

Bevn had begun to understand their strange dialect a little. Tetaris didn't believe that Eyri existed. It wasn't surprising, because the ruffian probably only knew of the forest, and the wastelands at its edge.

"We are from Eyri," Bevn said, "and I am to be king." His swelled his chest out proudly.

Tetaris regarded Bevn critically. His eyes were a bright brown colour like polished chestnuts.

"Kinge? Is ther kinge squarelish in your tribe?"

Bevn wasn't sure what 'squarelish' meant. "I shall be the ruler. This crown proves it!" He lifted the Kingsrim slightly.

"Ther tattinhat a rulermark, where your tribe hunts?"

"It is not a hat, you meathead! It is my crown, it shows my power."

Tetaris took a step back, a wary expression on his face. "Ye are the oldest in your land, menninman?"

"I–"

"Oh, shut up," Gabrielle said, in a low voice. "You're just making things worse. They know nothing of Eyri. We're the first to come from there."

"But how can they not know what a king is?" Bevn asked dejectedly.

"I can see you are an intelligent man, and understand the value of what we might have to offer," Gabrielle said to Tetaris, ignoring Bevn again. Her voice was all honeyed cream. "Can we travel under your protection?"

Bevn didn't like the way Gabrielle had upstaged him in front of all the rough men, but she seemed to know what she was doing. She was using her charms to draw their attention, and it was working. They were so stupid.

"Ye willerwalk with us to Bradach Hide," said Tetaris. "Kulomb our elderman will wisher na 'scuss your trade an a'tribe." The commander issued a few short orders to his men. Four archers came into close flanking positions around them. Bevn could see how sharp the tips of their arrows were—bright metal points with mean barbed heads. What was Gabrielle thinking, lying to these wild men? They would find out the truth, wouldn't they? They had nothing to trade. He wondered if the Lûk still tracked them. If they caught up with the Hunters, they would tell them how Bevn and Gabrielle had murdered their men and run away, but the more he considered it, the more he realised how clever Gabrielle had been. The Lûk were obviously not popular with the Hunters. If there was a feud between the Lûk and the Hunters, then the Hunters would believe the lies which painted their enemies in a bad light. They might even fight to protect them.

As the morning went by, he began to realise the Hunters might have protected them already, just by being there. The Lûk might not have dared to follow them into the forest at all. This was Hunters land, the commander had said, and the Lûk had no right to be there. The Hunters looked to be dangerous men. They were all armed with bows, and Bevn guessed they knew how to use them. There had only been five Lûk following them in the cutter. They might well have reached the edge of the forest and come no farther.

"How far is it to the edge of the Lûk's land?" he asked.

Tetaris's expression hardened at the mention of the Lûk. "Rôgspar is a daily march on away, wherebegins ther sixlanderside Lûk. We patrol to keep it thatter way."

Rôgspar, that was where the Lûk captain Jek had been aiming for with the cutter. Hopefully that was where he had gone, after losing his chance of catching them.

Bevn smiled at Tetaris. He decided he liked the Hunters, despite their silly way of talking and their rough appearance. As Bevn's fear of pursuit eased, so he became more aware of how much his feet hurt, but he couldn't let the tough men know.

He didn't want to see what his toes looked like inside his boots. His feet had gone all burny and slippery again when the blisters had burst during their run. He struggled to match the Hunters' swift pace as they led them on the faint trail. Some of the men ranged wide in the forest. The tangled growth did not seem to slow their pace and they made little noise. When Tetaris noticed how badly he was limping, he ordered half-pace for his men, which was only slightly better, in Bevn's opinion.

The Hunters were generous with their water and food though. He gulped gratefully at a bladder until he was full, and munched on some honey-flavoured bread thereafter. Gabrielle took a big chunk of bread herself. She kept up a soft conversation with the commander, endearing herself more with every sultry smile and sideways glance, no doubt.

The forest smelled less of the desert wind now, and more of itself, which was a pungent leafy living scent mixed with the darker smells of compost, mushrooms and bark. Now they were far from the edge of the wildfire waste, he saw none of the deadly metallic leaves driven into the soil. The canopy above was green and light, but all was not peaceful in this place. They passed a line of trees that might have been wrenched into whorls by a monstrous wind. Broken limbs littered the path. Fresh sap still oozed from some of the shattered boughs.

"What breaks the trees like this?" Gabrielle asked Tetaris.

"Nephilim," Tetaris replied. "Here he ran a'quarter moonlish hence. We felled him at Rellowvine."

"A what?" Bevn asked.

Tetaris just shook his head at Bevn's ignorance. "Once like you an me, but betaken by the firewyld."

"How big do these Nephilim get?" Gabrielle asked.

"Twicetalled the tree, but ee die so soon. The worst is ther one smaller, askin akin bubble, they liver year on year an remember therold life."

Bevn snorted. A creature that big was impossible. The trees were more than forty feet high.

He trudged after the Hunters at the unreasonable 'half-pace', and a bitter mood settled upon him. He worried how they were going to find Black Saladon now they weren't in the land of the Lûk. Saladon had been vague about their journey. They were supposed to travel north, but he'd lost his sense of direction under all the crooked trees. Saladon hadn't even prepared them for the desert and the windrunners. He'd said it was a test, to prove Bevn was ready for power, but it was an unfair test, Bevn decided.

He was tired of walking, tired of adventuring, tired of being scared and sore. He was tired of being scorned for not *really* being a king and being too young to command men's respect and fear. He had believed it would all end soon after his triumphant exit from Eyri, but it seemed his test had only just begun. The Sorcerer Ametheus was still far away in some distant lowland, Bevn didn't even know where he was himself, and Black Saladon had insisted that they could say nothing to anyone of their quest, so how was he ever going to find his way?

It was all miserably unfair.

He deserved more help than he was getting from the wizard.

As he moped along behind Gabrielle, he wondered idly what was going on beneath her tight, black leather trousers. How many of the Hunter men wondered the same thing? To them she must seem exotic and intriguing.

But she was *his*. They had no rights to her. They had better not think they had.

They would laugh at him. They wouldn't fear him—these tough militant men. He wished he was *older*. He wished he had power. He would show everyone just how tough he could be.

Night fell upon the forest far earlier than Bevn expected, and in a patchy way as well—full dark clutched at the leaves above, yet in other places the light of the setting sun still lingered among the tangled roots at the base of the trees. Bevn was glad to see the Hunters were stopping. They turned aside from the faint path and took them to an enclosed shelter made of rough untreated timbers. It was basic, but then it was only a patrol-house, Tetaris said, and they would soon be at Bradach Hide, the grandest of all the settlements among the many tribes of Huntersland. Bevn only listened with half an ear, for he could see the other men building a fire for supper. A deer carcass was produced, skinned and spitted.

There was a washing hole, which he was going to use until he discovered there was only cold water—and no soap. He soaked his feet in the spring and didn't bother with the rest. Nobody would notice because they all stank. The men gave Gabrielle her own private time at the hole, and they spoilt the fun by standing guard far out from the spring—too far for Bevn to see. They were a bunch of twits.

At least the Hunters ate better food than the Lûk. He devoured everything they gave him, and fell asleep while he was chewing, where he sat beside the fire.

CR80CR80

They reached Bradach Hide late the following day. It was nothing like what Bevn had imagined. He had expected at least a mighty fortified manor, where the people who faced the threat of the Lûk spears might defend their settlement in times of invasion. Instead, there was a settlement which looked so temporary it could have been raised in under a week and dissembled in even less time. It gave him the sense of a community hiding in the forest, rather than occupying it. There seemed to be too few shelters for the number of women, children and elders who flocked through the trees to greet them, let alone for the returning patrol themselves.

The more he looked at the shelters, the more he doubted they were for people to live in. Smoke curled through the slats of the one slanted roof, another low structure had water trickling over it and down the thin fabric walls: a smoking room and a cool-room, for meat and food.

If the lean-tos were stores, where did the Hunters stay? He gazed around the glade, from hut to hovel to lean-to, all centred around a green hill with a massive tree on top.

The shape of the real Bradach Hide appeared. It was not a hill at all. The slopes were too steeply canted, and ridged in ways earth would not ridge. He picked out a slit in the structure near ground level, then another—entrances. The hill was made from some kind of fabric hung from the tree to form a massive tent. The scale of it had made it difficult to recognise. The apex of the tent spiralled upward around the mighty centre-tree high above the ground, wrapping around the trunk tightly like a serpent's tail. Smoke billowed out the top. The fabric was deep green, and its surface glimmered as if jewels were sprinkled upon it. He recognised that glimmer—it was similar to the colour of the boards the Lûk used to cross the wildfire. The marquee's skirt came down to shoulder height, where the green roof was bound to the sharp tips of trimmed poles, which jutted outward in a prickly rim. The walls, set deeper under the overhanging roof, were made from dark, spaced uprights. He supposed such a wall would allow the Hunters to shoot arrows from within the protection of their hide. The transition from green slope to walls to forest floor was so disguised by leaves and woven vegetation it was difficult to find the openings. Unless he had been brought to this place by the Hunters, and turned to face the hide, he wouldn't have noticed it, despite the fact that it was greater in size than a great hall.

"May 'er spirit yonder Bradach fly over our allerways, may he keep us halerhale!" exclaimed Tetaris.

"Longendure, Bradach," the Hunters rejoined, pushing open palms against the air, as if reaching for the apex of the hide.

"We shall acclaim the homercoming after yon sun fallen under!" announced Tetaris. "For now I know ye bewish to be innin forest an be bind ye bonds wither family. May there be smoke and fire!" This comment drew cheers and chuckles from the Hunter folk all round, and most of the returning patrol dispersed with partners. A few children chased around the adults and swung into the trees.

Bevn's attention returned to the roof of Bradach Hide. That great sweep of material gleamed in the late afternoon sun, looking harder and more intricately constructed the closer they came to it. It looked almost metallic, the way it shone.

"What is it woven from?" he asked.

"Not a'woven," Tetaris answered, "it is Bradach. His a'hide."

"Bradach's skin?" Bevn said incredulously, staring at the immense stretch of roof above him. "All of it? What kind of creature was Bradach?"

"A dragon, that he was," answered Tetaris.

Bevn must have looked particularly blank, for the commander laughed. "Do you not have dragons in your parts?" he asked. "Maybe ye ken their kin by another name? They be Draak in 'er Lûk. Morkenn?"

"Dragon?" repeated Bevn, still not knowing what kind of creature it was. "All of the roof comes from one dragon?"

"Older as a mountain was he, an bigger than ther cloud bethundering when he died. It tooken best cut of 'er year to skinnin, an three season to return 'er hide from under yon Winterblades."

"How do you hunt something as big as a dragon?" Gabrielle asked.

"Hunt dragon?" Tetaris repeated, raising a mocking eyebrow. "I see ye have na begun to explain 'er sheltering yon Ayreeland must have. Ye nay hunt 'er dragon, ladyfair, there's na bow with fearsomeness enough and na hander strong enough to pull it gainst such a'mighty beasts as they be dragons. No nano, they be indeed creatures fiercely, and mostly more dangerous forbeside with wit and 'membering. Bradach was a rare one to die on alone 'fore returning to their ever an forever place of passing. Sooth say they be flying upper high white peaks of 'er Winterblades to be dying, where man na can tarry, an they be falling 'ponner summit. Their lifebreath stays to beblow 'er clouds to the fourfar corners of Oldenworld."

"And Bradach? Why didn't he make it to the peak?"

"He was old, an given gluttonly. Comes he descend upon 'er Lûk while they be engaging spears against Clanlees metal in 'er battle pon northborderland, near Muriah. Had he na sense for waiting, when dead be stiller an feeding easy. Mayhap was metalry of 'er Clanlees that kill the Bradach, mayhap 'er Lûk spears withinnin meal pierce his belly. We the Hunters hide an waiting, an fought who survived, an saw it too that there great dragon never bewoke." He looked proudly toward the tent. "The firewyld does na ever penetrate that there hide. But we must move if the strike comes near, for the ground is a ruin, and the forest is alive with firespawner. Good Bradach has formade us a home at many places."

"A dragon," Bevn muttered to himself, regarding the sloping roof. "Weren't the Nephilim a tall enough tale?"

He hadn't kept his voice low enough. Tetaris scowled at him. Bevn shrugged and lifted his nose. He didn't really care what they thought of him. They were tent dwellers. In Eyri, people who lived in a tent were less than poor—even swineherds had hovels—no, these Hunters were more like the beggars around Slurryrig, or the outcasts at Rotcotford. They did not deserve the royalty of his presence.

Outcasts nonetheless, most of them had bows, so Bevn followed the commander. Tetaris led them into the hide, through a reinforced archway made from heavily carved pillars, where names had been cut into the wood in rows. More than half of them had been crossed out. They passed into the strangely lit interior, a corridor formed by uneven nets of woven leaves. The woodchips were springy underfoot. The corridor ended and they emerged into a great circular space left clear around the roots of the central tree. A border of leafy curtains defined the outer edge of the communal hall-space. Overhead, rough ropes ran like spokes of a wheel to join against the trunk.

The roof was incredibly high. Pale golden-green light filtered through the translucent fabric. The central hall extended all the way around the base of the tree and was filled with a smoky meaty aroma. A small fire was burning in an open hearth, and the smoke curled upward. A long wooden table dominated the central space, long enough to seat at least fifty people. Seats were ranged around it, simple slices of timber, roughly finished but heavily carved.

Bevn and Gabrielle were seated at the end of the long table, under guard, and told to wait while the elders were assembled. The Hunter patrol had been fairly relaxed on the trail, but now they were in their own home they seemed distrustful and nervous of the newcomers.

"This is where they find out you lied about trading," Bevn reminded her, in a whisper. "What am I supposed to say?"

Gabrielle gave him a hard look. "Just shut up and let me talk to them."

"Do you think they'll let us go?"

"They shouldn't want to keep you. You've been such a rude brat."

"Hey! That's only because they wouldn't carry me. My feet were sore, they still are!"

"You think too highly of yourself, princeling. You are not in Eyri any more."

He ignored her after that, but what she had said stayed in his mind. She was right about one thing. If he was really, really rude, they'd want to get rid of him.

The elders arrived, some emerging from corridors and curtained-off living quarters within the great tent; some who had been summoned from outside. They were hard-worn folk, both women and men grizzled and scarred by the years, the most ruffian-like being the leader, Roherro, a barrel-chested slab of a man with leather bands on his tanned wrists and a wide-shouldered leather coat. His grey beard was trimmed in the narrow fashion of the Hunters, and his hair was tied back severely with a thong. He was clearly the oldest, and Bevn had learnt that among the Hunters age dictated rank. If it was really true what they'd said, that thirty years was a long life for a Hunter, then their tough old leader looked as if he had lived a life almost twice as long. His face was deeply lined, his eyes hooded yet strong and dangerous.

Roherro drew a wide-bladed hunting knife from his belt and stabbed it into the table before he sat, and all present at the table followed his example, including Gabrielle, although Bevn knew she had two knives upon her body and she'd only stabbed one down. Bevn couldn't tell whether this was a show of strength, a warning, or a custom intended to show their weapons had been set down. The serrated knives looked terribly close at hand, standing to attention on their tips at various angles, like a formation of drunken Swords in a courtyard. They were old-looking knives, worn on the blade as if they'd been passed down for many generations and sharpened many times. Gabrielle's blade drew more than a few glances, being sharp and newly forged.

Tetaris presented the tale of the two Eyrians, then Gabrielle told the same lies about their foray with the Lûk, further embellished with details of the items they had been bringing to the Hunters. She knew what they would prize; she had gleaned those details from the Hunters during their march to Bradach. Bevn stayed mostly out of it. She had a better ear for their strange dialect than he did.

But, after an hour, the story was growing stale, and greater holes were being picked in it by the distrustful and sly elders. How did they walk on wildfire? How did they know to come trade with the Hunters if they lived in a sheltered kingdom where the Hunters weren't known? If the boy was a ruler of some kind, then why was their party so very small? The questions carried on and on, and Gabrielle invented clever answers to them all, but Bevn could see she was growing more frustrated. The elders didn't believe Eyri existed, and so they returned to the same question, over and over. Where did Bevn and Gabrielle come from?

Then the elders stopped speaking to Gabrielle. They just argued among themselves, and Roherro pounded the table with his fist before adding his own comments to the ruckus. Bevn was tired of their distrust. They were low-born peasants. They should believe him. He was a king.

Bevn shouted to be sure he was heard over their senseless babble. "Eyri is a secret place hidden by magic. You're never going to know about things like that hiding in the forest. What is wrong with you leaf-heads! Can't you see we're not like you?"

Roherro and the other elders turned fierce glares on him.

"We brought gifts for trade. They were stolen by the Lûk. We can always return to Eyri and bring a great deal of those things you need. I am the king. I have command of a great wealth. We came to see what the Hunters could offer Eyri before we return, but it seems all you have is hot words and unfriendliness. Give us a meal and send us on our way, and we'll bother you no more. I am sure there are other tribes in this forest who would be intelligent enough to understand how important an alliance with us could be."

No one in the hide spoke. He could almost feel the hair rising on the necks and arms around him. They hadn't liked what he'd said. Too bad. These people were behaving like idiots and it had needed to be said. Gabrielle was trying too hard to be diplomatic and polite. She appeared just as upset by what he had just said.

"Big in 'er words for one so small in 'er years," Roherro said at last. "Sooth say ye can bejudge man in man by 'er enemies he holds. If ye have so much cleverinnin then answer a'this. Who is your enemy?"

"The Lûk!" he exclaimed at once. Roherro was surely trying to establish if the Eyrians were friend or foe, and the Lûk were an obvious enemy of the Hunters. A big man would have big foes—what other people were the Hunters pitted against? Bevn didn't think any other adversaries had been mentioned during the walk. Then suddenly he remembered one name which would be a sure-fire winner—everyone feared him.

"And the Sorcerer Ametheus!" Bevn declared.

The men jumped back with startled cries, as if a shock had passed through them. Bows were drawn, instantly taut, the points of too many arrows aimed at Bevn. Some of the men backed out of the hall and ran for the door, the rest tried to scan the sky through the narrow apex hole of the tent as if they expecting something to fall upon them. By Fynn, he'd swear these forest folk were scared of their own shadows! He'd just spoken the name and they reacted as if a whole army had attacked them. They were afraid of Ametheus, mortally afraid.

Bowstrings creaked. Tetaris held up a gloved hand, poised as if about to order the men to loose the arrows. He watched Bevn intently. "Ye holler to he who should na ever be hollered," Tetaris accused. "Ye harbinge a darkly tong. If ye namer name atwice, ye be killed, or threw upon a firewyld afor ye blame a strike pon our people."

Bevn swallowed. It would only take one slip on a bowfinger for him to lose his life.

"He seech 'er namerless name!" objected one of the archers. "He be lower lander! With 'er ruins an festid ways! Given word, Tetaris, given word an we loose 'er bolts!"

"Wait!" boomed a voice from the door. A mantled form strode toward them along the leaf-lined corridor, his footfalls so solid they seemed to set a pulse through the floor. He carried a tall weapon, and h. e was *heavy*; his presence pushed against Bevn even though the distance between them hadn't closed yet. "Hidesman Roherro, he has value to me!" That voice—Bevn knew that voice.

"An who are ye?" demanded Tetaris, squinting at the figure whose dark features were hidden by shadows, backlit as he was by the afternoon light falling on the ground beyond the door arch.

"Your sight grows weak, Tetaris of 'er Bradach. Do ye na ken your ally? Even one ever as black as I?"

"Saladon!" the commander exclaimed. A sigh passed through the Huntersfolk, just as Bevn's heart leapt in his chest. It *was* Black Saladon! The wizard had come to save them from the ruffians! They were saved!

The wizard was formiddable; his dark features were tight and hard, his plaited moustache tails quivering beside the rigid line of his lips. He was anything but glad to see Bevn. He came up to the prince and glared at him through smouldering eyes. Bevn had forgotten how heavy the wizard's presence was. He felt squashed and small before him.

"This littleratter is dangeroos," said Tetaris. "He call pon he who can na be called."

"Then we shall have to keep him silent," said Black Saladon. "Put ye a blade pon his neck while we parley. If he utters a word, ye slices 'cross that idiotic throat."

Bevn looked wide-eyed at the wizard. He understood the order despite the wizard having reverted to the Hunters' strange dialect. What was he doing? Why was Saladon so angry with him? Wasn't he glad to see them safely across the wastelands?

A cold blade touched his skin, and he knew then that he had missed the opportunity to ask anything. The rough grip of the Hunter behind him told him the man was braced and ready. He would not be shy to pull that weapon as instructed.

Bevn was horrified. Maybe he wasn't as important to the wizard as he'd originally thought. If that blade was jerked across his neck... It would be horrible, like when Gabrielle had speared the Lûk, but instead of some savage's blood spilling upon him it would be his own blood that would gush warm down his chest and onto his lap. His knees started to shake and he couldn't stop them.

Saladon stepped up to the table beside the elders and addressed Roherro.

"I can bring better gain to ye an Bradach under such amatter. Allow that I offer 'er saltweight for captives two, to be servants pon 'er road."

"Ye come a'lasting, trader Saladon. One breath a'later an dead would he have been."

Saladon nodded. "Boyer is as foolish as 'er frothjawhound, but I need him halerhale, he is part a'pact I maker familymine."

"Ah. We ken ye to be true, Saladon, but these two be full a'tales an twisted tongues. They bespoke a realm pon 'er waste's east. Ayree. Be there such land? Have ye trade betaken ye 'cross 'er dry an deadly wastes?"

"Ayree?" Saladon replied, mispronouncing it just as the Hunters did. "Might be that mighty Bradach saw such a place," he said at last. "I have heard it bespoken by other men; else where, else when."

"Saladon, your word-betold helps none to end this dispute!" Roherro said.

"I can na settle muddle-matter of where become," Saladon answered, "but I can settle where begone."

Roherro considered this. "Glad we be to see yon foolish-tongue begone," agreed Roherro. "But 'er vixen be a different tale, she be worth many times more than 'er pup. Ye can see for yourself. Bradachin is ever drained of womenkind. An she have 'er generous form, of nature pleasing to menninmen. Truthbetold!"

The commander stood forward. "I took her from 'er forest, an would have more than salt to bring level pon 'er scales."

"An I would put precious blades an whetstones in its place!" called out another Hunter.

Cheers ran through the men present in the hall, and whistles.

"Feify would put his'er wife on the scale," a gruff-voiced man joked, and the Huntersfolk all laughed heartily. Gabrielle indulged them with a wicked smile.

"Laugh pon your own time, Roherro," said Saladon sternly. "I have already named my price, and ye ken it is fair."

"I am not so cheaply traded!" Gabrielle objected. "You must outbid the others, that is the way it is done, and that does not make me your servant. You still have to negotiate with me, settling with the others merely eliminates your competition." She was enjoying this.

How many times has she played this game in the tavern in Fendwarrow, and how many men have lost their gold or teeth to rivals, only to meet with her clever tongue?

Saladon turned upon her, clearly unimpressed. "I thought you were wiser than the princeling, but I begin to wonder. Don't you understand, woman, you are not free anymore? Besides, I have already bought you. Now I must pay more?"

"That's life. Get used to it," said Gabrielle. She held the wizard's attention with a level gaze. Bevn wished he could be that brave against Black Saladon. She was daring him, resisting him, *showing off* to him.

Why did she never do that with *him*?

Saladon didn't answer her, but his dark gaze told Bevn that Gabrielle was in trouble with the wizard as well. Saladon turned to face Roherro once more. "Saltweight an a'halves," he offered.

"Sooth say they walk onna firewyld," one of the elders said, a craggy-faced woman with wispy white hair. "Such skill has value to Bradachin, witherso many burns a'forest."

"Double weight then, but na push me further, I warn ye."

"Na need for 'er threatening, friend Saladon, your price is goodly, we na stand in ye way. Take them as ye will." Roherro rose, and extended his hand. Saladon shook on the deal, in the manner of the Hunters.

The rest of the elders rose, and Bevn was lifted to his feet by the guard behind him. The man kept his blade across Bevn's throat. Gabrielle retrieved her dagger from the table.

"Come," ordered Saladon, striding away toward the exit. Bevn was pushed roughly forward by the knife-wielding Hunter. Gabrielle hesitated before following.

"Don't expect any more than you've bargained for," she called out.

Saladon gave a short, humourless bark of laughter. "That will be *your* pleasure," he said loudly over his shoulder.

"Follow me if you wish to live as well."

18. SILVER SAND

"Change the world and a person will adapt or die;
Change the person and the world transforms,
in the blink of an eye."—Zarost

They followed the new pass out of Eyri. They rode up the avenue like pilgrims about to enter a holy land, eyes wide with wonder despite their aching bodies. Tabitha rode at the head, with Garyll close behind on his roan stallion. The mist swirled at the crest of the Penitent's pass, billowing and disturbed as it was from the spell Tabitha had cast to break the Shield.

Something slithered around her neck. The clasps on her necklaces had lost their seal. She caught the heavy crystals and slipped them into her pocket. She turned to see if the same thing had happened to Garyll, and saw him looking down to where his stone had fallen to the ground. He left it there.

The pressure of the Shield had gone. Tabitha spread her arms and felt her presence spread outward, upward; released. She could breathe. There was slight warmth to the air, and a scent of burnt cinnamon. They rode downhill, into the grey and swirling mist, over the bare, rocky ground and onto silver sand.

Her brown mare jumped and skittered nervously, but she kept spurring her on to avoid backing into the others behind her. The mist began to break into shreds pierced with sunlight. As Tabitha rode into one of these clear gaps, the light caught her full on her shoulders, casting a shadow onto the horse's neck. The light was unusually bright. She glanced quickly at the sun, gasped and turned away. The sun was a crisp orb, blinding and powerful. It had lost its corona. It was intense. She turned her palm to the sunlight and felt the rays tickle her fingers—rough, raw, the sunlight felt *unfiltered*.

The sky above was blue but strangely disjointed, as if divided into great mismatched panes. Her mare took a few steps forward but slowed, unsure of finding its own way. The ground was silvery, covered in a metallic dust that crunched under the horses' hooves and sparkled in the sun.

There was a faint persistent sound. Tabitha cocked her head. A river running over rocky shallows? No, it was a rougher sound; it set her nerves on edge, like dry leaves scuttling in a breeze. A scratchy dissonance, a hissing screech, and yet it was also a rippled sound like water running over the bones of the earth.

Her horse shifted beneath her.

"Do you hear it?" she asked Garyll. "Do you feel it?"

He shot her a quick glance of concern. "There's something coming though the mist?"

She shook her head. No, she should have known he wouldn't hear what she heard—it was the elemental music that had altered. The crackle and screech came not from ahead of them, but underneath them. The earth was different to the soil of Eyri—it gave off a unique sound. The last of the mist rolled aside, and there, before them, lay their first view of the land beyond Eyri, their first view of Oldenworld.

"Oh mercy, it's a wasteland!" she exclaimed.

The ground sloped away, bare, barren, stripped to the silvery-white skeleton of the rocks, as if a great fire had raged across it and left only a swathe of ash in its wake. The morass stretched as far as she could see on the plains, a featureless expanse of lifelessness. Only on the far horizon did the landscape hold a narrow stroke of green—possibly a forest, but many, many leagues away.

"For shame, the horses! They'll die out here!" Ashley said. "There's not a blade of grass... Not a blade for them to eat."

"Fool!" said Garyll, to himself. "We should have brought a pack horse with grainmeal and fodder. I've never seen a place where grass did not grow. Even Slurryrig isn't this bad. Ah, this is a cruel twist to our fate."

Tabitha's mare twisted beneath her. She tightened her grip on the reins.

She scanned the wastes for signs of life. Nothing. Except for twinned tracks that led away across the sands, two widely spaced grooves. The tracks curved in toward them, turned behind them then curved outward again in a second line. Something had come past and gone away again. A coach? Tabitha didn't think so, because there were no hoof prints. No footprints either. The footprints she had been tracking ended beside the groove closest to Eyri, at the edge of the silvered soil.

Bevn had found some means of transport. Someone had collected him. That was worrying. Someone in Oldenworld had known he was coming. This might not be as haphazard as it seemed; it might be a planned expedition. They might be up against more than a runaway prince.

Garyll's stallion tossed its head, and Mulrano's whinnied.

Did the Sorcerer know about Bevn? With the Shield broken, Eyri was vulnerable.

With a great squeal, Ashley's mare jumped away. Garyll reached for the reins as its head passed him but missed. Ashley leant close to its head and seemed to regain some control, but then Mulrano's black stallion ran with a strange sideways gait, and Tabitha's mare shook its head as if trying to rid itself of a wasp. Garyll's stallion stamped and reared, stamped and reared again. Every hoof-fall raised a puff of dust around its hocks.

"It's something in the ground!" Ashley shouted, guiding his grey closer. "They don't like it. It's as if it stings their hooves, I'm not sure how. Uhhh, not again. I can't hold onto them!"

The ground? It was still, just as silvery-grey as ever. Tabitha realised too late what that might mean.

Across Oldenworld shall his wildfire spread. Sorcerer of the silver fire, thrice-dreaded.

They were standing in wildfire! The Sorcerer's magic, the touch of Chaos.

The horses took off, galloping and bucking, outward onto the silver sands.

"No!" shouted Tabitha. "Get them to go back! Turn them back!"

Was this whole wasteland filled with the Sorcerer's power? They would never survive it. She hauled hard on her mare's reins, but the mare Sharrow just fought her, panicked, frantic. The others tried to turn their horses back as well, but none of them obeyed. Every lurching sideways lunge took them further into the silver sand.

"Something's happening!" shouted Ashley. "There's a change... a *wrongness* in their minds!"

Garyll's stallion reared, and he was almost thrown.

"Stay on!" Tabitha shouted. "Whatever happens, stay on the horses! The ground is tainted with magic, all of it is tainted. Oh mercy me! Ashley! Can you calm them? Can you make them go back?"

"I can't... They're going mad!" he cried as his mare spun him in tight circles.

Tabitha looked in horror at Sharrow's pounding legs, stained silver from the dust. Thick worms crawled under the skin, bulging, growing; then they were as thick as writhing serpents. Sharrow's hair fell away like chaff. Her skin became tough and leathery. The girth burst and the saddle loosened between Tabitha's legs as Sharrow's back broadened and her limbs thickened. Her nose became more rounded, her muzzle wizened. She rolled a terrified horsey eye at Tabitha.

Chaos was upon them, a rampant curse, a poison that inflicted change. The living flesh was taking new forms. Tabitha was too scared to do anything but clutch to the neck of the beast beneath her. She couldn't afford to fall off.

Garyll's horse reared again, pawing the air with its forelegs, balancing there as its legs thickened and bulged with muscles. It lost its roan coat just as Sharrow had; its skin became as shiny as lacquer. All at once its hooves changed. Vicious, splayed talons grew through the old horny casings. A hooked barb thrust through the skin at each knee. The elegant lines of its head became warped and flattened, and the skin pulled back from a mouth of elongated teeth. It glared from suddenly predatory, slit eyes. It gave a sibilant cry—half horse, half monster.

Sharrow bucked and arched beneath Tabitha, probably trying to get away from Garyll's altered stallion, which lashed out with its taloned forelegs and almost caught Mulrano's stallion in the throat. Mulrano's stallion answered with a high unnatural squeal. It shrank, growing smaller and more hound-like, and blacker, if that was possible. It was like watching darkness concentrate itself around two evil eyes.

"Catch him!" Garyll shouted to Tabitha, who was nearest. "He's going to touch the ground!" There was a hint of panic in Garyll's voice. She grabbed for Mulrano. As she caught his arms, the saddle fell from under him. The tack clattered to the ground as the shrunken creature shook its head. The bridle smoked in the ash. Mulrano struggled and kicked his way onto Tabitha's thickset beast, and almost pulled her loose from the shifting saddle. Behind him, his shrunken animal fled. It was no bigger than a hunting dog.

Ashley's horse squealed and reared. Tendrils of silver shot up its legs and spread quickly over its body like a rampant creeper. The mare grew thinner, but something bulged from its shoulders, stretching the grey coat outward. The horse squealed and bucked, but the touch of Chaos was impossible to refuse. With a sudden tearing of skin, two limbs protruded through at the mare's shoulders, thick-edged and covered with bloody feathers.

The mare became thinner in body as its wings grew wide and strong. It tossed its head, which became thin and avian around its startled eyes. Its muzzle became elongated and hardened into a horny beak. With a leap and a surprised cry from Ashley, his transformed horse took to the air. He clung to its neck and whispered in its ear, but it beat the air with its new wings and rose in a frantic flutter.

"Ashley!" she cried out. "Ashley!"

"They still believe they are horses!" he shouted down, rising ever higher. "Give them clear commands! Ride them!" Ashley was soon too high above them to speak to, and the winged creature that had once been a horse lurched away on the upper winds.

"Garyll! I don't want to die!" *Oh Ethea, don't let me be changed like this!* The world had become unutterably strange.

Garyll's creature roared. Her own beast shuddered beneath them then ran. She clutched tighter to its neck, and Mulrano gripped her waist with desperate strength from behind. They galloped away, holding on for dear life. Heavy hooves thundered on the shifting sand. Although they plunged through thick banks of silver, they did not alter any more. Sharrow's legs remained thick and leathery, as if by changing she had developed an immunity to further change, if only for the moment.

The bridle bound the creature's nose so tightly it looked about to burst. Tabitha tried again to rein her beast in. It's Sharrow, Tabitha thought, she's still Sharrow inside, she just looks like a beast. She had to believe that. She had to believe that part of what she rode was still a horse, or she would go mad with fear. Garyll's taloned horse galloped close on their tail. It was harder to believe that the predatory creature had ever been a stallion. A *whorse*, Tabitha thought. It was a horse, now it was…something else, far worse.

She let Sharrow run. She suspected that Sharrow's mouth had grown too hard to care about the pull of the reins anyway. The saddle wanted to slip under Tabitha's legs. She gripped as tight as she could with her knees, but it was awkward to sit upon the wide back, and Sharrow's heavy gait was unsettling. Mulrano knocked into her with every step.

The wind whistled in her ears. The ground flew by in a metallic glistening blur. The danger lay in front of them. The plains stretched away in bright undulations, league upon league of wasteland. A ridge passed by on their right, growing larger as they descended beside it. These must be the back of the peaks they could see in Eyri, Tabitha thought. They looked so different on the Eyrian side—lush, carpeted in green trees. On this side of the Shield, the ground was barren, the rocks streaked and scarred and the slopes dry and empty of any life. Some clouds lingered on the border of Eyri, like ugly tongues jutting out toward the plains, twisting upward toward the brightness of the morning sun. Farther ahead, a brown-tinted thundercloud grew stacked and knuckled above the desert plains. The sky still looked as warped as ever, a montage of lopsided squares of uneven blue.

In some places the ground was silver; in others it was grey. Tabitha wondered whether there was a difference. The sound that came off the desert changed subtly when they galloped over the darker soil. The screeching hiss of wildfire became more like the soft hiss of a pot just beginning to boil. She didn't think it was much better, but if she was going to fall, she decided she would choose the grey sand over the silver. Maybe the wildfire had already done its worst there.

Her thighs ached. Her waist was bruised from Mulrano's fierce grip, but she couldn't ask him to ease his hold. She knew how desperate he must be to stop himself slipping. He was seated further back on Sharrow's leathery rump, and he was having a worse time with the whorse's lumbering gallop. She turned to look at him.

She caught a fearsome sight past his head. A jawful of teeth was opening wide just behind him, straining to reach his back. Garyll's beast was galloping flat out, trying to close the gap between them. Garyll was smacking it on top of its head with his left arm, but he could not use his baton—his right hand was holding tight to a fold of skin on its neck. He had lost his reins. There looked to be scant purchase on the beast for a rider.

"Mulrano!" she cried. "Mulrano!" In her panic she couldn't find the words to tell him what was happening, but he read the expression on her face and turned.

"*Hua!*"

He released her waist with one hand and fumbled for his weapon. The whorse snapped at his shoulder. Sharp teeth pierced his jacket, and a chunk of fabric was ripped away. The beast tossed its head and stretched its gait for a few thundering paces. Then it was close enough.

Mulrano swung his axe. "Don't kill it!" shouted Tabitha, but too late, the axe had already fallen upon the beast's snout. The whorse shrieked and reeled back. Blood stained its teeth—its own blood. It didn't try to close the gap again.

They galloped on, the landscape blurring by in low ragged spines that looked like scalloped shells. They crossed a dried rocky wash that might have once been a river. They ran across a wasteland filled with shattered rocks, then a more disturbing patch of whitened slivers that looked like broken bones. They passed the dark mouth of a great cave buried beneath an overhanging slab of rock. They crested a ridgeline and dropped into a hard-packed sloping valley. The sun burned down on Tabitha.

Her thighs ached, her throat was dry and her mouth tasted of dust. She shook with the strain of trying to avoid falling. She was growing weak, but so was Sharrow beneath her. Then something boomed, and her beast stumbled beneath her, and she was almost thrown out of the saddle.

The distant boom was repeated behind them, and she felt the ground move through Sharrow.

It was like a hammer blow.

Boom! The ground rippled again. A boulder rolled down the spine to their right, crashing into smaller rocks on the way and setting them tumbling in its wake. Tabitha could make no sense of what she could feel. A place filled with discordant elemental music, sounds and breathing, a moving mountain. The rocks shivered with the rhythmic pounding, shaking in their places, jumping clear of the surface, slipping down into the hollows.

The whorses took off. The ground lurched with great shuddering jolts, like the tread of something massive approaching. A figure crashed over the ridge-top behind them. Tabitha's whorse ran sideways to see what it was, four legs stumbling awkwardly across the grit. A wild man, but so big he looked taller than a tree. It had to be an illusion caused by their position, looking up to where he stood, momentarily outlined on the ridge. Maybe something distorted their view—he couldn't really be so big, so colossal. He shielded his close-set eyes with his great hand and looked from side to side. His hair was wild and matted, coiled like ropes upon his shoulders. His massive knees were covered in tattered leather, his thick legs ending in huge boots. When he took another step, the ground heaved.

The world had become altogether too strange. They fled from the walking nightmare on weird creatures across the deadly plains. A horrible realisation pressed in against Tabitha and clenched her stomach in fear. They were going to die out here. They would trip and fall, and tumble headlong into a patch of silver ash and one or all of them would be changed forever. Tabitha squeezed her eyes shut. This was Chaos—this land of nightmares, this horror of altered reality.

Above them the blinding sun skittered across the broken sky, like a mad god peering down upon them through shattered panes of glass.

The ground jumped up and down under their galloping steeds. The wind whipped in Tabitha's hair. The whorses ran at the leading edge of their own cloud of metallic dust. Tremors passed through the earth like waves that ran ahead of the company. The giant was gaining on them. Tabitha knew they wouldn't be fast enough. Rocks began to roll around them. The whole slope would soon be moving. The giant's great boots crashed into the barren land, lifting his own plumes of dust. Every stride brought him closer.

Tabitha gripped Sharrow's neck fiercely as she careened over loose rock. "Run, Sharrow, run!" she cried, her stomach clenched even tighter in fear, but the beast was already galloping flat out. They approached a semicircle of white pebbles. Something was different about the desert beyond, something about the light. Tabitha had only an instant to wonder what it was before she hit something hard. It felt as if she rode into a wall, or passed through one.

Her breath was knocked out of her chest, her stomach was left behind. She tried to draw air.

Nothing happened. A deep hum resonated in her ears.

She began to panic, but then the first warm thread of air entered her lips, a breath so slow she would surely die before she filled her lungs. She tried to rise in her saddle, but the movement took forever.

A deep, slow impact sounded below her, then another a long time after. *Fwa...dooff.*

Hoofbeats, she realised, stretched out in time.

There, another.

Everything was occurring in slow motion.

She tried to call out to Garyll, but her words made an endless groan. Her voice was so deep and slurred she couldn't recognise it herself. The air hardly moved—the dust hung in nearly static swirls around the whorse's hooves. She began the turn to look over her shoulder, but that took longer even than her first breath. It was as if they had ridden into a place where time was stretched out.

The giant wasn't yet in that place, and he was unhindered. He was suddenly right behind them. His great boot crashed into the place where Garyll's whorse had left its last clawed print. He towered above them. He reached for Garyll with a hand big enough to crush him, big enough to gather his steed up as well.

The Lifesong, she needed to sing the second stanza! But there was no time.

Another single hoofbeat sounded clearly in her ears.

Fwa-dooff.

Tabitha tried to cry out, but the slowed time prevented the sound from escaping. The giant began to close his fingers. His fingernails were jagged and stained with earth.

Suddenly they were released from that strange place of altered time. The deep elemental hum became a high-pitched whine. Their cruel crippled pace became sudden speed, a manic rush, as if they had been fired from a bow. The giant's hand closed on thin air. Garyll was ten paces clear, then twenty, then more. Their hoof beats sounded like a frantic roll of drums in Tabitha's ears. The wind shrieked by. Her breaths came like the beats of a hummingbird's wings.

It was too fast. Tabitha's breath was a maddening in-and-out. She felt like a shaken ragdoll. Everything flickered and jerked past, the whorses moved like shooting stars, the world flashed by in a silver-grey blur, the sounds of hooves and breaths blended in a jumbled babble.

The giant was trapped in the place where they had been, immobilised by the lethargic time of that strange space. They raced away from him at breakneck speed. The giant soon become a distant stationary figure.

They burst through another transition and her stomach was left behind again. The whorses galloped with a regular cadence. She could breathe evenly, slowly.

"What the hell was that?" shouted Garyll from behind her.

"Something the Chaos-magic has done," she guessed aloud. "It's changed time. How can it do that? The giant is in the slow-time now."

"He'll find the fast section as well then. Tabitha! Can't you do anything with your song? Can't you strike at him? We aren't going to survive!"

Garyll was right. She had to prepare a spell.

What could she use? Her first act in Oldenworld could not be to kill. Had the giant once been a man? Maybe he had just stepped in the wildfire, like the whorses, and been transformed. Maybe they would become like him if they fell off their beasts. Like him, or something worse.

Spriteblind! If he couldn't see them he wouldn't chase them.

She had to draw clear essence to her hands and coax it to become

Light essence. There was something nagging to do with wildfire, but she couldn't remember what it was. She had no choice. The giant had escaped from slowed time, into fast. His accelerated footfalls shuddered through the air. There was no time for doubt. She started the Morningsong and reached out to the clear essence. To make sprites was just a twist in her mind, a simple movement according to the pattern.

The ground trembled. The clear essence rushed to her hands.

The sky grumbled overhead. The earth shuddered around her.

She drew more essence, and it came toward her like a torrent. Something had changed—her power was easy to summon, there was nothing holding her back. She felt as if she was linked to everything, touching everything, in everything. The air vibrated with her voice. The sunlight became brighter, flickering. The silver sands around them began to shiver and shift.

The giant boomed toward them. He passed out of the speeded area, staggered, then carried on running.

"Quickly, Tabitha!" Garyll shouted. "He's almost on us!"

The ring burned like a bright star on her finger within the mass of Light essence that coiled around her hand. She tried to perfect the pattern of the Spriteblind before releasing it. The silver sand leapt into the air all around them, forming a strange pattern of little jagged ridges that pointed inward. The hairs on her arms stood on end. A queer tension filled the sky, and the giant loomed over them, his angry face impossibly high above them.

Tabitha released her hold on the Light and sent it rushing away. Her magic took effect with a resonant rush. The giant reached up to his face, staggered, then fell to his knees, and the ground heaved. A hollow terror gripped her stomach. Something was wrong.

The air crackled with sudden charge as above them, jagged lines of electric fury ran along the edge of one of the tilted panes of sky, and where four lines joined at the nexus, a sudden point of brightness arced, brighter than the sun, too bright to look at. The shimmering flare shot towards them, shrieking as it drove downward upon its intense glare, a fireball.

"Ride!" she shouted. "Ride, ride, ride!"

The wildfire. The wildfire had targeted her spell, it came for the magic. She remembered the warning all too clearly now, in the words of the Revelation.

Across Oldenworld shall his Wildfire spread, massing Chaos upon every spellcaster's thread.

Sharrow swerved aside and Mulrano pulled at her. She clung on. The wildfire screamed downward at their backs. The air was lit with a bright flash. Incandescence rushed past them then a clap of thunder hit them. A wall of ash followed them like a wave. Garyll's beast leapt past Tabitha into the lead, driven by the fear of the strange swirling dust grasping for its whipping tail. Chaos licked at their heels. Sharrow couldn't run any faster.

All was still behind them. The whorses beat a quick rhythm on the steady earth. Garyll's beast slowed to a lumbering canter beside Tabitha and Mulrano. "He's gone!" he announced. "He was blasted!" Tabitha looked back. All that was left of the giant was a single rough white boulder resting upon a silver mound amid a great, sparkling cloud of dust which rolled slowly outward in a settling ring. If they had not ridden so fast, the company would have been incinerated, whorses and all. At last the rush of the tainted ash-plume slowed, and they drew farther away from its threat.

Tabitha felt numb. She didn't want to think about what had just happened. The giant hadn't had a chance to escape. He'd been blinded by her spell.

She groaned as her whorse slowed to a jolting trot, then a walk. Tabitha's legs and arms were so cramped she couldn't straighten them. She leant against Sharrow's neck and hoped she wouldn't fall. Was the Sorcerer aware of her presence already or had the wildfire just reacted to her spell? Tabitha looked up, dreading what she might see, but no second strike was arcing down upon them. Only a single tall column of cloud mushroomed upward through the panels of rich blue sky.

The whorses plodded on, exhausted but driven by some remnant of their fear to keep moving.

She could never heal the whorses, she realised. The wildfire strike had made that obvious. If the wildfire came down upon her with any more accuracy, she would die. Tabitha couldn't even create grass for them to eat–the wildfire would burn it away. She couldn't make water either, or they'd disappear in a puff of Chaos. They needed a trough or stream to drink from but in the scorched plains there was nothing. The poor animals hung their heads low as they plodded along and they snorted from time to time against the dryness deep in their nostrils.

As they proceeded at a walk, Tabitha watched the greying hard-packed earth pass by. She would fall, she knew she would. Mulrano held onto her for now, but she could feel his grip was weakening. An hour went by in agony. There was no wind, and the disturbed metallic dust hung in their wake. The dusty plain offered no shade, no water; no respite from the endless dry brightness. The sun beat down until it was obscured by the great massing cloud which built above the place where the giant had fallen.

They encountered an abandoned ruined town. The closer they came, the greater the town appeared to be. It was completely desolate, only ash inhabited the ruined buildings. Blocks had tumbled into the bare narrow streets. An empty river course wound through the town like a dead serpent; the stone-bordered hollow was choked with grey ash. They were glad to be past the dead town's marker stone: Eastmark. A short strip of road led out of town to the north-east, but the grey dust soon reclaimed it.

Later on they passed through rock formations that cast long shadows, and yet still the heat radiated from the plains as off a furnace. A fitful wind brushed them but it brought no cooling. It only served to drive the dry heat deeper into their lungs. Small whirlwinds snatched the dust into tendrils that rose high around them, sometimes twisting into the base of the swelling thundercloud before dispersing. The dust devils spun with erratic tracks that worked on Tabitha's nerves. She could never tell when the silver column would bend toward the company. When the ash was lifted into the air it sparkled erratically, as if diamonds were caught in it, and they had to dodge the malignant threat for fear of being touched by Chaos.

The whorses weakened. Garyll's plodding beast led. Sharrow was taking on more dust than she could bear to think about. Her own boots were caked with grey. The orange sun sank toward the level horizon on their left, casting a glistening ruddy trail across the silver wastes. Some whitened pebbles passed beneath Sharrow's hooves, like markers on the edge of normality.

Suddenly, a high-pitched whine surrounded them, and they were galloping.

And yet they weren't. Tabitha hadn't spurred Sharrow, and she suspected she was still walking, but the hoof-falls sounded in staccato in her ears, and her breath was as rapid as the beat of a hummingbird's wings. They had entered another place of hastened time. On the distant horizon, a thin green line appeared, then grew, as if they were racing towards a forest. Tabitha couldn't believe they were approaching that fast. Everything beside them was a blur. Only the sun stood still.

Tabitha's strength drained away. With a gut-wrenching lurch, they crossed the transition into normality. They had covered more than a league yet the orange sun still sat one finger off the horizon, bathing the silver wastes in its fading light. Tabitha didn't know what to make of the time-gap. Time shouldn't be different in two places so close beside each other. In the desert, the day hadn't progressed more than a minute, but they had endured almost an hour's worth of riding. It was fundamentally upsetting. Life was measured out by steady beats, the regular tempo of reality, but here beyond Eyri things followed a different law. If time wasn't constant, what was?

The silver earth beneath them gave way to a grey hardpack. Scraped scars appeared on the surface, as if a great clawed hand had raked the desert to its bones. The dull hissing screech of wildfire dropped farther behind them. As the dusk gathered over the distant western horizon, the whorses crossed the edge of a rocky scoured valley, but as they moved onto the hardpack, they let them stray too close too each other.

Without warning, Garyll's stallion lunged at Sharrow, raking her with its wicked talons. Sharrow squealed and spun to defend herself, and Tabitha slipped from Sharrow's back. Mulrano tried to grab her, but he couldn't stop her slide. She fell upon the hard earth. The whorses went wild above her, stamping, slashing and fighting. She was so scared she didn't move. She just lay upon her face where she had fallen. The ground was warm against her cheek, but she felt the violent pounding of hooves.

"Be damned with you!" shouted Garyll. There was a scuffle, a tearing snap—a squeal, a roar then the sound of hoof beats.

Then, it was quiet beneath her.

Tabitha cried softly. She was utterly spent and terrified. She didn't want to turn to see who might not be there. It was a horrible mistake to leave Eyri. She was not ready for this. It was too much, the Sorcerer's power was too great; this world was too strange. When Tabitha failed, Ethea would die, and everything would be lost.

Footfalls sounded beside her. Hands reached for her, pulled her upright. Both Garyll and Mulrano were there. The relief made her cry even more.

"I think the bare rock is safe," Tabitha said in a whisper.

Garyll had only one saddlebag. He fell down beside her and lay on his back. Mulrano tumbled down and didn't move.

"They're gone," Garyll said at length, to the darkening sky.

Thunder rolled in the distance, once, twice. Again.

"I know."

Tabitha stared along the flat-bottomed mass of cloud. Far away, lightning seared the horizon, a short stab of silver light. Lightning, or wildfire? She couldn't tell. She wondered if they were really there, or if she had fallen into a nightmare. All of it was so strange—the wastelands, the altered horses, the giant pursuer, the wildfire. And Ashley, poor Ashley, borne away into the sky. Could it get any worse? This ruined realm, this altered land, this Oldenworld, so disordered: ruled by Chaos.

Apart from the thundercloud, the sky was empty.

"Oh Ashley," she whispered. "You didn't deserve this."

None of them did. She couldn't see how they would survive in this cruel land.

"Maybe his beast carried him to the forest," Garyll suggested quietly.

She knew he didn't believe it, he was just saying it to ease her pain. She laid a kiss upon her fingers and pressed it against his cheek. At least she still had Garyll.

಩೮ಲ಩೮

Just don't fall off, Ashley told himself. Hold on, hold on, hold on!

His eyes were shut so tightly his cheeks were sore. He knew the ground was so awfully far away. He wished he had jumped from the horse's back when it was changing, on the ground, but that would have put him in the silver dust, and he'd had no desire to test his resistance to it. So he had kept himself firmly in the saddle through the mare's wild bucking and rearing. He had watched with horror as the strange growths had become wings in front of his knees. He had never suspected they would actually work.

Then, after the first lurching flaps, he had believed Sugarlump would only flutter a short way and he would be able to slip off. But the wings had lifted them higher. The horse had flown on, until his friends were far behind, until his friends were gone.

Empty air yawned below him. It was a long, long way to fall.

Ashley kept his eyes closed and gritted his teeth. *Think, lummox, think! It can't be the end.*

Sugarlump was just as terrified as he was. He had been linked with the animal's mind all day, keeping her calm through all the terrors. Her thoughts were clear to him. She still knew she was a horse—nothing had changed within—but she had sprouted wings; she was a thousand foot up in the air! She was frightened, and so she ran, but running only agitated the great wings. And so they rose, higher and higher, as Sugarlump's hooves lashed the air and her eyes rolled wildly.

Ashley didn't want to die. He soaked the mare's mind with soothing thoughts, crooning and whispering to her as he clung onto her neck. After a terribly long time, he felt the wingbeats become slower then they stopped altogether. He forced himself to open one eye. He expected to see the horizon tumbling, the ground rushing up at them, but they weren't falling, at least not yet—Sugarlump had discovered that flying felt better if she splayed her legs, which caused the wings to be held rigid and outstretched. They glided.

Ashley breathed out.

They were spectacularly high. The land below them was vast, bigger than anything he had imagined possible. It stretched to such a distant horizon it made him gasp. Behind and below him was the great mottled wasteland. He searched in vain for Tabitha and the others, but they were lost in the vast expanse. He didn't know where to look. Toward the sun lay a small ridge of mountains, made insignificant by the altitude, but he recognised the proud spire of Fynn's Tooth— the unmistakable curve of ice, the skirt of snow before the stepped ridge. Beyond the ridge he should have seen the realm of Eyri, but the shimmering air only held the image of ranks of greater mountains. A circle of devastation surrounded the shielded realm.

Four rivers threaded through the hills, heading north, away from a rugged escarpment. Beyond this, to the south, were pale golden sands of another kind of desert. To the north and west of Ashley, a green carpet of vegetation rolled on and on, dense growth pocked-marked with random silver and grey craters. It might be a forest. From so far up it was difficult to tell. A great mountain range cut through the lands with its white peaks in the distance.

Sugarlump faltered in her flight, and Ashley clutched at her neck to steady himself. She wobbled and veered, flapped for a while, then settled into a glide once more, heading toward the white peaks in the distance. He whispered reassuring words to the mare, and watched her feathers flutter in the wind. Feathers. That still terrified him, that she could have been altered so much. He wondered if she would change again. If she lost her wings, they were doomed.

He knew she would grow tired, anyway. Those wings would fail. He rubbed her coat. It seemed unfair to call her Sugarlump now they were traversing the sky. He decided he would call her Princess. She deserved to have a good name, in her last moments.

"Just keep your wings spread out, Princess," he whispered to her, combining the words with a simple mental image. She was instantly confused. She gave an unsteady pace in the air, which tilted her wings awry.

"Legs!" he corrected, "keep your legs splayed out!" He gritted his teeth against their sickening yaw and roll. She didn't understand how she had changed. Princess was still a horse.

The glide steadied again. Ashley guessed that because they weren't flapping, they would slowly lose altitude, but it was difficult to tell anything from this high up. They seemed suspended over an unmoving landscape in an endless moment of breathless perspective.

They flew a long way. By the time the forest was beginning to expand and Ashley could make out individual trees, he was shivering from the wind and the fear. A tree shot by underneath them. Ashley gripped Princess tight. From high up it had seemed they could land anywhere in the soft forest canopy, but down here the trees were huge and they thrust up like spears planted in readiness. They were going to die. After all that flying, they were going to crash against one of these colossal trees and die. Princess knew his terror. She whinnied in fright, tried to rear, and everything went topsy-turvy. The glide became a sudden upward swoop that left Ashley's stomach behind. Then the wind stopped in his ears, and there was a terrible moment of weightlessness. He should have been happy they had slowed, but it didn't feel right, not right at all. Just as suddenly, they fell, straight down toward a great spreading tree.

The first branch cracked and tore away under their weight. Princess squealed, and kicked at the air with her hooves, which caused her wings to flutter wildly against the desperate fall.

"Gallop! Gallop!" Ashley shouted at her, as they tipped off another branch and burst through a thick spray of leaves. Somewhere below them was the ground, and it was coming up too fast. Princess ran upon nothing. As she did so, her great wings beat the air, but she failed to right herself. They rolled nose over tail, and the branches beat them as they passed. They came down in a tumble of hooves and wings and flailing arms. There was a matted cluster of great ferns. Strange, he thought, the way everything seemed to spread out suddenly in his vision as he fell at the ground.

19. CROOKED COVEN

"When you double-cross a double cross
You get a sixteen-pointed star."—Zarost

The wizard led them away from Bradach Hide, onward into the surrounding forest, through belts of stringy-barked trees which were so tall they leant on each other for support, past giant baskets of roots where the late afternoon shadows clustered as if waiting impatiently for nightfall, when they would escape. Black Saladon stormed on, his cruel battleaxe slung over his shoulder, drawing Bevn and Gabrielle in his wake over patches of open ground where hard shells of earth cracked underfoot, over a rough plank bridge that arched above a creek choked with sharp-edged grasses, across mushroom-littered swathes of loamy earth. Where was the wizard was taking them? He dared not ask. If his pace was any measure of his mood, he was very, very angry.

At last the wizard stopped on a ridge where the searching branches of the surrounding trees cut the sunlight into thin shreds. He turned. His eyes were burning. The walk had done nothing to cool his anger. If anything, it had become more intense. Bevn didn't want to cower, but Saladon had an overwhelming kind of presence that got inside his body and pressed on his heart. Even Gabrielle looked nervous.

"You idiots! You empty-headed imbeciles!" Saladon clawed the air in front of Bevn's face. "I laid a route through the six-sided land! All the way to Slipper! And you have ruined it! Ruined it! What in the Destroyer's name were you thinking? You killed two of the windrunners! The men I hired to see you safely through the wastes! That story will get out despite their code. Soon nowhere in the Land of Lûk will be easy for strangers to travel through!"

He stamped the blackened heel of his bladed staff down, and the ground heaved.

Bevn felt suddenly hot in his cheeks.

"We... I... It wasn't my fault," he stammered.

"You pushed one into the wildfire, and killed another before fleeing, and it wasn't your fault? Do you take me for a fool? Do you?"

Bevn wished he could become small and vanish into his own boots.

The angry wizard was close, so terribly close, and he had gathered that bladed staff to him in that knuckled hand as if the solid shaft and heavy metalwork weighed nothing at all. The wizard could probably scythe through him in one blow, let alone what he could probably do with his magic.

Please don't let him hurt me! prayed Bevn. *Don't let him hurt me, don't let him hurt me!*

"And then you call to the Sorcerer, you cross-eyed cussing *kont*! The one word you have to keep silent on, the one word that shouts your ignorance to the skies, and you have to let it out!"

How did Saladon know what he had said? He had only arrived afterward.

"That name disturbs the threads of Chaos. It aggravates the web. You almost triggered the junction above their settlement, you fool. You would have burnt them all out! If you'd called any louder, the wildfire would have struck like lightning. Don't ever do that again! His name is forbidden!"

Then why did you tell it to me? Bevn thought bitterly. He hadn't known it was dangerous. It wasn't his fault. He blinked away a hot tear. Right there in front of Gabrielle, the wizard was making him look like a baby. It wasn't fair.

"Oh, for shame! You have no strength to hang power upon! That crown should have stayed on your father's head."

Bevn wanted to object, he wanted to say something to explain what he'd done, but he was scared his lips would just quiver and his words would come out all garbled and he'd begin to blubber. The wizard was just too strong and angry; he was overwhelming, dominating, as if he was a beast standing over Bevn, considering how to kill him. Bevn couldn't face his raw power. Saladon drenched him with fear. Yes, that was what Saladon was like, a big black wolf, with great big teeth, and he made Bevn feel weaker than a naked little lamb. It was far worse than the coercion the Darkmaster had exerted through his Darkstones. It wasn't persuasive, cajoling and irresistible, it was a brutal irrefutable order. The wizard wielded a more fundamental power, and it upset Bevn to his core. He began to shake in his boots again.

"You aren't so spotless yourself," Gabrielle said tartly, addressing her challenge to the wizard.

"What!"

"You could have saved us a lot of pain at the Shield if you'd mentioned he was supposed to wear the crown. And you gave us no warning about wildfire! You didn't tell us what could happen when it touched people. I could have been killed. Bevn could have stepped into it without protection. How was Bevn supposed to know?"

Bevn looked to Gabrielle in amazement. She was standing up for him!

"You, you... Incompetent harlot! I charged you to escort him. Instead of being safely in the Lûk tunnels, halfway to Koom, you have him in the cursed Hunter's hall, a blade at his throat, about to be dispatched for stupidity. What kind of ingenuity does this display, I ask you? What half-brained plan would you have used if I hadn't arrived?"

"You didn't tell us about the danger! You didn't explain the wildfire, or the web above us. You didn't tell us anything! You are at fault, not us!"

Bevn's heart swelled. Gabrielle was fighting at his side.

She would show the wizard!

Black Saladon brushed her off with a snort. "Do not be surprised, princeling, she is compelled to defend you by the Order-field of the crown. I would not pay her words any heed. She is a woman and will always take the bait of scorn. She remembers her old ways and believes she still has some importance, but she is sadly mistaken."

Gabrielle had a knife in her hand, held by the blade, tilted and ready for throwing. "Don't you dare talk of me as if I am not here!" Gabrielle's voice cracked like a whip. "I am compelled by neither of you. Respect me, rude wizard, or I'll give you a reason to regret it."

Saladon turned his formidable attention upon Gabrielle; his eyes dropped to consider her whole body. "Do not overestimate your worth, woman. You may have some outstanding features, but you are not that desirable if you act like a brainless, bitter slut."

Gabrielle tensed to throw. "Correct those words or I'll pierce your heart, you bastard!"

Saladon held up his free hand, as steady as stone. The more he watched that hand the more he felt it *collected* steadiness to itself, until it seemed steadier than the world itself, and everything around them had some movement except for that point. The air *tightened* around that hand, as if unseen patterns of control emanated from it.

"That is a very stupid thing to do, Gabrielle Aramonde. Put your butter-knife away. If you try to use it on me I shall be forced to cast my magic outward to protect myself, and that will call the wildfire down, enough to lay waste to this place. A simple Transference will see me far away. I won't be here anymore, but you will."

Gabrielle hesitated. She was probably watching the wizard's hand as well, but Bevn couldn't tear his eyes away to check.

"I am stronger than you," Black Saladon said.

"I know that, but I can still fight you!" she snapped.

A faint expression flickered across Saladon's face. "Don't expect mercy, just because you are a woman. You have jeopardised my plans. You have compromised my secrecy and you have caused me much risk and delay! I cannot afford for the Kingsrim to fall into the wrong hands. After the mess you've made of the first leg of the journey, I have to guide you directly."

"You caused the mess, by leaving out the details."

"I told you enough to work from, but you failed the test of wit. I must have overestimated you."

"No, that is unfair! I accepted your charge in good faith, but you did not tell us what was expected of us."

That wry brief twist to his lips came again, as if he knew something she did not. "Fairness *and* faith? A strange foundation for a Dark mage."

"We were not prepared for this place!"

"Well *this* is life. Get used to it."

He stamped the heel of his battleaxe into the ground and turned upon it. As he spun Bevn caught a glimpse of mirth on his face. Then Black Saladon strode off, his shoulders shaking, leaving Bevn and Gabrielle to decide what they would do.

Bevn tried to catch Gabrielle's eye, but she followed Saladon without a backward glance. He had to trail along behind like an abandoned pup, and he hated it at once. One minute she was fighting for him, the next she pretended he didn't matter. The hope and hurt was driving him mad. He lagged behind, sulking, and watched as he walked.

She was impressed with the black wizard, Bevn could tell. She soon tried to walk ahead of Saladon, even though he was leading, as if to prove how independent she was, but never so far that she couldn't listen to him when he talked to her. She even laughed at some comment he passed.

Curse him! He was so self-satisfied, so…powerful. Bevn wished he had that sort of power.

Bevn limped along for what felt like hours. He was sure the wizard could have healed his feet in an instant, and every painful step just made him hate Black Saladon more. As night fell unevenly upon the forest, Bevn reluctantly decided to stay closer to the others. The shadows had a way of looking at him that he didn't trust. Gabrielle must have grown tired of the wizard by now, although they were still talking.

"Hunters live ever more scattered, in ever-weakening tribes. Their culture has tended toward Chaos for some time. That's why they fear it so much."

"Why do they speak so strangely?" Gabrielle asked.

"One of the Sorcerer's many delights is to tamper with the fundamental patterns of language. The more wildfire and Chaos a culture suffers, the more the pattern of their language is dismantled and its development regresses toward earlier and more basic forms. There are tribes in the lowlands who can only communicate in gestures and others who just hit, sneer and bark at each other to get what they want."

"Yet you speak as we do."

"Eyri inherited its language from the exiles of the Three Kingdoms. So did the Hunters. That language is called the Old Tongue now. It is what I learnt when I came to study at the college in Kingsmeet. Apart from you sheltered Eyrians, only the Korinese and the seafarers of Kaskanzr speak the Old Tongue properly. And the wizards. Each Hunter tribe loses something of the sense and integrity of the language with every generation, each tribe in a different way. You cannot teach them the original—they are losing the sense of it from their blood."

"And the Lûk? They speak an understandable version of it."

"The Lûk have retained the most order of any nation. They have been altered. They have their grey skins, and they are hot-headed and prone to fight, but they have an obsession with keeping relics and traditions, which has served them well in some ways. They keep records of the spoken languages and they learn every tongue of the upper lands before they are ten years old. It is sad that such effort will go to waste, but sadness comes with the bitter wisdom of seeing so much lost and knowing where it will end."

"You have been changed by what you have seen," Gabrielle noted softly.

"As have many others and many things. Little here lives as it used to anymore, and it will get more severe as we head north. Things that were once more like men have been turned to be rocks, and things that were once children buzz about in the mouths of sap-spiders, waiting to die. Though the people resist, much of this land belongs to the Sorcerer. The lowlands have long been his playground. All of Oldenworld will be his in the end. It really is just a matter of time."

"Then why have you joined him, if he brings such ruin? Why do we work on his cause?"

"It must all be ruined before it can be rebuilt."

He couldn't mean that. The way he'd said it, he seemed to believe the whole world had to be destroyed, but the certainty in his voice worried Bevn.

"Isn't there any alternative?"

"The alternative is death, a final end without renewal. This way we earn ourselves a chance to continue, albeit in a changed form."

"There is no way to beat the Sorcerer?"

"There is no one powerful enough to conquer him, alone or united with others. I do not come close to his level, and I was the best of the Gyre."

"You surprise me. You struck me as the kind who would never give up."

"I don't. I have chosen to change my strategy of attack by changing my enemies."

"You are a dangerous man, Black Saladon."

"You're not the first woman to have said that. You'll not be the last."

They came to a grassy hillock with a stream which gurgled its way down a gully. The first stars were pricking through the darkening sky. A blackened tree had tumbled into the ashes of its own fire. A few flattened willows were collected in a heap against the slope, in a way that didn't look quite haphazard enough to be natural.

"The Nephilim are long gone. You'll camp here tonight," the wizard said, in a way that didn't suggest he would be joining them. For the first time, it struck Bevn that they had no supplies of any kind, nor had they taken anything from the Hunters. He'd been so worried about not displeasing the angry wizard that he hadn't thought about it. He hadn't eaten since a midday meal offered by the Hunter patrol prior to reaching Bradach.

"Drink, princeling, the water is untainted here. Gabrielle, see if you can get a fire going. Stay clear of me for a while, both of you. What I must do must be done without interference."

Bevn went to the stream. The wizard was going to do something magic, he just knew it. He wanted to drink like a greedy horse, but he made sure to keep an eye on Black Saladon between gulps. At first he didn't seem to be doing anything but pacing around. Then he drew three intersecting lines in the ashes around the fallen tree, using the tip of his battleaxe. He set the tall weapon aside, and made some odd gestures in the air over the lines. Then he sat quietly.

Bevn was disappointed. His head itched. He took the crown off and set it carefully on some soft grass beside the stream, then bent down and splashed the cold water through his hair. It felt good to rub the sweat away.

There was a little shockwave, as if the world had been pushed aside to make space for something. Bevn jerked upright. The sky grumbled overhead, but went quiet again. Beside Black Saladon was a neat pile of goods. A blanket, a pot, a bag, some small sacks, a pile of fruit, a loaf of black bread and a great block of cheese.

Bevn just stood there, water dripping off his chin.

Saladon hadn't moved. He'd just plucked their supper from the air.

He ran to make sure it wasn't just an illusion. When he kicked the pot, it bounced and gave a hollow ring on the ground.

"You *are* a wizard! You made all of this with magic, didn't you?"

Saladon appeared slightly bored. "You can either make it or move it. Moving it is simpler, and much quieter. Creation of matter is a high-magnitude twist on the second axis and would trigger the wildfire, but a Reference spell is more like shuffling pieces of the world that are already there."

Bevn picked up the block of cheese. It was coated with red wax, and it was heavy. "Where does *this* come from?"

"All of it comes from the Gyre stores. The fresh-looking stuff has been preserved for a time with Order-spells, so it might taste a bit funny, but it's nourishing and clean."

Bevn was amazed. A storeroom in the air, where he could reach in any time he wanted. "Can you get anything you want from there?"

The collected food looked like Sword-rations. He could think of a better meal already, the kind he'd enjoyed in the palace when his father entertained important guests. Roasted duck with apricots and jam, fluffy pastry and gravy, slice-fried potatoes and stuffing and those little eggs you only got in Bloomtide-month done in herbs and butter.

Saladon picked some stray hairs from the end of his long plait.

"Pretty much, but only what you've put in, over the years. Think of it as having a very deep pocket."

Gabrielle came up to join them. "Can you move *people* with the same kind of spell?"

"Ah, you are quick—a similar spell, not the same. It requires far more...concentration...to cast a Transference than a Reference."

"But you could just magic us somewhere else, couldn't you?" asked Bevn excitedly. "We wouldn't have to walk! Why don't you just send us to the Sorcerer?"

But the wizard was shaking his head.

"You are worthless to the Sorcerer without the Kingsrim, and the amount of magic I would have to use to move you when you are wearing it would need the entire Gyre. I've already told you, that crown makes you the most slippery thing in the magical universe. Besides, trying to move you would alert everyone to where we are, and it would bring so much wildfire down the land would light up like a bloody mountain of burning magnesium."

"Oh," said Bevn, feeling his brilliant idea scattering like ash.

"We're actually very limited in what we can do underneath the wildfire threads. Cast a metal-weave, and you get wildfire. Cast any kind of essence flux, and you get wildfire. Even Chaos spells trigger the stuff, even simple Lumen spells, that's how critical it is. It's wicked stuff, it's indiscriminate, which is why it's so quick and so devastating and why the Gyre has never been able to eradicate it from Oldenworld. If magic was a tilled field, then wildfire is its weed—the weed that fights back at the farmer."

"What can I do with these?" asked Gabrielle. Her hands were covered with tiny black flies. Motes! Bevn realised. She had found some motes!

"Apocalypse! Go easy! Even that movement could have been enough to trigger a strike. Girl, you don't need so many in one place, haven't you Eyrians developed a multiplier pattern yet?" He studied her for a moment. "No? Well, even more reason to go easy with Dark essence. We may be serving the Sorcerer's ends, but it doesn't mean we're protected against wildfire. It is beyond his control. Most things are. That is the fundamental of his art."

"I will not be powerless! You can wield some of your magic. There must be something I can do that won't upset the web."

"Very little, with such a basic form of essence. You're using first-axis magic, for crying out loud! Trying to protect yourself with that is like trying to stop a falling rock by blowing at it." Saladon watched the motes on her hands then reached across and plucked a few off the tip of her finger. He allowed them to circle over his upturned palm. "I used to play with this form, a long time ago." The motes spun, chased each other then settled into a symbol like a five with a crossed tail. Saladon tossed his motes onto Gabrielle's and they scattered, forming little clusters of the five-pattern themselves before falling to the ground. Gabrielle cursed under her breath. She had lost command of her essence; Saladon's little spell had run through all of it.

"That's a multiplier," said Saladon.

The sky grumbled again, and Saladon nodded. "So I thought. Even the small spells are dangerous. Keep your Dark essence close. Don't try to project anything beyond the reach of your hands unless it is very small. You might be able to get away with a very thin shadow-shield, small patterns of mood, paralysis, illusions—things like that. Don't try complex patterns like soul-stealers or summonings, or you will be burnt." Then he shook himself, "Bah! I am not here to teach a wilful woman how to play tricks on the *lumen* axis. Don't use the Dark, you'll make a mistake."

He rose and retrieved his battleaxe. "If dawn comes and I have not returned, keep the sun on your back and head north-west. You are making for Willower. We'll have to stay in the Hunters' lands now, all the way through to Slipper." He looked none too pleased about that. "It'll be slow, but at least you'll be unknown. The Hunter tribes don't talk much to each other, what with their language problems."

"Where are you going?" Gabrielle demanded.

"I have a better place to sleep."

She threw her hands into the air.

"Your task is unchanged, Gabrielle Aramonde—to protect the bearer of the Kingsrim. I cannot be here all the time to hold your little hand. If a Hunter comes upon you, show him your palms, or your blades, and he might leave you alone. If it is big and has teeth, it is dangerous. Use your wits. What little you have."

He spread his arms wide, looked at them hard, barked a sudden laugh then he was gone.

Gabrielle cursed under her breath.

Bevn stared at the place where the wizard had been. He went over to swish his hands through the empty air. He wanted to have powers like that! Black Saladon had just vanished, and left them alone.

A little twist of night air brushed against him, cool and dark.

Gabrielle stomped to the pile of kindling she had collected earlier, and lit a fire using a small flintstone with angry strokes against her dagger. When the flames were was crackling through the dry wood, they sat by the gathering blaze to eat.

The royal King of Eyri positioned himself on an old stump, beside and above Gabrielle, so that he could catch a peek down her generous cleavage when she wasn't looking. She stayed close by, at his feet, with her back partly toward him, staring over the flames. She rubbed her one finger absently, but her finger wasn't where Bevn was looking. He chewed on an apricot while he watched, and explored its soft flesh with his tongue. It was sweet and juicy, but Saladon had been right. It didn't taste quite like the real thing.

The fire warmed him, and with the food came a flood of vitality. The night settled down like a soft silk blanket upon the tall upright heads of the trees, folding quietly into the protected glade where the grassy hillock rested under the sky. They were alone, in the wilderness. Was this the kind of place where young lovers *did* it? He didn't know, but he wished he did know. His father had always taken his secret women to his bedchamber. He'd spied on them often enough to know, but Bevn suspected from what he'd been told in Ravenscroft that Gabrielle had a taste for things beyond a brief bouncy four-poster bed. He reached out then clenched his fist. She'd call him an idiot.

She leant back against the stump he sat upon, and he could see right down the gap between her breasts to the small folds in her belly. Such smooth skin between her breasts. What would it feel like? He wanted to put his hand in there.

Was she just tantalising him to mess with his mind, to manipulate him? He knew her old ways among the Shadowcasters. The Darkmaster had told him all about her. Sex was her weapon, a web of lust which she wove around men. But if she was weaving it around him, didn't it mean she liked him? Well he had a weapon too. He wondered how long it would take for her to be compelled to obey him because of the Kingsrim, or whether he could command her already. She had fought for *him* when Black Saladon had put the pressure on.

He tried to tear his eyes away from Gabrielle and the flesh she flaunted, but even looking at the hot flames he still had to sit in that awkward way, holding one knee up to hide the bulge and trying to make it seem a casual pose. He was as hard up as a stallion in spring.

Maybe he should just try, before Black Saladon got her.

He'd never get to be king if he didn't learn how to command. One day he would rule so many people. He would have so many women. He would begin with her.

Tonight.

Now.

He let one hand drop to her bare shoulder. Touching her sent a shiver through his arm. He held on long enough that she could have shrugged his hand off, but she didn't, so he let his hand slip.

She spun. The slap was loud, and made his cheek burn cold.

"Take your hands off me! You arrogant little boy."

The words made him reel more than the blow. He had been so sure she was on his side. She had called him—

"Oh Bevn Mellar, how are you ever going to learn to be a king?" she said, laughing. "You have no fight in you. All your bravery goes out of your head with the first strike."

His blood pounded in his ears. His eyes were smarting. He felt so stupid now, stupid and cowed. He got up to run away, despite the shameful bulge, but Gabrielle grabbed him by the wrist and wouldn't let him go. He didn't miss how her eyes dropped then her sardonic little grin as her hand opened. He felt a chill, as if a cold mist had touched his forehead. She dropped her gaze again.

"What are you looking at, bitch?" he demanded.

He almost died with fright at his own words. He was angry, but he shouldn't have...

She slapped him again and caught his wrists before he'd even thought to back away. "Watch your tongue!" His cheek stung like cold frost.

Fight, a little voice in his head said. Fight fight fight fight fight!

"Watch your own tongue, trollop, unless you want to feel a blade across your throat when you fall sleep. I've had enough of your scorn, witch-woman! I am the King!"

"You are far too young to want what you were reaching for."

"You'd be surprised what I want!" Bevn retorted.

Butterlegs! I'd do that thing to you right now if I had someone to hold you.

"Are you feeling alright?"

"What's it to you?" Bevn snapped.

"You want me, don't you, you sad little wretch."

"I'll rip your tits off!" he shouted at her. Bevn didn't know where he had come up with such a curse, but he liked it. The dark anger was exhilarating. It pounded through him with iron strength. He took one hard knock, then ducked when she swung at him again and ran clear.

"Come back, princeling." She was laughing. "Come back. You have spunk. I like that in a boy." She came after him around the circle of ash to the far side of the fire.

"I was just playing," she said softly. Her eyes glistened wetly in the firelight. "I had to know that my essence works. Come here." Her voice was like honeyed cream. Lust, shame, excitement and anger warred in a whirlwind of emotion. She came closer. Her breasts swelled within the tight thongs of her halter, right there before his face. He wished he could bury his head in them.

"It is good to know you have a mighty manhood for your age," said Gabrielle, wetting her lips with the tip of her tongue. He could believe in that moment that anything might happen between them. A voice within his head screamed she was manipulating him, but he didn't want to believe it, just then.

She gripped his arms. Excitement shot through his skin. She leant close, peering into his eyes.

"Have you heard the tale of Ferrik's son in Fendwarrow?" she asked. Bevn shook his head. "They tell it to caution young bucks who are too eager for pleasure. Ferrik's son was the first conquest I made after I had learnt to master the Dark. I seduced the farmer's boy in exchange for access to his family's wealth. I took the boy to pieces with pleasure, and he was so entranced he gave me the strong room key. Of course I stole it all, but as I left with my takings, the boy's mother arrived, the stupid sow. She attacked me, so I snapped her neck. The boy was too late to avert the tragedy. He could do nothing to me, because his seed was full of the motes I had driven there and he was too afraid to fight. When I was gone, he realised it was all his own fault and, rather than face his father's wrath, he fell onto a pitchfork and ended his life."

Her eyes were hard now, boring into him, piercing him like a sharp skewer through a bursting sausage.

"That is what I am capable of," she whispered, up close. "Never think yourself immune to me, no matter how strong your crown might make you."

An icy sensation passed through his groin. Bevn yelped. Gabrielle let his arms go, and turned away. "Don't act on any of your fantasies tonight," she said over her shoulder. "I'll not be as gentle with you the second time."

Bevn pulled a rude sign at her back as he sank to his knees beside the fire. The lust drained out of him, agonising and slow, but the anger remained, his own anger, welling up through the fading influence of the Dark. He'd only just realised the terrible mistake he'd made. The Kingsrim was not on his head. He had left it on the soft grass beside the stream before he'd run to Saladon. While he was unprotected, she had used her motes on him. He should have been able to recognise her Dark-spells. He'd been taught some of the basics, but she had been so quick, and he'd been so distracted by her body he hadn't recognised his danger. She'd played him for a complete fool. He gritted his teeth as he went away to find his crown.

He *would* find a way to get her back, and as soon as he reached the fabled city where the Sorcerer lived, he would discard Gabrielle. He wouldn't let her learn the things he would learn. He would apprentice himself to the mighty Ametheus, just as he had been apprenticed to the Darkmaster. He would grow in knowledge and power, and when he was ready, he would return to Eyri as the great, unassailable and terrifying King. Ametheus would make him stronger than Gabrielle.

Ametheus would show him how to overpower her, and everyone else.

CRINKLE

A time passed in Oldenworld when nothing was heard nor seen of the fearsome monster that was Ametheus. Far be it from the minds of men who tilled the fields to know, far be it from the hearts of their toiling wives to care. Rows of corn were planted. Rows of stalks were ploughed under beneath the slowly gathering clouds. Chaff was shaken to the freshening winds, and wheat was milled and bagged, and set upon the fast-moving carts flowing along the thickening veins of the state, those slick slipways which distributed the bounty of hard labour away from the rural estates to those who had less in its making and more in its taking. The same exchange could be seen a hundred times over in places as distant as western Wor Cannint and far northern Yd—the goods flowing away, the reward returning, and to most people in that time it seemed a fair exchange. They earned gold for their labours, the good gold of the Three Kingdoms, with the kings' heads stamped upon it, as minted by the wizards in the college in Kingsmeet.

The monster Ametheus was far from gone; the truth would have made those ignorant farmers stand up clutching their hoes and harrows, looking west to where Orenland ended, looking west to where he had made his home.

Turmodin.

He had claimed a large headland that thrust into the sea amid the thrashing waves of the shallows, where the great Cascarrik River, carrying the effluent of its long journey, stained its delta with layers of silt. There he had fashioned a refuge from mud and rock, and therein lay his treasure. Few would have considered the restless roiling nebulae to be treasure; none would have exchanged good Kingdom gold for them, but in the end that might have served everyone better, had the people of the lowlands known what was to come.

For there, in his cavern that would one day be the basement of his mighty Pillar, lay the nodes of Chaos.

Ametheus had spent the years before his fateful visit to the wizards' college collecting the nodes, according to the vision of his dream. The nodes were easy for him to find but as scattered as windblown seeds. Wherever there was strife, fire, quakes, conflicts or even quarrels, a node was present—a cluster of energy invigorated by the many battles and wasted blood that had twisted around them. He plucked them from the sites, as unnoticed as a beggarman collecting litter. Where he passed there was sickness and strife, but where he had come from the land was healed, and peace descended upon people who had never known it. In a way his work allowed Order to spread, for he took the nodes away to his refuge.

In Turmodin alone, the raw Chaos mounted, waiting for Ametheus to be ready to wield it upon the world. Thus it had been when he had left the refuge to find Annah in the college. When he returned, he was ready.

Brother Seus experimented with the silver essence, and brother Amyar began to break things with their fists in rage, but he didn't try to stop Seus for he understood their need for power to exact revenge. The two brothers became closer, and Ethan was dominated by old anger and visions of impending doom.

He tried not to think about what he was doing, instead he thought of the effect he wanted, and allowed the inspiration from another time to come through Seus. It was rare for the three of them to be so unified, to be sharing a task without fighting, but the common enemy bonded them. They worked upon a spell to end the wizards, to destroy those who wielded magic, a spell that would be reactive, and permanent, and self-seeding. The wild animals of the delta suffered greatly as Ametheus tried time and time again to understand his unruly efforts, but perfection was not in his nature, and after many attempts he realised he should leave control aside. The spell should be raw chaos, infused only with the desire to spread. When it struck fertile magical soil it should multiply, when it found anyone using power it should link them to a node. It would be like a plant, it would be a vine, with its roots in his refuge and its feelers creeping outward through the traces of Order, along slipways, through village streets, up into the air, wherever it wished to seek for magic-users.

He knew what he was devising would ruin the face of Oldenworld. It would live by its own rules; it would run and run as long as there was magic in the world to nourish it. He might never be able to stop it. It might even turn upon him, in the end.

Then he thought of the target, and his mind was made up. He howled with rage.

He raised his arms to the sky, and sent the first wildfire upon the college in Kingsmeet.

After that, he hunted the remaining wizards.

At night, a fearsome fire-dappled face spoke to him, and he dreamt of falling cities and countries aflame and broken roads and dead people carried upon the rivers of his tears. He dreamt of destruction.

20. A RIDDLE IN THE WOOD

"If you understood everything that I did,
then I would not be a riddler, would I?"—Zarost

Ashley came to with a strange hot breath in his ear. He was lying in something soft and wet with dew. His shoulder ached and he was cold. He looked up. A horse was close, or something that once was a horse.

He sat up in alarm, and tumbled out of the ferns onto a swathe of grass. The creature shied and tossed its head. It sensed his surprise. *It's okay, it's okay*, he reassured her. *You're just a horse with a beak where there shouldn't be one, and wings, great big white feathered wings. A gryphon, of a kind, a legendary monster that shouldn't be real.*

It all came back to him. They had crashed into the forest canopy. It was a miracle they were both still alive. He checked himself over for injuries, but apart from the stiff shoulder and a stabbing discomfort in his chest that might be a broken rib, he was hale.

Sugarlump—Princess—hadn't fared so well. A great red slash stained her white coat, but the blood had stopped running from the wound. He hoped it would stay uninfected. As if sensing his concern, she came close again and pushed her nose into his hand. He stroked her forehead, and rubbed the edges of her beak. She whickered, obviously pleased with the sensation. But the bit and bridle looked painfully tight, wrapped around her snout like a baling wire. As if becoming aware of it only as Ashley thought about it, she bit down and there was a sharp snip. She bit right through the steel and spat the pieces out. The bridle dangled loosely beside the deadly beak.

"What are we to do with you?" he asked. His pack was still fastened behind the loose saddle. He worked the girth free, and untied her load. She nudged him gratefully. He supposed that he wouldn't need a halter to catch her if he needed to ride her. She was so close in his mind he could almost see the world through her eyes. Just a thought from him and she would come to be ridden. She blew heavily through her nostrils then ambled away to crop the grass nearby. Her tail swished lazily, a tail of barbed silvery wires.

Something had changed with his ability, he'd felt it when they had emerged from Eyri. It was as if a lid had been lifted off his head, and he could reach out far and wide with his thoughts. He'd never known what it was like to be a horse, but now he knew. Princess felt that he was her friend. He had helped her when things had become scary, and so he was a good man. And now… grass. Life was simple, as a horse. Except that with her new beak, trying to crop grass wasn't working very well. Ashley wondered if she'd have to find something new to eat. What did gryphons eat?

A good man he may be, but he was a cold man. The flight had chilled him to the bone, and the huge trees of the forest kept the air cool and damp. Ashley scratched through the disturbed contents of the pack and found the tinder and flint. A few leaves that looked dry lay around the bole of the nearest tree, as well as a pile of bark which had fallen from the scabrous white trunks. Once the moisture had dried from the kindling, he had a great blaze going. As he thawed out he chewed on some dried meat Mulrano had supplied. It took some chewing, but it was good. He washed it down with water from his skin.

Some time had passed since the morning, he supposed. The odd ray of sunlight lanced down through the great trees from above. He had no way to orient himself in the forest. He couldn't tell if he was facing east, north, south or west, toward Tabitha and the men or away from them.

He had to rejoin the group. There was too much about Oldenworld he didn't understand. Ashley had expected to be part of Tabitha's group all the time. She knew where she was going. He had only joined her quest because he'd wanted to help, and he'd hoped to spend some time with her, apart from learning some of her magic. She was the Wizard. She would have devised some protection against the strange wasteland, but he didn't even have one sprite.

Something cracked and rustled in the forest. Princess lifted her head from the turf, her ears pricked forward.

He tensed.

Silence again.

His thoughts drifted back to Tabitha again. He was sure he would be able to sense her presence if she was close enough, maybe within a league. Ashley leant back against the tree trunk, and tried to reach out with his mind—out, out, outward. Trees trees, trees, a river, trees, a collection of unfamiliar people. At least the forest was inhabited. He took a deep breath and tried again, opening himself to the fluctuations of mental energy.

Princess stamped and breathed heavily at his side. He sensed a creature who was hunting, an angry simple mind who was busy tearing through the forest, looking for the food that always ran and hid beneath the vegetation. It was close.

With a squeal and crackle of broken twigs, a boar rushed from the undergrowth beside them: a mean-eyed brute with horrible tusks. Ashley shot to his feet. The tree at his back was too smooth to climb. Princess was already shying away on the far side of the clearing. Only his was pack close at hand, with the wooden staff looped through its straps.

The boar made directly for him with lowered tusks, which appeared wickedly sharp, the ends stained a reddish brown. Ashley hoped it was from earth, not blood. He lunged for the staff, snatched it up, and ran. The boar was aiming for his heels. Its angry thoughts were plain to read—it knew that when things were running, they couldn't attack, and so it could run all the way into those soft legs, and tangle the tusks in them.

Then, the goring run. Then the feeding.

The cruelty of the pig's thoughts curdled Ashley's blood. He had known of the forest boars around Llury. They were dangerous if angered, but they ate roots, compost and waste. They'd eat anything, really, but he was sure they did not hunt people. This pig was different. Its skin was scaly and rusted, and looked as hard as iron. It ran fast. It was only five paces behind him, then three. He knew it wanted him to carry on running, for then it would win.

He turned, and brought the staff down upon its head with a double-handed swing, but he was too late, the pig was upon him. The staff rebounded from the iron head. The boar took both his feet out from under him. He hit the ground hard. By the time he had regained any sense of where he was, the boar was returning for another charge.

Soft flesh blood.

He knew where it was even though his back was to it. He crouched, and at the last moment, he leapt into the air. His ankles hurt. The boar surged underneath him and squealed in frustration. No blood, Ashley thought desperately, putting the suggestion into its mind the way he did with Princess. No blood, no food.

The pig slowed as it turned.

No food? Still can kill it, kill it, kill! Its mean little eyes glittered. It lowered its head and trotted closer. This time it was going to make sure he couldn't escape. He backed away, prodding at it with the end of his staff. It wasn't scared of him. Yet.

Ashley planted a suggestion deep in its mind. *The man is danger, great danger.*

The boar tossed its head, and grunted in disgust, but it stopped advancing. Ashley stared into its eyes.

The man likes to eat pig.

Its nose wrinkled as it scented him.

The man is hungry now.

It stamped its hooves.

The man has made a fire to burn the pig on.

The boar made a querulous noise in its throat. It didn't like fire.

Run run run! he told it. The thought was deep in its mind. *Burning pig, squealing pig, dying pig!*

It turned and bolted, running before it knew why, then only knew that it must run. There was a bad man behind it, a deadly man—a hunter. *Pig with its head hacked off! Pig roasting on a spit! Pig with an apple in its mouth!* Ashley projected the thoughts until it was far away, so far he could sense it no more. Then he sat down heavily.

His mind was fizzing, he was so lightheaded. He laughed with relief. It had been simple once he'd got the feel for it. He had shaped the thoughts from the raw stuff within the boar's mind. It was a simple mind, no doubt, but he had controlled its thoughts, planted ideas in its silly head. He called to Princess, and added a reassuring thought to calm her. She trotted to him from nearby in the woods and snorted nervously.

"It's all right, he's gone now." He scratched her neck. She rolled a doubtful eye at him, but settled down soon enough.

Ride? she wondered.

"Yes, let's find out what kind of a place we are in."

೮೩೮೦೮೮೦

In the narrow windblown neck overlooking the lakes squatted a hard stone stronghouse, much aged, its garrets crumbled and ill-repaired, its heavy slate tiles moss-filled and uneven, and the low stacked walls of the sheep-pens hiding under brambles. The outlying buildings were abandoned.

Passover had once been a vital link between the sovereign state of Korin and Moral Kingdom in the lowlands, and it had flown the flags of the Six-sided Land and the Amalgam of Lakelanders too. Trade had flourished, for it was here that the dissident Cleric of Qirrh had settled after he had walked the world. It was here that he had put his hand to map-making and founded a legacy on the strength of his penmanship and clever bartering, continued by his descendants. It was to this trading station that Twardy Zarost came, to find the last copy of the Book of Is. He was a backward forecaster, walking through his own work of prophecy and watching his visions escape ever more like desperate rats from a sack. He'd got it slightly wrong. A prophet should never doubt, he knew this, for then the vision of other prophets would come to pass instead of his own. But once one doubted, Zarost thought, he doubted that doubt could be undoubted.

It was dark and acrid in the old trade hall.

A moth *zuzzed* over Twardy Zarost's head, wallowing like a wide-bellied ship on high seas. After regarding him for a moment, it continued noisily through the gloomy room. It was huge. If it grew anymore, it would be a bird, but it still had the same mothy brain. It was heading for the light, Zarost mused, as they always did. The streaked cresset had a tall flame dancing on its end. The moth bashed into a low beam on the way to its target. It sank to the floor in dizzy spirals, temporarily thwarted on its holy quest for the light.

A man watched Zarost. Clumps of lanky black hair hung low over his rough face. He sat at a single table under the light. He was drinking from a cloudy bottle; he was drinking alone. Zarost didn't expect he ever kept company for long. One could tell a lot about a man from the kind of boots he wore. These were dirty, scuffed boots—fighter's boots—the kind that would have metal sewn secretly into the toe.

The man flicked his foot gently under the moth. It fluttered upward. Zarost was surprised at the gentle gesture, which seemed odd from the owner of such a crusty boot.

Flash! A winged blackened shape fell from the flame overhead. The man put out his hand, and the dead moth landed in his palm. He dipped the crisped husk into a dish of sticky liquid then threw his head back and dropped the appetiser into his mouth. He stared at Zarost as he munched. It was no accident that his table was positioned directly beneath the lamp. There was a more sinister effect too—whoever approached the table would be looking directly into the flickering light, and would find it difficult to see into the gloom on either side. Zarost waited just inside the doorway. He wanted to be sure he had counted all the henchmen before he stepped up to bargain. Things had changed in the House of Rohm.

The Passover trading post was under new management.

A lanky redhead stood in the corner, oiling a chain. He fretted over each link as if to clean it of a persistent stain. Zarost noted him as a danger. Someone who took such loving care of a weapon was usually someone who would delight in using it. The man was pretending not to watch the room.

Three others were rummaging through assorted caskets. One was a visitor, a heavy-set grey-skinned Lûk. The two men who accompanied him showed him something, and he shook his head. The visitor would likely not get involved on either side should there be trouble, but his attendants were part of the house crew.

The bigger of the attendants flashed an angry glance at Zarost. He looked to be as strong as an ox. Beside him, the last crew-man looked harmlessly small, with furtive, delicate hands. Zarost was not fooled. These men were mercenaries. The small man would use a throwing knife, whereas the brute would prefer to use his fists or a heavy weapon. A chain, a club, a knife—the most dangerous man in the house was the small one, because he would attack the fastest.

The place was decrepit. A tattered shroud flapped in a gaping window. A sagging door at the back of the room showed the flicker of candlelight beyond. Some busted furniture huddled against a wall, waiting to be burnt in the cold hearth. The seats had been replaced with upended wine barrels. A pile of feathers lay in a corner. Zarost didn't want to guess what it had been.

Passover hadn't looked so bad the last time he'd been here. The trading post had always been rough, that was the nature of dealing in such an outpost, but now the House of Rohm had a hungry feel to it. The current management were more interested in collecting money than generating it, Zarost guessed. They had overpowered the old traders and were failing to succeed at their new profession, because they were really just thieves. They had strangled trade through their greed, and the fewer the traders who came here, the poorer their information would be, and so the poorer their maps. The Passover trading post was doomed.

All things changed, Zarost noted, even in the places which had been spared the direct touch of Chaos. He approached the seated mercenary.

"Welcome to Passover, *friend*," the mercenary said without rising or smiling. His accent was thick and grating, not true Korinese—a

Lakelander then. "I am Drakk, and everything you see here is mine. I will trade nothing except for gold."

Zarost nodded. In the old days, the head trader would have been willing to trade for a variety of things. He had been right. They were raping the last of the stock before abandoning the place.

"I am looking for a chart—" Zarost began, using the language of Korin as well as he could remember it.

"Bargh! I don't speak with beggars!" Drakk growled. He extended his left hand. Zarost was about to shake it, but the mercenary withdrew his hand again, his black eyes full of malice.

"Pay," Drakk said. "I want to see the colour of your gold."

Why did distrustful men always think they could be good traders?

He drew a coin and placed it on the table. The mercenary picked it up and sampled it with his blackened teeth. He seemed surprised when he inspected the dents in the soft metal.

"This is too pure to be from around here. You from Kaskanzr?"

Zarost played along. He had been born in Kaskanzr, many many years ago, so there was honesty in nodding. Drakk sat forward on his chair, his face alight with greed. "What you want?"

"The Book of Is, and a map drawn in the latest year, from Highbough west, to the border here, from Slipper in the north to the six-sided land's tip, across to Qirrh, if you have such in a strip."

Drakk rolled the coin. "You are a far-travel one. Such things would be costly. Twenty of these outland golds, thirty if they are local Korin coins, sixty of those rubbishy Lûk gemknots, if that's what you'll use to pay."

"I have enough. All of it will be outland gold."

Drakk raised an eyebrow and then glanced aside. One hand slipped beneath the table and the mercenary shifted, as if to scratch an itch, but Zarost knew better.

"I have nothing more with me, it's hidden in the woods," Zarost announced quickly, "but I can retrieve the payment once I have seen the goods."

The redhead henchman who had been approaching faded into the shadows again. These men were too greedy by far. They would steal whatever they could get their hands on. Were any charts remaining in Drakk's palace worth buying, or had corpse of Passover already been picked clean?

The mercenary turned in his seat to address the slanting door at the back of the room. "Hulio. Hulio, you miserable turd! There's a man here, wants a map—a specially expensive map. Bring your Farlander chart. And a book. The book that is. What? The book of ease!"

A faint sound of disturbed parchment came from the back room.

"A moment," came a muffled voice.

So they still had a scribe-in-service. That was good. It meant the maps might be updated with news sold as traders passed by. A tall man emerged from the back room with a scroll in hand. The wretched and downcast expression he wore as he shuffled slowly to Drakk's table told Zarost everything. The old scribe probably wanted to leave his current 'employers', but had discovered how convincing a blade to the throat could be. The man was pale and gaunt. He probably didn't even earn a wage anymore.

"Here, Master Drakk," he said tiredly, laying the scroll on the table. "This is my best piece." He looked toward Zarost with a pleading expression, as if imploring him not to damage the work. With a careful gesture, he unrolled the vellum.

It was a beautiful chart, one of the best Zarost had seen. It would make a good gift. The old scribe must have laboured over it for months. Zarost ran his fingers gently along the illuminated border. The vellum was still soft. Zarost suspected it was a masterpiece from a man seeking to cleanse his soul of torment, seeking solace in his work, seeking peace.

Then he produced an ancient manuscript, wood-bound, yellowed with age but well-preserved. It had been carefully smoked and sunned throughout its long life. He rippled through the pages, showing Zarost the border-flourishes. As Zarost had expected, the copy lacked the stress patterns. The ancient language came before writing; without the phonic harmonies marked up, it was ineffective. He would have to find an expert in the spoken word to calculate the missing marks from first principles, but he could recognise the manuscript's authenticity. When he compared the diagram for the invocation of the God Zorsese to the torn page he had pocketed in the Gyre Library, he knew it was an original. The text would have preserved the deeper metaphysical instructions perfectly. It was exactly what he needed.

"This book is not for sale." The scribe closed the book and pushed it across the table toward Zarost.

"Yes it is!" Drakk exclaimed. He swung a fist at the scribe, and Hulio backed away hurriedly. Drakk laughed harshly. "Don't mind Hulio, he is just too proud of his own work to be any good at trading. So, friend, you have seen it, let us see your gold." The mercenary watched Zarost with feigned harmlessness, but behind Drakk, the old scribe caught Zarost's attention.

The scribe's eyes were full of warning. "Not for *sale*," he mouthed.

Zarost understood. The scribe had seen this happen before, too many times. "Those who are proud of their work should consider what their ink would do on blotting paper," he declared. "In a moment."

He took notice of where the four crew-men were positioned. He didn't like their kind, or what they had done to the good Rohm's trading post. In a way these bandits represented what had been done to Oldenworld, the corruption of the old order into lawlessness. It was people like these who caused the solid systems of trade to fail; it was people like these who took the world backward into ever more impoverished states of existence, into dis-union, into Chaos. They preyed upon the industrious fellows like the poor scribe, never caring that without such gentle, hard-working folk there would be nothing in the world at all.

Yes, these bandits deserved a little extra from this trade. It was time for a lesson in the danger of greed. He had to be very careful; he didn't want to be forced to use magic, because magic would bring Chaos, and this place already had enough of it.

Zarost pulled a heavy bag from the folds of his cloak—he had carried it with him all the time. There were many coins within it, brought to his hand from his private store in the Gyre Sanctuary by a Reference spell. Too many coins, over fifty Kaskanzan golds, but there was no time to separate his wealth now. He placed it on the table, like a declaration—a prize for the best fighter.

"Count yourself twenty out," he said.

Drakk could not resist fumbling with the knot to see his treasure. The distraction would keep him out of the first round of combat. Zarost sensed a disturbance pierce the edge of his aura. Zarost fell. Not a moment too soon, something whipped past his head—the knife, thrown hard. There would be a second.

He grabbed the edge of the table and sprang up from the ground, somersaulting over to Drakk's side. The mercenary tried to back his chair clear, but he was too slow. Zarost's boot found his face, and the mercenary toppled backward in his chair.

The second silver flash crossed the room. Zarost drew the table with him as he landed, tipping it over to fall upon Drakk. There was a solid thump from the underside as the thrown knife struck home.

Drakk thrashed, but the weight of the table kept him pinned. The bag of gold was close to hand, not yet fully opened. Zarost scooped it up and swung it against Drakk's temple.

The greedy trader got more gold than was good for him.

Zarost grabbed the chart and the book, and stuffed them into his shirt. He ran for the window, where the ragged curtain flapped but the lanky orange-haired fighter danced into the way. He spun his oiled chain with a deadly familiarity. He was going to be very hard to beat, with only the bag of gold as a weapon. Zarost dodged clear of the first whistling swipe, but he was forced away from the window, toward the jumble of furniture. There was a low beam overhead.

The big brute was coming from behind him—his heavy movement was easy to sense. The knife-thrower was running from Zarost's left side. He probably didn't trust his throwing hand anymore, and would want to wield his last blade directly.

The chain-fighter lunged at him. Zarost jumped. The chain whistled under his feet.

They had him trapped against a sagging bench. Zarost backed onto it and twisted the knot of his moneybag free. The bandits circled closer, the big brute in the lead, wearing a hungry smile. He carried a mace the size of a small tree-stump.

Zarost threw the coins at him. They showered over the brute's head. The glint of gold caught the bandits' attention for a moment, just as he'd expected. Twardy jumped for the low beam, caught the rough wood between his hands, and swung quickly up.

The chain-wielder thrashed out, aiming to take out Zarost's hands and ankles. Zarost almost rose and ran in time, but the chain flailed around an upright, and clipped his heel a painful blow. Bebittered bloodhounds, but the chain was a cruel weapon! Zarost hobbled swiftly along the beam, glad to see that the chain had hooked around an exposed nail. The orange-haired mercenary cursed as he tried to work it free. For the first time, Zarost considered that the lesson he hoped to dispense might turn against the teacher. He hurriedly prepared a Transference spell, just in case, but he didn't want to use it, not with the scribe still in the building.

When he swung off the beam, the knifer was there when he landed on awkward feet; the man was too fast. His blade flickered crisscross through the air. The knifer drove him back. A low grunt of exertion warned him of the brute at his back. Zarost couldn't guess where his blow was aimed. He took a chance, and fell flat to the floor at the knifer's feet. The mace hurtled by, brushing his hair. The brute had been intent on clubbing him to the other side of the Winterblades. The big man was carried onward with the momentum of his swing, and the knifer jerked back to avoid being caught on the tip. Zarost saw his opening.

He grabbed the little knifer's ankles, lifted him and swung him in a quick circle. Then he threw the small man against the brute's legs. The knifer cried out, some bones cracked, and they tumbled onto the floor. Zarost ran for the open door. His right foot protested.

A loosely dressed figure stepped from the shadows and blocked his exit with the point of a long spear. Zarost cursed himself. He had forgotten about the Lûk merchant, wrongly assuming the man would leave the violence well alone. The merchant pressed the tip of the spear against Zarost's throat.

"*Ght! Ght!* I cannot allow that you go, stranger. That's a mighty pile gold there. If I these men don't help to hold you, how could I my share claim?"

"Thank you, Rengwaam," someone called out from behind Zarost in a thick voice. Curse his luck! Drakk had recovered. "Hold him, and you'll have your share," the leader promised.

Behind him, Zarost could hear the big man dragging his mace across the floor.

"Wait! Let me end him," a man with a reedy voice said. "Please, let me end him."

"Make haste, Crellaine!" replied the Lûk, squinting suspiciously at Zarost. "This one is slippery."

Rapid footsteps approached, accompanied by the faint clinking of chain links. Zarost knew he would have his skull crushed if he stood still; he would be skewered by the spear if he moved. There was no time left for lessons.

Beyond the corner of the flapping curtain he saw a tiny figure in the distance. Nobody else would see the scribe who had solved the riddle. Like ink on blotting paper, he was running. That was good, he had a chance then. That was all Zarost could offer him, and he couldn't extend the scribe's lead any further.

The chain came with a rush of air, falling from behind and above.

Zarost spread his arms and cast the Transference spell. He reached out with his awareness, beyond the limits of beyond, and spread himself throughout. He was all, he was everything; he was unlimited. He embraced infinity, and was gone.

Zarost spun through the vastness of infinity. He was made of galaxies and dark, dark emptiness. He was safe—relatively. He cursed Ametheus for the end of the lesson. In the old days, Zarost would have been able to wield his power without causing indiscriminate damage. Ametheus had robbed all the wizards of the pure fun of using magic. In the old days he would have bound the bandits to each other with a Circle of Sin, he could have even placed a compulsion upon them to serve the scribe as their lord. That would have been fun! Instead, all Zarost could do was run, because fighting with magic would draw wildfire, and fighting the wildfire strike would do no good at all. He supposed the fighters would taste the gravy of their greed in the end; someone would replace them on the point of a blade. The days of the House of Rohm were truly ended, but his journey there was not wasted—he had the book and the map. What one carried into Transference, one could carry out again. It had to be so, he supposed, or wizards would always appear without their underwear, and that was a thought not worth lingering upon.

He needed to have the accents in the Book of Is marked up properly. He gathered his attention from the limitless backcloth of eternity and chose his destination with care. There was only one choice for such a scansion—Tattler Jhinny in the Lûk down of Koom. She was an expert in languages, she had studied all of them, and she would be quick. He supposed that the Gyre's Lorewarden could scan the ancient text as well, but with the way things were in the Gyre at the moment, he wasn't sure whom he could trust in the circle.

Better that he get the truth himself, before presenting it to the others.

Jhinny. It had been twenty years since he'd last seen her. She would be old by now. Still in that read-room in the Koom down, no doubt, whipping another generation of students into shape, cackling as they struggled to pronounce old Koramani words like *fløs* and *ÿgådnishir*, cackling again when they asked her what those words meant. He was looking forward to meeting the old Tattler again.

He considered the settlement of Koom: best for him to appear on one of the smaller casts, and work his way inward from there. No need to make a spectacle of himself. The eastern side-cast, where the red-leafed heart-creepers hung like quilts over the woven walkways and the dyed silks were hung upon the long-lines to dry in the breeze. He held that place in thought, and he was there. He appeared as he'd disappeared—fast and furry. The wind from the parting strike toppled his hat from his head. He dusted it off and looked around.

The capital of the six-sided land of Lûk had changed very little in twenty years—on the surface, at least. The vegetable gardens were still thriving between the golden soap-berry bushes, reed fences still threaded in curving patterns across the bowl. The smoke still billowed from the bakeries in the face of the Koom hills. Everywhere the vents poked up through the dry grass like the stems of a felled forest. The scent of thyme bushes lingered in the air, warm and dry. The Lûk were as scarce as ever, hidden in their burrowed settlement, safe from the dangers of dragons or wildfire.

They were the wisest of the survivors. It didn't pay to be seen in Oldenworld.

Zarost looked nervously to the sky. He didn't want to be out longer than he needed to be either. There was a *kazunderstorm* building, spreading out from the south and leading toward the Winterblades well to the north of Koom. It commanded the sky, and its edges grew at an alarming rate. This was not a simple nuisance-cloud with rumbles, turbulent winds and the odd sparkle of lightning. This was an unnatural column of bulging wrath towering across the heavens, blocking out the world below with its dark shadow, its face straining towards the edge of the sky where the air was so thin no creature could breathe it and where everything froze. Whipped with vicious winds, it would collect its ice into fists, and strike down at the earth. It would give forth shouts of thunder that would shake the mountains to their roots.

It was just the kind of cloud that would form after a major wildfire strike. With so much Chaos at its heart it would attract the Sorcerer's attention. He would be drawn to it; he would take more power from it. What had triggered it in the first place? He had been far away in Passover. It couldn't have been his spell. Never so quickly. It looked like it had built over something out in the wastes near Eyri. Had one of the Gyre wizards been careless with a spell? If so, what were they doing out there?

He headed for the main hatch along a bamboo pathway. Sometimes the tortured things that wandered the wastes could trigger the wildfire themselves, he supposed. He was glad to be getting out of the way of the storm. He arrived at the rounded lid of reinforced rush-weave set into a wide bamboo frame. The small pattern of an oat stem in its centre told him that it was safe, not a trap-hatch. He stepped onto the woven surface, and the weave parted in a slit in the centre. He slipped into the woven chute that was the entrance to the east sidecast of Koom, and slid down to the eye chamber. The spicy smell of Koom met him, and with it came the distant sound of the moaning singers and the blurts of reedy message-pipes. He had entered the realm of the Lûk.

ଔଞ୍ଚଔଞ

The forest was familiar, in the way of all forests. Green things grew in clusters; the loamy earth was littered with bark chips, broad leaves and questing roots; and the great trees reigned supreme over everything—mostly redwood, or something equally aged and tall. The air was cool and moist, and smelled of old flowers. Ashley followed a rivulet to a slack pool where he let Princess drink. A family of bright yellow frogs hopped away across the lily pads. A mist oozed onto the pond's surface. It seemed to follow them when they left, tracking soundlessly through the forest, always keeping its distance, always slightly behind. Ashley shook his head, he knew it was nonsense—probably just a breeze, pushing the moist air through the trees. He ranged out with his thoughts anyway, but he didn't sense anything close by. In the distance, he encountered the sensation of a community of people, but he couldn't tell where the thoughts were coming from, they were just voices, in his head not in any particular place. He passed a bridge made of cables woven from a kind of knotted fibre, and a disused pile of slender poles.

They rode into a glade where golden sunlight filtered through a gap in the trees to strike a wide bowl of grass. The forest was strangely quiet. Only the delicate *frrrt! frrrrt!* of a small bird broke the silence as it flitted from bloom to bloom along the edge of the hanging creepers. Then even that was quiet, hanging from a branch, watching them. Princess slowed uncertainly at the edge of the glade.

"Come on, it's only grass," Ashley reassured his mount.

They moved out into the glade. The air held a scent of sweet blossoms. It was warm.

But at the limit of Ashley's vision, something moved.

He spun in his stirrups to look—a swinging vine, dappled brown and gold. He eased back into the saddle. There were many vines like that. He'd seen them everywhere, woven through the creepers. They swayed in the breeze, appearing to be much lighter than they should be. He urged Princess onward, to get a closer look.

Then his heart dropped. He didn't need to bring Princess up short;

she was already prancing backward, away from the threatening, weaving obstruction. Not vines. Snakes! They were entwined with the vegetation. Their camouflage was clever. The first snake dropped to the ground and slithered toward them. Princess reared and squealed. Ashley had nothing to hold on to except her wiry mane. He urged her to turn around, and she obeyed his thoughts. They leapt away, but they hadn't gone five paces before Ashley saw the movement in the grass ahead of them. Another snake reared beside the path and Princess skittered to the right. There were snakes there as well: Ashley could see the telltale disturbance in the grass. The hunting was clearly good along this game-trail. It was a trap, and Ashley was in the middle of it. The snakes came at them from all sides. He wondered how the snakes would divide a prey as big as a horse, but he didn't have time to complete the thought. A serpent reared out of the grass and Princess leapt.

They never came down. They were flying again.

Princess floundered, unsure of her movements in the air. Ashley looked down and wished he hadn't—it seemed that as soon as they had launched, he was too high to jump down to the ground. The snakes met below in a writhing heap. Princess lurched through the air toward the high curtain of vines. There were snakes there too, ones which had not yet dropped to the ground. They waved about in the air like tentacles, hungry for flesh.

"Right, right!" shouted Ashley, wishing again the had reins to pull on. He discovered the first hard lesson of steering a flying creature. Pushed by a powerful stroke on her right wing, Princess went left.

"Left, Left!" he shouted.

Princess gave a stronger beat with her left wing. He was almost tipped off her back and into the snakes. As they brushed the lowest leaves of the creeper wall Ashley's legs tingled. He'd been bitten by a snake once, a little coppercoil, and it had hurt for days. He couldn't guess how much worse a bite would feel from one of these big Oldenworld vine-snakes. At last Princess gripped the air with her wide white wings and began to fly properly. Ashley was pushed down into the saddle as his mount flapped hard, escaping the clutch of the forest and its deadly inhabitants.

They were free. The matted green canopy fell away below his feet.

Flying!

Princess maintained a steady rhythm with her wings, beating her way higher. He held onto her mane for dear life. He was scared, but by flying they would cover a lot of ground. He would try to backtrack and find Tabitha. Once they had gained sufficient height above the forest he could see the wasteland, which judging by the sun's position was due south. He guided Princess that way. A great channel lined with dark and jagged rocks cut through the forest and headed out across the wastes. The whole of Oldenworld spread out before him again like an arcane tapestry, waiting for him to learn how to read its patterns.

They rose and rose, flying all the while under a high-knuckled mass of cloud that reached out from the grey wastelands all the way to the great white-crested mountains to the north. It looked to be over thirty leagues to the beginning of that distant range. One knotted carpet of clouds shadowed all the land.

It's only a cloud. Stop worrying. If they stayed below it they should be fine. The sun was hidden from view, only the ground far to the east and west was lit. The under-surface of the cloud was like an inverted saucer, and it had grown little dark hooks of mist on its belly. He'd never seen a cloud like this before. Princess nickered. Her flying was growing more uncertain. Ashley sent her reassuring thoughts, but lacking conviction.

A gaggle of banded geese joined them, straggling out in a ragged 'V'. Ashley watched in fascination as they crossed under their feet. They had such glossy, smooth feathers on their backs and along their wings. He watched them grow smaller as they dropped away toward a shadowed lake on a plain to the east.

It took a while before Ashley realised that the wind was doing strange things to them. It whistled steadily in his ears, and Princess was beating the same rhythm, but they didn't seem to be moving over the ground. Ashley squinted down at the forest below. There was a wide river which was easy to reckon on. They were drifting backward, in the direction of the distant mountain range, whose white-capped peaks were now hidden in dark cloud. It was impossible, they couldn't be going *backward*! Princess was flapping with a regular beat, and he could feel wind in his face, so they had to be flying forward, but it seemed that the headwind was just too strong. They were being drawn up toward the great brooding cloud at their backs.

Stop, Princess. We must go down.

She trusted his inner voice completely, too completely. One moment they were flying, the next she had folded her wings against her body, and they were falling. Ashley yelped in fright. Princess splayed her legs to steady herself, and her wings snapped hard back in a widespread gliding position.

"Keep them like that! Keep them like that! Don't do a thing!"

They were gliding, smooth, calm and majestic.

"Just stay like that, sweetheart," he whispered.

It had helped them down last time; it should do the same again. Ashley looked nervously over his shoulder at the brooding thunderstorm. It had grown blacker and bigger, and it had spread out on either side of them. He leant close to Princess's neck and peered down to where the trees of the forest ended and the wasteland began. It was very difficult to tell if they were going down or up. The ground was so far below them now that it seemed to be a flat tapestry of greens, blues, greys and browns. He hoped they were going down.

The strain of catching the wind so suddenly had hurt Princess, deep in her shoulders, where the wings joined her body. It was a strain to keep them outstretched. She whinnied plaintively. Cold fear turned in Ashley's stomach. *Down, down, down, we have to get down!* He couldn't think of any quick way to do it that would not strain Princess's wings.

The ground went all misty, then all of a sudden, was gone altogether. They were in the clouds.

It was quiet. The wind became a hushed whisper in his ears. He was sure they began to tilt to the left, so he compensated by guiding Princess to the right, urging her to shift the angle of her wings. He still hoped they could outrun the storm. If they kept heading south, for Eyri, they should come out of the cloud in the end, shouldn't they?

A fine mist collected on his eyebrows and on the hairs on the back of his hands. Princess's mane began to bead with moisture. She whinnied louder and louder—she didn't like this place, the gut-tilting sensation of it, and the way the world had been taken away. They couldn't see more than a yard in front of them. It could have been ten yards, Ashley couldn't tell, it was just a grey featureless mist, all around; underneath them, above them. The sunlight faded away to nothing as it became darker and wetter. Rain began to sting his face and he stayed close to Princess's neck. There was a horrible sensation of the power all around him, the hunger of the cloud which drew the air to its mouth, feeding it with moisture. It had taken up twenty leagues of sky, and still it wanted more.

The wind shrieked at them and tore at Princess's feathers,

wrenching and twisting her wings. Such immense strength. Was it more than just a cloud? Ashley strained to see into the mist, to pierce it with his mind. If there was some presence, it was hiding, with fangs and talons, twisting the cloud's gloom against them and reaching for them with fear alone. The cloud spun about them, swirled and rushed, boiling upward in angry coils.

They tumbled as the air was sucked out from beneath them. Princess flapped in desperate lunges to recover her balance. Just fly straight and level, Ashley prayed, just straight and… level. But there were no reference points to tell up from down. They tumbled, nose over tail, as Princess beat furiously against the broken air, falling with a downdraught, then—slam!—lofted from underneath, as the air currents switched.

Princess floundered, her wings were wrenched forward. She gave a forlorn cry. Muscles tore in her wings, Ashley suspected, but there was nothing he could do to help her. Slam! They were tumbling again, up became down, sideways, backward and the wind was tearing at the roots of her feathers, roaring past their ears. Princess's majestic wings were turning to sodden clumps of feathers on bone.

They fell into a maelstrom, tumbling out of control. Something hit Ashley hard in the back; something else thudded against his head. Hailstones. The air blackened, thick and seething with a fearsome presence. Something was building around them, he could feel the gathering charge… all the air seemed to be rushing forward, pulling them into a deep and waiting silence. He tried to make himself very small against Princess's neck.

The strike was swift, and it passed them in a forked flash, blinding and intense. Time seemed to stutter and repeat. Then they fell.

A careless calm settled upon him and he stopped shivering. He couldn't feel his arms or his legs any more. His face felt like solid ice. It didn't matter. They couldn't fight the storm anymore. It began to seem funny, in the end. He'd wanted to fly all his life, and here he was, in the realm of the gods. It didn't pay to play in the realm of the gods unless one was a god, Ashley decided. Only gods had the power to be up here. Only the gods could save him, but they wouldn't, because he was falling, cast out of the realm of the gods, an unworthy human, sent back to the earth where he belonged. A peaceful way to die, in the end. Would their bodies eventually come down to earth in some exotic corner of Oldenworld, where strange and beautiful people lived? It was a sad thought, because they'd miss seeing it, Princess and he. They'd be dead for sure.

Only the mournful shriek of the wind and the sting of rain in his eyes told him he was still alive.

"No!" he tried to shout to Princess. She hadn't wanted to be with the gods; she didn't deserve to die. "Life is worth living! Save yourself!" His lips were frozen and he made no sound, but he *thought* it loudly.

A strange face appeared in the cloud, a distorted face that flickered through the mist, enlarged around the right eye as if the watcher was peering through a bulge of glass. The watcher reached out and the cloud bent outward as if it were a membrane.

The Sorcerer. Ashley knew it the moment he saw him. Even his stomach turned cold.

The Sorcerer watched them with that unnervingly enlarged eye. Then he raised his hand and slapped the open palm toward them. The outline of a great hand ripped through the cloud above them, a handprint traced in silver. The sky was ablaze with lightning. Bright bolts shot at them. The image of the watcher was lost in the raining chaos. They fell through crisscrossed crazy light, stuttering and exploding. Stuttering and exploding.

Threads of Chaos tangled upon them then were suddenly wrenched away, by the cloud's power, or by some vagary of magic. Had the Sorcerer changed his mind? Either the Sorcerer had a terrible aim, or he had aimed to miss. They escaped from Chaos.

A scene flashed into view; a patch of sky or water of the palest blue; and a speckled green rim around it, and mountains, which jutted up at odd angles. The perspective was all wrong: the scene was swirling, spinning. He could see they were out of the cloud though. Its dark base stretched away like a tilted wall of dented iron.

Ashley adjusted to the new jagged horizon. The widening oblong of light blue below them really was water, a high alpine tarn, the white-flecked green its snow-covered banks. They were spiralling toward it at great speed, and the way he could see the individual ripples probably meant...

Spla-doosh!

Icy water closed overhead, and they were driven deep below the surface. He lost his breath. He kicked away from Princess, fought against the weight of his clothes. He thrashed at the water, struggling to propel himself upward, kicking for the surface, but he was too weak. He fought the overwhelming desire to open his mouth and draw in all the water of the lake to satisfy his burning breathlessness.

Slower than the dawning of the morning sun, the translucent surface came closer. It was patterned with circular ripples from heavy raindrops. Ashley broke through and heaved in a desperate breath, then sank, came up for another breath and sank again in the icy water. His strength was failing. Princess broke the surface beside him, snorting and spluttering through her nostrils.

Help me to the shore, he thought. *Help me. I can't paddle anymore.*

Princess came close. He tried to grip her mane as she passed but his cold hands were useless and had no strength. She came around again and nudged him from behind, edging him forward, even though it caused her to snort desperately to avoid drowning herself. She ducked her head under his body and heaved him upward, so that he could draw breath. He slid across her back. They emerged thus from the blue waters of the tarn, crawling out of the shallows and falling heavily upon the ground.

Princess lay on her belly with her sodden wings splayed to either side, blowing gusts of steam. Ashley remained where he was, lying on her back. He hung his head down and wept. Relief flooded him. They had survived.

After a while he realised that they could not stay there, with the waters lapping at their legs, exposed in this cold wild place. He crawled away to look for shelter, and urged Princess to follow him.

The vast cave he found had a funny smell, a carrion scent, but there was no rain inside. A great tumbled pile of bones littered the floor. Something big had died there long ago and had been picked clean. A small charred tree grew in the entrance, its blackened limbs struggling toward the sky. The way the rain was falling meant the tree was protected. Ashley guessed it would make good firewood, but he couldn't finish the thought before losing consciousness for a time.

Before nightfall he roused himself again. He was shivering uncontrollably.

Move, you fool, move. He hung on the weakest branches of the blackened tree until they cracked and tore off. That was the easy part. He searched in the damp saddlebags, and retrieved the tinderbox from the pile of salvaged supplies. Getting a spark to catch on the sodden slivers of tinder with the flint and steel was impossible. His hands were so cold they hardly worked at all. Only when he found some old grass and fluff in a nest among the shelved rocks did he have his first hint of smoke. Eventually the grass took, and he added kindling, then the branches caught ablaze. At last he began to feel some hope for living through the night.

Thawing out was more painful than the growing cold had been.

Princess was nervous of the flames, but he did manage to convince her to bring her sodden body close enough that she was out of the coldest draughts. She would not come close enough to be dried by the flames, though. He rubbed her down as best he could, but he knew she was going to have a cold night.

There was little to eat. Most of his supplies of drybread had floated away upon the lake. What remained was sodden. He squeezed it into a fist-sized lump, pierced it with a short stick, and stuck it over the open flames.

The wet bread turned out to be as awful as it looked. Even though he'd crisped it to black on the outside, it was still soggy in the middle, but it was food, and he knew he needed every scrap he could get. He was in trouble—he was in the mountains, in a grey, cold and bitter place, with a horse that wasn't a horse anymore and might not make it through the night. At least she might be able to tear up some grass in the morning; there was enough of that between the clumped snow, but what would he eat? He might be able to hunt. If there were things that built nests among the rocks, there had to be ways to catch them.

Ashley lay down beside the fire. What kind of a beast had owned the bones which lay scattered at the mouth of the cave? He closed his eyes—he was truly too fatigued to care. The warmth of the flames was heavenly. The warmth was everything.

21. A LOOK INTO THE FOREST

"Isn't it odd, what different cultures
can ferment from the same brew?"—Zarost

The storm broke above them, and the night fell heavy and wet upon their backs. Garyll got them to their feet. Despite their fatigue, they had to go on. There was no shelter where they had fallen, and no way to keep warm except to walk. Mulrano shouldered their meagre supplies. The water puddled on the bare grey earth, soon forming pools, then running under their boots in a sheet of liquid whispers. The hardpack became slick and treacherous. Garyll led them over the lip of the rocky gorge they had been lying beside and they descended into the scoured channel.

The sides of the gorge rose.

The rocks were jagged, they chewed at the soles of Tabitha's boots, but at least they offered a solid grip and kept out of the water, which sloshed down the sloping rock-fields in hundreds of rivulets. The occasional silver sparkle lit the waters like lost fireflies, but for the most part the runoff from the desert plains above was dull and harmless. The rocks underfoot were all compacted like ragged crystals. Tabitha picked one up. It was extremely heavy, and bluish, but in the dark it was hard to tell for sure. It was composed of a solid sound, a blue bass note in the chiaroscuro of raindrops and silver silence. The rain sluiced down, and they picked their way carefully through the scree until they reached an overhang where they could huddle together and escape the worst of the storm.

Tabitha didn't remember much of that horrible time, except that she shivered, on and on. Garyll held her tightly all through the night, but his body heat didn't help much. She wasn't shivering because she was cold. The rain came down, washing down on the corpse of the day, and they waited upon its resurrection, but it never came. Night stole into their souls. Beyond the protection of Eyri, they were small; the world was vast.

At last the grim dawn became strong enough to see in, and they pressed on, if only to stretch their cramped muscles. They had all seen the forest on the northern horizon the previous day. There should be some better shelter there. It hadn't seemed too far off: three, maybe four leagues?

They followed the course of the wide gorge. The water had pooled in the base of the channel, but it wasn't flowing anywhere. Tabitha had assumed they were in a river course, but the stagnant water proved otherwise. But if it was not a river course, what had carved such a massive channel out of the desert? The question returned to her many times as she followed Garyll along the alternately scoured and encrusted surface. After a while the channel sloped up and ended, and they had to shuffle upon the hard-packed mud. Then the channel began again, dipping then rising, dipping again, as if it was a trench made by an erratic hand or the random trail of a hungry worm. They walked along the line of its devastation.

When the rain abated, they climbed to the trench's rim to see where they were heading. The forest was barely a league away; the trees could be identified individually. Towering and yet strangely buckled trunks held up a deep and mottled canopy. The trench carried on into the forest, and on either side of it the ground was scoured and bare, the trees were stripped of leaves, and those closest to the trench had fallen flat to the ground, as if a great wind had tried to collect them as it passed.

Another hour and they'd be there.

And then what? Tabitha thought. She was deathly tired. Her boots had begun to wear through on the sharp rocks and she could feel the cold mud seeping in at her left heel. She sat on a boulder and held her head in her hands. She had hoped to find people in Oldenworld, people who could help her to find Ethea. Instead, she had led them into the deadly wastes, she had lost them the horses, she had lost Ashley, she had nearly killed them all, and now that she could see the forest they had been striving to reach, she realised it was not the end of their troubles. It was just a forest, another wilderness in this strange and ravaged land. How far would they have to tramp across Oldenworld before they found any hint of where the Low Lands were? And how would they ever find Bevn? Those tracks that had led off across the desert from the top of the Penitent's pass were long lost. Now, after the rains, there would be no way to find them.

"Here, have something to eat," Garyll said at her elbow. He offered her an orange.

She ignored the food. She wasn't hungry. How long would their meagre food last? Three days? Four? Then they'd die, and it would all be her fault. She was terribly ill-prepared. She had assumed that because she was the Wizard of Eyri that she could do anything. It had begun to feel like that after all the miracles she had performed in Levin. Fame had changed her, she realised. It had made her foolish. She thought too much of her own abilities, and now that she faced real hardship she realised how hasty she had been in setting off on this quest. She should have studied the Revelations more; she should have waited until Twardy Zarost returned.

"Eat," Garyll insisted. "We're all feeling a little low because we've used up our fuel."

A little low? That didn't begin to describe how she felt. She allowed him to slip a segment of the peeled orange past her lips. It burst in her mouth, sweet and juicy. It was better than she'd expected. She took another piece.

Her mind lingered on Twardy Zarost. She wished he had told her more about what to expect in Oldenworld. She wished he had told her more about magic. She wished he had come back.

"Whok hu fink abouk?" asked Mulrano.

"Magic," she replied. "I wish I could heal our pains. I wish I could make us dry and warm."

Garyll gave her a consoling squeeze. His sodden loden cloak had begun to *smell* green.

"Can't you do anything?" he said. "Not even a little sustenance for yourself?"

"Something in this world out here doesn't like wizards," she answered, staring across the wet surface of the desert to the misty trees. "I don't think we'll survive the next spell, Garyll."

Garyll's strong arm felt good around her. His cheek was rough beside her face.

"Your casting—provoked—that strange lightning, didn't it?"

"I think so," she replied.

"Does the Sorcerer know we are here? Can he sense our presence?"

"I don't know. I don't think he's aware of us. He can't be. If he was, we'd probably be dead already. He'd just dump a sky-full of Chaos upon us. The way the energy seemed to gather above me, it's like it's part of a web the Sorcerer's built to react against magic, to burn out a wizard, or to touch magic-users with his power. Maybe he doesn't like competition."

Garyll watched the clouds with her for a while. They both knew what hid in the heights beyond the mists—that strange network of cracks in the sky which had spawned the wildfire strike.

"It is an effective deterrent to using magic, isn't it?" he said at length.

"Either I'll have to learn how to combat the wildfire or I must stop using my power altogether." Maybe she could just use a trickle of the Lifesong. Just a murmur of her magic, a soft whisper of song. Maybe, unlike the Light-spell, the song wouldn't be noticed, but she couldn't risk being wrong.

What could drive a man to cast such a horrible web of magic, in place just to bring ruin upon others, to blight so much land, to leave places so ravaged that even time was twisted upon itself? Why would someone with so much power want to break everything? What drove the Sorcerer to such extremes?

A-m-e-t-h-e-u-s.

The mud swelled against the writing she had made with her finger, as if the living earth rejected what had been placed upon its face. The single word faded quickly until it was gone.

After a slow trudge that seemed to last forever, they reached the edge of the first of the great trees.

They searched for a pathway, working their way northward into the mighty forest. It had seemed a hopeless task, for the ground was littered with bark and leaves and showed little in the way of traffic. Garyll picked a careful path between the detritus of the fallen limbs that plagued the border of the forest. The farther they went, the tighter together the trees grew. The canopy drew closed overhead so that the morning sun cast only a dim light ahead of them.

The forest was humid and rich with the scents of wood and earth. They passed clumps of mushrooms, white, orange and pale pink. Lichen grew in scalloped shapes in the crooks and curves of the trees. The trees were similar to oaks, but everything was oversized—the first boughs were twenty feet above the ground, the second, thirty. It made her feel very small. It also made the Great Forest of Eyri seem like a pale joke. Those trees were dwarfs in comparison.

"Over here!" Garyll called out. "There's a trail here."

A kind of hardy moss had been cultivated in parallel strips to form a green-and-white carpet leading through the trees. At its edge lay a border of giant leaves, planted into the earth so they stood upright. Some of the leaves had their centres hollowed out from decay, but their bright red or yellow rims remained. Tabitha went up to feel the strange shovel-sized blades. They had fleshy centres, but their edges were as hard as metal.

They walked on the carpeted trail for some time, which was easy to move upon, adding a slight spring to her steps. It was almost straight, except for where it wove around the roots of the larger obstructions. Most of the trees seemed to have been coaxed to lean and grow away from the road. Tabitha saw a few saplings bound back on twisted vines. Someone had worked on the forest, tending the trees. There were people here.

The forest was silent. She stayed close to Garyll, having developed a queer sense of being watched, but she couldn't place the cause. The air was still, trapped within the endless trees, filled with an expectant hush. Even her footfalls and those of the men alongside seemed to be absorbed by the soft earth.

Something whistled out of the air and struck the ground with a thump. She spun around.

A bird called from high above. "*Lwhoo-lululululu!*"

Another whistling impact. Something rolled away from close by her feet, a big nut of some kind. Tabitha craned her neck, but the bird was hidden among the great canopy.

"*Lwhoo-lululul!*" Gay and cheeky.

Tabitha wondered if the nut might not have been dropped by accident.

"*Lwhoo. Lwhoo!*"

A third nut whizzing down, like a stone shot from a sling.

"Watch out!" she cried, but too late. The nut smote Mulrano on the back of his head as he ducked. It bounced high into the air. A cackling call from above identified the culprit.

"Wek-argh whorefung!" he cursed. He shot a glance at Tabitha and reddened as he rubbed his head.

With a flash of colour, a feathered form dropped toward them. The bird swooped then beat its brilliant crimson wings to hover at head-height. A pair of humanlike eyes peered at Tabitha out of a parrot's face, blue eyes, shocking in their demanding intelligence.

Tabitha yelped in surprise. The bird opened its hooked yellow beak wide, and shrieked in shrill laughter as it beat the air and flew away.

"*Hoh hoh hoh hoh hê!*" it called out. "*Hoh hê!*"

It was an upsetting creature. Its sudden closeness and escape left her feeling strangely violated. It had a human presence, yet it was clearly a bird. It had laughed as it escaped.

"Did you see that?" Tabitha asked Garyll.

"This is a very strange place," Garyll replied, eyeing the trees. The bright bird was perched high above them. It bobbed from side to side. It was still watching them. Tabitha was about to dismiss it and continue when it leant down and screeched out loud, "Don't know who ye are, don't know ye are, *hoh hê!*"

It seemed to be aware of their rapt attention, for it spread its wings out wide in a shivering display, and gave two low bows. "*Whooop! Whooop!*" it called. "Born inner fire!" It hopped along its branch toward the outer leaves. Small round objects were clustered among the foliage.

"Nuts!" she warned the others. "Get moving!"

The trees began to close in on them, and although the bird followed them, issuing shrieks and jeers, it didn't make another clear shot. Such a dense canopy of vines linked each towering tree that in the end the sunlight was cut off altogether. The lowest boughs reached out like frail and naked arms, skeletal memories of an older time when the sun had shone upon the dark loamy floor. The earth was wet, and it oozed where they trod upon the mossy road. The air was thick with the scent of mushrooms and mould. Great spider webs dangled slackly beside the trail, and there were more, still whole, strung deeper in the forest, great nets hoping for a catch. The spiders Tabitha saw were as big as her head, and as black as pitch. Thankfully they seemed content to sit in their webs, waiting for prey to be foolish or panicked enough to venture in where they shouldn't.

A cool wetness brushed her head. She looked up and the next beard of lichen caught her directly in her face. Garyll pulled her back, too late. It stung; it felt as if the slime was eating into her skin. She smeared it from her face with her sleeve. The lichen was difficult to discern in the gloom, but once she looked for more, her eyes picked out the prolific hanging garden ahead, a greyish green mass growing upon a latticework of ropes stretched between the trees. Somebody was cultivating the slime. For what?

At the far end of the hanging garden they encountered a tree which had been carved upon. It was a marker of some kind, white-barked, free of lichen. Large symbols had beenccut in a haphazard hexagonal pattern. It was no language she had ever seen before. She had been taught some runes in the Dovecote, but these weren't spell-runes, they were more like little clusters of pattern. Each raised symbol was linked to the others by a system of lines, worked into the wood. A map, perhaps, or a register. Below the carvings, the pale exposed bole was stained with spirals and twisting organic designs, marked out in a dark fluid.

"*Wooo! Izzit Hunter? Izzit? Brrrradach! Izzit traderkind?*"

The bright bird had returned to plague them. As before, it swooped down and hovered just ahead of Tabitha in the clearing. It looked directly at her with those terrible eyes, tilting its head from side to side as if trying to make up its mind what she was.

"*Ki-oo, ki-yoo,*" it screeched, then more clearly, "Kill you. *Rrrrround!* Look kill you." It beat the air and rose higher, flying around the carved trunk before finding a perch in the boughs.

A shiver passed down her spine. It was eerie to hear a bird speak, even if it was in a screeching avian way.

"Do you think it's dangerous?" she whispered to Garyll.

"The bird? Not up there it isn't, but it will alert anything else in the forest of our presence."

"Hoh hê! Look coming, look coming! *Krooooookrookrook!*"

The bird danced around in an agitated manner. It swooped down from its perch again, this time harassing Garyll with its piercing litany. Garyll swung his baton, but the bird tumbled in the air and easily avoided his swipe, banking up and around to come at them again. It strafed low over Tabitha, and pulled her hair as she ducked.

"*Zrreek! Dumbich! Dumbich!* Whatarewhee? Firewyld?"

"Will you shut up?" Tabitha shouted after it.

"Angry now!" it called out. "Fly away. Hoh hê!"

Its screeches might not be random nonsense, Tabitha realised. It might be trying to tell them something.

"What is coming?" she asked the highest branch, where the bird had hidden. It was not likely that the bird would understand her, but something about the strange human awareness in those eyes made her persist. "What are you trying to warn us about?"

"Look. Rrrround. Look kill you," came the hidden taunt.

"Look where?"

"What if it's saying Lûk?" Garyll cut in. "As in the people, the barbarians. The Lûk."

It clicked into place. Tabitha had read it, in the Legend of the Forming, how the Eyrians had battled the fierce northern men with shaven heads, the northern Lûk, whose pointed staffs and great woven shields made them difficult targets, and whose devious throw-nets were said to grip like iron cables.

"This is the land of the Lûk?" she asked of the bird.

"*Lûklûklûklûklûk!* Killer hunterkind."

"Hunter kind?"

"*Brrrradach!* Find Brrrrradach!"

"How do we find Bradach?" Tabitha shouted to the trees above.

"Brrrrradach! Hoh hê!"

"How do we find him?"

A bright beak jutted over the branch, and those wet eyes watched her.

"Setsun, setsun, *lwhoooo!*"

"We follow the sunset?" she asked, but the bird just squawked and took to the wing.

It was going to be impossible to follow the sunset in the forest, what with the overhanging trees and the mists above. Maybe the bird had a better idea, as it could rise above the canopy. The bird had darted off back the way they had come.

"I think we should go back," said Tabitha.

"You believe the bird?"

"It couldn't gain anything from lying."

"It also threw nuts at us," he reminded her. "It's just as likely to send us over a cliff!"

The Lûk were ancient enemies, but war was a fire that needed constant feeding. After four hundred years the fires of the Lûk hatred toward Eyrians must have long since burnt out. Surely they didn't have anything to fear from the Lûk?

A haunting sound came from deep in the forest ahead, a horn, perhaps. The gentlest of breezes pulled through the lichens, a damp spicy breath. Tabitha strained to reach out with her hearing. There were many small sounds, creatures in the undergrowth, birds flitting through the trees. Underneath those sounds she heard a trampling, like a herd of cattle on the move. Or people. The horn sounded again, a hollow woodwind tone. It was answered by another, closer, higher pitched; a few loose notes drifted past her. Then a flat drumming sound followed, slightly mistimed.

"Do you see them, Garyll?"

The gloom hid much of the forest on either side of the trail, but far away down the corridor of trees she could just make out the pale shape of another marker tree with its stained base, and around the tree poured figures, men with shields, bristling with spears. They came like ants from some secret chamber, a steady stream that diverged around the pale divider. They wore scarlet-and-orange headscarves, and their clothing fluttered as they ran. Tabitha couldn't be sure from that distance, but it appeared to her from what she could see of their faces and arms that their skin was grey.

"Do you see them?"

Garyll looked hard, but his expression remained puzzled.

"Where?"

"At the next marker tree!"

She had forgotten to allow for the advantage she had with the wizard's ring. It was warm on her finger; she drew on it without even thinking, it was a part of her now.

"Men?"

"Sort of. They move like men, they have spears and shields, and coloured headscarves."

"Ah, I see something now, just a bit of colour."

"How mengy?" asked Mulrano.

There were too many to count. The stream of warriors flowed past the pale tree and poured toward them on the mossy road.

"An army of them," she replied. "Two hundred, maybe more."

"Have they seen us yet? Are they running, or walking?" asked Garyll.

"Loping, I think."

"Then there's a hope their eyesight is as poor as mine," said Garyll, "we can still hide. Come, let us get off this trail."

"No, wait, Garyll." She tried to put her feeling into words. If this was the grey-skinned people's territory, hiding would do no good. She needed the help of the people of Oldenworld, to find where Bevn had gone, to find Ethea. They couldn't run from every danger; they'd just as likely stumble into some other threat in the gloomy forest. Besides, she was simply too tired to run. "I think we must meet them. We must stand."

"In the face of an army?" Garyll objected. "We shall be defenceless before them."

"Then they will have no reason to harm us. We have done nothing," Tabitha answered, feeling the deep truth of her words. She hoped her truthsense still worked, out here in Oldenworld.

"We did nothing to that colossal man in the wastes, and he was none too friendly," he reminded her.

The drumming sound was repeated, they were hitting their spears upon their tall curved shields as they ran. The leader raised a pipe to his lips; a few moments later the mournful call reached their ears.

"Stand by me, please," she implored him, holding onto his arm. He only met her eyes for an instant.

"I'll stand by you," he answered, "but I think you're being too trusting." He began to loosen his baton from his belt, but stopped. It would be useless against two hundred spears.

The tramping of many feet became louder, until it was more than near enough for the men to hear. The approaching warriors were chanting a song, one which passed backward through the phalanx as they jogged along.

"*Jorek, kahn, mirid, bakir—*" called four men in turn.

"*Jak jin jeer,*" they chorused.

"*Mrekken, tosti, ahhai, lôth—*"

"*Jerrik vinn nageer!*"

Their voices were strong and jubilant, if somewhat out of tune. Their faces were grey, with jutting chins and high-bridged noses, and their skin looked stony. Their foreheads shone like marble. Tabitha wondered if it was a kind of grit they pasted on their bodies. Darker whorls adorned their cheeks and necks. Their arms were marked as well. Their clothing was colourful and loose; their trousers ended in plaited tassels that flapped against their wide-toed boots.

The Eyrians stood side by side on the mossy road and awaited their old enemy.

The lead warriors became suddenly alert and the piper issued a sharp note. The warriors slid to a halt. Those farther back bunched up upon the lead members, jostling and muttering among themselves, but when they saw the Eyrians they become suddenly organised, their spears held ready, their shields covering their right flanks from ankle to shoulder. The piper disappeared through the front rank of warriors. The leaders were big, broad-shouldered fellows with heavy bands of black streaking up and away from their eyes.

The warriors approached slowly, like wolves that had sensed a hidden threat. They scanned the trees.

Tabitha spread her hands outward to show them she was harmless.

"*Yo chi carom!*" shouted one of the big leaders.

"*Bali beg skik elekelen?*" asked a second warrior, one who carried a bunched net in his free hand instead of a spear.

"*Isye hunterkinned?*" demanded a third.

The words sounded somewhat familiar, but the pronunciation was incomprehensible.

"*Whattaree beplace sofarrinnin llanderlûk?*"

The warrior shook his spear at them. Tabitha's heart sank. They spoke another language! How was she going to convince them of anything?

"We come in peace!" shouted Garyll. "We seek to talk with you, not to fight you."

The warriors paused, surprised.

"We have come from the desert," Tabitha added. "We are looking for the low lands."

"*Yo cajrek skol Koramandin?*"

"*Bridlok!*" a man with a thinner voice scolded from behind the leaders. "*Stan camtonden!*" A craggy-faced man pushed through the front rank. He wore a headscarf that was more gold than red, with heavier knots than the others. He brandished a finger at the warriors. "They use the tongue of the kingdoms three. Old tongue! You would this better recognise if you your full ten years with your tattler spent. *Dûnmarken!*"

The warriors looked belligerently at the elder but parted for him as he approached.

"Come you from the lowlands?" asked the elder.

"No, we come from Eyri, across the desert," answered Tabitha.

"South by two days, maybe three on foot," Garyll confirmed.

"Eyri! So the windrunners' tale is true!" the elder exclaimed. "But now you are in the land of Lûk!"

"*Ba tektek,*" he said in a low voice, and the warriors tensed.

Tabitha's heart began to flutter. The elder signalled and before Tabitha could do anything, a fine net whistled upon them. Even Garyll was caught by the speed of the cast. They tried to escape, but the double-layered net tangled them tighter with each movement. The grey-skinned horde encircled them quickly, their sharp-tipped spears angled toward the trio. Tabitha stopped struggling.

"On the knees," demanded the elder.

"Please, we haven't done a thing," she cried, "We come in peace! We weren't there when you fought in Eyri. We weren't there! Please, that was hundreds of years ago!"

The spears were so close. Patterns ran down the shafts, all the way to the hollow angled points. The tips were dark-stained. They had been used before.

"Jek? *Musti kan!* Are these the strangers for we looking are?"

A stern-looking fellow came up to look at them. His face was weathered; the whorls in his skin really did look as if they were carved in stone. The short sleeves of his shirt were tied off with loose ribbons at the elbows. His eyes held a smouldering anger, but he was restrained by a hard discipline.

"Boh! These are new to me." He bent close to Tabitha. "Do you know Bevinn and Gabreel?"

Tabitha looked at the man in surprise. He knew of Prince Bevn! But who was Gabreel? None other than the Shadowcaster, Gabrielle, she realised. They must be travelling together.

"Yes, I know of them," she said with guarded care. "Bevn is the prince of Eyri." So Bevn travelled with the Shadowcaster. She remembered the tracks across the desert, and wondered if the stone-skinned folk had helped Bevn and Gabrielle pass across the wastes. If that was true, then she shouldn't tell them that they were chasing Bevn. They should say that they were his friends.

"Are you with him, or against him?" demanded their stern-looking interrogator.

She paused, uncertain. Did the Lûk support Bevn? What if they were against him? Then lying wouldn't help her at all. She chose the truth.

"We are tracking him, we came to catch him. We must take him back to Eyri, before it is too late."

Their interrogator straightened. "Rook!" he exclaimed. "They carry justice! They are my friends!"

"Wait Jek, we know too little," said the elder. He faced Tabitha but didn't approach any closer. "Who are you in the land from where you say you come?"

"My name is Tabitha. I am a singer, I work with…magic." She waved her hands as well as she could, to indicate casting a spell.

An immediate tension ran through the men. The spears snapped into place, sharp points at the ready.

"*Daa! Bakrekishan!* You have been touched by the *dorra*?"

"No!" Tabitha answered, afraid to provoke them. "What is the dorra?"

"She is a healer," said Garyll. "A wizard."

"Wizzard?" said the elder with a hint of trepidation in his gravelly voice. "Alike the Sorcerer?"

"Like the Gyre, but not so strong, I am…new to it." Twardy Zarost hadn't spoken much about the Gyre, but she knew she didn't have anything near their level of power.

"Gyre," he said, rolling the word as if tasting it. "That's a word not many would know, or dare to speak, and so you prove yourself in the naming." He squinted at Tabitha. "A new wizard? There are only seven *mahgu* we know of, eight if you count the one who makes a riddle of them." The elder took half a step forward, and peered down at Tabitha as if she were a fascinating but deadly snake. "It is unexpected." His eyes narrowed. "The strike in *dorra* yesterday, the *sosisshon,* did you call that down?"

"The wildfire? I...didn't expect it. I didn't know it worked that way."

The elder looked puzzled. "Yet you say you are alike the Gyre? The *dorra*—wild fire—does not do this in Eyree?"

"Eyri has a shield...or it used to, until Bevn stole the crown." *And then I blew the Shield into the ever-and-never.* "We do not have this wildfire in Eyri."

The elder shook his head slowly, as if what she said was incomprehensible. "I cannot tell if you are a good thing for us, or bad," he said at length. "Who are your companions?"

"Garyll is—"

"I am her guardian," said Garyll from beneath the net. "And this is Mulrano, a fisherman. We come in peace."

The elder considered them for a long moment.

"It is strange in our land for a fisherman to have such a big axe," the elder commented.

"We have big fish in Eyri," Garyll replied with a knowing expression.

The elder laughed then, and the heavy knots of his golden headscarf danced. "You protect her," he said simply. He jerked his hand up and one of the warriors whisked the net away.

"Forgive us for the rough beginning." He helped Tabitha to her feet. "I am Spearleader Sihkran, from the Fifth *Dja*, or the Fifth *spoke* if I the right word have. I will allow passage through the six-sided land for those who know the business of the Gyre. We would not in their way get. Forgive us, we have strangers seldom in our land whom we wish to welcome, and your Bevinn has a bad introduction of your kind left."

"What has Bevn done?" Garyll asked.

A sadness shadowed Sihkran's stony face. "He killed two men. Captain Jek and his windrunners were hired for them across the wastes to bring, and so Jek would have, had the *bogadin* not pushed one windrunner into the *dorra* and let his woman the other kill. They escaped from the captain as well. I suppose that puts you in the same position as Jek here. We march now to Rôgspar and then into the Huntersland, to demand Bevn handed over be. We know that they have him. Jek tracked the boy and his woman to the forest, but only a fool would go into those parts with a small crew. The Hunters are savage with their arrows, but we have a full *Dja*. We are ready. We go."

They were going to seek out Bevn! Tabitha was overjoyed. "May we come with you?" she asked Sihkran.

Sihkran considered them for a long moment. "I believe not that you should the six-sided land alone wander. You will most likely for Hunters mistaken be. We almost that mistake made. It was a good thing you spoke in the Old Tongue when you did. We thought you part of an ambush were. We would have killed you."

He turned to the many warriors assembled around them, and addressed them in rolling Lûkish for some time. The men farthest away tried to peer over the shoulders of those in front to better see the strange trio from Eyri. There was much nodding and shared looks, then Sihkran raised his fist and the men slapped their spears against their shields and the piper blew his mournful tones.

"Come then," said Sihkran. "We run our justice into the Huntersland."

ଔଐଔଐ

Prince Bevn, *King* Bevn, was bored. They had been in the rank and dripping tent all day long, sitting out the rain, waiting for the Wizard Black Saladon to return from his "urgent matters", and now it was well into the night. All of the previous day, he'd just wished to reach the promised Hunter settlement, wished for a pause in Saladon's relentless pace, for shelter as the great cloud built over the forests and the heavy rain began to pelt down, but now all he wished for, was to leave.

Bevn sniffed. He'd thought Bradach Hide had been primitive. This place, Willower, was pitiful by comparison. It reeked of tar. The apex of the tent was only fifteen foot up the gnarled trunk they'd built it around, and it was made from patched hides sewn with thong stretched over curved saplings. The floor was mud. The fireplace was cold. The Hunters had told him it would remain so while it rained, for with fires you either got a closed tent with too much smoke, or an open-topped tent filled with rain and wet logs on the hearth. Bevn wished he didn't need their shelter, or he would have told them what he thought of their slack-wit architecture. Surely somebody in their in-bred family could work out a way to make a wretched covered flue. These people were dumb, they were ugly, and they were uncultured, the lot of them.

The only light came from three blackened oil lamps, which they hoarded at the main table around their game of *knuk*. It was a strategy game played with carved knuckles of wood. Bevn had been useless at it. After losing his blanket in his wager, he'd cursed the stupid game and had gone to sulk at a crumbling table with stumps for seats. A girl too young to waste his time on had given him a meal, but he'd left it half-eaten. The smoked meat he'd stolen from the shed outside had been better. She returned with a mug of juiced water, and he'd sent her away to get him the "heartwoodbrew" everyone else was drinking. He had no time to be treated like a child, especially by a scrawny maiden.

He was a grown man, he would be king. He was a king, he corrected himself. Blasted commoners!

He tried to drain the mug when it came, but it was too strong and bitter for him to stomach. He belched like a soldier and asked the girl for something wicked, like jurrum leaf, but she grew more and more puzzled, and he couldn't make her understand what he was asking her. Her affected language drove him mad.

She understood some of the names he called her well enough though, because she left in tears.

Stupid wench. She should learn to speak properly then he wouldn't have called her a cleft-tongued flat-chested hellhag. He wished the Hunter men would leave the main tent and go to their own hovels. He wanted to be left alone, so that he could try his luck with Gabrielle. She had drunk a good quantity of the heartwoodbrew, he had counted the servings—five whole mugs, and he knew now that it was heady stuff. Surely she would be pliable. In Ravenscroft he'd heard that if you made the women drunk enough, they would do anything. Anything!

He shifted on his seat; his trousers were uncomfortably tight again. Across the tent, Gabrielle laughed, and the lamplight caught her throat, her opened shirt. She had loosened another button, be damned if she hadn't! Men were gathered around her, watching her play *knuk* against a well-muscled veteran. The man made a move on the table and he took one of Gabrielle's pieces. The other Hunters cheered. Gabrielle smiled and slid her hand into her shirt. She slowly, slowly, let the button loose. Some dirty hunter woman scowled and left the tent. The men laughed and leant eagerly forward again to see what Gabrielle's move would be.

Bevn understood that the veteran was wagering mugs of ale, and she, the buttons of her shirt. She was teasing them, he could see it, the glistening interest in the men's eyes, their fascination. She was playing them; she would probably take the highest bidder to her bed, or name a price only an enthralled man would consider. There was something about her that made him want to compete too, and he couldn't figure out what it was that she did. It made him want to fight her. It made him want to own her.

The brew buzzed through his veins. The rain hammered with a hundred little fingers on the tent.

Why should *they* have her? It couldn't be too hard to convince her to lie with a king. He dwelled on that thought, over and over, as his courage swelled. He took another glug of drink then slammed it down. He *wouldn't* be afraid, not of a woman.

"Gabrielle!" He raised his voice to carry over the conversations at the main table.

She turned. Her dark eyes looked into his soul.

He swallowed. "It's time for us to go to bed."

Some of the men chuckled.

"Really?" she asked. Her eyes were girlish for a moment, but then she measured him with a level gaze.

"We...have a long way to go, tomorrow," he said.

She smiled a little smile. "That's sweet of you Bevn, to look out for me, but I can keep my own bed time. I'll be strong in the morning, ready to travel at Saladon's hard pace." She watched him still, but Bevn's eyes dropped to the open invitation of her shirt. One more button and her breasts would be properly exposed.

"I'm going to bed, then." He hated the way he wasn't saying what he wanted to say.

"I'll see you at dawn then." She raised her tankard to him.

Her knowing smile made his knees weak. *Ask her, damn it! You carry the command of the Kingsrim.*

"Join me." There, he had said it.

She smiled and looked puzzled for a long moment then her smile became a little twisted. "What do you have to offer in return? I can choose from many fine men tonight," she said. There was a spontaneous laughter from the Hunters. "Why should I choose you?"

She'd said that, out there in front of all of them. Bevn felt his ears warming. How dare she?

A few more men looked his way. Some grinned, some even laughed.

Damn her! I am the King! King! King! He clenched his teeth against the growing laughter. *I wear the Kingsrim! I should not be so challenged by a woman!*

"You shall earn my favour," he said, as regally as he could manage. When his father spoke like that, all manner of people would scuttle and fawn about. But the smile dropped off her face, and her gaze became cold and…sober.

"My price is far higher than that."

Money, money, all she thought of was money! Well, his family had lots of it, didn't they?

"I know how to get into the treasury in Stormhaven," he said.

"If it must still be stolen, then it is not yours to bargain with." Her voice was like ice.

"I will pay you a full gold now, then!" He had only a few Eyrian coins in his pocket. He didn't really know what one paid for a woman, but he guessed that was a fair exchange considering it was only one night.

Gabrielle's glare pinned him to the wall. "Even a bearded crone has more pride than to accept such an offer," she spat. "Your gold is worthless out here in the Huntersland. Run along to bed, little boy, and take your need to your palm."

His eyes stung with unshed hot tears, and a whispering anger rose on shadowed wings within him. She mocked him! She was making him look like a fool in front of these rough men.

He raised his voice. "You're just a greedy slut who is a few ruts short of growing deathrash!"

Gabrielle was up on the table and leaping for him before he could turn to run. She flew toward him, feet first. He tried to stumble out of the way, but she caught his head between her thighs and bore him down. He was trapped in a crushing grip, his head off the floor, looking up at Gabrielle. His crown slipped, and struck the ground behind him with a dull thud. She squeezed the life out of his neck. Her thighs gripped him like an iron clamp. Her cold fury washed over him.

"I was a Vortex of Ravenscroft, second only to the Darkmaster, you little worm! You apologise for what you called me, or it will end right here, right now! I don't care about the quest! I will not be called a slut! I choose who shall please me. I name the price. The pleasure is mine and not the other way around!"

He struggled against her grip. She was using this confrontation to make a point to all of the men present. He thrashed his legs, but could find no purchase. Then he saw the effect the Kingsrim had upon her, a shift in her eyes, one he recognised from the Penitent's pass. Even though it lay on the floor, it was close enough to affect her. His mistake had been to try to command her from across the room. He ripped at the back of her shirt, and she did not fight back. He clawed at her chest, pulling the shirt open to fully expose her breasts. Her face was a frenzy of anger and dismay. She slapped him, half-heartedly, but did not close the shirt. He panted from the panic and the rush of delirious excitement at what he could see. Her eyes were dark. He was between her legs. Her scratched breasts rose and fell above him, the nipples wide and protruding.

"Apologise," she said, in a quivering voice.

She was just a woman; she should pay for his humiliation. He was king!

"What's the difference?" he croaked belligerently. "You're either a slut or a whore."

He reached for the Kingsrim, but his crown, as if betraying him, rolled slightly farther away on the floor, and Gabrielle suddenly caught his right hand, and drew one of her knifes from the sheath on her hip. The blade was cold and sharp against the inside of his wrist.

"I will twist it once it's in. You will bleed to death slowly." Her words were as hard and certain as the blade. He looked into those dark eyes. She really was going to run the blade into him. He suddenly didn't want to fight her anymore. He knew that if he didn't plead with Gabrielle, right now, he was going to see his own blood. What had he been thinking? He didn't want to bleed.

"I'm sorry...I'm sorry, I didn't mean it, you're not a whore, I was just teasing, I've had too much to drink, I didn't think I'm sorry all right, I'm sorry!" He squealed as she gripped tighter with her legs. Something popped in his head, and he feared she was going to squeeze his neck right off. He couldn't breathe. He couldn't breathe!

She stepped away suddenly, and he fell on his back beside the toppled log.

"Don't you ever think to scorn me, or use me," she threatened. "It will cost you too much." She gathered her shirt across her bosom, and strode from the room. He almost puked, he was so relieved, humiliated and angry all at once. He just stared at the floor as the blood pounded in his head. When he stood at last, he tried to feign an indifferent air. He collected his crown from the floor, but his hands were shaking. Bevn righted his seat, but he was too hasty and the stump toppled over the other way. He left it and made for the exit.

"Ahey youngerly!" shouted a forester, "ye pickerwrong the night. She not inner vein fer randy."

The jest produced howls of laughter from the men.

"He gotterwhat he yen, didnatee? Kadam! right 'tween legs an lillies!" joked a scrawny grizzled fellow.

"Hayha, betruth! He gotterwhat he yen!"

Bevn tried to face them down with a glare, but that just produced more laughter.

He didn't have to take this from commoners! "Good night and good riddance," he said, but it was he who left the room. The laughter followed Bevn out of the door. He walked away, into the rain.

Cursed tent-dwellers, cursed tents. Compared to Willower, even Fendwarrow was a centre of high culture. These people only knew how to hunt creatures in the forest. They were primitive barbarians. What did he care what they thought of him? He didn't care. They were commoners. Hang them all! His cheeks cooled slowly in the wet gloom. He walked for a while without noticing anything, just seeing it all playing over and over in his mind.

He should have drawn that knife himself, the one in her belt—pushed it into her kidneys, sliced her belly, or found the softness of her loins. He'd reacted too slowly, because of the heartwoodbrew. Gabrielle should be crying now. She should be begging for his mercy, not laughing at his impotence. He would make her sorry she'd scorned him.

Bevn strode onward through the gentling rain. The humiliation followed him like a damp shadow.

The Kingsrim wasn't working the way he'd expected. He'd wanted a powerful domination of the kind the 'stones had offered the Darkmaster, but something had gone wrong. It seemed he couldn't just wear a talisman and have power automatically. He still lacked the kind of mightiness his father had, a presence that made people do things just because they'd been asked to serve the King. Maybe he had to act more boldly, more violently, to earn her fear then her respect. Maybe he had to be more of a man. Then the Kingsrim would work properly. He spat into the drizzle, like they used to in Ravenscroft after eating jurrum. He wished he was stronger. He wished he was older. He wished he was a Sorcerer already.

Life was so unfair.

He trudged on through the drizzle.

Voices came to him, voices out in the dark forest. Bevn slowed. The drizzle stopped, but water dripped off everything, making a random pitter-patter upon the leaves of the forest floor. The air was still thick with moisture and threads of mist, full of softness, which muffled the words. He strained to hear. He had to get closer. He sidled to the nearest great tree.

What would drive people to meet outside in such foul weather? Only secrets, or dark deeds.

He edged past the spreading roots. The voices came from beyond a cluster of moss-covered boulders, where a light flickered against a lopsided tree-trunk. Bevn moved as silently as a mouse to the closest cover. Then he recognised one of the voices, rumbling and deep, powerful despite being hushed. Black Saladon was back! He would tell the wizard what Gabrielle had done to him. No, the wizard would just laugh at him.

He listened. The second voice was weird and textured, almost gristly.

"I am b-busy w-with the G-Goddess, shhhe will sing for me s-s-soon."

It wasn't a nervous stutter. It was unsettling in a shivery way.

"Comrade, you shall have no interference," answered Saladon. "The Gyre is without the knowledge it needs. I have covered all the places where the book might be. The lore is destroyed."

"D-d-don't be too sure of yourself, that's open t-to failure, like all ordered th-things."

The stranger Saladon was speaking to wasn't a Hunter, because he didn't speak in slithery-blithery dialect. He pressed himself close to the boulders. The light thrown against the trees changed, bright then pale, grey then green then dirty yellow. Little patterns danced upon the bark, faint moving images. He wanted to look over the boulders, but he was scared Black Saladon could sense the Kingsrim. That was how he had found Bevn in Ravenscroft. He supposed Saladon might even sense him behind the boulders—he wouldn't be able to hide near the wizard for long. His curiosity burned like hot rum within his belly.

"They are caught flat-footed right now, the Writhe took their strength."

"You are s-so certain that the crown shall b-be their unwinding."

"It has a trace of each of their souls, yes. It is the symbol of their hope."

"But y-you must bring it to Turmodin, or it remains that w-way. I w-want to work with that boy b-before they know that anything has happened."

Was 'the boy' him? Was it the crown of Eyri they talked about? He was suddenly breathless. He had to know. Who Saladon was talking to? He eased slowly up to see over the mossy barrier. In the angled hollow beneath the lopsided tree was a sphere of watery silver light. Black Saladon stood between the light and Bevn, the sharp cut of his mantle raised across his broad shoulders, his single plait falling from his shaven scalp and his battleaxe tilted to one side. Saladon steamed as if he had made his body hot to dry himself from the rain.

The light swelled, dancing over the leaves and roots, delicate, searching. Bevn couldn't see all the way around Black Saladon, but there was a shape there, formed within the watery light, part of a face, many times too big—a hideous face, pasty white, pinched beyond ugliness. The single eye was greatly distorted, as if it was pressed against a glass ball, and the eye was unsteady, quivering yet intent. There was a horrible sensation, as if his body had been rippled by a passing wave in the air. Bevn's knees went weak; he slipped down behind the boulders.

Bad things had leaked out from that wobbling gaze, very bad things.

Whoever it was, wasn't actually there. Saladon was talking to him through a spell.

"How close is the moment of the invocation?" Black Saladon asked.

"Soon, soon. The bird shall s-s-sing, to be done with her m-misery; her b-bloodbath has reached her knees, and she has b-begun to understand what it is for. When the Goddess c-c-cracks, the fires shall be lit."

"Have the clerics from Qirrh built the pyre?"

"They have d-done up to the arms of the w-wicker man. A few days m-more."

"Still they do not understand?"

"Understanding is n-not everything. They will be g-g-grateful to perform the final ceremony, to f-f-find peace. Where are the other w-w-wizards?"

"I watched them today. Three are in the Sanctuary, three are still recuperating in infinity, and the Riddler is abroad. I suspect he is following the trail of the book. He knows how important that missing knowledge is to the Gyre. He went to Qirrh, but I lost his trace after that."

"H-he m-may have returned to his student in Eyri."

"I don't think so. He believes her to be safe there. He does not know about the crown yet, or he would be here in Willower."

"You are c-c-confident you can h-handle him if he comes?"

"The Riddler?" Saladon snorted. "I can handle him. That was the plan."

"You believe too s-s-strongly in plans."

"This one is infallible."

"Then tell me about the young man who rides in the sky."

"Who?"

"Something t-t-triggered the wildfire, s-something near to you in the m-midlands, maybe the w-w-wastes."

"I guessed that from the clouds. I can't say what set the web off. I wasn't here at the time. It might have been any one of the wizards. It might have been nothing. What man?"

"He was y-y-young, he r-rode through my cloud on a w-winged creature. He shouted at me. At me!"

"So what? Many things you have touched take to the air before they die. He was probably the spawn of the wildfire strike."

"Yes, but what tripped the wildfire? Someone was using magic! Are you sure it was n-n-not your little thief from Eyri?"

He's talking about me. I'm not a thief! The crown is mine! My father set it down.

"He has no mage skills yet," answered Black Saladon. "So far he is just proving to be an idiot."

Bevn almost jumped up to challenge that. *How dare he? I'm not an idiot! Who is he to call me an idiot?*

"Stupid is b-better than b-bright, then he won't get c-c-clever ideas of his own."

"He's not stupid," Saladon disagreed. "He's idiotic, wilful. He behaves like a child."

Bevn did jump up this time. "I'm not a child!" he shouted at Saladon's back. He leapt over the boulders and ran down to the wizard. He slapped Saladon's mantle aside. He didn't have quite enough courage to actually hit the wizard himself. "Take that back! I'm not a child!"

Saladon stiffened. In front of him, the white-faced apparition looked up in surprise, then horror. The silvery light turned golden, shrieked like hot metal being suddenly cooled, and was gone.

Saladon's backhanded blow lifted Bevn out of his boots. An impossible weight in his head swung him away. The thunder of the blow shook his body like a rag. He hit the ground and skidded into the mossy boulders.

"Bloody imbecile!" Saladon shouted, moving closer, towering over him. "You pissing ignorant prawn!"

Bevn could taste blood in his mouth. Some of his teeth were loose, and his lips trembled. A horrible unstoppable wail welled up from inside him. *He's hit my teeth out! He's hit my teeth out! He's hit my teeth out*, Bevn thought in a screaming panic.

"What are you doing spying on *me*?" demanded Saladon. "Do you know how rare an audience with the Sorcerer is? Do you know how difficult it is to set up a link to Turmodin from here? You blasted faecal idiot!"

That was the Sorcerer? That hideous pasty-faced stuttering creature? The freak appeared to have only one eye. Bevn gulped down a breath and tried to deny the second sob. "But that couldn't be Ametheus. He was as ugly as a boiled bullfrog!"

Bam! Saladon rapped his head on the ground, again and again.

"Don't say his name! Don't say his name. Don't. Say. His name."

Bevn burst into tears, shameful hot, weakling tears, but Saladon carried on beating him. *Ametheus is an ugly freaking bastard*, Bevn thought, as his tears burned down his cheeks. *Ugly, ugly, ugly, and Saladon is a stinking mean bully who doesn't have any friends*. He cried and cried until Saladon finally dropped him in the mud.

The wizard left him. As he passed the boulders, he threw Bevn a parting comment. "I'll make you look far worse than him if you don't follow my orders. Don't *ever* spy on me again."

Bevn pressed himself to the ground, expecting a final blow, but the wizard's footfalls faded into the dripping sounds of the misty forest.

He spat out a tooth with a mouthful of his own blood, and cried some more at the horror of it. The ground was wet, and his tooth glistened in the muck like a ghostly root. He was changed forever now; he'd never get that tooth back in his head. He was disfigured! The forest was dark, now that the strange sorcerous light had gone. He wanted to puke. Was he going to die, with all the blood that was coming out of him? He had had enough of this adventure, altogether enough. He just wanted to go home. He'd even give the stupid Kingsrim back, if he could. Just to be home. Life was too strange in Oldenworld.

22. THE MUSIC, THE RHYTHM

"Love leads a dance to a secret end
and you cannot see around the bend."—Zarost

The Lûk took them to the border town, a woven and wonderful *down* known as Rôgspar. It was like stepping into a festival in a rabbit hole. The gaiety in the spicy underground air seemed at odds with the weapons stacked against the walls. The warriors expected to confront the Hunters from Bradach after only a day's march, but here, for a brief precious night, they could relieve the tension of the impending battle.

They were celebrating, yet their expressions remained stony. The Lûk's features were difficult for Tabitha to read. There was so much about the Lûk and their world that was strange—the sensuous flex of their fabrics, the curling aromas of sharp herbs, the patterns which covered everything in sight from the carpeted floor to the clay-fired cups to their curved eating utensils. The Lûk women had colour painted around their eyes, a twisting stripe banded with gold. Their faces seemed even more elongated than those of the men. In profile they looked like crescent moons, and the light glinted in their eyes like little stars. Even the radiant purple *mishkr* criss-crossing the roof had been smeared in lazy loops and spirals instead of straight lines. Firefly tubes sputtered on the woven walls and along the radiating passageways. The central chamber was warm with bodies, the air close with the bearable stink of warriors, incense and spice. Sounds were softened by the curving walls and layered mats.

Lûk musicians played pipes, chanted and beat upon paper drums. Their music was lilting, arrhythmic and discordant; mournful, yet enchanting. Passion wove through the air.

Tabitha took a sip of her mulled wine. Some of her strength had returned. They had given her one of their daft knotted headscarves to wear, the *bong*, except that hers was a plain earthy tone, with no patterning but for a small twist of orange on the hem. Sihkran had assured her that the lack of pattern on the *bong* was a sign of courtesy not of disrespect. They couldn't write her story upon it because they didn't know her yet and couldn't tell what pattern she represented or where her pattern might lead. It was a gift; it had fresh herbs in the knots. Sihkran had insisted that she cover her hair in the central chamber; Mulrano and Garyll had been obliged to do the same. Hair was considered to be an item of great value, and to expose one's hair in company was considered rude among the Lûk, especially for one with such a wealthy head of hair as Tabitha. The warriors, she discovered, were all shaven-headed beneath their ochre bongs.

Sihkran extracted a scroll from the wall. He laid it open on the table, revealing intricate artwork which glistened in the light—the villages and towns rendered in fine detail, the graphic landmarks, the winding rivers and trails.

"This came with a runner from Koom today. It is a great gift. It is one drawn in this time, it has things… Jhanmestikan! Look for this! It has the line of the *dorrabalaan*."

The tall warrior beside Sihkran peered over his shoulder, his eyes poking at the map like a man searching for a fish with a spear.

"I do not know this picture."

"Yes, Jhan, it is new! See, the Sorcerer's…worm…through from here to here ate."

"*Ai-oi!*" the warrior exclaimed. He began to quiver with excitement, looking from the map to Sihkran and back again. He clasped his shaking hands quickly behind his back and thrust his nose at the vellum, closer than he needed to be, dragging his eyes across the page.

"I do not know it!"

He was horrified by it, not excited, Tabitha realised.

"Have you forgotten?" Sihkran asked in a soft voice. "Jhan, have you the skill lost?"

"I…"

The two Lûk shared a long moment.

"Ah, Jhan, that is too sad. You have still your words, *nê*? So all is well. Feast well tonight! In the morning can you your anger to the battlefield take."

Sihkran clasped the man's arms. Jhanmestikan broke from his hold and hurried away through the clustered crowd who brushed him with their outstretched hands.

"And so the Sorcerer more from us steals. Oh! How we him hate."

"What happened to Jhanmestikan?"

"It is most sad," replied Sihkran. "He has forgotten…how to read it."

Tabitha saw a fire in the Spearleader's eyes that was shared by many throughout the chamber. The Lûk down had become suddenly hot.

"Yes, Tabitha Mahgu, we lose our talents to *him*." He punctuated the word with three raised fingers jerked into the air. "We write the history on the walls, we record our culture in the story-patterns. We write even *how* to write, in case that is from our minds next taken, but the Chaos erodes everything like water that through saltrock eats. We write our name-stories upon these bongs...so we do not forget. We will not become like the Hunters, broken into tribes, no! We bind ourselves together. We learn the ten tongues. Yet nothing in this world can be relied upon. We do not know where the wildfire will strike next, what will stagger out of the wastes and fall upon us, who within us will be struck by the silverblight. We live under the scourge of the Sorcerer."

"Do the Lûk ever use magic, Sihkran?" she asked. "Do you have wonder-workers?"

"Well no, not within us, but we have the *Mahgu*, the wizards. We see little of them. The wizards are not Lûk. They are an unchanged race, more like you than me, yes indeed. They have been with us since the old times, but they have done little to stop he who can not be named. They merely seem to limit his effect."

"But where are they?" Tabitha asked. "Can they be found?"

If she could just contact them, any one of them, she could find out so much; the Riddler most of all. Twardy Zarost would know what she should do, or he'd ask her just the right kind of infuriating questions to drive her to find the answer herself. Had the wily wizard returned to Eyri and found her missing? Would he look for her? She had thought of sending a butterfly to find him, as she had done before, but that would require using the essence, and that seemed to trigger the wildfire. She desperately needed to know how to use her power in this hostile world.

"In Koom, in the capital of our six-sided land, there know they such things as wizards," answered Sihkran, "but I think not they can ever be summoned, they just come, usually when we don't want them to. Always are they harbingers of coming sorrow. When the Writhe came through they appeared, to warn us of the path of destruction. I suppose we did save much due to their efforts. Nonetheless, one does not usually look forward to meeting a wizard."

"What was the Writhe?"

"The *dorrabalaan*? You told me of the valley you walked in the wastes. The shattered rock? That was the tail of the Writhe. That is the remains of the spell. It was the worst that the Sorcerer has unleashed upon us in all these years. It tore through the length of the Six-sided Land. Even farther than that! It punctured the Winterblades before it struck upon our homeland, so it must have crossed the lowlands too. Some say it stretches back all the way to the Pillar. Who knows where it ended?"

The Pillar in the lowlands! Sihkran knew of the Pillar, where Ethea was confined.

"How far is it to the lowlands? How far to the Pillar?"

"To Turmodin? No one knows for sure, no one has the lowlands for centuries travelled, no one would want to. It is a wild place with the worst *dorrakaan*—silverspawn—deadly, vicious beasts. But Slipper at the border to reach would take a runner on the woven roads near to a sevenday. Longer, now that so much of the weave has been damaged. Beyond Slipper? Who knows. Another sevenday? Two? Who cares? You can not in that land travel. It belongs to the Sorcerer."

Tabitha glanced down at the chart. "Is that why there is nothing marked in the lowlands?"

"The land changes too fast there. Nobody can it chart. Who would want to?" Sihkran turned to give her a hard look. "Nothing there but Chaos. Nothing but death, for all of us."

Tabitha began to appreciate the scale of what she was attempting. They had walked a tiny portion of the distance to the Winterblade mountains, and beyond that there was a vast area of uncharted land, before Turmodin. She slumped against Garyll. Ethea didn't have weeks left, she had days, possibly only hours. But if the lowlands were so far away, and so dangerous to travel through, how would they ever save the Goddess in time? They might catch Bevn, but what then? Without the Goddess Ethea, there would be no Lifesong. Tabitha was certain the whole world would begin to crumble and die without Ethea's vital power.

Maybe she was wrong; maybe the world would carry on, without the music. Most people didn't even know there was a song beneath the surface of life. She hadn't really known herself, until she had become a wizard. Maybe, even if Ethea died, life would persist, but what kind of life would it be, without the Lifesong? It was too sad to consider.

"The Sorcerer is everywhere in Oldenworld. We have a hard enough time surviving here, so far from Turmodin," said Sihkran.

"Is that why you live underground?" asked Garyll. "Because of the Sorcerer?"

"Because of the *Dráák*," Sihkran replied, looking puzzled. "You don't know *Dráák*? Ah, they were *dragons* in the Old Tongue, they are *kriklik*—hated—things spawned in the lowlands at the end of the time of Kingdoms Three. Their only value is in their scales. It can shield against wild fire. It is why they survive. They cannot be changed anymore, they are resistant to the Sorcerer's magic. We get our scales from the northern settlements like Kah and See'gi. They get the worst of it when the Dráák down from the Winterblades swoop, but at least they get a shower of scales to trade with. We see seldom the Dráák this far south, it is too warm for them here so close to the wastelands, but it never pays to be complacent with such creatures, especially in winter when the air is cold enough their roaming range to extend. The Hunters have the forest to protect them but most of our Six-sided Land is grassed and open to the sky. Only along our western border have we the sheltering trees, but there is just as much danger within the tangled undergrowth as there is within the Winterblade dragon-caverns."

"Now after so many years of underground living, it seems strange any other way to live. We have perfected the ways of constructing downs. We have a network of woven roads, underground, that link the heartland together. Only outlying settlements like Rôgspar and Graa have surface roads. Many Lûk need not go outside at all."

"Yet you warriors risk it, to face down the Hunters," Garyll noted.

"That is another matter! We avenge the death of our windrunners. They have sheltered the murderers who came from your land. They will regret it!"

"Show for us this Eyri," he demanded.

"Where are we now?"

He stabbed his blunt finger down on a bright dot.

"That's Roguespar?" she asked.

"Rôgspar, Kurum, Spek, Flek, Sark, Kem." He worked his way around the hexagonal land of the Lûk, "and Koom at the heart. The wastes you passed over are here. The Winterblades here, on our northern border."

The highlands and lowlands were spread out before them. Eyri was not marked on the map; Tabitha supposed that for most people in Oldenworld it did not exist. She could guess where it lay, near the bottom of the page, beyond the swathe of contaminated silver-sands. How long before the Sorcerer's influence crept into Eyri and stole the Order and the Eyrian culture with it, now that the Shield was broken?

She touched her finger to the vellum, just west of a great range of mountains, south of wastes.

"Jek-ai!" Sihkran called out. The windrunner captain came close. "Jek? Is this the place?"

Jek nodded. "As near as a cable. You say your land lies beyond it? I saw nothing but sands there."

"It was hidden by a Gyre spell," Tabitha offered.

"I do not understand such things," Sihkran admitted, "but maybe that magic is to blame for all the wild fire that comes upon the wastes. It is said that magic draws magic upon itself."

Tabitha had never thought of that. There were a great many things she would ask Twardy Zarost when next she saw him. Too many mysteries were unexplained, not least of which was the Gyre.

They spent a long time over the treasured map, exploring its arcane knowledge until the meal was called. The scribe must have been paid handsomely for the map. It was a wonderwork of detail cleverly layered in subtle colours. The sheer scale of Oldenworld took Tabitha's breath away. Her homeland was a fold in a great page of humanity.

There was much to eat, for the men of the Fifth Dja had brought supplies from Koom and See'gi to replenish the depleted Rôgspar stores—flour, oatcakes, sugarcane, fruit, wine and barleybree. Something they called *takatakêk* had been unlucky enough to linger in the warriors' path.

"We have a saying in Lukish," said Sihkran. "*Takatakêk maradin lek, basti kum kerêk*. When a... pheasant...speaks of its own greatness, it will soon be crowned."

After a moment of puzzlement Garyll replied "What does it mean?"

"It ends up in the pot."

Mulrano burst into laughter, and after a surprised silence the Lûk joined him. They delighted in the sound of the fisherman's laugh. Every time he laughed they responded with a greater roll. Theirs was a deep and different sound, like river-pebbles being rolled in a drum, a rumbling *hoklok-hoklak-hoklok*.

The *takatakêk* was very tasty.

Skewered mushrooms followed the stew, a twisted bread called *magding*, and a pale mash of *nobki* that arrived in warmed clay bowls. It was spiced with a sweet cinnamon flavour and it melted in her mouth. And they loaded it in. Garyll grinned at her as he accepted a third bowl of *nobki* from the tireless serving-man. Mulrano was not shy either, but even he pushed his bowl away at last.

Lûk children came to clear away the remains of the meal. They seemed to know how to behave without becoming noisy, but a young rapscallion tried to feel her arm. He seemed puzzled by her soft skin. "*Watai!*" Sihkran scolded the boy. He dropped his hands and backed away at once, and the adults clicked their tongues like mocking crows.

An old, grinning woman began to tap her palms against a set of small tubular drums. A flute joined her in a minor tone. The Lûk musicians played a short piece, lilting and arrhythmic. Then someone called out, "A song from land Eyri!" and other voices joined in chorus. "Singsong! Singsong!"

"Will you for us sing?" asked Spearleader Sihkran.

The room grew still around Tabitha, and she set her sharp-edged spoon down beside her plate of food. A *kutl*, they called it. Tabitha wondered if they were expecting a demonstration of magic from her or just a melody.

"Can you?" repeated Sihkran. "Something from your homeland."

Tabitha hesitated. She'd told them that she was a singer; she hadn't explained about the Lifesong. Singing that was out of the question. "Can it be a simple song, not one of my special art?" she asked.

"Yes, Tabitha *Mahgu*, whatever you are happy to sing. We will like to share your culture."

Singing to the Lûk would be a small way to repay their hospitality. A ripple of excitement passed through the gathered Lûk. Garyll handed her lyre to her, one of her few things which had been saved from the saddlebags. "A moment, please," she said. Tabitha spent a few minutes tuning the strings, which had stretched badly during the rains. With each note the Lûk leant inward to capture the sound, then muttered and whispered among themselves, jostling to get a closer position without crowding her. She managed to find a serviceable chord, and tightened the strings on their keys. The body of the lyre was true—the strangle-oak would hold its shape forever, she suspected.

She chose an easy melody to warm up her voice, a joyful madrigal known as *Rain upon Barley*.

From the moment she began, she could see that the Lûk were more fascinated with her music than she had been by theirs. Even the giggling children fell silent, rapt. Her fingers danced over the lyre strings. She was glad to be playing music again, ordinary music, with no magic apart from the special joy of being a singer. The song made the world more familiar, filling the air with ordered rhythms, the culture of Eyri. Her homeland surrounded her.

Tabitha expected some kind of applause when she brought the song to a close, but her final note faded into a dense silence. The Lûk watched her. Tabitha's attention flickered through the chamber—not a single brightly scarved head moved, not a single body shifted. A toddler cried and ran for its mother's arms, unsettled by the tension in the air, the strange vigil of the adults; it was settled with a quick "*osh!*" from its mother.

She smiled nervously, but nobody smiled back. They appeared wooden, shocked, their expressions unreadable, implacable and terribly sober. It must have been a lyric in the *Rain upon Barley*, she decided, she must have offended a custom or rule through her ignorance. She was about to apologise when the elder Sihkran raised his hand.

"Another?" he asked, in a whisper. "Please, another."

They were awed, not offended. She saw the sparkle in their eyes now, the anticipation. They wanted her to sing. Tabitha settled the lyre against her shoulder again, and the Lûk breathed a communal sigh. She played *Haven from the Storm*, *I Come Home*, and *Love is in the Air*. The warriors and womenfolk were transfixed. If anything, their rapture grew as Tabitha gave more heart to each song.

"Sings Garyll?" asked Sihkran.

"No," he answered curtly.

"Oh, come on!" Tabitha cajoled. "You can sing the tavern-song *Fynn Fell Down*, at least."

Garyll tried to hold a stern expression, but the Lûk began to clap in time and stomp their feet, and his scowl faded. Tabitha played an introductory bar on her lyre, and let her voice fly.

Mulrano began to hum a counter-harmony to the song in a deep bass tone, surprising Tabitha. They sang *Fynn Fell Down* together, and toward the end even some of the Lûk joined the chorus once they'd learnt the words.

When Captain Jek requested a tenth song, Tabitha had to decline.

"My fingers ache," she explained, raising her voice to carry throughout the chamber. "Please, that is all for now. I must rest my singing voice. I hope you all liked it. I would love to hear more of your own music tonight."

That broke the spell. They applauded her in the Lûk way, with whistles, yelps and trills, which filled the down to the far ends of the passageways. The children danced about and began to chase each other.

A serving-man appeared at Tabitha's side with some goblets of dark brew. She sipped at the spicy dark fluid. It did little to soothe her throat, but it shot warmth and excitement through her blood.

Sihkran came forward.

"Thank you, Tabitha *Mahgu*, thank you! Tonight, have you shown us something we did not know."

"I enjoyed your culture and your music just as much," she replied, bowing gratefully.

"It is more than culture," Sihkran insisted. "No, it is far more than the joy of a tradition from a place we did not know existed to taste. Your music brings for us a gift that we can not equal."

"It was not the Lifesong, they were just traditional Eyrian ballads—many other singers sing them."

"Then must Eyri a truly blessed place be to live, to have such tradition."

"But you have your own music, quite beautiful itself!" Tabitha objected.

"Ah, but some of us the difference recognise. Yours is truer, it is older, far older than ours. It stirs something in our blood, an ancient memory. Something we knew, but have forgotten. Something we once had, but have lost. You gave it back to us, in the moment of your singing. Your music is together in a great pattern tied, a regular pattern, a...*now* and *then*."

Sihkran's brow furrowed as he searched for the right words to express what he was thinking.

"You mean rhythm?"

"Yes!" he exclaimed. "But it is more than that alone. Everything is in the place wherein it should be. You share something that structure has. Orderliness."

"That is what we have in Eyri: Order."

"I fear we have all but forgotten what that is. That is why your music us so moves. In my blood, I remember a time of order. We thought we had much of it retained, but when we your first song heard, could we hear that we had lost it long ago."

"We have been protected from the touch of the Sorcerer, but without the Kingsrim that Bevn has stolen, the spell cannot hold together, and our king cannot maintain his control. The wildfire will touch Eyri."

"And so turn it also to Chaos," finished Sihkran. He stood silently for a moment. "This Bevn must be stopped, if the last place of Order shall be lost to the world without the Kingsrim. Such a rare thing must be preserved. We have heard its value tonight; we have the product of such a place in the three of you seen. The world would poorer be, without your kind."

"Don't judge us all by her perfection, Sihkran," Garyll interjected. "Tabitha is not...typical of Eyri. Very few have her heart, or her talent."

Tabitha shot him an admonishing glance, but he held her eyes with a confident gaze. She turned back to Sihkran.

"I see you are weary, Tabitha *Mahgu*, forgive me. We have talked too long and hard on sober matters. This night is meant for celebration! Enough! We must be strong for the morning. Would you like to rest, now? *Sunni! Musti kan!*"

A girl came forward, her grey skin as smooth as polished marble, her rounded cheeks marked with red circles. She had a sweeping stripe above and below her eyes, and a pale flaxen headscarf with rounded knots.

"Please, take our guests to a *kott*, see that they have all they need," said Sihkran. He turned back to Tabitha and Garyll. "My daughter will show you to a place for the night."

"Thank you, Sihkran. You have been very generous."

"As have you. I shall your special songs in my head for many years keep."

"Good night, Spearleader," Garyll said. "My thanks as well."

"*Moji jan kerilak*, may your bed warm be." He smiled, and his stony skin folded in deep seams beside his eyes.

Tabitha looked around for Mulrano. He was the centre of an animated group of Lûk. A stout woman was showing him a system of hand-signals, among much disagreement and laughter from the cluster of Lûk men. He saw Tabitha and Garyll watching him and he waved them on with a big grin.

Sihkran's daughter led them away from the central chamber along a gently sloping passageway. She gathered a glowing tumbler of purple liquid along the way, which she held high as they walked, casting a pool of hazy light that picked out the rough threads and reinforced ribs of the corridor ahead of them.

Tabitha reached for Garyll's arm, and pulled him closer to her side. The sound of merriment floated after them, fading, until it was as soft as a murmur. They passed woven circles of colour, doorways into private rooms, she supposed. She hoped she would share a room with Garyll. She didn't want to be parted from him tonight.

Their *kott* turned out to be a private space no bigger than standing room for the two of them, and an alcove hidden behind a patterned silk curtain with a steaming washing bowl. The bed was a tunnel, set at waist-height in the wall. A wide reed mat supported an arrangement of fluffy blankets of beautiful colours. A long roll of stuffed fabric formed a soft pillow. Tabitha wondered if all the Lûk slept in such cosy cubicles. They thanked Sihkran's daughter and bade her good night.

The pale light, left in the corridor outside, did little more than throw a mauve colour upon the curtain. Inside, their room was almost dark, warm and scented. Garyll shed his heavy cloak, kicked off his boots, hesitated for a moment, then took off his belt as well. "You wash first. You're the smelliest!"

"I am not!" But she knew she was just as ripe as the men. It had seemed to be Lukish culture to eat first and wash later. She began to undress, and her pulse thundered as she considered how far she would go in front of Garyll. She wanted to tease him; she wanted to watch him undress too. They were alone at last. She drew a shuddering breath and took her jersey off. She watched him watching her in her criss-crossed halter top and rough riding leathers. It was hot in the Lûk down. She stepped up to Garyll.

"Here, lose this funny headscarf," said Tabitha. It was white with amber knots, just a pale shape now in the darkness. "It makes you look like the court fool."

"A fool for your beauty," he replied. "Your singing was special. It helped me to remember as well. This world is so…different, in many ways. It is good to know you haven't changed."

"Liar," she teased, running her fingers through his hair. It was short now, it had been so ever since he'd cut his soldier's tail off and set aside his great sword. "You're enjoying watching me change."

She pulled him down and kissed the corner of his mouth, where he was laughing.

He tasted faintly of the Lûk's sweet *nobki* dessert, slightly spicy from their wine, but mostly like Garyll.

She stepped out of her trousers, letting them lie on the floor. She pulled him gently toward the bathing room then reached up and untied the braid which bound her hair. It cascaded over her shoulders.

He watched her for a delicious moment then lifted his tunic over his head. Tabitha's heart raced. She knew they shouldn't be together, but thinking about that only seemed to make it more exciting. There were rules to follow, especially since she was a lady now. Lady Tabitha.

Silly titles. Silly rules.

She reached out and touched his chest. His skin felt smooth under her fingers. They weren't in Eyri anymore, they were far beyond it. She could live her life differently out here. She didn't need rules to live her life by. The rules were empty things, she decided, it was her pounding heart that mattered most.

Her resistance slipped away as easily as her own halter top fell off her shoulders as she undid the knot.

The steam of the bathing bowl caressed her back. She reached back and dipped a cloth into the water, soaking it wet and warm. She explored her man with her hands as she washed him. His body was so much bigger than hers, his chest so wide—his arms so full and firm. Tabitha kissed him in the centre of his breastbone, where his muscles formed an indentation above the ridges of his stomach. He smelled of the soapberry the Lûk had dissolved in the water, a pungent scent, refreshing, like the juice of a burst orange.

She coaxed him further against the wall, letting him push against her, until his weight was wonderfully heavy against her hips, trapping her. He kissed her, and she gripped his head with her hands, pulling at him, wanting him, needing him. Garyll dragged a wet cloth up her back; the warmth washed her thighs. He drenched the cloth and soaked her shoulders and neck, turned her so the soapy water ran down her body, glistening like a statue in the summer rain. When he slipped his hand up her wet chest, the weight of passion felt heavy in her breasts. He brought his breath down upon her skin. Tabitha was aware of nothing except the way the skin tightened so eagerly in anticipation of his lips and his tongue upon her. A growing breathlessness spread through her like an intoxicating paralysis.

"We have to stop," Garyll whispered.

"Ohhh," she said, closing her eyes, shuddering against him. "We don't *have* to, do we?"

"Yes, we have to." Uncertainty choked his voice and he pushed her gently toward the bed. The passion hung in the air like smoke against a windless sunset, red and clustered upon itself. Garyll joined her under the covers. She still wanted him terribly, but he was holding back. She could feel the tension in his body. He wanted her too; the pressure of his need was fierce against her back when he held her.

"Why do you deny yourself what is offered?" she asked into the dark.

"It is not mine to take," he answered in a low voice. "Only a weak man would take advantage of your innocence."

"I would not offer myself to a weak man."

"I am trying to be strong, Tabitha," he said through gritted teeth. "It is harder than ever before. I don't know why, but I feel the passion of ten men tonight. Please, I don't want to fail you."

"I'm scared of you Garyll, when you do that! It is not strength, it is punishment, as if you have done wrong by thinking of loving me. You cannot fail me by loving me. You hurt me when you spurn me so. Why do you do it? Why do you do it?"

Garyll was silent in the dark for what seemed like forever.

"I don't deserve you, my beauty."

"If not you, then who would be worthy? Who must I love? By the sun and the moon and the stars, Garyll! You are everything I want."

His shoulders were firm against hers. "Maybe I am not ready to stop punishing myself." Then there was a warm wetness upon her cheek, a tear fallen from his eyes. He whispered, his breath moved through her hair, his words soft against her ear.

The wildness of that gentle hand
The pain! Oh love! You do not see!
You reach within my stubborn heart
And touch me with your peace.
A violence done unto my soul
Fury, fire; sweet release.

Tabitha lay still. The beautiful words lingered in the dark. "What was that?" she asked in a quivering voice.

"A poem," he said simply, kissing the edge of her ear.

"You wrote it?" The words were so powerful, so personal, heartfelt.

"I did," he answered. She turned in his arms to look into his face, and he caressed her shoulder absently, running his hand down her arm, over her hips. "During the days in Levin," he continued. "I couldn't bring myself to show it to you. I don't know why."

Tabitha lay there, entranced by all of him. The poem was what she wanted, what she needed so much from him, access to the depths of his hidden soul—his trust. "It's not much of a poem, but it's the truth," he said.

His words led the passion that surged through her body. She hoped feverishly that Garyll felt what he was doing to her.

"What truth?" she asked, breathless, wanting to feel the vibration of his deep voice again, that masculine resonance that made her shudder.

Something had changed in his eyes. A shadow had left from behind his gaze—that haunted aspect of his expression; it had been replaced by a furnace. His fingers touched her breast. Hot anticipation flooded through her, filling her mind, gathering her soul.

"That I love you," Garyll said. "That I cannot live without you. That no matter what I believe of myself, I will always love you. I want to be your man, your protector, your strength."

"Wanting me is enough," Tabitha whispered. "All the rest just makes me love you more."

"Help me to be strong," he said. The way he kissed her showed her the depth of his desire. Their dammed-up passion broke. Their hands led the rush of their ardour, exploring the nakedness of their open fields, moving into channels denied, breaking through shallow walls of gentility, running through every vein and filling every crevice with the fertile flood. Currents of agonising delight twisted around them. She forgot duty, fear, wizardry, crowns and kingdoms. Everything was washed under in the flood of love.

It felt as if she was being dissolved in pure music.

Pain was drowned in pleasure. She did things she had never dreamt of before, but she knew she would dream of those things in nights to come. She would dream of him forever.

There was a moment when she felt broken and made whole again in the same moment, where she wept, utterly bereft, with tears of joy. She had become something…more.

She dreamt she sang the Lifesong, a single verse that was all the verses.

But maybe she hadn't.

23. TELLING TAILS

"How tall a tale can a teller tell
When the truth must tie it tight?"—Zarost

The world had forgotten about Ashley Logán, it seemed. He was abandoned, in the high cave, huddled against the cold rock beside his dead fire, and he awoke to the squeals of a panicked horse. A strange rank smell filled the air. It was gloomy inside the cave and bitterly cold. He struggled to react, but his thoughts were scattered, like hailstones on a frozen lake. There had been a lake, hadn't there? Swimming. Drowning, almost.

Where was he? He pushed himself up beside the ashes of a dead fire. He groaned. Why was he so very stiff? It felt as if a herd of horses had trampled his body all night.

The storm. He remembered the storm, its raging icy fury. They had flown, Princess and him. They had crashed. They had come to this place, this refuge, this dark and sheltered cavern. The winged horse clattered past him. The ground heaved, and the faint light from the mouth of the cave dimmed. He turned.

Something blocked the exit. Something very, very big.

He scrabbled to his feet.

A great head dipped into the mouth of the cavern, long and triangular, covered in hard black-veined scales. A shaft of morning light caught a ridge of spikes, which flashed, greenly brilliant. White teeth glistened like wet icicles in its jutting snout. Then the shaft of light was gone, blocked by the creature's advancing bulk. Only the massive slit eyes were visible, green and glowing like sentient jade— hard, predatory and pitiless. The creature loosed a cry that was so loud it made Ashley's teeth rattle. He fled with Princess deeper into the cavern, into the unknown blackness.

Princess slowed and neighed in fright ahead of him. She might kick backward if he pushed into her. Ashley was trapped between the two dangers in the dark. Instinctively he reached for Princess' mind, to let her know he was there. Princess was so panicked that she didn't know what she was doing, and kicked out anyway. Luckily she missed.

The rank smell washed over them from behind, and the great cry thundered in their bones again.

Closer...it was so much closer.

Ashley ducked past Princess and scrabbled along the damp wall, pulling Princess after him by her mane. They went deeper and deeper into the cavern, through a narrow section, then a turn. After that Ashley couldn't move freely anymore. He felt to the left, then to the right, but the walls drove into a tight wedge. They had gone as far as they could; they were trapped in the small chamber, a cave within the cavern. A breath, a rumble, a *wind* was coming from behind them.

Suddenly Princess thrashed beside him. He threw his arms around her neck and smothered her with reassuring thoughts. If he lost control of her now, he was sure she would trample him with a mad flurry of hooves. It took all of his concentration to keep a grip on Princess's mind. She was panicked by the tight space, by the darkness, by what was approaching them with an impossibly heavy tread.

Little by little, he calmed her mind, and she stopped flailing, but she breathed in panicked snorts, and his own heart was hammering in his ears. A low, grumbling purr measured out the time, an endless rolling wheeze of the mighty creature in the cavern. Slowly Ashley's eyes adjusted to the darkness. They had backed into a narrow cave guarded by a ragged crevice. The bulk of the creature filled the cavern outside. A big eye peered at Ashley. It was emerald green now, as clear as a jewel, and filled with a terrifying intelligence.

He was drawn closer by that eye, entranced by its magnetic beauty. He wondered why it glowed faintly.

COME A LITTLE CLOSER. I WANT TO EAT YOU.

A vast thought, it drove against him like a gale. The image had an unfamiliar scale and construction, a rhythm like language.

Ashley staggered back to the cold wall of the chamber.

WAIT UNTIL YOU RUN OUT, I WILL, I WILL, OR YOU'LL BE FIRED IN THERE WHERE I CAN'T GET YOU.

The thoughts were so large, so intimidating in their proportion, that he lost his balance and fell to the ground. He grappled for a mental purchase, fighting in the vast consciousness filling the cavern.

Fired? Where is the fire?

PATIENCE PAYS IN MEALS, IT ALWAYS DOES.

The eye withdrew. The great, snakelike snout thrust into their chamber instead. Teeth like giant swollen swords clashed against each other as its jaws closed in the air. But it could not reach them;

the snout could push no more than a few yards through the crevice. Princess had run in through that crack, and yet the creature couldn't get more than the first part of its head through it. Ashley began to fear how big the rest of it was—the bit they couldn't see.

The creature snorted, and a terrible wash of hot foul air passed over them. A rank smell hit them; the stench of a hundred carcasses burnt on a pyre, or spoiled leather mixed with tar and ash. It stung his nostrils, making his eyes smart. The creature croaked an angry roar then pulled its snout free with a scraping of scales against rock. Pale light played in the rock dust in the gap, a hint of the impossible freedom of the morning outside the distant cavern mouth. Ashley wondered if he'd ever get to see the sun again. A slithering, shifting sound came from outside, and the clicking of rocks pushed aside, then silence.

Time passed slowly in the dark. Only a subdued rumbling hinted that the creature breathed nearby. Ashley reached out with his thoughts again, carefully, hesitantly, not wanting to be overwhelmed. He could sense its great mind and something of what it was doing. It had eased its great head down on its forepaws like a dog watching a rat-hole, prepared to lie there all day for something tasty to run out.

Princess grew restless again, tossing her head over and over. Her eyes were wild, showing too much white. She had taken on too much terror; she could bear it no longer. She broke out of his grip, rearing and pawed at the air.

"Princess, no!" he shouted. He knew what she was thinking.

No, wait here, no! He tried to lasso her with his thoughts, force her to halt the mad charge. *It's still out there, it's just waiting for you.* But her mind was closed tight on her panic. She galloped through the ragged gap, tearing her shoulder on the rock, smearing blood.

She leapt forward then, seeing the way open to the sunlight at the distant mouth of the cave. Toward the light she ran, in a panicked kicking of hooves that prevented Ashley from holding her back.

No, no, no, thought Ashley in despair, *not Princess, not after what she has endured for me.* She cleared four strides, five. Princess galloped, her hooves a storm of stone chips. The brightness at the mouth of the great cavern highlighted her for a perfect moment, a winged horse in the moment of taking flight. Just a few beats of her wings, and she would be clear of the cavern.

He sensed the sudden alertness of the great mind, and he clenched his stomach. The floor of the cavern uncoiled. The terrible scaled head emerged. Its jaws were drawn wide, exposing the wicked teeth. Trails of fire spilled over the creature's snout, lighting it to glistening iridescence. The great eye was intently focused. His precious Princess was going to die.

"No!" he shouted, wanting to run out from the crevice.

Stop! he tried to command the creature, but either it didn't sense him, or it cared nothing at all for his puny mental effort. The creature launched its bulk from the floor with the practiced lunge of a predator. It was carried on mighty wings; it stretched its head forward upon a sinuous neck. All of its mass passed before Ashley in an instant, before a wild high squeal and a terrible crushing sound was heard. A great gout of flame burst forth, a flickering trail of bright golden fire that tore through the gloom.

Ashley looked away. He sensed her intense pain, her final moment of mortal terror. Then the life was snuffed out of her in one swift twist of the jaws upon her head.

"You big ugly bastard!" he cried, before he could think, but he backed away into the cave again, through the protective crevice that would keep the creature from reaching him. Already, as it devoured the winged horse, Ashley could sense waves of attention scouring the cavern, searching for him. It was too aware for him to risk bolting for the gap. Beside, what were his chances of surviving beyond the mouth of the cavern? The moment he got out there he'd just be searching for a crevice to back into again.

Princess was gone. *Eaten.*

He retreated in the darkness until his back thumped into the wall, then he hunched down and covered his ears. He couldn't bear to listen to the crunching sounds which came to him from the main cavern. Sweet Princess, so trusting of his lead, so ravaged by the strange magic, so terrified by this strange new land. She could have run away before, when they had crashed into the trees in the forest, but she had stayed with him, she had been faithful to him, and he had led her here, to this place, to this predator's lair, to be eaten.

Ashley put his head between his knees. He should have been more careful. He had seen the signs the night before: the bones piled at the mouth of the cave; the rank smell; the charred tree. He had used that wood to build a fire, yet he had never thought why it was burnt to begin with.

He could never have guessed what was going to return to the cave. He would never have imagined such an awesome creature. Even in his worst nightmares, no such beast existed. Then again, neither should a winged horse exist. The final cracking sounds told him that she didn't, anymore.

He shivered. It didn't seem he was going to last for too long in Oldenworld either. It really was ruled by Chaos.

After a while the beast returned to the crevice. It snuffled and snorted when its snout was as far in as it would go. It sent a tentative blast of golden fire licking toward him that singed him with a rotten carrion stench. Ashley found a boulder to cower behind, in case it blew a worse blast of fire the second time. The creature had its great eye stuck up against the crack again. The green iris glistened, fascinating in a deadly way, cunning intelligence shimmering in its depths.

Could it smell him in the chamber? Princess had given herself away with all her stomping and whinnying, but he was sitting as still as a mouse. It shouldn't be able to see him in the gloom, for it blocked out the light every time it leant close to look inward. It wasn't stupid. It knew he was in there.

After a while, it gave up and retreated, probably to the same hiding place it had used to ambush Princess. The sound of it sinking to lie down was like chainmail settling on stone. The silence returned to the cavern, except for that distant rumbling that grew slower and slower until Ashley couldn't be certain that he still heard it.

Was he imagining that it was still there, or had it dragged itself outside?

It was awfully quiet. The cold numbed Ashley's bottom to creep up his spine. He didn't dare move.

He waited and waited, his guts a tight knot.

An hour passed, then two. Every minute was an agony of suspense. How much longer would he be trapped in the chamber for? Until starvation took him? The daylight faded, the night came, and the silence stretched on like an oiled tightrope across the abyss of fear.

By the next day, he couldn't bear it anymore. If there was a chance to escape, it was worth taking. Ashley reached out with his mind, but this time there was nothing to sense apart from the empty walls of the cavern. He made as little noise as possible stretching and trying to work some blood back into his numb legs and feet, but he was as stiff as a corpse, and deathly cold. He tiptoed towards the crevice.

As he neared the mouth of the chamber, the grinding respirations in the cavern became clearer. He pressed his shaking hands against the rock face, and leant past the corner. The creature's breathing was a steady rumble, one slow breath for every twelve Ashley took. He hoped that meant it was properly asleep, digesting its meal. Ashley searched the gloom for the lurking shape, and found it by the telltale glimmer within its nostrils, a faint hint of the fire it contained. It was deep in the shadows, far from the mouth of the cavern, but its head was pointed directly at Ashley, as if it had lain down in position to leap. The creature's eyes were closed. It drew another slow whistling breath and then exhaled with decadent, sonorous purr.

His heart pounded. Maybe he could sneak past it. It lay in a hollow, under an overhanging ledge. Maybe it wouldn't have enough clear space to use its wings at first. No, he mustn't wake it at all, for he had to find another hiding place once he had escaped this cave. Ashley tried to gauge the distance between the creature and the beckoning glow of the cave mouth. Sixty, maybe seventy paces? The creature was just as far away to the side, but he had no illusions about its speed. He had seen it leap before. If it was awake, it would be upon him long before he reached the exit.

What am I doing? By Fynn, what am I going to do if I get out there with it on my heels?

He was so filled with dread that he could hardly balance on his legs, but somehow he forced his hand to push the wall away, and he tottered a step into the main cavern. He stood there, his throat dry, his jaw clenched against the sound of his own breathing.

The beast didn't move. The deeper shadows were still. The beast's feral scent filled the cavern, carried upon another slow reverberating exhalation. He took another unsteady step away from the safety of the crevice. Another. The cavern's floor was more uneven than he remembered. He came halfway to where his campfire had burnt away to ashes.

He stopped.

Something was not right. Beyond his panic, he knew he was missing something. A horrible premonition that he was being very stupid churned in his stomach. He tried to see inside the dragon's head again, to sense any thoughts, any images that would betray its intentions, but there was nothing there, nothing at all. That was what was wrong. It should be thinking something. Even if it was asleep, it would be dreaming. Yet he could sense nothing. It was almost as if it was hiding: hiding its thoughts from him, so he would be lured out from his safe cleft.

The dragon drew another slow breath. The twin fires glimmered within its nostrils. Then he saw it—the fraction of movement at the base of its lidded left eye, a brief glimpse of green. It was watching him!

He ran for the safety of his crevice. The creature came at him with a leap that carried it halfway across the cavern. It roared—an ear-splitting thunderous wail—but Ashley's potent fear lent speed to his legs. He reached the ragged opening in the cavern wall. Flame singed his back as he ducked into the chamber. He dived down behind his boulder. A scraping sound suggested that the great snout had been shoved into the crack again. He flinched as rank hot breath washed over him. He gagged, but remained where he was. There was nowhere else to go.

THINKS IT IS CLEVER, IT DOES, IT DOES. DRAGONS ALWAYS WIN AT GAMES OF PATIENCE.

Thoughts as thick as castle walls, images as tall as trees.

When his heartbeat had steadied a little, he peeped over his boulder. The great green eye was blocking the exit. *No food,* he tried to convince it. *Bitter ugly food, poisonous food, not worth hunting.*

It pulled abruptly away, and Ashley felt a moment of triumph.

But it was not over. A great barbed tail slithered into the crack, its thickened end searching the air like a blinded fighter swinging a club. At full reach, it smacked into the rock above Ashley's head then twitched away to slam into the other wall. He was grateful for his boulder's shelter. Without it, he would have been squashed like a fly against the wall.

He might have convinced the creature he was not worth eating, but that was not enough. If it wasn't going to eat him, then it would kill him instead. He was in its lair and he would be punished.

Wham! The tail clipped his head on the next pass, leaving a ringing dizziness behind. He ducked between his legs, and heard the next swipe connect with the rock overhead. The creature thumped away at his refuge for some time. The air filled with dust, and infrequent showers of stone chips rained down on his head. At last the creature grew tired of its failure to squash him.

It thrust its snout into the crack instead, and let off a frustrated blast of fire. The air was unbreathable for a few moments, so hot and dry. The creature seemed to sense his discomfort, for it fired him again and again. The back of his hands were singed, his hair curled and his thick travelling robe began to smoke. He kept his head tucked down. His lungs ached for clean, cool air, but there was only the foul exhaust from the stinking furnace to breathe.

UNGRATEFUL MIDGET! MY BREATH IS THE FLOWERS OF SPRING.

Ashley sensed something beyond the curse as well, deep in the patterns of that great mind: a sense of hurt pride. Ashley looked up in wonder. The beast cared what he thought. The beast was vain. Even though he was to be killed, his opinion mattered to it. It was actually upset that he considered its breath foul.

And it had sensed his thoughts, he realised. It had his talent.

HEAVEN'S SCENT! BLESSED WITH MY FIRE'S KISS, THE BEST OF ALL THE DRAGONS, AND HE THINKS IT FOUL, HE DOES. HE'LL BE BETTER OFF DEAD, THE RUDE LITTLE HUMAN. NOT EVEN WORTH KEEPING AS A SNACK, NO.

Another roar of golden heat washed overhead. His boots issued a puff of greyish smoke. He slapped at a flame that had caught on his knees. It went out, but left a black scar in the fabric.

Too close. The flames would soon burn him.

Ashley gathered courage for what he would have to do. He knew he would not be able to dominate the creature's great mind. It wasn't like the wild boar in the forest, but maybe flattery would work. He was desperate enough to try anything.

"Great Dragon!" he shouted, not moving from his place of meagre protection. "Please do not kill me. I wish to behold your beauty for a moment longer!" It was easier to focus on the thoughts when he spoke them aloud, and he wanted to be sure it understood every word. Ashley strained to imbue each image with as much clarity as possible. It was the equivalent of mental shouting, he supposed. The beast sensed something of it, for it paused and didn't loose another burst of flame.

MY BEAUTY?

He could only hope it understood the mental images he offered in its own terms. Its thoughts were vast, so wide, but they were becoming more understandable to him. Most of his own thoughts were probably inaudible to it, like the small squeaks of a mouse, but if he concentrated really hard, he could amplify the thought enough for the beast to appreciate them. The thought about its bad breath must have just slipped across in the ether. Maybe it was oversensitive to criticism.

"Great Dragon, I wish to behold your true wonder, but I am scared you shall burn me before my eyes rest upon your loveliness. This dark cavern does your beauty no justice. I have seen the morning light glitter against the tips upon your head, but I suspect that your skin must look majestic in the full light. Please, let me live a moment longer, so that I might see you more."

A considering rumble came from the far end of the corridor. The creature's huge eye was up against the opening again. A slit green eye. A squinting eye. A thinking eye.

THIS LITTLE ONE IS NOT AN ORDINARY MAN. HE SPEAKS AS A DRAGON. HE HAS SEEN ME GLITTER?

A dragon? "I have travelled from afar, and nowhere have I seen such a magnificent creature as you."

I AM MAGNIFICENT? I *AM* MAGNIFICENT. I TOLD THEM I WAS.

"What is your name, great dragon? Tell me what they call you, so that I might have a name to place beside the memory of your exquisite bejewelled eyes."

He encountered a strange thought-form, a sound or symbolic image in a language he could not grasp.

"What would that sound like, if you were to call it out to—the others?" He suspected there were others of its kind. The dragon threw its head back and issued a piercing sibilant cry.

Ashley did his best to interpret the sound. "Sassraline?" It sounded like a jewel. The dragon clicked its teeth. "Is that...a girl's name, or a boy's?" he asked. The dragon's eye became suddenly hooded, dangerously so. It thrust its snout into the crevice and spewed out a blast of fire over his head. He fell to the floor, and scrabbled backward to his boulder.

SILLY SWEETMAN. HE REALLY DOESN'T KNOW MUCH ABOUT DRAGONS.

Heaven's breath, heaven's breath. It's the scent of spring flowers!

The dragon made a kind of coughing sound. After a while he realised that it might be a kind of laughter. The dragon had only intended to warn him with the blast. It could have fried him easily, it could do so at any time, but it waited for him to find his feet. His hair was singed worse than the last time.

A girl then, he decided.

"Great Sassraline! You bless me with such an honour, to live a moment longer in your presence. Your breath is like a blazing forest, so rich with scents. Please forgive my rudeness, for I am but a little man, and am awed by such a dazzling creature as yourself. I was blind to not know the truth at once, but I am not accustomed to such wonderful ferociousness in a female. You are so strong and terrifying to me."

There was an awful moment when he thought he had guessed wrongly, but then she sighed and sank to the floor again, her eye up against the crack. She waited for him to talk.

"Great Sassraline, your eyes are more dazzling and beautiful than all the jewels of the world."

HE IS VERY CLEVER, THIS ONE, BUT HE DOES SAY SUCH NICE THINGS.

The dragon settled down, slightly further away from the crevice, where he could see most of her head. She closed her eyes. Ashley continued his litany of praise until her breaths were slow and deep, and the fire in her nostrils was only a faint glow. He couldn't trust that she really was asleep; the only thing that could keep him alive was to continue talking, to flatter the scales off her belly, and to give her no reason to feel threatened.

"Your tail is so graceful, your talons so strong. It is truly a wonder that such a fearsome hunter as you can have such great mercy to allow me to live, miserable wretch that I am, but I can see that you are very wise, and must have lived a long, long time."

"Not that it shows in your scales," he added hastily, "they are as bright as a maiden-dragon in her prime, and no less alluring."

It was exhausting. The longer he spoke his praise, the more outrageous he had to be to add anything new. He was terrified he might offend her odd sensibilities with an ill-considered word, but she didn't blow fire at him again, or even snap her teeth. She seemed content, for a while. Later, much later, the faint light from beyond the mouth of the cave began to fade.

He earned every breath of that long, long day, stealing moments of life from the dragon's vain heart.

24. BATTLE CRY

"In the dead marshes, don't follow the lights;
When the dead marches, don't follow their fights."—Zarost

Flowers grew everywhere outside the Lûk down. They wreathed the short slope with colour, brilliant under the morning sun, dancing against the darkness of the forest nearby. Nobody knew how the blossoms had come to be, for they hadn't been there the day before, and Rôgspar wasn't known to have fertile soil. Little white snowdrops and fuzzy mauve velvet-flowers grew among clusters of lilacs, the thyme bushes were smothered in pink and the sorrel in red. Flowers, thick in the hollows, all the way up the mound of Rôgspar's cast where the earth ejected from the down over the years had raised the spiralled exit path above the surrounding meadow. From where she stood, Tabitha could see a few of the trapdoors that marked the many entranceways to the settlement; most were indiscernible among the grasses. The occasional ventilation pipe protruded clear of the surface, marking the limits of the hidden habitation below.

The sunlight danced upon Tabitha's smile. . The colours of the flowers reflected what she felt inside. Alongside the descending path, even goldenbells dipped their heads in the breeze.

She squeezed Garyll's arm and he hugged her tighter.

"Sihkran thinks we may encounter more trouble than we are looking for," he said, as they followed the departing Lûk patrol. "He thinks you should stay here, with the other women."

"No!" Tabitha objected, looking up to read Garyll's face: those dark eyes that entranced her, those lips that had kissed her, so strong and yet so tender. She felt as if he was a part of her, as if their bodies were still linked. She could *feel* his smile hiding beneath his sober expression.

"What if we must go into the Hunterslands to follow Bevn?" she added. "No Garyll, we must stay together." She didn't want to be separated from him, not this morning, not ever.

"Sihkran thinks it will be dangerous." At the mention of his name, the leader of the Luk glanced their way. He looked concerned.

"So will it be for you men if you try to get me to stay," replied

Tabitha, planting her feet and facing Sihkran down. Sihkran raised his hand in mock surrender.

"It was a suggestion," he said.

"Well it was a bad one. We're all in this together."

Garyll hesitated. "If we are attacked, promise me you'll fall back."

"You'll not make a coward out of me," she answered.

"No! You are not a warrior, Tabitha. The Lûk are better prepared for this."

"It is our crown that we seek, not the Lûk's. We should be at the front of things."

"The men are preparing for a fight."

"They expect blood to be spilled," added Sihkran. "They shaved their heads this morning."

"A battle is no place for a woman," said Garyll.

"Then today I am not a woman, I am a wizard!"

Sihkran's expression became as blank as stone, and he nodded and strode away. Garyll didn't look happy, but he could think of nothing to say. Tabitha looked around among the men. She hadn't noticed their haircuts, for all of the warriors still wore their brightly coloured headscarves, but a warrior pushed his *bong* back to scratch at his head, revealing a scalp that was bare and oiled. The grey skin glistened like steel.

"Why do they do that?" she whispered to Garyll.

"Sihkran told me that their hair is plaited and kept here at Rôgspar. If they do not return from a foray beyond the border, the hair is sent to their families in Rek, or Koom. They do not wish to die in the Hunterslands and have such wealth go to waste."

The men were grim-faced, restless; ready to set off for battle. They all carried spears, hardened long-shields of woven cane, ochre-coloured breastplates of a tighter weave and sling-shaped bags which fitted close on their backs. Garyll had been given a shield himself, which he had strapped to his left arm. He had declined the spear they had offered him, preferring his short baton that hung from his belt. Mulrano had his woodsman's axe and a pack of provisions. From the boisterous welcome he received as they joined the ranks, it seemed he had made some friends the night before.

The Lûk were a good people. They had given her a flaxen-coloured dress, short-cut in the Lûk style, and she wore it to honour them, although the coarse fabric scratched her skin in places. At least the patterned ribbons were soft where they crossed between her breasts. They had also given her a pair of *salakan* boots, to replace the ones she had worn through the wastes. They were hard-edged, besides being a bit wide in the toe, but once Sihkran's daughter Sunni had shown her how to bind her feet with an inner wrap she had found that the boots were comfortable and warm.

Sihkran met them again where the men gathered into loose ranks at the edge of the forest.

"Beyond these trees lies the land we call the *brdaki*, the blood-belt," he explained. "It belongs to neither the Lûk nor the Hunters. It is where we fight. I see you are determined all the way to come, Tabitha *Mahgu*. That is brave, but when we through the bloodbelt move, you will to the centre of the group keep. You are not as well-protected as us or as accustomed to the Hunter's way of battle. I will not allow one of such great stature to fall prey to a hateful arrow."

"Are the Hunters that bad?" Tabitha asked. "Can't you talk to them without a fight?"

"Know that for over two hundred years, the Hunters have waged terrible war against us. They take the lives of our women and children. They are scavengers, they steal whatever they can lay their hands on and kill whoever tries them to stop. We, the Lûk, make things, we weave; we grow. They are hunters, they only take from life; they never give. My father at the hands of the Hunters died, my father's father before him. There is nothing that a Lûk more hates than a Hunter."

Men swore in Lûkish all around them.

"Have you never known peace?"

"Peace?" Sihkran repeated, rolling his tongue in his mouth as if tasting the unfamiliar concept. "That is an old word, from the myths of the Old Tongue that you speak. Peace is spoken of in the tales we tell to our children, but in our lives? No. There is always war. Our task is to see it in the blood-belt is kept, and not in our Six Sided Land."

He drew himself up to address all the assembled warriors.

"Let the Fifth Dja seek out the murderers! The ones who our windrunners slayed shall find no shelter in the Huntersland."

The men beat their spears against their shields.

"Spearleader!" Garyll called out. "With respect, Sihkran, but we need Prince Bevn alive."

Tabitha had been thinking the same thing. King Mellar would

never forgive them if they allowed Bevn to die.

"Alive?" Sihkran repeated, incredulous. "What justice would it be to keep him alive? One who kills should be killed, just as one who steals should have everything stolen from him. No! *A'Lûk telamenn im!* He and his bitch have killed our kind. I am Spearleader Sihkran, and I will see this Bevn dead." Sihkran came closer, his demeanour suddenly threatening. "If you are truly against Bevn, then you will prove it by fighting on our side."

Garyll held Sihkran's eye for a moment, but then he turned aside, to Tabitha. He nodded his head a fraction, and she could guess what he was thinking. They were in the Lûk's land now, and could not dictate to the warriors how they handled the matter of Bevn's treachery. They were lucky enough to be included in the march. If Bevn died at the hands of the Lûk, it was a fate he had brought upon himself, Tabitha decided. They would still be able to retrieve the crown, and that was what mattered. She nodded back to Garyll.

"Aye, we are with you," Garyll said slowly. Maybe he had a plan, for Bevn.

"We move!" shouted Sihkran.

He turned and led them into the forest. They followed, and the Lûk warriors settled into a steady lope, keeping Tabitha, Garyll and Mulrano in their midst. Jek, the craggy-faced captain of the windrunners, took a position close on Tabitha's right.

"We shall meet many Hunters before we find Bevn and Gabreel!" he said. "You do not move toward their lands without them knowing of it and so we make no effort to conceal our approach for that will only delay the meeting. Prepare yourself. The Hunters are known for surprise attacks. They are cowards."

The forest drew them in, with all its strange organic scents, unfamiliar birdcalls and sounds. The trees closed behind them, the coloured flowers of the meadow of Rôgspar lost to view. The air was still in the forest. The first trees were healthy, but after a while they began to appear more gnarled and sickly, with growths bursting through the flaking bark of their trunks. There was no road; only a faint game trail, a narrow channel through the undergrowth. The Lûk crashed through the creepers and beds of lichen and brittle leaves, apparently unconcerned about their noisy passage. Tabitha was glad she was deep in the column—the many feet ahead trampled the worst of the thorny creepers and clusters of sharp twigs flat.

They crossed a narrow, white-stained stream upon stepping stones, careful not to let it touch their feet. The current frothed and foamed, and it gave off a gritty jangling sound to Tabitha's ear; she could sense the Chaos essence within it. Soon afterward, they skirted a ruined ashen circle where the dry scent of wildfire lingered. Despite the rain of the days past, she could smell it, the fatal magic; the Sorcerer's scent.

They passed other places that had been struck by wildfire that morning. The growth in the forest alternated between areas of health and places of sickness. The trees got taller the farther west they travelled.

The Lûk men chanted as they loped along.

"Bakti, Benna, Jallen, Paduk—" called four men in turn.

"Jak jin jeer," they chorused.

"Likwhan, Yud, Runkkn, Brât—"

"Jerrik vinn nageer!"

Tabitha turned to Jek beside her. "What is that song about?"

"We sing whenever we are heading beyond the Six Sided Land. It is a way of remembering, letting everyone know they are seen, that they are part of the Fifth Dja, and the greater weave of the Lûk. If there is a battle, the memory of the song will carry on in those who live. They call out their names: Bakti, Benna, Jallen and Paduk, those four there, strong as stone. Then the next four, they carry the might of their ancestors."

The plainsong passed back through the moving ranks, until it was Tabitha's turn to add her own name to the chant of remembrance. "Tabitha!" she called out. It felt strange to call her name into the expectant hush which had fallen upon the Lûk.

"Garyll. And Mulrano," said Garyll beside her.

"Ralok krn ros keer!" the Lûk sang gruffly, from ahead and behind.

"Brave to the end," Jek translated, in a whisper.

Tabitha wished it hadn't sounded so much like a final pronouncement. They would be remembered, in the Lûk tradition, in the plainsong. The chant moved on through the men behind her.

They entered a darker part of the forest. A chill passed over Tabitha. Something had changed—something within the background sounds had altered. The blood-belt—it was a terrible name. Through the trees on their right, a loop of river lurked, sliding by like a great and swollen grey serpent.

When the song reached through the soldiers behind her, to the rear of the company, it stopped. The army loped along, the shafts of the spears glistening as they crossed a narrow gap of sunlight. The ground levelled out in a broad swathe between the giant trees. In a brief moment of stillness, when even the breeze seemed to pause around them, Tabitha heard the pitter-patter of running feet, but when she listened harder for it, there was nothing. Her mind was playing tricks on her.

Sihkran slowed at the head of the company, lifting his hand. The forest seemed to be filling with awareness, movement unseen. What Tabitha could see of the trail ahead was empty, but she had come to recognise the capering sound of living things amid the music of the elements, and she sensed that something lived nearby, spread out, approaching with hushed footsteps.

"Garyll—" she began.

He tensed beside her, reading her apprehension. The mounting presence was undeniable, playing havoc with her nerves. Ahead. To the sides. Behind? Mercy, Tabitha thought. Had they circled them already? Could they move that quietly? She caught a flicker of movement, nothing more. A flap of fabric off to the right. No, it was a motionless tree, when she looked. Then another, farther off to the left. Then she saw them.

They came from between the trees, running light-footed and swift, and even as she watched, they seemed to fade in and out of view, so well-camouflaged were their garments. They covered a great area and although she could not count them, she sensed at least thirty figures approached in a tightening arc.

Sihkran gave a sharp command, and the Lûk readied their shields and formed up, shoulder to shoulder, in a broad wedge. Tabitha was shuffled into a space behind Garyll, many places back from the front line.

A tall man with white hair stepped out from a tree not thirty paces ahead, and as he did so, ten others with drawn bows came out from behind him. They had narrow beards, just a stripe upon their chins. They looked like rough men accustomed to hard living. Most of them wore assorted leathers—thick doublets, wristlets, breastplates or collars. Some wore low-browed helms, smeared with muddy colours. Their clothing blended into the colours of the forest; their cloaks had russet-coloured leaves sewn into them.

The tall man drew his great whitewood bow, and he held the arrow as steady as if he were merely pointing at Sihkran with his finger.

He made some challenge, but his speech was difficult for Tabitha to understand. There were few recognisable words within the brogue.

Sihkran shouted something back, using a similar accent to the Hunter.

The white-haired Hunter shook his head. "Lûklings, belay yer weapons pon where ye stand onnin loudfeet!" he commanded.

"Notnay a'likely," responded Sihkran. "We willer spy yor shaft bedowned a'first."

"As well as can be, then we yock over mine arrow bepointed. Why are ye inner Hunterland, Lûklings?"

"Blood-belt, na Hunter's land, ya canna claim ground before yon river beside Bradach," argued Sihkran.

The leader shrugged, as if he didn't care where Sihkran thought the Huntersland began. "Why are ye not innin cozened hole inner Sixersides?"

"We beseek newacomers, they owe a'Lûk two that were living. A boy that a'walk ponner firewyld, he an he woman. They come of a'place named Eyri. We seek justice pon them."

A flicker of colour drew her eye upward. A man in the tree pulled his bow taught, his balance steady; his aim intent. Once she'd seen him, she spied ten others among the boughs. Tabitha felt the points of many arrows, kept from falling upon her only by the interruption of the tenuous negotiations.

"Why should we cannacare about yor justeece?" the Hunter's leader demanded, his expression implacable, his bow steady. "Why should we waggle tongues pon those from Ayree?"

"Ye begiven us they that are murderers, or ye let us pass to Bradach."

"What makes ye say a daredevilfoolish thing as that? Why should we let er Lûk innin Hunterland? So ye can betrample onner hunting ground, and soiling innin brook? Be away with ye all!"

"Are ye asimplemind? We have more inner number than ye can hold. Ye bespeaken er truth about a'two newacomers, or ye for treachery die."

The Hunter didn't seem intimidated by Sihkran's threat. He spat upon the ground then backed away, and his men fanned out around him. "We shed na tear if he killer two Lûk," he called out. "The riddance be good!"

"They were treasured men!" roared Jek, just ahead of Tabitha.

"Majar!" shouted Sihkran. The Lûk rushed forward as one.

A bowstring pinged, and her quick eye caught a movement against the darkness of the forest, a single shaft, moving fast, its tip a rusted brown triangle, its fletching dirty red. A moment later the heavy-shafted arrow quivered in Sihkran's shield. The Lûk bunched tightly together, their shields already raised. Then there was a sound like a flock of low-flying doves. A staccato of impacts followed as arrows struck into the company hard and fast. Some of the outermost men yelped, one warrior fell, a red bloom on his chest. Then everyone was roaring and running.

The battle unfolded around her like a strange vision she couldn't believe. It had begun so quickly; so stupidly. Garyll and Mulrano stayed with her, framing her on either side with their shields, immobile in the sea of chaotic activity. The Lûk fanned out in multiple wedges, their shields held together like carapaces. Between the volleys of arrows, they advanced, and the Hunters retreated. The closest archers fired. As the Lûk advanced upon them they turned and fled through their own ranks to take positions farther away. A Lûk warrior fell hard, an arrow driven through his chest. Tabitha cried out. The foremost Lûk faced a barrage of arrows shot from extreme angles. Their shields were long and hard enough, but when they lifted them to cover their heads from the tree-borne archers, their legs became exposed. Men fell from the front edge of the formations, clutching arrows, as the remaining Lûk warriors hurried past.

Tabitha was sick to her stomach. She had no quarrel with these Hunters, but the Lûk had vowed to help her and they had drawn her into this battle. Tabitha might have to fight beside them to survive. She had to call upon her power.

What could she do? Heal the Lûk as they fell, so they could rise and fight again? Kill the Hunters with the terrifying resonances of the second stanza? What use was there in being a wizard if she couldn't bring peace?

What was worse, she might bring wildfire down upon them all if she tried anything. The Sorcerer's bane might be less reactive over the forest than the wastelands, but she couldn't be sure. Could she risk moving the clear essence? She knew too little about the workings of wildfire. She was too scared to try. The flowers, there was something about the flowers that was important, but she couldn't *think*. Violence seethed all around her.

As she focused on her dilemma, the perspective she yearned for began to flicker into her mind. Wildfire was drawn to the movement in essence. If she could sing but not move the essence, just *change* it, there might be a chance. The flowers outside Rôgspar had been changed, whether in her dream or not, she had done something to the world beyond the down, she was certain of it…yet the wildfire hadn't struck them down. Her understanding was too vague, the solution too complex, and it was coming too late. She had to do something at once.

She heard the chilling wails of injured men, and the strident howl of Lûk in battle-fury. She drew on the ring's arcane lore. The Hunter's bows were the most noticeable danger. Those weapons gave the Hunters too much of an advantage. If the bowstrings were to split, the archers wouldn't be able to nock their arrows. When the next archer pulled, from within the boughs to her left, she extended her awareness and gathered the elemental sound that the string gave off, the fine frequency that described its presence in the world. Tabitha imagined the fibres fraying and tried to predict how the sound would change if she used her music to alter the world to her liking.

As she reached for her power, the Lifesong overwhelmed her. She lost all sense of her own body. Time seemed to shake free from her shoulders, and she was filled with air. Harmonies and melodies rose around her, rising in volume and complexity as her awareness expanded. There was so much to the Lifesong, so many cadences and layers beyond the element she had chosen for her focus. She wanted to heal all the wrongs, to let life flood through her, to let her voice echo through the stars, but she couldn't afford to let the full power escape, for fear of triggering wildfire. The music she was seeking came to her, through her.

The horror of Ethea's condition hit her, like a sliver of madness cut into her mind by an axe blade. She had known it was coming; she had to work around it.

She sang, following a wordless melody, as the tears streamed down her face.

The world softened before her eyes. The forest became hazy.

Flames and fire, screaming children, , and the beating of drums.

The forest surrounding her was a living tapestry of sounds, and she considered the element that she wanted to change. She thought only of the bowstrings as she spread her awareness through the glade. Clear essence swirled like a river through the trees. She was careful not to move it…only, to change it; to be aware of it.

She took another strike, like an arrow driving into her mind, a birdlike face that screamed at the red sky, shackles that bit, pain that flooded her with horror; raw unguarded emotion.

Tabitha fell to her knees, but she completed her musical pattern. There was a frame of wood, and the children...the children were trapped inside. She couldn't think on it, she could only let it wound her. She released the vision she wanted. The sky tightened.

A stuttered snapping came from all around and sudden cries of dismay. Hunters threw aside their bows, and drew ragged-bladed knives. Some of them dropped from the trees. None of them fled.

A man screamed as a spear skewered his throat. Wherever the Hunters clashed with the Lûk at close-quarters they lost ground. The grey-skinned warriors had a deadly advantage with their long spears. Hunters began to fall, blood rushing from gaping wounds. Men fought on blindly, never turning to run away, hacking and slicing with their knives even when they had been driven to their knees. It was turning into a bloodbath.

Tabitha felt sick. She had merely turned the tide of battle, she had not ended it. She had done nothing to bring peace. She reached for the Lifesong again, without thinking, plunging through the music, into power. She wanted the battle to stop.

Flames and fire, and the screaming of children, and the beating, beating, beating.

She yearned to sing to the sky, to give voice to all of the Lifesong which she felt, to answer the powerful need to express it. The flux of the universe was there for the wielding. Remember the wildfire, she told herself desperately. Remember the wildfire. Don't make the essence move; use the song to *change* the world.

All the while, the Hunters darted in and out of the Lûk, slicing at their legs, but the Lûk were tougher, their thick skins protecting them. Hunters hunched over upon thrust spears. Hunters were slapped down by whirling shafts. Hunters were stamped into the earth under heavy boots. Tabitha had never seen such a frenzy of killing, so violent, mad and bloodthirsty. It was as if everyone in the battle was possessed.

She had been wrong to focus on the weapons, she realised. Even without any weapons, these warring peoples would fight. Those crippled Hunters who lay on the bloody ground still tried to slash their opponents. Dying Lûk warriors pulled arrows from their chests and threw them at their enemies.

The fight was in their hearts. She had to change what they felt.

As she considered what emotions might rule the men, she began to see the world in a different way. The fighters had writhing outlines and their bodies were filled with threads of coloured light. Moving threads coiled outward from hearts and danced between them in shimmering cords of emotion, like a ruby essence, flowing in curving, waving channels, but such clean bonds only joined the Hunters to Hunters, and the Lûk to Lûk.

The currents between adversaries were dirty red streaked with grey, covered with hooked silver barbs. The dirty tendrils were prolific, like vines, splitting and multiplying at many nodes, choking the space between the fighters with silver-tainted hatred, pulling them toward each other, binding them tight, clutching at their hearts with those wicked thorns. Wherever a tainted tendril gripped a heart, silver ugliness bloomed across the red. Chaos drove this battle on. A desire for destruction infested their emotions. The Sorcerer's touch ran deep; it seemed he could influence more than the physical world.

She had no idea how Ametheus had achieved the effect she could see, but she suspected that if she could link them all with a purer emotion, just for a moment, they might be released from their madness. They needed to feel something beyond hatred for each other.

Love, she needed love. Tabitha touched Garyll. She drew on her feeling for him, gathering the music of their bond and giving it a voice. As Tabitha sang each note, she felt an answering vibration in the clear essence throughout the glade. She gathered it without thinking and as she sang, something came free within her. The simple melody opened her awareness and she was swept up in the torrent of sound, of music, of emotion, of voices that sang multiples of supporting harmonies. She was made sensitive.

The spearlike vision of Ethea's agony pierced her heart: the priests had come, the priests had come, with their bitter words and madness in their eyes, in the flames, in the sacrifice.

She reached for more power and her spirit soared. A current of glory flowed through her as she spread her arms wide to encompass everyone.

The priests sang in a circle, and the fires burned, and the flesh became flame then flesh again. Their breath was taken away; her breath began.

She sensed the men spread out in the forest. They were like stars, and she would be the light that danced between them. What was it Sihkran had said? They only take from life, never give. Well, she could give, but before she had completed her song, the Hunters attacked the trio of Eyrians. Some of the archers must have replaced their broken strings, for a sudden volley of arrows rained down upon them. Garyll moved with lightning speed and caught the first arrow before it had struck the ground, but Mulrano fell back, two shafts in his shoulder. Garyll danced over him, using his baton to swat the next three arrows from the air. He moved in a blur, but he could only do so much. An arrow struck the ground between Tabitha's feet and another brushed her hair as it whipped by.

"You must fall back!" Garyll shouted at her, as she sang. "You must run, Tabitha! Run!"

"Give me time!" she cried, panicked by the discontinuity in her song. Garyll seemed to understand, because he turned to face the battle again as she sang louder. She could not run because she would lose her connection to the quickening spell and her link to the essence. Tabitha could feel the emotion spreading through the people, swelling as her attention expanded, reaching in secret through the tangled tension of the fight. If she ran now, she would lose any hope of stopping them. The Hunters would surely follow them if they fled, and hunt them down. She had to stand against this hatred and change it or they were all done for. Tabitha backed slowly away to give herself a few more seconds to sing. Things happened fast around her.

Four Hunters ran through a gap and came for them, running hard. Mulrano staggered to his feet behind Garyll. He pulled the arrows free from his left shoulder. Blood spilled down his arm. He grunted as he lifted his axe with his right hand and stepped up to cover Garyll's flank.

A vision struck her like a warhammer—dead birds fell from the sky, their heads torn from their bodies. Tabitha stumbled backward, singing desperately, giving life as part of her died, driving her melody to completion. The advancing Hunters veered to follow her.

Oh Ethea, do we both die now? Is this end of the story? Is this the end of the Lifesong?

It was all happening too fast, she needed to find the end to her song, but she couldn't tell where the end was until she reached the notes perfecting the pattern. The song had a progression that couldn't be hastened if it was to be true. She was the descant worked over the driving theme the hidden voices sounded in her ears—she was the witness, not the source. The approaching blades rose, their motion slowed, and her soft music flowed against the chaotic currents of dying, hatred and violent abandon that rushed at her. She felt so terribly exposed, like a single flower, a delicate lily standing in the trampling madness of the battle, a little songbird vying against a howling storm. It was useless.

Garyll leapt to block the first Hunter's lunge and he dropped his shoulder hard into the man's chest. The Hunter was thrown toward the second charging man, who vaulted clear. Garyll met that Hunter's blade with the edge of the Lûk shield he carried, then whirled and struck the assailant's knee with the baton. Beside Garyll, Mulrano swung his axe in a similar low arc, missed then found his target with a reversed strike. That Hunter screamed as he clutched the axe lodged in his groin, his voice tearing through Tabitha's song like a bitter banshee. How could she sing of love in the face of such horror? But how could she *not* sing against it? She could not afford to falter.

Mulrano struggled to pull his axe free but the Hunter fell and he had to abandon it. He plucked an arrow from the ground as he staggered back, waving it desperately in front of him, but the fourth Hunter advanced on him. The man whom Garyll had shouldered down had regained his feet. The two Hunters grinned cruelly as they closed on their prey, their hatred boiling forward like a cloud of bloodied tendrils.

Garyll worked with feverish intensity to keep the two blades from penetrating his defences while he retreated, protecting the weaponless Mulrano with his shield. He didn't see how the tainted cloud of hatred swept around him, past him.

Did it drive him to fight too? Five more Hunters came at them from the left, savage men, leather-armoured, their hair wild, their bloodied blades raised. Garyll would not be able to face them all. Tendrils of silvery red reached out from their tainted hearts. They were all going to die here.

Tabitha sang against the hatred, holding onto the idea of love until it overcame her. She reached the climax of her song. The pattern felt true at last, balanced, complete. The essence changed as her spell engaged. Her awareness grew in scale—she felt like the earth and the sky in the same moment—then she threw her heart out wide and released her intent, touching them all with her love. Light bloomed in the glade like the burnished copper fire of a desert sunset.

In the pool of blood, Ethea turned her head toward her, a glimpse of hope upon her strange, beautiful face. Then with a whipcrack in her mind that vision was gone.

The men who charged toward her cried out. They stumbled to their knees and turned their faces away from her, raising their hands as if to fend off a terrible brightness, or a sudden burden. The two Hunters Garyll had fought stood motionless. Their weapons slipped from their hands. Beyond them, the Lûk warriors had turned from where they had engaged Hunters—the knotted mass of fighting bodies was suddenly still. All around the glade, men turned to her, Lûk and Hunters alike.

The sky shivered, but when she looked there was nothing but a brilliant blue beyond the canopy.

A soft silence settled upon the forest as the resonance of her song faded away. Even the wounded men had ceased their cries to look upon her. She had not expected such a profound effect. The men were linked in a glowing web of emotion, heart to heart, ruby red, with her at the centre. They seemed entranced by her and could not take their eyes off her. She couldn't guess how long the enchantment would last.

She raised her voice to carry to the farthest of the men. "Set down your weapons," she said. "There will be no more fighting here."

Men separated. Despite their dialect, the Hunters understood her, for blades dropped from slack fingers just as spears fell from the hands of the numbed Lûk warriors. Lûk and Hunters alike seemed to be in a state of momentary awe.

"Gather your wounded and bring them to me, I shall do what I can to take their pain away," she declared. If she didn't offer healing, they might resume their fighting. The coloured currents of emotion faded as she released her demand on the burning ring.

She had done it! She had worked a miracle, and the Sorcerer's magic had not touched her. She had power in this place. Pride swelled in her chest. She raised her voice again, louder this time.

"You need not fear Ametheus! I have found a way to work around him!"

They stopped, and as one their faces fell. The men looked at her with abject horror, Lûk and Hunter alike.

"She has spoken his name! *Dorra kan balaan beshiru!* She has spoken his name!"

"Allerall ye frommer Eyree so blanbrainen!" cried a Hunter.

There was a sudden movement, a ripple in the ground. Her stomach gathered in a tight knot. She knew what it meant. His name? Ametheus? She was not supposed to say 'Ametheus'? Too late she remembered the warning in the Revelations. Too late.

across Oldenworld shall his Wildfire spread
massing Chaos upon every caster's thread
ending the work of the wise and the ordered
till Eyri alone stands protected, shield-bordered.

hold still your tongue when you translate –
each founding letter of these verses eight
uncovers the provoking name of that capricious-headed
Sorcerer of the silver fire, thrice-dreaded

The provoking name. Too late she understood the Riddler's warning. Oh Zarost! He had expected too much of her! The earth stood in little ridges, all around the glade. Shifting, feathered ridges, pointing inward towards her, through the men who stood motionless; struck still by horror. The air tightened.

It would come from the sky. The wildfire was gathering, and it had marked its target.

Tabitha threw her head back. A harsh light fractured the sky beyond the broken canopy. The fracture-lines joined at a node high overhead, where silver burst forth. A cluster of wildfire threads spat down toward them, a many-tentacled writhing mass that lit the river white.

They were going to get many wildfire strikes, all around them, all at once.

It was all her fault. It was coming too fast; there was no time to run anywhere. Tabitha fell as her legs collapsed. She had allowed herself to feel pride at her achievement. Like the pheasant that sang its own praise, she was about to end up cooked, by Chaos.

Oh mercy! Now that the men had had a change of heart, they were all going to die.

She took a last look around the glade. The awe had faded from the faces. There was only stark horror now, as the men turned their eyes skyward. The Lûk Spearleader Sihkran, much bloodstained, was one of the few still watching her.

"What have you done?" he shouted. "What have you done? We can't outrun *this*. You seemed like an angel, Tabitha *Mahgu*, but you have brought the *dorra* upon us. This is no way to end!" He raised his fist at the sky and repeated defiantly, "This is no way to end!"

Some men scattered into the forest, but most understood it was too late.

A heavily injured Lûk, his bald head glistening with blood, sank to his knees, reaching his arms to her, imploring her to save him, but she didn't know what to do. A silver light flashed into the canopy. Bright flickering lightning snaked down one tall trunk. The stricken tree cracked and shattered where it stood, disintegrating upon its own collapsing carcass. Then another strike came, and another. The undergrowth heaved in a wave of altering form. All around the trees screeched and imploded as the impacts of the wildfire rushed inward. The river exploded into spray.

Closer, closer; and she, alone at the centre.

Men screamed. Life flashed before her eyes.

Life, and all she had learnt from it.

25. A FAR AND DISTANT PLACE

"As soon as you can touch the stars
You'll need to be everywhere at once."—Zarost

Twardy Zarost paced among the Lûk children, where they sat dabbling with symbols they would soon forget, drawn in coloured inks. They were assembled in a neat spiral on bright cushions, on the floor of the readroom, deep in the down of Koom. He had enjoyed teaching the rules of logic to the *bogadins* while their Tattler Jhinni had worked on the translation of the Book of Is for him. He hadn't planned on spending so many days in Koom, but there were worse places to be, and Tattler Jhinni could be very insistent once she'd decided what constituted a fair trade.

Despite all the spicy comforts and foreign delights of being in the Six-sided Land, he couldn't stop thinking about Tabitha Serannon. He had been away from her for too long. True, there was little of danger in Eyri that she couldn't handle, now that the Darkmaster and his minions had been conquered. Zarost couldn't relax, because a singular truth kept turning over and over in his mind.

Young wizards had a habit of getting themselves into trouble.

He knew, because he had been a young wizard all of his life.

He was her Riddler; he should be getting back to Eyri. The Gyre could deal with the issue of the traitor, and work on meeting the challenge of Ametheus. They could summon him when they had need. Now that he had collected the fully translated manuscript of the Book of Is, the Gyre should have an advantage against whatever spell it was Ametheus was devising.

He paced his way back to the oval slateboard, where he chalked up a riddle in orange.

I can be big, I can be small,
I poke through trousers before they can fall
I can curl like a snake, yet I cannot see
I have only one fang—what can I be?

He sat down on his own cushion, and riffled through the pages of the Jhinni's translation. One last lesson and he'd be gone. How long would it be before he'd be in a Lûk down again? Some of the children were giggling and whispering. They were older than he'd thought.

One brave little bogadin had his fist raised in the Lûk manner.

"Yes, Jikjak."

"A belt, Twardy Mahgu, it's a belt!"

"Very good. Who else thought of that?"

After a telling hesitation, all the hands went up. The Lûk were compulsive liars, and the children had learnt the tradition. No one wanted to admit to being slower than little Jikjak, especially since he was the youngest.

"My, my, my, what a clever lot you are," Twardy Zarost said. "Always remember, he who thinks in little steps can often answer big questions. Tell this riddle to your parents, and see if they are as quick as you are."

That would provide some reddened faces in the family cots tonight.

He was about to pose a more difficult riddle on the board, when a sweet and beautiful distant voice came through the earth, so delicate it would be inaudible to the children, but it made him stop dead in the action of cleaning the board.

Had he really heard it? Or was it an echo of his concern?

No, he could have sworn on a double-headed dragon, he had heard the Lifesong!

An improvised stanza.

Tabitha?

It could not be her! If he heard her voice, she would have to be beyond the Shield of Eyri, in Oldenworld itself, and that would be a bad thing, bad for her, bad for the Gyre. She might be a wizard, but she had no preparation for the dangers of Oldenworld—no warding skills, no understanding of second- or third-axis spells, not even the Transference to escape the worst trouble. The wildfire! She would trigger the reactive web, and be ended.

He had to leave at once.

Twardy Zarost swiped a cloth across the board. There was a sudden indrawn breath from the doorway. Tattler Jhinni was there, looking at the slateboard over the heads of the seated children. Colour was rising in her old grey cheeks.

"Zarost!" she exclaimed. She clicked her tongue at him as she advanced into the chamber. "You should not be teaching such—"

"Tattler Jhinni," Zarost cut in, "So I have taught them more than you traded for? Surely then you are in my debt again?" But he could see by the hardening in her hard jaw that Tattler Jhinni was about to give him a piece of her mind. He didn't have the time. Although he was fond of Jhinni, she had a particularly *long* mind, especially when she was angry. "But I'm in a generous mood," he added hastily, "because you've been so kind, so I'll leave you with a gift, a problem for your mind."

He snatched up the orange chalk. On the slateboard, he drew a one, a line, and the symbol for infinity beneath it. Beside it, the equals sign and a question mark—the formula for the Transference spell.

Then, as an afterthought, he drew a head, arms and legs upon the one. That was him. He gave the little stick figure a tiny hat.

Then he spread his awareness, as fast as thought, which was always faster than the speed of light, but often not quite as direct. He drove his being in a rush, outward to the non-boundary of infinity.

He was the tunnels, the grass, sky Earth space stars galaxies universe…

He touched infinity, and vanished from the Lûk down, right before the delighted audience of *bogadins*.

As he flashed through in the limitless backcloth, he wondered if any of the Lûk children would work it out.

One over ten was a tenth, one over a million was a millionth, but one over infinity was so small it was nothing at all. And so the template of his body, attempting to contain everything, ceased to exist. The whole spell was founded on a paradox, but if he thought about it too long and hard, he'd just lose time and get nowhere at all. The Transference spell rewarded leaps of thought.

He considered where he wanted to be.

Somewhere closer to the source of the singing than Koom, the closest place he could remember well enough. He chose the down of Rôgspar. He had seen it marked on the map, beneath Koom, at the southern limit of the Six-sided Land, on the northern edge of the wildfire wastes. He had been in the area before, but so many, many years ago. He hoped his visualisation was complete enough to take him there.

He returned from the crossing point of infinity. His body pushed the world aside.

At once he knew he had made a mistake, but a hasty departure meant a hasty arrival, and there was no time to adjust his position. He was in Rôgspar all right, literally. He had not expected the level of the cast to have risen so much. Successive generations of Lûk inhabitants had burrowed farther underground, and the earth had been ejected upon the conical mound. Although Zarost had chosen to arrive near the top of the cast, he was chest deep in the soil. He flapped his arms to free himself, but only managed to flatten the flowers on either side of his shoulders. He was stuck.

A sweet-scented blossom tickled his nose, another brushed against his beard. There were flowers everywhere, surrounding him at eye level, sweeping down the cast and spreading across the meadow in a hovering tapestry of colour beneath the open sky. Glistening insects buzzed from bloom to bloom, feasting in the many nectar cups. Vermilion butterflies flitted about, overwhelmed with choice.

Rôgspar had changed. This had used to be a hard Lûk outpost, a staging point for raids into the Huntersland, a base for collecting whatever the windrunners had mined within the wastes. The Lûk were made tough here by their work with the vicious garspider silk and cultivating the stinging strands of light-emitting bacteria. But Rôgspar had changed—instead of tough and embittered it felt young and joyous, full of life.

A Lûk maiden, kneeling in the field nearby, stared at him with wide eyes. She had frozen in the act of weaving a garland of flowers. He was about to call out a greeting to her when the Lifesong swept toward him a second time. This stanza was of an altogether higher order than the first had been, drowning his senses, filling him with rapture and ruling him with a single emotion—love, so pure he felt as if his heart would burst. The emotion thrilled through him, the music rushing on by with the faintest of rainbow shimmers.

A breeze pulled across the flowers in the wake of the song. Peace came upon that breeze, balance and harmony, healing and hope, so much latent potency that he wanted to spring into the air.

He would have done so, had the earth not gripped his body so firmly. He was certain. The beauty of the melody was unmistakable. That voice belonged to the young wizard of Eyri, Tabitha Serannon. She was outside; she was beyond the Shield of Eyri!

She had sung. By the stars! She had sung. The Lûk maiden walked over to him, watching him with a dreamy smile. She placed the garland on his head then walked away and began to collect flowers for another one.

Tabitha was somewhere in the forest to the west, somewhere in the bloodbelt bordering the Hunterslands, no more than four leagues away. How had she made it through the wastes? There were so many dangers in the terrible spillage, so much malignant silver essence. Why was she out of Eyri in the first place? He'd put so many warnings into the prophecy, but maybe she hadn't read them yet. She was supposed to be accompanied. Strangely enough, her singing hadn't drawn the wildfire. It had felt so different. It had *changed* things, without moving the essence. How had she done that?

But then he felt the horrible rupture. The world jumped. Something else had come after her spell and triggered a terrible consequence. The sky fractured overhead, a jagged crack that tore through the disjointed clouds and the varying blue panes of sky, marking the running passage of the deadly charge. Many erratic lines converged over a place a few leagues away in the dark forest. The tightening web arced and spawned a bright knot of threads in its centre, which fell upon the forest, its many tentacles searching the air ahead of it—a multiple strike, a super-cluster of Chaos.

Twardy clutched his hat. Wildfire fell upon the Lifesinger.

Would she be able to outrun the strike? Surely not. There was little chance of escape for her if she was on foot. Sometimes the wildfire strikes were prone to be inaccurate, especially so far from the Sorcerer's Pillar in Turmodin, but he wouldn't bet on it. He wouldn't bet on anything when playing against the Sorcerer.

Tabitha needed him.

His transference was quick, for he could see where he wanted to be—beneath the shrieking fall of Chaos-essence, where the ground had most likely ridged up in anticipation of its coming. He was gone from the flower-strewn meadow of Rôgspar in a mental jerk that caused his awareness to whip outward to the immeasurable ends of infinity and return, in the flickering of an eye, to a single place in the forest.

He found her in the middle of a trampled battleground, where dazed Lûk warriors and wounded Hunters stood among discarded weapons, fallen bodies and blood. She was with two Eyrian companions—Swordmaster Glavenor and the fisherman Mulrano. Mulrano! What was he doing in Oldenworld?

The Swordmaster had raised a long shield over their heads. Lûk-woven cane, hardened, strong against arrows—the wildfire would burn through it as if it was made of paper.

"This is a merry fix," he said, ducking beneath their shield's useless canopy.

Three startled faces looked back at him. Zarost recognised the glazed expression of helpless panic. Even Glavenor was affected. That was something new—the man had changed, he was wiser; older. Zarost turned his attention skyward. There was no time for a complicated spell like the multilaced backbraided dispersal shield or a slow spell like a reference. He had two options—a transference, or a spell of reflection. His thoughts split upon the probabilities. Success with the transference would be unlikely. He could take Tabitha away, but many others would die. He wouldn't be able to move her companions in such a quick weave, because they weren't wizards. Their minds would cave in under the vastness of infinity, and he'd never be able to bring them back. He followed that line of prophecy for an instant. He would lose Tabitha as well. She would mourn the loss of her precious Garyll and forever search in the stars for her love, like the legend of Erill and Gamede. No, reflection was the only option. Funny how it always remained as the last thing in the smelting pot, when all else was burnt away. The power of reflection, he reflected, was in what was reflected.

Even as he breathed the words of the spell, he knew there would be further consequences. The Gyre didn't approve of the spell, it wasn't *classified*. Most of the wizards felt it was closer to the Chaos end of the third axis than to any other pole. It would act as a mirror. It did nothing to alter the wildfire, or even to diminish it—it would drive the falling Chaos essence back upon itself. Thus the disorder would be multiplied as particles collided against each other with even greater vigour. There would be more Chaos in the universe, not less, but it was the only solution.

The sky fell with a whining screech. *Keep your hat on. Can't afford to lose your head.* He considered the simple algorithm that would flip the velocity of the wildfire, if he could reach enough of it in time. The pattern formed a little half-sphere in the air between his hands. In its convex surface the approaching wildfire shot out around the reflected image of Garyll's raised shield and the small worried faces beneath it. Silver light danced upon the spell's curvature. It would draw the wildfire faster. It *did* look like a Chaos-spell, now that he saw it like that. It took its nature from what it faced.

Out in the forest, a tree flared, then imploded as the advance strikes began to fall.

"And the multiplier pattern," he explained to Tabitha, hastily scribing a pattern upon the liquid clarity that looked like a minus one. It would bind the spell to its own reflected light and so travel outward at great speed, reversing any moving particles it met along the way. The simplest spells were always the fastest.

He released his hold on the essence. The domed Reflection shot away in all directions, spreading as it rose, rushing through the men then the trees just as it passed upward through the raised shield and raced to meet the wildfire. Its surface, as delicate as the skin of a soap bubble, carried shimmering images of the people it might save.

Zarost held his breath. If the spreading spell encountered a gap in the essence, it might develop a lesion at that point, and the wildfire might pierce it there. He hadn't had enough time to *gather* the clear essence before beginning. He hoped Tabitha had activated enough of it.

Wildfire filled the collapsing sky, rough and ragged, as if heavy clumps of silver rock plummeted toward them. The Chaos essence, so bright before, seemed dull when seen through his expanding spell. Zarost wasn't fooled. The wildfire was as potent as ever. They were merely inside a mirror, so there was very little light.

The wildfire struck.

Silver essence screeched away into the sky, a scattering of deadly mayhem. It would bring worse destruction on Oldenworld where it fell. Some of it would even spread out into the stars. Despite the filtering effect of the Reflection, it grew brighter and brighter in the forest. A blinding hole burned through in the membrane. A finger of Chaos shot down, and a tree on the edge of the glade burst into a multitude of experimental forms, splitting into a haze of fibres, recombining into broken spines, then a black and sickly skin, sinking upon itself with each alteration, until it was a globular heap steaming in a patch of burning soil. Another tree lit up, spread its limbs, and screamed with an eerily human voice as it fell back into the undergrowth.

The Reflection spell reached the edge of the available clear essence, and it faded away. The light returned in full to the forest. Zarost peered out from under the shield.

A thousand tails of Chaos chased each other away into the sky.

Zarost breathed out. There was nothing left of the wildfire strike. It had been turned, cast outward upon the rest of Oldenworld. Much devastation would come of it, more than before, but Tabitha Serannon was safe. A tinking sound, like cooling metal, told him they were all safe. He turned to face the young wizard of Eyri.

"What in the blue blazes are you doing here?" He was still struggling to get used to the idea—the raw graduate was outside, in

Oldenworld. He was shocked, challenged and immensely proud. He jigged from one foot to the other.

Tabitha just mouthed on empty air, and looked at him with brimming eyes.

"Oh Twardy!" She threw her arms around him. "I'm so glad you're here!"

He flapped his hands helplessly behind her back for a moment then returned her embrace. Her presence was a warm blessing of tenderness and youth. She smelled of Lûk crumble-spices and pollen. She felt good in his hands. Her hair had caught in his stubbly beard.

Garyll Glavenor looked upon him with unnerving steadiness.

Some things about the man *hadn't* changed.

"Careful," Zarost said jokingly. "Your protector will think I've caught your eye."

"Little fear of that," Garyll responded. "No, I was wondering why you only arrived so late, but well met, Riddler, you are most welcome! It seems you are more than just a riddler." He extended his right hand, and Zarost ran the gambit of gripping it as he and Tabitha parted. Thankfully, the shake was no more than firm. More than just a riddler? The man had no idea what a riddler truly was.

Zarost turned to Mulrano. "My friend, they have roped you into this crazy journey as well!" He wanted to slap him on the back, but the poor fisherman had wounds in his shoulder, ones that could be healed.

"Egh!" said Mulrano. "Cahnk go back engy more." He winced. "Cahnk go ong ngow, eiver."

Zarost looked at the three of them. "Well this is going to take some unriddling," he said. "It seems I have missed too many chapters of the story." He surveyed the carnage. "Which side of this battle were we on?"

"The Lûk's," Tabitha replied, looking horrified and ashamed. "I was trying to stop it."

"While they were fighting?" Zarost asked. Trying to stop a battle between such arch enemies was like trying to separate a pack of rabid dogs by waving a piece of meat at them.

"They did stop," said Garyll.

Zarost hesitated. What had Tabitha learnt to do in his absence? Whatever had she used that beautiful new stanza for? She was not the same wizard he had guided back to Stormhaven.

He eyed his charge critically. "Why did you join the battle in the first place?"

"The Lûk were coming to find Prince Bevn," she replied. "So are we."

"Prince Bevn, King Mellar's son Bevn? But he is no mage! How in the Destroyer's name did he pass through the Shield?"

"I don't know, Twardy, but he has stolen the crown. King Mellar sent us after him."

Zarost felt the weight of all his eluded years press suddenly upon his heart.

The Kingsrim had left Eyri!

If the prince was wearing the crown, if it had accepted him, he would have been able to walk through the Shield as if it wasn't there. And Zarost, the one wizard who should have prevented such a disaster, had done nothing. He had been following the trail of the missing Gyre text.

A trail, or a distraction?

"By all the black-hearted crows! I take it the king is none too well? Dear oh dear oh dear! This is no good at all."

The Kingsrim was the anchor for the Shield of Eyri, it was the crux. Without it, the Shield would be weak, and the king would be tripping headlong into madness.

"If you came after Bevn, and not with him, how did you cross through the Shield?"

Tabitha looked down and away. "It got hardest right at the edge, where the essence was bound so tightly. I...I grew a little cross at being denied." Her voice grew small. "I think I might have broken it."

"Oh merry me! It gets worse every time I ask a question!" Zarost exclaimed. "And the wastes, however did you cross them without being killed?"

Tabitha closed her eyes.

"It was a bad journey," Glavenor filled in. "We lost our horses. We lost our companion, Logán, the young Gifter. The wildfire struck down on her once, and we outran it. We found a scoured valley that was clean. I think we were lucky."

"Lucky? Lucky! Nobody has ever crossed it on foot, nobody in unaltered form. You have the luck of all the Gods and Goddesses combined."

Tabitha looked at him in horror. A shadow seemed to cross her face.

"Well. Not really lucky, I suppose. Blessed, then?" No doubt the wastes had been a horrifying experience.

"I've just been trying to survive, so far," she murmured.

"And yet you have perfected the art of being at the centre of every conflict. What were you planning to do with all the Chaos you had summoned? Did you have any plan at all?"

"There wasn't much time. I had thought—maybe—the Shiver note would do something?"

"And so spread the wildfire like a fine dust upon everyone?" He gave a nervous little laugh. "Very effective. You would have had time to appreciate each monstrous form you took, instead of burning away instantly."

Zarost shook his head. She was so impulsive. She never thought things through. So much like himself, all those years ago, in the college in Kingsmeet. Tabitha was going to be very, very dangerous to be around.

"Never mind, that subject fills half of the Gyre's library, and still we are not wise enough to answer it."

"I didn't know his name would summon wildfire, here in the forest!" she exclaimed.

"It will happen everywhere in Oldenworld, wherever the wildfire web has grown."

"Then why didn't you warn me?" she challenged him.

Zarost laughed. "I did that, I did indeed, and yet you have found a way to work around his web! I heard your song, dear Tabitha, it was a wonderwork."

"But what am I to do, Twardy? We must find Bevn, we must retrieve the crown. Will you help us?"

"Have no fear, I can do nothing else. The sooner we can find the Kingsrim the better. You said the Hunters knew something of where Bevn is? Well, then we shall ask them."

So many dead. Bodies littered the forest floor. Most of the remaining Hunters had fled into the forest while he'd been speaking to Tabitha, but he spied a ragtag cluster of wounded men moving slowly, supporting each other. He walked in their direction.

"Spearleader Sihkran tried that," Garyll called after him. "They weren't very forthcoming. That's what sparked off this whole battle."

"Surely so," Zarost acknowledged, "but it is mostly how a question is asked that determines the answer."

He strode off after the ragged bunch of leather-clad men. The Eyrians trailed along behind him.

"Men! I can help you, if you tell us some things."

They looked over their shoulders, and the more agile among them ran away, shouting.

"Wait! I shall not fight you!" But Zarost understood. They were afraid of magic, not weapons. After the quantity of wildfire Tabitha had summoned, he wasn't surprised. They must have seen him appear, and had marked him as a magic-worker, one to avoid at all costs.

One Hunter could only move at a slow hobble. He had nasty gashes in both of his legs, and he held his one arm cradled in the other. He kept his head down, even when Zarost stopped him.

"Do yer ken wherebegone a Prince Bevn?"

The man slowly raised his head. He looked back at Zarost with blank incomprehension. The Hunter language had changed again since he had last been among the south-eastern tribes. He made a stab at a likely degeneration.

"Telleroos wherebegone a boyden Eyri. We kennernow he par thoo a'huntersland."

He seemed to understand some of that, because he snarled and said, "The owing be a'settled ready all with our lifewater!"

"You paid that debt to the Lûk, not to me," said Zarost. He bent closer. "If ye come back upon yon querrying, I taker pains. I make a'foot running."

The Hunter jutted his chin out stubbornly, waiting for Zarost to step out of the way.

"Please," said Tabitha, brushing gently past his shoulder. "We need your help."

The Hunter's eyes widened as he looked at her then he knelt suddenly, despite his evident pain.

"Ye touch my heart with asingsong, ladyfayre, ye touch my heart."

"Where is the Prince from Eyri?"

"The bratling is as gone, he left the Hide an bin running northwards from three days hence. 's no loss to Bradach! We be glad to see him gone. He namer name of yon silversoul in a'hide, as'er yee."

Zarost tensed. "Bevn spoke the name out loud as well?" He named Ametheus? The prince knew of things he shouldn't know, coming from Eyri. It was unnatural. "How does he know where to go? Who is with him?"

The Hunter's uncomprehending gaze swung from one face to the next.

"Who strays aside a'boy?" Zarost tried, using his best imitation of the Hunterly brogue.

"He be with a fiery wench, she inablack leatherly, a fighterly girl na querry. Anner ally, he giddey all onbeyon' Bradach."

"An ally? Who was the ally?"

The Hunter's mouth made a little "O" of horror, and he looked suddenly inward, as if he'd wished he hadn't said anything.

Tabitha squatted in front of him, her eyes at his level. "We need to know, goodman. We have to track these two, they are thieves. Who do they travel with?"

"I cannerna say! Yoch, ye canner ask me! He willerdo thinge terrible a'me!"

"Who will do these things?" asked Zarost.

"The ally! He is na ever angered!" The Hunter swung his panicked gaze from one face to the next. He tried to struggle to his feet, and he cried out in agony, but he rose nonetheless.

"Let me take away your pain!" Zarost offered again. "Or the lady Tabitha can heal you, if you'd prefer. Just tell us who the ally is."

"Nay, I willna be drawn inneryor world so full a'treacherly. The ally helped a'Hunters first, an I'll na betray him to another magickan, no matter the bargain be."

The Hunter backed away, stumbling. Zarost looked at the man in amazement.

Another magickan, he'd said. The Hunters' ally was a wizard, a male wizard because he'd said "him".

Zarost tried to fit the pieces of the puzzle together. There were only four male wizards in the Gyre, besides Zarost. The Senior and Mentalist had been present in the Gyre Sanctuary when he'd left there recently. That left only the Lorewarden and the Warlock at large in Oldenworld.

"Does he have red eyes? The ally! A red that holds gold?"

The Hunter looked more horrified than he'd ever been. "I did na say that! *I* did na say it!"

But by denying that *he'd* admitted it, he revealed too much.

"Black Saladon," Zarost declared.

The Hunter turned and fled, with hobbles, jumps and cries.

Tabitha made a small sound beside him. She couldn't bear to see the poor man in such pain. Before she could try to do anything about it, Zarost sent a small spell of his own after the Hunter, a little stitch of nine—a blend of Order and Matter-magic that would encourage the loose threads of flesh to knit together. It probably wasn't as good a healing as Tabitha could achieve with her Lifesong, but it would do. The hole he'd blasted in the wildfire web gave him a temporary freedom in the use of his spells. Nevertheless, he didn't want Tabitha to use her magic again, not here, not until she had some understanding of what she was doing.

The Hunter stumbled then gathered speed. At this, Glavenor tensed. Zarost could see that the Swordmaster wanted to go after him.

"Let him go," Zarost said gently.

"But he will lead us to Bevn!" Glavenor exclaimed. "Or at least to where he was. We can track the prince from there."

"You'll not follow them quickly through the Hunterslands," Zarost replied. "Not if Black Saladon is leading them. No, we must use our wits if we are to stop them now." He raised his eyebrows in the Swordmaster's direction. Glavenor gave him another of his characteristically hard looks.

Zarost considered their predicament. Why was Black Saladon leading the renegade prince? Was that really the truth of the matter? Maybe Saladon had discovered the prince and his consort in Bradach Hide, and he was luring them away from whatever devious plan they had been trying to complete.

Zarost hoped that was the case. He wanted to believe that the Warlock was still on their side. If he'd joined Ametheus then there truly was little hope left for the Gyre, but then he remembered the trail of blood he'd seen in the Temple of Qirrh, and a cold chill crept up his spine. If the Warlock had been responsible for that...

Oh, of all the wizards, why did it have to be Saladon who had been turned?

The more he considered it, the worse it became. The Warlock was also a master strategist. He would know there was a chance his movements would be discovered. He would expect someone to try to follow him. He would have laid traps to slow down pursuit, or eliminate it. What was Saladon trying to achieve by leading the bearer of the Kingsrim north through the Hunterslands?

North, toward Slipper. Then the lowlands, and Turmodin.

No, it could not be!

If Ametheus got his hands on the Kingsrim, he would have a hold on every Gyre member. A part of their life-force had gone into the making of that crown, a part of every soul, woven into the threads of metal; it had been the only way to achieve the Kingsrim's lasting effect. The aura of grandeur surrounding the crown and the longevity of the Shield anchored upon it relied on that secret link. So long as the wizards of the Gyre were alive, the Kingsrim retained its power, and while it retained its power, it held onto a thread of their souls.

"I must warn the Gyre, at once!" Zarost exclaimed then, aside, "We'll be run through the miller if it reaches the Pillar."

Tabitha snapped her head around. "Pillar? What pillar is that?"

"It's where the Sorcerer dwells, in Turmodin."

"You know where it is? Twardy, will you take us there? I must reach the pillar, before it is too late!"

"Are you mad, child? Nobody goes there. It is the centre of ruin, the source of all disorder. It is the very aperture of the apocalypse. Even fools do not go there willingly. You do not come back, if you go to the Pillar."

Tabitha seemed forlorn, even desperately sad. "But I must. Oh Twardy, there is so little time left!"

Zarost couldn't fathom why she wanted to die. She was so young, so talented, and yet she wanted to go to Turmodin? "Why do you want to rush to such a certain end? Was the wildfire not evidence enough of his power?"

"But he has Ethea! He has trapped the Goddess."

All the doubts and worries that had plagued Zarost during his search for that missing lore torn from the Book of Is found a terrible conclusion in Tabitha's announcement. He couldn't understand how she knew it, but she was certain of her words. The ceremony of invocation was for Ethea, to bring the Goddess of Life into this world, to bind her, to trap her. It was a diabolical plan.

"She is going to die." Tabitha spoke softly, looking at the ground.

No. It could not be. "How did you learn of this?" Zarost asked.

"I have been with her, Twardy. When I sing, I am taken closer to her. There, where the sky is red and the wet air smells of salt. I have seen what he has done to her."

"You have *seen*? You have pierced the veil of Turmodin? You must take your vision to the Gyre! They must know what we face is dire."

"Will it help Ethea? Will they do anything to save her?" Tabitha demanded.

"They must," he answered. "You cannot succeed alone, Tabitha! What will you do against the Sorcerer, if he has wielded the power to bind a *Goddess*? I've never heard of such might, he is too powerful to oppose alone; we shall need our combined power to match him. Besides, if Ethea is in danger now, you'll not *walk* all the way to Turmodin in time to save her! There are quicker ways for wizards to move. Come with me to the Gyre. Many things will be clearly clear to you, once you have met the other few."

"Will they show me the way to Turmodin?" she asked.

"That, and much more," Zarost answered. "There is so much you can learn, now that your own lore has emerged. Come, we must travel by transference. We must travel at once."

"Wait! What about Garyll?"

"The Swordmaster cannot come where we shall go, Tabitha, he is not a wizard."

"No! If I am to go somewhere, Garyll must come with me, and Mulrano."

"It cannot be done, Tabitha. Do you remember what it was like?" She wouldn't have forgotten the time when he had saved her from the last Morgloth, those long moments when she had been suspended in infinity before he'd managed to gather her awareness and return her to Stormhaven.

"The stars?" she asked uncertainly.

"Yes. We must go through them and beyond, to reach the Gyre. You have...advantages...that they do not have. They cannot come with us. They'll lose their minds."

"Is there no other way to reach the Gyre?"

He shook his head.

"Then I shall not come," she stated flatly.

Glavenor touched her shoulder. "If it will help you understand, then go with him, Tabitha."

"But if I leave here, how will I find you again?"

"You'll always find him when you're apart, you'll find the man within your heart," Zarost reassured her.

"Go, Tabitha, we are beyond the danger, Mulrano and I. We need answers, and only you can get them for us."

She grabbed hold of Glavenor. They really had become attached to each other—love sparkled in their eyes, and its dark twin: the fear of losing love.

"I will give you some many moments, to say goodbye," Zarost said. A goodbye was important, more important than a hello. It created the shape that the next hello would fit into. He gestured to the fisherman, and they walked aside, away from the bloody battlefield, toward the river. The Glimmershot was polluted, Zarost noted, full of fallout from the Chaos strike. They stood and watched the water flowing by.

"We fign Bevng?"

Zarost nodded. He appreciated the bluff fisherman. The man had bad arrow wounds, he'd just survived a battle, and yet he moved on, practical as ever. They had cut out his tongue, and he moved on. Like an ox. Like a river. Zarost liked him immensely.

"I must help Tabitha with her Goddess-relief, but you can help the Swordmaster catch the thief," Zarost agreed.

"Woo have ung igea weh vey ahh goink?"

"Indeed so, they would scuttle for the lowlands. They'll make for Slipper, in the gap in the Winterblade range where this river falls away and becomes the Caskarrik. But you'll not have a chance of catching them, even if you run on the Lûk roads."

"Wo' abouk rivah?" asked Mulrano, jerking his thumb in the direction of the frothing river course.

Zarost nodded, glad that Mulrano had chosen correctly. It was simple to guide a man like Mulrano. It was just a matter of placing the next practical solution ahead of his feet. The river would be the quickest. The Glimmershot River ran past Slipper. After the recent rains it was swollen and swift. It was what they might find *in* the Glimmershot that was not so helpful.

They watched the water for some time as it slid by in stretched grey ripples, like landscapes passing under a winter sky, like patterns in time. He couldn't see anything moving within the liquid, which just proved that there wasn't anything that was visible.

Would Saladon not have thought of using the river as well? He tried to think like the Warlock. Strategically it would be the best way to Slipper; it would avoid most complications that settlements and people introduced, but there was something menacing about it for the Warlock, very menacing indeed.

Water, especially flowing water, held bad memories for Saladon, phantoms that would wail at him from their graves. Zarost knew something of the Warlock's childhood, and he knew it had ended with water. His parents had been swept away in a time of flood, and the young Saladon, a child of only six, had clutched onto the tree that had ultimately drowned them. It had rolled over his parents in their struggles. In the years that had passed, he had grown strong, and he had become a formidable fighter, and finally he had studied to be a wizard, but he had never outgrown that secret terror carved upon his spirit. Water drowned, water destroyed and water would take his life away. He controlled his fear well, and he probably thought his weakness was unknown, but Twardy Zarost knew how to infer things from the littlest signs, and he saw things that others did not.

Yes, the Warlock would have preferred the Lûk tunnels, or the cover of the deep forest. He would not have tempted the uncertain currents of the Glimmershot, and if he was escorting the Kingsrim, moving via a Transference spell was impossible.

Tabitha and Glavenor approached in silence and joined them beside the river.

"I must wizard Tabitha away, but she will come back," Zarost promised. "While we are gone, the Kingsrim must not get to Turmodin, or we will lose everything. We are going to need your help to catch the thief, Swordmaster."

Garyll looked up. "I am not the Swordmaster any more," he corrected.

That explained the absence of the sword Felltang. "You have forgotten yourself? That is most difficult to do, most difficult."

Garyll gave Zarost a level stare. "Forgetting is not the same as forgiving."

"Ah, but remembering yourself again, that is the hardest of them all," said Zarost.

"Riddler! Don't vex me with your wit, give me some knowledge I can use to catch the crown thief! You think we'll have a chance tracking them through the Huntersland? Is there somewhere we can intercept them?"

"Mulrano has already guessed upon the river. Run with the Lûk to Firro, it's a riverside settlement to the north. Take a boat from there. It'll be hard work on the upper reach, but hellish fast, three days at most. If you can reach Slipper in time, you may be able to intercept them. We shall join you as soon as we can. Look for the three spires of rock. They look like fingers, on the right on the final approach. You do not want to pass Slipper by mistake, the rapids beyond are too treacherous. Follow this river long enough and you'll find yourself with the Sorcerer, at its end. Come, it's time we went to the Gyre, wizard of Eyri."

"Now?"

"Yes."

She turned to Glavenor, planted a slow kiss on his lips. "I'll come back soon, my love," she said.

"Come back when your questions have been answered," he replied. "Don't worry about us, if Bevn gets to Slipper after us, we shall stop him."

"Goodbye, Mulrano."

The fisherman bobbed his head. "Hmh."

A good man that, Mulrano. Zarost wished he had more time: time to stop and talk with him, time to fish with him on the Amberlake. When this was all over, he decided. He'd arrange for something large to bite his hook, just for the pleasure of seeing the joy and determination on the fisherman's face as he was pulled off his boat, fighting his line. Zarost whispered the words for another Stitch in Nine spell, and guided the tight weave of essence to Mulrano's wounds. Mulrano rocked back on his feet as the essence struck him, but he grinned and shook his head, as if enjoying a private joke.

"The Lûk are used to taking arrows," Zarost added. "Ask them for some foaming salve. It'll clean those scars out nicely as they knit."

Tabitha turned to face Zarost, her lyre in hand. She squared her shoulders. "All right, I am ready. What do I do?"

"Nothing," he said, touching her shoulder.

His awareness expanded in a cosmic instant, and they were gone.

Two divided by infinity was just as thinly spread as one had ever been. With their coupled awareness they spanned the stars, the galaxies, and spread across deep space, to the end. It seemed black, utterly black, until Tabitha finally let go and the colours came out, the finest jewel-dust scattered upon a sea of blue-black velvet.

26. OITAMBAKALKALISSEMI

"If the end had your eye and you were the tool,
You'd gibber sometimes, and act like a fool."—Zarost

Ametheus looked up at the endless stars. The winds spiralled around him, guided by his need. A vortex had opened in the low belly of the clouds. It allowed him to see all the way up to the night sky. He reached out his hands and sifted through the heavens, searching for the movement that would show him where the wizards might be. The winds pulled at his clothes—the forces were unbalanced, never under control. The encrusted surface he was standing upon shifted under his feet, and the Pillar below tilted with a shuddering groan.

He was frustrated, angry, impatient and scared.

Brother Amyar was the one who was angry—he always was. He remembered the early years, when destroying Order had seemed so certain. The whole terrible system of control had toppled, piece by piece, shot through with his wildfire. The structures of civilisation had crumbled under the raw force of Chaos like sandcastles before the tide, but as time had passed, the task had become more and more of a burden to complete. To eliminate Order altogether, to crush the final resistant strain, was fiendishly difficult. The smaller the source of Order became the more difficult it was to isolate and target. The Gyre of Wizards! For too long had he chased the last eight, the wicked spider of spells; for too long had he searched for their sanctuary. Seven now, considering the leg he had already broken off the spider—the traitor. He only had to find them once, and the game would be ended.

Brother Seus knew the wizards moved through the stars but he could not mimic their spells. He didn't need to. He could snap off a piece of space and transport it whole. He never moved to the places himself. He simply moved whatever had piqued his interest to Turmodin, swapped it with a useless piece of coastline or sea or sky. The citadel below was an accretion of collectables, torn from the landscapes they had originally inhabited. He collected many things to his lair, some for their beauty, some for their company. Half of a bridge from Azique, with its spangled shroud-lines and scalloped copper plates, lay submerged in the clutter of the Pillar's eastern foot. Smooth holed boulders from the riverbed near Fairway formed a root which jutted into the turgid seas to the north. Those boulders had supported a foaming green waterfall when he'd chosen them, but the river hadn't survived the move. Upon the current roof he had planted some slender blue-leafed trees from the forests around Oren Lees, but since they had come with too little soil most of them had fallen over, breaking the coloured glass sculptures he'd wrenched from the ruins of Wrynn. Most of the towering building below was made of dark, rusted metal, pitted and bent, gathered by the waifs within the Pillar in the hope of preventing slippages and structural collapse. Such efforts were wasted, but the inhabitants of the Pillar never understood that. They were too short-lived to learn the futility of their actions and too fearful of his wrath to leave. So close to the Nodes of Chaos, trying to build structure into anything was hopeless. If there was order to the construction, it would fall apart. Only haphazard, careless placement allowed the Pillar to grow, the new elements balanced impossibly upon the layers below. And so the Pillar had grown and grown, a monumental mass of Oldenworld's prettiest scraps, added to year by year, until now it thrust him up to the very base of the clouds. It should have collapsed centuries ago, and yet it clung to its many pieces, erect, hollow, with a flush of false vitality within it.

Yet it had no life of its own—the life that moved within it was taken from Oldenworld too.

Girls whose faces mirrored the sun, boys whose bodies were lithe; the best examples of beauty he could find. He couldn't resist their allure, the chance to discover the secret of their form. Like a magpie, he stacked his nest with those attractive treasures, but although they were living when they arrived, they always ended up dead. Their sparkle went out. Then they would be tossed out by newcomers, those who sought to appease him.

Fools! His brothers could not be appeased, not until the wizards were all dead.

Ethan looked down at the ground behind his feet—he had no choice, because his brothers looked up at the stars. Clumps of white hair swirled across his vision like old smoke. It was sad, Ethan thought, nothing lived for long amid the disturbance caused by the Nodes of Chaos. Always, among the slouching columns and crumbling walls, through the flooded basements and the polluted canals, there was fighting, bloodshed, disease, filth and death. Nothing he worked upon could retain life. He could alter their form, over and over, but beings of flesh turned to creatures of wilder forms then became plant-like or wood-textured, until they finally became rocks or a speckled kind of ooze that did not respond.

He *would* find what it was that made things beautiful. He *would*. Then he would change them all, and they would be glad. It was worth a few dying to learn that secret. Surely they understood that. They would, the ones who were made beautiful. They would understand it in the end. And while they didn't understand, it was best for them to stay in the Pillar, and the higher the better, where he could keep an eye on them.

He did what he could for them, but they always died.

And now there was that bird-creature, the goddess, so pitiful in her chains, so strange and beautiful it made his heart ache to look at her, and yet he had to take her to the very brink of despair, or she would not perform her function and call out her enchantment. She wasn't a wizard, he was all too painfully aware of that. She was a spirit being, she was Life, and he was forcing her to perform a terrible thing. It made Ethan want to throw up, yet his brothers wouldn't hear any of his pleas—she was a means to an end. She was the means to *the* End.

It was his Father's will, and so it would be done. Nothing could stop what they had set in motion.

Ethan was scared. What would become of *him*, once her song was sung? *All* life ended? His Father had assured him that it would lead to glory, but when he tried to think about what could lie on the other side of the ending, he just got a headache. It made no sense. If everything was shattered upon the Destroyer's anvil, where would he and his brothers live? What would *living* mean, if there was no universe and nothing to *experience*? That would be the result if the goddess sang her song—the End, the final apocalypse, with only timeless nothingness thereafter. Suddenly it clutched his gut with its thrill. It revealed its promise to him. He was so tired of being here. It would wipe away all of his tears. The End would be his release.

Oh Father, you understand me too well.

He had had no choice in the matter, anyway. Once he had been shown the opportunity, his Father had demanded that it be done, and so he had worked the mighty spell upon the goddess, changing her spirit to flesh, capturing her essence with the aid of the willing clerics. Now she was trapped in her body and she clung to her manacles, watching the bloody waters rise, the poor creature. He was torturing an innocent. Instead of studying beauty, he was breaking it. Again. And if she sang her song, everything would die, even the little forest things.

"Oh, we should not have done it," complained Ethan.

"Shut up, you!" answered Amyar.

"It is our Father's will," added Seus, loftily. "We live to serve him, our power comes from him."

"I never wanted power," mumbled Ethan, but the others ignored him.

How had it come to this? What they were doing was worse than what had ever been committed under the name of Order.

"It's the wizards fault!" Amyar shouted. "If they had let Order die, we wouldn't have to do this."

Amyar was right. That was why he had to search for them. If he could gather them all up and crush them in time, maybe his Father would let him release the goddess. Chaos would have no opposition, and there would be no need to destroy this flawed and miserable universe.

Ametheus knew that when the black-faced wizard brought the crown to him, he would have a better grip on them all, but he was impatient, he wanted them ended *now*. And so he searched the stars, for the trace of their spells, hoping to follow them to their source, to find the location of the Gyre's keep. He knew they convened somewhere and yet it remained beyond his grasp.

Some were abroad now, he had felt disturbance as the faint trace of Order had cannoned through him, spreading outward, rushing away to the far limits of space. They would pass by again, soon. Maybe he could catch them on the return-stroke.

And so at last, Ethan reluctantly joined his brothers in their search. It was time to work with magic, or at least, against it. He looked up, through his brothers' eyes, at the endless stars.

The stars were not eternal, he realised. They, too, would be gone, if the Destroyer had his way.

THE THIRD MOVEMENT

THE TURNING OF THE GYRE

He will chase the gold and find the red
Chase the tail and find the head
Chase the song and find instead
the tangled weaves of magic thread

—*Wry Tad Zastor, Prophet*

27. A CRACKLING GOOD TIME

"When two people are right, yet neither agree,
then the truth's of a kind they cannot see."—Zarost

It was like breathing cold air through every part of her body. Her mind had *expanded*; she was spread throughout the vast expanse of the universe. Tabitha was *everywhere*, all at once. Her omnipresence threatened to overwhelm her.

She had been here before. Infinity, Zarost had called it.

Tabitha tried to hold on to her identity, but it was difficult knowing where she ended and anything else began. She was part of everything, and everything was part of her. Shifting currents of energy and matter moved within her, light radiated into darkness, great clouds of pale coloured gas billowed around bright fragments and slowly turning systems collapsed inward to spiralling foci of chaos.

She was far more than she had thought she was.

Somebody tugged at her awareness, but she was too absorbed in her reverie to pay the interruption any heed. Tabitha drifted on a dark star-studded sea, and she could feel everything within her vibrating in a regular rhythmic pulse. A sound flowed in her reverberant veins, carrying strength, carrying vitality. She recognised the exultant chords: the Lifesong. It was immense, it governed so much life.

Suddenly, giant fingers raked over her, as if someone was trying to gather her from the cosmos. She was dragged downward. The harmonious sound of the Lifesong was smothered by a jangling discord. The grip of the giant unseen hand strengthened, and her awareness of the universe and all its immeasurable beauty gave way to the demanding presence that pulled her down. An image formed under the star-scape, as if she was seeing through water and something was rising through it. A figure stood upon a tall, misshapen building, his head bent to his chest, a fringe of white hair hanging down like a beard. He watched her out of a single dark eye set in a pasty white face. His head seemed to be upside down. Was his neck broken? The incongruity of his posture made Tabitha dizzy. He should not be able to see her in that position. It was as if he had a face in the back of his head, and it had been tilted over to reveal that silver-patterned eye. His gnarled, broad-fingered hands clawed the air, and a horrible sensation of raw power wrenched through her.

"Turn away, Tabitha, turn away!" whispered an urgent voice from afar. "Come back to me. Listen. Follow the sound of my words."

Twardy Zarost, she remembered. He was with her, in infinity.

Below her, the forbidding figure roared; his clamorous din threatened to drown out everything else.

"Quick! Follow the patterns!" ordered Zarost. "Keep your sight on the stars."

But she couldn't see anything, apart from the entrancing intruder. She knew who he was—Ametheus, the Sorcerer.

Waves of heat came off him. A crumpling, caving, collapsing feeling engulfed her.

"Tabitha! This way!" Something grasped her from behind.

She felt as if she was being stretched between two opposing forces.

Not a moment too soon, she reached for the Riddler in her thoughts, and as she did so his voice became clearer.

"Spread your mind out, spread out! Don't allow yourself to become focused on that place. Disperse, reach for the outer limits of infinity. If you are *thin* he will not find you."

She tried to release her focus, as Zarost had instructed, but it wasn't easy because she was scared. Slowly, a cluster of bright stars became visible, superimposed upon the vision of the Sorcerer upon his Pillar, then more stars, and the deepness of space.

"That's better," said Zarost. "Now hold on! We shall have to shake him off. This will feel a little strange."

He guided her away, along a glistening trail of stars. Tabitha was glad Zarost was keeping a firm grip on her awareness, because without him she would have been hopelessly lost. They shifted inward to a particular point, then shot outward again, only to converge in another place. Faster and faster they moved, spanning galaxies the one moment then converging upon a single star in the next, zigzagging through the universe until Tabitha had lost all sense of direction or dimension.

She felt dissolved in the vastness. Tabitha wanted to close her eyes and shut it all out, but she couldn't, for in this strange dimension she had no eyes to close. She was aware, and that was all.

"Now we are ready to transfer," whispered Zarost, his thoughts echoing through her. "To the Sanctuary!"

As the thread of her consciousness drew tight, so she became aware of where she was being guided to. Somewhere in a desert—a tiered stronghold, surrounded with arching loops of clear force, layered magical shields.

With a sudden jolt, she was in her body again.

She gasped and staggered, using a wall to steady herself—a deep blue marble wall that had not been there a moment before. Great columns of braided metal threads rose around her, supporting a high detailed ceiling crisscrossed with arcs of gold and strange symbols.

The Riddler let go of her shoulder and spun away, hopping from one foot to the other across the white rough-tiled floor. "Who-ho-ho! That was close, by djinimy djin, closer than a hair! I did not expect *him* to be able to find us in infinity! The Sorcerer, lurking in the crossing point!" He turned toward her. "Forgive me, Tabitha, that must have seemed too fast, but I couldn't risk him following us, finding us at last."

Tabitha was too stunned to answer. She had been everywhere, and now she was—somewhere. The sudden shift from energy to matter took some getting used to. She had been moving so quickly, racing; now she was perfectly still. She felt displaced.

This was the Gyre Sanctuary? Unfamiliar objects covered most of the floor, and metal panels holding moving inscriptions ran along one wall. There was no dust, the air was clear and dry, and light seemed to drift through the room of its own accord, for there were no windows or obvious light sources.

Zarost was looking at her and grinning from ear to ear. "Ah, but your attention is so strong!" he exclaimed. "I had to fight to lead our movement during the Transference. You have developed, my young wizard of Eyri. You don't realise how compelling your presence has become."

"I don't feel very powerful," Tabitha replied. She felt more confused than ever.

"Don't worry, most of the Gyre members don't fully understand infinity. We use the knowledge of it, but we don't truly understand it. It's a paradox, and you can never get to the bottom of a paradox. You'll get used to it, with time. Think of infinity as a big idea you can bounce off."

Tabitha settled for just trying to adjust to where she was. Did the room really exist? An awesome silence surrounded her.

"W-what is this place?" she whispered.

"This is the lowest level of the Sanctuary, the Reliceum. We'll not be disturbed here. I wanted you to have a few moments to adjust to being here, before we meet the others. I'm expecting it'll be quite rowdy, quite rowdy indeed. They'll be a little surprised, and they hate surprises. Oh how they hate them!"

As Twardy was speaking, something moved on the far side of the room. A tall sculpture of glass, a great swan, spread its translucent wings. It scooped its neck, twisted its head then settled, only to begin its sequence again. Its many parts moved soundlessly. Beside it, a coloured ball spun rhythmically above a golden sphere. A suit of plated armour rested on a stand, and a glistening robe hung on a frame to its right, balanced above their reflections on the dark polished floor.

"The weaker armour's on the left," Zarost commented, seeing where she was looking. "It doesn't look like it, but the robe has Moralese higfibre in the weft. It's an Order-forged composite that will turn blades, and bows, even a strike from a lightning-rod. But it has become a deadly garment now that there's wildfire around—it soaks up the flux as fast as the dead wizard who's wearing it and lights up like a beck-beacon. At least it's a quick way to go. A bit…dramatic."

An angular sphere with dials upon its surface hung on a cable, motionless. A rack of slender instruments glinted in a circular recess. A collection of banded rods balanced in a neat triangular stack. There were a great many things Tabitha couldn't identify, shapes of smooth material, bulbous items with jewel-like skins, oblate screens of etched glass, things that were unidentifiable in the distance.

"Everything you see comes from Oldenworld," Twardy explained. "No, not the Oldenworld you have experienced, not the Lûk-downs or the savage forest or empty wastes, oh no, this all comes from an earlier time, when Order was at its height and the Three Kingdoms ruled the lowlands. These are the products of genius and industry, the most significant inventions of the Ordered civilisation. Or at least, the ones they could save. These things are kept in the hope that they can be returned to the world when the time is right, when Order can reform. When Chaos is ended."

Twardy snorted then, as if he did not believe such a time would ever come.

"The plans for most of these things are encoded in the masterlores in the library, but in truth they cannot be replaced, for we have lost many of the specialised processes needed to build them. Such works of high art are priceless, and they mark more clearly than any tome of history the ascendancy of the mages—ascendancy, or arrogance, perhaps."

Tabitha ran her hand along a smooth railing. A pale blue light ran ahead of her fingers. It vanished when she pulled her hand away. The hall was vast, and crowded with silence.

At the end of the railing was a shallow recess covered by a silk curtain. The fabric moved gently with the subtle pressure of her arrival. A woman stared at her from beyond the curtain—proud and aquiline. Her figure seemed almost lifelike in the eerie three-dimensional image. A statue? Symbols and diagrams seemed to float in front of the figure and behind it as well, as if there was a great volume beyond the curtain. Tabitha reached out to move the curtain, expecting to find the figure behind it, but she found that the statue was swept aside. It wasn't behind the curtain, it was *within* it, etched upon the thin sheet of material. Other sheets hung behind the first, different figures, each on their own curtain of diaphanous silk.

"Maytric sheets," offered Zarost. "They copied some of the greatest men and women of the college into these using a dimensional compression algorithm. They are supposed to hold five, even six dimensions of information within the clever patterning of the weave. The basic mind plan and physical identity of these revered mages is stored here, but their trace essence is missing, and without that they'll never be reformed. The research on maytrics was ended with the collapse of the original college in Kingsmeet, when the Sorcerer first moved against the wizards. Most of the lore was lost in the wildfire, but we keep these relics, in case we can devise a solution. For now, these wizards will be limited to two dimensions."

Zarost flipped through the hanging sheets with casual indifference. "Mame Peligreeve, Magister Thuran, Archor Mephissachary. And Boldigar. Boldigar! Hah! Some of these fellows developed questionable arts."

"What did he do?"

"Let's just say that mistakes made in the past should be left in the past. Most of these fiddlers would be better off made into robes." He bunched up the sheet he was holding, and the haughty face upon it began to resemble an angry cabbage.

Tabitha stifled a laugh. He was so irreverent.

Zarost let the sheets fall back into place. "Come. There'll be ample time to explore all the many wonders of the Sanctuary, but first we must face the fearsome creatures that inhabit the upper levels."

"Creatures?" Tabitha looked around nervously.

"Why, the wizards, of course! Be prepared for a rumpus." He strode away toward the door.

She hesitated. "Twardy?"

"What?"

"Do you think they'll help me to save Ethea?"

"I can't see that they wouldn't try, but first, they'll all need to talk about it. The Gyre is a council, after all. Come, they will be most excited to see you. They've been wanting to meet you for over four hundred years. Some more than others."

They left the Reliceum, with its precious relics and its atmosphere of perfect stillness, and passed through a long hall with doors leading off it. Zarost led her up a spiral stairway and along a curving corridor. There were windows on this level, tall slits of gold-tinted glass. Warm sunlight spilled down onto the patterned floor. The sound of voices came from ahead of them. They rounded a bend where the inner wall tapered off to nothing.

The air was full of clear essence. The sense of power was palpable.

They had arrived at the Chamber of the Gyre of Wizards.

Five council members were busy arguing from their places around a pool. They were seated on a circular bench that was backed with gold-filigreed greenstone.

"A normal day, in the Gyre," whispered Zarost. "A committee of wizards; more opinions than members."

A severe-looking woman stopped in mid-tirade. She turned her cold, grey gaze upon Zarost.

"What are you doing here!" she demanded.

"I missed you, dear Cosmologer, and so had to return." He led Tabitha by her hand through a gap in the circle.

"What kind of an answer is that? You are not excused, Riddler! You are supposed to be in Eyri! And who is your companion?" The woman whom Zarost had named as the Cosmologer reached out with her scrutiny. Tabitha felt as if she was held between two mighty pincers.

"This is most ill-advised, Riddler!" exclaimed another wizard, a balding, bearded sombre-looking man. "A worldly woman here, and one so young! You risk us all!"

"Wait, Lorewarden! Isn't that—?" began a white-haired woman.

"Good grief! She has command of her own essence," exclaimed a smooth-faced man whose eyes were as blue as ice on fire and whose black hair radiated like quills on a startled porcupine.

"The Eyrian?" asked the eldest among them. His eyebrows rose amid many wrinkles.

The five wizards sat forward. Tabitha felt interrogated by their unified gaze.

"But then why is her aura so small?" asked the Cosmologer. "Riddler, you said she was a wizard. She has hardly any power."

"No, it's there, on the spiritual plane," corrected the white-haired woman.

"And a touch on the mental plane, too," said the shock-haired man.

"You underestimate her, all of you," said a young woman who sat curled up upon her seat. She had an otherworldly cast to her features. She was pretty, her hair was short, and she had the most clear green eyes Tabitha had ever seen. "There is more to her than what is present this moment. Her fate is entwined with Chaos. She brings a great danger upon us!"

The eldest member stood up abruptly. "Wizards of the Gyre! We are getting ahead of our heads. Let the Riddler speak, and announce his guest. I think we are forgetting ourselves. This is an auspicious moment."

"How can she be presented to us before we have decided that she is ready to be presented to us?" demanded the Cosmologer. "I don't see her power, Senior, in any of the three axes. Her prime circle is too close to the origin to be a wizard."

"Cosmologer!" said the elder, grasping the air with his fist and shaking it. "Your sense fails you! I am sure the Riddler has proof enough, or he would not bring her here."

The Cosmologer pressed her lips together and said nothing. Tabitha did notice that the Cosmologer was being rocked in time to the movements of the elder's knuckled fist. At last the Cosmologer looked away.

"Might I extend our *combined* apologies for your introduction," the elder offered. "Riddler, let us begin again."

Twardy Zarost grinned. "Behold!" he announced. He winked slyly at Tabitha and waved with a dramatic flourish. "The talisman has drawn a new apprentice through the mysteries. At long last, one bearer of the ring has seen the path through to the end and apprehended her own nature. If some of you have not seen the extent of her power, it is a reflection of your lack and not hers. Let none doubt her power.

It is different to yours, it is different to mine, it is different to any of the wizards in the long history of the college. Oh compassionate and exceedingly wise fellow Gyrends, swallow your mischievous tongues before they betray you anymore, and cast your serene gaze upon the talented wizard of Eyri. I give you the Lifesinger, Tabitha Serannon."

Tabitha stood there, before the five silent wizards, feeling her cheeks heating up. She bent one knee in a shallow curtsy, unsure what would be appropriate.

The eldest member of the Gyre cleared his throat. "H-hm. Yes. Thank you, Riddler, for that... illustrious... introduction. Well, I think we should all rise and return our visitor's courtesy, yes?" He stood and the others followed his lead. They bowed, some deeper than others, then returned to their places.

"I am the Senior," said the old wizard. "Here beside me are the Lorewarden, the Mentalist, and Spiritist." That accounted for the bearded balding man, the suave shock-haired one with the icy-blue eyes, and the white-haired gentle-looking lady in the soft purple silks. "The Cosmologer has already made her name...and her nature... known. And the pretty one across from you is the Mystery, but don't mistake her smile for sweetness. She's likely to be your biggest foe if you mince your words."

The Mystery watched her with feline inscrutability.

"The only member of our octad who is missing is a rapacious fellow with dark skin named the Warlock. You'll recognise him when you see him. He has a martial manner."

"If I might intrude, Senior, he shall continue to be missing, I fear."

"What! Riddler, this is foul news. Foul news! He has not fallen, has he?"

"In a manner of speaking."

The Senior blanched visibly. "Oh by the light of all the stars! You mean he works against us? No, we cannot have this now, when the Sorcerer is stronger than ever."

"Aspersions! Lies and aspersions!" cried the Cosmologer.

"What proof have you, Riddler?" demanded the Mentalist.

"You hide the truth in your words, Riddler," the Mystery accused. "Say what you mean!"

"The Warlock was here not two days past!" said the Spiritist, before Zarost could answer. "He helped us to restore the Sanctuary's outer skin. There were some loose threads that he reworked. He can't be on the other side. He can't be against us, after so many years. It doesn't make sense!"

"Riddler, you have no proof!"

"Order. Order!" shouted the Senior. "We shall hold council on this matter, but we must have order, and the first issue we must decide is the wizard of Eyri's place in our circle. Forgive me, Lifesinger, but we cannot continue to discuss these matters with you present if you are not part of the Gyre, and if you are to be a part of the Gyre we must have proof of your ability."

"Proof!" exclaimed Twardy Zarost. "I found her in the bloodbelt, between the Lûk and the Hunters, *dispersing* the rage of men upon a battlefield. She emerged from Eyri, she crossed the wastes unaided. She followed a reintegrated Transference with me on the thirteenth meridian to reach here. What more proof do you need?"

"You did not pluck her from Eyri yourself?" asked the Senior, clearly surprised.

"No!" Zarost threw his hands in the air. "I have been in Azique, and Korin, and in the Lûk downs. I had no idea she had emerged until I heard her spellsong altering the world. If I'd not reacted then and there we would have lost her to the wildfire!"

"Ahh. Forgive me, Riddler, I jumped to a conclusion, I think we all did. I assumed you had returned to Eyri and grown impatient. If she was already beyond Eyri, without your assistance at all, then she has surely transcended all the conditions of her test. She has outgrown her sheltered cocoon."

"This all sounds very impressive, Senior," interrupted the Cosmologer, "but it is still an account told by the Riddler of his own protégé. I would still prefer a demonstration, if it is not too great a request of the wizard."

"I must concur, Senior," added the Lorewarden. "If the Lifesinger is to join the Gyre for this council, I would see a demonstration myself. I've no suspicion of your talent, Tabitha Serannon, so take no umbrage at my hesitance, but if you are to be the ninth, I need to understand what I'm dealing with at my side."

"Is this the Gyre's consensus?" The Senior looked around the circle and counted the nodding heads. "Lifesinger, is this too much to ask?"

Tabitha felt their eyes upon her again. She didn't want to let them down, but she knew her power was limited because of Ethea's plight.

She wanted to tell them about her fear for the Goddess, but she couldn't think of how to begin to explain that without it sounding like an excuse, a way to avoid being tested. They would think she was inadequate.

She didn't want to seem like a failure before these high wizards. Twardy might make light of their grandeur, but Tabitha could sense they were very powerful. They had formed Eyri, they had created the Shield; they had been there at the beginning. She couldn't tell them now that her ability wasn't really her own. She would win them over, she decided, and maybe then she could demand their support in saving Ethea.

She turned to Zarost. "Is it safe? The wildfire…"

"Oh yes, we are beyond his grasp here, too far south, more protected than you ever were in Eyri. This is our sanctuary; you can summon or speak as you will. If you're sure it's what you want to do."

"Yes. I'll be fine, Twardy, I won't reach too deep."

He nodded. He seemed to understand her dilemma and her decision to meet the Gyre's challenge.

She slid her lyre around her shoulder and lifted the strap over her head. It had come with her, through infinity, she realised. She wondered about that briefly as she tuned the strings. The Gyre grew silent and attentive. The air seemed to thicken.

Tabitha noticed how still and lifeless the chamber was. Apart from the gathered wizards in their various colours, it was all stone and architecture, elegant but dead. There were no plants, no woven fabrics and no works of art. The small pool encircled by the bench was dark blue, empty, like the night sky without the stars. Nothing moved in its sterile heart.

She stepped up to the edge of the pool.

As she stroked her lyre, the familiar wonder of the first stanza flowed into the air. Tabitha reached for the symphony beyond the words she sang, and it was there in her voice at once. It was so easy now, and yet so treacherous. The Lifesong pulled at her with the allure of its depths of wonder, and she had to resist the higher movements to keep her creation simple, to keep from being drawn toward the source of the power, to keep herself separated from Ethea and her plight. She felt like a thief, sipping from the vitality of the Lifesong when she knew how desperate the Goddess was, chained to her rock below the Sorcerer's Pillar. But to use it was the only way to gain acceptance among the Gyre, and she needed their help. She couldn't face the

Sorcerer on her own.

They were all watching her, each in their different way, and it felt as if invisible fingers picked over her thoughts as she gathered the clear essence. They were trying to understand what she was doing. She ignored them all and focused on her creation as her song reached its climax. Bright colour flashed in the pool.

She extended her thoughts further, and sudden life spilled down the walls, vines of deep green, with bright golden blossoms spilling like bursts of sunlight upon the verdant drapes. As an afterthought she set a clutch of butterflies dancing through the air to play above the pool.

The last note dripped from her lyre. One of the fish, bright, wet and shiny, flipped high out of the water, its little tail wriggling, before it splashed down, to slip into the depths.

She set the end of her lyre on the floor.

Only then did she notice the Riddler, who spun and spun, his arms pounding the air as commanding an orchestra to play in time to the echoes of the Lifesong's rhythms. He slowly wound down and down, until he was standing before her, breathless, his eyes shining.

"Haha!" He embraced her quite suddenly. "Haha! Haha!" He danced away along the edge of the pool. "And there is life in the centre of circles, when the true Lifesinger sings!" He stared into the waters, and Tabitha feared he might topple in, but all around him was silence.

It was difficult to read what the other wizards thought of her performance. None of them had spoken, and they seemed startled. Their eyes flicked around the room, from the vines to the flowers to the fish, looking, measuring, analysing. Then they moved.

"Remarkable!" whispered the Senior.

The Mentalist had covered his mouth with his hand. The Lorewarden whistled through his teeth.

"Even the butterflies have unique souls," whispered the Spiritist. "It's all new. It has never *been* before."

"But the fish will foul the water!" exclaimed the Cosmologer. "And the butterflies will lay eggs, and they will die!"

"Oh Cosmologer!" Zarost cried.

"The vines will litter the floors. Who will clean them?"

At this, Zarost scowled, paused, then burst into laughter. He laughed and laughed, and as he did so the wizards lost their restraint and began to clap their hands on their knees, stamp and hoot themselves. The

Cosmologer's further objections were drowned out by the rumpus.

When the merriment had finally subsided, Zarost said, "Sometimes, Cosmologer, I really wonder if you have a sense of humour at all."

"Humour is not a constituent of Order, Riddler. It is not necessary in a structured defence against Chaos."

"But humour is necessary for life."

"In your kind of life, maybe. Not in mine. You should wait until we have conquered the Sorcerer before you laugh. There will be ample time for playing the fool once the Chaos is ended. This is a mess!"

"And it is alive," chided the Mystery. "It is alive."

"I have seen nothing like this in all my many years," stated the Senior. "Tabitha Serannon, you are most uniquely talented, and we are honoured to have you here in the Gyre. Well done, Riddler, your patience has paid off a thousand-fold."

The Lorewarden cleared his throat. "The Cosmologer did raise an important point though, Senior. This will not last. It is not truly like Order at all. It is impermanent. Wonderful, but impermanent."

"Lorewarden, you can cast your own stasis spell upon it if you wish to keep things as they are," said Zarost, "but that would only diminish the beauty, not enhance it at all. And consider how impermanent Order can be."

"Riddler, you misunderstand me. What I mean to say is this. How are we to work with this brand of magic in our midst?" This gave Zarost a moment's pause. "How do we link our flows of essence with something so different? I was expecting Eyri to produce a purified strain of Order-magic, not something so ancient and wild. I'm not even sure we could guide her power with steering flows."

"If we cannot enforce Order upon it, is it not then a form of Chaos?" asked the Mentalist in a hurried voice.

"No, this is not what the Sorcerer wields," answered the Mystery. "That much I can tell."

"I see now why her power was so difficult to apprehend at first," said the Mentalist. "She wields neither Chaos nor Order then, her power is balanced somewhere in between."

"Is this upon a fourth axis? Is there such a thing?" pondered the Senior.

"A fourth? I don't believe it!" scoffed the Lorewarden. "We know there are only three. Where would you *fit* a fourth axis in?"

"No, consider it, Lorewarden," said the Mentalist. "Think laterally. It could be. Life is balanced on the first axis, between Light and Dark;

it is balanced on the second axis, between Energy and Matter; and here we can see it could straddle the third axis of Chaos and Order. Either that puts the Lifesinger's power upon a fourth axis, or she is at the very centre of us all—inside the prime circle."

Tabitha had little idea what they were talking of. She watched the fish turning in the depths.

"You might name the moon a ball, but that won't mean the moon must fall," said Twardy Zarost.

"What do you mean, Riddler?" the Mentalist asked.

"You are wasting time, arguing about such things. You try to fit her into the confines of our knowledge, when before you stands a miracle."

Tabitha kept her gaze down. It was the Lifesong that was the miracle, not her. She just gave it voice.

"Quite so, Riddler," said the Spiritist. "Quite so!"

"She is a wizard, no doubt there," said the Lorewarden.

"And an incredible singer," added the Mystery. "You touched me in my bones, Tee."

Tabitha looked up with surprise at the pretty green-eyed wizard. How did the Mystery know her nickname? Only her mother and her friend Lyndall had ever called her that. The Mystery winked at her, as if they shared a secret, then said, "You bring upon the Gyre the greatest threat it will ever face. Yet face it we must."

The words had the underlying solidity she could recognise as truth. "I-I don't mean to threaten anyone," Tabitha said. An awkward moment of silence followed. The Senior was the first to speak. "Yes. Well. I believe the matter of her power is undisputed now." He looked around the circle of wizards, ending on the Cosmologer. The Cosmologer opened and shut her mouth without making a sound. The Senior's expression darkened. "Riddler! Have you taken the words out of her mouth again!"

"I just sent them somewhere where they wouldn't be heard." He looked as innocent as a boy with stolen sweets in his pocket.

"Let them out," the Senior instructed.

The Riddler reached reluctantly for his hat. As he lifted the brim, a babble of sounds tumbled out, like a crowd of petulant children all speaking at once. The Cosmologer coloured, but didn't launch into a tirade against Zarost. Perhaps she was surprised at the petulant tone of her own voice. When heard in that strange manner, all jumbled together, it sounded particularly silly.

"Now. Would you join us, Lifesinger?" The Senior pointed to an empty place between Zarost and the Mystery. Tabitha noticed that each seat in the Chamber was surrounded with inscriptions, and each had a distinct colour. There were only two empty seats—the unadorned one the Senior offered, and another, placed between the Senior and the Mentalist, marked with barbed script and red-bordered symbols. She guessed that was usually the Warlock's chair. Her seat was blank, just a curved outline cut into the stone, with nothing inscribed upon it except the twinned wizard's rune she recognised from Eyri, the heart rune.

"The ninth seat in the Gyre," said the Senior. "We hope to find that you will take a permanent place in the Gyre. You have caught us a bit unawares. We shall have a… ceremony, yes! And an inauguration, with the oaths and odes and awards, but such things take time to prepare properly, and we had not quite expected… Anyway, I hope you'll stay with us, now that you have reached the Sanctuary. Now your training can begin in earnest."

Stay with them? Tabitha didn't know if she'd understood the old wizard correctly, but she wasn't going to stay in the Sanctuary. She'd promised Garyll she'd return to him as soon as she could. Tabitha didn't know what to say, so she just smiled at the Senior and eased into her seat. It gave slightly under her weight. The stone was pliable and resilient. She guessed that it wasn't stone after all, but some magical composite.

"So tell us of the Warlock, Riddler," began the Senior. "Why do you suspect such a failure? He has been a cornerstone of our Gyre. I find it hard to believe that *he* has fallen!"

Zarost held up his hands. "That story begins with the Lifesinger's account. Let her tell how she came to be in the Hunterslands, and then I shall tell you what we discovered there."

So Tabitha began her account. She told them of how she'd been summoned by the ailing King Mellar, and how she'd tracked the thieving prince and his consort through the Penitent's pass and into the wastelands beyond Eyri. She spoke of the terrifying passage across the silver desert, of meeting the Lûk and hearing of their bitter experience with Prince Bevn, of the blood debt he owed for the Lûk men he'd caused to die. Finally she told them of their march westward through the forest, and the battlefield in the bloodbelt, and how she'd tried to lift the stain of hatred from the men's hearts.

"Then I made a terrible mistake. I called out his name. The Sorcerer.

The wildfire came upon us, so much I knew we'd never run away. I believed we were going to die. That was when the Riddler appeared and turned it away."

"Afterward I asked a Hunter if he had seen the Eyrian Prince, Prince Bevn," Zarost added hastily. "He knew of the boy, he'd seen the crown, and he knew who had taken them onward from the Hunter settlement at Bradach Hide. Though he tried to hide the truth from me, I fished out the details soon enough. He had seen Black Saladon. The Warlock."

Stunned silence filled the chamber.

"What is he doing with the Kingsrim?" said the Mentalist. Then understanding dawned upon his face. "Oh no! No, no, no!"

"Yes," said Zarost. "He is heading north with the Kingsrim. He'll hand it over to the Sorcerer, I'll bet my best boots he will! And if you think about it a little longer, you'll see that he must have planted the idea in the boy's head in the first place, for there is no other explanation for the prince's journey through the Shield than that he was told there was something beyond it to strive for. Saladon has made a pact with the prince, and he is using the boy to further his own plans. Why would he do such a thing, you ask? The Warlock must be allied with Ametheus. He is working to spread Chaos. He is taking the Kingsrim to Turmodin as a gift, in exchange for some kind of amnesty."

"Eyri will be lost!"

"More to the point, Spiritist, *we'll* be lost! You of all wizards should know how deep those soul-threads go into that crown. Oh, we never considered this! We can't let this happen! We can't!"

"How can it be that none of us were aware of this?" asked the Senior. "How can the crown have moved so far from Eyri without even one of us knowing of it?"

"It is by its nature invisible to sensing," said the Lorewarden.

"I know that!" snapped the Senior. "And we have deliberately kept our eyes averted from Eyri. No, I aimed that challenge at the Riddler, because that is why we placed you there. Why did you let this happen, Riddler? Where were you?"

Zarost didn't look up when he spoke. "I was chasing a trail of clues in Oldenworld. Oh, the Warlock set this up very well."

"And most of us were recuperating from the damage the Writhe did to us," added the Mystery. "Little thought was given to other matters, but can we be certain of the Warlock's intentions? All we know is that the Kingsrim is abroad in Oldenworld, and that the Warlock was seen travelling with the crown thief. Maybe he intends to mislead him."

"Yet when he was here yesterday, he mentioned nothing of it," said the Mentalist.

"He's as guilty as sin!" exclaimed Zarost. "Why do you think he didn't stay here?"

"I think we should all remember who was entrusted with the preservation of Eyri in the first place." The Cosmologer looked directly at Twardy Zarost. "You're very keen to shift the blame away from your own head, Riddler. The Kingsrim is lost, you say, and you think the Warlock took it? Why would the Warlock have risked coming to the Sanctuary, if he were guilty of such traitorous deeds?"

Zarost threw his hands in the air. "He must have come here to see if anyone had spied him out! He can travel faster if he knows he is not being watched. Already, the threads of the Shield scatter on the winds. Soon Eyri will be defenceless. How can you believe what he has done is anything but betrayal? He has fooled us all, and were it not for the Lifesinger, we would not have known until it was too late."

"But where is your proof that it is the Warlock who works for Chaos?"

"Who else could it be?"

The Mentalist cocked his head to one side. His eyes glittered dangerously. "Tell me, Riddler, the rescue that the Lifesinger mentioned, the spell you used to avert the wildfire strike, that wouldn't happen to be a Reflection spell, would it?"

Zarost picked at a fraying thread on the brim of his hat.

"We condemned the use of reflection, Riddler!" the Senior barked.

"That is a Chaos-spell!" declared the Cosmologer. "Clearly it is!"

"More particles in motion does mean more disorder," the Lorewarden agreed.

"And by that logic a sneeze would be a Chaos-spell!" objected Zarost. "Reflection is not always Chaos—it depends on where the energy has been taken from, or what has been avoided by its use."

"What was avoided, then?" demanded the Cosmologer. "Surely not the Lifesinger's death? If you were there to cast the reflection, you could have used transference at once."

"There were others involved," admitted Zarost. "Others I couldn't transfer. I had to save them."

"Save them? How many others have you condemned?"

The Gyre members looked hostile. Tabitha hadn't realised Zarost had risked anything to save the ones who had stood beside her in the forest. He had saved Mulrano. He had saved Garyll. She wanted to jump up and hug him.

"Well, Riddler, it is now noted that you have wielded a megaflux of Chaos. Time will tell if you can swing the balance, but for now, I'd consider you more of a threat to Order than the Warlock."

"I hate you!" screeched the Cosmologer. "I'm going to be chasing outbound trajectories with their squared random velocity for months!"

"Be careful, when you do, my dear Cosmologer. The Sorcerer is too lucid for you, right now."

"How can you know that?" Her cheeks coloured dangerously. "Are you trying to make fun of me?"

"We met him on the way, lurking near the crossing point of infinity," Zarost replied in an off-handed manner.

"And you came here? You fool! He will track you. He will find us!" The Cosmologer was spitting fury.

"He will not find us. I zagged and zigged all over the thirteenth meridian."

"Our Sanctuary is too fundamental to jeopardise with your games!"

"Maybe you should begin chasing those reflected threads now," suggested Zarost quietly. "Every moment you wait, the Chaos will spread, and you'll be running out tracers until you are dead."

The Cosmologer didn't appreciate the limerick. She was on her feet in an instant. The air crackled with power as she swept across the intervening space. She didn't even bother to walk around the pool— her power supported her in the air, so tight was her grip on the matter in the chamber. The air became thick and violet-tinged. Tabitha felt herself bound in the magnetic weave, even though the Cosmologer's attention was upon Zarost. The Cosmologer's eyes were narrow slits, her eyes like chips of stone.

"Are you playing the fool, Riddler? Are you trying to anger me just for fun? Because if you are, you miserable rotter, I shall invoke an execution myself."

Zarost sat quite still, and didn't answer. He was lifted from his chair.

The Cosmologer swung around to face the others. "I demand a trial of this member!" she spat. "He does not answer my charge, and so admits his guilt!"

"I am true to my oath," Zarost said simply from behind and slightly above her.

The Cosmologer came closer to him, so close her face was right up against his feet. Her magnetic presence intensified throughout the room. Tabitha gasped. It was like being crushed from all sides at once. Twardy Zarost hung in the air, forced by the Cosmologer's ire to swing slowly around, until his face was level with hers—level, but upside down.

"Liar!" the Cosmologer shouted into his face. "You have been dismantling things, haven't you, taking out your strand of the weave, now that you know the crown is in jeopardy? Trying to extricate yourself from the mess you've led us all into!"

"I have never worked against the Gyre," answered Zarost.

"You lie!" she screeched.

"I cannot lie and be the Riddler."

"I am not sure that you are, any more. I *question* your ability to follow your oath!"

"If it is just a question, then you must accept the answer. I have kept my oath."

"You stretch my tolerance of you past its limit!" She brought her fist down as if pulling against some invisible resistance. Zarost was drawn through the air and over the pool. Then he was plunged beneath the waters and held there. He kicked and writhed, churning the water around him, but he seemed unable to break free of the mad woman's grip. His hat floated to the surface amid a froth of bubbles.

"Enough, Cosmologer!" boomed the Lorewarden. He spoke seldom, but it seemed when he spoke, he was listened to. The Cosmologer turned, uncertain. The Lorewarden continued. "We have already lost one member from our octad, and see how that has unbalanced us? We are divided against each other. Chaos has even begun to drive into the heart of the Gyre."

"But we don't need the Riddler!" The Cosmologer's chest heaved. "I vote that he goes!"

"No, Cosmologer," the Senior cut in. "You cannot deny the Riddler his place in the Gyre. For our structure to work, we must all be free to do our work, each to our own talent. You cannot hold two positions in the cube alone. It shall fall in upon itself."

"But why does he have to be so contrary!"

"He must be *different* to you, that is our strength. We are all vastly different but our goal is common—to put an end to Chaos. The Riddler is just as valuable as you are—remember that when you allow your frustrations to rule your judgement."

"But what he does affects us all! He taints all of our efforts with his frivolity. How can there ever be Order, with his disruptions? When are we going to recognise his danger and banish him from the collective?"

"When he sides with Chaos, and not before. Until then, we support each other."

Tabitha couldn't stand to watch Zarost fighting for the surface any longer. "Take him out! Take him out, you wicked witch! Take him out!"

The Cosmologer turned on her. "How dare you, you little brat! I am dispensing discipline here!"

"Then why are you trying to drown him? That's not discipline. It's murder! He can't breathe!"

"Yours is not to question us," the Cosmologer retorted. "He is a wizard. He has many ways to survive. Until you understand how the Gyre works, you will keep silent!"

"If you don't let him go this instant, I will never join the Gyre." Tabitha held the angry woman's eye. "I will never use the Lifesong to help the Gyre."

"But you *must* join us, you *must* take the oath! The skills that you have are due to our work. Your entire realm was created by us. You owe us your allegiance."

"You expect me to use my power according to your demands?"

"My demands are those of the Gyre! The will of the Gyre *will* rule you. It rules us all."

"I will only consider it once you release him! Release him!"

"You have no choice!" exclaimed the Cosmologer. "You were grown to serve us!"

"Not so, Cosmologer," said the Senior, as if he had all the time in the world, and his voice seemed to make it so, to make a space in time. "She is a wizard, and an equal. You all know that the offering must be of her own free will, or the skills will not be pooled. Your negotiations raise an interesting question. Will you link with us, Lifesinger, and complete our circle? Because if you won't become the ninth then you have nothing to bargain with."

No bubbles came up from Twardy Zarost anymore. Tabitha became desperate.

"What is wrong with you? He's dying!

"I doubt it—"

"This is not a negotiation, it is an assassination!"

"The oath," stated the Senior in a strong voice, "is to fight Chaos, in every form, forever. We are sworn to Order."

"If I swear your oath will you release him?"

"Yes. Swear it. Now!" screamed the Cosmologer.

Rage flared in Tabitha, filling her with its Dark extremes, with strength, with hate.

"You torture Twardy to compel me? You are evil! Damn you!"

"How dare you!" screeched the Cosmologer. The air became horrendously *tight* around Tabitha, and she was crushed and lifted at the same time. "You can not deny us! You are what you are only because of our work. We have the rights to your talents!"

"Cosmologer! That is enough!" barked the elder. A whip of twisted blue light split the air, striking the Cosmologer with a crack across her back. She yelped, and Tabitha fell to the floor. Tabitha's ears popped with the sudden drop in pressure.

"How dare you strike me!" cried the Cosmologer. She faced the elder. "Old man! You are unjust!" She raised her arms, but the others reacted instantly, drawing together in a united front, facing the Cosmologer down. They seemed to move over the floor without walking.

Twardy Zarost broke the surface, spluttering and gasping for breath.

"Enough!" the Lorewarden warned the Cosmologer. "Now is not the time to separate the Gyre."

"Find yourself, Cosmologer," the Senior reprimanded. "Find yourself."

The tension crackled through the air. The six wizards seemed to be poised on the brink of a cataclysmic show-down. So much power waited to be released. Tabitha had no doubt the Cosmologer would be the primary target, but she might be caught in the crossfire. She didn't know how to protect herself. The silence was painful as the wizards stared each other down.

Zarost hauled himself from the pool. He didn't look so chirpy anymore.

"Riddler! Have you lost your mind?" asked the Mentalist.

"Why? Have you found a spare one lying around?" He sloshed over to his seat.

So this is the Gyre—the legendary union of wizards. They were not at all the serene figures she had imagined. At last the Cosmologer turned away, a disgusted look on her face. "You tempt ruin, all of you. I am not at fault."

"Cosmologer," warned the Senior.

"The Gyre is only useful if it is wise. Look at the evidence before you!"

"Cosmologer."

The Cosmologer looked as if she was chewing on a lemon rind. She took a slow breath. "The dratted girl insulted me. I shall reserve my judgement upon the Riddler until you have all had a chance to come to the inevitable conclusion. In the meantime, I must attend to the mess he has left behind him with his reckless Reflection."

She strode from the Chamber, taking a good portion of the tense atmosphere with her.

The Mentalist blew his cheeks out with a long sigh. "Well, that was a crackler."

The Spiritist shook her head and returned to her seat. "Do you have to push so hard, Riddler? You practically dared her to drown you."

"It is my task in the Gyre to stir things about. It is hers to take the sediment out."

"You were a little too enthusiastic in your duty," said the Mystery. "She is still badly shaken by the Writhe. It damaged her confidence. She feels vulnerable and on edge."

"As do we all, Mystery," said the Senior. "As do we all."

Tabitha slipped into her seat beside Twardy Zarost. "Why was the Cosmologer so angry?" she asked. "Is that normal?"

Zarost laughed, and made to say something, then seemed to think better of it. But when nobody else filled the silence, he bent his head to the side, to whisper to her. "A long time ago, the Warlock took her to his bed. She's been hoping he'll cast his roving eye toward her again, even though he has made it clear that his tastes lie in other directions. He has her enthralled, and she did not like hearing that her tittilator is a traitor."

He'd spoken in a low voice, but not low enough to escape the senses of the wizards. The Spiritist shot him a disapproving glance. "Riddler! That's scandalous! You cannot know that."

"Ah, but I can puzzle it out, not so? We know our balance always skews if we place them too close in a joint spell, and it always skews in the Warlock's favour."

The Mystery grinned and looked away, as if she found the idea of the Warlock having anything to do with the Cosmologer very amusing.

"Nonetheless, it seems the Warlock's roving eye has roved too far of late," said the Lorewarden. "We shall have to find him, and if the Riddler's guess is true, we shall have to end his treachery."

"Wait! We must capture him, we cannot kill him!" exclaimed the Senior.

"Why?" asked the Lorewarden and the Mentalist at once.

"We cannot risk that crown being loose!" exclaimed the Spiritist. "Ametheus will turn us inside out! With the seven strands of our blood twisted through the gold, it is the most powerful weapon in the hands of our enemy. Only the Riddler is spared from that weave. He could pull us to pieces. We *must* blast the Warlock from the face of Oldenworld."

"No! Think, and think as the Gyre!" commanded the Senior. "We cannot harm the Warlock. The ninth member of our circle is essential. If we cannot expand, we are too weak to resist Ametheus at his peak. His last spell was an eighth-level weave of Chaos. That we know. We need a Gyre of nine wizards to beat such magnitude. We need the balance point in the cube to perfect order. We have the Lifesinger now, or so we hope, but we need the Warlock too. If we kill him, we lose our chance at gaining the upper hand. Nine is the number; it is infinitely more powerful than eight."

"Oh, this will be most tricky," said Zarost. "He knows we will come for him, he knows we won't wish to harm him, but he might not have the same restraint in return. It is not wise to stop a man armed with a sword if you face him with empty hands."

"Indeed, Riddler, indeed," said the Senior. "Except in this case, it will be a damned big battleaxe he carries, and we know that's not the worst of his weapons."

The wizards brooded on that, and the Chamber seemed to darken.

"I have an idea! Oh, this will be a good surprise!" said Zarost.

"I don't like your surprises," the Mentalist muttered. "Last time I was stuck here on the roof for weeks, before I could break the bond you placed upon me."

Zarost looked at him blankly then his eyebrows hooked upward. "Aah! My trick with the Transference. Maybe that wasn't such a bad skill to have found, to know how to vanish before you've hit the ground. You will need that talent if things run foul with the

Warlock." Zarost turned to face the Mystery. "Cast a seeing spell for us, Mysterious-Miss. We must find the Warlock, and we must find him fast. Let us begin where the Hunters hide at Bradach."

The Mystery didn't leave her chair. "Will we be able to see the Warlock at all, if he's so near to the crown? It is the best shield-core we've ever made. Once beyond its holding pattern in Eyri it would be impossible to track."

"Oh, we'll not be looking for *him*," said the Riddler. "We'll be looking for a special kind of spy. We might not be able to sense the thieves through the cover of the Kingsrim, but they're still visible to the eyes of those whom they pass. I think it's time to commission the aid of a *sha-lin*, to take a challenge to the travellers."

"Why don't we just transfer there ourselves?" said the Mentalist. "We could go to Bradach Hide right now, and search the different trails. We'd find him soon enough."

"What, split up?" Zarost asked. "That's precisely what he wants us to do! Think about it. He will take us down, one at a time. Our only hope is to be unified when we face him."

"But if he does have the Kingsrim we must not dally about!"

"How do you rate your chances then, if you caught the Warlock in a dark corner of the forest?" Zarost asked.

"I would have a chance!" replied the Mentalist.

"How much of a chance?"

"Oh tosh, Riddler! What if we were in twos?"

Zarost just left that question resting gently in the silence. They all knew how dangerous the Warlock was in open combat.

"No, the Riddler is right," said the Senior. "We must know where he is first, so we might trap him together."

"Mystery, would you at least do us the honours of scrying before seeing?" the Mentalist asked. "We should have some idea if this is a likely path, or a right royal balls-up."

"It will work, I'm telling you!" Zarost objected. "The *sha-lin* is all we need."

The Mentalist bared his teeth at him, like a warning from a wolf. "I'm happy for you to riddle us out of a problem, but I'd rather you didn't riddle us into one."

"Very well." The Mystery rose from her chair and approached the pool. Her elegant green garments glistened as she moved. "I will pull what I can from the future." She shivered, like a cat flicking rain off its coat, and the surface of the pool was distressed with ripples. Light danced in the water. It calmed as the Mystery spread her hands with fingers splayed. Then she explored the air with her fingers, and the threads of light moved, forming networks, forking, branching and rejoining, pathways of possibility in the restless fluid of reality.

"I sense a parting in the future," she said. "You see, we shall meet again here." She pointed to a conjunction of threads. "It would be quicker for us to take *this* path that the Riddler has chosen, leading through to *that* meeting, than to go separated like *this*, and end up *there*."

Tabitha didn't understand what they were looking at or how the Mystery could be certain. How could one take a short-cut to an event in the future? "Can you see if you will find the Warlock?"

"Our future would not be so bright upon that path if we were likely to fail."

"What is that massive cluster up ahead, Mystery?" asked the Lorewarden.

"That? That's something I cannot see beyond, a knot of futures clustered on an improbability."

"Is that the Warlock's thread?" asked the Spiritist.

"No. I don't think so."

"Ametheus then?"

"Or the Riddler, making a bungle-up?" said the Mentalist hopefully.

"Or the Lifesinger," offered the Mystery, holding Tabitha with steady green gaze. "I can't tell."

"Looks like a hell of a mess," said the Lorewarden.

"Improbabilities always look that way. It will resolve itself, in time. Now, let us find our herald of woe."

28. THE INHERITANCE SAGA

"The present is the slave of the past
And the master of the future."—Zarost

Prince Bevn staggered along the forest trail. His feet were unbelievably sore, hot, blistered and raw. The wizard Black Saladon had collected them in the morning from the smelly Hunter-tent in Willower, and they hadn't slackened their pace since then, except to sleep in a hollowed-out tree-trunk for a few hours. The ordeal was made worse by the way his pack dug into his back. It was loaded with supplies. Saladon had said that they wouldn't be stopping at anymore settlements until a place called Slipper, which was many days ahead. The wizard didn't want to risk further contact with the Hunters.

"This is so unfair," Bevn moaned. "Why don't we use magic?"

"What, and light up a beacon for the others?"

"What…others?"

"The Sorcerer is not the only one who has power in this world."

"But why can't you just *magic* us—to—somewhere else? Like the way you get our food. The way you *go* somewhere else and then come back."

"You can not come with me the way I travel. You would lose what little mind you have."

Black Saladon squatted in the path, his battleaxe resting casually across his knees. Bevn gulped and tried not to run. "I can not take the crown you wear through transference. It is bonded to your bloodline. It is becoming attuned to you, young Bevn Mellar. That must be allowed to develop and to strengthen. Its aura has already doubled, since Bradach. Surely you want to be strong when you are presented to the Sorcerer. Neh? So here on these trails you get strong. We must reach Turmodin. Nobody can do this but you."

Bevn didn't know what an aura was, but he wouldn't be fooled.

"Why aren't we using horses then?"

"Did you bring one with you?"

"No! You know we don't have horses!"

Saladon shook his head. "I don't know how you expect to ride, if you don't have a horse."

"Can't we get any?"

"Have you seen any around to buy? Horses are plains animals. They do badly in such a forest. And a horse is too good a target for a Nephilim or a dragon. They both like horsemeat very much. Nobody would be stupid enough to stay close to a horse. If you see one, I suggest you run the other way."

"Why is everything so bloody primitive out here? Don't these Hunters have any means to travel faster?"

Saladon gave him a hard look. "You can thank the Sorcerer for that. Civilisation is built on the foundations of Order, but it does not take much Chaos to break it down. Remove the rules of governance, and men begin to take instead of make. They are easily driven by greed. Soon there is no wealth, and without wealth, there is often hunger. Desperation sets in, and desperate people will pillage with little regard for others, until in the end all the wealth is squandered, and all the systems are broken down. People forget how to be civilised when Chaos is in their midst, when they hate, when they are fighting for survival."

"But the Hunters had some things," objected Gabrielle. "Bread, mead, perfume."

Saladon snorted. "They cling to the eroding remnants of their culture, but it will not last. Nothing lasts against Chaos. You'll understand that, when you see the Lowlands." Saladon turned to look up at Gabrielle. She stood, poised as always, her hands in the small of her back, her breasts outlined against the morning sun. Posing to be screwed, Bevn thought. "You might have noticed the change in this Chaos-tainted world," Saladon continued. "The way your body feels. Ya? There is no greater force of Chaos than the surge of sexual tension. Lust is a great force of anarchy. It breaks through rules of marriage, tribal intolerances, family values, common sense and even pride and dignity, in the end. You will feel things will get—hotter— the closer you get to the Lowlands. It's why the things have survived so well in the Lowlands, despite their unbelievable violence. They are wild with lust, and their progeny is rampant."

"I feel nothing," Gabrielle replied, but Bevn suspected she was lying.

"You will, soon enough. You'll feel it in your sex…" He turned back to Bevn as he stood. "…if you have anything more potent than two peas and a carrot."

"Well do *you* feel it?" Gabrielle demanded.

Saladon didn't answer and he didn't take any more questions after that.

They walked, over crumbling mossy ridges, over stray roots, past cold-mouthed caves that smelled of lurking danger, around thickets of oozing thorn-weed that tore at his trousers and plucked at his shins, and all the time the weight of the pack grew worse and worse, biting into his shoulders, pressing him into the ground.

It wasn't fair. Gabrielle didn't have to carry as much as he did, so Gabrielle could keep pace with Saladon. He watched the muscles tensing in her leather-clad butt as she sauntered ahead. Bevn stumped along behind them, always just too far behind to be able to hear what they talked about, but he could guess, from the way the wizard began to look at her—those quick sideways glances that took in the shape of her body as she moved.

Saladon didn't have anything at all to carry, except his tall battleaxe. That was unfair too, but Bevn hadn't pointed it out to the wizard—Saladon's expression was still too dark when he looked at Bevn. He sucked on his loose tooth as he walked, and pushed his tongue through the bitter hole of the one he'd lost when he'd spied on Saladon talking to the Sorcerer.

Black Saladon was just too scary, too ruthless. Bevn began to wish he'd never become involved with him. The wizard led them with a fanatical urgency and he seemed to become more driven with every hour that passed. He kept them under the cover of the trees. They seldom walked across open wolds or on the hardpacked trails that Bevn noticed from time to time, trails that slipped over exposed ridges and vanished into the deep foliage on either side.

Bevn wondered if he could complete the quest, after all. He was tired, he was so ready to stop, but it sounded as if they had a long way to go to reach the Sorcerer and that their journey would get harder and harder the farther north they travelled. He was certain all this rushing onward was unnecessary. The wizard was doing it just to punish them. Gabrielle was pretending to be unaffected, but he'd noticed her favouring her left foot, so she must have grown some blisters too. Well, if she could pretend to be strong, he would be stronger. They wouldn't make him whimper, they wouldn't get him to cry. Not again.

But it was still unfair. He was a king, and his crown should be giving him power. Saladon was too mighty to be affected, and Gabrielle was just too stubborn. Bevn longed for some common Eyrian peasants to command. He imagined them bowing and scraping their faces upon the bare earth at his feet. The Kingsrim would work on them. Once the Sorcerer had shown him how to do magic, he would return to Eyri and be king. He'd get them to carry him everywhere on a bier, and he'd never have to walk again.

He reached a steep hill where the others waited for him on the crest, standing beneath a lone white tree whose bare branches extended like arms pointing to the four horizons. Gabrielle turned to look down at him. Was that a twist of approval upon her lips? Surely it was. Bevn gave her a sugary smile.

She looked through him, as if pretending he did not exist at all.

Sourpuss, he thought, as he laboured up the hill. As he came close he noticed that she had applied an alluring scent, one he recognised from Willower, a perfume they had called myrrh. She said that she'd acquired it in 'trade', but Bevn thought she must have stolen it, because what did she have to trade that the Hunters could have wanted?

He groaned his way to the crest, and released his pack. It dropped hard onto the ground. There was fruit in there, but he didn't care, he needed a rest. "Get me an apple out the bag," he commanded Gabrielle, without thinking. He was too tired to care what she thought. She bent to the bag and produced a hard green fruit, then rubbed it on her thigh to clean it before tossing it down to him. Bevn was delighted. Saladon pretended not to notice him; he continued talking to Gabrielle instead. "The whitened creature is a Ludertree. His kind are rare this far from the Lowlands, but my guess is we'll see more of them as we progress. This is what happens when wildfire gets into the groundwater. This tree has altered slowly and so it has survived in its new form. Don't ever touch it, for that will alert it to your presence and the bark will burst and the tree will spew a hideous sap upon you. They hunger for flesh as they used to hunger for sunlight, for a Ludertree has no leaves to gather energy. This is a carnivorous creature now. The resin will bind you where you stand, and the roots will search you out within a day. Once you are thus held, it will grow into your body, entering you at your toes."

The tree made a stark contrast against the deep blue sky, but it was still just a stupid dead tree. The wizard was talking nonsense, just to make them scared. Bevn scowled and looked outward instead. The mottled canopy of trees stretched away to the north and west. Some river or lake glistened far to the east, where the land was a paler colour. Bordering most of the northern lands were mountains, ragged ranges of fading purples, capped with a crust of white, the highest peaks lost in cloud. Streaks of feathered clouds crossed the massive sky, and once again he noticed those disconcerting crack-lines in the air that split the sky into panes of slightly varied hue. To the west hc could see no end to the landscape. The vastness of it pounded against his sanity—this was nothing like Eyri. The world here was just too big. The horizon turned to a blue haze so far away he could have ridden a horse for a month and still not have reached it.

"You can tell much from a Ludertree," Black Saladon told Gabrielle. "A sign of the times, indeed it is, though few folk care to read their fate in its arms. Their branches mark the comings and goings of men. See how most of the limbs point to Rek in the east, or to Willower behind us?" He laughed. "Bitter few toward Murkermark, or Slipper. Nay, none at all. The people retreat across their own heartlands to escape the growing threat of the north."

"How can the branches move?" Bevn asked, despite himself.

"It senses things it shouldn't be able to. It senses life. We shall bend a few boughs. Look again once we have passed."

They moved on, but Bevn wasn't ready to go yet. He had just put his pack down. He refused to go on until he was ready. Gabrielle was sweet-talking her way into the wizard's black heart, he could tell. They walked on, talking as if they were old friends.

Something moved above him, and he jerked his head back, grasping at the air in fright.

There was nothing there, just two white branches pointing away down the hill, in the direction Saladon and Gabrielle had gone. North! There had been no branches pointing that way before!

Or had there been? He couldn't be sure. The wizard had *said* there weren't any branches pointing north, and he hadn't looked. Black Saladon was messing with his mind. Trees couldn't move. Bevn gritted his teeth. They were both making fun of him, he was certain of it. He wanted to strike out at something. He almost kicked the roots of the tree, but stopped, uncertain. They were driving him mad! He slammed the pack onto his shoulders. Follow, follow, serve and follow. It was so wrong. He should reign. He should rule!

He pulled out his own dagger, a wicked little curved blade he'd stolen in Willower. It felt good in his hand; it made him dangerous. He walked over to the tree and stabbed his blade into the bark. He needed to hurt something, to relieve his anger.

He hacked at the tree until he had opened a hole in the bark. He wormed his dagger deeper into the trunk until a sticky pale fluid oozed from the wound. He turned the blade within the weeping flesh of the tree, and worked the cut sideways then down, sideways then down again until he had extended the damage into a rough-carved initial. 'K' for 'King'. Then he topped-and-tailed it with two quick slashes, to make the B. He would carve that initial upon the faces of those who displeased him, and those who were loyal would be allowed to use the scarred subjects as slaves.

He set off again, watching the tree over his shoulder, but it did not react to his passage. He checked it from twenty paces on, even from the bottom of the slope, but only the two branches that reached after Black Saladon and Gabrielle remained pointing away to the far-distant mountains. It was as if the tree hadn't noticed him at all. As if he didn't count.

"I am the king of Eyri!" Bevn shouted at the tree. "And I shall bring my army through these lands, and I shall cut you down!" But the tree looked dead already. It shouldn't have been able to change. Why did he care, anyway? It was just a stupid tree. And Saladon had lied. The tree hadn't attacked or done anything. The wizard was just trying to make his life a misery.

He staggered onward, his legs burning against the awkward strain of the descent.

Some time later, they passed a cluster of rotten pink flowers in the forest, each one growing in a tangle of black briars, each a haven for sallow flies and the scent of decay. Bevn couldn't shake the feeling that something was watching him from among the sickly blooms. He speeded up too much on the decline to escape, and the weight of his pack nudged him to ever-greater speed. He careened over roots and barely stayed upright through the trees until the slope eased, where he staggered on jellied legs until he'd crashed into the others.

His chest heaved, and he doubled over to rest on his knees. He didn't care about being stronger than Gabrielle any more; he couldn't go on.

"What was that smell back there?" he heard Gabrielle ask.

"Sapspiders," answered Black Saladon. "Young Bevn did well to run past them, for I think we had disturbed a few, and they don't like being disturbed."

"They were spiders?" Bevn gasped then remembered. "I don't believe it. They looked like flowers."

"They may look like flowers to you and the flies, but those are their mouths, thrown wide. They'll stay like that for hours, until dinner has collected in sufficient numbers."

"And then?" Bevn asked.

"Then they close their mouths."

"Why do they smell so bad?"

"You would too, if you left your food in your mouth until it had rotted enough to swallow."

The flowers had been wider than the span of his hand. If the pink bits had been only their mouths, that would make the spiders huge, big enough to catch up to him even if he ran.

He looked nervously back up the slope, but the spiders' patch was lost in a gloomy patch of trees. All those jumbled blackbriars had been legs, folded up around each flower!

"We want to be far from here by nightfall," Saladon added. "Sapspiders can be quite a nuisance at night if they are still hungry."

Bevn didn't believe him, but he suddenly found the strength to carry on.

 CBℰOCRℰO

The inside of the tent was rank and dark. Furs hung from the crossbeam. The hunter, a lean weathered man with bleached locks that clustered around his balding pate, worked on a pair of rough boots with needle and thong. In the corner, beside a saucer of ale, sat what Zarost had been looking for, surly-eyed and gaudy.

"How much for the parrot?" Zarost asked.

"Immerna for sale!" screeched the parrot.

"He's na for sale," answered the hunter, his voice like parched gravel. "Essa bitterparrot frommin Azique. Dyee kenner rare those things howbe? He's ma eyes inner forest."

"Imma rare! Wraak! Imma rare!" The parrot tilted its beak to look more directly at Zarost. It had those lidded human eyes that showed its mixed ancestry—another victim of Ametheus's manipulations. The empire of Azique had fallen recently, only a century past. It was sad to see the descendants of that fine civilisation reduced to servitude. Zarost doubted that the bitterparrot was loyal because it valued the human company. The ale kept the *sha-lin* bonded to the hunter—the ale it was addicted to.

"What's his name?" Zarost asked.

"Querrihim yerself." The look the hunter gave him told Zarost that he was only tolerant because he wanted to sell some furs. Zarost approached the perch. "What's your name, little one?"

"Brreek! Zaul. Noo little one, nooo sweet beak."

"Breekzol?"

"Aaak!" the parrot shouted, his beak wide. "Getit rrright, herrychinchin! Zaul. Zaul. Zaul!" He shook his feathers.

Zarost chuckled. The bitterparrot had a fine temper. "Well, Zaul from Azique, I'll pay you directly if you work for me," he offered. "A fistblock of salt a day, which you can trade for ale, or whatever you want."

"Oy!" shouted the hunter, throwing his leatherwork from his lap and rising to his feet. "Oy! What a'strange words ye bespeakin to him? Aye a'say he's na for sale."

"Then I'll not be buying him," answered Zarost. "I have offered Zaul a job."

"He has a job! Hesserna working for ye."

"Whatizzit, pay?" asked Zaul from the corner. "Be a'salt mine? Mine? Kroo."

"Get a'ye out!" ordered the hunter. A wet-tipped arrow pointed at Zarost. His bow creaked. "Get. A'ye. Out."

Zarost nodded politely. He turned to leave, but as he ducked beyond the tent-flap he said, "A fistblock a day," over his shoulder. He danced aside, just in case, but the arrow did not fly fast enough to catch him.

If the hunter had been sharper of wit, he would have loosed a whole quiver at Zarost, for Zarost had offered the *sha-lin* enough to make even the most hardened of its kind think twice. A bitterparrot was an intelligent creature. After all, it wasn't really a parrot. The first of their kind were descendants of the resistance fighters of Azique, proud warriors who had faced the onslaught of the Sorcerer's invasion into their land. When the harbingers of Chaos had toiled through the gap from Koraman in the north, dragging the net of tangled spells behind them like a dirty train of silver filigree, the warriors had stood firm on the borders of Azique, their feathered head-dresses ruffled by the dry wind of the storm's approach, their faces stern with the hard lines of battle paints, their deadly scimitars raised. What had come of that defiance, but ruin? How could men stand against a sorcery that hollowed out the bodies of bullgorgons and filled them with fire? How could the Gyre prepare for what Ametheus sent upon Oldenworld?

The Aziqueans had attacked the first line of fell beasts, only to be enveloped in the Chaos they had not prepared for, for the beasts were saturated with it. The men were scalded with change, as chips of randomite erupted in their faces. Gravity was reversed and the warriors were thrown into the air, their feathered headdresses exploding around them. That was probably how the genetic material of parrots had become mixed up with men, but no one truly understood what had happened that day, for they faced Chaos, and Chaos often defied analysis. One way or another, those men had been altered, into multitudinous forms. Those few who remained airborne were spared from death, and so in a way, it was a blessing to become a bitterparrot. But their new forms were useless in battle. They had to flutter around, hopeless, ineffectual, watching their own people being ravaged, watching their comrades fighting on, falling to the ground, writhing and dying. It was understandable that they harboured bitterness so deep that it spanned generations.

Zarost guessed that Zaul was fourth- or fifth-generation *sha-lin*, which meant there was still much human blood in his veins. He would have no problem understanding the principle of trade. Salt was a prized commodity within the Hunterslands. With a fistblock of salt, Zaul could buy the ale he so desperately depended on *and* have salt spare to trade for food. There would be more to his life than spying on game for a hunter who only paid him with a dirty puddle of sour grog.

The *sha-lin* would understand that it had been offered its freedom.

Zaul would find him.

The bitterparrot would be a valuable ally. Not only would he take the challenge to the Warlock, but if he was smart he would be able to escape and bring back word as well, of where Black Saladon was, and what he was doing. Zarost strode quickly away from the low dwelling at the edge of the Hunter settlement, up to the ridge, away into the forest. The day was cooling in the long shadows of the trees. The forest smelled of wet wood. He whispered the words of a small Reference spell, drawing the small block of material he needed from the Gyre stores.

Zarost remembered how he had been called from Eyri to watch the fires rush across Azique like a shimmering flood, driven onward by nodes of Chaos that rolled into the raised plains, fanned by great winds, attended by colossal smoke-filled thunderclouds whose low black bellies dragged over the altered landscape.

The only thing the Gyre could do was to drive the Great Rift all the way around Azique, to split it off from Oldenworld, to contain the disaster and prevent it from ruining everything. It was no solution, it was just a limited failure, and Azique was now a wasted land. It would never be the same again.

Ametheus. His ideas were always unexpected, his designs so horrific—sane minds could never conceive of such diabolical manipulations, and thus they could put no plan in place to combat the next assault, until it was upon them.

෴෴

The wizard Black Saladon commanded their halt with a raised hand. He stood, a tower of brooding silence, looking past the shaft of his battleaxe as if something in the forest was moving, up ahead.

"Why have we stopped?" Bevn whispered to Gabrielle.

"Because he says so, my lord," Gabrielle said then looked suddenly away. Bevn narrowed his eyes at her. The golden morning light shimmered on her skin. Bevn didn't understand what he felt when he looked at her. Something like anger and hunger; something like anticipation. Her hair cascaded in loose dark locks over her shoulders.

Had she just called him 'my lord'? He couldn't be sure. Was the crown finally starting to work? It was weighing down on his forehead, but at least now that his hair was matted and curly, it didn't slip down over his ears so much. He wedged it back into his tangled hair.

Black Saladon pointed down the trail. "Look, by the tree. We must wait."

Bevn couldn't see anything that way until he squinted against the sun and looked far ahead to a distant copse, where a group of brown piglets foraged among the undergrowth, beside a larger sow.

"Ironpigs," said the wizard. "We'll be run down if we come too close."

Honestly, Bevn thought, he's stopped for a grunt and her litter! *He* knew how to deal with pigs. He'd seen his father hunting them from horseback, and the one time he'd even managed to kill an old sow. His father had wounded her by mistake, but he had finished her off. It was easy; he just had to jump on its back, grip its shoulders between his knees as he faced the tail, reach down and around and drive a long-bladed knife in between its ribs, hugging it tight to press the blade in deep. There'd been nothing as exciting as that feeling—the pig squealing and thrashing beneath him then writhing together with him on the ground, and the hot warmth and shuddering sigh as the creature died. His father had never taken him on a hunt again, but he remembered everything about how to kill a pig.

They were scared of a pig! He would show them both what a man he was. Gabrielle would see it, and be properly affected by his manliness. Then the Kingsrim would definitely be able to work its magic.

He pushed past Saladon. The wizard struck his chest and lifted him by his collar in the same movement. Bevn's legs dangled in the air. "Let go of me! I know what to do!" He swung his arms, but the wizard's arm was longer, and he couldn't reach him.

"Shut up," said Saladon, still not looking at him. "You'll be run through with their tusks. Those are ironpigs, not playthings."

Bevn couldn't see why they would be any different. A pig was a pig. Saladon was making up stories again, trying to make him seem stupid, when he was actually clever. He would show them!

"Then why don't we go around them!" He pried at Saladon's fingers to try free himself.

"We're downwind of them at the moment," Saladon said quietly, "but if we pass them they'll sense us and track us down. They can't see beyond fifty paces, but within that they're deadly. We shall wait here until they move off."

"Why can't you just cast a spell on them?"

"From this distance? It would trigger the wildfire. If I was close enough to use my magic quietly, they'd know I was there."

"So what? Surely you can kill a pig? They just look like a bunch of stupid porkers."

"Your brain is weaker than your eyes. Do you really think something would survive for long in this vicious forest without having a particularly good defence? You don't want to make those things angry."

Saladon dumped him on his butt, and there Bevn sulked. He hated the way Saladon treated him like a little boy, especially in front of Gabrielle. He wanted to kick the big wizard in his shins, or hang on the long tails of his moustache. He glared at the pigs. Stupid pigs.

He began to brighten as he realised that he could pull a prank on the wizard. The pigs might be good survivors, but he had his own particularly good defence. He knew how valuable he was to Saladon—so valuable that the wizard was accompanying him on foot across land he could easily have traversed in a moment with his magic. Saladon didn't want to let him out of his sight. The wizard would protect him against any danger. If he charged the pigs, the wizard would have to do something, and he'd get to see more of the magic Saladon refused to show him.

He needed to test what Gabrielle would do. Was she being influenced enough by the Kingsrim now, or would she side with Saladon? His blood pounded in his ears. Some inner sense told him she would side with him. The Kingsrim was warm, hot on his forehead. It made him strong. It made him King.

He stood and moved out of range of Saladon's long arms. He sauntered over to Gabrielle, where she rested against the bole of a tree, and squatted beside her, so the crown was right against her head. "Protect me from him," he said, with all the kingly command he could muster. Then he grabbed one of her knives from her belt, and he ran, before they had realised what he was about to do.

"Bevn, wait!" Gabrielle called after him.

He laughed and lengthened his stride. Let her run to catch him—that should remind her of a time before, in the Penitent's pass, when she'd recognised his power over her. Let her run. Let them both run. He sprinted down the trail, toward the rooting pigs, the knife brandished like a commander's sword. The air tightened for a moment as a strange pattern of glistening tendrils wove around him. Magic! It seemed to disperse around the Kingsrim, and he ran on unhindered. Black Saladon cursed behind him. Bevn whooped with delight. The crown gave him some protection from the wizard's magic. That was an unexpected bonus.

He made for the trees. Upon his approach, the sow looked up in surprise and waggled her tusks in his direction. The pigs drew closer to each other. They had seemed so very small in the distance, but something about the perspective of the downward slope had hidden their true size. The piglets stood almost waist-high, the sow came up to his chin. Still, she was just a pig. She would run, wouldn't she, if given a choice? He didn't turn to look behind him. The others were sure to be close.

Another pig burst from the undergrowth beside the sow. It had tusks as well, dark-stained at the tips and well worn. Both pigs had hides like rusted metal. Bevn felt a stab of alarm. He waved his arms at them. The pigs watched Bevn falter and come to a halt. Their little eyes were steady. Solid wet snouts tested the air. The daddy-pig, the boar, even had the nerve to drop its head, as if it was considering facing him down. At least the smaller critters had the sense to cower behind their mother, but they didn't run away.

They probably weren't sure what he was, the stupid things. Pigs didn't charge humans, did they? They were swine, not predators. No, he was not going to back down for a bunch of pigs! He was a ruler of men. He certainly ruled pigs. Besides, Saladon would save him.

Where was he? He had expected Black Saladon to be on his heels, but it was silent behind him.

The ironpigs stepped back a few paces, tossing their heads, swinging their tusks from side to side. The boar was wider than the sow. He seemed more like an armoured bull. His tusks were as long as Bevn's forearms. The boar bellowed, showing sharper teeth than Bevn had expected, more like wolves' teeth than the flattened stubs of a pig. Bevn kept his eye on the brute as he backed away, but it was the sow who charged him first. With a bloodthirsty squeal, she came for him. Those mean little eyes held no fear.

"Gabrielle," he cried weakly, looking for her as he stumbled away. With a horrible hollow feeling in his stomach, he realised where she was. Grappling with Saladon, back where he'd left them. He'd ordered her to prevent Saladon from hurting him, and she'd complied. She had listened to him! She was following an order of the king! The Kingsrim had worked, at last, but there was no time for Bevn to enjoy the triumph.

"Gabrielle!" he cried, as heavy hooves pounded on the turf behind him.

He'd meant for her to protect him *after* Saladon had saved him from the pigs, not before. He'd wanted her to be his shield when Saladon chastised him for the prank. Instead, she was preventing the wizard from getting into range. She might be obeying his command, but in truth she was using his own words against him.

There was a soft implosion, and a cry, and Saladon threw Gabrielle clear.

That was all he saw of Saladon's approach, for the sow scooped him up from behind with her tusks, and flung him back over her head. The tips of her tusks scored a stinging streak across his ankles. He cart-wheeled in the air, then he was tumbling headfirst, watching with horror as the ground came up. He was going to hit hard, and that was not the worst of it.

He was going to land right among the piglets. The daddy-pig

wasn't going to like that at all.

The leaves and humus littering the ground broke his fall somewhat, but he hit his head a dizzying blow and felt the Kingsrim tumble away, and with it, his courage. He reached for it blindly, and poked one of the piglets in the eye instead. It squealed. It was trampling the crown. He tried to slap the piglet aside and almost broke his hand its hide was so hard. The others piglets ran, jumped and grunted, and squealed around him in a maddening flurry of activity. They seemed excited, rather than scared. One of them nipped his thigh.

Where was the boar? He couldn't see it. Bevn staggered to his feet.

A horrendous impact took his legs out, and the world went topsy-turvy again.

He tasted wet leaves and earth. A tusk drove into his side, hard enough to drive the breath from his lungs. He tried to fend off the attack, but he was so dizzy and suddenly sick he couldn't tell up from down. He cried out and caught hold of a tusk on the second strike and clung on as tightly as the pain in his chest would let him. At least if he held on, he figured the boar could not run back for another lunge. The boar thrashed from side to side, dragging Bevn across the dirt, then it advanced again, pushing him backward. He thought he might have a chance to get to his feet then, and as his sight began to clear he shifted his grip on the tusks. Then Bevn heard a second low grunt from behind him, and the pummelling of hooves on the earth.

The sow was coming. He was going to be sandwiched between the two of them. Bevn knew already how hard they were. He was going to be squashed like a grape between two rocks.

"Stop them! Stop them! Somebody help me! Help!" he cried out.

He couldn't get free from the boar, he couldn't get free from the boar—the tusk had pierced his clothing. He looked desperately over his shoulder. The sow was charging at him, her brutal tusks lowered, a snorting charging thundering beast. He was terrified.

Saladon was there, just behind the sow, coming in from the side. At the last moment he dropped his battleaxe and dived, but the sow reached him, her tusks slamming into his back. He was done for. All the breath was forced from his lungs. Something crunched inside his chest.

Suddenly, the weight at his back was gone. The sow blasted him with frustrated bellow, but she had begun to back away, walking awkwardly on her forelegs. Saladon had caught up the hind legs of the sow. He struggled with her weight, but the way he had tipped her body up gave him some control. The sow could not reach Saladon without falling over, and her neck was too short to use the tusks upon him.

Then the boar, its snout close to Bevn's face, began to bellow as well.

Bevn looked up to see Gabrielle, at the rear end of the boar. Her expression was not kind.

"I'm hurt!" he cried out to her, gasping for breath. "I'm bleeding. I think something's broken!"

"Let go of the pig, you idiot," Gabrielle shouted. "Let go!"

He was too sore to care that she was ordering him around. He let go of the dirty tusk, and Gabrielle fought the thrashing boar on her own.

"Now get around the tusks and get the knife in it! Get in there!" Gabrielle commanded him.

Bevn groaned and rolled on the ground. She should be more sympathetic to him. He was injured. He couldn't remember where the knife was—he must have dropped it somewhere on the ground.

"Get up, you weakling. Get up!"

He tried to rise. A sickening pain stabbed through his right calf. He breathed in short little gasps.

"I can't!" he cried out. "My leg hurts. I think it's—oh mother it can't be! I think it's broken!"

"I don't care if you have to crawl on your belly, dandyhead!" shouted Gabrielle. "Help me finish this brute off. You started this, now end it. We can't hold these beasts for long!"

Bevn staggered to his feet, crying out with the pain, but even so he managed to hobble away. It was amazing what he could do if he tried. He had to get away from the ironpigs. He had to get away!

"You come back here, you horrible boy!" Gabrielle demanded. "Come here!"

She was holding on to the back end of a wild and angry pig, and she couldn't let it go. One of the piglets butted into her legs. Two more were harrying Saladon.

"You don't command me!" he announced in a high voice. "The king is leaving."

He hopped and stumbled away. The wizard should have warned him more thoroughly. Gabrielle should have been more humble. They were big enough to look after themselves. He lurched down the trail, moaning every time his right leg took too much of his weight. He had to get as far away as he could. They would find him later, he was sure, but he didn't care. The wizard thought too much of himself, and if Gabrielle wanted the protection of the Kingsrim, she would have to beg for it.

The Kingsrim! His guts made a sickening lurch. He'd done it again, that's why things had gone so wrong. It had fallen off, right at the beginning. He'd left it behind! Bevn turned, but he couldn't see it anywhere.

A piglet got in under Gabrielle's feet. She went down onto her knees, struggling to keep control of the boar she held. Saladon was trying to steer the sow closer to where his abandoned battleaxe lay, but the sow resisted. Why didn't he use his magic?

There! The Kingsrim—it lay among the leaves, between the two struggling figures, where it could be trampled. The golden crown glinted. He watched with horror as first Gabrielle then the wizard were drawn against their will on the hind end of the angry pigs, stomping the leaves all around the crown.

They wouldn't forget to bring it to him, would they?

What if one of them picked it up, and decided to keep it?

He started forward, but couldn't bring himself to return to the melee.

Saladon dropped the sow's legs, and ran. The ironpig didn't waste any time in following him. Saladon ran straight for a big tree. If the wizard was intending to climb out of range of the wicked tusks he had chosen badly. The tree was broad at the base, and rose for twenty feet before spreading into branches. The bark looked gnarled and soft—it would most likely come away in chunks if he tried to scale it. But Saladon didn't change his course, he ran as if he was going to dive *into* the tree. The sow thundered along behind him, narrowing the gap as her hooves tore at the roots. Bevn watched with morbid fascination.

The sow was about to impale Saladon against the trunk when something peculiar happened. The wizard was there one moment, and then he wasn't. A booming clap sounded in the air.

Magic! He'd cast a magic spell! Bevn was delighted.

The sow, blind with rage, drove her full weight behind her tusks, but her target was gone. Only the bole of the tree blocked her path. With a surprised squeal and a thump, which shook the leaves overhead, she impaled her tusks deeply into the soft bark, and there she remained, her hind legs scrabbling at the roots, her forelegs splayed. No amount of heaving was going to get her free, not for a while, at least.

Gabrielle was struggling with the boar, trying to keep a hold on its hind legs, and wrestling with the brute to avoid his tusks. As Bevn watched, she lost her grip on one of the legs, and the boar found a better footing. She clung onto the last foot at the ankle, but it was too awkward to grasp, and with a sudden cry she let go. The boar twisted, bellowed and turned on her.

With a quick fluid motion, she drew one of her knives from her hip, and plunged it downward into the boar's blunt head. The knife bent, and Gabrielle cried out, cradling her hand against her body. The boar drove forward and she was forced to back away. She kicked out with the sole of her boot, a stamping kick which landed right between the boar's squint eyes, but it just shook its head and continued its advance. She fended off its first lunge with her left hand, catching at the tusk before it could impale her. The boar drove her back, toward a tree, just as its mate had done to Saladon.

He was sure Gabrielle couldn't perform Saladon's vanishing trick. She was going to get skewered.

Bevn hobbled over to the Kingsrim, where it lay among the leaves.

She called out to him. "Bevn! Quickly! Get its legs! It's going to pin me here."

He ignored her and dusted off the crown. "Let's see," he said in a loud voice. "She tried to command me, she hasn't made any effort to please me, she spurned me that night in Willower, made me look a fool before all those men. She doesn't want to lie in the bed of a king. So be it. I think it is a good time to get rid of her, I don't need her, do I?"

The ironpig would be occupied with mauling her for long enough to allow his escape, he was sure. It might even eat her. Who knew what these creatures of Oldenworld were capable of? The Kingsrim fitted snugly, despite being slightly bent. He could even hold his head upright, and look down his nose at the woman.

The ironpig had her trapped against the tree. She grasped for the tusks, but one-handed. Her right hand was still cradled against her chest. The boar thrashed its head, the tusk slipped in her grip. The boar braced itself, and with a ferocious heave of its head, broke completely free.

"Goodbye, Gabrielle," Bevn called out. "You really should have been more willing to obey your king."

Fifty paces, Saladon had said. He could get that far away before the boar was finished with her. The ironpig hooked her legs out from under her then, throwing her on her side. She caught a tusk again, but the beast had the advantage now, and she would not last long against it.

"You little bastard! You are not going to leave me here!"

She hadn't learnt. Even when her own end was upon her, she was trying to tell him what he would and wouldn't do. He would show her just how wrong she was. His back would be the last thing she would see.

He turned and walked straight into a heavy fist. The surprise blow lifted him off his feet and threw him far back before his bum hit the leaves. With horror he realised that the crown had been plucked from his head as well.

Black Saladon. The wizard stood there, crown in hand, his eyes blazing red, his face so dark and dangerous. He made a strange gesture in the air and Bevn felt terribly heavy. Saladon thrust his arm through the crown and moved so quickly Bevn's eyes couldn't quite follow him. He rolled over the ground in a blurring tumble, to where the battleaxe lay. Then he was at the tree, beside Gabrielle. His axe shrieked, and it tore through the air in a disturbing way that left a visible arc after it had passed. Saladon's weapon passed through the ironpig behind its shoulders, cleaving the animal in two. The rear half of the pig flew away, smoking, and when it struck the ground it burst into blackened chunks.

Then a shockwave slammed into Bevn, leaving his head ringing.

Saladon leapt away, swinging his battleaxe. He fell upon the other ironpig, where it was still lodged in the tree trunk. He smote it with a double-handed overhead strike. The air split again upon the curved blade; the ironpig was divided. The ground heaved and opened along a narrow fissure. Chips of stone spat outward as a wave of force rippled through the earth. The grit stung Bevn's face. He felt hollowed out. The immensity of Saladon's power made him weak. The fury of those two blows awed him. The piglets scattered among the trees. Saladon let them go, slowly prising his weapon from the ground. Then he turned and his gaze found Bevn.

Bevn panicked. He still couldn't move. The wizard was a going to kill him, and keep the Kingsrim! He knew it! He didn't expect any mercy from the wizard. Saladon came closer, with slow, steady steps.

Bevn's legs wouldn't move. It was as if they were tied to the earth, but there was nothing trying them down, nothing but air. He began to cry.

"Put this on." Saladon threw the Kingsrim toward Bevn's feet as if it was a dirty old hat. As soon as it rolled against his leg, the strange bonds which had immobilised him fell away. Bevn was so relieved. He scooped up the crown and crammed it down upon his head at once.

He looked up at Saladon through a haze of tears. He didn't understand what was happening.

"You are needed, because of that," Saladon stated bluntly, pointing at the sky. "I'll not have her turned into silverspawn just because you're a witless runt, and you're no use to me as a patch of fungus. You will wait here."

High overhead, even more brilliant than the harsh yellow sun, was a ball of silver fire. It hurtled down toward them as if aimed at his heart. Bevn clutched onto the Kingsrim, and watched the imminent comet with quivering dread. It was huge; it grew with alarming speed as it neared them. It brought a rumble with it, which became a roll, then a roar, then a whip-shriek. He wet himself.

Saladon dragged Gabrielle nearer to Bevn. The howl of the comet was suddenly deafening. It hit them and everything exploded into silver. The ground was lit by brilliant white, a light so intense there were no shadows. He would have run, if there had been anywhere to run to, but Saladon's iron grip on his wrist kept him pinned to the ground. It seemed that the safest place was where he was with the Kingsrim on his head. Saladon and Gabrielle were within the sphere of the crown's influence, inside a curtain of silver particles that flared to gold before vanishing. Saladon was doing something to the magical essence as well, standing with his arms spread wide, pronouncing an unbroken chain of words in an ancient language.

The forest sizzled, the ground shook. A wave of ash and dust encircled their place in the forest, washing away through the trees, consuming everything in its path. The sound of destruction filled the air, as the vegetation issued tortured screeches, like wet logs on a roaring fire—a great hissing, splintering eruption of sound. Random trees burst into dazzling outlines as the wildfire touched their stems and raced through the life it found there. As the wildfire spread farther outward, its potency reduced and things remained standing, but they were warped, twisted, altered in place. Bevn saw a tree sprout roots all up its trunk, toppled over and run away. An area of underbrush writhed, bulged and spewed out a plague of fat locusts. Change rippled through the forest, until the wildfire had reached its limit.

Then, at last, all was quiet. It seemed as if the forest itself breathed a sigh of relief.

It was not over for Bevn. Saladon turned toward him, with Gabrielle at his side. Bevn lurched to his feet. His right leg was throbbing, but he would run, if he had to. Gabrielle leant heavily on the wizard's shoulder for support. She was concentrating on the ground. Saladon, however, looked straight ahead. His gaze was steady, and more threatening than ever. Bevn began to regret what he had done. He regretted many things, but he wasn't about to admit to any more than he absolutely had to.

"Is she—all right?" he asked, backing away on unsteady feet. He exaggerated his own limp. Maybe they would feel sorry for him and go easy on him.

"You shall have to ask her yourself," said Saladon.

"Gabrielle?"

Her legs were a mess. Blood soaked from multiple wounds. Her right hand looked bad as well.

She looked up then, and he was caught by those dark eyes, so deeply mysterious. He had expected her to be spitting fury, but she was strangely calm. She smiled at him, a broad smile that made his heart turn in his chest. How did she do that? He knew he should be afraid of her, but she was smiling. He faltered, and didn't bother to back away any more. The Kingsrim had pacified her again. She was his subject. He was her king.

"I didn't really mean—" he began, but he didn't finish his sentence. Gabrielle's eyes held a sudden glint. Her left fist came out of nowhere, straight into his jaw, as hard and straight as a charging ram. His head snapped back on his neck. He tasted blood and stars. He fell.

29. EYE SPY WITH MY LITTLE I

"Riddlers are measured by what they say;
spies by what they see."—Zarost

When the bitterparrot found him, Zarost was far from the Hunters. It had been part of his plan to see how good the *sha-lin* was at tracking. If he couldn't find Zarost in the forest, he would be no good at finding the Warlock. Here he was, in a sudden flurry of feathers and gaudy colours, complete with a flurried landing. Zaul tried again for the low branch he'd missed, gained a perch then wobbled around to face Zarost. Zarost suspected he'd passed by the saucer of ale before escaping.

The bitterparrot glared at him out of his black-lidded human eyes. "What ye belooking? Kraak! Ye gotta cheek comin innas Callum tent. I were happy til'ye came. Riches and rewards! Bribery, corrupt! Show see what ye haver paying."

Twardy Zarost held out the chunk of salt. "This one's for coming. Another for every day I need you."

The parrot hopped along its branch, coming closer to Zarost. He extended one foot, but stepped away again.

"How a'long I spy with my little eye? How a'long ye pass me pay?"

"As long as I need to you to track for me. It might take you a day, it might take a week. Once I'm done, you'll be free."

"Free? Ye bemeaning na job. Na salt, noo drink anymore for Zaul. Rukukurruk! Roo!"

Twardy Zarost nodded. "I can't promise you a future.'

"Ten, I take a ten blocks 'pon finishing. If I be quick, so good for me. Ye dinna like it, ye can go shunt a sheep."

He pitied the bitterparrot. Zaul had no idea how easy the salt was for Twardy Zarost to acquire. No matter, it had value to the *sha-lin*. "Eight," he said, knowing that if he did not haggle, the *sha-lin* would not trust him.

Zaul shuffled closer on his branch then reached for the lump of salt with his beak. He snatched it away, and took to the air. "We na trust menner who are na frommin Azique!" he cried.

"Water upon you, heat taken from you," whispered Zarost, twisting his fingers in the air to create a blend of two small second-axis spells in the clear essence. The second pattern would release the energy needed to form the matter of the first. Zaul disappeared in his own little cloud then plummeted to the ground.

He landed with his beak in the mud, but he kept a firm grip on the salt nugget.

"Bloody feathers be now so soaked!" he croaked, speaking around the obstruction in his beak. "Wraak! Colder than a corpse. Becussedy, cussedy, stranger. Ye be wizardly, ye be trouble," he scolded, hopping in a circle. "Stirring the silverness, bringin a'ruin. Cussedy, cussedy, cuss."

Zarost quickly scanned the sky, just to be sure, but his limited activity hadn't registered upon the wildfire web. He squatted beside the bitterparrot. "Consider this, little friend. I found you first, so I can find you again. If you take the payment, you take the job."

"Noo! Firs' salt is a'for coming t' find ye. What iffa noo want to spy for ye? Puckpraak! Wizzard!"

"Have you ever considered how stupid you'd look without your feathers?"

Zaul dropped the salt nugget upon the ground. His sad eyes were wide, the small feathers on his head raised in panicked tufts. "Wloo! Kibbit! I dinna want a'nothing to do wither ye!" But his left foot betrayed him, for it reached for the discarded nugget and drew it under his chest.

"I thought as much," said Twardy Zarost.

"Nine fistblocks?" asked Zaul.

"Eight," Zarost corrected. "*And* one a day, until you're done."

Zaul rolled his head to the side, to better take in Zarost's face.

"Whatter ye want me be do?"

ഒ൦ൟൟ

Bevn must have been knocked unconscious for a long time, because when he came to, it was dark. His mouth tasted like glue. His head pounded, his jaw ached; his whole body ached, especially when he breathed in. His lips were thick and split from where Gabrielle had hit him. He was instantly embittered, but he remembered enough of what had happened to know it would be wise to keep his complaints to himself. He lay still and listened instead.

They were arguing nearby, their voices low. Something was

roasting—he could smell cooked meat.

He slowly rolled his head to one side. Gabrielle and Black Saladon sat beside a fire. Gabrielle had tied her hair into a braid again. Saladon stirred the coals with a finger.

"They will investigate the strike-point, it's a beacon for wizards," Black Saladon said. "We must move on! We must pass through Slipper before the Gyre discovers what we are doing. If we are too slow, we will have to fight all of them."

"No!" Gabrielle exclaimed. "I understand that *you* need to move, but *I* don't. The agreement is off! You asked me to be an escort, but I cannot travel with that brat any farther. He is not worthy of any respect, yet that crown of his erodes my resistance, and it gets worse every day. Why do you think I always stay away from him? I find myself wanting to lower myself before him, damn it, to obey him! And he's just a stripling! I couldn't stop myself from turning on you when he ran for the ironpigs. I was compelled to fight on his side by his command. That crown affects something in my blood. It rules me when he's near. I have spent years living with a Domination spell, I know how it works, but I have some influence over the Dark. I have no command over the ruling force that reaches out from that golden coil. It is subtle and strong, so strong. Hitting him at the end was hard to do, even though I wanted to so much. No, you will be better off without me, Saladon. *You* can resist that spell. If I stay in his company any longer, I shall kill that boy, before it is too late for me."

Bevn was delighted. She *was* being affected.

"You will just have to deal with the effect of the Kingsrim until we reach Turmodin," Saladon said. "You cannot break your word now. If I must leave him at any time, he will be alone and defenceless."

"He can die, for all I care."

"I cannot afford that," Saladon answered. "He is too valuable to me."

"I will not be forced to become servile," Gabrielle said. "Either you give me some defence against the Kingsrim, or you lose me."

"There is no defence I can provide against it, it is a seventh-level Order spell. It would take nearly all the members of the Gyre working in unison to alter the pattern."

"Then you shall have to chain me and drag me beside you if you want my company. I'll not willingly allow myself to be influenced by that back-stabbing little prat."

"You expected honour from a thief?" he asked. "Thieves have no honour."

She stared at the fire and did not answer him.

"You will come, because I need you, Gabrielle."

"Then I want more from you in return," she answered hotly. "Healing my wounds was not enough."

"What do you want?"

She looked him over. She seemed about to say something, then hesitated.

"A position of power in the Sorcerer's court."

Saladon roared with laughter. "You should have asked what first crossed your mind. The Sorcerer has no court. There is no organisation in Turmodin—he despises structure and governance. No, Gabrielle, you cannot bargain for a position. The Sorcerer rules because no one can challenge him, not because he is supported by the people of Turmodin. You can only gain his favour by being useful to him in the present. Your usefulness might be forgotten by tomorrow."

"But you must have some alliance with him! You must have a position of power yourself."

"Only because I bring something useful to him—the Kingsrim, with the true-blooded royal to enliven it."

"Then I am useful to him as well, so long as I accompany you toward Turmodin?"

"Yes!" Saladon agreed. "That's exactly how it works. When you assist Chaos, you gain the most for yourself. If you break away now, you will gain nothing, and if you work against Chaos, you will lose everything."

Bevn was stiff. He straightened his legs carefully, but discovered that he was hobbled and tied onto something. He rolled awkwardly onto his side to see what had been done to him. His broken ribs gritted in his chest. He moaned.

"Ahh, the golden calf awakes," said Black Saladon, turning.

Bevn struggled upright. At least his hands were free, but his feet were tied together with a length of cord and secured to a gnarled root. The cord was slippery and tough and seemed to have no knots in it at all. Bevn couldn't see how to free himself.

"My body hurts," he complained.

"It'll hurt even more if you even think of repeating a stunt like that." Gabrielle's quiet voice ran up his spine like a chilled blade. "I'll make sure you feel everything before I slit your throat."

Saladon came over. He squatted at eye level, blocking the firelight with his body. He looked at Bevn intently. "You're lucky to be alive. Don't try my temper again. I shall have to kill you."

But Bevn had heard what he'd said about taking him to Turmodin alive, so he knew the big wizard was lying.

"Mm," he said, pretending to agree. He glanced around, but they were not where he'd expected them to be. There was no sign of the ashen destruction of the wildfire strike. Instead, the trees loomed tall and straight around them, their distant tops indistinct against the dark night and tiny stars.

"Where are we?" His swollen lips made his words come out sounding thick and stupid.

"Far enough away from prying eyes."

"How did I get here?" His jaw hurt savagely.

"On my shoulder, you lump of lard." Saladon rose and pointed to a stain on his bronze shirt. "Your blood." He brushed at the stain with a finger. With a puff of smoke it burnt off the fabric. "I'll carry you to Turmodin, if you give me reason to believe you will run off again and put us all in danger, and believe me, I'll make it as uncomfortable as all hell. You'll ride like a sack of oranges, not as a king."

Bevn checked himself over. The back of his right leg was a huge, purpling bruise. He supposed it wasn't actually broken, because it felt straight when he probed it with his fingers. His ribs, however, hurt like hell. The bones gritted with every breath.

He balanced and stood, moaning, to show them how very sore he was, but they didn't seem to take any notice.

"Is there anything left to eat?" he demanded.

Saladon pointed to the fire, at a great carcass hung skewered over the coals. Ample pickings remained, more than they could possibly eat. Strips of meat had been cut to hang over the far side of the fire, where the logs still flamed and smoked.

"What is it?"

"One of the piglets."

He hobbled over. His tether was barely long enough for him to reach the meat. He was tethered! Like a slave! Like a prisoner! Like a dog. It wasn't fair. He tore a long rib from the carcass. His jaw ached terribly when he tried to bite the meat off the bone. His split lip stung. He sniffed loudly and hid his tears by scratching at his nose.

"Did you kill it?" he asked Saladon.

"No, no, it was Gabrielle. I just mentioned to her where she could strike. It's a soft place every man should protect; especially from one as talented with a knife as Gabrielle."

She was pretending not to listen. He shifted uncomfortably on his feet. Gabrielle had retrieved the blade he'd stolen—two hilts protruded from her belt-sheaths. He was about to take another painful bite of supper when he heard wing-beats in the air above, coming down upon him. He ducked, instinctively, but then there was sudden added weight upon his crown. He twisted his head. There was a flurry of wing-beats and a scratchy-voiced curse.

"Idjit! Skraak! Keep yer pip still, or I'll beshitten yer ear."

There was something on top of his head! Something that spoke like a Hunter. Had it just threatened what he thought it had threatened?

"Saladon?" he said, cowering under the uncertain threat. "Saladon?"

"Don't move," answered the wizard. "What do you want, *sha-lin*? We have no drinks among this party."

"We're na all drinkers!" the whatever-it-was screeched. Bevn reached up tentatively to remove the crown and its load. He yelped as something bit his finger, hard. The creature gripped his hair fiercely.

"What is it? What's on my head?"

"I be deadly, tattinhat, my beak be sharp. Ikkin pecker eyes out."

"Just stand still! It's called a bitterparrot," Saladon explained. "It can be a right nuisance if it wants to be."

From the weight of it, Bevn knew it wasn't that big, but he knew it wasn't lying about its sharp beak. His finger had been savaged, it was bleeding. The threat of having his eyes pecked out was too vivid. He stood dead still.

"What do you want?" repeated Saladon, facing Bevn but looking over his head.

"Izzard! Gizzard! Rukatukatoo!"

"If you want some meat, go ahead. We have eaten our fill."

"Wizzzard."

Saladon grew suddenly alert. "What gives you that idea?"

"Hoh he! Wizzzard, an tattinhat boy, an ladyhunter, travelling north from a'Bradach. I see! I see! Na better tracking-eye than Zaul."

Saladon moved fast, with that disconcerting speed Bevn had witnessed before. One moment he was close to the fire and Gabrielle, in the next his chest was in Bevn's face. The creature squawked as it was lifted away. Something warm and runny trickled through Bevn's hair.

"Na shoot a'messenger!" the bitterparrot cried, struggling

helplessly in Saladon's fist.

The bird was the oddest thing Bevn had ever seen. It had gaudy feathers and a hooked beak, but wide, wet human eyes. It tried to bite Saladon's hand, but the wizard squeezed, and it threw its head back, squawking. It had a naked, fleshy neck.

"Oohk! Messages, I have a'messages for ye!"

"From who?" Black Saladon asked. "Who is sending me messages?"

"The Riddler!" the bitterparrot shrieked. "The Riddler! Elp! Ye be a'breaking my neck!"

"So they know," said Saladon quietly, looking off into the distance. The bitterparrot issued a gobbling croak.

"All right," Saladon said at last, opening his palm. The bird fell to the ground, where it hunkered with its brightly coloured wings splayed wide. It coughed and coughed.

"Talk fast, little spy."

"Sed nothing 'bout danger," the bird muttered between coughs, its gaze downcast.

Saladon lowered his battleaxe until the long blade was almost touching the back of the newcomer's head. The bitterparrot flipped onto his back in surprise. His eyes were transfixed by the deadly edge.

"Talk," said Saladon.

"It a…he a… All right! I talk! I was set to talk anyway! Yihdy wizzards be nothing but troublers. He say ye be welcomerman. Bloody hell! Na so, na so. Skrooskra! Riddler spoke in manner strange, an' he want me be repeating with na mistook. He telltold that ye be found, for he holds the far end of the essence thread attached to me, and he can read the length an direction of it. If I be harmed, the thread willer snap back to him, and he will ken where ye are. So ye can na hurt me. If ye wish to remain hidden, ye must a'parley wither me, an' truthbetold. The Riddler laid these terms. Bury the Kingsrim here, show me the place, then run free, all three. Ye will na be followed. Keep the crown, and ye be soon found, and captured by the Gyre, and the boy be killed."

Saladon looked down at the messenger for a long time. "Very clever, Riddler," he said at last. "Very clever, but you have forgotten, I walk toward Chaos. I will not do what you expect me to, or even what would seem sensible to you. *Sha-lin*, you can tell your director that he should not trade lives for a hopeless cause. Order has been surpassed. Those who continue to support it only make themselves clearer targets."

"What ye meaning?" croaked the bitterparrot. "Cannint make beak nar feathers of yeba oddly words."

Saladon lifted his battleaxe away from the bitterparrot, and leant it against his chest. "It means just this." He gestured with splayed fingers toward the fire. Ten flames spurted out from the coals, ragged-edged and hot. Saladon lifted his fingers, and the flames rose, diverging, searching.

Saladon glanced down at the bitterparrot.

The messenger looked back, and his eyes went wide. In that brief moment, Bevn understood what was about to happen. The ten loose flames converged upon the little figure, enveloping him with a sudden searing roar. There was no time for a leap, or a curse, or even a final cry. The strange gaudy-feathered wet-eyed visitor vanished in a blast of fire.

Bevn moved back, away from the sudden heat. The fireball compressed upon itself then ran away in a single smokeless jet that moved as if tracing a thread, running like a fuse, Bevn supposed, back along the route the bird had approached upon. Bevn looked down at the charred remains, just a few bones in an ashen heap. A smoking feather, its filaments glowing, rode upward on an air current.

Someone had badly underestimated Black Saladon.

"That trace-line will arc as soon as it crosses under a wildfire node," said the wizard, more to himself than anyone else. "Damn, I should have thought of that. Blast you, Riddler, you are too tricky!"

"What does that mean?" Bevn asked.

"It means the race is on. They have our position, or near enough to be dangerous. Now we must move, and faster than anyone expects us to. The wizards of the Gyre are coming for us."

Saladon looked down at Bevn's tethered feet and frowned. Then he hefted the battleaxe, balanced it, and swung it hard, straight down for Bevn's head.

Bevn fell back with a cry of surprise. The blade whooshed toward him.

It missed his head, only because he'd fallen, and severed the fibres of the cord binding his ankles together. Rocks cracked beneath where the battleaxe had struck. A plume of dust sucked up past his feet. Bevn sat in mute shock. He thought Saladon had decided to kill him as well. The wizard glared down at him.

"Now if you so much as think of disobeying my orders, I will cut your head from your shoulders. Get up, and stay close to me."

Bevn obeyed, despite the pain in his body.

Gabrielle gathered their bedrolls and stuffed them into the pack. She shouldered the load as she came up to Saladon.

"Who is the Riddler?" she asked.

"He's a wizard, one of the eight Gyre members," Saladon answered, while leading them away from the temporary camp. "You should try to stay away from the wizards of the Gyre. They are more dangerous to you than the Sorcerer himself."

"Why?"

"The Sorcerer just kills his enemies. The wizards of the Gyre prefer to keep their enemies alive, and turn them to their own ends."

Bevn had heard of a Riddler before. There had been a Riddler in the Darkmaster's service, in Ravenscroft, an advisor of sorts, a wily man. Bevn had met him, but he had never seen his face. Saladon couldn't be talking about the same man. That was impossible.

"This Riddler," Gabrielle asked, "Was he ever in Eyri?"

"Oh yes," Black Saladon replied. "He's been in Eyri since the beginning. He has the most to lose if the crown reaches the Sorcerer, because it will destroy everything he has worked for. She is their last hope, and she will belong to Chaos, no matter how they try to prepare her, she will belong to the Sorcerer, in the end, because his new wizard is an Eyrian, and so the Kingsrim commands her."

He turned to Bevn and held him with that gaze that made all things seem possible.

"You will command her," he said to Bevn.

30. THE SCALES OF HONESTY

"Lying for a living gives a man
a great hunger for the truth."—Zarost

In darkness he composed his litany of lies. It was freezing—the cold of ice, the cold of altitude, the cold of midwinter night. The cavern was a temple that arched over Ashley's thoughts as he considered his survival.

One of the great pillars of his life was truth. He'd always believed in truth; that no matter what, it was important not to deceive people, to be honest and to deal with the consequences—no matter how difficult it made his life. He'd been held back in the Dovecote because of that. Shamgar hadn't taken kindly to his direct and honest observations, but Ashley had always felt right when he spoke out against untruths. Did that make him better? Such holiness seemed hollow now. What was holiness, but a particular kind of vanity? What was honesty, but a luxury of the man who wasn't truly at risk?

If he was dead honest with the dragon, he'd just be dead.

Her breath stank; she was as brutal as a barbed mace, as weighty as a falling boulder. She stretched across the cavern like a lethal guardian, like some nightmare hammered out of an old mountain.

He couldn't tell her that, and so the truth became mutable in his hands.

He found small things that could be distorted by close attention. If he ignored his opinion of her as a whole, if he ignored his feeling that she was a killer that farted noxious gas which exploded when she blew angry flame into it, he could notice the details that could be used to his advantage. Her scales shimmered when they caught the sudden flare of yellow light. Her breath formed swirling puffs of steam. Her rumbling purr, when she was happy, was like a great orchestral roll of drums.

He found that the truth was a tool for one wise enough to use it. If he could guide *how* he looked at things, *where* he looked at them from, the truth could seem very different. Every awareness took its own position. The position determined its truth, but that position could be *moved*.

He began to consider the ways in which he could move the position of her awareness.

The first challenge was to get warm. He was freezing. An icy breeze came down the cleft in the wall of his damp antechamber. He didn't want the dragon's fiery breath in his chamber again—better to keep her eye upon him and the fire pointed the other way. But, in a moment when she snorted an irritable gust of crimson flame, he saw what he needed. Against the rocks, near the mouth of the cavern, was Sassraline's midden, a spiked heap of skeletons and discarded trophies. He was shivering to his bones, and there, upon the heap lay a piece of pelt, feathers along its edge—the last remains of a devoted pony.

Ashley covered his mouth with his hand. Could he actually bring himself to use it, the skin of his dead friend? He shifted his point of perception around the idea. Yes. It would be warm. *That* was the truth.

"Sassraline, oh immense figure of awe, so filled with colours I have never witnessed in my brief and miserable life, your grandness will surely endure for longer than I can survive. You are a great lady, and it is your right to be praised, and it is surely my duty, but I could perform my duty for longer if I were warm. No! No! I do not have the wondrous skin that you have which protects against fire, and I have no protection from the biting cold. I am weak beside your grand strength. If you would give me just one thing from your pile of treasures, I would be warmer, and desperately grateful for your serene mercy."

WHAT DO YOU WANT FROM ME?

"The leather pelt, the skin there, with the feathers on it," Ashley explained.

Sassraline shook herself, as if suddenly realising she had made a mistake.

WHAT? HE WANTS TO STEAL MY TROPHY?

She drew herself up.

"I don't want it for myself, I want it for you!" Ashley added hastily. "I am your servant. I belong to you already. I live by your whim. Surely you can pass something of yours to a servant? It will still be yours, because I am yours."

Sassraline paused.

YES, HE IS MINE. IT IS THE SAME, WHETHER THE PELT IS HERE, OR THERE. EVERYTHING IN MY CAVE BELONGS

TO ME.

"I will live for longer, and you will hear more truths about your wonder."

Sassraline turned to look at the midden.

With a sweep of her tail, she hooked the pelt from the pile. She swayed across the cavern and stuffed the pelt through the opening. Ashley fell flat to avoid the hooks and barbs. A shower of bone splinters fell off the leather bundle. As her tail pulled back through the crevice, a scale sheered off with a ping! A disc the size of his palm, green and sharp-edged, rolled across the floor.

"Thank you," he called out to her retreating bulk.

I DID IT FOR ME, NOT FOR YOU! She stamped the floor and Ashley jumped with the shock. Her great eye jammed up against the hole, and it went totally dark.

That was her truth. He'd work around it. Everything was about *her*. What was important was that he made it seem to be for her benefit.

"I need—" he began and then corrected himself immediately, "You would be better served if your servant had light to see your colossal beauty. With your eye so close, although it could hold things more entrancing than the most splendorous vision in a crystal forest pool, there is not enough light to see it, and I am left with only the horror of losing the sight of your exquisite iris."

She gave out a bellow, long and loud, and raked her forelegs across the rock. Then with a shriek she was gone, away from his chamber, across the cavern, a flash of wings, gone. Ashley held his breath. What had he done? He was worried that he had made her too angry; that she had leapt away only to gather her anger and her fire, that she would flame him to death on her return. But he needn't have worried. She returned soon after with a dead sapling in her talons, and she stomped over to the mouth of his cave and planted it, flaming, in the boulders clustered there.

She had brought him a light. She lay down and snorted, looking across the cavern, away from him, pretending not to care, but her eye snapped back to him the moment he spoke.

"See how great she is!" he cried, as if to an audience of thousands. "A merciful heart beats in her jewelled chest, she who can crush her foes with one talon and yet gives of her gifts to others, she who lies like a living blade in her secret and most special retreat and yet can be gentle to those whom she trusts, she who is kind-hearted, compassionate, she!"

Ashley continued his litany for some time then crept a little way into the opening to gather some of the heat. Sassraline seemed content to lie and listen to him. He worked the leather flat with a pebble. It was dry and supple, with a fine crust of fire-damage which came off when he scraped it. He didn't waste any time; as soon as it was clean enough, he wrapped it around himself. It was larger than he'd thought, and wonderfully warm. After sitting before the burning tree and thawing for a while, he turned his thoughts to what he could do with the leather. The fire would soon be out, and darkness would return. While he had a chance he should use the light.

He used the dragon-scale to cut his outline on the leather, twice. The scale was ridiculously sharp on the lower edge and it had a circular hole near the top. When he scrutinised Sassraline he could see the hole was the way her scales locked in place, like plates of metal, studded together. She would be impossible to spear or pierce with arrow.

With the ragged tails that remained of his pelt he made as many thongs as he could. Then using a sliver of bone as a needle, he sewed up the jacket and pants. He made a mess of it because his fingers were so cold. The skin was a bit chewed in places, but it only had three puncture-holes, and it was strong and flexible. He tied a bunch of thongs around his waist to hold the trousers up.

I must look like a winter hunter from the snowy wastes. He looped the last piece of thong through the dragon-scale and hung it around his neck. It was too valuable to discard, but he'd have to be careful not to cut himself on it.

None too soon. The tree-torch, now a rude finger of black coal, guttered, and went out.

In the darkness, he realised the second challenge was to get some food. He was starving.

That was considerably harder, and it took him two days. Two days of flattering, cajoling, coaxing, instructing and nudging her viewpoint closer and closer to his way of seeing the truth, until Sassraline finally could stand it no more—the truth that her servant was starving and that he had to be fed, had become *her* truth.

Ashley waited for her. Her trust was more important than his freedom. He knew she would find him if he ran, find him and punish him for abandoning her. Fleeing would prove him a liar. Staying would make her believe.

He had much time to reflect on the value of his life, for he had to convince her of it if he was to win this contest of wills. What was it that kept him wanting to live? It seemed an obvious question with no obvious answer. Because he hoped it would get better? Because there were times when life made him joyful? What was that part of him that wanted more?

Life itself?

The dragon brought him a great lump of meat. She even fired it for him when he persuaded her that he would be sick if he ate the flesh raw, but then, as if sensing his jubilation, she exposed her teeth at him.

DON'T THINK YOU'LL EVER GET ANOTHER! I DON'T HUNT FOR OTHERS!

He didn't ask her what it was because he didn't want to know. He was so hungry he had considered eating his clothes. Ashley munched on the meat, aware that he was eating something that had been living only moments before, yet he realised another truth. When he was hungry enough, he'd eat anything. He chewed on the gift of life.

What was life, if not a gift? A gift from something else, always—a gift from his parents, a gift from the land, a gift from the world that had come before. Something had died, that he might live. Every day he was alive, things died—living things were ended, to fuel his insatiable hunger. In many ways, people and dragons were the same. They lived. They ate. Things died because of them. He should not feel the nagging guilt, and yet he did.

Humankind always felt the guilt, he decided. No matter how small the feeling was, it was there in the depths of their minds. Maybe that was why everyone did good deeds. They were trying to pay back the debt of all the lives they'd taken to be alive themselves—their life debt. Some people denied it, some ignored it, but everyone was nudged by their life debt toward good deeds. A dragon had a greater life debt than most. He wondered if he could work with that truth, whether a dragon could be persuaded to perform a greater service because of all the killing.

It was true that she wasn't a dumb animal. She had a highly developed consciousness. No, what was he thinking? She was a predator. Her highly developed consciousness was so wrapped up in its own importance it saw little else. It was going to be a real challenge to get her to care about his life. He rose and followed the sound of the drip to his clear puddle at the back of his cave that periodically quenched his thirst.

It took him many days to get food again. Slowly the dragon began to trust him, but all the time she kept him in her lair, and never once did she allow him to enter her great cavern. He followed the thin trail of hope. His beard grew in the gloom as he worked with the truth, and the many ways it could be used.

31. A PERFECT SLICE OF PI

"In the absence of wisdom rely on knowledge,
Without knowledge, principles;
with no principles, good luck."—Zarost

The wizards of the Gyre took their places around the black stone dining table—an oblong slab that dominated the narrow room. Sprites glowed in bulbs upon the walls, reflecting off the polished stone, making the arcane gold designs within the table stand out brightly. Silver cutlery gleamed. Tall glasses glinted. Outside, a red-fired desert sunset was fading over the distant dunes, visible through the open west wall. The Sanctuary was a beautiful place, Tabitha thought, but most of it felt surreal, as if it was too clean, too sterile—too ordered. She wanted to fill the dining room with plants, colour and life, as she had done in the meeting chambers.

The wizards themselves seemed comfortable in the strange space. They bantered away to each other as they shared out the food. Bread was broken in the hand, plates were loaded with hearty portions and a decanter of pale blue drink they called *aluvir* was passed around freely. The meal was borne on platters which the wizards guided to speed around the table.

Tabitha tried a little *aluvir*, but found that it tasted too strongly of fennel, and it seemed to stretch the inside of her head in all directions, somewhat akin to the beginning of a Transference spell. She ate a small portion of fruit and cheese instead.

The Mystery, seated beside her, offered her a different glass. "Fallwater," she said. "Much less punch." It was cold and clear, with a minty aftertaste. It turned her breath to a little cloud of mist when she exhaled. Tabitha put her hand to her mouth. The Mystery smiled.

"It must be wonderful to have an ear for the Lifesong," said the Lorewarden from across the table. He had dressed for dinner in an elaborate orange shirt covered with spiralling black script, a language that was twisted upon itself like a struggle of snakes. "Where did you learn the words for your verses?"

"My mother wrote some stanzas, but I heard them first in a dream, sung by many voices. I still hear those voices when I sing, the voices of the harmony."

"The echoes of Ethea? I remember… I read about that long ago. Something…"

"Lorewarden?" The Mystery looked at him askew. "You have forgotten something?"

"No! I…ah… Yes."

The remaining wizards exchanged concerned glances in silence.

"Did you have time enough to complete your rest?" asked the Senior.

"I think so…yes. I can't…remember all of that either. How strange."

"Lorewarden!"

"You never forget anything!" exclaimed the Spiritist softly.

"Maybe something was done to him while he rested," ventured the Mystery.

The Lorewarden looked at her in alarm.

"Relax, old man," said the Mentalist, "it's probably nothing fundamental. There are always a few loose connections in a mind."

"Ah so! I remember. The echoes of Ethea run through all time. They are ancient omnicursors like the Word, and three point one four one five nine two six five three five eight nine seven—"

"Lorewarden!" warned the Mentalist.

"Ah, yes, forgive me. The song is an irreplaceable aspect of this existence. We exist, therefore there is a Lifesong; there is a Lifesong, therefore we exist, but there is so little recorded about the lore! They knew of it in the time of the bards, but nothing survives of their knowledge because it was an oral tradition. The Goddess Ethea has been absent from our world for so long."

Yet now she had returned, and somewhere in the lowlands, far, far away, the Goddess Ethea was chained to a wall in a rising pool of blood and rain, her sodden wings dragging her ever downward, her face shadowed by grief. In a way, Ametheus had tied Tabitha to that rock. Time was running out and instead of racing to save Ethea, Tabitha was dining and making polite conversation. She felt like a traitor, all because she hadn't wanted to let them know how temporary her power as a wizard might be.

The Mystery cast a sideways glance at her. "You keep something hidden in your heart, Lifesinger, something that greatly pains you. We can speak in private, if it will help."

Tabitha gathered her nerve. She would do it now.

"I am going to need your aid, all of you. The Sorcerer has captured Ethea, and I need to save her."

The silence was complete.

"Why didn't you say something before?" the Mystery asked her at last.

"You were all arguing in the chambers, and I didn't know when I should speak of it."

"Good Lord!" exclaimed the Spiritist. "But such a thing is impossible! The essence of the Gods is not on the physical plane. You must be mistaken, Lifesinger!"

"Ethea is ethereal, she is not incarnate, she has no flesh!" argued the Cosmologer. "She is a principle. How can you trap that?"

"And when the principle begins to identify with the flesh it is in?" asked the Senior. "You *can* violate a principle."

"But giving form to spirit? Changing it? That is an impossible achievement!" replied the Cosmologer. "Isn't it, Spiritist?"

The Spiritist held her hand to her mouth. "If he considered the spirit, in the past, present and future, and exerted his power equally through a range of time, he might be able to change spirit to matter. It could be a second-axis spell, linking energy and matter on the *animatus* axis, but way out on the chaos side, for it bends time to achieve it. and somehow, it traps life in its coil as well. No, I cannot believe it."

"Save us! Is this his first ninth-level spell?"

The Mystery cocked her head to one side. "If the Sorcerer did have the Goddess, he would have killed her, and the Ending would have come and passed. We are still alive, so it can't be true."

"No, that's not correct, the song would linger even without the Goddess," said the Senior. "Everything we have learnt about time points to it being a circular pattern and not finite. It cannot end as you suggest, Mystery, it can only pass into a new cycle. However, such philosophy is irrelevant. I agree that it is impossible for the Sorcerer to hold a Goddess like Ethea."

"Senior, can you be sure?" asked the Lorewarden. "We don't know this lore, we are guessing in the dark."

The Mentalist chuckled. "Listen to yourselves. The Sorcerer has captured the Goddess? How would he do such a thing, eh? Even with the greatest ninth-level spell Oldenworld has seen, he could not achieve it. Ethea is God-kind, just like the others, she exists beyond the Veil of Uncertainty. She could never be trapped by the Sorcerer, she does not possess dimensions of the kind he could manipulate. The God-kind are beyond our influence, they span all existence. Ethea must have been there at the beginning and must be there at the end, or we would not exist at all. The Sorcerer could not threaten the Goddess Ethea without threatening his own life. I'll tell you what has happened, Lifesinger. You have been given a sending by the Sorcerer. You have been made to see something which is not there. You have been fooled."

"Ah, yes, the Mentalist is right!" the Senior agreed, visibly relieved. "You have been sent a vision, a false vision, to disturb you, to destabilise your power. It is an old trick of his. Don't believe what you have seen. It is impossible."

But she had been there. She had seen the floating feathers, felt the water, smelled the smoke and heard the clamorous sounds. She had read the anguish on Ethea's beautiful face. Tabitha knew it was true.

The Mentalist rocked backward in his chair and clasped his hands behind his head. "What bothers me more is how has he managed to get a hold on the Lifesinger already? How does he know?"

The Spiritist looked angry. "The Warlock! He must have betrayed all of our secrets! May he rot in the lowest chamber of the Pillar."

"You don't know that!" spat the Cosmologer.

Tabitha shivered. The Pillar, in the lowlands, where Ethea was held.

"I have to go there!" she whispered.

"To Turmodin? Don't be mad!" exclaimed the Mystery. "No, no, no, that would be the end of you."

"None of us would survive being there, Lifesinger," said the Senior. "The Chaos would tear your mind apart! No magic works there, only the kind of disruption that the Sorcerer employs. Anything you do there would be turned to serve him. You will not be able to think clearly, you will lose all sense of your self and your purpose. You will be ravaged by the nodes of Chaos. He has them amassed in Turmodin like a clutch of eggs, and he sits and broods upon them until they hatch another rotten and corrupt idea. He would take delight in reaving the talent from you and silencing the last note of your song. Do not even consider going to the Pillar. We would not venture there, not even protected as a full Gyre union. We would be devastated."

"But I must! How else am I to help Ethea?"

"Why must I tell you again, Lifesinger!" exclaimed the Mentalist. "You have been fooled! Whatever you have seen is not real!"

"I spoke to the Goddess. I made a promise to her. She needs our help."

"I am not going to argue against this-this-*ignorance*," declared the Mentalist, pushing his chair back loudly. "Lorewarden, the Lifesinger clearly needs to be instructed in some of the basics of what is possible on the three axes. I have more important matters to pursue. A Goddess cannot be magicked into being, just as a mage cannot be magicked into a God. If that were possible, we'd have a new kind of chaos altogether." With that, he departed, his spiky locks pulsing like an angry porcupine. Just after he had left the room, a bowl of stewed prunes vanished from the table.

The Senior cleared his throat. "Turmodin is an altered realm, Lifesinger. It is the eye of the Sorcerer's storm, the crux from which his power spins. You cannot go there."

"Don't feel bad, Lifesinger, a *sending* is a common ploy," added the Spiritist. "He tries to lure us to Turmodin all the time."

"Why can't we go there just to see if it's true? We could transfer back to the Sanctuary at once, and be in no danger at all."

"No, Lifesinger, you cannot wield Order so close to Chaos," said the Senior. "You will have no command upon the essence. You cannot use a Transference spell. You cannot escape. The Pillar is the heart of Chaos, it *is* Chaos. If you went there you would not come back."

"I'll go there on my own if I have to. I will not rest until I know that the Goddess Ethea is safe."

The Lorewarden gave her a pitying glance. "Do you even know where it is? Lifesinger, hear me now. You can only transfer to a place if you can visualise it perfectly, and to do that you must have been there in person. We have all walked Oldenworld far and wide to extend our range. You only know Eyri, and the narrow track of your first passage to the Six-sided Land of the Lûk. You could not use transference to reach Turmodin until after you had traversed the entire route on foot—northward first through the forests of the heartlands, to the fortress at Slipper, through the gap in the Winterblades, down into the Lowlands and all the way north and west to the coast. That would be an epic journey, considering the present dangers. In the older days of Order even western Orenland was unsafe to traverse. Nowadays, that land is a waking nightmare, filled with the worst of the chaos-spawn, those who have survived despite what has been done to them by the Sorcerer—the strongest, meanest, most lethal beasts. Nothing human remains. Those that appear human are not. Bloodbirds prey upon anything that moves, there are swamps that will grow around you as if they are conscious, there are freaks there we have no name for—ever-hungry, ever-mad. Even the lands of once-mighty Moral kingdom are given to ruin, teaming with bullgorgons, vandals and the roaming Scalard. Wildfire threads through the boiling clouds like a net of malice, lower and more deadly than anywhere else. You would not survive unless we were with you all the way, and we would not undertake such a foolish quest. There is nothing to find in the Lowlands but misery, there is nothing to find in Turmodin but your own end."

"I know the Riddler would have an answer when he comes back," interrupted the Mystery, "but how can the Warlock be attempting such a quest for the young prince of Eyri. Is he mad?"

"Or totally ruthless," said the Lorewarden.

"Maybe he's trying to lure the Sorcerer out of his lair. Do you think that's possible? Could the Warlock still be working on our side?"

"But there are eight of you in the Gyre!" objected Tabitha. "How can the Sorcerer be so much more powerful?"

The wizards looked at each other. There was an uncomfortable silence.

"There's only one right answer to that, and it's the long answer," the Lorewarden said. "Let us finish the meal first. You'll have much to consider in the library."

CʒꙄꞳCꞳꙄꞳ

After the meal, the Lorewarden led Tabitha away. The Mystery joined them, following like an inquisitive cat, her green eyes watchful. They descended to a cool level deep in the Sanctuary building, and passed along a brown corridor. The Sanctuary was quiet, the patterned floor absorbing the sound of their footsteps.

Tabitha kept her thoughts to herself. She would listen to what the Lorewarden had to teach only because she wanted to be prepared for her journey to Turmodin. She did not believe the vision of the Goddess was false. The 'sending' had been too real, she was certain that Ethea was in danger. If the Gyre would not help her, she would learn whatever she could about the Sorcerer and his magic then she would try to go there herself. She knew it would be dangerous, but to allow the Goddess to die at the hands of the Sorcerer would be unforgiveable.

She knew little about the balding bearded Lorewarden, and even less about the Mystery at her back. Could they be trusted? She didn't know if they could sense something of what she was planning.

"Don't worry, you make us just as nervous," the Mystery said suddenly from behind her. "Sometimes I wonder if you don't make me more nervous than the Sorcerer himself."

"You can't mean that, Mystery!" The Lorewarden swung around.

"You don't see what I see around her," answered the Mystery. "So many futures cluster upon her like butterflies upon a bright flower, yet she is unaware of them. Don't hear me wrong, Lifesinger, I believe your heart is good and you have a warmth and beauty in your manner that I wish I could match, but you are both powerful *and* ignorant, a dangerous combination. It's what you *don't* know that makes you dangerous to me, dangerous to the world. You might destroy things you don't even know are there."

Tabitha couldn't defend herself—she could understand the Mystery's concern. The Lifesong led her beyond herself, allowing her to wield a power she didn't understand. She might well strike a wrong note some time, and cause something she hadn't intended.

"That ignorance might be what allows her to act, where we have not had the courage," commented the Lorewarden. "Maybe we have too much knowledge in there, Mystery." He pointed ahead to an archway that led into darkness.

The Mystery laughed gently. "That is a bold statement for the keeper of the lore."

"Well maybe so. Maybe that is the effect of the Lifesinger. I like her. She lets me see things in a new light." He smiled at Tabitha. "She gives me hope."

"And so your future is tied to hers," the Mystery said wistfully. "I daresay mine is as well."

"Come, Lifesinger," said the Lorewarden, "You wanted to learn about the Sorcerer." He led them through the archway into a gloomy room. He gestured to the low roof, and a strip of light split the darkness, running away to fill a grid of lines. The light shimmered and pulsed in a fluid current. Sprites, Tabitha realised. The Lorewarden had sparked them in an instant. "Behold, the collected wisdom of the ages, well, some of it, at least."

Shelves and shelves of books fanned outward from where they stood, separated by narrow corridors. The near end of each shelf held a diagram with intricate patterns upon it, full of meaning but too complex to understand at a glance. Tabitha had never seen so many books in one place. The collection surpassed the Stormhaven Library a hundred-fold.

"Twardy Zarost said that you had lost most of the precious lores when your college was destroyed."

"That is true, but we have gathered what little remains."

There were thousands of books.

"The Lorewarden forgets to mention that his pen has been busy too," added the Mystery. "The three shelves on the right have been entirely rewritten from first principles."

"Writing helps one to understand," he explained. "It helps to bring order to one's thoughts. So I write that I might better understand that which I write about."

The weight of the accumulated knowledge pressed down upon Tabitha.

"Who reads all these books?"

The Lorewarden regarded her with a serious gaze. "Why, you do, of course."

Tabitha looked at him with wide eyes. It would take hundreds of years to turn all the pages, let alone absorb the knowledge upon them. She tried to imagine what books she would want to read, if all the knowledge was laid out before her. Where would she begin?

"Did you ever write about Eyri?"

"Most of the study of your realm has been completed by the Riddler. He dropped his books off from time to time and I read them with great interest. All of us read them."

"I don't understand why the Gyre made the Shield around Eyri. If you had all this knowledge at your disposal, why didn't you train someone here, in the Sanctuary?"

"The arrival of the wildfire cut off our chances to recruit new apprentices. It is very difficult to find someone who is willing to learn a profession when they know that their first successful work outside of the Sanctuary is likely to result in being struck down by flux. No, to even begin on the path to finding another wizard, we needed to find a place where the people cared not at all about the Sorcerer. That is Eyri. We had hoped that the Shield would encourage a new strain of magic to develop, one untainted by Chaos, one that had grown out of pure Order. After the Shield was erected, the memory of Chaos faded, and the people of Eyri grew pure and strong. If any of us had visited Eyri after the Shield was up, our presence would have influenced the developing mages. Even so, your Lightgifters and Shadowcasters were far from unique, basic lumen-mages. We'd given up hope, until you."

"But what about Twardy Zarost? He was there since the beginning, wasn't he?"

"The Riddler is skilled at hiding his talents. It is far easier to copy what someone has demonstrated than to invent something new. He took an oath of abstinence. His role was to be the guide for the Seeker. It seems he has done well, very well indeed."

"How did you know you would find a wizard in Eyri?"

"We didn't know it would be you, and we certainly didn't expect the lore to be the Lifesong, but something of the sort was inevitable, given a long enough time. What do you know of your ring? How much did the Riddler explain to you?"

"Twardy? Explain? He never explained anything. He always forced me to solve things."

"Yes, yes, he would, wouldn't he? Maybe for once he took his role as the Riddler too seriously. Without knowing anything of its origins, you have nothing to piece together. See here, the rings were forged in the height of our ascendancy, in the time of Order. They were designed to accelerate the development of second sight. A ring will bring out your capacity for magic, and draw the challenges upon you to test the new skills. It is partly a trial, partly a tool. We all bear them, they aid us, they link us and they store our experiences. The older the ring gets, the more knowledge it holds in its layers, knowledge that the bearer can draw upon. When it is being used well, it is warm and tight on the hand that bears it, but whenever the bearer ceases to add new knowledge to it, it grows cold and eventually becomes unbearable. In that way it will move to a candidate with potential. This process helped us to eliminate the unfit apprentices from our college. Even now, after all these years, we Gyre members must continue to learn if we want to retain our rings. They are the mark of our class, and we bear them proudly. To be wizards, we must be wise, and to be wise we must always be learning. We must always gather new knowledge."

"Have you read all of these books?" she asked, half expecting him to laugh.

"But of course. We all have."

How did he hold all that information in his head?

"Remember, thought is beyond the physical plane," said the Mystery. "It has no dimensions, it occupies no space. It has no limitations. It need not take time to be completed."

"Is there anything written about music?" Tabitha asked.

"Now there's the pity," replied the Lorewarden. "The one lore we have so little of is music. It has never been considered much of a carrier for essence. You have opened our eyes, young Lifesinger, you have shown us all! We knew of the Lifesong, to be sure, but the lore was lost in the myths, it was too old to have survived in any texts. Without a true living bard we have had no one to draw our knowledge from. I hope you shall be adding many books of your own to our collective."

"Why is it that you have all this lore, yet you cannot beat the Sorcerer? Does he know more magic than all this?" Tabitha swept her hand around the Library.

"Ah yes, the Sorcerer. You cannot compare our arts so easily. Our magic is far more advanced than his, more sophisticated. The Sorcerer knows very little. He spurns all knowledge, burning any book he comes upon, but his Chaos is like a thunderstorm unleashed—he reaches a level the equal of all of us combined. By that I mean the magnitude, the power within the spell, the level-count. A singular wizard has a maximum reach of one level from the *origin*—that is where essence is at rest. Two wizards working in a perfect union would attain a fully realised second level spell. We have found no way to surpass our individual limits, yet the last spell the Sorcerer cast was a mid-eighth level. That was the Writhe, and it almost killed us. We are being stretched too far, and now, with the Warlock missing, we are reduced to a weak seventh-level defence, assuming we were all present and unified in our purpose, including the Riddler. Eighth-level, counting you, but I do not know if we can safely include your lore in our constructions yet. None of us understand it."

"You have come to us in a desperate time, Lifesinger," said the Mystery. "If we wait for the next attack, we might be overwhelmed, and yet we dare not seek him out with our own spells, because we might not be the equal of his counter-strike. We need to build our own strength before we can be effective."

"Have you never hurt the Sorcerer? Is there no way to weaken him?"

"Oh we have wounded him many times. We have blasted his Pillar to pieces and we have tamed some strands of the wildfire. But the wildfire swells with a new season of growth, a taller Pillar arises from the ruins of the old, and the Sorcerer himself becomes stronger. He seems to gain a level with each survival, as if the ordeal has forced him to reach deeper into the source of his power."

"And so he gets worse," continued the Mystery. "He cannot be reasoned with. He is irrational, often insane. He has a terribly strong imagination, and he devises the most convoluted and savage spell-patterns ever seen in Oldenworld. He never repeats a spell. We think he actually forgets it the moment it is cast. That is what makes him so difficult to predict. We never know what curse the Pillar will spit out next, and every time we must study it intensely before we can devise a counter-spell. We cannot even discuss a treaty or compromise with him, because he does not value the stability of peace as we do, and he is too fanatical to be convinced that some order in Oldenworld is useful to us both."

"But if he is so ignorant, how does he wield magic?"

"He is a Sorcerer, not a wizard," answered the Lorewarden. "He draws his inspiration from a hidden source."

An uneasy feeling passed over Tabitha. "Is that the same as the way that I draw my inspiration and power from the Goddess Ethea?"

The Lorewarden frowned. "I suppose…in a way…yes."

"Oh dear," said the Mystery. "Could there be a link between them?"

"No, Mystery, I know what you are thinking, but we have seen her spells. They are not clustered anywhere near the Chaos pole."

"And yet we are not certain where the root of her magic is. There may be similarities between them that we cannot apprehend."

"Does it matter, Mystery? Whatever they achieve with essence shall be constrained by the immutable laws of the three axes. So long as the Lifesinger uses her power against Chaos, she must be a channel of Order."

"Please, what are the three axes?" Tabitha asked.

"You do not know? How on earth do you balance them so well, without knowing? That is remarkable! Remarkable indeed." He observed her for a while, his head tilted to one side. Then he smiled. "Let me explain. The three axes form the structure in which all magic can be placed. It has to do with the orientation of the essence. You are familiar with the Light and the Dark?"

Tabitha nodded.

"Well that is *lumen*, the first axis," he said. "Dark is the one pole, Light is the other. In the centre, at their balance point, the essence is at rest, it is clear. We call that place the origin. The second axis, *animatus*, runs through the same origin, but at right angles to the first axis, one could say it runs forward and backward instead of to the left and the right. The violet essence of Matter is the one pole of the second axis, the red essence of Energy the other. Finally, the third axis, *struct*, intersects the others at right angles through the origin; you could say it runs upward and downward relative to the others. We have dedicated our entire lives to spreading the golden flax of Order, because there is altogether too much flux in the world—that silvered essence of Chaos."

"So a spell runs along a different axis depending on the colour of the essence used?"

"Not really, the colour is a simplification, a codification. A spell can be confined to a single axis, or it can be positioned anywhere within the sphere defined by the three axes. A spell can begin near the Dark pole, curve away toward Energy, and end with its tail wrapped around Order. You have already experienced a second-axis spell with a third-axis definitive—the transference shifts Matter to Energy and Energy through an Order-matrix to Matter once more. There are many patterns one can draw, and each one has a different effect. That is what makes three-axis magic so complex. That is why we need to study so hard. Without knowledge, we might cast a spell which backfires or collapses and turns into Chaos. We must know precisely what the pattern will do before we can wield it. We must understand the mathematics. We must resolve the equation and define the outcome before we cast every spell."

"Which is why your rainbow essence worries us so, because it is such a unique state," the Mystery explained. "We cannot yet determine what your spells really do, whether they enhance Chaos or Order, Dark or Light, Energy or Matter."

"It seems your spell spreads as a wave, rather than as moving particles," said the Lorewarden. "It is most bizarre. Most paradoxical."

"And then you've twisted life into your pattern as well," added the Mystery. "Now that's a miracle that none of us have ever achieved."

"But you must have some power over life. You're all...very old, aren't you? And you look young."

"Oh no," replied the Lorewarden, "that is just the Restitution spell. It is merely a re-ordering of matter into a memorised state. If one of us had to die, none of us could bring that wizard back to life. We are old, but we are not omnipotent. We cannot pass life on to anything."

"Neither can the Sorcerer," the Mystery added. "He only has a talent for taking life away."

And he would take Ethea's life away. Tabitha needed to learn the secret of how to reach Turmodin.

"I'm still not sure I understand what you meant about the three axes," Tabitha said. "Could you show me what you mean with something like the Transference spell?"

"Transference?" The Lorewarden shared a glance with the Mystery. "I'm not sure that we should begin with something so grand. That one takes years of practice to perfect. I doubt you'd apprehend the pattern quite right."

"You would need foundation classes too," added the Mystery. "To be sure you understood the forms."

"Well how am I ever to return to Oldenworld without the Transference?"

"You are in the safest place you could be, right now."

"You have so much to learn," added the Mystery.

"I didn't come here to study! Twardy Zarost said I must present my problem to the Gyre. I must save Ethea!" Had Zarost really helped her by bringing her to the Sanctuary, or had he merely found somewhere to contain her and keep her out of trouble?

"You are too valuable to risk in Oldenworld now," declared the Mystery. "We'll not permit it."

"Be patient, Lifesinger," added the Lorewarden. "You must be prepared first."

"I will not stay in this-this-monument!"

Tabitha felt the walls of the library closing in upon her—all those shelves and shelves of books, that immense weight of knowledge. It pressed upon her. It contained her, limiting her. The Gyre wizards would probably expect her to learn all of their wondrous lore before considering her to be ready, even though they admitted that her power was different. She would be trapped in the Sanctuary of the Gyre until she learnt the Transference spell. They would teach it to her last, she realised, last of all the lores.

"Where is Twardy Zarost?" she demanded.

"The Riddler? He is abroad. He has been put in charge of tracing the Warlock for us."

Had Twardy Zarost brought her to the Sanctuary to deliver her into captivity? He had encouraged her to come; he had separated her from Garyll and Mulrano. He had promised her that no harm would come to her, but could he be trusted? He was, after all, a member of the

Gyre. He was, after all, the Riddler.

Even Zarost might not be willing to help her escape.

"Can you show me how the three-axis system works with the spell you all used at the dinner table, the one which moved things from one place to another?"

"That is the Reference," replied the Lorewarden. "Yes, that is much simpler, and it doesn't matter nearly as much if you get it wrong. I can show you the Reference, but don't ever presume you can use it on a living body. It only works on inanimate objects." He gave her a warning glance. "A Reference would move the body without moving the being, and both would perish instantly."

Tabitha tried to cover her disappointment.

"Come," said the Lorewarden. "Not in here, the books are too precious. We go to the asylum." He led her through the long library then through three heavy doors to an adjoining hall. It was a thick-walled circular enclosure with a domed roof and a slightly dished floor. Although it was clean, the walls and floor were pitted and scarred. The Lorewarden sent Light essence blooming in a grid across the high roof. They stepped out onto the bare stone floor.

The Lorewarden made a gesture in the air with some clear essence. It shifted to gold and a small cube of sugar appeared in his hand. "That's from the stores. So, if we wanted to move this cube from here, to there," he said, pointing to a point a few paces away on the floor, "we would have to define the start and end-point in our Order matrix. All you are doing is moving an item relative to the space in which it is placed. You do not need to alter the item itself, just its placement. And so it is a simple movement of essence on the Order axis. What you are modifying is the arrangement of things. See?" He made the same gesture with his hands. His fingertips left a faint pattern in the clear essence, but because of the pale floor and dim light it was difficult to see.

"What is it? I can't make it out."

The Lorewarden paused. "You can't see the pattern?"

"Well not all of it. I can see the clear essence moving, but the design is too fine and too small." She drew on her ring for clarity, but even with its assistance she couldn't discern the detail of the Lorewarden's fading spell. "And I don't see what you mean about the Order axis. How do you know which way it's going? Where is the third axis? Where are any of the axes?"

"She should have an eye," the Mystery said. "She's not going to apprehend the third axis without it. Her art uses different sensitivities."

"Mystery, she should have no special treatment," the Lorewarden replied. "An eye was always earned, in the college, and only when the wizard was ready."

"And I maintain that she is an exceptional wizard, and needs exceptional treatment. If she can see things as we see them, it will help her to understand. I feel it is important. Here." The Mystery held out her hand. On it was a small blue box with a gilded design of an eye in a circle.

"You have brought one with you?" said the Lorewarden, incredulous. "You knew that this moment would come!"

"Yes."

"You are certain that the Lifesinger needs this?"

"The futures where she has the eye seem better than the ones where she does not have it, yes."

Tabitha accepted the slim box from the Mystery. It was so light she thought it might remain floating in the air if she took her hand away from underneath it.

"Which version is that?" asked the Lorewarden, looking at the box suspiciously.

"The final Screed, Lorewarden, the *ogle-i*, the one that includes the parameterised induction lore just like the ones we wear. I have always kept a spare eye safe."

The Lorewarden looked surprised. "I thought that the others *ogles* were all lost. Ah, I see, you kept it hidden because you knew it would be needed much later. This is one of your *moments*, not so, Mystery?"

The Mystery held the Lorewarden's gaze. Her green eyes blazed with confidence.

"Well then, it seems the Lifesinger is to be awarded a rare privilege," he said.

Tabitha opened the box. It was empty: just a shallow tray, with a blue velvet lining. Tabitha looked up at the wizards, but they were still looking at the box, so she dropped her gaze again. Was there something in it that she couldn't see? She moved her palm, and light glinted off something that rested inside the box, on the velvet. She was about to reach into the box when the Mystery stopped her.

"Careful," she warned. "Watch."

She placed her finger over the mysterious object. A sudden star of golden threads bloomed within it, a pattern of light that defined a circle and left traces swirling upon its surface when it cleared. Symbols flickered to life briefly, like a scattering of arcane letters reflected upon the surface of a small lens. Then something strange happened to the light within the room, as if the colours were draining out of everything nearby, running inward toward the small circle within the box. Tabitha was drawn forward, as if the circlet was *gathering* a part of her.

The Mystery lifted her finger again, and the disturbance ceased, the patterns vanishing. Just a clear empty circle rested on the velvet. Tabitha now knew that there was something there, but it was even clearer than the crystal clarity of her wizard's ring.

"Your turn," urged the Mystery. "Don't touch it, just activate it. I must see your reflected potential before I can be sure you can bear it."

Tabitha reached out with one finger. The images raced across the surface of the lens again, ghostly faces crisscrossed with faint tracelines and symbols that pushed upward in a bright fountaining rush. A golden star bloomed brightly. Then the star faded again, and patterns moved within its depths; faintly-scribed lines that rose through the liquid clarity. Its strange beauty intrigued her. It was gathering the light again, draining the pigments from the day. Variable hues danced upon the convex surface, like oil upon water.

"My word," whispered the Lorewarden.

"Why did you call it an eye?" Tabitha asked.

"Because that's what it is," the Mystery replied. "That's how you wear it."

"I don't see."

"It is a lens, Lifesinger. It goes in your eye. You've seen the power flower, so it is activated. You will see things through it that will enhance your talent. You will come to see things the way we see things, and so you will understand."

"Gather it up," encouraged the Lorewarden. "Gather it up."

"Are you sure?" The idea of placing something in her eye seemed strange to her. "Won't it hurt?"

"It will be soft, it adjusts to the shape of your eye," answered the Mystery. "The wizard's eye is from the height of the Three Kingdoms, it is the most sophisticated example of Order-forged technology. I have worn one for over five hundred years, Lifesinger. It is an invaluable tool. I would be practically blind without it."

Tabitha looked uncertainly at the Mystery. If she looked into her right eye, she could see faint golden lore dancing over her green iris. The more she looked, the brighter the scribe-lines became—tiny threads of information, crossing the Mystery's sight. She realised she had seen the golden flecks in every wizard's eye. All of them had that glint in their right eye. Especially the Riddler, now that she thought about it.

"Your ring works, doesn't it?" asked the Lorewarden. "That is much cruder than the Eye. The lens is a tool of a much higher order."

Her ring was warmer than ever on her finger. It had changed her perception of the world, and she had been better for what she had discovered. The eye was a masterpiece in comparison to the ring? Tabitha felt a thrill of anticipation. What would she see when the lens was in her eye?

"Balance it upon your fingertip," instructed the Mystery as Tabitha reached for the wizard's eye.

Strange symbols fluttered within it, coming up toward her, gyrating patterns and structures of light. She raised it slowly, watching the images. The little lens shimmered, almost vibrating with a flood of rainbow colours.

The lens jumped to her eye. The contact was sudden. She blinked in surprise. It was all a blur in her right eye, full of light and shifting patterns. Then suddenly everything came into focus.

"Oh!" she exclaimed, for the Lorewarden had become entangled in a network of threads. The Mystery was also surrounded by a swirling halo. Lines and arcs crossed Tabitha's vision, as if a mad draughtsman was sketching over everything she could see, marking off measurements, outlining elements, highlighting lines of movement and areas of force. The two wizards backed away from her as if to give her space, and as they did so, symbols trailed off them like thistledown. Tabitha looked up and down and around herself in amazement.

She had entered a world of arcane knowledge, encoded in the *ogle-i* and released all around her, floating in her vision like a translucent shifting painting. She reached out to touch the filaments of golden light, but there was nothing there to touch, and her hands did not disturb the designs. Instead, new lines converged on her hands, concentric circles ran off her fingers, and her ring blazed within a cluster of runes.

She looked across the pitted floor.

The two wizards jumped toward her as she looked at them. She fell back, startled, fending them off with her hands, and the wizards jumped away. She concentrated on the wizards again and they were suddenly close.

"Steady," said the Mystery. "It will take a little while to get used to it. Your intent drives the field of view." She realised from the distance of the Mystery's voice that she was confused. The wizards weren't any nearer, they were just closer in sight, although she could see the stubble on the Lorewarden's chin clearly, she was aware of the distance that separated them. It was just like the way the ring had enhanced her senses, but it was a hundredfold more powerful. It was the strangest sensation. If she concentrated on seeing him through her right eye, he seemed within arm's reach, but if she looked more *leftly* at him, he seemed to retreat again, and the scribe-lines faded.

There were lines below the floor. She couldn't be sure that it was solid any more. She was standing on an ocean of lore. The world was a composite diagram that showed her the inside of things as well as the outside. She began to feel horribly queasy.

The door of the hall, the serpentine Light upon the roof, the stitching around the toes of her boots, all responded in the same way when she turned her gaze upon them, sliding nearer, slipping farther away. She looked at the sugar cube the Lorewarden still held in his palm, and tried to hold her gaze steady on that alone, trying to settle her rolling stomach. Two faint lines ran away from her on either hand, like a scratch-line scribed on glass, curving to converge and cross on the sugar cube.

Then she saw his spell, the design in clear essence that he'd completed but not released. The pattern came closer and closer the more she willed it to. She saw that the clear essence was now surrounded by series of delicate lines which described its movement. As she centred her sight upon that, she noticed three axes dividing the spell, forming a grid in three dimensions, allowing her to pinpoint where the Lorewarden's pattern flowed. She followed the light-lines, letting the strange moving guides lead her attention along the arced and crisscrossed course of the spell, and slowly she began to understand the pattern. It looked like a piece of fine string looped randomly around the third axis, some way from the origin, but she knew it wasn't random or tolerant of any inaccuracies in the positioning of the individual loops of essence. She didn't know if it was the suggestive power of the strange symbols, or whether it came to her from some other aspect of the eye, but the knowledge seemed to flow into her mind, filling her with a gathering weight, like a sponge growing heavier as it absorbed water: the Reference spell, this was the Reference spell, and it was a third-axis manipulation one third of a *struct* toward the Order pole, with a secondary feeding loop of one seventh of an *animatus* on the Energy side used to dislodge the spatial inertia of the objective.

Tabitha squeezed her eyes shut. She was learning things she should not know how to use, and yet she did.

It was blissfully dark behind her eyelids. Simple. Empty.

She opened her eyes. The lens overwhelmed her with details again. A shimmer of scribe-lines hovered at the limit of her vision, just waiting for her to focus on something so they could pounce upon it and separate her sight into the many layers of arcane symbols. The lore was too detailed, too rich; too complex.

Tabitha tried to ignore the details and focused instead on the sugarcube. She gathered clear essence to her hand then watched the Lorewarden's spell pattern where it turned in the air just above the cube, and she copied it using her own essence, weaving it around the third of three axes which appeared in her vision. She tried her best to be precise, copying every curve, bend and twist of the design. Then she released the clear essence.

Clusters of illuminated squiggles rushed away from her. They swept over the sugar cube, converged, and dissipated. Nothing else happened. The sugar cube was still visible in the Lorewarden's hand. The Lorewarden smiled.

"Why hasn't it moved?" she asked.

"Because my spell is over-riding it. You see, you cannot have two spells like the Reference targeting the same point in space. How could two objects exist in the same place at the same moment? Build your pattern and try it again."

This time when she was ready to release her spell, he erased his own, letting the essence disperse.

Those strange guide-marks converged on the sugar cube a moment after the essence. They described the outline in light briefly, just lines in empty air, for there was no sugar cube.

Tabitha was delighted. She had cast a successful Order-spell.

"Where has it gone?"

"You don't know where it has gone?" the Lorewarden asked, "See if you can discover that for yourself."

She focused on the fading spell trace that surrounded the space where the sugar had been. Runes, numbers and lines came at her thick and fast, but none of it made any sense. Something pressed against her mind, but she couldn't accept it. Tabitha was overloaded with information, and suddenly very tired. She closed her eyes.

"I don't think you'll ever find that sugar cube," said the Lorewarden. "You sent it to three different places at once. You need to learn how to read an ordered matrix. You need to understand how the inertial calculations are made, and how the distance of your Reference influences the effective speed which can in turn bend the space out of shape and cause the Reference to fail." He looked at her knowingly. "You see, there is much you need to learn before you are ready for something as complex as the Transference. You can join with another wizard for a jump, but to do it on your own is just too dangerous. So I'm afraid you're just going to have to wait, before charging out to face down the Sorcerer."

Tabitha knew what they were trying to do. They were inundating her with knowledge, to show her how ignorant and unprepared she was. They were trying to keep her away from danger. She should have been glad for their concern, but they were trying to control her, and all she could see in her mind's eye was Ethea's face, growing smaller and smaller, lost, forlorn and abandoned. She gazed at the pitted stone floor, and watched the frantic patterns of encoded lore that flickered across her vision. The patterns seemed to respond to her thoughts, throwing nets and graphs across whatever she saw or imagined—categorising, ranking.

"What are you doing?" someone demanded. Tabitha looked up to see Twardy Zarost standing behind the Mystery and Lorewarden, bobbing from one foot to the other. The two wizards turned, surprised.

"Why, hullo Riddler," the Lorewarden answered. "That was a very subtle entrance for you. We're trying to help the Lifesinger understand the Gyre's magic. I'm not doing too well."

"But what are you doing?" the Riddler asked again.

"Passing on lore, Riddler. It is my role, remember?"

"What are you doing?"

"You and your three questions! I am filling in the chasms in her knowledge caused by your vague tutelage, Riddler. It is not wise to leave everything to guesswork. The Lifesinger is ill prepared for her place in the Gyre."

"She has her own lore, her own talent to follow! She should not be encumbered by our knowledge. That is the whole point! The Sorcerer has surpassed every lore we have. We need new wisdom." He turned to look at Tabitha, stiffened, and came up close to her. "Why, oh why, does she have an eye?"

"So she can see as we do, Riddler. You are very wrong—our lore is not worthless. We all have a part to play in shaping her future."

"But we should not shape her at all!" Zarost exclaimed, moving on the Lorewarden. "She must seek her own truth. Oh, the eye is the last thing she needs. You have cursed her with our limitations."

"Riddler, you insult me, you insult us all! This is our *lore* you are looking down upon. There is nothing greater than our lore. It is the *truth*. It is above *all* of us!"

"Lorewarden, hold! Tabitha has already gone up against the greatest combined spell the Gyre has ever created, and she broke it. The Shield of Eyri is cracked along every meridian, I've just checked. Have you not considered what it means? How can she be so good, so soon? She has none of the training of the fundamentals, she doesn't even know of the balancing of the axes, does she? We are unlike the Lifesinger. None of us has succeeded in balancing all three. She has a way of working the essence that does not bring down the wildfire! She must be allowed to grow on her own!"

"She can work around the wildfire?" The Lorewarden looked shaken. "Maybe…maybe she... How is this possible?"

"Maybe it is because she hasn't had the disadvantage of our education. She sees things in a different way. She sees sound instead of theory."

"But she might be a danger if she sees us in a different way to the way we see ourselves."

"That is the whole point, you fool!"

"Riddler!" The Lorewarden warned raised a finger in his face.

"Warden!" The Riddler raised two.

"Men! Stop it, you are both right," declared the Mystery. "Don't forget that she is the one who chooses where she walks. It was my gambit, Riddler, I have played this piece into the pattern."

"But what you have just done will only allow her to see one path, Mystery!" exclaimed Zarost.

"What is wrong with *seeing* Order, Riddler? This path leads to a brighter future than the path where she is blind."

"Then you gamble against me, Mystery. I would see it done another way."

"Would you rather she follows Chaos?" asked the Lorewarden. "Have you lost your mind again?"

The scribe-lines burned in the air between the two arguing wizards, lines of potential; lines of danger. Jagged arcs of anger crackled overhead, billows of symbols and diagrams surrounded the two wizards, until they were obscured by the bright gathering of tension. Tabitha was submersed in information. She knew what kind of magic each wizard was likely to use, what the blast radius would be, the precise fraction of time she would have to cast a Transference to escape—the knowledge came at her with all the other data. It was too much to look at, and again there was that hollow nausea. Tabitha blinked the tears out of her right eye.

"I did not bring her here to have her abused!" Zarost exclaimed. The Lorewarden backed away from the Riddler; his hands spread ever so slightly as he moved, but Tabitha could see the sudden gathering of essence. The air tightened as Zarost readied himself too.

Someone needed to diffuse the argument or there would be a disaster. She didn't think the Lorewarden had intended to abuse her—she had been the one asking the questions, driving them on. "I asked to have this explained to me Twardy! I accepted the eye myself. I never got answers out of you, only riddles. The Lorewarden has been answering my questions directly. I am glad that he has."

The Riddler turned toward her slightly while still holding an illuminated segment of attention on the poised Lorewarden. "Oh Tabitha my young friend, it is not *answers* you should be seeking, but the questions—those questions you need to ask yourself. When you seek answers from others you just delay finding your own truth. He can give you no answers. The *ogle-i* can give you no answers. *You* are the answer. You must *be* the answer."

"You expect too much of me, Twardy. I know so little of your three-axis magic, the forms of essence, the effects of casting a spell, all the knowledge you take for granted. Sometimes I just want a straight answer."

"Ah yes, but the *ogle-i* will burden you with more than you need to know."

"If it will help me to understand you all, then I can deal with it." But she had to close her right eye altogether when she looked at the Riddler—the flood of images was now too intense.

"I believe you shall learn to deal with it, given enough time," he said, his voice softening. "But I had wished that you wouldn't have to. The eye is not like the ring. It will become a part of you, a part which I do not believe that you need as the Lifesinger."

"Pah!" exclaimed the Lorewarden. "We all have one eye on power, Riddler, it is our way. If she is to join the Gyre, what can be wrong with following our customs?"

"Our mistakes are encoded in our customs. What if she should be leading, and not following?"

An awkward silence held them enthralled, making the force-lines Tabitha could see become jagged and unbalanced around the Riddler. His answer scored a five for relevance, a four for content and a poor two for logic. She blinked, and he scored an eight for intelligence, six for constitution, ten for charisma, but to confuse her further, the numbers weren't fixed—they shifted second by second.

"I shall not pay too much attention to it," she said, in a small voice. She hadn't realised that the lens was permanent. "I can still look at the world normally, can't I?" She had noticed that if she *willed* the lines away, her vision cleared. But the lines came back with the slightest hint of desire for information, as if it was activated by the *idea* of a question mark.

"We shall see, we shall see." He stepped away from both Tabitha and the Lorewarden. "I might have read the riddles wrong." The tension between them eased. "Now is not the time to dwell on regrets. Gyrends! I have found the Warlock! We need to plan our assault. Come to the chamber, all of you." He twirled, and bounded from the hall, as if by his movement alone he would sweep them up in his wake.

"What?" exclaimed the Lorewarden. "Riddler, wait! The Warlock? Where?"

But Twardy Zarost had gone.

"Confound that man, he can work on my nerves!" the Lorewarden exclaimed. "But he has done well if he has found the Warlock already. Lifesinger, would you go on ahead? I would have a private word with the Mystery before we reach the Chamber."

"I... Certainly. Thank you for spending time with me, and thank you Mystery, for the eye. I will try to use it. I want to learn as much as I can."

"Don't mind the Riddler's comments—we all see things in a different way, regardless of the knowledge we have available to us. That is important to remember. Knowledge is a tower we can look out from, not a prison."

Tabitha headed for the exit. As she passed from the hall, she caught a snatch of the Mystery's quiet words to the Lorewarden.

"...you and the Riddler were badly divided there. This is the second time since the Warlock stepped from the circle. I have never sensed so much Chaos among us before. It's as if the Sorcerer is here, in the Sanctuary. We must be very, very careful. If we are divided a third time, something vital shall break."

"Then we must find the Warlock," answered the Lorewarden, "before it is too late."

32. THE WIZARD'S WAY

"Be sure you want a snake in your hands
before you reach for a serpent's tail."—Zarost

Prince Bevn gripped on for dear life. The big dogs were running wild. The sled careened over a ledge, slapped down upon the flat rocks and slid into the coarse grass again. Black Saladon shouted at the dogs. One tossed his head and snarled back at the wizard, dirty foam flying from his jagged teeth.

They had been marching along a forest trail, the big wizard demanding ever more speed, when the sled and its team of dogs had come upon them from the north. Two Hunters rode within the sled with a load of skins.

"Bow your heads and stand aside," Saladon had hissed.

Bevn had been reluctant to drop his gaze. The dogs were so strange looking, fell-eyed and fierce, and the two Hunters intrigued him. They were tough warriors, heavy and square-jawed. There was something different about them. The driver had both hands on the reins, but his companion held his bow ready, two shafts nocked.

Black Saladon gripped Bevn's hair and pulled his head down. The sled scraped past and continued on its way southward. The Hunters had let them be.

Saladon waited a moment longer then he ran after the sled, blurring with speed. He leapt upon the Hunters, his battleaxe raised, and the two men fell before they had even turned, cloven through by the butcher at their backs. They had never expected such a fast attack from a man on foot. They had not expected such a ruthless fighter. They should have paid better attention to the tall battleaxe.

Saladon hauled on the reins and turned the dogs around. When they passed the bodies of their dead masters, the dogs became frenzied, barking and baying and biting each other, but Saladon boomed some commands from his position behind them and he bent low and gestured across the pack. They howled and began to run again in a pace that didn't slacken for anything, not for hills or roots or rocks, not for fallen trees or gravel or broken marshy ground. Bevn wished he had never jumped aboard. He'd been eager to take the exciting ride. He hadn't expected such jarring, crashing, shuddering, slamming agony, on and on, hour after hour. The wizard wouldn't let them stop, not even to water the dogs.

Bevn's fear of crashing had filled his bladder to bursting. At last he could hold out no more. "I have to pee," he said.

"Then go off the side. I won't stop until we are at Slipper, because they might turn on us. For now, their fear drives them, but fear grows old and bitter in the end. These are marrow-wolves. They're never kept in the villages, they are too aggressive. The fur-traders keep them tied up to separate trees when they are at rest. I've heard of a team that killed an entire Hide before. They are vicious beasts, but there's nothing better than a marrow-wolf if you want speed."

Bevn decided it might be better to keep the hounds running. He waited until Gabrielle was looking the other way, before peeing over the back of the sled, clutching on with one hand. He complained about his broken ribs, but Saladon had no sympathy for him. "The present was built in the past," was all he said.

Much later, when Bevn was a pitiful shuddering heap, cowering against the low rail of the sled and whimpering with every bump, they crossed a relatively smooth plain. Through bleary eyes Bevn saw that a wall of white-capped mountains rose ahead of them, blocking their way northward, but for a single gap. Saladon guided the sled toward that place. They travelled for a league on hard-travelled trails that cut into the foothills, and then made a long descent to the bridge on the western bank of a great river.

Tall cliffs rose on either side of the gap. In the centre of the river, built upon a wedge of land which split the falls, crouched a great fortress town. It divided the flow like an axe head, its great grey walls polished by the current, its ramparts crossing the town, reinforcing it, level by level. But for all its defiant geometry, even from a distance Bevn could see that its former strength had been eroded. The hook of the docks on the western side, where many small rowing boats were tied, was washed away in many places. On the eastern side, another dock held barges with cables running over the water toward the eastern bank, but cables dragged in the water and the ruins of some tall structure lay in the water. The lower levels of the town had a twisted look, although they were the northerly districts and were barely visible over the rise. From what Bevn could make out, the last two walls were just piles of rubble, stained silver.

"See there, that is Slipper," said Black Saladon. "Watch your tongue when you get there. They have fought a bitter war against the creatures of the lowlands since it all began. They hate The One Who Can Not Be Named more fiercely than anyone. One mention of our plan to reach Turmodin, or the Sorcerer, and you will find yourself blowing red bubbles. The anger runs deep. They will take your head off at the shoulders and nobody would stop to question the murder."

Gabrielle looked unimpressed. "That tumbled-down sprawl is Slipper?"

"The greatest defensive city of the heartlands, yes. Slipper is like a tongue thrust into the cleft of the Winterblade mountains. This is where the Alliance launches desperate forays, down the tongue and into the throat of the Sorcerer's lowlands."

"It looks like a ruin," said Gabrielle.

It looked like a dead end, to Bevn. "If they are protecting against things coming up from the lowlands, how are we going to get past their defences?"

"We shall pretend to be resistance fighters," answered Saladon. "There is a stair down to the advance garrison posts on the spine north of town. We shall wait until the early hours of morning. I shall find a place for us to rest and eat first."

They left the dogs near the river, in a place where the road curved in behind a spur just before a settlement. The hounds were so thirsty they didn't realise their captors had jumped from the sled; they ran down to the water instead. Saladon considered the harnessed hounds for a moment, then snapped his fingers at them and turned away. "Chaos allows for interesting freedoms," he said with a small smile, and led Bevn and Gabrielle quickly along the road.

They came to a great bridge that sat low over the speeding river. It ran over to the western edge of the promontory that was Slipper. A burly soldier challenged them, but just as Saladon was answering his questions, a commotion broke out in the riverside settlement below. Screams, shouts and barks, then a high piercing trumpet call, sounded over and over. The soldier ran to answer the frantic call. Another three ran from within the guardhouse.

There were people down there, running in a panicked knot, men and women, children too. There was a commotion upon a landing stage. A hairy beast was mauling a man, and three men with poles were trying to beat it off. More beasts entered the fray, one of them trailing a sled. The marrow-wolves were upon the people, marrow-wolves, wild with hunger. "Come," said Saladon, and led them across the long bridge to Slipper. No soldiers remained to challenge them. Bevn realised just how good the wizard had been at setting up the diversion.

They arrived in Slipper with the setting sun. The blank outer wall rose before them like a wave, rippled and uneven along its crest, poised in the moment of breaking. They passed beneath the arched stone and into the town. The streets were busy, all manner of people pushing to and fro.

"They drink a lot in this place, they smoke a lot," said Saladon. "They also fight a lot. It's probably because they are so practiced at fighting each other that they can hold firm against the invasions from the lowlands. Don't look for trouble with anyone tonight, and be alert. The Gyre might not have been fooled by our speed. They might be here already, waiting to trap us."

"But if you think they will trap us here, why don't we go somewhere else?" demanded Gabrielle.

"Because I am prepared for them, my dear vixen. Just be alert, that's all I ask."

They passed a clump of shaven-headed men who were passing the other way. They wore fibrous green armour and carried their wooden spears casually over their shoulders. They were laughing and jostling each other, and one brute knocked into Bevn. Bevn was thrown aside into a fruit-sellers stall, where most of the stock was rotten. The armoured men didn't even seem to notice. Bevn bit back his curses. He had learnt to listen to what Saladon said. Sometimes.

"Those men!" said Bevn to Saladon when he'd caught up again. "They are—aren't they—"

"Lûk, yes!" said Saladon, and Bevn jumped. That had been loud enough for them to hear.

The muscled fighter turned to scowl back at them. One of his companions slowed with him.

Bevn tried to sink into his boots.

"Good evening, shiyaman!" Saladon greeted. "Strength to your spear arm."

The Lûk raised a reluctant fist in the manner of their greeting then turned to join the others who had already turned away.

"But that was a Hunter guard at the gates, wasn't it?" protested Bevn. "I thought this was a Hunter town."

"Then you should be careful of what you think," said Saladon.

He soon noticed that there were other kinds of people there

too. They passed a group of small men who occupied a doorway, chattering away to each other in a strange guttural tongue. They wore a lot of metal.

"They're not Hunters either, are they?" he said aloud to Saladon.

The small figures fell silent. They jutted their bearded chins toward the newcomers, their eyes like chips of stone. Someone had understood him.

"*Achna grakena!*" Saladon said, raising his hands in an apology. "*Kchek tizkekkn bigar, yo kelikille ght.*"

"What did you just tell them?" Bevn asked.

"That you are a fool boy and wet your bed more often than a rock-rabbit."

Bevn reddened. "But I'm not—" he began.

"Silence! They would have cut your legs off at the knees, had I not insulted you. Don't underestimate them. You develop quite a strong axe swing when you're picking at the rock for most of your life."

"They're miners?"

"Clan Lees, I believe. There are many people here. Miners, Lûk and Hunters, and the Lakeland Drells and the desert Armads. All may fight each other, but their hatred for the Sorcerer is greater. They gather in Slipper to answer that hatred."

"But how can you fight against someone else when you fight against yourselves too?"

Saladon waited until they were out of earshot of the miners before answering. "Do you begin to understand the power of the Sorcerer? The essence of Chaos is everywhere. The differences between these people are caused by Chaos, yet they do not recognise it. They are all silverspawn, yet they believe themselves pure. That is the most ironic fact of all. They are allied against the enemy in the lowlands, and yet the enemy is within them already."

Bevn thought about that as Saladon led the way farther into the town of Slipper. At the end of the canted street, they turned left along the first of the town's fortified inner walls. They climbed a ladder, passed through an archway and emerged on the north side of the wall. There a raised street clung to the outside of the buildings. The boarding shifted with every step. In places, great cloths covered the walkway, flapping against their tethers. Odd pennants, suspended on rope, hung out over the street, old battle standards and faded imagery and plainer fabric with unfamiliar inked words. A cool wind pulled over the tiled roofs, dragging the smoke from spired chimneys.

"Come," said Saladon. "The best food to be had in Slipper is in this district." He crossed a narrow bridge to another boardwalk. It became more difficult to pick a way through the crowds as they progressed, as more and more people milled about, talking, smoking from pipes. The pipe-smoke was strange-smelling and made him giddy, but it was the scent of cooking that really made Bevn's knees weak. They rounded a corner, where there were the vendors, their cooked fare laid out for all to sample.

Bevn approached the first stall, where something like noodles was frying in a dished pan. It smelled deliciously spicy. Saladon dragged him away. "You don't want to eat that. Come, I know where to arrange a good meal."

"Why? What was that?" Bevn asked.

"The brain of a dog. As I said, there are many types of people here, and many kinds of tastes. It's what will keep you protected; no one will recognise you as a foreigner, unless you open your stupid mouth at the wrong moment. Now be silent."

A crush of men occupied a wide door: big, brutish men, some with scarred faces. Lively clapping and boisterous singing came from within, and not a few screams and laughter.

"You would earn a handsome fee there," Saladon said over his shoulder to Gabrielle. "It is what they call a *hurry-hurry*."

Gabrielle didn't answer at once. "They have some unlikely customers," she said.

"They have even more worrying girls inside," Saladon replied.

Bevn craned his head as they passed the door.

"Nasty girls, bad girls, cheap girls all."

Bevn pretended to be disgusted. He marked the location in his mind.

Saladon took them down a narrow staircase to a crowded hall on the ground level. He muscled his way through the people toward a counter where a blunt-faced innkeeper stood. The wizard fished in his pocket and produced a sapphire-encrusted ring which he laid on the counter. "I'm looking for two rooms, and three portions of your breadmeal."

The innkeeper didn't touch the ring, but his eyes didn't leave it.

"Unruhmer," said the vendor, holding up a finger. "Wido areeng?" He shrugged.

"It's a Moral kingdom treasure. You would impress any woman with it. One room and a round of ales, as well as the meal."

The vendor looked up. He smiled and extended a beefy hand. The ring disappeared into his pocket. "Ruhmark," he said, giving a dirty red feather to Saladon. He pointed to a door at the back of the hall. "Nosh kibbit."

He busied himself throwing things together in the secrecy of his worktable then ducked into the cookhouse.

"What did he just say?" asked Gabrielle. "I couldn't understand a word of it."

"Neither did I," replied the wizard. "But I think he's given me a pass to one of his 'daughter's' rooms and not a room for the night. No matter, we'll throw the hussy out. Here in Slipper you often have to improvise and respond to what you think the other person is saying. Very few people actually understand each other. The languages in Slipper are the worst in all of the heartlands, for they bear the brunt of the Sorcerer's influence. The people lose more of the memory of their culture every year. When you speak you might as well say anything at all. It's what you mean that matters most."

"But that's—madness!" Bevn exclaimed.

"No. It's Chaos." Saladon shook his head. "And they believe they are resisting it," he said to himself.

Bevn wondered what would have happened if Saladon hadn't been able to produce from his pocket just the kind of ring that the innkeeper had wanted. It seemed a stupid way to trade. "Why doesn't anyone use gold?"

"They've lost the system of accounting for values. It was one of the first Ordered systems to decay. Every exchange here is based on a swap, a need for a need, a cow for three sheep, a barrel of wine for a slab of cheese, that sort of thing. More often than not, there is a discrepancy in the values being traded. That's why there is so much fighting. But still, it's nothing like the raging anarchy of the lowlands."

Chaos was like a disease, Bevn realised. It ate away at civilisations, causing one system after another to fail. What was the point of ruling a kingdom where everything was dying? He wanted power, he wanted magic, but he wasn't so certain he wanted everything to go to ruin. For the first time, he wondered if he was doing the right thing, taking the crown to the Sorcerer.

But what were his alternatives?

"Threption, hot as!" the innkeeper called out, having returned with top-heavy cylinders of bread stuffed with spicy fruit. At least a part of

Saladon's demands had been understood.

A chewy meaty delicacy was hidden in the meal. Bevn didn't ask what it was.

ଓଃଠଠ୧ଃଠ

Twardy Zarost watched the Prince of Eyri. The youth was tired, and he hadn't washed for days. Not that Twardy could smell him, for in Slipper one couldn't discern the scent of one unwashed body from another and that stench was always covered by someone smoking Bane, but Bevn Mellar had a telling crust of dirt on his arms, and sweat-stains around the neckline of his tunic. His lip was split. The way he sat, hunched over, suggested other injuries. The Warlock had been pushing him hard. No surprise, considering what balanced upon the young thief's head.

The Kingsrim glinted, projecting Ordered spheres of protection. The spell was anchored upon a callow king. Bevn Mellar was way out of his depth. He was caught in a treacherous plot. He had surely been misled, lied to, manipulated and had no idea of how deadly Chaos was and what he would be used for, in the end. Zarost almost felt sorry for him.

The Warlock could have healed the youth with a simple spell, so Zarost guessed that the prince had angered the Warlock and he had not been forgiven. Zarost picked at a speck on the rim of his tankard. The truths one could unriddle from the little things. Like the way the Shadowcaster Gabrielle had thrown her hair over her left shoulder, to divide the Warlock's attention from the prince and keep it focused rather on her. As it was.

The Warlock leant closer to her as she spoke then he threw back his head and laughed. Gabrielle smiled secretively. She cast a glance his way and Zarost stiffened. Her eyes were upon him; her dark attention lingered for a sultry moment. She was working him over, just as she worked upon everyone in the room, teasing him with her wicked allure.

She wouldn't recognise him. None of them should.

Gabrielle gave him a twisted smile and her gaze slid by.

Zarost lifted his tankard to celebrate the success of his disguise and knocked his long chin against the rim, spilling foaming green *kanush* into his lap. That was the problem with being a Lûk; nose like a dagger, chin like a boat. He had to pour his drinks down his throat rather than sip from the vessel. He tried again in the proper Lûk manner, and managed to swallow most of what he tipped back.

He was disguised as a Lûk marauder, complete with a time-worn coppery headscarf, facial tattoos, badly healed battle scars and an indigo eye patch over his right eye. He had cast the spells hours ago, and the alteration had had time to settle. He had even shed his aura of essence, which left him vulnerable, but made him indistinguishable from a commoner. The Warlock wouldn't have expected that. He probably couldn't conceive of being so vulnerable. The Warlock wouldn't know him if he stood beside him. Twardy Zarost could watch him in secret from his seat, but as soon as he drew on essence to cast a spell, the Warlock would know there was another wizard nearby.

The Gyre had infiltrated Slipper because they had calculated that the Warlock would pass through the fortress town to reach the lowlands. The Mentalist, in the form of a Hunter soldier, had first spied the trio as they passed his post at the west-bridge. Now that the Warlock had arrived, they had to wait, for there were too many people close by, too many innocents whom the Warlock could use to tip the scales in his favour.

The Gyre had expected it to be that way. They had established a perimeter, and they planned to draw the net slowly inward, filtering out the commoners and discouraging any new patrons from entering the area, until the pressing crowds had cleared. Then they would strike. Twardy Zarost was to keep the trio in sight, and if they moved before the Gyre was ready, he was to create a disturbance that prevented them from leaving. It shouldn't be too difficult, considering how crowded the ale-hall was and how boisterous everyone in Slipper was. Already most of the men were shouting to be heard. A fight would knot up the crowd quicker than a dog in a blanket.

Zarost looked at the Warlock again. He was amazed at how brazen the wizard was. The rogue had made no attempt to hide himself or his companions other than to use the protection of the Kingsrim. He had travelled fast to reach Slipper so quickly, but now he had placed himself in the open, and he was languishing in a public place. It was almost as if he wanted to be found. It was an unexpected move, and it gave Zarost cause for concern.

Did he want the confrontation? Did the Warlock believe he would have the upper hand when he met the seven of them? Seven against one were bad odds to gamble on from the minor side, especially when the players were all equally powerful. The Warlock must have a hidden advantage, some weapon of Chaos. Or he was bluffing that he had one?

The woman? She was a Dark mage, an ordinary Shadowcaster, she wouldn't get anything out beyond the first axis, and she would probably draw down wildfire as well. She would easily detract from the Warlock's strength. And the youth? He had no magical ability whatsoever. He was a pawn, placed in harm's way.

Then again, Zarost knew that a pawn in the right place could topple an army.

The Warlock was planning something, but Zarost could not pass up the opportunity. The Kingsrim was within reach. Zarost looked to the hag at the door. The Mystery had taken the form of a hatchet-faced half-Lûk wrapped in dirty shawls, the kind of beauty who would give children nightmares. Zarost made a dividing gesture. The Mystery would understand that he meant to split up the trio, to separate the Warlock from the other two. He tapped his head and nodded her way. She would be responsible for lifting the Kingsrim in the moment of division and bearing it away. They could not afford to have the crown disrupting their main spell.

The Mystery gave him a gummy grin. She knew she had the easier task. He would have to face the Warlock, who might have anticipated that Zarost would make the first approach, because as the Riddler he was usually the risk-taker. The Warlock might be prepared for him. Whereas Twardy Zarost wanted to keep the Warlock alive, the Warlock would have no such restraint. If he truly adopted Chaos as his guiding principle, he would have no restraint at all.

Clear essence swirled around the Warlock in restless coils. His battleaxe was near at hand, angled against the wall. Zarost would have to be quick. The challenge was to separate them without the Warlock realising it was a wizard who was doing the separating.

The other Gyre wizards were stationed outside the ale-hall at the five points of a pentagon, hidden in their disguises, deep in meditation. To be quick enough to catch the Warlock they had to be focused on the pattern of their spell alone, so that the essence would collect immediately when they needed it. They had prepared a fifth-level clustered containment that would hold the Warlock in place, but it would only succeed if he didn't cast his own Transference first.

Just then Bevn rose, and said something to the Warlock. The Warlock gestured to Gabrielle at once, and she rose as well. The prince objected, but the Warlock raised a finger in warning, and the prince dropped his head. Zarost strained to hear what the Warlock was saying to them.

"You'll only find bog-rocks on the eastern edge of town. Follow your nose. And Gabrielle, that time we talked about, it has come. Watch your back. You know what to do."

The prince and the Shadowcaster departed. As they left the room, the ugly half-Lûk slipped surreptitiously from the crowd. She would follow them, but she probably wouldn't act until she sensed the Gyre's spell engaging behind her. She would give Zarost time to act.

Zarost couldn't believe his luck. The Warlock was alone. He only had to clear the area of bystanders, and the Warlock would be isolated. The Kingsrim was gone from the room, so he could use his own magic without the risk of interference.

It was too easy. What was he missing? He scanned the hall for signs of trouble: Hunters, Lûk, soldiers, tough-looking men, all drinking, all shouting to be heard, and in the centre of the commotion, the Warlock, sitting calmly in his chair, rolling a small stoppered brown bottle in his right hand. And in his left...

The beginnings of a Transference spell.

Zarost shot to his feet. They were going to lose their opportunity if he didn't act.

He entered the Warlock's blind spot, gathered the essence, stepped forward, gripped the Warlock's plaited tail and said one word.

" ."

The word that was no word—the silent syllable. It had taken him so many years to master the powerful spell known as The Space; now it seemed as simple as taking a sudden breath. It was an almost pure Order manipulation. The gaps between the particles of air surrounding him expanded a thousand-fold. The people nearby would feel nothing, but in an instant they stood twenty paces from Zarost and the Warlock, and there was a great empty space between them.

Zarost dropped with the Warlock and landed on the frozen earth of the shallow crater in the bedrock—the alehouse had been shifted outward from the centre, the floor and foundations had been pushed aside. The roof was open to the night sky—exposed beams and broken tiles faced each other around a ragged circle. Dust and grit rained down past the stunned crowd, into the fighters' pit.

It was bitterly cold in the centre of the circle. Zarost kept his grip on the Warlock's plait. If he could anchor him with his touch, just for a few moments, he could prevent his Transference from engaging.

The Warlock spun and lashed out fiercely with his left foot, sweeping Zarost's legs out from under him. Zarost swung himself up on the Warlock's plait and sprang onto his shoulders, where he clutched the Warlock's head between his knees. The Warlock roared and fell backward. Twardy Zarost dropped clear and allowed the Warlock to fall then he jumped upon his chest and pinned him down, using the long plait to hold him across his throat. The Warlock writhed on the floor but didn't break free. Twardy wondered why the Warlock wasn't attacking him with his magic. In his right hand the Warlock still held the brown bottle, in his left the unfinished pattern of a Transference spell.

Tight cords of gold-tinged essence whipped down toward them; the Gyre had arrived. The essence converged on the Warlock from five sources. Pressure cracks formed in the air as the spell struggled against the limits of the Warlock's aura. Heat burst against Zarost's face, and Zarost leapt back to protect himself. A boiling surface of flame shed a shower of sparks as the first heat-skin formed around the Warlock then the second and the third. The clustered containment spell tightened like a shimmering net of golden wire.

The Warlock was held.

The patrons stared dumbly at the spectacle in their midst, then all at once they began to run. Magic was being used, and the result was inevitable. Twardy Zarost expected his hair to stand on end when the receiving-point gained charge. A rumbling thunder should come toward them soon then the silver threads of light would snake inward to meet at a bright confluence high above Slipper.

The wildfire would react to his use of magic, as it always did. Change would come upon Slipper with devastating intensity. The Gyre could not abandon the spell that held the Warlock captive; only the Riddler was free to act. But even as he began to cast the planned lure-spell to divert the strike toward the lowlands, he realised that something was amiss. There was no gathering tension.

The air was calm over Slipper.

It made no sense. The containment that held the Warlock was a mighty Order-spell; it combined the essence of five wizards. It should have triggered a massive wildfire strike. They had planned for it, they had expected it. The night sky was empty. A few stars twinkled innocently overhead, visible through the gap in the damaged roof of the ale-hall.

The Warlock seemed unsurprised by the lack of wildfire. He broke the small bottle that he held by crushing it in his right hand. The glass shattered and a puff of brown gas escaped, billowing to form a lopsided circle. It was filled with a strange light, as if it was a dirty window into another world. The Warlock whispered to himself.

"Hold him!" Zarost shouted to the distant wizards.

"We are! He is going nowhere!" the Mentalist answered. The cords of the Containment thickened, wrapping the Warlock in tight cocoons of force, Order-magic strong enough to hold a herd of angry bullgorgons. The Warlock could not possibly escape from the net.

Yet still he completed the Transference spell in his left hand. He did not release the pattern upon himself—with the bonds it would have been ineffective—instead he guided the coiled essence towards the tainted gap in the air. His arms were held, he could not move, but he could still use his mind to command his essence, in a limited way. The spell vanished as if pushed through a curtain. He had sent his Transference somewhere else, despite the Containment which should keep things exactly where they were. The window-space popped like a soap bubble. A wisp of brown gas curled in the air, faded, and was gone.

Zarost blinked. Something had just happened that he didn't understand.

They couldn't afford to have the Warlock cast any more spells—Zarost extended his hand and drew his personal essence away. The Warlock didn't resist.

"Now we have you," said Zarost.

"For the moment," the Warlock replied. "But once you understand what you have done, you will release me."

Zarost looked down at the traitorous wizard, into the dark holes within those red eyes. The Warlock had betrayed centuries of trust. His soul had crossed a bridge; he was no longer on their side. He was alone. Under pressure, he would always lie.

"Your treachery is ended, Warlock. You may as well speak the truth."

"Treachery? Treachery!" He laughed, a small sound in the amphitheatre of the broken inn. "No Riddler, you are mistaken. Everything I have done was for our cause, for the triumph of Order. Are you too blind to see that? I have worked hard to get close to the Sorcerer, to convince him of my allegiance. I have endured great perils, taken great risks, but never did I abandon my oath to the Gyre. What I did was a cover to get close to the Sorcerer, to gain his trust.

It might seem to you that I am a traitor, but in truth I have ever been loyal. That is why I do not fight you."

Zarost considered the Warlock's words. His calm expression was difficult to read.

"Explain the Kingsrim then. How could it possibly benefit us to have the anchor point of Eyri's Shield loose in Oldenworld?"

"Do you think the Sorcerer would have believed me if I had done anything less? He is impressed with extravagance, with daring, with risk. I am so close to gaining his favour. I have done more in the last few weeks than all of you have achieved in a hundred years. Who among you have even talked to the Sorcerer, who among you has discovered his weaknesses? Only I have done this, and I have learnt that we were wrong, we always fought against Chaos, pitting our strength against his. That only makes him stronger, for he draws upon his source only in moments of need. But hear me now. If we work with him, if we support Chaos, if only for a short time, he loses the focus for his hatred. He becomes weaker. The only way to conquer Chaos is to become it. Once I have gained his trust, I shall be close enough to tame the beast, to pacify him; to end his threat."

"You can't influence the Sorcerer. Even the Sorcerer cannot control his power. That is what Chaos means! The absence of control. You will never have any influence over him."

"I already do," the Warlock replied. "Did you fail to notice that the sky above Slipper was drained of wildfire? That was at my request, so that we might have this discussion in peace."

Zarost wondered if that could be true. It was more likely that they were under a faulty area of the wildfire web. "If taking the crown was a cover, why did you never tell us?"

"Come now, Riddler! If I had told any of you, you would have tried to stop me. Not so? This plan is too daring for a council of timid old-timers to consider, but I could wait no longer. The last conflict with the Sorcerer was dire—something had to be done. To act on my own was better than waiting for a false hope, and the crown of Eyri was a small sacrifice, because Eyri was already a failure. Can't you see that your new pet wizard is too inexperienced to make any difference? She will be swept aside; we shall all be swept aside unless we change. To triumph we have to get our hands dirty: we must get close to Chaos. That is what I have done, that is why you must release me, so I can press on with my task."

Zarost should have known that the Warlock would break out on his own, he had ever been ambitious. Black Saladon didn't see the big picture as Zarost could see it, wrapped in prophecy, beauty and betrayal. He would never see it that way, because Zarost couldn't share that vision with anyone.

"You underestimate the Lifesinger," said Zarost. "She carries a real hope of renewal for all of us."

"She is nothing but a channeller. The Sorcerer has already captured her Goddess, she will be silenced, and you will have nothing except for a fading memory of that song. Do not gamble our lives away on a false hope."

"The Sorcerer only knew how to trap the Goddess Ethea because of the lore you took to him, stolen from the Sanctuary. *You* caused the Lifesinger's power to be threatened, *you* jeopardised our hope!"

The Warlock shrugged. "Some sacrifices had to be made. It had to seem to the Sorcerer that I had turned my back on Order. He was quite convinced."

The Warlock had traded the Lifesong for the Sorcerer's favour. Zarost could not contain his anger. He grasped the Warlock by his moustache. "Such a sacrifice is unforgiveable!"

"I do not need your forgiveness, Riddler."

Zarost hit him then hit him again. There was little permanent damage that Zarost could do to the wizard, but it would hurt the Warlock until he had healed himself, and it helped Zarost reign in his fury. The Warlock was held immobile by the Containment. A fiery anger swelled in his eyes.

"You play a dangerous game, Riddler," he warned, through bloody teeth.

"And I will play it to the end. You will tell us what the Transference spell you cast was intended for."

The Warlock flashed him a humourless smile. "It shall be my pleasure to tell you, to see you understand the depth of your dilemma. The bottle contained a small discontinuity."

"Where from?"

"Turmodin, of course."

A chill ran down Twardy Zarost's spine. The Warlock had sent his spell into the brown haze, and his spell might have appeared in the Pillar.

"What use is a Transference spell to the Sorcerer? He would not use an Order spell."

The Warlock looked away from Zarost, into the night sky. "You understand so little about Chaos. He will use anything, if it will bring him the prizes he seeks."

"Where will that spell guide him to? Where did you send him?"

"Think about it, Riddler. To keep me contained, you must all remain here, not so? You are trapped by the trap you have cast. Wouldn't you say that is a perfect opportunity for someone else to break into a protected place? When you realise where that is, it will be too late. Ruin is upon you! Release me if you wish to save what you hold dear from the wrath of the Sorcerer."

33. AN AWFUL APPRECIATION

"How often the wise words we need
lie in the writings we are forbidden to read."—Zarost

Ametheus—three thirds of a man that didn't match.

Amyar, the scarred face, looked down upon the Goddess. She was still chained to her rock. The bloodied waters had risen far up the sides of the amphitheatre. The broken crescent of the moon's reflection danced in the surface of the pool like a dervish dancing for the dead. Quivering ripples moved outward from the prisoner—the Goddess was whispering to herself. She wouldn't stop. Yes, she understood her dilemma. The watery tomb would soon be sealed and the immortal would taste mortality.

All that power, yet she was so helpless. According to brother Seus, the Goddess Ethea was responsible for the life in every living thing. She was the current which ran through everyone, a song which resonated in the blood. She was life, and she was his to command.

He and his brother Seus weren't planning to kill her. They only wanted her to believe that they would. In the moment before her death, when she was truly desperate, she would give life to another. He had prepared the vessel well—the Wicker Man was ready, and the clerics would make the perfect sacrifice. They would provide the flesh for his father's coming. All that was needed was for the Goddess to begin her song, and he would light the fires at his father's feet. Into flames he would come, born within the screams of death, smoking flesh and wildfire. The Goddess would fill that Chaos with life and the Destroyer would step into the world.

"You will sing!" Amyar roared. He leant hard against the boulder. It crashed down the short slope and struck the water with a great splash. The wave washed against her feathered shoulders. She turned her head away to protect herself then she cried out. Somewhere under the surface, the boulder had settled against her. She was trapped by many boulders. Ametheus had rolled down every one, and each time the water level had risen. Another few boulders, and a bit more rain, and she would drown.

Yet still she refused to sing.

Brother Ethan regretted what he was doing. The Goddess was beautiful, she was gentle; she was kind. He wished she would just sing, so he could stop tormenting her. She was a creature of air and the water held special terror for her. Ethan thought they should stop, perform the ritual from the book and release her, but the others didn't agree, so he hid his own tears, crying silently in the shadow of his brothers, as Amyar set his hand against another boulder. Ethea pleaded to him from the watery prison below. Amyar gathered his weight.

Just then, something in his pocket exploded. He stood still, puzzled. His brown bottle! He shook out the shards from his pocket in an excited flurry. A sickly pattern of Ordered essence turned in the air before him. He raised his hands, shrieking with alarm. Why was it here? Ethan wondered. Then he remembered, or Amyar did. The dark-faced wizard had told him it would be so—a special spell to move him to the Sanctuary. The dark-faced wizard had promised him the place would be abandoned. He could destroy it and be there to destroy the Gyre when they returned to save it.

It took him a moment to remember the plans he had laid for the Sanctuary. Sometimes there were so many ideas in his head he couldn't count them, so many paths to follow that he got lost.

They were going to walk straight into the Sanctuary?

"Yes," Amyar reassured them, "we have thought about this before."

"What will we do?" he asked Seus.

"We will take a Node with us and release it in their den. Then we shall get creative around it. We shall destroy what we can and divide them as they come. The Gyre is like a tree with too many branches and only one root. They rely completely on their store of knowledge. We shall demolish their books. The tree can not stand once we have broken out its foundation."

Ethan smiled. The wizards and their Sanctuary, now *this* he could do.

"We must leave the Goddess and face the wizards," he said.

"Yes," whispered brother Seus. "Tonight is the night."

They contemplated the turning pattern of pale gold essence—a gateway to the place of the wizards' power, hidden from them for so long.

"Can we trust the black-faced one?" Amyar asked.

"We don't have to," Ethan replied. "He wants to gain our Father's favour, so he can't do anything to hurt us. If we can finish off the

Gyre before our Father comes, just imagine how proud He will be!"

Ametheus left the boulder where it was, poised on the brink of the slope above the Goddess.

The Sanctuary.

He summoned a Node from the Pillar. It came slithering across the ground with a sputtering sound like a phlegm-choked death-breath. He gathered it up, stepped forward into the twisted oblate swirl of golden essence, and the Transference spell took hold of him.

ॐॐॐ

Tabitha was alone in the Sanctuary. The wizards of the Gyre had gone to capture the Warlock. They had feared she might be exposed to dangers that she couldn't handle, so they had left her where it was safe. If it was possible for a building to have emotions, she would have said that the Sanctuary *sulked*, alone in the desert beneath the silent stars. The building was as cheerless as a tomb.

She sneaked down to the library and wandered through the books until she came suddenly upon Ametheus, standing in a dark corner. The book on the reading stand was old, really old, or it had aged faster than the other books she had seen. The pages were brittle and randomly holed, as if something had found the writing tasty, or the writing had eaten through the pages.

Thricety, said the cover, *An Awful Appreciation of Ametheus*, by Annah Nerine Good.

Unclassified! bloomed the lens suddenly. *Unclassified! Unclassified!*

She looked more *leftly*. The book groaned as she moved the heavy pages back. On the first page was something titled a 'Claimer', written in a scratchy handwriting, little letters that tilted at odd angles. 'If you die because of this it is my fault and I am sorry. If this writing leads you to him but he is unwelcoming and wroth, say his name once, and you call on all three, and being conflicted he cannot get free. His name will bind him for a moment. That is the only defence I can offer. Be honest. I don't fear Ametheus. I fear those who try to control him. ANG.'

The following pages were works of art. A story was told in images, little boxes of sketched faces and figures frozen in their actions, arranged in patterns, sometimes in sequence, sometimes overlapping, so that it took quite some time to apprehend the flow, which one led to which. It seemed that the writer had a mind that didn't run in straight lines. The thoughts ran obliquely at times, from left to right, from right to left, up and across and down, and words danced in curlicues over the images, expanding the tale with information and exclamation, sometimes coming from the lips of shouting faces, sometimes forming poetic associations drawn in the background amid the notations, lines of force and patterns that seemed drawn for the pure pleasure of their design. The holes in the pages made it even harder to follow. It was entirely fascinating.

The Wonders of Childhood told a story of deprivation and desperation, a little figure clinging to the fur of a goat, a little figure looking up at ripe fruit on a tree too tall to reach, waiting for the fruit to rot and fall to where he sat among his tears, a little figure huddled against his goat as rain lashed his rags. His face was never shown, there was just an outline of his head in every frame as if the writer didn't know what he looked like, or wanted to keep her knowledge hidden.

The First Encounter told a story of a child hunted by tall thin creatures with bright sticks and dogs. It ended in a forest, where flames spread gleefully up the page and consumed the last of the attackers.

The Watcher in the World told the story of a man hidden behind a veil that separated the world beyond from the world within, and every time that man reached out through the veil he was met with horrified faces, fear, revulsion and violence.

There were many stories, episodes then, abruptly, it ended. There was an illustration of a chalice then… Nothing. She wanted to know more. She wanted to know what had happened to Ametheus. She wanted to know what had happened to the writer.

Terminated! flashed her eye. *Terminated! Developing Chaos lore. Reclassified: book equates to Chaos lore. Alert!* Bright lines skittered across her vision, throwing information at her faster and faster, formulas and metrics, three-dimensional explanations that made no sense although the understanding was imprinted on her mind. Her right eye was tearing too much, she had to stop reading. She couldn't look at the book any more.

Tabitha couldn't stay in the Library—she went back up to the chambers and sat by the pool, where the dangers in her wizard's eye slowly faded, but the memories didn't. Ametheus, alone against a world of hate, and a writer, killed for her creativity, or for her compassion. She was beginning to understand the Riddler's reluctance about her exposure to their lore—their way. The Wizard's way.

Tabitha hummed the Lifesong to keep her spirits up. She drew the Light from clear essence with a simple command and allowed the glimmer of sprites to drift over the water before her. She was beginning to understand how to use the principles of the three axes. The essence changed nature depending on the pole she directed it toward. It was driven by her *intent*. When she thought of a clear question, the lens presented information to her through symbolic shapes and force-lines that scampered across her vision and impressed the distilled wisdom upon her. She could learn their lore simply by watching, by looking through the *ogle-i*.

She played with the patterns that she knew, the simple Heal-all spell, the dove-shaped Courier, the Spriteblind. Then she turned the essence as black as pitch and worked the Silence and Freeze and Seduction spells with the Dark. It was interesting exploring the limits of her magical ability, but she knew she was just distracting herself from her real problem. She was worried about Ethea. Too much time had passed and nothing had been done to save her. Ethea did not have time. Tabitha could hear her whispered call, the plea for help, over and over in her mind. It felt wrong to be safe in the Sanctuary. She was a wizard, and she should be in the midst of things. She should not be in hiding.

Something fell in a room nearby, probably the night wind, gusting through some scrolls.

She should not allow the wizards to dictate how she used her power. Tabitha hummed the Lifesong a little louder, determined to shrug off her sense of helplessness. She would find a way to reach Ethea. She wished she knew how to cast the Transference spell. The wizards had forbidden her from following them up to the roof-quad when they had departed, so she had been unable to examine the pattern they used. She needed the pattern because if she lost her way in the awesome expanse of infinity, she might never return.

The surface of the Gyre's pool rippled. Probably her fish, she had glimpsed it turning in the depths.

She contemplated making up her own kind of transference spell. The second stanza of the Lifesong turned flesh to clear essence. If a person was disintegrated in one place, and recreated in another using the first stanza, would they really be moved, or would they die and would another soul be born? Tabitha couldn't tell. She supposed it might be possible to do such a thing, but she couldn't see how she could sing *herself* to life again once she was disintegrated. She supposed that she would be able to learn the secret from Ethea.

Was Ethea's plight still so desperate? Did the Sorcerer still torment her?

Words, whispered words, barely audible over the Lifesong stanza she was humming.

"*Oh little Singer...*"

Although her lips were closed she heard the words again, carried on the bars of her own music—whispered words full of sorrow.

"*Oh little Singer, I have found you!*"

Ethea?

"*I have reached for you for so long, and you have hidden.*"

Ethea's voice was carried in the music like a melodic resonance.

"*Why do you never sing? Are you ashamed of me, of my weakness? Why do you hide from me? Help me, oh help me, I grow weaker, so weak, he will make me commit a horror. I cannot allow it, but I cannot escape. Oh Singer come to me!*"

The words wrenched at her heart. She was ashamed at herself for not having the courage to face down the wizards and demand they save Ethea. The Gyre had left—how was she to help the Goddess now? She continued the Lifesong melody on her lyre and whispered her own words into the hollows in the music in the hope that somehow they would be carried to the Goddess. "I am in another place, trapped in my own body. How can I come to you? Is there a way to sing it so?"

The Lifesong themes swelled within her. Ethea's whispers were clearer this time, floating on the notes. "*The song moves through all of it. The song is here, the song is there. Be the song and nothing more, give yourself to the music. A-way-a-lay. Come to me.*"

"I did that before, my Goddess, but my body stayed behind. I need to be whole to be able to help you. How will my body move?" But the Goddess did not answer. Tabitha played on, hoping for some whispered guidance. Maybe Ethea had no answer. Maybe the Goddess did not know how to work with the strange limitations that flesh imposed. She was about to ask another question when a frightened cry came upon the carrier notes of the Lifesong.

"*The water! The water! It is upon me! He threw another rock down. Now it rains. Oh, the weight of it! He breaks me, he breaks me...*"

Ethea gave a forlorn wail, and the Lifesong came to an abrupt and discordant end on Tabitha's lyre. She had come upon a gap in the music and could play no further. The emptiness she sensed in the song was worse than any vision of torture. There was nothing to reach for, nothing to sing. The Goddess was losing the fight.

"No! Ethea! Hold on! I am coming!" She cast around in the room, desperate to find something to assist her. The chamber was stark, empty. She would have to make her own spell. There was no time to waste anymore. Ethea was dying.

What she really needed was the Transference spell, but she didn't know how Zarost had done it, except that her awareness had spread until it was everywhere at once, and he had whispered a word, a single word.

"Infinity," she tried.

Her ring flared with heat. A memory flashed across her mind. A tingling pain shot through her palms and she spread them wide, in case that helped her reach outward, but she knew at once that she had made a mistake with the spell. Between her hands was an inky void filled with stars, as if she had peeled open the air to reveal the midnight sky beneath it, or within it. She had summoned something very strange—the space between her palms exuded a feeling of vastness that was unsettling, almost dreadfully huge; Tabitha felt so very small. She was scared she might fall into the ragged hole which yawned and whispered at her. She clapped her hands, and the air returned to its correct place in the ordered reality of the Sanctuary. A boom of thunder exploded above her palms.

Well *that* hadn't worked. Tabitha closed her eyes and searched for clarity. She could move essence anywhere on the three axes, but she knew very few spell patterns. The most advanced Order spell she knew of was the Reference spell, but she had been warned about the consequences of using it on anything living because it was designed to shift matter from place to place and it did not cater for the soul. She wondered what would happen if she used her rainbow essence in the spell, instead of the golden essence of Order. Would the Lifesong carry the soul along the threads of music while the pattern of the Reference produced the shift from place to place? It was terribly risky to cast such an untested blend of spells on herself, but if it was the only way...

She opened her eyes. The fish flashed in the pool beneath her.

The fish. She would send one of them to Ethea, and if it worked she would cast the spell again on herself.

A high-pitched whine sounded outside, like something tensioning.

Then there was a hard pop. Lines of disturbance skittered across her vision as her lens went wild. Something was happening to the essence outside. Were the wizards returning with the Warlock? She couldn't afford to be distracted. Not now. They would want to keep her in the Sanctuary, like a prize; just another treasure hoarded in the Reliceum.

She struck the strings of the lyre, playing into the gap in the Lifesong, filling the silence with her own music. Clear essence gathered around her. She sang a wordless accompaniment. The essence shimmered with dancing colours, a silken cloud of iridescent hues. She set the lyre down but did not release the essence. She worked it into the Reference spell pattern, using the grid that the lens scribed upon her vision to guide the shift from the Order axis down to the origin. That was the balance-point where the Lifesong essence usually collected. Finally, the tail of the reference pattern had to be aimed to the target. She had a moment of panic as she realised she had no idea how to define the Pillar in the lowlands. She only had the vision of that place, the pool and rock and cliff she had seen. As she thought upon that place, the tail of the pattern moved and came to rest at a particular point. She had been there, with the Goddess. The memory of it would have to be enough.

When the spell was prepared as a tight net of colours in her hand, she looked upon the pool, where the fish turned in the depths. One finned its way closer to the surface and, as it swept past, Tabitha cast the spell upon it. "Begone, and live with the Goddess." The pattern pierced the water and wrapped the fish in a rainbow of light.

A puff of bubbles rose to the surface. The fish was gone.

She had to know it had reached Ethea. Striking the theme of the Lifesong on her lyre, she searched with her music, but had to strain against a persistent silence, as if she grappled against void for each note, forcing her way through a howling emptiness toward the Goddess and the source of the Lifesong.

The ground shook. A moment later an explosion pressed against her ears. Outside, the northern sky was suddenly bright. Something about the sequence disturbed her. Had the wizards returned? Were they fighting the Warlock?

Her right eye was a fury of symbols and lore, blinding and intense. It frightened her, but she knew she had to remain focused on reaching the Goddess.

"Do you see a silver-blue fish?" she asked the air. She hoped Ethea was listening; she hoped the Goddess would turn away from her despair for just a moment and hear the message carried on the notes. She couldn't commit until she *knew*. The music began to flow more easily and familiar warmth filled her heart.

"Goddess, do you have a fish?" she asked.

Outside, the night sky was split again with jagged lines of light, silver light, deadly light. A sharp scent was in the air. A rush of silver spilled in the window and burned through the floor. Tabitha cried out. She recognised that silver dust. Somehow, the Sorcerer's wildfire had reached the Sanctuary. This wasn't the wizards fighting among themselves, it was Chaos.

A faint whisper came upon the threads of music, small beneath the shrieking and spitting clamour which approached from outside. *"I see a fish, it flashes bright within the pool! Ay-lis-ay-lee."*

At once, Tabitha repeated the preparation of her spell, collecting clear essence, activating it, moulding it into shape. She couldn't do it quickly enough. Something broke downstairs. A great smashing and rending force shook the building. The magnitude of the approaching power was terrifying. Tabitha reached for Ethea through the song and used her memory to guide her to the place where the sky was red and the warm rain fell upon a bloodied pool amid smoke and clamour. The Goddess should not be abandoned. She prayed she had not made a mistake with the pattern; she knew she was pushing her luck.

She released the net of bright colours upon herself. "Begone, and live with the Goddess," she whispered. A terrible ripping impact shook the Sanctuary. The floor cracked open, and the waters of the pool fell away. There was a moment of bright pain then everything was music.

34. RELATIVE INSANITY

"An advantage, well concealed
Can tip a hasty battlefield."—Zarost

The Gyre was in a right royal bind. The Warlock had told them that the Sorcerer had gone to the Sanctuary. They had to save the Sanctuary. Too many precious things were preserved within it, and nothing so precious as Tabitha Serannon, thought Twardy Zarost. But to go to the Sanctuary they had to release the Warlock from the clustered containment spell they held. They could not transfer with him and still *contain* him, because the Transference spell used the crossing point of infinity, and it was impossible to contain something of an infinite size.

They had to choose between the Warlock and the Sanctuary.

Zarost knew what the Gyre's decision would be, and he suspected the Warlock knew it too—he had planned it this way. What made it was worse was that it could all be a bluff. They might go to the Sanctuary and find nothing amiss. The Warlock would laugh at them from afar. The Gyre was crippled by the lack of information. They had to go to the Sanctuary to verify the truth, but if the Sorcerer was at the Sanctuary, it would not be safe for one wizard to transfer there, even momentarily. They would need to go together, as the Gyre—which left the problem of what to do with the Warlock.

"We *could* kill him," suggested the Mentalist.

They considered this for a long moment.

"No, we need his skills," the Senior disagreed. "We are forever weaker if he is dead."

"But he uses them against us, for crying out loud!" the Mentalist argued.

"I agree with the Mentalist," said the Lorewarden. "He is too great a risk to have as an adversary. He knows too much. Let us end him now and if it turns out that the threat to the Sanctuary was a lie, then it shall be a lie that costs him his life."

"No!" the Cosmologer objected. "I will not stand for it! Have you heard nothing he has said? He is pretending to be allied to Chaos only to earn the Sorcerer's trust." She had taken the form of a sickly violet-spotted child in a bilious green dress for the purposes of the ambush. It was a truer representation of her character, in many ways, thought Zarost.

"Oh, come now, Cosmologer!" exclaimed the Mentalist. "He has led the Sorcerer to the Sanctuary! What more could he do to prove his guilt?"

"He's just saying that! I don't believe he has done it."

"Yet you believe the other things he has said?"

"Your judgement is clouded, Cosmologer," said the Spiritist.

"You cannot redeem him by protecting him, Cosmologer," Zarost added. "He has been corrupted by Chaos."

The Cosmologer turned on him. "You! You have no right to speak like that! I will still spend days chasing down the Chaos you reflected with your ill-considered spell. Should we kill you too, then? The Gods know I've wanted to, but I vowed to protect you as I vowed to protect the Warlock. We are the Gyre. If we turn upon ourselves, then we fall apart."

Words she could well consider herself Zarost turned away from the Cosmologer. There was no use arguing—it would only escalate, and as they argued they lost time. What could they do with the traitor? The Warlock still couldn't move, he continued to face the sky. He had known they would be divided. He had known he was safe from execution.

"We'll just have to leave him," said the Mentalist. "He'll stay pinned down."

"Not for long," the Senior noted.

"Yes, but long enough!" said the Mentalist. "We shall return here once the Sanctuary is safe."

"Yes, very well," said the Senior. "Spiritist? Cosmologer? You agree with that?"

They nodded, but Zarost knew that without at least one wizard to tend the anchors, the flows of essence would weaken with time. The Warlock would be able to chip away at his prison, layer by layer, until he was free. Was that a glimmer of a smile on the Warlock's dark lips?

As the others disengaged from the containment spell, the Lorewarden stepped forward. Zarost watched with interest as he drew designs over the Warlock with his fingers, leaving puffs of white in the air which sank upon the Warlock. Oh, *that* was a good idea. The smile slipped from the Warlock's face. He tried to hold his breath, so Zarost gave him a hard kick in the belly. The Warlock gasped and fought against the gas then, but at last his eyes rolled back in his head and he slumped against the earth where he was held within a net of golden essence in his hollow in the centre of the ruined tavern in the fortress town of Slipper.

The Mystery was still retrieving the Kingsrim, but there was no time to track her down. She would look after herself. The Gyre had to save the Sanctuary and Tabitha, dear Tabitha! Zarost chose his destination point carefully, so that he would appear in a hidden corner of the chambers. Infinity came and went in a flash of consciousness. Like falcons fired from the sky, the wizards of the Gyre came upon their temple of collected knowledge, the vault of civilisation and the guard-house of Order.

Instead of the austere room, Zarost found empty air. The collapsed remains of the building, awash with fatal wildfire, far below his feet. He had already fallen half the way to the ground before he snapped his attention back to the crossing point of infinity.

Chaos! Upon the sacred chambers! The Warlock hadn't lied, and it had happened so fast. It had taken them all by surprise. Chaos! He re-emerged upon the sand, clear of the deadly waste. Zarost's stomach drop away in horror. Thick black smoke hissed through the jagged combs of the splintered walls. Clouds of ash idled upward into the low and brooding sky. A brittle moon rode on the backs of the shredded clouds, throwing dirty silver light upon the sands. The air was tense, too dirty. The wreckage of the chambers hadn't settled yet. Something organic had been made amid the wildfire—such an acrid stench would not come off the shattered masonry alone. In places, the earth bubbled and spat.

There was no sign of the Lifesinger. She would not have survived against this. Ametheus was too wild, too reckless—too angry. Remorse flooded Zarost. *Oh Tabitha! We should not have abandoned you!* And yet, they could not have foreseen the attack. It was unprecedented. The Sorcerer had not abandoned his power seat in Turmodin for centuries, yet he had used the Transference he had been offered by the Warlock. He had come upon the Sanctuary. He was close. Where was he? Zarost tried to see in every direction at once.

A figure appeared over the ruins. The Mentalist. He had been dressed as a Hunter with a tangle of braids, but like the others, in his haste, he returned from infinity without the disguise, reformed upon his residual self image, dressed in his hempflax garments. He ran on the floor, which was no longer there, then the Mentalist was falling. A moment later he was gone then Zarost felt the gentle pressure of his arrival behind him.

"Living hell, but it was made of fortified stone!" exclaimed the Mentalist. "How does he burn it?"

"If you change stone to wood then it will burn well and good."

"If he can strike this far from Turmodin, he can strike anywhere," the Mentalist said in a hushed voice. He came up beside Zarost and scanned the wreckage with a skittering gaze. The Senior and Cosmologer were there, approaching from some distance away.

"We should split up!" the Mentalist called out. "We are too vulnerable—all of us could be wiped out in one single blast! We must leave!"

"Wait, Mentalist, before you transfer yourself to safety!" the Senior urged. "We have a chance to capture him here."

"We only have a chance if we are alive! This place is rife with Chaos. He is too close!"

"And so he has extended himself too far," replied the Senior. "He cannot summon much of his power here. Let him meet our full Gyre."

"We are only four! We are too few!" cried the Mentalist. "The others aren't coming!"

As if to prove him wrong, two figures appeared above the ruins, the Lorewarden and the Spiritist. They began to fall then slowed and glided aside as they took command of the forces acting upon them, but even that minor use of essence disturbed the wildfire on the ground, and it rose in restless ridges, preparing to strike at the source of magic.

"Transference! Use the Transference, you idiots!" shouted the Cosmologer. The wildfire arced upward from many different points, hungry tendrils searching for prey. The Lorewarden and the Spiritist vanished. Two bright flashes of silver marked where they had been. The two wizards reappeared on the ground between the others.

Something tightened through the brooding sky. The billowing smoke was wrenched upright into a single plume which shot up to the concaved base of the cloud, sucked into a dark and hungry maw. Zarost guessed what Ametheus would do—a great strike of wildfire through the concealing column of smoke would explode within the waiting reservoir of fatal tainted ash in their centre and would cause a wave of Chaos which could overwhelm the six wizards. However if he was close enough to trigger Chaos in that way, he was close enough for the Gyre to reach him with their own spells. He was there and, for the first time in years, the Gyre could face him directly.

A subtle charge rushed under Zarost's feet, away from the ruins. It puzzled him—the surge usually led toward the trigger point. Maybe Ametheus wasn't going to use the ruins after all, maybe...

"Outward!" he shouted. "Face outward! We are within it. Chaos comes upon us!"

The air was perfectly still. The clouds sank and drew the dark night down upon the world. Then lightning broke in painful brilliance; fractured lines fell everywhere. Zarost linked his attention with the others to form the union of the Gyre. They augmented the Cosmologer's skills to redirect the strikes and the air was shattered around them upon their protective sphere. Roll after roll of thunder hammered at their bones. Where the lightning found purchase, it lived, connecting earth and sky without fading. Some of the deflected strikes were so close Zarost could smell the meaty cinnamon scent of wildfire in the shivering air.

Within the pooled attention of the Gyre, they shared a moment of doubt. They should escape to the crossing point of infinity, while there was still a chance, but the defiance which held them there was stronger—they could weather the storm, they would turn the Sorcerer's game upon himself.

They would end him.

The ground lurched. The strands of lightning forked horizontally all at once, raking the air with a thousand claws. Zarost regained his balance and strove with the others to deny the advance of the wildfire. Ametheus would not be able to sustain the multiple flows. Chaos never endured. Change was a rapid force, it corrupted what it touched, but the power itself always faded—only Order lasted. The Gyre would have a chance to retaliate, if they could just hold on for long enough.

The whirling lattice of lightning ignited in one horrendous incandescent flare. A great cracking sound assaulted them, riding the crest of a shockwave that blew them toward the ruins at their back. They almost lost the Spiritist in that moment. She tumbled to the edge of the contaminated ash before the others grounded her and parted the elemental forces to allow her a moment to rejoin the collective. Then they stood firm. The flow of Chaos was poorly directed and the rushing force passed them by.

It became darker and darker, until the only light came from the failing threads of charge which lingered around the perimeter of the Gyre's defended area, and from the wastes behind them that gave off a sickly smoky glow. Zarost tried to sense where the Sorcerer was hiding. His presence would be revealed for an instant as the assault waned. Zarost spread his awareness, outward across the dark sands. He met a strange wall beyond which his mind could not go. It was impossible—he should be able to extend his consciousness through everything in the universe, all the way to infinity. He tried again, searching upward then behind, hoping to find a gap.

The limit was complete. A skin had formed around them; impenetrable, absolute. Where the lightning had raged it had burnt emptiness. It was as if something was missing from reality, as if an invisible trench had been cut across it. Like a gap of nothingness, Zarost realised, that paradox they had used against the Writhe. The Gyre had used the dimensional anomaly in desperation to end the previous spell the Sorcerer had unleashed upon Oldenworld. Now he was using it against them, but in a way that defied belief. A sphere of nothing, with their little world contained within.

As Zarost knew, so they all knew. The other members of the Gyre groaned.

They really were trapped. By breaking a piece of reality out of the pattern, Ametheus had ensured that there was no escape. Even with all the cleverness beneath his hat, Zarost could not understand what had happened. The Sorcerer had enclosed them in a new dimension, a *converse* less than a quarter-league wide.

The Mentalist was the first to panic and let go of the Gyre, to try to transfer out of their prison. He went nowhere; he didn't even begin to fade. Without his awareness touching infinity, his body would not dissolve. As he knew, so they all knew. The Cosmologer had discovered the reason for the darkness. It was as if the sun had ceased to be part of their reality. In the tiny world they were in, there was no sun: only the fire, the sand and the ruins of their tradition. The Gyre turned to Zarost. He was the Riddler, best suited to solve such a quandary. As the Gyre members directed their intent to Zarost, his concentration sharpened, and his mind staggered with the combined intelligence.

Ametheus had unleashed a spell of unprecedented magnitude. He had *contained* his Chaos, which in itself was strange. The vital seeds of wildfire were locked in this small place. Whatever happened in this sealed world would remain here. Zarost had never seen a spell cast by the Sorcerer which sealed Chaos off—that was typical of an Order spell, not Chaos. Was the Sorcerer learning to use their own power against them? No, Zarost remembered, he had been *advised*. The Warlock had planned this, down to the panicked beating of their hearts. He had done more than point out the Gyre's weaknesses. He had strategised their responses and wielded the wildfire against them all. He had learnt how to use Chaos.

Zarost could almost understand the Warlock, a man who saw life as a power struggle, defecting to join the greater power. In many ways it was an old story—a man of frustrated ambition turning to treachery to reach his goal. He was simply a traitor, and so, *human*. To endear himself to his new master, he would employ his knowledge to bring about the ruin of his old house. Why had Ametheus *listened* to him? It meant that Ametheus was *in league* with an Order wizard. It was contrary to his nature. It was unexpected, and so Zarost solved the riddle. The Gyre's mistake had been to expect Ametheus to behave as he had in the past.

"Chaos is never predictable," he stated simply.

They had lost the age-old war in a most bizarre way. They had been *taken out*. They weren't part of the right universe any more. They couldn't fight the Chaos in Oldenworld, because they couldn't get *into* it. They were in a world that was no world at all—a dead end. To escape from the separated sphere, they would have to create a bridge of substance through the void of nothingness. When the Gyre had used the nothingness before, they had each held a corner of a rectangle. They had been able to stretch the gap wide then close it again because they could each anchor a corner point and direct the transition along straight divides. But with a *sphere* of nothingness, there were no corners. There was no place for them to get a hold on the transition point. It was a horrendous spell. Zarost did not understand how Ametheus had been able to create it. He should not have been capable of disrupting reality so perfectly. There was always a flaw in his manipulations, it was the fundamental truth of Chaos—perfection of any kind was impossible.

None of them had the power to fill Nothing—not even together. They could manipulate what was there, but not what wasn't. None of them could *create* a reality. Even the Cosmologer was an assembler, not a maker. She needed the raw materials of essence to begin with. In a space without essence, they were powerless, just as the Sorcerer was. He could break and separate but he could not heal such a rift in space.

Zarost realised what they had really lost. He knew of one maker. Oh how that stabbed him in his heart, through and through. The Lifesinger was the only one who could bridge a gap of life, who could heal a broken circle. Tabitha could have *created*. She had been destroyed first, somewhere in the dead ash, in the ruins of Order.

He considered his many mistakes. He had laid the right pieces of the puzzle of prophecy, but his adversary had reordered them and created something so strange it could not possibly lead to the moment of truth.

Laklødder skran ðzak dehr nihil bloşnihil.

Nothing but madness, when the end is played against the end.

There was only one consolation. If Ametheus wished to finish them off, he would have to enter the separated world. In so doing, he would breach the gap between worlds himself, and come he would. He would not be able to resist the temptation of six wizards all in one pot. When he came, they would leave. There was no question of facing him down anymore. He had demonstrated his ability, he was surely at the apex of his cycle of madness. The flames that licked through the ruins of the Sanctuary rose higher, throwing a baleful light upon the sand.

They had to prepare a strategy.

"Analyse this, Lorewarden!" he said.

"F equals m a," the Lorewarden replied.

"And easy emsy squared?" ventured Zarost

"Exactly my point. So energy is proportional to force over acceleration. If this truly is a separate system, the energy we can draw on is small and constant, due to the limited amount of matter, and the more we try to accelerate ourselves, to escape, the greater the force against us will be. We have to be calm, as calm as possible."

"But that assumes energy is constant in the universe."

"But energy *is* ultimately finite, Riddler. There is only so much matter available to convert."

"Ametheus isn't bound by that assumption."

"It doesn't matter how much you tip the second axis, you get to the same end of the rod. Convert all the matter to energy and you still have a finite total."

"Ah, but what if you increase the force *and* cause the acceleration to decrease?"

"Don't be a fool!" squawked the Cosmologer. "How would you would you do such a thing?"

"Apply the force from all directions at once. Compress this space until there is nothing to compress anymore. Isn't that what he will do? Crush us into oblivion. He would harvest so much energy he could use it to create anything."

"But the matter would resist such compression!" objected the Cosmologer. "You would *require* an immense amount of energy!"

The Lorewarden concurred. "You can't compress your hands together because your left hand fights with your right hand for the space. Matter resists." He clapped his hands to make his point.

"But if you take enough of the spaces out, doesn't gravity do the job all on its own?"

The Lorewarden was silent. The Cosmologer's lips worked like a fish out of water as the awful idea assaulted her mind. "Oh," she said.

The Gyre turned slowly on the dangerous thought.

"This is true, yes," said the Lorewarden. "If you removed enough space, the matter would collapse upon itself."

"You'll get some horrible time compressions too," said the Senior.

"Blast it, Riddler, will Chaos be the end of us?" demanded the Mentalist. He looked at Zarost with haunted eyes. "What do you propose?"

There was no time.

"The ground!" the Mystery cried out. "Out there! The air as well!"

Zarost spun around. A crumbling, breaking, crushing sensation came at him from within the gloom. A jagged crack whipped past him on his right side, skewing the sand beyond at a horrible angle as if what he saw was a scene in a tilted mirror. Another crack passed between Zarost and the wizards to his left, as space folded. The Lorewarden shouted something, but Zarost couldn't hear him.

His link to the Gyre was suddenly severed, and in that moment he knew the true terror of his isolation. He had only his own skills to draw upon. He was alone in his sliver of reality, and he could not escape. Silver raindrops began to fall, dangerous wildfire, each droplet burning with Chaos. It would change his flesh if it struck him, altering him with random mutations until he lost command of his body altogether. He mustered all his concentration and danced beneath the assault, throwing small hooks of Dark essence at each droplet to freeze them before they struck. If he used a more sophisticated spell to defend himself, the wildfire would be drawn to him too quickly.

The rain fell faster and faster. *Pit-pat pittat pittit-pittat.*

Despite his caution, his Freeze spell attracted more and more droplets, finally so many that he missed some of them. Poisonous liquid stung his face and shoulders. He abandoned his frantic attempt to alter the rain and concentrated on resisting his own alteration instead. Change rippled over his skin. His hand turned black and dripped like sponge. He resisted. Fifteen eyes burst through at his wrist. He denied them. He held his own image firmly in mind—Twardy Zarost, with a bristly beard, a wiry mop of hair and his favourite striped hat upon his head and his indigo pants. He refused each deviation of form as it came upon him: his leg swollen with elephant skin; red scales that ran up his arm; and barbed whiskers upon his face. Resisted, refused, repelled. Gradually, the cancerous growths and painful crusts washed away in the steady flow of Zarost's revisualisation.

He was the Riddler. He was the Riddler.

He was still the Riddler, despite the Chaos working upon him.

Zarost recognised the assault for what it was. The rain was only a trickle of power, it was not devastating. The raindrops had made him panic and prevented him from focusing his attention on the real threat. Ametheus had done it to all of them. The neighbouring scene tilted toward Zarost, as if a piece of the mirrored world was falling inward along the line it had cracked upon. Within the warped window of reality, Twardy saw the Lorewarden changing earth to laval fire to burn the frenzied silver ants that crawled toward him. Farther away, in his own separated space, the Mentalist was on his knees, his arms spread wide, shouting like a madman. Whatever he was being subjected to was overloading his attention. Zarost couldn't see the Spiritist anywhere, but a glimpse of an oblique scene told him that the Senior was surrounded by clouds of swirling ash. All the while, the real threat was disguised—every one of their little worlds was collapsing, crumbling, fraying at the edges. Zarost guessed that each wizard would end up in a tiny shard, isolated and trapped, dodging and weaving until there was no more space to hide. A crack would eventually find every one of them, pass through their bodies and divide their attention. They would be divided and divided, until they died.

He had to find a way out.

The Chaos-formed rain continued to beat down on him, but he denied it. He refused to be erased.

It made no sense—reality would not break apart on its own, but how could Ametheus manipulate this collapsing world, if it was fully separated from the realm which he inhabited? A link to the Sorcerer had to exist, there had to be a cord of attention along which Zarost could escape.

"W-what if there is no c-c-cord, b-because I am h-h-here?"

Twardy Zarost jumped, the voice was that close. He spun to face the flames. Only a portion of the ruins remained. The rest had broken off into the scenes in which the other wizards battled, canted off at odd illogical angles. There was no sign of the Sorcerer, though Zarost was sure Ametheus had spoken. The voice was full of the stuttered words that characterised the inner turmoil Ametheus endured.

"You-you d-d-don't see me because you d-d-don't want to believe I can do w-what you are seeing." The Sorcerer's deep voice surrounded Zarost.

"If you showed yourself in a way I could understand, would you and I ever come to the same understanding?"

"C-clever riddle, Riddler. B-b-but before I reveal myself, I-I and I wish to e-explain something to you all. I h-hold the vital access to each of your worlds. If any of you t-try to harm me now, I sh-shall abandon you to this c-c-current fate. If by some m-miracle of m-magic you injure me, y-you will still be trapped in your shard of reality. You will n-never escape it, for your w-way back will be gone. Your salvation is through me."

Things were worse than Zarost had thought. Not only was Ametheus in the height of his cycle of Chaos, but he was in control of his magic as well—for the moment. He had separated the six wizards, but from the way he spoke Zarost had to assume Ametheus was heard by all of them, which meant he existed in all of their separated worlds. He was the one common element, the centre-point, the crux. Their lives relied on the concentration of a man who was at best unstable; at worst, utterly insane.

Zarost tried to get his lens to reveal the Sorcerer's position, but there was so many warnings coming at him he could not find Ametheus amid all the stroke-marks. The silvered rain continued to fall in the strange little world. The sand was pitted and strangely coloured by the impacts. The flames continued to blacken the few remaining columns of jagged stone. Zarost clung to a single hope—

the Sorcerer wanted something from the Gyre or he would have ended them already. If they talked, they might have a chance to delay him long enough for his concentration to slip. Then again, maybe Ametheus was simply toying with them. Zarost watched the flames. He was sure the Sorcerer was concealing himself somewhere in the fire. It was the only common point of all the wizards' shards.

It had been a long time since he had been so close to the Sorcerer. He had forgotten how disturbed things could become.

"I understand, I will not try to strike you down," he said simply, indicating his compliance with open palms. "I will see you."

The rain slowed. Each droplet tumbled languidly through the air, as if gravity had eased its pull. Zarost knew that was not the case— Ametheus was stretching Time. The fires burned too slowly, swaying instead of flickering. Zarost caught a glimpse of a figure standing in front of the flames, a fleeting shadow, but it was gone. Time slowed further. The figure reappeared, pale metallic clothes shimmering for a fleeting moment.

The instant passed. There was nothing again.

The raindrops hovered in the air, silver jewels hanging on an invisible web.

In the slowed space, nothing seemed to move, but Zarost was aware of time crawling forward. The figure reappeared, blocking the flames, and as Time halted, so the Sorcerer remained. Zarost understood why he hadn't seen him before. He had been looking too *fast*. Ametheus was only partially present in Zarost's world, one fraction of an instant in many. He was cycling from one broken world to another, keeping himself in all of them, and in none.

He was as heavy-set as ever, broad-shouldered, clad in a fraying cloth shirt with a great tooth-studded belt. His trousers were woven thickly to appear as chainmail, or perhaps it was chainmail which he had tried to change to silk. His boots were made from a strong glistening skin, but they were already split at the toes. His red mantle was torn in places. Only his oval headpiece was undamaged, hammered as it was out of bronze. It framed a countenance both handsome and cruel—Seus, the most reckless aspect of Ametheus.

"Well, brother Seus, what do you have to trade?" Zarost asked by way of greeting.

Ametheus smiled. His teeth were white and sharp. "Apart f-from the lives of your f-f-fellows? I have a r-r-riddle...for you." The Sorcerer's stuttered words were distorted by an uneven rhythm, something to do with the warped time. "I t-take a th-thing apart, and k-k-keep all the pieces, yet w-when I put them together again there is always s-s-something missing. What is it?"

Twardy Zarost considered the riddle for a moment. "Anything which lives," he replied.

"V-very good, Riddler. Now tell me, w-why is that so?"

"Life is not like Matter, it is indivisible. It can only inhabit things which are whole. You cannot dismantle them."

"Yet we can c-cut off your hand, and y-you will still b-be just as alive."

"True, but you cannot cut off my head."

Ametheus looked at Zarost speculatively. "S-so your head holds m-m-more life than your hand?"

"Some things are vital to life, others are not."

"W-we shall change that."

"It is impossible to change such rules of life."

"Hah! W-wizard! Always denying, limiting, p-prohibiting! What if what you s-see is only one k-k-kind of Life, the k-kind which has been imposed upon this universe? I have the m-means to break the rules. Life is about to change and a new God shall have dominion."

"Who might that be?" asked Zarost, not really wanting to hear the answer. What horror did Ametheus reach for?

"C-count yourself lucky that you w-will be dead before he w-walks Oldenworld."

"You speak of the Destroyer?" It was as bad as Zarost feared. Ethea had been trapped to raise an even more fundamental God. He had to convince Ametheus that he was wrong. "You believe he will stand beside you? You are wrong. He can never have dominion here. He is a Principle, separated from this plane, with no bridge to cross the divide."

Ametheus chuckled. "We shall see. We shall see." His eyes wobbled slightly from side to side, a barely perceptible movement which made Zarost want to look more intently at him—blue eyes, the colour of the sky in spring; beautiful bright eyes. No. He would not allow the Sorcerer to hypnotise him. Madness lay on the far side of those eyes—a mind ruled by Chaos, a place of warped dreams and living nightmares. He shifted his gaze to the Sorcerer's chest.

"What do you need from me?" Zarost asked.

"I n-need nothing from you, w-wizard!"

"You would not be trying to enchant me now if that were true."

Ametheus bellowed with laughter. "H-how do you think it is possible for me to m-m-manipulate the world this way? You...are already enchanted. You believe you live *now*, but there is no *now*, no present moment, only before and after. We experience a subset of those times."

Beyond the edges of the space in which they stood, five shards of altered reality tilted at awkward angles, running from the flames into the surrounding blackness. Six wizards trapped in mirror-glass. Time had halted. What he saw was impossible, but if he was already enchanted, then Ametheus had control of his mind, and that was too terrible to believe. The Sorcerer was feeding on Zarost's doubts. Zarost found himself focused on the Sorcerer's blue eyes again. He looked away. "Your power has grown," Zarost muttered.

"And y-you have grown weak-minded," Ametheus replied. "Your friends d-d-defend themselves better than y-you do. You are lucky that I am f-feeling generous. I shall g-grant you a dying man's w-wish. If you could save only one of the w-wizards, who w-would it be?"

The Senior? The Lorewarden? Zarost himself? It was too late for the one who really mattered. Ametheus had taken too much already.

"That choice is no choice at all," he replied. "How can I choose one wizard over another? Either we all go free, or none of us do."

"What if it c-could be Syonya?" The world hissed with the static hunger of Chaos. "Yes, I know about S-s-syonya, Riddler. A...f-f-friend...told me about your dead s-sister. I have a p-p-piece of time in my c-collectibles that would be v-vvery interesting to you, I th-think. The t-t-time of the election of the second coterie of Kaskanzr."

Ametheus knew too much. If Zarost could just go back in time to before his sister Syonya was murdered... That was a dream he had tormented himself with forever. He had first studied in the college purely to gain that skill, but discovered to his dismay that shifting time backward would be utter Chaos. How had the Warlock discovered his secret? Zarost was certain Ametheus hadn't discovered such a personal *get* on his own. He never took the time to study his enemies, but the Warlock was a different matter altogether.

"I c-can't g-grant life, but I c-c-can turn back t-time."

The temptation was terrible. Zarost was trapped in indecision. If Tabitha Serannon had already died then Syonya was the only Lifesinger he could use. Her time was past, but he might have a better chance playing the fates of that time again. He hadn't done very well with *this* time, not very well at all. If he could go back, before Syonya's death, he could have her sing the song differently. Maybe he could save her. Just maybe.

The uncertainty made his toes crawl in the sides of his boots. What if Tabitha had escaped the Sanctuary? He didn't know enough to risk everything. He couldn't embrace Chaos the way his adversary could.

Ametheus snarled. "You f-fool, you throw away your last chance. You see, that is the problem with Order. You always try to think for others. You should concern yourself with yourself. You should have p-pleaded for your own life, I might have s-set you free. See how your stupid p-principles work against you? I may return, once I have s-spoken to your friends. If you are still alive, you may wish to b-b-beg for mercy."

Time turned on fraction of a second forward, and the Sorcerer was gone.

The Lorewarden and the Cosmologer were visible in the nearest shards, where they battled manifestations of Chaos. As Zarost watched, the ends of their jagged slivers of reality shattered into flakes which spun away into the black surrounding mist.

Suddenly the Spiritist was torn in two. The Spiritist, her soft hands thrown up to shield her face, a matronly face, one he'd gown to love over the centuries, painfully innocent in her final moment, her pale eyes wide, her mouth a silent 'o'.

Then the Senior went down.

Zarost couldn't watch. The Sorcerer was taking the Gyre to pieces. The Senior had been the head of the Gyre, the Spiritist had been its soul and, just like that, their precious heritage of lore was gone. Gone the library, gone the Reliceum; gone the prized examples of Oldenworld technology the Gyre had preserved in the sanctuary. All that the Gyre had valued from the time of Order lay in ashes. Order itself was being broken by the brutal fist of Ametheus.

Zarost's hope slipped away.

Was this really the end? Would all the centuries of learning and lore end as useless grey dust?

What of the song? Would it ever be sung again?

The offer to return to the time of Syonya was so very tempting. He could play the fates in another pattern and beat the Backcaster, but if there was one thing he *had* learnt from his years of studying the cards, it was that he couldn't win with a hand chosen for him by his adversary. He had to play the cards he had. His hand seemed empty. What was he missing?

Laklødder skran ôzak dehrer nihil bloşnihil.

35. A MOMENT OF LIFE

"A cluster of days to call your own
is just a whorl in the giant wind."—Zarost

A concert played upon a thousand instruments would have sounded poorly beside the depths of the Lifesong Tabitha experienced. The harmony rose to resonant crescendos then dropped to faint whispers, elusive and yet all around her. Each voice followed its own thread of music, and yet it was part of the whole, linked to the Goddess at the Lifesong's heart. Moving through the song toward Ethea was like being transported along the fibres of a great tapestry, in the way that a dropped stitch might undo itself all the way to the origin. Tabitha felt as if she was moving, but she wasn't made of anything. She was just a pattern in consciousness.

She was a great mountain, white-crested, immense, thrusting a sharp and perfect outline against the sky. She was a flower opening to the sun. She was a field of flowers, yellow-faced, dancing above a dry land, wanting to live. She had been in the rains that had come before; she was in the rains that would come after. She was an oryx that fought another over its mate, battling on a high slope of rock, life pounding in her veins. She was a lone tree, many arms outstretched, waiting for the delicate touch of pollen from a far and distant other. She was a forest slumbering upon the hills, her feet wet with the decay of growth. She slithered through the leaves, searching for life, and yet she was life, searching, in a million ways, along a million threads. She was carried on the river over great falls and through the lands beyond, she flashed as fish in its depths, and slipped over chuckling rocks, slowing elsewhere on the sucking mud, where an army of worms wriggled through the slime, labouring upward, yearning, striving, to become food for the long-legged storks wading eagerly in the shallows. She was the joy of uncountable births; she was the agony of all their deaths.

She was the end of a beautiful day, and the dark beginning.

Every event could be seen as a sound and as she moved at the right pace, from place to place, from face to face, from bright acts of anger to pale perfected grace, she could suddenly appreciate the rhythm and harmonic resonance of life. It formed a single song: the Lifesong. She lived, she lived everywhere; she lived in all things. She lived because she could live, because there was nothing, besides living. Life was everything, life was all. She sang and, as she sang, she formed new patterns in consciousness.

She was many people, she was a few. She was a boy, breathless, running from danger. She stood in a forest, a spear in her hand and blood at her feet. She rowed a boat in haste, strength flooding her arms. She lay beside a great green creature and felt its hot breath. She laughed at a lover, she scolded a foe. She touched too many lives to comprehend. She gathered it all up and sang a bright melody into a crisp dawn, a little song that was ever-changing, and yet always expressing the secret. And she flew from a branch into an open sky. She flew. She flew.

Tabitha passed beyond the world into the seas of emotion below, so tangible within the music they were colours—a pale and pearly compassion, an aching indigo love, a faint and purpled sadness. Deeper and deeper she went, toward the source of all the songs. She knew a vast melancholy, she knew a great and overwhelming sorrow; she knew loss, dark and intense. Heaviness gathered around her soul and she was besieged by the deepest despair.

The Goddess: her misery like black fire, an assault of raw emotion, an agony to endure in the spirit world. Tabitha fled from the terror. She tumbled from the abstraction of entrancement to the steady forms of the physical. Tabitha found her own body, waiting for her where she'd sent it with the Reference spell. She remembered the familiar comfort of flesh. She had got her life out of order and back into order again as chaos and impossibility had whipped at her heels. Incredibly, she had soul-travelled upon the music and survived the transition. Tabitha gasped as a new assault of sensations rushed at her.

It was dark. The heat was intense, the air clammy. A moaning, wailing, keening, chittering sound filled the air. Beneath her feet the earth shivered with churning, clashing, bashing impacts. Spiralling corkscrews of force rushed hither and thither across her vision, faster and faster, brighter and brighter against a leaden sky. Her lens detected wrongness, dissonance, disorder, pushing against her in a nauseating wave of warnings.

Tabitha was overwhelmed—she wasn't ready to see the Pillar yet. She couldn't face seeing the Goddess. She had reached Turmodin but she had to find some calm place within herself or she would go mad.

Tabitha breathed in slowly. The air smelled of wet ash. The hot wind threw her hair awry.

> *three brothers, 'midst fire and smoke and blight,*
> *all of Oldenworld scoured by their dreadful sight*
> *the sky bleeds with wildfire seeds and beasts unholy roar*
> *until the Pillar in the lowlands claims life evermore*

The wry prophet of the Revelations had known what it would be like. She could hear the cries of the beasts amid the distant horns and clash of metal. Unholy beasts—if they saw her, they would fall upon her, rend her with their teeth and tear her limb from limb.

Calm yourself! Find the silence between the sounds.

No silence existed in Turmodin, no pause in the ruckus—it went on and on, an ever-changing cacophony. Tabitha felt her will crumbling under the assault. What hope did she have of resisting the Chaos, if the Goddess couldn't fight it? The wizards of the Gyre had warned her that she wouldn't be able to cope with it. She hadn't believed them because she had had no idea of how distressing the collected Chaos could be. She felt it now, all around her—the Chaos—trying to get in, trying to tear her apart. Her own body felt wrong. The space around her felt warped.

The pace of the discordant sounds gathered speed and the earth shook to a frantic rhythm.

Tabitha needed something true and constant to hold onto. She tried humming a single note. The disruptions seemed to settle, but as she allowed her note to fade, Tabitha realised someone was singing softly nearby—softly, oh so softly, as if she didn't want anyone else to hear her. Tabitha knew at once who it was. She was ready to see, at last, as ready as she'd ever be.

The sun was rising into a red sky. It had been a dark night when Tabitha had closed her eyes; a moment that was a lifetime ago. She blinked. The Goddess was revealed in profile, outlined against the sudden brightness of dawn, trapped against the rock wall with her body entombed in water. Only her head and her shackled hands protruded from the pool. The foul waters had risen that far. The tips of her wings, which extended beyond her shackled wrists, were plastered to the cliff face at her back. Birds circled the pool, swooping low past Ethea's head with forlorn cries. A few white-stained boulders stood poised at odd angles around the rim like old teeth. Overhead, a ribbon of pink cloud turned in the air like a serpent; the slow eddy of a disturbance passed.

Ethea trembled as she stared vacantly across the rising sun, blinded by the light, uncaring.

"Goddess!" Tabitha cried out. She tried to run toward Ethea but fell at once. Black mud clung to her feet, gripping her knees and hands as well. Something like an eye opened beside her, a saucer-shaped watery orb within the muck. Tabitha yelped and pushed herself away.

The mud resisted.

No, this is not happening, Tabitha thought. Mud does not try to trap people.

Her feet came free with a loud suck. The eyehole closed over.

"Goddess! I have come!" Tabitha called out as she struggled closer to Ethea.

She had underestimated the scale of things before her. She was some distance from the pool. Ethea was larger than she had thought. Her feathered crest, the only part of her that extended above the rim of the pit, would be at least twice Tabitha's height. The scoured earth was flooded in front of Ethea, so Tabitha veered toward the higher ground.

"...dess! God! I have come!" came her own voice like a slap in her face, a mocking echo. "Come I! Have come! I ha-ve!" it continued, never really fading, overlapping, destroying itself into a lingering yabber-yammer of disconcerting broken syllables.

It was already warm, despite the low angle of the sun. It would be hotter than a furnace by midday, Tabitha guessed, as hot as a baking house. A surge of warmth passed her by and the ground cracked underfoot. Steam rose around her legs. What had been mud a moment earlier had become a brittle crust of black glass. She took a step forward and the crust splintered again. Tabitha had just *thought* of heat and the ground had cracked with it, as if her thoughts had some strange power in this place. It couldn't be true, but she guided her thoughts toward a cooling earth, a *solid* earth, just in case. Was she losing her sense of reason? She hurried toward Ethea. Tabitha couldn't trust the altered skin of rock to hold her weight, but there were lumps within it, boulder-sized crystallised knots. She jumped from clump to clump. Some of the edges looked sharp—sharp enough to cut, and she was grateful for the Lûk boots she wore.

Tabitha had almost reached the crest of the cliff when a figure loomed out of the fire-coloured mists at the edge of the pool. He faced her across the water, a great blocky beast of a man, larger even than Ethea. Tabitha slowed, her heart pounding. Was it the Sorcerer? She had hoped she could remain hidden from him. If he *was* there, in the mists beyond the pool, then she didn't have much of a chance, but it wasn't how she remembered him from the Revelations. The figure stood unmoving, but his outline shifted and writhed as the sun's rays filtered past him. His great shadow fell upon her for a moment then the orange mist hid him again.

She stood dead still, watching the mists, but the figure did not reappear. Could it have been a shadow in the mists? Her vision was disturbed by the lens—so many warnings flashed across her right eye she was almost blinded. How much of what she saw was real, how much imagined? Her *ogle-i* seemed to be suggesting that there were many people in the mists and not just a single figure. The scribed images were confusing, clustered, conflicting. Things near Turmodin could obviously not be represented very well in terms of Order.

She crept to the edge of the cliff and looked down, her heart still thundering in her breast. Ethea, the source of life, was close enough to touch. She was wrapped in filaments of power, shimmering with delicate colours. Millions of life-threads terminated in Ethea. The vital currents became enhanced by Tabitha's lens as she focused upon them. It was like looking at the centre of a song, a vast and timeless song, a sad song—a heartbroken song.

"Goddess!" she whispered. "I am here." The ruckus of lingering sounds drowned out her announcement. She tried again in a louder voice. "Goddess! I have come, as you asked." Ethea twisted her head to look up at Tabitha, her feathered crest dragging on the rock. Her great green eyes were dull, her falcon-face drawn and her smooth lips blue-tinged—fatigued, weak and helpless, a principle of life trapped in fleshly form. "My singer? Is that you? *O-ay-o-ray.*" Her voice was like a breeze upon broken wind-chimes.

"Oh Ethea! What can I do? How can I release you?"

Her indrawn breath caused a small gale. "If I knew that, little sister, I would have escaped, escaped this plane." Her exhalation rumbled. "Her voice, only a whisper, rolled like distant summer thunder. "Everything is so *heavy*. The thing that binds my limbs is called iron, it is stronger than my body and if I try to pull my limbs free, the flesh breaks. This is distressing, so distressing. And I have cravings, cravings I do not understand. I wish to consume things, *eat* things. Why is that? I am the Goddess. I do not eat, I sing! They feed me when the sun is high, and after I have eaten I feel stronger for a little while. *Oh-ay-to-day*. The strength always fades, it fades and passes away and the craving returns." She looked away from Tabitha. "Everything here is so *temporary*. Especially *me*! I know that the liquid which rises and rises at my throat is thicker than the substance which I breathe. I will come to an end here, unless, unless... I perform for him. But I cannot. *No-no-no-nay*." She looked down into the ruddy water. "I cannot!" she whispered. "Yet I must, to save myself. Oh, how can he make me choose such a thing?"

Tabitha tried not to look at the pool, the dirty slick polluted with the corpses of birds that touched Ethea's neck. "What does the Sorcerer want from you?"

"I must sing, sing a life into existence, sing the bridge for a terrible one. Only I have the power to summon Him. He is Apocalypse. He is the Destroyer." She shuddered then looked away.

"When I sing the Ending, I pass all of Creation to Him, to break it, to reduce it, reduce it to Nothingness. When a full cycle of life is done, a new song must begin, and the old must perish, this is what happens during the Ending. Everything is destroyed so that everything can be created anew. I sing Life into the new universe that the Creator produces, as I call upon the Destroyer to break the old one down."

Ethea looked down at her again. "This is how it has been for all time. This is how it must always be. Life continues, *moving* from cycle to cycle. What the three brothers want me to do will disrupt this order, disrupt it forever. Don't you see? There would be nothing that the Creator could make which Apocalypse could not instantly destroy. He will never again need to wait until the time of Ending to begin his work, for he will be *here*, in this plane, on this side of the bridge, waiting. I see it now, the horror and the ruin. It will be worse than this place of Chaos, far worse. Worlds shall be pulverised in His fists, blood shall run out between His fingers like an ocean tide, until there is nothing, nothing left to infuse with Life...except for Him."

Tears trickled from her great hooded eyes. "Oh, it is a horror! He will not break me—he will release me first, as they have promised, so that I can fill things with Life only to appease his insatiable hunger. He will do it so he can draw on my power. I cannot deny my song, even if it was only Him. I must sing or Life ends and I cannot finish it with *Him* in this plane. Oh it is wrong, it is wrong! Then, when all is broken here, and He has gathered all there is to gather, He shall stride across the bridge and face the Creator. There will be a war between them as there has never been. I might remain. I cannot tell. It is a mystery to me. It might herald the End of all Ends, the ultimate triumph for Apocalypse."

She looked off into the mists. "That is what will happen if I sing life into the effigy. Yet if I do not sing such a song, I will die here in this pool. The Lifesong will be interrupted. This universe shall be the last cycle of Creation with life in it, with only fading echoes of my song as its theme. Who knows how long life will continue in such a world? And it will be the very last world with life. Oh, it will be so empty, after all!" She raised her voice to the sky, and sang a slow lament.

No sun—no moon!
No morn—no noon—
No death—no dust—
No love—no lust.
No life—no leaf—
No joy—no grief—
No song—no sound—
No glimmer to be found.

Ethea's sorrow overwhelmed Tabitha. "I cannot escape by singing," Ethea added. "I have tried, the music goes awry. I am limited to this place. I need to span all time and space to wield my power. I must be free, but I don't know how to reverse the change, to return from this heavy flesh to the music, from now to eternity. I have fallen too far. Oh, I have fallen."

Tabitha wondered what would happen if she dispersed the great avian form using the second stanza of the Lifesong. Would anything be left of the Goddess? Dealing with Ethea was complicated. She was so otherworldly. She tried to think through the problem slowly. The Sorcerer had captured Ethea's soul and *changed* it to flesh, drawn her down into the world. She knew that her own soul and body could be separated, but did the same apply to a Goddess? She was God-kind, she didn't ordinarily have a body and had only the one eternal presence. That presence was now contained by the great spell that had been wrought upon her. If Tabitha sang the second stanza upon her, would she destroy the source of the Lifesong instead of just the body holding her captive?

"Can I sing something to release you, if you taught it to me?" Tabitha asked.

"Our songs do not work here. The sound of this place disrupts everything. The only one who can influence the prison woven around me is the Sorcerer, and he will only do so if I bring the Destroyer to him. I must call to Apocalypse, I must grant Him life, and then the one I summon will grant me freedom."

Apocalypse. His name alone sounded terrible enough—the destroyer of worlds.

"But will the Destroyer not simply kill you once He is here? Won't he destroy everything?"

"He will covet the life He has been granted. He has raged against His isolation from the Universe forever. He has tried to enter this plane before. His survival here will depend on my song flooding through His veins. For Him to live in this world, He needs me to be in my power."

Tabitha was puzzled. "If the Sorcerer could bring you from the plane of the Gods into this world, why doesn't he summon the Destroyer himself? Why does he need to torture you?"

"The Destroyer is a Prime. He exists beyond the confines of the Universe. He is like the Creator. The Sorcerer could never reach that far into the higher dimensions on his own, but through me, the demi-urge, he can."

"And yet if you die from his tortures, he loses his chance?"

"The Sorcerer is a—complexity. It is as if part of him doesn't want to succeed, and that part fights against the others."

The ground trembled. One of the boulders poised beside Tabitha above the pool, was dislodged by the tremor. It slid down amid an avalanche of stones and plunged into the pool. The sickening impact threw a wave toward Ethea and, for a terrible moment, the Goddess was submerged. When she emerged again, her eyes were wide. She spat out a mouthful of bloody water then coughed and coughed.

"Not like this," she pleaded softly. "*Ae-oh-fa-ray-oh.* Not like this. I don't want to end, in this plane. I must call to the Sorcerer. I must call to him and perform his ritual!"

Tabitha began to sing and gather essence. She didn't care if she drew wildfire upon herself—she couldn't watch the Goddess drowning, or witness her abandoning hope and acceding to the Sorcerer's request. She would alter the water—she would turn it to air, or break out the walls of the pool—anything to divert the danger away from the

Goddess.

"No!" Ethea cried out. "You will give yourself away! He will sense that you are here, and then he will come to kill you!"

Tabitha stopped. "But Ethea, what else can I do?"

"You cannot save me. This I understand now, the Chaos will not allow it. My only hope rests in the Sorcerer. Only he can grant me freedom. I wanted you to come to me because I need you to learn a verse, the most powerful stanza of them all. It is a great burden I will ask of you, a task beyond your duty."

"I will do it! Anything! I will sing it for you!"

"Oh my singer, you are so young, you are such a beautiful bird. Maybe it is best that it ends on such a note." She looked away. "The Sorcerer has promised that he will release me if I bring the Destroyer into your world, but what if he doesn't? What if the Destroyer doesn't allow him to? I will be trapped here, out of my power. There will be only one way to right such a terrible wrong." She turned back to face Tabitha, her green eyes burning. "You must close the cycle of Life by singing the Ending."

"The Ending?"

"It will be the End of everything. It will threaten the Destroyer with his own end, and he will flee from this plane to take his proper position in the cycle."

"But why? Why won't you let me free you instead! I can change things, Ethea, I can sing away your bonds."

She shook her head. "Your song won't work here, it will go horribly awry. You must go elsewhere to work it. Besides, it proves nothing to unshackle me, to free me here. I am still trapped in this body. What should I do? Walk the earth in this form? This body is falseness! I am a principle, I am eternal. I should not be here. If the Sorcerer fails to return me to my plane, if I *die* here and the Destroyer is present in this world, then you must end it."

"Why can't *you* sing the Ending now?" Tabitha asked.

"I am separated from my power here. You have more power than I do in this plane. You have learnt how to reach beyond it."

That was a surprise for Tabitha to hear. She didn't know what to say. As she felt Ethea's grief, rain fell upon them, warm rain, like the tears of the world, washing their pain into the rising pool. She sat beside the Goddess, a small figure in a wet dress, and she sensed the faint sad melody of time fading, and everything, everything, coming to an end.

"What will happen to me if I sing the Ending?"

"I have never passed the Ending to another, so I do not know, but the Lifesong will endure. There will be another Cycle."

"But what will happen to me?"

"I imagine that you will become a Goddess."

Tabitha was stunned. The Goddess was sacrificing herself and expecting *her* to replace her?

"The Ending drains the entire Universe of life," explained Ethea. "When you sing it, you will gather all that power and own it, ready to infuse the next Creation. You will take my place. You will keep Life and the Destroyer will have to flee and break what is left. It is what he does. This world, this Universe will be gone, and you will sing your own Beginning, in the new Universe made by the Creator."

Ethea was expecting her to become a Goddess?

"How will I know what to do? I need you, Ethea… I have only just begun to sing the Lifesong. How shall I know all the things I will need to know, without you there to guide me? I'm a singer, not a Goddess."

"You will learn from yourself, as I learnt, when I was young."

Tabitha looked away. How could she admit to Ethea that she was not up to the task?

"Oh, little sister, I should not be asking you this," Ethea declared from below. "Would you really be able to sing the death of all those whom you love? Think hard upon it. This world shall cease. Everything you know shall be gone, but it is the only way to save them from Apocalypse and, because of what the Sorcerer has done, I have no choice but to ask you."

"I-I could do it, if I had to," Tabitha declared bravely. She knew at once that she had spoken too soon. *Does she really mean the Ending? The life recalled from all living creatures? I'd have to kill Garyll! And Mulrano. And Twardy Zarost. All the wizards. Everyone in Eyri too; everyone, gone, in a wild climax of the Lifesong. And then?*

It seemed too extreme. It was a Goddess's solution, one of ultimate sacrifice and rebirth. Tabitha tried to think on more human scale. What could she do to change things? Could she stop the Sorcerer from completing his mad plan? Better still, could she convince him to change his mind? She knew so little about Ametheus and his ways. She wished she had someone experienced with her, like Twardy Zarost.

"You said part of the Sorcerer doesn't want to succeed. Is there a chance to talk him out of summoning Apocalypse?"

"Oh my singer, I doubt it. The brothers have already made the effigy and peopled it."

"The effigy? What is that?"

"Wait for the mists to part. You will see the scale of the madness."

The mists did recede then as a gust dragged them away toward the sun, and the looming figure Tabitha had seen before emerged, clearer than before. It was much farther away than she had thought. A thick-hewed figure, ominous, huge: it seemed to be a great structure of interwoven branches, a colossus of straw and wood. A crude face watched her, a great black mask with an open mouth. It was not the Sorcerer after all. It was not to be feared, she realised with relief. It was just a statue.

But, as the light shifted, Tabitha saw the legs that dangled from within the structure, the arms which waved like hairs, the hands which clutched the framework, the faces pressed up against the bars. The moaning, wailing and mournful cries she had heard since her arrival found a focus. They had not been made by any kind of beasts, but by the occupants of the effigy.

"But there are people in there!" Tabitha exclaimed.

"Yes, that is a Wicker Man," Ethea replied. "The sacrifice to make the flesh of a God. The Destroyer will stand taller than the greatest tree. There are hundreds of priests in there. They called me with their ceremony. I came to answer their call. That was when the brothers cast their spells upon me and tore me from my place. Those priests served the Sorcerer first and now they will be sacrificed, to form the flesh of the Destroyer. They believe it to be an honour, as do the children they have convinced to join them. The others...are captives."

Tabitha just stared at the structure of imprisoned people. How many days had they been trapped in there? What madness was this?

"Apocalypse shall be born of blood and flame," said Ethea quietly.

She fought to keep her gorge down. They were to be burnt alive? The Sorcerer was truly insane.

"How did they make you, Ethea?"

Ethea choked on her reply. She looked at Tabitha in pleading and terror, like a trapped thing sinking in mud, like a murderer drowning in grief.

"Ethea?"

Great tears ran on the Goddess' cheeks.

"Oh my life! Ethea, no! How did they make *you*?"

She understood Ethea's despair and it became her own. The rain came harder for a time, stinging her face, driven by the incessant winds that drove distant things around and around in the air, clanking and tinkling, as if everything was whirling in a circle around the twisted heart of the Sorcerer's domain.

"Teach me the Ending," she said.

In case I fail to release Ethea. In case I fail to stop Ametheus. In case those people burn and Ethea is forced to call the Destroyer and witness the devastation He brings. It would not be worth living in a world ruled by such a God. She had to learn how to end it.

Ethea sang a soft and complicated melody, a bittersweet madrigal, one that reached to the depths of Tabitha's soul.

All creatures in this world and Time,
be they hidden from our sight,
all motions in all earths and oceans;
gathered by this might.
All creatures of the air will fall!
All beasts and beauty slain!
The strings of Life shall be made still,
only silence shall remain.
The strings of Life shall be so still,
until a Singer sings again.

The enormity of the stanza weighed upon her. She sensed there was a great depth to it, a dimension beneath the words that would become accessible to her when she sang it. She knew its result would be final. The death it caused would be universal. It would be almost as much of a disaster as having the Destroyer loose in the world. There had to be another way.

"Where do I find the Sorcerer?" she asked Ethea.

"He comes, he goes. You will hear him when he approaches, he brings his terrible minstrels. He usually comes from behind me, from his tower."

Tabitha rose from her position on the lip overlooking the pool. There was so much tension in the air, so much lethal energy waiting to be released. It pressed upon her from all sides, the imminent Chaos, waiting to obliterate her. There was only one way to save Ethea. She had to convince Ametheus to change his mind.

"Hold on, my Goddess, hold on! I have an idea."

"Are you thinking to confront him? No! You must escape! You must go back the way you came, now I have shown you the song and made you understand. If you are killed, who shall sing the Ending? Who shall begin the next cycle?"

"If I can reason with him, I might not have to sing the Ending at all."

"Little sister, you can see his madness! It surrounds you."

"And maybe he doesn't want it to be like this. Maybe he wishes it was otherwise. You said yourself that part of him fights against this."

Ethea paused for thought. "But he *must* like it like this. Why else would he have made it so?"

"Why else would he be summoning the Destroyer? Why else would he want it to end?"

Ethea was silent.

"Maybe I could offer him an alternative, a kind of peace," said Tabitha. "A kind of healing."

"You risk many things if you approach him now," warned Ethea.

"I would put more at risk if I did not."

She would talk to him, she decided, and if he was too mad to listen she would call out his name and escape. *Say his name once, and you call on all three, and being conflicted he cannot get free.* It was a slim chance of safety but at least she had something to use in her defence. Tabitha would approach him and if he attacked her, she would call his name and flee with her song-spell, somewhere; anywhere.

She turned and she saw a thousand faces, watching her. She had noticed some of the figures before, scattered around the pool, but they had crept closer while she had been talking to Ethea, and many more had joined them, standing on the slope, jostling in clusters on the hillocks, climbing on each other. They were frightening in their diversity: faces with shocking eyes, faces with lopsided snarls, with slick dark skin or too much hair, faces red with rot, faces with too many teeth. Skin that looked like scales, figures with fists like clubs, tall creatures with sticklike legs that stood swaying in the crowd like windblown trees—blunt things that should be animals but for the intelligence in their eyes.

"*Ulaäan ma maar!*" shouted a man with a red-tinged helmet, the kind she had seen before on the sacrificers. A piper blew a jarring blast on his horn. The wind whipped it away. "*Ulaäan ma maar!*"

The crowd went wild, shouting, barking, clashing metal against metal, metal against flesh, hitting, slapping and throwing things into the air and at each other. *Yop yip yee* they shouted, and there was something that went *boomghara*, frightening in its brutality.

Then they fell to the ground. The sacrificer led; another five red-helmeted figures fell in random places in the crowd. Then all of them did it, falling with arms spread, onto their faces, onto the rocks, onto the others who had fallen before them. Then they picked themselves up and did it again.

"*Ulaäan ma maar!*" shouted the sacrificer triumphantly.

A pit opened in her stomach. It was as if they recognised her, somehow, they recognised her, as if she had been expected. They were worshipping her, and it wasn't the worship that was shocking. It was that they had known she would come. Someone had prepared them for this moment.

Ametheus! She had to get to Ametheus.

She took a step and the creatures backed away, as if there was a holy circle they feared to enter.

The sky was moving in a circling storm, swirling over the heads of the multitude. Broken bits clanked and tinkled past in the air. Whirling air currents roamed across the ground, lifting dust, scraps and flocks of tumbling birds.

A great building rose against the sky to the west, a lopsided veined tower with tendon-like protrusions of brine-coated metal that splayed outward through the piles of debris massed around its base. It was built on the shore of a great restless body of water, which threw tall green waves of scum against the litter-choked groynes. A harsh and salty tang filled the warm air. Every time a wave fell upon that broken shore, the strange clang and crash of metal and glass sounded—a regular discordant cacophony.

There seemed to be no end to the water—the blue-green horizon was unbroken. The foaming waves were huge things, a hundred times bigger than the waves Tabitha had ever seen on the shores of the Amberlake in Eyri. They made a thump that shook the earth then they hissed as they drew back upon themselves.

The tower's many spires and levels were completely off-balanced, stacked atop one another with no guiding geometry. It should have collapsed upon itself, yet the rust-streaked walls rose beyond the base of the low driving clouds. The many odd-sized windows which studded the walls reminded Tabitha of a spider's hungry eyes. She clenched her stomach against her fear.

The Pillar. Ametheus should be there, probably at the top. She had seen him there when she'd travelled with Zarost through infinity and he'd tried to draw her down. She'd seen him there in the vision in the Revelations. His chamber was nestled in the clouds.

Light shifted overhead. Tight balls of lightning seared the air and where the charge struck ground beyond the Pillar, it bloomed silver and rippled like boiling liquid. The wizards had warned her. She was not ready to face the Sorcerer, but she had no choice. Tabitha ran toward the Pillar.

Heaven help me let the earth be made to run upon; let the Pillar remain standing while I am within it. Let the crowd part and leave me untouched.

The ground crunched underfoot. Jewels! Obsidian pebbles, jade nuggets and blue tumblestones lay in a thick channel like a solidified river. Rubies, moonstones and garnets were strewn over the underlying rock. A purple boulder as tall as her shoulder could have been amethyst, a glittering column sapphire. The crowds thinned as she progressed. The figures became more hunched, misshapen—miserable. They noticed her less, reacted less, until they stood, staring, like clenched threats carved from the rock.

She concentrated on finding a way into the Pillar. A narrow ridge angled steeply upward, entering the Pillar via a fissure which might have been formed by a collapse. She followed the ridge and was soon high above the ground. Below she could see Ethea, trapped in her pool, and the waiting Wicker Man beyond.

Ahead, the Pillar reared to the sky, dark and stained, tilting its many eyes toward her.

36. THE RULER OF THE REVERIE

"A man awoke in a place he had dreamed,
and learnt that his life was not what it seemed."—Zarost

The wind whistled through the teeth of the high mountains outside. Ashley Logán jerked awake. He had dozed off on the stone floor of the lair. An odd smell hung in the air, sweet, warm and tasty. The cave looked smaller and the ground farther away than it should be. A small leathery figure was curled up against the wall, a figure containing a soft glowing coal of life. A compulsion swelled through his vast stomach—he was ravenous. The little creature before him would make a small morsel, but it was better than nothing. He took a step forward and covered a greater distance than he would have expected. It puzzled him, so he looked down at his feet. They were green and covered with scales.

All at once, Ashley knew who the little figure was against the wall, and who was approaching him with dreadful steps. In his sleep, he had drifted deeply into *her* thoughts. And somehow he had crawled from his sheltered cubicle, into the main cavern. To get warmer?

"Stop!" he pleaded. "Stop, Sassraline, it's me! Don't eat me! Oh great and beautiful dragon, your glistening scales will not protect you, you cannot eat that morsel, it is made of poison."

She eyed the glowing figure against the wall, but did not step any closer.

AAH, SWEET TALKER, I HEAR YOU LOUD, I REMEMBER YOU, BUT YOU HAVE CEASED, CEASED TO PRAISE ME. DO I PALE, PALE IN YOUR EYES, HAVE YOU RECONSIDERED MY BEAUTY?

"No, great Sassraline, you are gorgeous—a feast for the eyes." He remembered now, he had been exhausted by hours of praise and yet still she had demanded more, to be appeased. He had worshipped her until he couldn't any more. "I must sleep, great Sassraline. I must rest."

NO EXCUSE FOR NOT PRAISING ME. CAN YOU NOT SPEAK, SPEAK WHEN YOU REST?

"Speak? When I sleep, I must be still. I close my eyes and I can not see your beautiful body to describe it."

WHY DO YOU NEED TO CLOSE BOTH EYES WHEN YOU REST?

"How can I do otherwise?"

Sassraline tossed her great head. Ashley's view swirled then grew clear once more.

YOUR KIND IS STRANGE. WHEN YOU REST YOU MUST LOSE YOUR VIEW OF THE WORLD? HOW DO YOU PROTECT YOURSELF?

"We don't protect ourselves, we—dream."

Sassraline tossed her head again.

DREAM? WHERE IS THAT?

"It is seeing pictures and hearing sounds. Imaginings. When we wake up, we forget what we were seeing. This world takes over and the other vision is gone."

Sassraline considered this for a long dragon moment.

HOW DO YOU KNOW WHEN YOU ARE AWAKE, AND WHEN YOU ARE DREAMING?

Ashley paused. How *did* one know?

"The real world always begins again where you left off. You wake up where you lay down. Dreams just begin anywhere and end off suddenly as well. Strange things happen in dreams, things you can't explain. The real world is ordered." But as soon as he'd said that, he realised it was no definition at all. He was talking to a dragon, a creature so vast, mighty and utterly alien it confounded his logic, yet he knew she was real. He was somewhere inside her head, using his talent to communicate with her. It was probably the strangest moment of his life, and there was no way he could explain it. Ever since they had crossed the border of Eyri, the world had been one long weird tale—the wastes, his transformation of horse, the ironpig, the dragon. His days had little order. A queer uneasiness crept up his back.

"Dreams change quickly," he asserted. "Ordinary things look different in dreams." His view was still the strangely altered vision of Sassraline. He saw himself as a warm glow curled up against the boulders.

He reached out, in thought, for his own body. He opened his eyes and looked up at the fearsome head which peered down at him. He was Ashley again.

SO WHEN DID YOU WAKE, IF YOU HAVE BEEN SHARING WORDS WITH ME ALL THIS TIME?

"I'm awake now. I was...almost...dreaming before."

I SEE. IF I ATE YOU THEN, YOU'D STAY IN MY HEAD. IF I EAT YOU NOW, YOU'LL DIE?

It was a shock to be reminded of the terms of their relationship. "Oh great Sassraline, please I beg you to extend your mercy." He reached out to the place where he had been, so deep in her mind. He concentrated. "Wonderful dragon, your teeth are as white as snow, as sharp as the jagged peaks of my homeland."

I HEAR YOU, LITTLE THUNDER! BE STILL OR YOU'LL AWAKEN EVERY DRAGON IN THE WINTERBLADES. I'LL NOT BE SHARING YOU WITH OTHERS.

"My words are too loud?" Ashley asked. She usually complained he was too quiet.

"YES!" she answered, with such intensity he was forced to his knees under the weight and volume of it. ONLY THE ELDER MAY SPEAK THUS.

AND I another awareness announced. Sassraline pulled back from Ashley and flapped her wings in surprise.

FOOL HATCHLING. NOW YOU'VE DRAWN THE WRONG KIND OF ATTENTION UPON US.

"Who was that?"

HE'LL BE HERE SOON ENOUGH NOW THAT HIS INTEREST IS PIQUED.

"Who?"

AKONISS. HE IS AN OBSIDIAN OF THE WORST KIND. HE IS A GREAT DANGER.

Sassraline turned to go, but then looked back at Ashley in his hollow.

I SHOULD HAVE EATEN YOU WHILE I HAD THE CHANCE. She looked almost sad. Those great emerald eyes glistened like wet jewels, polished and perfect. They were truly beautiful. STAY OUT OF SIGHT.

She moved away fast, slithering her great bulk with a fluid grace over the rough stone floor. Even so, she had not quite reached the mouth of the cavern when the newcomer announced his presence with a thunderous roar that rolled through the rock like an earthquake.

WHAT TREASURE DO YOU HIDE IN YOUR NEW LAIR, SASSRALINE?

The voice seemed to fill the cavern, ominous yet insidious. A great wind blew in from the mouth of the cave. The ground lurched then lurched again. Sassraline arched and spewed a vicious spout of fire, but the intruder advanced through the flame. For all its searing heat, her fire caused the other dragon no visible harm. He looked like living rock. Ripples passed along the length of his body as he flexed his scales.

He was a head taller than Sassraline, his high crown of blade-like spines scraping the roof. He was dark, brutal. The edges of his massive shoulders were jagged, his legs facetted, curved and wickedly sharp. Sassraline blew her fire against the roof and rock fell upon him. Flakes of his body fell from his back, scattering on the floor like discarded sickles, and still he advanced on Sassraline, and she was forced to retreat.

WHERE ARE YOUR WHELPS, SASSRALINE? I EXPECTED TO FIND MY CLUTCH WITH YOU BY NOW.

Sassraline leapt suddenly, swinging and twisting in the air, using her outstretched wing to pivot upon, bringing her mighty tail to smash down upon him. She sloughed a spray of chips off his back, but he caught her tail as he fell back and gripped her hard with both forelegs before ripping his talons aside in a slashing movement.

Sassraline squealed and jumped around to face him again as she backed away.

I ATE THEM, Sassraline replied. I WOULD NOT SEE YOUR SPAWN SURVIVE IN THIS WORLD.

Akoniss stamped his talons into the rock and this time the quake lifted Ashley off the ground.

THEN YOU ARE MORE STUPID THAN I GAVE YOU CREDIT FOR. I WILL TAKE YOU AGAIN, AND AGAIN, UNTIL YOU HATCH ME A HUNTING PACK. THE OTHERS ARE NOT SO WILFUL. WHY DO YOU PRETEND TO BE SPECIAL?

Akoniss towered over Sassraline. He had cornered her against the wall of the cavern.

WHY SHOULD I OBEY YOU?

BECAUSE I AM AKONISS!

Sassraline snorted. YOU OBSIDIANS DON'T LAST. I HAVE SEEN YOUR KIND BEFORE. YOU COME AND GO LIKE THE SEASONS. MY KIND LIVE FOR HUNDREDS OF YEARS.

Akoniss snaked out a foreleg and snatched her by the neck. She thrashed against his attack, but he was too strong, and he pressed his talons in under her scales. A fiery orange blood oozed down over his limbs, hissing and smoking as it was exposed to the air.

DON'T TELL ME MY KIND IS NOT TRUE! YOU HAVE INCLUSIONS ALL OVER YOU. YOU ARE WEAK. I AM FURY AND FIRE!

He breathed his own fire upon her then, a blinding red vomit of heat. It hit her in the face, but he held her neck firm, and Sassraline couldn't escape from the barely gaseous assault of magma. The air was too hot to breathe and Ashley cowered to defend himself. When he looked up again, he saw the dark dragon strike Sassraline on her snout. His fire dripped from her head. It left an ugly blue scar down her neck when it cooled.

Her left eye was fused shut and a livid wound ran across her nostrils. Yet still she pretended to be undaunted by his violence. She stood tall and proud, but her voice quivered.

YOU HAVE LESS APPEAL TO ME THAN A LITTLE JASPER.

Akoniss laughed, a menacing and heavy sound, like a slide of boulders.

YOU MAY CALL OUT TO YOUR MOTHER NOW, AS YOU DID BEFORE. THE ELDERS WILL NOT HELP YOU.

Ashley clenched his fists. He couldn't just sit there, while she was— broken. He sent his awareness probing into the black dragon's mind. He was instantly amazed. The obsidian was not nearly as intelligent or complex as Sassraline. He was a beast, young and inexperienced. His was a simple world, of violence, feeding and fighting. And fear.

The obsidian had a mortal fear of water. It corroded his skin; it could destroy him. His body was a brittle mass of mineral plates and water was his nemesis. He lived in the desert; he didn't belong up here on the Winterblades. He was on a mating rampage. He had only dared Sassraline's mountains because the rain-clouds had cleared. To be caught in the rain would be the death of him. At once Ashley knew how to beat him.

A sudden leak in the roof allowed a small rivulet of water to fall upon Akoniss. He flinched away from it and, giving it a wide berth, rounded on Sassraline on the other side. Then he gripped her with his talons and flipped her over in a violent wrestling mass of twisting tails and jaws.

Ashley rejoiced. Akoniss's reaction to the jet of water confirmed his theory. It had been a trick, no water dripped from the roof, it had not been real. It had been the *idea* of a rivulet which he had projected at the dragon. It was a simple thing. Once he was in the dragon's mind and he imagined a thing well enough, it was as if the thing became real for the dragon—it believed the projection, particularly so with a dragon as simple-minded as Akoniss. He was big and brutal, but he didn't have a mind to match. He crouched over Sassraline, his tail thrashed in the airthen whipped out straight.

Ashley stood from behind his boulder. Sassraline was on her back, her head nearest to Ashley. Over her, the dread dragon Akoniss lurked like a vulture, his prey between his knees, his speckled wings covering her like a dirty tent. His ragged teeth were exposed in a snarl of domination and lust, and it was to this snout that Ashley spoke.

"No," said Ashley. Speckles of fire dripped from Akoniss's maw. He didn't raise his head, only his red eyes flicked upward beneath encrusted lids. The split in his irises drew closed as he focused hard on Ashley.

There was a long, slow intake of breath.

Ashley threw his vision at Akoniss. He imagined a crack opening in the roof of the cavern, a waterfall rushing down upon them. Water sluiced down in an unbroken sheet, like the falls above Fendwarrow in Eyri. He used the memory of piercing that waterfall to envision a cascade that pulled at his hair and foamed at his feet. Akoniss howled, his nostrils flaring so wide Ashley could see the fire deep within him. The dark dragon reared back on his hind legs, but his wings fluttered, betraying his fear. Akoniss blew a gout of flame at the waterfall, hitting Ashley with terrifying heat. He almost lost his concentration then, as his hair crisped and his ears stung, but he allowed the waterfall to expand in a great cloud of steam that billowed forward, moist and searching, and behind it he intensified his vision, allowing boulders to tear from the roof as water gushed and sprayed in all directions.

As Ashley advanced with his vision, he drove the dread Akoniss back.

Ashley sent a giant crack zigzagging through the roof of the cavern past Akoniss. New geysers spurted and spat like a breaking waterpipe under pressure. The dragon issued a high whine and fled with his long neck outstretched, like a swan trying in vain to launch with wet wings.

Ashley followed him, being careful not to step on the shards the dragon had discarded on the floor. He carried his vision out through the mouth of the cavern. Akoniss was airborne, but not yet away. Ashley thought the clouds should darken somewhat. A heavy brooding mass of cloud spread across the sky, driven by an impossible wind. The fringes whipped by like a ragged blanket, the dark base sank until the peaks dragged through the currents of his imagination.

For good measure, he made it rain in the lee of the nearest peaks. Sparkling swarms of cold droplets drove down the slopes. Akoniss became a bolt, fired from the mountains, flying out to the distant sunshine.

He was gone.

Ashley sank down beside the mouth of the cavern and buried his head in a clump of snow. He laughed uncontrollably as the shaking took him. He had saved one dragon, from another. What had he done?

HOW DID YOU DO THAT? asked Sassraline, emerging from the cavern to stand at his side. HOW DID YOU BRING DOWN THE WATER?

She had seen it too. He must have projected his thoughts harder than he'd realised. He'd been desperate to save her, because he'd known if he hadn't, he would have been next on the dark dragon's menu.

THE WATER HAS COOLED HIS FIRE IN MY SKIN, Sassraline said.

Ashley didn't try to explain that it wasn't real. If her pain had been eased, then let her have that small mercy. For someone as proud as Sassraline, to be assaulted by a ruffian like Akoniss must be deeply humiliating. She stared off into the distance, beneath the clouds that were already evaporating from Ashley's mind. The sunlight returned to dance on her sinuous green neck, highlighting the high points of her folded wings. She was truly spectacular in the sunlight. The scars of the recent battle did little to mar her beauty.

HE IS AS COMMON AS A CORUNDUM, she said, then turned her great head to look down upon Ashley. YET YOU ARE SOMETHING QUITE SPECIAL. NO ONE HAS EVER STOOD UP FOR ME BEFORE. NO ONE HAS EVER RISKED THEIR LIFE FOR ME.

She contemplated him for a long time with that penetrating gaze, and he sat in the snow, wondering if she was going to change her mind and eat him after all. At last she dropped her head close to him, her eye almost level with his head. She blinked.

WHAT IS YOUR WISH? YOU HAVE EARNED A FAVOUR.

Ashley reeled as he tried to find an answer. She was offering him a wish? She would *do* something for him? He had finally succeeded in making her think about someone beyond herself, of making her *care*.

He sat for a long time to consider his answer. He thought at once of leaving the frozen heights of the Winterblades, but where would he go? Eyri? That train of thought led at once to Tabitha Serannon and the others. Had they made it across the wastes? What had happened to their beasts? Was she still pressing on with her quest? Were they in danger?

A drab little bird fluttered onto the branch of the dead tree. It sang a bright melody into the crisp dawn: a little song that was ever-changing, yet expressed a secret. And it flew from the branch into the open sky. It flew.

"Take me to my friend," he replied. "I must find her."

YOU HAVE A PARTNER?

"No, she is not mine, she is a...fellow."

BUT STILL SHE IS THE KIND YOU WOULD SEARCH FOR?

"She already has a man," Ashley explained.

SHE HAS AN AKONISS IN HER LAIR?

He thought of Garyll Glavenor. "Not an Akoniss, no. Her man is hard to fault."

AHH. WHY DO YOU SEARCH FOR HER THEN?

When Ashley did not answer, she nudged him, gently, and he was pushed backward through the snow a way. Pale colours adorned her snout. He ran his hand over the polished curves, careful not to touch the acid stains that were drying around her wound.

She eased her head away from him and stood tall again.

I MUST LEAVE THIS LAIR ANYWAY, NOW THAT HE HAS FOUND IT.

She lifted one great foot and extended it toward him. Her toes were flexible, her talons like spear-tips at their ends. Ashley realised she expected him to step into her grasp, and she would lift him.

"Won't it be easier if I climb on top?" he asked.

ON TOP? THAT IS MORE THAN I AM OFFERING!

The prideful creature! She wouldn't allow him on her back. Yet. He would have to be beneath her, like captured prey, or he would not be flown at all. Ashley probed her thoughts. He could trust her, it seemed, although there were hidden places in the dragon's mind that he didn't understand. He stepped into her grasp. The sharp talons closed around him. She held him gently, cupping her foot around him to make a loose basket with her toes. Before Ashley had a moment to consider his precarious position, she leapt into the air, beat her mighty wings, and they were airborne.

37. THE CURSE OF CHAOS

"Like to know what Chaos is like?
Catch a cat after a lightning strike."—Zarost

Prince Bevn woke, scratching. A cheap scent clung to him. Dirty sheets were tangled around his legs. He sat up abruptly. There was a second depression in the pillow, a hollow in the sheets that was undeniable. His stomach rolled.

The woman was gone, not Gabrielle—someone else, a woman who had seemed to be attractive in the dark, but had turned out to be a nightmare. The memories assaulted him: the hot and smoky pub; the burning feeling of that strange smoke called Bane, as he had inhaled from the shared pipe, again and again; the veiled woman dancing on the table, full of such urgency that no one in the pub could ignore her. At the time, he'd thought it strange that none of the men had taken what she so obviously had to offer. Men had howled and jeered at her instead, and someone had emptied a tankard over her head. Bevn had gulped at the revelation of her swollen wet breasts. She had beckoned to him, yes, and drawn him from that place. By the stars! There had even been a fight to keep her, in the alley outside—a fight to keep her, or someone trying to stop him, he couldn't remember which. He sucked at his lip, and found it was split. He'd really wanted to discover the forbidden delights of her sex, and yet when he had, it had been too late to stop.

Why oh why had he done it?

He remembered the strangely slack folds of skin in the place where her breasts should have been. They were flaccid in his hands, not at all like the generous curves he'd expected. Those green beady eyes had watched him with a wicked glint. Her bare skin was more like porridge than silk, her body grown soft and pock-marked. Beneath the false colouring on her cheeks, her face was like a paper bag, crumpled by time. She'd growled in his ear like a dangerous dog. She wouldn't let him go, even when he'd fought against her, even when he'd tried to escape. It had gone on and on. She'd pressed him down with her body, trapped him, her loins like gravel against his traitorously rigid member. She made a hoarse and throaty moan all the time until it was over. Toward the end it had even seemed like she was crying, as if she was doing something that appalled her just as much as it did him.

That had not been the worst of it. Once she had stolen his seed, she had reached out and taken his crown. He remembered the look of delight on her face, and the way her skin had shifted, revealing something almost beautiful for a moment before the hatchet-faced Half-Lûk visage returned. "Our fates are a mystery again," she whispered to the air then she had touched him on his forehead and a star had burst inside his mind.

Bevn scratched again. He'd never felt so unclean in all his life. He rose from the bed and kicked the sheets to the corner of the room. It was over, he promised himself, over and done with. He would never want a woman again. His head pounded. He put out a hand out to steady himself. His crown was gone, and he didn't know what to do about it.

Bevn washed himself slowly at the basin. He was tired of the strangeness, of having sore feet, and of being bullied by Gabrielle or Saladon. His head felt like a swollen melon. He wanted to go home, but there was no point in going home unless he could be king, and without the Kingsrim that wasn't going to happen. The Sorcerer had promised to give him the power to rule, but Bevn knew that the Kingsrim was a vital part of it.

His crown was gone and it made him feel so sick. It felt as if he'd eaten a bucket of slither-eels, those slippery spotty ones you got in Fendwarrow, down between the reeds. He staggered out to look for Gabrielle, emerging onto a high boarding and following it until he came to a strange open area amid the wreckage of the buildings. Some of the buildings had collapsed into the open space in their middle, but the Slipperfolk had improvised supports and patch-boards. Lûk cable-weavers were running lines to link those levels that had been separated and new ladders joined the levels with those below. It seemed that the people were accustomed to change. Most of the Slipperfolk were clustered in the upper galleries, tense, watching, and there, below him in the circle of scraped bedrock, he saw the wizard and Gabrielle.

Black Saladon was contained in a net of pale golden threads of light. He was tilted back as if he had been frozen in a moment of combat—his body almost horizontal and his arms thrown back. The wizards had got him.

The mob parted nervously as Bevn drew near. He guessed they

recognised Bevn as part of Saladon's crew—so much for remaining hidden in Slipper. They feared him because of who he was associated with. It was a kind of power, dependant on their fear of magic and wildfire strikes. He realised with sickening dread that he had no protection any more. The Kingsrim had protected him, before. He looked nervously to the sky. It seemed clear of the tell-tale cracks of Chaos. Or were there fine filaments of disturbance returning?

His hands shook on the way down the rickety ladder, and he almost threw up, but he managed to make it down to ground level without slipping. He waited for the pounding in his head to subside before shuffling over to Gabrielle and the wizard.

"Gabrielle—" he began.

She didn't turn. She was concentrating. Flies buzzed around her, tumbling in the breeze, and Bevn swatted one away. It was icy cold. Motes! She was using magic, but she was trying to hide it from the Slipperfolk. She was trying to pry Black Saladon loose from his confinement, but where Gabrielle's flies struck the golden restraints, the motes hissed and disappeared with a puff. Her magic wasn't strong enough.

He glanced nervously at the sky again. What if she couldn't get Saladon free in time? They needed Saladon—they were totally dependant on him.

"Gabrielle—" he repeated.

"Not now, I'm busy!"

"Gabrielle, they've stolen the crown," he said.

"What!" She whirled. "When? I hardly left you! I checked in on you moments ago. When did they steal it?"

"Um, last night?"

"You had it just now!"

"No… I didn't."

"Yes you did! I sat with you all through last night. You were fast asleep with the crown on your head. You know that!"

Gabrielle had been with him? The last he'd seen of her was… Leaving the first alehouse, he remembered. She'd wanted to escort him to the toilets… And then? There was a fuzzy place in his memory, then the other alehouse, the one with the smoke and the dancing woman and the terrible acts.

It was a dream? It couldn't be. There was no crown on his head and she could see that.

"You weren't with me last night," he corrected her. "I wasn't in our normal room."

She gripped him by the shoulders and shook him hard. "Stop jacking around, Bevn, this is no time for jokes! We're in serious trouble here!"

"I'm not lying to you! I wasn't in our room. I was with—another—woman. I've just come from—up there," he ended, pointing to the high boardwalk. There had been something very strange about that half-Lûk hag. Gabrielle followed his gaze.

"She took it and then put me to sleep," Bevn wailed. "There was nothing I could do!"

"Damn it! How could this happen? What did the thief look like? Oh forget it, it doesn't matter. Saladon showed me a way to trace the crown, but I can't believe it. I saw it not half an hour past! I was in your room with you, and I can see the door from here."

If that were true then something had happened Bevn couldn't explain. He was certain he'd just walked down from the higher boardwalk, and he'd woken in that room with the dirty sheets and washbasin. Whoever Gabrielle had watched in their rooms hadn't been him.

"I'll search faster alone," Gabrielle said tersely. "Wait here and watch him. Don't let any of these hotheads do anything to him while he's vulnerable like this. Tell them he will break free soon enough, because he will, and he'll be angry with anyone who threatens him. I've bust some of the threads, but there're still too many holding him, and he seems unconscious."

Bevn nodded. He felt so stupid letting Gabrielle go to find his crown, as if he were a child who had lost his toy bear in the hayfield. At least she had a chance, with her magic. He didn't know where to look. The hag could be anywhere.

He waited beside Saladon and tried picking at the wizard's restraints with his dagger, but the magic made the blade hot and stung his hand. Nobody approached him and, after a time, the Slipperfolk went on about their business. Black Saladon hung in suspended animation, a moment short of falling on his back.

Bevn hated him. Even with his eyes closed, the wizard had an arrogant air, as if he thought himself superior to the other lowly mortals. Bevn sneered. Saladon was clever and he may have learnt a lot, but he didn't have the blood of kings. He was just an underling. The Sorcerer Ametheus was the real ruler, and it was Saladon's fault he had lost his crown—the wizard should have protected him.

He kicked the wizard on his shins, but the big man didn't react at all. He was comatose, locked in stasis by the spell placed upon him. Bevn sulked. He couldn't do anything but wait. He was bursting for a pee.

Gabrielle was still gone. He had a sudden idea. He slipped his willy out surreptitiously, and wizzed away merrily on Saladon's leg. The brute would never know who had done it. He'd come around and find his boot wet. Bevn chuckled to himself. Served him right for bullying him, and for leading him to this forsaken crumbling city where the women were ugly, mean and dirty. It was all Saladon's fault.

"You should be careful who you insult," he told the wizard.

Bevn was just shaking the tip when two things happened at once.

He saw Gabrielle fighting against a burly man who forced her into the open area on his left. Her hands were at her throat. Beside her, a man paced toward him, a face Bevn recognised instantly—Garyll Glavenor, the retired Swordmaster of Eyri. He had caught them.

At the same time, on his right, Black Saladon's eye jerked open, the nearest one, looking right at Bevn.

"Eek!" exclaimed Bevn and wet his own foot. He ran.

Something whistled through the air. He was hit and pain exploded in his head.

He tumbled to the ground. The Swordmaster had downed him with something. He couldn't run, his legs wouldn't work. Bevn began to wail.

Glavenor came up behind him, gripping his collar. "Not another step, Bevn Mellar. You are under arrest." Glavenor dragged him upright then pulled him backward past Saladon. His single eye was still open, fixed, staring. Had he seen what Bevn had done? The wizard's right hand moved. Three fingers flexed and came together. One of his restraints snaked away and struck the ground then the essence recoiled and flew at the man who held Gabrielle. It wrapped around his head in a single band. It didn't seem to have any effect on the man, but then Bevn felt a horrible surge pass underfoot and the dust stood up in little ridges. He knew what that meant even as he looked up at the sky and saw the gathering of charge.

"It's back," he said, feeling suddenly very small. He had no protection. None of them did.

Glavenor halted.

"Mulrano!" he cried out. "Run! Above you!"

Gabrielle's captor looked up, saw the approaching wildfire, and loosened his grip in a moment of indecision. It was enough for Gabrielle—she twisted, swung her elbow hard against his head then dived away, free. She came past Bevn and Glavenor.

"Let him run, or you're both done for!" she shouted at Glavenor. He hesitated then turned and pushed Bevn roughly ahead of him. They ran, but they hadn't covered more than a few steps before the small hairs on his arms stood on end. Bevn knew an awful moment of premonition.

A bright flash came from above as if the morning sky had ignited. With a whining shriek, the wildfire fell upon Slipper. One tail of lightning burned fiercely in a roof. The whole building hissed and shook. The roof-panels crackled. A second fork of silver lightning as thin as blade-grass snaked down upon the marked man. "Mulrano! No!" Glavenor cried out, but it was too late for him.

The wildfire grounded itself and he disappeared in a cloud of sparkling dust.

All around the open area, people were shouting, pushing and wailing. Things were toppling. A stampede had begun, to get away from the Chaos. A stuttering light came out of the dust-cloud, and Bevn saw the horror. The Eyrian man was lit from within like a paper lantern. Random shafts of brilliance escaped through rents in his clothes and breaks in his skin, around which the flesh boiled, smoked and turned black. His eyes were wide white orbs. He toppled forward onto his outstretched hands, hitting the ground with a shattering like a breaking plate. His arms were crushed then his head disintegrated across the stone, leaving a scattered pile of jagged pieces. Elements of the man's body lay amid shredded remnants of his clothes. His blood looked as dry as dust, red crystals mixed with darker reds and pinks. White bones like crisp chalk. Brown and blue stones cracked and popped with heat. The black stones marking a broad perimeter smoked gently.

Glavenor had slowed, his attention lingering on the oblong scattering of coloured grit, where two round white pebbles were all that was left of the eyes which had once looked out of Mulrano's face.

Gabrielle was suddenly beside him, and Bevn saw her gather motes to her hand. She slowed as they entered an alleyway. "Keep running!" she shouted at him. "My spell will call the wildfire again!"

She threw a net of darkness behind them, across the end of the street, a fabric of shadow that wouldn't hide them very well. It didn't have to. Already a second strike of silver fire streaked down at Slipper, triggered by the movement of the essence. The eerie whistle filled the air. The tail of Chaos plunged into the buildings. A great light swelled from within the structure and burst through the suddenly transparent walls. For a moment everything was clear—the boxes and barrels, the tables and chairs, the people outlined brightly in the gambling den. Then the vivid moment was past, and a cloud surrounded the building, obscuring it within a roiling, hungry billow of ash. Thunder clapped like a stroke of iron in Bevn's ears. His bones shook. His vision blurred.

They ran.

CRSOCRSO

Garyll Glavenor reached down slowly and picked up the two white pebbles. They were smooth and warm as if they still contained some life, but Garyll knew that Mulrano was dead. Mulrano, who had run with him and the Lûk escort all the way to Firro, Mulrano who had hauled on the oars the hardest as they swept downriver. The two Lûk windrunners who led the search, Jek and Kal, had done what they could with the sails of the sleek *korakli*, but it was Mulrano who had got them to Slipper so quickly, refusing to wait for the whims of a fickle wind.

Only to find his end. It was like a spear through his heart. Garyll closed his fist upon the pebbles, and turned to pursue the fleeing prince and the Shadowcaster, only to see the wildfire streaking down again. Terror clutched at his guts. He could not fight this magic with his blunt rod. All he could do was run, away from the Chaos blooming in the street ahead. A short fork split from the main strike and cut across the space ahead of Garyll, terminating on the restrained wizard. It whipped around him like an angry vine.

"Go for the princeling, we will this wizard guard!" Jek shouted to him, backing away from the roiling mass of silver that was the wizard. "We will words with him have, if he survives this *sosisshon*."

The Lûk windrunners had their spears ready to throw. They had history with the man they called Black Saladon. Within the Chaos, the wizard still seemed to be restrained, but his fingers jerked and twitched as if he cast hurried invocations. His eyes were wide. Garyll had heard something of what Black Saladon was capable of, and he wasn't a man one wanted to try stop. He suspected that a mage who had survived for so long in Oldenworld would have some defence against the wildfire. Garyll wished the Lûk luck as he ran after the prince and Gabrielle. The prince was just a youth, and Garyll understood something of the Shadowcaster Gabrielle's power. He had the easier task.

The people of Slipper had no defences against the wildfire. He passed the building which had been hit. A screaming man stumbled from the wreckage, and yet it was not a man. His face was altered. His bald head had become a smooth and sightless dome. Only the howling orifice of his mouth remained. He staggered blindly into a silvered wooden upright. The upright shivered, but stood firm and the man recoiled, clutching his head with grossly deformed hands. Too many fingers clustered together like a clutch of swollen sausages. Silver threads ran from his hands over his body like worms, writhing in searching patterns. Wherever the threads touched, the man changed. His clothes smoked away, exposing purpling skin. He shrieked and beat at his body, but he lost his balance, and toppled headlong into the bright ash. As the silver dust spilled over him he arched his back in a violent spasm. His skin seemed to swell. He issued a hollow moan then split down the middle, like a caterpillar that had been trodden upon, his innards spilling strangely yellow over the ground.

Someone emptied their stomach behind Garyll. He ran on. People emerged from buildings ahead of him. Most of them were armed, their weapons drawn. They looked at him warily, but dismissed him soon enough when they recognised that he hadn't been altered by the wildfire. He passed them where they stood—they were resolute, holding a stern vigil, waiting to cut down anything unnatural trying to escape the wildfire. There was no escape from the Chaos once it touched flesh—either the wildfire was fatal, or friends finished one off.

Garyll threw a parting glance at the site of the second strike. Even the building had been affected; those parts of it that were still standing writhed as if they were no longer made of treated timbers. One pillar spread dark, sickly branches over the ghostly glow of the ash. Ahead in the street Garyll caught a fleeting glimpse of what he thought was the prince, but when he reached the end of the street he found a mob scattering through the three divergent ways—Lûk, Hunters, all manner of Slipperfolk. He moved with them, scanning every alleyway, but there was no sign of the Eyrians again. They could be anywhere.

Then the air tensed, and a flash came from the west. The

Shadowcaster had used her magic again and triggered the wildfire. He ran against the flow of humanity, along a soiled street, and encountered another ruin. A figure emerged from the ash, a delicate serving girl in a red dress. She was crying hysterically. Searching silver tentacles gripped her legs. The girl leapt as if dancing on hot coals, but the tentacles only spread further up her thighs. She ran, but she could not escape the wildfire. When she had reached the edge of the ash she was stained to her waist by shimmering coils. Her dress began to smoke. Her shins glistened blackly, as if the skin had hardened and grown bristles.

The victim of the wildfire lurched straight toward Garyll. "Help mee, help mee, gerrit off!" cried the girl. She reached for Garyll, but he sidestepped her clumsy grasp, letting the girl stumble to her knees. He hated himself for doing so, but the wildfire was too deadly to touch.

An elderly woman staggered past him. "Oh Maryna, my Maryna!" she called out.

"Daan toucher, Debaleen!" someone shouted from within the crowd, but the warning came too late.

Wildfire snaked up the girl's body, over her darkening arms, and onto the old woman who held her. The woman jumped back in alarm, but she did not succeed in breaking free. The girl's swarthy hands were clasped upon her wrists.

"Muthr forgive mee! Muthr!"

Wildfire crossed the link between them, and the flesh where they were joined seemed to melt and ripple. The old woman cried out. She heaved on her trapped arms, but only succeeded in pulling the panicked girl upon her. They fell to the street, and a web of silver wove around them both. Garyll backed away, wanting to howl against the torture he was forced to witness, the torture he could do nothing to avert.

"Rleez mee, Maryna!"

"I kaan stop it, I kaan stop it!" the girl cried, kicking at the ground with legs that seemed too long, too thin and too black to be her own.

"Rleez mee! Letter ga! Letga!"

The two women rolled over and over in the street, like two wrestlers locked in combat. The silver threads burnt their clothes away: they weren't women anymore, their bodies were joined at the chest, the elderly woman absorbed into the growing shape as she was infected with the blackening disease. Her limbs grew long and thin too, and she scrabbled ineffectually at the dirt. The silver threads danced with frenetic activity, and a new form took shape: one low black body, a swollen glistening abdomen between tall jointed legs. Only the misshapen faces of the women remained at the front of a hideous body. Their cries became unintelligible, more animal-like, until they ceased.

Nothing of the two women remained, only a row of mean little black eyes—a horrible creature. If Garyll were to give it a name, he would have called it a spider, but it was bigger than a big dog—a hungry hideous thing. It scuttled toward him. A rock whistled over his head, striking the creature a glancing blow. The creature jumped back.

"Stones on it!" someone cried behind him. "Before it away! Dorrakaan! Stones on it!"

When the creature rushed forward again, stones struck its head, raining upon its body. A burly Hunter man swung his club as the spider passed and caught its grizzly leg. The limb snapped with a sickly sound, but the creature had seven other legs to use. It jumped over its attacker and jumped again toward the safety beyond the crowd. A tumbling knife followed it and struck its abdomen. Black fluid oozed from the wound, but the spider ran fast, and escaped toward the north, leaving only a stain upon the wall to mark its passing. North, thought Garyll, toward the lowlands and others of its kind. The Lûk had told him about the dangers of the wilds north of Slipper, where the influence of the Sorcerer had ravaged the ordered civilisations that had once graced Oldenworld.

The prince and his companions had brought wildfire upon Slipper. They must pay for their crime. He saw them then, running on a lower level, heading for the river, to the boats. Garyll jumped down a wall to a lower roof, jumped again to the street, and ran.

CABACAB

Bevn scrabbled into the small boat as Gabrielle pushed it out. They had to get away! Saladon could find them later, but for now, they had to escape from Garyll Glavenor. Bevn still couldn't believe it. The Swordmaster of Eyri had tracked them. How had he crossed the wastes? How had he made it through the shield? That was enough to make Bevn scared of him. If he was strong enough to endure that pain, he could endure anything. He would have no mercy when he caught them.

They had lost Glavenor in the crowds, but it didn't make the shock any better. Just having the Swordmaster near made him feel like a thief. He knew Glavenor knew the truth—that Bevn had stolen the crown.

As Gabrielle dipped the oars into the water, Bevn saw him, running down through the storage sheds.

"Gabrielle! Gabrielle! He's coming!"

She pulled hard at the oars, but the boat was a sluggish craft. They'd only chosen it because it had been left on the water's edge. Now it was letting them down. Glavenor reached the tilted slime-covered slipway, but instead of tripping as Bevn had hoped, he just ran faster. He hit the water in a dive.

"Cast a spell! Cast a spell! Do something, Gabrielle!"

Glavenor stroked out toward them. He only had one hand, his left arm ending in a stump. Bevn hadn't seen that before, but it didn't matter, Glavenor could still swim fast enough to close the gap on them.

"I can't use my magic out here!" Gabrielle answered. "Where would we run to? We'll be sitting ducks for the wildfire." She heaved on the oars, faster and faster, but it was not going to be enough. Glavenor was too close. She lifted one of the oars out of its rowlock and braced herself as Glavenor neared the transom.

Bevn clambered further into the bows and the movement tipped Gabrielle off-balance. Her first strike went wide and slapped the water and Glavenor caught hold of the oar.

"Sink him, sink him, sink him!" Bevn cried, but Gabrielle couldn't dislodge Glavenor from the end of her oar and he yanked hard and pulled himself at the boat. She stamped down on his hand as he gripped the rail, but he grimaced and hauled himself in nonetheless, blocking her attempts to strike him with his blunt arm.

Then he was inside their boat, right there, dripping, deadly and furious. Bevn edged right to the very point of the boat. He wanted to jump out but he couldn't swim well enough to get back to shore. They were drifting with the current already. There was nowhere to go.

"Shadowcaster," said Garyll.

Bevn could almost feel the hackles rise on Gabrielle's neck.

"And so were you, our dear *failed* Swordmaster," Gabrielle retorted.

His expression hardened. "Nevermore," he asserted, looming over Gabrielle.

She took her seat, acting casual. "Once you have tasted the dark, you know its pleasures," said Gabrielle, reclining against the rail.

Garyll didn't respond to her; he turned upon the prince instead. "You have a debt to Eyri. You have betrayed your father." He was determined not to whimper, because Gabrielle was watching.

"You are no better, you betrayed him as well!" Bevn accused.

Glavenor flinched, as if stung. "I was not myself! I was under the grip of an evil spell. You have a choice. You do not have to seek out the Sorcerer and bring ruin upon Eyri."

"But I am not myself," mocked Bevn, pretending a faint with an affected wrist pressed to his brow. "I am under the grip of an evil spell." He had got Glavenor. He tittered. "You can't prove I'm not."

A bone cracked in Garyll's clenched fist.

"You will turn this boat around and take it to the shore," he commanded Gabrielle. "The prince will return with me to Eyri, to face his justice there and to pass the crown back to his father."

"I don't have the crown! It was stolen, you big lump-head! Why do you think I'm not wearing it?"

Glavenor looked at him hard. "You're just lying to try and earn some respite."

"No, it is gone! The hag took it last night! Where do you think I could hide it, in these clothes?" A wonderfully clever idea formed in Bevn's mind. Being caught by Glavenor might be useful after all. "There's no point taking me back to Eyri without the crown. It's the crown my father needs. He'll not think much of you if you come back without it. You must help us to find the crown again!"

Once they'd found the crown, Bevn could worry about how to escape from the Swordmaster. He was certain Gabrielle could be helpful in that regard.

"You lie!" Glavenor lunged at him and caught him by the front of his tunic then pushed him back over the rail.

"Gabrielle! Help me!" Bevn wailed, but Gabrielle didn't even get a chance to rise from her seat. Glavenor threw Bevn down, pulled his baton from his belt and angled it to meet the underside of Gabrielle's chin in one fluid move. "You will tell me where he has hidden it," Garyll warned her.

"What happened to your big blade?" Gabrielle asked, unruffled by the sudden challenge. She seemed to have taken strength from the conflict, from Garyll's direct attention. "You weren't shy to show it off before."

"Don't try me," Garyll warned.

"I would love to, but I'll wait until you're in a better mood," she answered. "You can put your piece away now. You've made your point, and the prince is telling the truth. He covets his crown more than his own head. He would be wearing it now if he had it. It really has been stolen."

Garyll stared at her like a hawk.

"Just remember I will not hesitate to strike you." He stowed the baton once more.

"That's good to know," she retorted. "I'm sure we'll have a great time travelling in each other's company."

"Now start rowing," he ordered. "We've already lost ground. Get moving!"

Bevn noticed how far they had travelled downriver already. The current was strong; they had been drawn away from the shore. Gabrielle would have to row hard to get them back to the same slipway. Slipperfolk clustered on the jetty, a rowdy bunch, gesticulating at them. They looked none too friendly. Someone nocked an arrow; a second later it hissed down at them and splooshed into the water.

A sudden gust of wind slapped Bevn. It pulled their bow skew. Gabrielle pulled hard on the oars to keep their heading. Another gust tore at the water, and threw spray in their faces. Two more arrows came at them, but the wind snatched the shafts in mid-flight and tossed them far downriver. Then a wall of wind came at them, tumbling down from the tiered city in streaks of mist, scraping the water into waves and making the air white.

"This wind is unnatural," Glavenor cursed.

"You shouldn't have angered my boyfriend," Gabrielle said with a smirk, and then Bevn understood. It was the wizard helping them. Somehow Black Saladon had escaped from his confinement.

"Move over, give me the right oar," Glavenor said. He sat down beside Gabrielle. "Now pull, on the left!"

He leant so hard away from his oar he lifted his body off the seat. His pull was much more powerful than Gabrielle's and the bow slewed off across the current. The wind caught it and turned the boat even more, and they drifted faster downstream. "Pull! Pull!" Garyll shouted at Gabrielle. "We can't go down this river! We must make for the jetties."

"Why would I do anything you want me to do?" Gabrielle asked him archly.

"Because you don't want to die?" Glavenor hauled hard on his oar to force their nose to swing all the way around. "Row, you stupid woman! There are deadly rapids below here. The Lûk told me about the Knarles. Even the daredevils among the windrunners won't risk this run."

At that, Gabrielle began to row again, but they were losing ground nonetheless. Glavenor began to angle for the shore instead of the jetties. As it was, they would only make ground in the rough rocks at the edge of town. Bevn became suddenly nervous. Maybe it wasn't Saladon helping them, maybe it was another wizard, and maybe that wizard wasn't trying to help them at all. He looked downstream, where the river narrowed between the rising cliffs and the flow became swifter.

"There's a cable across the river there," he told them. "Maybe you can catch it."

"Those ratlines," said Glavenor. "We pass those and we're done for."

The ratlines came up quickly—great woven cables strung low over the river, like a bridge turned on its side. Bevn supposed it was a safety net for wayward watercraft. The bottom line skipped and tugged at the surface of the swollen flow.

A sullen roar echoed off the cliffs and the wind whipped at their backs, driving them downriver.

"Take my oar!" Glavenor shouted to Gabrielle. "Keep rowing upstream!"

But their speed increased without Glavenor pulling on the oars and the current swept them swiftly on. Glavenor hooked the line perfectly, but the force of the entire river dragged at the boat, and he was pulled to the bows, squashed hard against Bevn as he fought to keep hold on the cable. "Hey!" Bevn cried.

Glavenor strained against the river. He moved his hand along the cable, trying to pull them closer to the shore, but it was awkward for him with one hand, and he wouldn't hold them for long. Gabrielle left her oars and jumped up to help him, but then the cable snapped. It writhed like a snake in Glavenor's hand, and he lost it as he fell hard into the boat. Bevn ducked just in time. The ratline clipped the top of his head then it splashed into the river.

Bevn couldn't believe their bad luck. They weren't going to make it to the riverbank at all.

A lone figure stood beside a stone guardhouse where the cable had terminated, low on the cliff. With the low angle of the sun and the way the driving mists streaked by in the wind, Bevn couldn't be sure, but it seemed to be a dark-faced figure, broad-shouldered and grim.

The wind shrieked and they were driven into the head of the Knarles.

"Turn it, turn downriver," Glavenor told Gabrielle. "We'll drown if we go over any rocks facing this way. You, sit in the middle of the boat." He pushed Bevn away and braced himself in the bows, a short pole in his hand.

Bevn tried to make light of the situation, because of his fear. "Don't be such a scaredy-cat. It's only a river. How bad can it get?"

ༀ৪ণ୦ঙৱ୦

Garyll knew there was deadly white water ahead. They had to go fast, it was the only way. It was useless for him to try row with only one hand, and he didn't trust the boy to navigate, so he had to trust Gabrielle to the oars.

The river had lost its slick appearance. Streaks and eddies plagued its surface, restless heralds of what was to come. The river narrowed. The roar became a thunder, and the air became moist, filled with the spray of the imminent violence. The spur of Slipper rose on their right, the receding walls so far above on the imposing cliff face. Then the cliff cut the town off from view altogether.

"I can't believe Saladon has abandoned us to this," Gabrielle said quietly to the air.

The current took them swinging right up to the cliffs and then swept around the tight left-hander. The boat rocked over a series of deep furrows, then tipped again into a rushing pace. Gabrielle cursed as her oar struck an exposed rock.

"Mind your bloody oar," Bevn cursed behind him.

A hard slap and a thump described the prince's fate. Garyll didn't need to turn.

The boat lurched over a hump then wallowed in a depression. Garyll reached out to fend them off the rock. "Left!" he called to Gabrielle.

The boat began to swing.

"Other left!" he shouted. "Go right!" He'd forgotten she was facing the stern.

She reversed her input. She trusted him, because she didn't want to die.

"That's enough. Now left!"

They shot past a cluster of jagged rocks. The river foamed around them. The boat dropped and juddered, then slewed wildly.

"Left! Left!" he cried to Gabrielle. She grunted against the sudden pressure in the oars. A second later she fell back off her seat as the oar was plucked from the water by the canting boat. Something ground against the boat, and Garyll dived over to force it away with his pole. A large scarred rock shot by, trimming shavings from the boat. Close, too close. He had almost lost the pole altogether. The boat bucked again, and slewed left. Garyll looked ahead with dread. The river, so deep and blue above Slipper, was now a white churning mess, marked by jagged black pillars of defiant rock. The rapids stretched far ahead, a rumpled surface of treachery.

They dropped with gut-wrenching suddenness, and ahead the water loomed in a feathering crest. They were swept into the standing wave and through it. Garyll was knocked from the bows again, but this time he held onto the bow-rope, and was able to haul himself back to his post.

Gabrielle's next oar-stroke found mostly air. She timed her next stroke to coincide with a trough, and she found purchase this time.

"Left!" shouted Garyll.

The rock was a submerged beast with a razor-sharp fin along its back. It would split them down the centre of the hull. There was no time for a good stroke from Gabrielle. Garyll dug his pole in, and leant all his weight against it. The wood creaked, his feet slipped and his legs flailed against the rails. The boat turned, but they slowed, and were more at the mercy of the wild current than before. Gabrielle cursed as she fended off with her oar, and Garyll heard the sound of splintering wood. They scraped past the obstruction, and tipped into the trough in its lee.

They topped three rapids which lifted them like a bucking horse. Then a wave leapt high in the sudden confluence of currents. Cold water swept over the bow and slammed into Garyll's face. The boat was awash and reeled drunkenly under the weight. They began to spin out, side-on to the current. Gabrielle fought the oars to regain control.

"Bail, or we drown!" he shouted at the Prince. The prince stared at him with wide eyes.

"The bucket, you fool!" shouted Garyll. "Under the seat. Take it, scoop the water out!"

Bevn just stared at him with his saucer eyes and clutched hold of his heels instead.

It was then that Garyll realised that they were doomed. His strength wouldn't last in the fearsome rush. Gabrielle couldn't row effectively, one oar was shattered already. Ahead, the passage to the lowlands roared its hunger: huge, leaping waves; deep, sucking troughs; and all around, the rocks, sticking up like hungry teeth, waiting in the churning water for a chance to shatter the little boat and its occupants to pieces.

"I hate you. It's all your fault," Bevn cried out at his back. Garyll didn't recognise the danger in time. As the boat pitched down and Garyll reached forward with his pole, the prince slammed into his back, pushing him over the bow.

"No, Bevn, we need him!" cried Gabrielle, but it was too late.

He lost his balance and plunged in. The boat rode hard over him and smote his head. Glavenor sank.

༼༽

Prince Bevn sat in the bows, dejected. The Swordmaster had spoiled everything. They hadn't seen him again after he had tumbled into the river. Bevn couldn't understand why, but he was sorry for what he had done. He shouldn't care, but Glavenor was different. He was strong. He was good. Too good, surely, but somehow he was a *real* man. He had tried to capture them, but he had only been following his duty to Bevn's father in doing so. Bevn knew he hadn't done it because he wanted the crown for himself, or for money. He wasn't like Saladon, or Gabrielle. Glavenor did what he did for justice, and that was what made the man so hard to fault. He was more than just a man. He didn't deserve to die, did he? Bevn had just wanted to escape from him, but now he wished he hadn't done what he'd done. He hoped the Swordmaster had survived, but the doubt dragged at him. The water around the boat was too polluted; streaked with milky ghosts. Glavenor had fallen right into it.

The air was humid and hot. The river flowed swiftly, swollen by the tributaries they had passed after they'd shot out of the rapids. It didn't matter that the wind had slackened as the strange storm had passed, for the current was strong enough, and there was a strange force at work on their boat, as if an unseen hand guided the craft and caused it to find the right currents. Gabrielle didn't bother to row. The shattered stumps of the oars weren't even worth keeping for firewood.

"When is Saladon going to come to us?" Bevn asked. Gabrielle ignored him. It was only the fifth time he'd asked.

"When he's finished punishing us for your foolishness," Gabrielle finally retorted, her words slurred with fatigue. "Here, sharpen my blade if you're bored. I'd like to know it'll cut when I stick it in your back."

Bevn was about to reply with some acid remark then thought better of it. He extended his hand but didn't get up, forcing Gabrielle to accede should she want the favour. She placed her hand on the rower's seat midway and leant far forward to pass the knife. His eyes dropped as he took the knife. With her low-cut halter, he had a great view. A small gust of wind tugged at her hair.

"Oh, for crying out loud, you're hard-up," exclaimed Gabrielle. She gripped the knot of her halter and pulled it free with a swift jerk. "Is this what you wanted to see?" she shouted out, louder than necessary—a shout that would reach to the riverbank. Her clothing dangled from her shoulders as she stood upright. Bevn gawked. "What more do you want from me, you bastard!" she shouted.

He admired the way the sunlight caught the swell of her breasts as she faced the shore. Perhaps she wasn't addressing him. She was challenging the wizard. He scanned the shore quickly for what Gabrielle had seen, but he couldn't find Black Saladon anywhere. "Show yourself!" she demanded.

The flame-leaved trees on the riverbank shook their dry leaves upon the water. Bevn grinned and turned. While Gabrielle searched the shore, he could search her body with his eyes, but it was over too soon. Gabrielle recovered from her passionate outburst, fastened her clothes and sat without a second glance at him.

The river soon brought them to a great orange hill, which proved to be a great pyramid of clay, bare and fresh as if it had been scoured from the earth somewhere nearby. The river turned brown as it cut past the new soil. Disturbed eddies plagued the water at its base. They scudded over a few rapids, but the flow was deep, and the river soon smoothened again in a straight channel between the hills. Great roots and branches thrust up through the water, some borne on the current; some stuck, straining the flood through rigid arms. They rounded a lazy corner and there, at last, they encountered him.

Black Saladon stood on the shore, his great axe planted like a declaration upon the bluff. The metal fibres in his flared shoulders glinted. The boat heeled over on a stiff breeze, and they were driven toward him. As they approached, his gaze remained hooded, hard. He didn't help them to disembark, waiting for them to walk to him.

"You come at last to the hardest part of your journey," he stated.

"How dare you put us through that? You risked my life!" Gabrielle accused him.

"And you failed me," he replied. His presence seemed to gather the air until little remained to breathe. "Was your task not to protect the prince and to ensure that he retains the crown? *Retains* it! Yet you allowed them to take it. It was time you learned the cost of failing me."

"You did not need to be reckless with my life," Gabrielle said bitterly.

"You had a strong man with you. I took a strategic decision—that you and he would want to live, that you would find a way to survive the Knarles. And that you did."

"We *had* a strong man, until piddlewit here pushed him into the drink. I could have died in there, you pig!"

"Watch your tongue, hex, or I'll strip it from your head. Do you think the risk is any less ahead? That has always been the price of a mistake."

"And you!" He turned on Bevn, who tried to shrink away, and Gabrielle pulled Bevn back toward her. "What have you done? Nobody should be able to carry your crown away from you. It is bonded to your blood. It will resist any thieves, It will burn their hands and break their minds. Only someone with the blood of Eyrian kings may bear it. What did you do that they thieved it from you?"

Bevn could feel Gabrielle's breasts pressing against his back. They were firm, as he had expected them to be. Despite his pounding fear of Saladon, he squirmed against her to better feel her body. Gabrielle shoved him roughly aside. "Away!"

Black Saladon stepped close, and Bevn realised he couldn't delay the tale any longer. Saladon was ready to rip him apart.

"There was a woman," he admitted.

"What kind of a woman?" His eyes were dark and alive and something hid there, waiting to burst out and seize the world.

"In that place you showed us, the hurry-hurry."

"And I say there was no woman!" Gabrielle interjected. "I watched over him in our room all night. His crown was safe, I left him for a minute in the morning, yet he came down without it."

Saladon regarded Bevn intently. "What did she look like?"

"She changed! She was good-looking, to start with. Well, a little."

"How bad was she? What was her price?"

"Price? She never... I... How would I know?"

"They wear their price on their necks in Slipper. The whores all have copper bands. Did you count them?"

"She... I don't think she had any necklaces on. They threw beer at her, and it made her wet."

"Then she was so bad she hadn't earned a price yet. What did she look like?"

"She was a half-Lûk." He looked down. "She was a hag."

"And how is it that this half-Lûk took your crown?" Saladon demanded.

"She—took me," Bevn replied, in a small voice.

"She did what?" Gabrielle exclaimed.

"We had sex."

"Oh lord," said Gabrielle.

"And then she took my crown. She stole it! There was nothing I could do."

"What did she say?" Saladon gripped his chin to force his head up, his face so close to Bevn's he could count Saladon's twirling wiry whiskers. "Did she say anything at all when she left you?"

"I can't remember! Something about the fates, that they were a mystery."

"Mystery. Mystery! Aargh!" Black Saladon threw Bevn aside. He paced away. He smacked his fist into his palm then considered things for a long moment. "She has made a dangerous play. Oh, I see what she is doing. She will attempt to save the others, the fool. She will go to Turmodin. The race is on! She cannot use transference with that thing on her head. Yes, we must move! If I can get you near to the crown I may be able to wrestle it back from her, or compel her."

"But how can she wear my crown?" Bevn cried. "You said it was only someone with the blood of kings who could wear it. She's not from Eyri, she was like the Lûk; she was ugly."

"Ugly? She disguised herself well, but you are right, she is not an Eyrian. She is a wizard of the Gyre. She carries your seed, you fool. She is pregnant. So she carries the bloodline of your ancestors and she can wear the crown. Oh Mystery you take a most costly gamble."

"She is—pregnant?" Bevn repeated. "But she can't be! She can't be! I'm just a boy! I can't be a father!"

"And yet yesterday you were demanding that you were a man," Gabrielle commented quietly.

It hit him with the full force then and his stomach rushed up at him. He went down on his knees and puked on the spiralweed. He was going to be a father with a hatched-faced half-Lûk. She was a wizard? It didn't make him feel any better. He felt violated. She had stolen his crown.

Black Saladon squatted on the weeds in front of him, his big axe resting casually across his knees. There was nothing friendly about his demeanour. His eyes burnt with a dark fire. Bevn could believe that worlds could begin and end in that gaze. His words seemed to pull power from the ether and wrap around Bevn's mind like cables. "Now understand this, Bevn Mellar. The only value you have left to me is in your blood. I can use the Mystery just as well, for my purposes, although she is harder to control. Do not think to defy me anymore, because I do not much care if you live or die. You will come with me, because if you do not, neither of you will survive a day. You don't want to be near the river from here onward, the water is too tainted. It's far too dangerous in the Merewraith lands, but the hinterland is not safe either. So stay close and obey me perfectly, or I will trim your head off at the neck."

38. A TROUBLED WORLD

"Evolution is the slow murder of tradition."—Zarost

The monster floated in the deep. The water was cool against its burning skin. The world was slow, moving—fluid. Things had changed, it knew, important things, but for now it was strangely content, to drift, to watch the light play through the facetted surface above. Amber trees spread searching branches across the yellowed sky and tall clouds boiled at the fringes of the tilting liquid panorama.

It found a rough rock and it rolled and rolled to clean the old scales from its sides, the ones that itched so terribly, the ones that itched so bad they hurt. The ones that kept its memories. The ones that spoke of ravage, responsibility and failure.

The monster shed its skin, and sought solace in simplicity. There was only the slow climb to the surface for air, the long descent into the darkness, and the wild hard imperative of survival ahead.

ଔଞ୍ଚଔଞ

The crack in the sky was close, a jagged junction running like a mad painter's spasm. On the left of the line, a bank of thunderclouds massed in knots. On the right, the pale dusty-coloured sky stretched away in an arc. The crack terminated in a tight angle, where four more cracks joined on a wedge of red clay. It was like looking at badly arranged mirrors. Smoke escaped from the clay and coiled lazily along the seams of the cracks.

"What is that?" Gabrielle asked. "There's a growing strangeness in this air, Saladon."

"It's a gate, a discontinuity. It is our way forward. What you sense is the Chaos essence it throws off just by existing. For every league we travel closer to Turmodin, it will get worse." He glanced at Gabrielle. "You'll get cranky, erratic, impulsive and unavoidably erotic. The creatures survive in the lowlands because they are crazy with lust. Otherwise they would have died out long ago with their violence. Chaos is a dangerous, destructive, wrecking force and the Gyre was right to try contain it, but you can feel how it stirs the blood!" He raked Gabrielle with his gaze. "Everything becomes possible, the rules split upon the infinite chances it creates. Spontaneity, surprise. You can never predict what a person will do next, when they are under its influence."

"Where does the...discontinuity...lead?"

"We shall see. I think this one is a pointer to somewhere far from Turmodin, but it matters not, for it is a maze, and if you calculate your sequencing correctly you can move fast and far."

"Don't you have a map, or something?" asked Bevn.

"Little use a map, when the land changes with every strike the Sorcerer makes."

"It...changes?"

"Moves, shifts, transforms itself! Every hill and mountain has been transplaced and every river course diverted at least a hundred times. He Who Can Not Be Named plays with the lowlands as it were clay and he the sculptor."

"Then how do you find your way around?"

"I don't travel here much. A place is called a name because of what it is, not where it is. There are signs, to find what you seek, if you know what you are looking for."

They approached the red clay, but just as they were about to walk upon it, Saladon held up his hand. The wizard bent close to the ground. Then he swirled around, and swirled back the other way.

"Hah! She has been through here," he announced. "She has hidden her trail well, but here at the gate her touch disintegrates. Oh you will run, Mystery, but you don't know the quickest way through this maze. I will pass you by! Then we shall see who is the master and who is not, when you come to Turmodin." Saladon holstered his axe on his back. "Come!" he commanded. "Be on my either hand. We must step into this together."

Bevn didn't like the way the clay smoked. His hand shook, but Saladon snatched it up and dragged him forward. They passed through the first discontinuity. He endured the feeling of waking up, over and over again, like rising through successive layers of consciousness. Each time, the volume of silence grew, until his breath thundered in his ears. He grew hot all over. The strangest was the sense of time. There was no time in which he felt all the sensations of change, it happened instantly that he stepped into the gate and was at his destination. It was as if the gate in the hills near the river and the new place they found themselves in were in fact one place—the same place.

The smoke dragged across the new landscape beneath red clouds.

Ash swirled, tendrils fought each other in strange vortex patterns. Blackened ruins towered all around them, a city of stupendous size, broken and tumbled by furious destruction. They were inside the city. Far away on the limits Bevn saw giant defensive walls made of plates, like monstrous overlapping shields strapped together. A tortured hiss filled his ears, an endless scream of a city burning. The heat was hard to bear.

"This was a centre of industry. It was known as Chagrim in old Koraman kingdom. It was broken three hundred years ago, but the fire is caused by the stasis that will not release the steelwork. It will smoke for a thousand years yet. There is nothing to fear here, except that it is all toxic and supports no life. Keep your hands off the surfaces, don't fall into any water. Keep on the plating and you'll be all right. We will be gone soon enough."

Bevn followed Black Saladon across the parched earth along a metal road. Huge pipes passed overhead in places, cables wound upon them in regular coils. They passed a tall building where gigantic mechanical humanoids stood in rows beneath a high roof. The wizard seemed to be reading the crack-lines in the sky, those parts that were visible through the random gaps in the low dragging clouds. They crossed the metal landscape like fleeing fugitives. Saladon strode fast, his cloak whipping in his wake, Gabrielle loped and Bevn stumbled, whimpered and ran, worried he would be left behind.

Bevn finally caught up to them at an enormous rusted road-junction. The road seemed to be made to carry a great load, and there were tracks in it, as well as regular hexagonal patterns scribed in green copper and something orange. "What did they make here?" he asked.

"Everything you could ever want in metal," Saladon replied. "They were becoming ingenious toward the end of the Age of the Three Kingdoms. Thinflex, pods, higfiber and carbonline. After Kinsfall, everything changed. They tried to make some defences against wildfire here—they lasted longer than most—but once you lose Order you lose commerce and you lose the trade that will support production, so Chagrim was strangled out of existence. They had limited success with silvertails, their decoy-launchers, but in the end they could not innovate fast enough. What you will see today is all the junk and trash of an ordered world gone to chaos. Such waste. Such a mess."

The wizard seemed saddened by what had been lost, and it echoed something which had been bothering Bevn for a long time.

"Then why do we side with the Sorcerer?" Bevn asked. "Isn't the world better with some order in it?"

"Yours is not to question why, princeling. For now you only need to know that we must support Chaos. The path we walk upon does not end with the Sorcerer ruling this world."

"Who will rule?" asked Bevn, already afraid that he knew the answer.

The wizard Black Saladon stopped. The dark sky swept over his head. "I shall," he replied.

ᏣᎬᏆᏁᏣᎬᏆᏁ

Later that day, Saladon led them to the second discontinuity and they passed from the martial industrial wastes of Chagrim through the *tight* moment to a rusty patch of soil at the edge of a settlement that was colourful, collapsed and crowded. People lived there, folk with sun-darkened skins and rough clothes. Flies buzzed about in the heat. Bright fabrics hung on lines and the tilting buildings had been smeared with colour, but the people had a pinched look about them. Their eyes were set too close together, thought Bevn. Some of them didn't even have proper nose bridges.

A few noticed their arrival and began to shout and wave at each other, but before they could approach the travellers, a column of hungry-looking figures shuffled between them. They were chanting and carried tall, spindly staffs with limp red rags on their tips, pennants to mark their common purpose, dark coloured like beet-dye, or wine. Or dried blood.

"Pilgrims," said Saladon, to himself. "So the word has spread even this far out. These people won't get there in time, but they will try. Never mind, I shall find a use for them all."

"Where are they going to?" asked Gabrielle.

"They are part of the great movement of people," replied Saladon. "The Last Pilgrimage. They go to Turmodin the long way, to find absolution for their sins, to find a promised release and an end to suffering. For them it is a chance to do something truly unforgettable, the great honour of climbing in consciousness. The Clerics of Qirrh are leading it, some of the best have already gone before and been transformed, and the ones left are desperate to gain favour and be in the head or heart of what is coming. So they spread the word, and collect more pilgrims, as if by numbers alone they can guarantee a better salvation."

Saladon watched them with a kind of satisfaction as the column moved off to the west. "The right words, Bevn Mellar. That is the secret to power. You must learn how to tell a good story. They won't stop. They will walk night and day. They won't stop walking until they die."

The clamour of the market returned. The villagers moved continually, even those with stalls tugged at their tables and moved their wares, as if too restless to remain in place. Bevn thought it was like watching an ants' nest he'd kicked open once. Everyone remembered a task, but their route had been taken away from them, and so they scurried about like idiots, among their peculiar name boards.

"What are the names for?"

"They label things, before they forget, but they argue all the time about those same labels."

The script on the nameplates was curly and difficult to make out, and he didn't recognise any of the words. People of all kinds were crammed together, talking in raised voices.

"Traders," said Saladon. "This place is called Merica." He kept them to the edge of the crowds, avoiding direct gazes wherever possible. "Our way leads beyond this town. I don't want to become embroiled in anything local."

However, a big man blocked their way as they neared a stairway, a heavy brute almost as wide as he was tall.

"Kirkajz?" he demanded.

"Let us pass," Black Saladon answered. He pointed up the stairway.

"Kirkajz?" the big man repeated, puzzled. He thrust a big board at Saladon.

"Ahh," said Saladon, taking a piece of chalk from the man and writing on the board. "They have lost their spoken word altogether then," he commented to them. "The spellingrot has hit this place hard since I was last here."

Saladon of Menerain, he had written. The big man read the board slowly then snarled. He smeared the board clean with the edge of his stained sleeve.

Spupiles, he wrote. "Zpli," he said. "Zmm?"

"I think he wants to know what we are trading here in Merica," said Saladon.

"What would they trade here?" Gabrielle asked.

"Serpent-dew from K, rare stones from the Fallen House, a vial of Myrki oil perhaps? It's difficult to tell what they would place value on here today, it is likely different from before. Food, probably, it all ends with food, when all else of value is lost. This man has one of the larger slateboards, so he must be important, or he believes he is so."

"We are not here to trade," Saladon said. "We are on our way to the gateway."

No trade, he wrote.

The big man seemed angered. He rubbed the writing out with his fist. "Pintly!" he shouted. "Pnit!"

peantly - ax or wmoan, he wrote, and thrust the board at Saladon again. People began to gather around them, drawn by the conflict.

"He is demanding a penalty," Saladon commented. "He seems to think my battleaxe or our vixen here will do him some good. Both will likely kill him, but he hasn't the sense to realise it."

"Penalty? Why does he write it so funny?" Bevn asked.

"Because of the spellingrot." He held up his hand to forestall the big man. "Observe what Chaos does to language." He cleared the board and wrote quickly across the slate, and Bevn read.

Aoccdrnig to the rscheearch dnoe by the Gyre, it deosn't mttaer in waht oredr the ltteers in a wrod are, the olny iprmoatnt tihng is taht the frist and lsat ltteer be in the rghit pclae.

Bevn couldn't believe he could understand what he was reading. When Black Saladon was satisfied Bevn had read it all, he smeared it clear with the back of his hand, and wrote again.

The rset can be a taotl mses and you can sitll raed it wouthit a probelm.

"This is so because you don't read every letter by itself but the word as a whole. Still, the Chaos takes over, and once they lose the anchor letters, they lose the words altogether. It begins with saying 'muvva' instead of 'mother'. It ends like this. Although they are descendants of the most literate class of Moral Kingdom, this is effectively a village of idiots. They cannot speak what they write, it makes no sense. You can only read it so. They shout at each other, yet understand nothing. Only in their writing does a little sense of order survive. Oh, it is far worse here than in it was in Slipper."

Saladon looked to the sky, where the crack-lines ran—warped assaults on reality. The Chaos broke the world here even more than in Chagrim. The wizard made a small gesture, and a ripple of disturbance passed through the air around him. Bevn held his breath. The filaments of wildfire moved, but didn't bunch and strike the way Bevn knew they might. Saladon reached into his pocket and withdrew a heavy book. When he passed it to the big man, the man seemed puzzled, but when he opened the cover and took in the first page, his face lit up.

"Tau, tau!" he exclaimed, nodding his head, and stepping aside to allow them all passage up the stairs.

"To him, it is a wonder," Saladon commented. "So many words, properly spelled. It will make him the richest man in this village to some, and the poorest, to others."

"Where did you get a book from?" Bevn asked.

"I know where to reference from," Saladon replied.

They left the big man to ponder his fortunes, but they hadn't walked three steps before the crowd of villagers closed their way. The closest three traders made a wall with their boards, their demands scrawled in hasty print.

Pnneal. Pty. Plenty.

"Ah, stuff it, I don't have time for this," Saladon muttered. He jumped straight up, and dropped with his great battleaxe in his hands, his hair flicking like a lion's tale. The vicious blade scribed a hot arc in the air and sliced hard through the closest trader's slateboard.

The man's arms were blown wide by the explosive force, and chips of his board rained out across the crowd. "Plhg, Plhg!" the man cried out, staggering away. The crowd broke and stumbled back away from the angry wizard.

"Right, now run!" he commanded Bevn and Gabrielle, mounting the steps three at time. "The worst insult in a place like this is to break their board."

The stairs opened to a short market street followed by a storage yard littered with abandoned wares and spillage. Birds exploded into flight as the trio ran through them. Saladon ducked into an alley, and they followed. Traders shouted at them as they ran. Some people tried to block their way, but upon seeing Saladon's battleaxe, they hesitated. Bevn tried desperately to keep up. Then five men in dirty clothes came running behind them, sickle-blades in hand.

"This is bad," Saladon shouted over his shoulder. "They are close to ruin here. Those are their robbers, sent to kill us and take whatever we have. I will kill them if I must, but I would rather not spill blood without benefit. So run!"

The men caught up to them before they had escaped from the village of Merica, because Bevn was too slow, and Saladon was forced to dive behind him, and dispatch them with his great blade, one by one. They didn't stand a chance against his martial art, yet they fell upon him with a total slashing frenzy and wild baying from the trailing villagers. They had lost their sense of reason, or the understanding of the value of their own lives.

Saladon's axe cleaved the last robber's body from head to tailbone in a sudden shocking cloud of blood. Before the body had even fallen to the ground, Saladon had gathered both Bevn and Gabrielle, and pushed them on. They ran until they were well clear of the border of the village, heading for a tight cluster of angles Bevn recognised as a Gate.

Saladon allowed them to halt, to gather their breath. Bevn's lungs burned, and his legs wobbled horribly.

"Why were they so crazy?" Bevn asked, leaning on his knees. "They could see they shouldn't fight you!"

"Chaos. It gets worse than this. These men only have their reason and language eroded. They are not ruled by it yet. Take away everything from a man, and what will remain? What makes a man a man, and not a beast?" He looked hard at Bevn. "When you speak in grunts and moans, when you can no longer remember the day before or think of the day after, who will you be? How much of what you are is what you have been taught, the culture of Order you carry with you. How much is merely your memories?"

It was a horribly *cold* thought; it sat in Bevn's head like a mute judge, forcing him to *consider* himself.

"How much is really you?" Saladon asked. "And is it enough to make you a man?"

"In chaos, is there any identity left at all?" asked Gabrielle.

"At the heart of it? No. I don't think so."

"Which shall you use? Chaos, or Order?"

"Whatever gives me the upper hand," Saladon replied. "Whatever gives me the most power, when I need it. It is time to move beyond the constraints of the third axis. That was our error in the Gyre. Thought should not be limited to a system, because that system is conceived at the limit of the wisdom of the time. The system can never incorporate thoughts that go beyond the system. It can never progress. I have seen the future. It is a blend of Order and Chaos. Neither must be supreme, but using both, I can be."

CRﾂꙨ

The monster rose from the deep because it was hungry. It broke the surface quietly, amid the watery weeds, as it knew it must, for on the shore was its prey. The green-skinned creatures lay upon the bank in the late afternoon sun. They looked warily at the river, but the river curved tightly behind them; they looked the wrong way. They would be too slow.

The monster reached the shallows, finding purchase on the rock; it gripped with a tough, webbed hand. It didn't wait for a better moment, it just launched hard and fast, using its powerfully hooked hind legs. It took the biggest one off the rock, talons piercing scales, jaws closing on the soft neck, twisting in the air to snap the resistant bones, falling to the river with a splash, taking the meat with it to the safety of the deep.

It was what its new body demanded, so it ate of the creature's flesh. The river ran red in the gloomy crevice, and the sky, so far above, was made red too for a time. The monster was a killer, and there was nothing it could do about it. There was no shame in surviving. Life was easier this way. It rose for a breath at last then thrashed its teeth through the water, cleaning them. It inhaled warm, forest-scented air. It heard bird calls in the woods. It floated. Much later, it saw the stars come out.

Only when it sank into the cool water again, did it disturb the scales of memory clinging to its back, in the places it couldn't reach. And it remembered. *He* remembered. The two white stones, they tumbled down, the two white stones, tumbling, into the cool green dark, past his outstretched hand. And he grieved for the friend who had come before those stones, he grieved and his heart swelled in his chest, and his tears were unto the water borne, and his body was carried on the current, downstream—down, down, to whatever distant end life would take him.

If there was one thing he would do before he died, it would be to avenge that single unjust act. The one who blighted the sky and ruined the earth must pay for the murder. There would be justice. He felt his body alter as his resolution strengthened. He would hunt his prey, and his prey had a name.

Ametheus.

39. AN EYE ON THE MOON

"Beliefs are breakwaters; they shelter me
from the fearsome seas of possibility."—Zarost

The world lurched around her. The sun had tracked too fast through
the sky; it stood close to noon. The angry red clouds wrapped upon
themselves, twisting and churning. From the high point of the Pillar,
a bright flash bloomed against the clouds.

Tabitha neared a strange archway guarding the protruding entrance
to a tunnel. It seemed to be a sculpture, but it was terribly lifelike.
Many human-like figures clutched hold of one another desperately,
joined in an arch well above Tabitha's reach. Their naked bodies were
silvered; their flesh looked as hard as granite. They faces were fixed
in agony.

Tabitha shivered as she passed through the tunnel. It seemed to be
a sculpture of humanity, as if real people had been forced to create the
structure, and once positioned, they had been altered to stone. Some
reached out in frozen gestures of appeal. Some of them looked down
at her with almost sentient eyes. She came to the end of the gruesome
tunnel, to emerge in the gloom of the Pillar.

The building groaned as it moved around her. Strange sounds
echoed through the corridors, the calls and taunts of its many unseen
inhabitants. Ruddy daylight filtered through irregular slits and gaps in
the outer walls. Her lens outlined each structure with scribed angles
and warnings of stress-points and overload. Danger was all around.
According to the principles of Order, the Pillar should have been a
heap of rubble. Tabitha ignored what her eye told her. She knew she
would become a nervous wreck if she clung on to Order here.

There was no clear path to the top. Some of the floors sloped
upward, some down. Wherever there was a choice, she took the upper
route. Higher and higher she climbed, scrambling up piles of broken
masonry and unstable metal plates in places, clambering up corded
vines dangling from higher beams, sometimes even scaling the
framework of the Pillar on the outside, where long pieces of lichen
slipped slowly down the walls, leaving wet trails. A dead tree had
been thrust through a broken window; Tabitha used it to climb to the

next level. There were staircases in places, but none of them were whole, and some had crumbled away so badly they ended in midair. The higher she went, the worse the fear became, hammering away at her gut, telling her the entire structure was about to collapse. The shifting strands of Chaos her lens outlined began to converge; they centred upon the peak of the Pillar, only a few levels above where she stood—the Sorcerer's chamber. She was almost there.

The swaying movements became more pronounced. A tremor shook the building and an untidy column Tabitha was considering for a stair broke away and took a floor with it, tumbling down, breaking patches clear inside the Pillar, tearing out hollow sections which shouldn't have been there; ripping out its own rotten core. She couldn't look down. Far below, things slammed into other things. It went deeper than she'd expected. Metal shrieked, living things screamed. She clutched at a railing, but it broke in her hands, crumbling to grey dust. The floor tipped, and she had nothing with which to steady herself. She took a wild chance and hummed a single note. The floor tipped back and she slid against the wall. The upheaval settled.

Had it settled because of the note, or had it just settled? She couldn't tell, but she was beginning to suspect things in Turmodin were somehow fluid and responsive to her thoughts. So many years of Chaos in one place had weakened the permanence of reality. If *that* was true, she would have to be careful what she thought; particularly, what she feared. *The pillar is strong, the way up is clear, and the Sorcerer will hear what I have to say,* she told herself. *The pillar is strong. The pillar is strong.*

In a way, the collapse of the column was a blessing, for it revealed the proper passage to the Sorcerer's chamber. Across the inside of the tower a scalloped membrane looped over the displaced beams. It looked like the husk of some worm, twisting upward through the jumbled architecture. The membrane was holed in places, and once she was inside the tube, Tabitha found the going easy. Each ridge of skin provided a step, and in the places where the sides had decayed, rope-like thews remained to be used for balance. Her boots gripped the surface well. The passage smelled like dry parchment, yet it gave under her weight slightly as if it were still elastic. The translucent tube spiralled upward quickly, spanning great gaps in the ruins, looping sickeningly between the main tower and a tilted side turret, out through wind that moaned with altitude, then back again, until she emerged upon the highest level of the Pillar. The sun dived toward the horizon, and the wind began to whistle.

The Pillar's pinnacle was a terrifying plate of rock, upon which a bulbous building squatted, a deformed thing, like some chitinous insect killed when the heavy roof had been slammed down unevenly upon it—the Sorcerer's chamber. It could be nothing else. Most of the windows faced away, into the clouds. A ruddy light spilled from the only doorway, on Tabitha's side. Tabitha heard voices, but with all the recycled sounds of Turmodin plaguing the air she couldn't tell if the voices were new, or just echoes. They rose and fell, as if people were arguing. A cluster of torches sputtered beside the open doorway, burning despite the weather. Great dead trees had tumbled against the one side of the building: an attempt at a garden, which had failed? Only blotches of moss grew upon the slab. She recognised the exposed area. Ametheus had reached for her from there; she had seen him standing where she stood now.

The clouds whipped by, pressing moisture into her clothes. The passing wind tangled her hair and caused the strings of her lyre to whine softly. It was almost as if the lyre played a tuneless music of its own. The light of day began to fade. It was too early for sunset, Tabitha thought, too early by far. She tiptoed towards the open door. The voices became clearer.

"Break them, break them all, Seus!" A barrel-deep baritone.

"Patience, brother Amyar." A clipped answer sounded in a cold voice. "This shard holds the wizard they call the Cosmologer, you can see from the violet colour. She might be useful to us if the Goddess fails to sing."

"She will deceive you! All the wizards have wickedness in their hearts. Have you forgotten what they have done to us? Have you forgotten the suffering? We must stamp out all traces of magic. They deserve to die!"

"Of course they do, Amyar, but we have broken the Gyre. On their own, they cannot harm us and they cannot escape. They are imprisoned. Think of it, brother. To take their lives now would be merciful, their suffering will end, but if we keep these shards, they shall live on, trapped in their slivers of reality. For longer than all the years we have suffered, they shall suffer, in isolation. We have shattered three of them already. These last few should serve an age of penance. Besides, there's the one who escaped. Maybe she is stupid enough to come here to save the others."

"It d-doesn't m-matter what you d-do," added a third man with a phlegmy voice. "If you idiots m-make the Goddess s-s-sing and you b-bring Him here, you will h-have little s-say in anything. It is all g-g-going to end."

"Oh shut up, Ethan!" ordered the man with a cold voice whom the others had called Seus. "You know nothing of the future!"

"And you remember too little of the past!" added the deep-voiced one, Amyar. "Who asked you to wake up, anyway?"

There was a groan, as if someone had been winded, or had fainted.

How many people were there in the Sorcerer's chamber? Should she wait for a better moment? She supposed there was no good time to approach the Sorcerer. There was no point in delaying the inevitable confrontation.

"Now, what about this indigo one?" said the deep-voiced man. "The Riddler. Father knows how many headaches this one has given us. Shouldn't we rather bust him? He worries me. He's too clever. He's not like the others."

Tabitha stepped into the room. Her mind was wild, unclear. She could not think or speak.

For a long moment she was disorientated. The space inside the building was much greater than the outer dimensions had suggested, greater than what was possible. Strange places existed where she couldn't even keep her eyes focused, as if her vision was repelled by the irreconcilable conflicts of geometry. The wide irregular windows, so far away, admitted a panoramic view of the ragged bottoms of the clouds. The real view was in the low roof overhead, contained in convex curves of glass. Images shifted across the ceiling: rumpled land, tilted at an awkward angle; shifting faces, crowds, beasts, villages, landscapes and starscapes.

A dirty carpet stretched away under a litter of debris and ash. The air was hot and potent, like a brewing house with an added metallic tang. Only one figure inhabited the room. At a bench at the windows, his back toward her, stood a large man in a divided robe, a garment of uneven texture made of thick threads like gathered snakes. His face was obscured by his red headpiece whose engraved metal wings came down to his collar. The back of his head was covered with a loose fold of black silk with spiralled silver patterns upon it. An ugly mallet was clenched in his broad right hand. He was looking down at something on a bench before him—three big shards of a mirror.

"I tend to agree, the Riddler is not like the others," he said in the cold voice. "He's nothing but trouble."

"Ametheus," she whispered to herself.

He turned his head slightly toward her, as if she had spoken louder than she'd meant to. His youthful face, bracketed by the strips of metal, was dark-browed, intense, with lips as straight as a cold blade. He turned further and his icy blue eyes caught her from far across the room.

Tabitha felt as if she was falling toward him. She had made a terrible mistake entering his chamber.

"Where are the other minstrels?" he asked in that smooth cold voice, which seemed to come from many different directions. There was nothing welcoming about the way he looked at her.

"I-er—" Tabitha stammered. She didn't know what to say.

"Well, play your piece. That is why you have come? To show off your talents? This is why they climb the Pillar. This is why they fall back down. You musicians seldom impress me."

"I haven't come to play," Tabitha asserted.

Ametheus narrowed his eyes, and the walls seemed to press inward, squeezing Tabitha where she stood. "Who are you? I don't remember bringing you here. Your looks are strange, unblemished. You are not from the lowlands. Where have you come from?"

"I come from a...long...way away."

"Yet you speak in the way of the Three Kingdoms, as I learnt to speak. How is this so?"

"Let me see!" the deep-voiced man demanded. That second person, whom she had heard before, was in the room, but Tabitha couldn't identify where he was hiding.

"Quiet, Amyar!" ordered the Sorcerer, speaking to the air. "No, you will not steal my attention. No! I am observing the newcomer."

"Let me *see*, Seus!" Amyar boomed in his deep voice. The Sorcerer jerked and twitched where he stood, but he kept watching her. Seus must be a nickname, a shortening of Ametheus, Tabitha decided, but who was Amyar, the man he was arguing with? And where was the third man, the one with the phlegm-choked voice she'd heard before she had entered?

"You are a very strong-willed woman," Seus said. "People very seldom find the door to my chamber."

Did he live entirely on his own?

"I draw people here whenever I want, but no one ever enters until I wish them to, because there is no door." He gestured behind her.

"Look." The red-plastered wall was continuous. No exits led from the room. Tabitha stared at the place she knew she had entered through. It was now solid stone. "Yet when you arrived, you found a door," Seus continued from behind her. "You intrigue me, woman. You have a gift for change."

"I will see her *now!*" shouted the deep-voiced man. Tabitha turned back quickly.

Seus had gone, and a different man stood before her. He was dressed the same, as large and stocky as Seus, but his features were completely different. Had Seus *changed* his face? He glared at her through bloodshot eyes. Fiercely ugly, a nasty scar cut deeply through his nose, pulling his lip into a permanent snarl. His cheeks were florid. He looked old but strong and embittered.

"Who are you, intruder. Who are *you?*" It was the voice of Amyar. Where had Seus gone?

"T-Tabitha, I am Tabitha Serannon, a singer."

"*Ulaäan?* Are you the one? No you're not, you're a wizard, aren't you? You're the one who slipped the trap. You're the Gyre's Mystery! Wizard-bitch, you are trying to trick me!"

He took a step toward her. Tabitha backed away from his fearsome anger, but he kept on advancing.

"I'm not from the Gyre!" she pleaded, but it came out with the sound of a lie. As he drew closer the space around her changed horribly, as if her own dimensions were becoming warped. Her composure eroded and the words tumbled out of her. "I know them, but I'm not one of them, I'm not the Mystery, I promise, I'm not the Mystery! I came here on my own. I came because my Goddess called me. I'm not here to fight with you, I just want to help my Goddess. Please, I'm telling the truth."

A heavy scent, like curing hides, washed against her. Amyar's heat burnt against her skin. He had trapped her against the wall. His strong hand slammed her head back. Rough fingers parted her eyelids.

"The songbird? I don't believe it! Let's see, what is your story?"

She looked at him through her tearful right eye. Her lens flared. He was such a mass of tangled warnings and lore-marks that he could hardly bear the brightness. Closer and closer he came, until his bloodshot eye was wide across her vision, demanding her surrender, pouring his angry intent into her, and as he did so she was drawn into his soul. She saw a churning pool of memory, brief images of torment, moments of heart-wrenching sadness, seconds of agony, loaded with the analysis the lens provided, scribe-lines, levels and lore that stuttered at her in a barrage of information and ideas.

"They gave me their lore," she tried to explain.

"There is no law!" he shouted into her face and her lens burst with light. In a horrible flash, she was blinded. Her Ordered sight had seen too much Chaos. She cried out and wrenched her head aside, and Amyar leapt back as if stung. He began to howl.

"No, Amyar!" said Seus, from somewhere. "You will not break this one yet!"

"She's a wizard! Wizard! I saw it! Her eye is full of gold! Treacherous, traitorous, lying bitch-wizard! Die, witch, die!" He lunged for her. Something caught his feet. He tripped and toppled headlong onto the floor. With his arms outstretched, he almost caught her. She couldn't judge the distance. She could only see out of her smarting left eye; her right eye smoked and spat with pain. Tabitha shook with terror as she stumbled aside and backed along the wall.

He lay face down on the floor, the black silk hood covering the back of his wide head.

"Seus you bastard!" Amyar shouted into the floor. "Seus! Release me! I will break you, brother!"

"Wait!" Seus replied. "She might be the songbird. She might know how to make the Goddess sing."

"I will kill you!" Amyar screamed. He thrashed against invisible bonds, as if he were trying to rise but someone else was holding him down.

"Amyar! Get a hold on yourself. We can overpower her. I see that we may yet need her talents."

"They must die!" shouted Amyar, spittle flying. "All of them must die! They force their Order upon the world."

"I am not here to bring Order!" Tabitha cried out, her voice small in the Sorcerer's presence. "I am here to help the Goddess."

"Lies! Wizards always lie! Let's burn her in the fire then she'll tell the truth!"

Amyar pushed himself up onto all fours. He glared at her. Madness swirled in his eyes, madness and bloodlust, but just when Tabitha thought he was going to leap at her, he shook, his head turned aside, and the other aspect of the Sorcerer was revealed: Seus, with his clear eyes and smooth, severe expression. The two brothers were joined. They were part of the same man, divided only by the headpiece he wore.

"How can I believe you?" said Seus. "Give me something to believe, and be honest. I can't hold my brother off for much longer."

Tabitha stared at the Sorcerer. Two brothers, in one body, yet their minds were separated—almost.

There were three brothers, she remembered, then she knew what must be beneath the black silk hood. The one called Ethan was asleep. They had forced him to sleep, she had heard his phlegmy voice protesting, and his groan when he had been subdued. There were three brothers in one body and they fought with each other. Ametheus was the intersection between Amyar, Ethan and Seus. No wonder the Sorcerer was so savage in the use of his power. Ametheus was a battle for consciousness between three brothers.

Seus was watching her. "You are not like the other wizards. None of them would have come here so unprepared. None would have taken such a great risk. You must have Chaos in your blood to attempt such wild things."

Chaos in her blood? That couldn't be true. Eyri had been protected from Chaos.

Tabitha wanted to curl up and cry. She wanted to hide from his attention. He had burnt the sight out of her right eye. He was too powerful, too dangerous; too mad, but she knew if she didn't speak she would have no chance; the brother Amyar would return and end her. "I am the voice of Ethea," she said. "I am her singer. I have come to beg for her life. Please spare her life. Please, I beg you." For a brief moment, the incessant sounds of Turmodin broke off then they returned, gathering, gathering, to a fever pitch.

"The singer!" He looked surprised. "What are you doing here, now? You have come too early!"

"You must listen, or you will get nothing from her!" Tabitha replied quickly. "She will die without performing the deed you want. Your tortures are wasted, they only give her pain. She can not give you what you want."

"How can you know that? You cannot know! I see the future, girl, I *see* it. I know that through her I will get what I want."

"She has no power because you have imprisoned her here. She needs to be in her godly plane; she should not be bonded here in flesh."

"She will call to Apocalypse. He will not be denied! He cannot be denied!"

Tabitha took a chance. "If you have seen that future then it is only with my help that you shall get there. Spare her life. Let her go free."

"Who are you, to make such demands? What are you?"

"I can sing her song, I am a Lifesinger."

"Ah." He regarded her for a long moment. "Yes, I discussed this with the black one, I...forgot."

"I have little to work with while you keep the Goddess here," Tabitha added.

"You wish for me to release her, so that you can grow strong, and then you will help me?"

Tabitha nodded.

"Pah! I am not a fool. What's to stop you from escaping as soon as she is free? Why would you wait around? Why would you ever bring the Destroyer to life?"

"Because I don't think that I can escape from this place unless you allow me to."

"Yes, yes, that may be true," he replied. Seus looked suddenly suspicious. "Either you are very brave and very honest, or you are lying."

"It is wrong to lie."

"Hah! An honest wizard! Hah! I don't believe it. Are you as innocent as you look?"

"I-I am seventeen," Tabitha replied.

He looked surprised again. "Well, Tabitha the singer, you have much to learn about the ways of the world. Everything can be changed, even fate, even history. Even the truth."

Truth and history could be changed? The man was mad. "Some things should never be changed," she said. "What you have done to Ethea is wrong. You made a mistake to bring her here. You must correct it."

Ametheus flinched and Tabitha felt that awful adjustment of space again. The Sorcerer drew himself up.

"Now *that* is the voice of a wizard, full of judgements and rules. I can do whatever I wish!"

"You cannot afford to let the Goddess die. The Lifesong will end forever. Her death will be your death as well as mine."

"That would please our solitary brother," he said quietly, as if to himself. Then he snarled. "Why do we need such a song, ruling our forms, dictating its patterns, over and over?"

"Without the Lifesong we shall have a dead world. The world

needs its pattern to grow upon."

"Pattern is Order! The world has never needed order! You've been talking to the Goddess, haven't you? And she just wishes to escape! She'll tell you anything to extend her life. She told me the same things. Your mistake was to believe them."

"But the Lifesong is her voice! It is her power that keeps you living! How can you deny your own existence?"

"You think I must release her, so that the song continues? Like the bloody birds. They sing! And they carry their song from generation to generation. There is always an egg somewhere, a new clutch of young birds to carry the song on from the old. So I must kill them. Life keeps on repeating in the same patterns, over and over. Somehow they carry that pattern. *They* are responsible! When they sing, they reinforce the pattern, but everything dies in the end, they all come upon starvation and sickness and death. Life is a misery, they must see that. Yet they sing! Why do they sing?"

"It is the thread of the Lifesong within them that inspires them to live," she replied. "It is beauty."

"That is why it must be ended. There is no beauty. There is no happiness. Only bondage and our Father, who will break us free."

"How can you expect to find happiness when you are surrounded by the creatures you have created, these tormented souls trapped in bodies they cannot love, in forms which demand violence for survival and can't speak of their pain."

"So what? Look at me!" screamed Amyar. "Nobody cares about me." Tabitha had forgotten he was still there, hidden by the divide in the Sorcerer's headpiece. He was waiting to overpower his sibling.

"Wait, Amyar!" demanded Seus. "I am not done yet. Quiet! Let us say I release the Goddess, and then you shall sing for me, and do my bidding, yes?"

She hesitated.

"Careful, Seus, she is messing with our head!" warned Amyar.

"Calm down, brother," responded Seus. "She is making some sense to me, even if you don't understand."

"She will trick you!" exclaimed Amyar. "Don't listen to her! You have forgotten that we drew her here, and you said we need the others to be here first! It is too early. She is trying to trick you!"

"I said that?" Seus looked frustrated.

"She carries their Order-eye!" warned Amyar. "She has a cursed vision of the world."

"It doesn't matter what vision she has. What *I* see is what will be. I am stronger than her."

"And I say no! Enough! Enough! You are fooled by her beauty. Just bind her, or break her!"

"What you are doing cannot succeed," Tabitha said. "You have made a big mistake."

"I will rule the future, not you!" Seus shouted and lunged toward her with an outstretched hand. Tabitha fell back, struck in her chest by the Sorcerer's repulsion. It felt as if he had gathered gravity and hurled it against her. She flew backward across the room and struck the wall. Her knees went weak, but she did not slide down the wall, rather she was pinned where she stood, pressed back like a leaf in a gale.

Panic gripped her. She had thought she was beginning to win Seus's support but he was attacking her. He stormed across his chamber, his arms raised, debris pulled along in his wake. Suddenly she recognised the moment. The Revelations had shown her this scene, all those weeks ago, in King Mellar's chamber in Stormhaven. She had stepped into a moment of prophecy. Something strange was happening to reality, with links to the past in the present moment, and links from that past to the present. She had the impression of being at a confluence of causal threads, and that her hand could change the weave.

Yet there was no escaping from the vicious pressure of the Sorcerer and his murderous intent.

Had she ever really escaped the prophecy, or had she just caused it to be? Here things were almost exactly as they had been visualised. It was a sudden thought, a flash, but for an instant she wondered... If she could visualise her own future well enough, would that be enough to change the present? She wanted to be free.

The sorcerous assault broke off and she toppled forward to the dirty floor.

"Run, girl, run!" cried Seus. "Amyar is taking my mind! He will kill you! Begone!"

But he was already upon her. He reached down with those strong hands and hauled her up by her collar. He drew back a massive fist.

"No Amyar, we can use her!" shouted Seus, out of view. "I see your memories now! We were going to use her! It was my plan!"

Tabitha twisted out of his momentary weakness, breaking his grip and running for the door. Tabitha slowed. She had forgotten. There was no exit. The Sorcerer's vision of the reality atop the Pillar was stronger than hers.

"Better to kill her!" Amyar howled.

She tried to believe an exit existed, a break in the smooth wall.

There was a door.

There was no door.

There was a door again. She ran for the gap.

She ran into solid rock and struck her face.

Tabitha bounced backward, and fell, disorientated.

The Sorcerer laughed from behind her. "You are ill-equipped to deal with the impossible," he said, in Seus's deep voice. "Your kind will always lose when the game is played upon my turf."

She twisted on the ground, looking up into bloodshot eyes. It was the cruel scarred face of Amyar that regarded her. She had only one last resort. She could name him, as the book had told her. Tabitha hoped that the word of power would inflict a long enough moment of paralysis for her to escape.

"Ametheus!" Tabitha called out. "Ametheus! Ametheus!"

"Damn you!" shouted Amyar. "Damn you, damn you, damn you!"

"The third one will be angered!" exclaimed Seus.

"You have roused our brother," they chanted in unison. "Ethan awakes."

The Sorcerer's body jerked. It jerked again.

Tabitha didn't wait to watch what happened to him. She turned to the wall again, and willed the door to form—an opening, a hole, a break, anything through which she might escape. She knew the pinnacle of the Pillar was outside, where the wind blew across the naked slab, open to the sky. She could see it in her mind's eye, so close, but she couldn't reach it.

Tabitha beat upon the wall with her hands, but the mortar was firm and unmoving. The Sorcerer might have been paralysed for a moment, but so had his vision. His vision was of a chamber without a door, and so it was.

Could she risk singing and using essence in this place? She had to try. If reality really was so fluid around the Sorcerer, she would create her own world, one in which there was a door to this high chamber. She began to sing her stanza of destruction, to tear a hole in the substance of the wall and convert it to essence. She sang, but her notes came out wrong. The awful arrhythmic beat of Turmodin disrupted her music, and she could find no harmony. Fragmented voices split and rejoined in an incessant cacophony. Metal clanked and groaned. Insects whined. The Lifesong died on her lips.

She hadn't managed to deal with two of the brothers. How would she survive three? She wanted to melt away and disappear. Tabitha pressed her face to the red-plastered wall, not wanting to see who was waking behind her. She should have listened to the wizards of the Gyre, who had known she could not survive in Turmodin. She had made a terrible mistake, and now, she would die.

"Wh-what has h-h-happened?" asked someone with a quiet, constricted voice.

Too late; no time remained to find an escape. The third brother was conscious.

"Wh-what has changed?" continued the new speaker, his voice a curdled whisper, the voice of a tormented sleeper, slurred and slow. "Oh my b-b-brothers! You are angry w-with each other, aren't you, y-y-you are d-divided? To s-sleep! You as w-well, b-brother Seus. I w-will enjoy my f-freedom."

"Beware, there is a wi..." began Seus, his voice fading.

"S-s-sleep! Yes. Sleep."

The Sorcerer shifted his weight behind her. The wind moaned softly by, carrying the cacophony of chaos in random gusts. The Pillar groaned and shuddered. She turned her head slowly, dreading what she would find.

He was close, looking at her from beneath the silk head-covering that he had lifted partially. Clumped strands of white hair obscured much of his pasty face, but one silver-patterned eye stared at her. The Sorcerer's body was facing the other way; she was looking at the back of his head, yet still it was a face, with a puckered mouth and stub of a nose.

"Who are you?" he demanded. "Why are you here?"

Didn't he know that already? His gaze was difficult to bear, but she resisted the temptation to look at her feet. It was important to pretend to be calm, or she would become hysterical. "I-I am a singer. My name is Tabitha."

"Oh. Oh! A new minstrel? You are beautiful, quite beautiful, my brothers have chosen well." His voice, so stuttered before, had gained clarity, as if he was more directly in the present. He took a step toward her by taking a step backward, and extended an upside-down hand. "I am Ethan."

"P-pleased to meet you," Tabitha stammered.

She didn't extend her hand. She couldn't touch him; she couldn't trust the brutality of those rough hands was under control. The Sorcerer dropped his hand, disappointed.

"Were my brothers misbehaving?" he asked. "I have slept too long. I am afraid my sibs are a bit dominant, one of the problems of having shared blood. It's been a while since I've been allowed to be myself. Excuse me if I appear a bit slow." He cast an eye around the room. "Why were they fighting?" he asked.

He really didn't remember! Maybe she had a chance. "Amyar wanted to kill me and Seus was trying to stop him."

"The bloody fool Amyar, he'll break anything he can get our hands on. Between them they have ruined so much. Talk about a chip on my shoulder; I've got a whole head on mine. Amyar just can't forget the past, it's all he sees. Damn brute. I'm glad he didn't kill you, Singer Tabitha. I'm sorry he tried." Tabitha was surprised by Ethan's behaviour. Despite his grotesque appearance, he seemed gentle, even polite. His dark singular eye, wet and tearful, wobbled slowly as he watched her. How could there be in one brother such rage, and in the other such meekness?

"You're all joined, and yet you're all so...different," said Tabitha.

"Of course we are!" Ethan exclaimed. "It wouldn't do to get right and left mixed up now, would it? We keep a separate house here, or try to. We each have our tasks to perform."

"What is your task?"

"Me? I see the present. Without Seus I have no magic and without Amyar, no strength." He leant toward her. "I'd like to talk with you and enjoy my freedom a while, but if you do anything to threaten me I'll have to wake up my brothers. Understand?"

To hold his gaze steady was like staring closely into a freshly cut onion.

Tabitha nodded. He wanted her promise of fair play. It was probably plain to him that she was some kind of wizard, yet he was still prepared to risk talking to her.

"Your eye!" he exclaimed. "It's all mixed up, gold and silver, just like the chalice! How did you do that?"

The pain of it throbbed in her head, and the thought of it made her want to cry. "I...didn't. Your brother Amyar has just blinded me. I can't see out of it."

"Oh dear. Dear oh dear oh dear. What a wonder it would be, if you could see from it. You would see things just as Annah wanted... Oh well, there's many things that are a shame in this world, let's not dwell on them. I am sorry for what he has done to you. Come, join me by the windows, I'd like to talk a while."

"How come you don't hate me, like your brother Amyar?"

"While my brothers sleep, their thoughts are hidden from me. I feel only the guilt from the past, without the memories. I feel only a foreboding of the future, without knowing the plans. It's when we're awake at the same time that we interfere. They will sleep now, until I grow tired or call to them. I don't hate you because you haven't given me reason to hate you yet. Very few people have ever held my gaze. So many people turn away..."

She couldn't sympathise with him, not when he was the one who had trapped the Goddess, and all the people in the effigy. "Maybe if you didn't terrify everyone with such awful spells, the world would be kinder to you."

"Oh! I see your anger," Ethan said. "Please, don't direct it at me, my brothers did it! They always do it! They brought the ruin, they wield the magic."

"Your magic," Tabitha persisted. She thought of the wildfire webs, spitting Chaos down upon the world.

"No! I hate magic. Magic gives men too much power. They believe they are greater than others, they do strange things, but Seus says that the only way to fight magic is with magic. I have to agree with him. How else could it be done? That's why there must be wildfire, to stop the magic. The wizards began it, by developing Order. We must end it, in Chaos."

"But what good shall come from that if life cannot continue!" Tabitha blurted. "The Goddess will die if you don't release her, and what can come after without her song? Nothing!"

Ethan looked sad. "The Goddess? What else can I do? My father has commanded it. I can't make a difference."

"Your father?" Tabitha asked.

"He sees the world through me. I am cursed with his eye."

"What? Your eye is..."

"Yes, the eye of the Apocalypse. He could see you now, if he chose to look."

Tabitha took a step backward. She understood how it was possible that Ametheus had trapped the Goddess, why he committed such atrocities—the son of the prime God, the *son* of the Apocalypse? The warnings in the book had been real. She had begun to think Ethan was the least threatening of the three. It was not true at all. He was the greatest danger. He was watching her with his silver-patterned eye.

"You are more than you appear to be, Singer Tabitha. What do you care about the Goddess?"

"She is my inspiration."

"So you are very much like me, then. You are a sorcerer."

Tabitha couldn't answer, because he was right. He drew his power from Apocalypse, her source was Ethea. They were both Sorcerers, yet he had the upper hand. He had captured her source, and he could break everything with the power he wielded. She could not save Ethea unless she convinced him of her value, yet without the Lifesong the world would end in utter desolation.

Ethan looked sad. "You wish to save her from death?"

"Yes."

"That is only possible if you sing the song she will not sing. My father must be brought into this world. The way to a new world is through Apocalypse." His voice altered, as if he spoke from far away. "Everything shall be destroyed and everything shall be made again."

"If you destroy the only one who can bring life again, then that is a lie."

"If I bring life to the only one who can destroy it completely, then it is not," Ethan retorted. "Just because you cannot conceive of an existence without life doesn't mean there isn't one."

"What do you mean?"

"Seus says that life is just one kind of existence, a passing phase. There are other states of awareness, other forms. This world must end."

"But you are condemning everything by summoning the Apocalypse! Why do you want to bring him into this world?"

Ethan gave her a haunted look. "Because I must be sure everything else dies when I do. There must be no chance that Order will be rebuilt from the ashes."

CRXOCRXO

"How much farther do we have to go?" Bevn asked, again.

The sun was warm, too warm. The air was sticky. It seemed to Bevn they had been in the stinking bog lands forever. He had seen an abandoned city of broken glass where the light had pierced his mind, he had seen places were terrifying creatures fed upon each other, but the bog lands were the worst, for here in the heat and filth, the ground itself seemed to be alive. It bubbled, burped and shifted underfoot, as if he was being led across a crusty skin. He was certain he was going to stumble into a festering sore in the land and plunge into some foetid liquid horror below.

"I don't know, fool!" Saladon replied. "It could take us another day, it could take another month. Everything depends on finding the Gate! We couldn't walk to Turmodin if we tried from this side, there's too much growing land around it, too much sea."

"Sea? What is that?" asked Gabrielle.

"Think of it as a very large lake."

Saladon led them up an incline, where the fruits were dark and heavy on the low trees. Bevn knew he wasn't to touch them. They were all toxic, poisonous or hallucinogenic, like the fungus that squelched underfoot. The air was thick with insects, ones that whined incessantly and bit Bevn all the time. Often they drew blood. Saladon didn't seem to care, for the insects didn't come near him. Those that tried, burned, the moment they touched his body. Bevn didn't have any protection from the cruel interest of his tormentors, and he was miserable, sick and afraid.

They topped a rise and the wizard stiffened beside them.

"There's what we've been looking for, all this time," Black Saladon announced.

Prince Bevn and Gabrielle followed his gaze. Reed huts spiralled outward around a great red obelisk, a carved stone that looked like a split tooth. Many were just wooden frameworks, lattice structures of saplings or planks, unfinished, but even from this distance, Bevn could make out the figures swarming over the constructions, and pilgrims, staggering through the activity with their fluttering red pennants, driven ever onward to find the promise.

"That's Kragha?" asked Bevn. "I thought it was a town."

"Sometimes it is, sometimes it isn't, but it's always at the final gate to Turmodin."

"How can it only *sometimes* be a town?" Bevn protested.

"It depends how long it has had to grow," answered Saladon. "I'd say it has been on that slope for all of three or four days, but it's been Kragha for many many years. Things pass both ways through Kragha. A lot of interesting things come to Kragha through that gate, and the closer you can build to the marker stone, the more risk you'll run, but the greater your reward. Sometimes they send raiding parties into Turmodin. It's very exciting to live in such a town, especially when it's on the move."

"The town moves?"

"The big guy moves the discontinuity. The people move quickly thereafter."

"Kragha wasn't here a few days ago?" Bevn asked.

Saladon shook his head. "The old site would have been wherever the gate rested previously. It'll be a ghost town now, whatever's left of it after the building strippers."

"But that's crazy!" Bevn objected. "Why break down a whole town and move it?"

"Change can be good," said Saladon. "The Kraghans get a chance to build again, exactly as they would like, so it's always very new, improved with each generation, or so they think, and it's not just the buildings that are broken apart and rebuilt. All the families, all the couples and brothers and sisters, all ties are broken when the town is moved. There's a lot of excitement going on up there. They have a culture of exchange and regeneration. Right now it must be at its peak."

"Beyond this gate we get to Turmodin? I get to meet the Sorcerer?"

"Yes indeed, unless we run into trouble."

Bevn felt his guts tighten. The Sorcerer's Pillar. They would be there at last.

THE FOURTH MOVEMENT

†HE †WIS† OF CHAOS

Where are we now, with all our deeds
behind us like the planted seeds?
How long can we reap this crop
before our life comes to a stop?

—*Bard Melic*

40. THE BREAKING OF THE WORLD

"They built themselves a golden cage
and threw away the key.
Who is left within the wilds,
to come and set them free?"—Zarost

*There came a time in Oldenworld when even the winter was driven
away. Every street had flax-domes, every town was contained within
a weather-ward, every city was shielded, sheltered and regulated,
provided it paid its triple taxes to the Three Kingdoms. No more the
snows driving hard out of the Winterblades, no more the rain slapping
against the powdered and painted faces. Rain was controlled,
diverted, guided into channels that spread like veins over the lands.
Sometimes the rain was allowed to wash the streets at night, when
the good folk were abed. Sometimes the winter chill was allowed to
refresh the stale and smoke-filled air; for the most part it was thrown
back upon the Winterblades, to maintain the temperature equilibrium.
As the cities became hazy and pleasant, the mountains and outlands
became harsher. In summer the store of ice and snow was tapped
to send cooling breezes upon the sweltering Moral streets. These
services were charged for as well, and so the wizards grew wealthier
and more powerful upon the shoulders of the kings.*

They devised a system of ownership in the Three Kingdoms, a
boon of freedom for everyone, or so it seemed when it was introduced.
Land, something that previously belonged to no one, was awarded to
every citizen, a portion according to their station, with a small annual
tithe attached to it. The people were ecstatic, and in their joy they did
not conceive how such a system could come to rule them. Borders
were defined, limits pegged into the ground with static-staves, and
citizens took ownership of the earth. Stands were defined on maps.
Larger titles were awarded to those of noble birth, or those who
were deemed noble enough by their associations or appearance or
cunning. A feverish time of politics ensued, with lies, schemes and the
transferral of favours occupying the courts of Kingsmeet and spilling

out to every borough and county in the Three Kingdoms. Once land was defined as something one could own, everyone wanted more of it. It seemed a person's worth could be measured by how much of the earth one could call one's own, regardless of the fact that when one died one would take none of it with one. Strange land-crimes began. People who lied about their origins, disowning their own fathers and mothers; documents that were forged; even wizards who were bribed to move static-staves from their defined positions. And murders, strange disappearances and accidents, impersonations, all centred on the new land documents, until the wizards devised the blood-deeds, an infallible proof of lineage. Only direct descendants of land-owners could inherit the land. Those who died without blood relatives forfeited their lands to the state, to be bought again by other nobles.

And so Order was enhanced; the kings and nobles became wealthier, and the wizards more powerful.

As the wealth flowed, it defined the classes more clearly between the deepening divides; the nobility who owned the land, the traders who had the savvy to pay rents and organise labour and still turn a profit; and the workers, who had ever less hope of escaping from their lowering position, as the price of property and food and travel rose, with the price of the annual tithe on their lands. In the end they were forced to sell their land to survive. The system of freedom slowly enslaved more and more of those who supported it—the foundation, the working class.

Then came the laws, written by the nobles, to restrict what the other classes might do, and where, and when, and how they would live, what education they were entitled to, whom they would marry, and where they may travel. Even the colours and fabrics they would wear in public were identified, to better declare their status. Ever more their lives were defined, and those who dissented were dealt with harshly. The enforcer class grew and grew, as more rules required enforcing. With their slotted blackvision visors the enforcers inspected every corner of Oldenworld. They became a latent presence much supported by the wealthy, much feared by the poor, for it seemed there was always some new law they had broken and some fine or tax to be paid.

Within each class, subclasses formed, as the citizens of Oldenworld became ever more stratified. One was defined by one's rank, and so were one's descendants. Life was ruled by Order.

And so it was in Oldenworld, until a man defied the system, a man who owned nothing, who could claim no royal blood, who demanded no reward for his efforts. He had no title to land; he did not wish to earn it. He had no allies, and no friends. He had nothing to lose.

Ametheus—he would be blamed by the wizards, cursed by the nobles and accused over many graves, but some of the poorest could understand. They knew his rage. They would become his army, swarming after the wildfire strikes and the searching spells, running through the cities to ransack and rape, to take back what had been taken from them. Once they saw that they could steal wealth instead of have it stolen from them, there was no going back, because upon their shoulders rested the ordered society of Oldenworld. Those who had risen up high plunged the furthest.

But Chaos was impermanent, and the rewards were short-lived, for without Order there was no system of wealth, there was no industry and trade, there was no system of reward, no privileges of class to steal, no value in the ownership of fallow land. The poor became poor and desperate again, but their belligerence born of Order remained. They would never go back to the old ways. Order was enslavement; they would rather be free. Free to be changed by the wildfire, free to forget the rules they had been taught, free to fight. And so Chaos reigned in the age of Ametheus, and Oldenworld was ruined.

ೞೞೲ

The images swirled in the roof of the chamber: rivers that ran red; forests that were on fire; storms of insects that flew in a plague, stripping the vegetation wherever they touched down. A monster passed through a swamp, parting the green scum as it moved by, eyeing Tabitha with a hungry stare. It felt to Tabitha as if the scenes might fall down upon her at any moment and immerse her in their horror.

"The nodes of Chaos, they are at the heart of everything," said Ethan, following her gaze. "See how restless they are in their containment? They search on their own when brother Seus is not using them. They reflect places where change is most active. They are the pulse of this time."

"Why must you change everything?" asked Tabitha. "Why can't you just leave the world as it is?"

"Because Seus has the power to change it."

"But you are ruining the world!"

"Some things are beyond saving," Ethan replied. "What's the point, anyway? We're all going to die down here. I may have a body that ages at a strange pace, but Seus has seen our end, he knows we are all dead in the end. We are dead! Nothing we do will have any consequence, everything will be gone. We will all end in dust when my father brings the Apocalypse. If that's how we end, then let it come sooner than later, because everything we do is a waste of time."

"How do you know it is true?"

"Oh, my father has told me, over and over and over, and brother Seus has told me. You can ask Seus yourself, if you don't believe me. So we must spread Chaos. The more we can free, the weaker the bonds in the Order of the universe and the closer it is to the day of the Apocalypse. We are very, very close now. My father will come, and then at last we can all burn."

"But you could stop it! You could stop breaking things, and maybe the Apocalypse won't come."

"What, allow Order to return? That will just bring slavery and injustice. They will find ways to prolong, protect and cosset their lives, and that will just prolong this stupid existence. No, Seus brings freedom to the world. I won't stop him doing that."

Tabitha was incredulous. "Freedom? You call this freedom? Your wildfire has destroyed everything. How is being altered into a freak a way of finding freedom?"

"You're-you're seeing things from the wrong side! When you see those changes, it is people's spirit breaking through. Brother Seus says it carries the genetics of whatever it strikes. It recycles, recombines. A man, who is really more like a dog, will become a dog. A woman who is poisonous liar will become a snake. A man who thinks himself a monster will become one, but a man who dreams of flying will take to the skies, and a person like you who sings will probably become a songbird. Don't you think that is a special thing? To live out your last years in the form you dream of, instead of wishing it and never finding it before you die?"

"But most people die from the wildfire!"

"Some of them can't handle the change," he said sadly. "I don't think you see what brother Seus is trying to do."

"Just because people have yearnings doesn't mean they want to change."

"Exactly! That's why he helps them. Why should things stay the same? The wildfire encourages change, invention, alteration. You must know. You have been touched by it."

"We don't have wildfire in my homeland. I was never touched by chaos."

"Yes you were. You must have been altered. No ordinary person has your powers."

"I became a wizard in my homeland," Tabitha asserted. "I was sheltered before. I was never touched..."

"Are you sure?" Ethan eyed her critically.

Touched by the silver dust, the dream, that afternoon, under the spreading tree at Phantom Acres. There had been a starburst, and a trickling of the dust had touched her.

"I—"

That was the moment when she had begun to hear the Lifesong; the moment when her power had been awakened. Then the wizard's ring had been drawn to her, and she had begun to learn at an accelerating rate.

Chaos.

It was within her.

She was the way she was because of Ametheus.

"You were begun with Chaos," Ethan asserted.

Tabitha had never considered the possibility. She might have a dual nature, and She was not the only one, she realised. If the book she read was true.

"And you were begun with Order," said Tabitha.

Ethan looked immediately distressed, and his eye began to wobble. "I have no Order in me!" he shouted. "They t-t-tortured me with it, but I f-fought them off! I d-ddon't have Order in me. I don't!"

"They say you were divided by an Ordered spell, in your mother's womb. The wizards showed the book to me."

"Hah! Wizards t-t-trust too much in their books. Even if what was w-written is a lie, they b-b-believe it. Which of the idiots th-th-thought they knew enough about me to w-w-write a book? Fools! Nobody knows m-mme!"

"She was called Annah Nerine Good."

Ethan froze. "Annah?" His eye grew moist. "Annah?" He wrung his hands. "Do you have it? Do you have the book?"

"It was in the Gyre Temple."

Ethan put his hand to his mouth. "Oh Annah! That is d-destroyed then, there are only the sh-sh-shards left." He looked immensely sad. "They killed her for her wisdom. She was too brave. Oh, I wish... I wish I'd seen that book! I had no idea… a whole book, about me?"

Tabitha didn't know what to say.

"Let me show you how Chaos works," offered Ethan, "maybe then you will understand." He shuffled away from Tabitha a few steps. "I will need to wake Seus to do this. Be careful now, he can be tricky."

"No, Ethan, don't—" It was too late. Before Tabitha could stop him, Ethan stiffened then his head swung around, and Seus became visible, cold eyes alert. The prescient aspect of Ametheus cocked his head like a startled raven.

"Who is this?"

"Our n-new ap-p-prentice," answered Ethan from the side, his face only partly visible to Tabitha. "D-don't you remember? Here, I'll rem-m-member for you. See? She is learning h-how to spread C-c-chaos."

"Apprentice! What need do we have of an apprentice?"

Ethan didn't answer.

"Never mind, I will indulge you, brother, since you have wakened me. Don't be stupid enough to give Amyar our blood. I can do without his ranting."

"Show her h-h-how it is d-done," said Ethan in a thick voice. "Show her how we b-b-bring freedom t-to them."

Ametheus took a position beneath a low bulge in the transparent surface.

"We will begin with a settlement then," said Seus, "somewhere in the upper lands, a place that clings to its Order." He reached for the glass-like dome. An image of dry and rumpled grasslands hung above him. Seus rolled his palms and the landscape moved away, as if they were travelling over the hills. They flicked over the high ground and encountered a partially tilled landscape beside a lake.

Tabitha felt swept up in the current of the Sorcerer's fugue. She was still reeling from the rapid shift of attention—one moment speaking to the mixed-up Ethan, the next in his arrogant brother's domain. She was incapable of resisting his raw coercive force. He rolled his palms and Tabitha was swept along in his wake. In the image of the world, a paling sunset touched loosely woven fences. They slowed over a settlement of grass-roofed huts ringed with sharpened wooden stakes.

"Ah, a good place to begin, a border-town. See how few Lakelanders they are, how empty the dwellings. They must have suffered a battle. There, see the mourning rites?" Seus pointed to a cluster of dark-skinned women milling around a smoking pyre. The women wore sleeveless shifts, their arms and faces smeared with ash. A few men stood with bowed heads around the blaze, their hands clenched on the shafts of tall spears, silent and unmoving. The women wove an intricate procession around them.

"If we stay in the smoke of the fire, they'll not see us," said Seus. "Look at their pallor, the gloom upon these people. They are so caught up in their loss, so trapped in their *personalities*."

The bodies swayed within the smoke. One woman stared at Tabitha suddenly, her eyes wide with fright. She threw up her hands and gave a soundless wail. Others beside her turned inward. A man lofted his spear.

Tabitha tried to shy away, but the Sorcerer's hand was firm against her back.

"Now they know they are watched," he said.

The man threw his long-spear. The tip of bone was jagged and sharp. Tabitha jerked out of Seus's steadying hand but the spear reached the edge of the sphere. The vision rippled, the spear vanished. There had been no need to avoid it.

"We are still in the Pillar, apprentice, nothing can come through unless I intend it," explained Seus. "Nothing can avoid the pull if I decide it must come. See how they tear grass from their roofs? They fear what they see in the smoke. Ignorant Lakelanders. Fear only drives Chaos faster."

The villagers threw bundles of grass at the fire. The flames grew higher.

"They stand around their dead because they tried to fight to hold onto their land, to defend it from the Lûk, most likely. They must learn to let it go, to be free of the need for wealth and possessions. Chaos will lead them to the truth."

"Why should they abandon their possessions?" Tabitha objected, struggling to follow Seus's twisted logic. "Things have value! Possessions will always have value!"

"No! Value is a crippling system of thought. *Things* should not be held onto. They are temporary, value is an illusion."

"But *life* has value. People will always fight for that. If they are threatened they will defend themselves. There are dead people there. Maybe they were attacked, maybe there would have been more dead among them, if they hadn't fought."

"What does it matter to the world that one man lives or dies? It is only the man in his conceit who believes his life is of value. Life has no value! It is worthless. We shall all be swept aside in the end."

"You would fight, if someone threatened you."

"But why do they fight when they cannot win? Why do they want to live!" he shouted, slamming his fist into the bench, breaking the end off.

Tabitha wondered about that for a moment. It was difficult to think clearly in the Sorcerer's presence, with the noise, heat and sickening *unsteadiness* to the world, but she could still remember the real world, her world. She wanted to see the clouds spilling down into Eyri ahead of the morning sun, she wanted to feel the joy of singing again; she wanted to watch Garyll's face as he slept. Moments of joy, high points that were gone in a breathless instant, yet they were the essence of her life.

"Because life is beautiful, at times," Tabitha said. "It is worth enduring hardship to touch that beauty."

It wasn't Seus who answered her then. It was Ethan, in his sleep-slurred voice. "No it's n-n-not... Life is ugly, and c-c-cruel, and violent. It isn't worth f-fighting f-for."

Tabitha craned her neck around to catch Ethan's eye, while Seus stood immobile. "Don't you see anything of beauty in your world?"

"What is b-beauty? *Show* me something b-b-beautiful."

Tabitha couldn't see anything in the Sorcerer's chambers that would qualify. "Beauty is... It can be a rare thing that is delicate or perfect, but it's also the feeling you get, when you see it. It's grace and joy and hope altogether. It's a song. It makes you happy just by witnessing it."

"W-what if you n-never get that feeling?" replied Ethan.

"Never?" she asked.

He didn't answer; he looked down instead.

Did he really not see beauty? Or did he refuse to see it. His immediate world was so responsive to his thoughts, and so there couldn't be anything of beauty in it while he refused to see beauty, but then how could she be in his chamber? She wasn't part of his world of violence and destruction. She believed in harmony and peace; he wouldn't have endured her presence for so long unless he was curious about her. Maybe her task was to show him something of beauty, to change his mind. Maybe he needed her, after all.

"Are you done with your snivelling, brother?" Seus cut in with his harsh voice. "Give me back my attention. I was busy educating the apprentice."

The chamber belonged to Seus once more and Tabitha was sucked away from her brief contact with Ethan. Seus stepped up to the orb and the image shimmered as he moved close. The Lakelander women fell back as he advanced the image through the crowd. He passed quickly through the village, turning the view from side to side as if he hunted for something.

"Feathers and tails," he muttered, "Feathers and tails! Your task will be to hold them when they come through." Seus homed in on an enclosure toward the edge of the settlement, where a group of rangy goats moved nervously against the fence. Speckled fowl scattered at their approach, but Seus struck like a snake. One instant a hen was running pell-mell across the dirt near the centre of the image, the next Seus reached into the image shouting, "I know where you'll be!" The hen fell squawking from the glass amid a flurry of feathers. When it hit the floor, it ran.

"Well don't just stand there, catch the damn thing!" Seus shouted. "I must ready the other elements."

The hen bolted for the far windows and leapt in panic. Its instincts were ruling it.

She had to obey Seus; she couldn't face his anger.

"It's okay, it's okay, shh shh shh," Tabitha tried to reassure it, walking slowly toward the windows. She jumped to the left but it jinked to the right.

"Don't be an idiot!" shouted Seus. "Catch it where it will be, not where it was."

Tabitha tried to imagine where the chicken would run to, but it was hopeless, the thing zigged and zagged all over the place as she ran after it. She tried to visualise herself holding the chicken instead, which brought a shift in the light and time. She scooped the chicken from the floor and it struggled in her hands, its red-rimmed eyes wide in fright. Tabitha thought it would be better if it was a calm chicken and it forgot its panic and eyed her quizzically. It nestled against her chest. She carried it back toward Ametheus.

"Very good. Right, now get the blade from beside the chalice."

"The...blade," repeated Tabitha, her stomach rolling over.

"Bring a few bones as well. There should be some on the bench."

Tabitha froze. This was some kind of sacrifice. It wouldn't be beneficial to the mourners at the fire or to the chicken.

"Let me explain something to you," said Seus, suddenly close. "I don't involve myself in dealing with threats, for my brother is far better than I. Are you a threat? I don't like to wake him, but I *can* wake my brother to deal with your dissent."

"Ethan?" she asked in a small voice. "Where is Ethan?"

"I'm not talking about Ethan, that half-wit is asleep," replied Seus. A cold smile twisted his lips. He turned and the scarred face of Amyar was revealed, the face of the bully, vicious and feral. A flicker of awareness twitched behind the closed eyes.

No. Anything but that. She did not want Amyar to wake. With Amyar would come the rage and violence. Her blind right eye throbbed as soon as she thought of him. His name alone made her knees tremble and her guts heave.

"I understand," she said to Seus, "I'll try to do what you want."

It seemed Ethan had lost consciousness again. Had Seus stolen his blood? How could she wake Ethan again without alerting Seus? The chicken nestled into the crook of her arm. She scurried away to find the blade and the bone. The dirty wooden bench against the near wall held jumbled piles of strange implements, a clutter of papers, pens and inkpots, stacks of carved tablets, many glasses, vases and gourds. A curved knife was stuck into the bench. She pulled it free. Its pitted edge didn't look very sharp.

She found a long bone under a pile of junk, wrenched it free and other objects tumbled from the bench. The chaos knocked another stacked pile beside it, and Tabitha caught a bottle on her elbow as she tried to jump clear. Tools clattered to the floor amid fragments of glass.

"Sorry."

"Sorry? No, no, no! Apprentice, you are spreading chaos, as you should. It is good to disrupt things. Stir them around, break them, lose them. Let them be found again! Come, bring that bone."

Seus had the image of the fire in the foreground again. "To me!" he commanded.

A burning log fell to the floor. It burst at his feet and sparks scattered in all directions. He did not seem to be affected by the heat. "The bone," he said. Tabitha handed it over.

"Now this, this is something my father has an affinity for," Seus announced as he gripped the bone-shaft at either end. "Inside every man is a dead man, waiting to get out. They will feel that now." He touched the bone to his forehead, whispered "Unbind," and the thick bone exploded to a gritty dust-cloud. Tabitha gripped the chicken tighter. She had thought Amyar the worst of the brothers. Seus was. He used his power in such a callous manner. She wished she was far, far away.

But *that* wish didn't work to change her reality.

What if he decided to *unbind* Tabitha, just to amuse himself? She tried to calm herself.

Seus leant over and plucked the knife from her shaking hand. "The blood upon the fire will stir in their blood also." Without warning, he sliced the blade through the chicken where it sheltered against Tabitha's breast. Blood splashed against her arms; warmth soaked through her dress. She cried out and dropped the chicken and blood gushed across her boots. The chicken ran off in a jaggy death-run even though Ametheus retained the chicken's dripping head. When the blood fell upon the burning log, the flames hissed. Acrid smoke billowed upward to spread over the image that curved over them. It was becoming a nightmare.

Ametheus made a spiralling gesture at the glass and the acrid smoke entered the image, roiling outward to enclose the mourning villagers, rushing through the huts to touch dogs, babes and the aged villagers who watched from the shelter of their doorways.

Before Tabitha could move away, Ametheus gripped her wrist and drew her close to the flaming log. The reek of attar mixed with cloying sweetness stung Tabitha's nostrils. She closed her eyes against her burning tears, but she was assaulted by a sickening swaying gyration. Then the heat hit her. They were standing in the fire, no longer in the Sorcerer's chambers. He had *moved* them. The fire flared up; flames leapt all around them. Ametheus stood at her side, as deep as she was in the coals. Tabitha fought a moment of panic as the sea of glowing embers shifted underfoot, but although the heat was intense, she wasn't getting burnt. She fought to free her trapped arm, but Ametheus held her in an iron grip. The air was almost too hot to breathe. A great wailing could be heard over the crack and hiss of the fire, dogs howled beyond it all, goats bleated, chickens clamoured and children cried. Stricken faces circled beyond the wall of flame.

She was *there*, in the village they had been watching, standing in their fire. She was inside the people as well; she knew their agony as her own. Tabitha felt their devastating woe, the fragility of their self-control. The people were close to the limit of what they could tolerate, a small step away from madness. They had lost so much of their family, the battles had gone on and on, for many years, and they were at the end of their wits, but they had held onto something through it all. They had held onto their village and the land they farmed. It was everything to them. It was their home, their security, their order.

Seus began to chant.

It was no language Tabitha could understand, if language it was. He drew some words out in sibilant moans and cut the next one short with clipped restraint, as if time wasn't constant through his speech, and his tone was staggered as if he drew on more than one voice in the same moment. Had he wakened some of his brothers, was he drawing on their voices? It was disturbing. Tabitha felt as if she should recognise the chants, they spoke to something within her, she could sense an awful shift within her body, a pulling apart, a feeling of disintegration, as if she would be blown apart should a wind press against her back.

His language was like the Lifesong, she realised, it had that fundamental effect, but it had no guiding rhythm, no beauty. It was weird, wanton and wild. Ancient.

From the folds of his robes, Ametheus produced a tubular shaker. Seeds or stones were trapped inside it, for it rattled as it moved: a dry, distressing sound. Ametheus tightened his grip on her arm and chanted louder, faster. With each pulse of the shaker, she felt her heart jump, as if her own pulse was being ruled by the random timing of the Sorcerer. Beyond the flames, a tall woman collapsed. Seeing this, a thin old man placed his spear before him, and tilted its tip at his own chest. A young woman cried out shrilly and stumbled toward him but she was too late to prevent the grip of the despair. Ametheus chanted, the shaker shook and the old man spread his hands wide to fall upon the spear. The jagged tip protruded from his back, thrusting upward like a red finger of accusation as his body slipped down the slick shaft. The young woman wailed hysterically and tried to lift him, but he was stuck half way to the ground. His legs kicked out and he slewed over to impact the trampled dirt beside the fire.

"Those who want to die will die now. Those who want to fight will fight. I hasten their fates and bring their freedom."

Tabitha held her hands over her mouth. The horror was too much. Seus was truly insane. The shaker shook again, and her grief burst through her veins like a sudden poison. Tabitha stepped away from the Sorcerer, but she was free for only an instant before he caught her wrist again.

"They must live to the extreme, live with chaos, or not live at all. They must work to enhance the spread of anarchy, or they are wasting their lives." The Sorcerer's fanaticism shone in his eyes. "I will clear apathy from the world. I will clear the dross and duller blood from life."

"But they were innocent! They did nothing to you."

"Hah! Innocent? They are alive and so they claim also the consequences of living. If they do not live out loud, if they choose to snivel and bemoan their lot, to mourn and weep, to be idle, then they forfeit their privileges. So do you."

"What were they supposed to do? How does it serve any purpose to punish the villagers for their grief?"

"They should be out fighting, not dripping tears into a fire," Seus snapped.

"You are a monster," declared Tabitha.

Seus stepped close, crushing the log underfoot with his weight. *It's going to end right now*, Tabitha thought. The Sorcerer had a gaze like thunder. He loomed over her and her heartbeat boomed in her ears. Ametheus held his shaker still and, for a terribly long moment, Tabitha's heart stopped. She closed her eyes against the intense fear shared through the whole village, the fear of being ended at the whim of the Sorcerer.

"A monster, you think me? You have much to learn. Much change will come to this place now, much intensity, fierceness that was waning, rage that had faded to discontent. Those who are left will wish to exact revenge for what was done to them, and who will they turn to? Why, their neighbours, the Lûk. The war in the upper lands shall find its heart again. We may even see the Lûk women taking arms at last."

He shook his shaker and life pounded in the village again. Tabitha gasped. His manipulation of them all was abominable; his plan for the villagers was worse. People shouldn't be driven to fight. They deserved to live in peace.

"You are evil!" she accused.

"Good and evil, why waste my time by making judgments? Order is served by having rules. For Chaos to thrive we must abandon judgments. Action is everything!"

"But you are forcing it upon people. They don't want what you bring!"

"The desire to run amok is always there, I just set it free. Chaos is unbinding life from the rules that would control it. The chaos is already there in the weave of the world, just pull the right strings in the right places, and the weave comes undone, as it must."

"You are no better than the Order you try to destroy."

His eyes flashed with cold fire. "You have seen but one minute of my life's work which Amyar tells me has spanned almost a thousand years. Do not be so quick to judge! No, best you observe, watch as I work and learn what you shall be required to do as an apprentice."

Tabitha watched the vision shift before her eyes. "You mean that figuratively, don't you?"

"What's that?"

"A thousand years. Nobody lives that long."

Seus raised an eyebrow. "Take what you know of the world, multiply that by the length and breadth of all the stars you can see in the night sky, and you would still have no concept of what is possible in my domain. Chaos is unlimited, apprentice. An ordered world is flawed, it can never be complete. That is what they don't understand, those stupid wizards in their Gyre. It ends in Chaos. I have seen it and it will always be true no matter what they strive to build. Nothing can prevent that end. Chaos is the natural state of the universe, Order is an abomination. I endure because I am meant to be here, they perish because they are not."

He was insane. She would have to flee. Her heart fluttered as she tried to gather her courage.

"You pull away from me and you'll burn in the fire," Seus warned in her ear. "I am your only protection. I am your only path to return from this alive."

The brief flare of fire against her legs announced the truth of that, but she couldn't endure the Chaos he was inflicting upon these innocents. The world swirled and swirled in her vision. Two women had begun to club each other with abandon, incited to violence by his strange rhythm. Another woman collapsed. A man threw himself into the flames, roaring as he leapt with outstretched hands. Tabitha staggered back as far as she could, trapped as she was by Seus's grip. The man screamed as the flames bit through his clothing, but his leap carried him all the way to Tabitha, and he fell upon her.

He passed straight through her.

A cloud of hot sparks burst over the man's back as he impacted the firebed and scorched at Tabitha's feet. It was difficult to reconcile what she saw and heard, but she understood they were not really there. Ametheus had immersed them in his vision, but both of them were also standing in the chamber in the Pillar. She hoped. She had lost contact with her body; all of her awareness was in the place of smoke and fire.

The man who had leapt at her rolled away through the coals and staggered a few steps before falling on his face. His hair was ablaze. The villagers threw handfuls of earth over him, trying to quell the flames "eating" at him, but Tabitha knew the man's pain, she felt his agony. He was too far gone, he would die.

Ametheus shook his shaker wildly.

"No!" she cried. "*No!* You cannot do this! You cannot do this!"

Her rage gathered and swept outward through the world ruled by the Sorcerer's vision, and the fire became suddenly dark, extinct. The smoke blew outward across the village and silence filled the air. She stood before him, a small figure before the great bulk of the Sorcerer, and she quivered with anger.

"Ah, do you feel that?" asked Ametheus. "The breaking of your utmost extremity. You are beyond your limits now. *That* is Chaos. You tried to measure my power and then you wallowed in despair and defeat. *Now* you reach beyond yourself, *now* you ride the winds of Chaos. You face your own ruin. *Now* we will see what you are made of."

Tabitha gathered her power, reaching out to all the essence she could grasp. She gathered her lyre and plucked the vital notes. The force of the Lifesong was a moment away. She could punish him for his vision. She could destroy him. Her essence began to brighten, turning gold and vital.

Ametheus backed away and raised his arms. The villagers fled. They faced each other across the dead fire, the Sorcerer and Tabitha, and the world spun around them. Night fell and the stars streaked across the dark sky like windblown tears. The firmament screeched as the Sorcerer pulled Chaos from the cracks in the air. Filaments of flux whipped around him, and his presence exploded. He was a mass of whipping silver tentacles. She gathered more essence, before he could, extending her will desperately beyond him, racing for power. And suddenly she understood.

"Ametheus!"

He jerked, his hands clawed the air, and his power tensed.

"This is wrong. If *power* is placed uppermost, there will always be battles... On and on, until *one* remains. Ametheus! This is the wizard's way. You are playing *their* game. You have always been playing their game."

He was compelled by her naming to listen, for a moment, but his anger was coming, like a storm. The air spat and crackled around him. He was mass of wildfire, a writhing seething fury of Chaos.

She did not need to defeat him. She would show him another way.

"Ametheus!" she cried again, waking the third brother, holding them all for a final moment before he fell upon her in fury. "Listen now. Listen!" And she sang, giving voice to the music she had used in the forest, the part of the Lifesong that was love.

The song swelled like sunshine in her heart, it made her blood burn like fire; it made her fingers dance. The world quivered with her spirit, and she played, in music. The Sorcerer's presence disturbed the rhythm, but now it only made it more strangely beautiful, throwing echoes on either side of the melody causing the Lifesong to pulse, pause, shift, backward and forward, the sounds tumbling around the aria like swallows diving through the wind. As she sang, so she was transformed.

> Fly with me now, into the night,
> Love! Take me from this place;
> the vigour of your precious touch
> sweeps me with sweet Grace.
> See how it brings these mighty wings
> that carry me toward the sun?
> All of my shadows fall away
> as I fly, as I come, undone.
> All of the shadows burn away
> As we fall, and rise as one.

Singing of love made her feel empty. She couldn't understand it. She missed Garyll terribly; he had become an ache in her heart. Colours shifted through the Sorcerer's essence, rainbows that rippled across the silver threads, engaging his silver in a dance with gold, fusing the flux and flax, calming the fury, resolving the imbalance, joining the powers, leaving him wrapped in the fading coppery haze of a fiery love.

"Without love there are no dreams," she ended. "Without dreams we fall apart at the seams."

All was quiet.

Ethan was watching her, his single moist eye wobbling in time to his bobbing head, as if following the memory of the Lifesong as it slipped from his mind into his brother Amyar. His mouth a small 'oh'. His white hair drifted over his face in sad strands.

Tabitha faced him. "If *love* is placed uppermost, there can be peace. We can live together."

"That was b-beautiful," he cried. "It was b-b-beautiful!"

"It is what you will take away from the world, if you let Ethea die."

"It is not f-fair. You c-c-can't show me that, a-after all these y-years. You c-can't! After all they have d-done!"

"I think it is a blend of Order and Chaos."

"An-nnah was right! It c-can be done. Oh, why did you c-c-come so late?"

"I am not too late, Ethan. I am not too late!"

"Ohh. You are, s-s-singer." He looked infinitely sad.

"It is *not* too late to change."

"It is t-t-too late for m-me."

"Let go of it, Ethan. Let go of the war against Order."

"I c-can't! You are the g-g-guardian of our f-father's c-coming. He w-will f-f-fight you and *end* you! Oh, b-brother Seus has s-seen it all! I c-can't stop it. He faces you t-t-tomorrow."

Tabitha reeled at the pronouncement. Seus had seen her being killed? "But I do not want to fight you. I want to heal you."

"Heal m-me? I will n-never be healed. There are *th-th-three* of me! If you want me to b-become one, which two shall you kill?"

"The...others?"

"Who, me?" demanded Amyar from the front.

"Who, *me*?" shouted Seus.

She had forgotten they were conscious; she should have known by the way he was stuttering.

"They are my b-brothers!" Ethan cried out. "They have b-been with mm-me since the beginning! And they are all that k-k-keeps Apocalypse from ruling my m-mind. I can escape to my p-p-past, I can ff-flee into the f-future. If you bring us all into the p-p-present, you bring my f-father here. This will h-h-happen soon enough, you f-forget, this is all my f-f-father's vision. You can d-disagree with *me*, but you can't ch-change what I do. "

"What I did!" argued Amyar, from the front.

"What I shall do!" declared Seus, turning on Tabitha and grasping the air around them with a jerk of intent. Something shifted in the air, it became suddenly warmer, and the night and the village were gone.
ᘓᔓᏳᘉᘙᔓᏳ

An image swirled in the orb overhead, choked with ruddy smoke. She was lying on the floor, stained with ash and blood. A charred log had burnt itself out at Tabitha's feet, beside the remains of the chicken. The Sorcerer's chamber was lit by the dull orange glow of imminent sunrise.

Ametheus lay on the floor beside her, unconscious, with a heavy arm across her waist. She didn't want to disturb him, she didn't dare to move. She watched the images in the ceiling instead. They were relatively calm, showing a small island filling with ever more clamouring seabirds, a termite mount being rooted up by a lop-eared boar and clusters of brown bison jostling on a migration. Tabitha watched ice break off a high slope, outlined in the first crisp rays of a high-altitude morning. The ice dislodged a ragged line of rocks, which tumbled down the black slope, gathering momentum. And, in the orb beside it, was that monster she had seen before, eyeing her hungrily as it swam downstream.

It sank beneath the surface, becoming a shadowy outline in the green flow. The river passed a muddy spur, where a spindly-legged calf was drinking beside its mother. The mother lowed and ran back from the river, and the youngster froze, uncertain, not old enough to understand the danger.

Tabitha tensed as the shadow rose fast. The monster burst from the river in a white spray, felling the calf with a vicous swipe before dragging it into the shallows, tearing the calf's head off. The violence of its feeding was awful. It didn't bite and chew—it ravaged and destroyed its prey. It lifted its head to look at her, as if suddenly aware of her attention and, with blood on its face, blood on its hands, it abandoned the evidence of its wild lust to dive headlong into the river once more where it sankdeeper below the polluted waters, out of sight.

Had it been changed by the flux? There was something piercing about its stare, a terrible intelligence. What had it been before it had been changed? The image flickered and was lost. She saw a river. She watched it for some time, tracing its course through heavy forest where trees thrashed in a great wind. Where the river ran over a rocky shelf, it moved strangely. Upstream. The image exploded to light, then became bubbles, shot through with silver tendrils, fibres of flux searching past a frantic paddling hand. A boat high above, on the surface, where the bubbles made circles. More bubbles, and an arm that ended in a stump.

"Garyll!" she shrieked.

Ametheus jerked awake. The images wobbled and changed. He rose to his feet.

It couldn't be true.

Yet, now that she had seen the image, she knew it might be. Something terrible had happened to Garyll.

Seus stared her down. "What were you doing? You called out to all of us, didn't you? That's why I've got this splitting bloody headache! Idiot! Are you? Who are you?"

Tabitha stared at him, numb with the shock of what she had seen. Did Seus have no memory at all?

"I am the Lifesinger—the apprentice."

"You are the apprentice! Whose stupid idea was that? I don't need any snivelling slave getting in the way of my work!"

He had no memory of the night of terror he had put her through. It seemed he saw only the future. Ametheus contemplated a thing with eyes glaring at him from within a glass bottle, a spider, of sorts. "What will I do? I will break the Gyre, yes! The wizards and their Sanctuary... Sanctuary no more!" He lifted the bottle and the spider scrambled to the end, away from the rough hand.

"You see, apprentice, the eight of the Gyre had me fooled for ages. Two cubed is eight! The number of building is eight! There are eight colours in the spectrum, if you count the purple! Eight notes in an octave! Eight legs on the spider. Eight! Eight! Eight! Balanced, stable and undying, but I've worked out how to kill it!" He smashed the bottle suddenly on the bench. The spider scuttled from the wreckage, but Ametheus caught it by one leg, reaching to where it would be. "It's the legs," he said, flicking the spider down roughly, breaking the leg off at the joint in so doing. "They're the easy bits to get at, and on their own they are weak." He caught the spider again, snapped a leg and set the spider loose. It scuttled as fast as ever, with the broken leg drawn up to its body. "If you break off the legs," he said, breaking another two, "it's a simple thing." The wounded spider changed its tactics. It sat, waving its remaining legs frantically about, searching for the hunter it could not escape from. "In the end, all it can do is watch the hammer fall." Before Tabitha could move beyond her horror, Seus had gripped his heavy mallet and brought it swinging down among the shards of glass and spider legs. "The Gyre exists in too many dimensions," he declared. He turned the mallet to reveal the squashed spider—an outline of colour and splayed legs.

"See? Two dimensions. Now, because I am in three, I can pick the legs off at my leisure." He lifted a leg with his dirty fingernail and popped it into his mouth as if it was a delicacy. He was dreadful, killing purely for experimentation, for explanation. It might just be a spider, but it had been a living spider. Tabitha felt no less sorrow for the small thing, dead.

"See you, these slivers each have a wizard," Seus announced, waving at the bench with his mallet.

There were small panels of mirror-glass on his bench, jagged-edged, arranged in a loose fan. In each, an image was reflected, but when she looked to the roof she couldn't see the corresponding image in the bulbous nodes of chaos. The reflections were from another place, another world. Then she saw a face she knew, a man fighting for his life against an onslaught of Chaos, his hat clinging to his head as he danced against the silver death. Zarost!

The wizards of the Gyre lay before her. There were only four mirror shards. Either that meant he hadn't caught them all, or worse, he had. Tabitha wished Ethan would return. Even Amyar would be better than Seus. Amyar was violent and domineering, but he had reasons to be angry and frustrated. Seus was too deeply advanced in his own psychosis. He was going to break the mirror shards! Maybe if she got him to think about something else for long enough, he would forget his current intention. Maybe she could trick him.

"When will Ethan come back?" she asked.

"Why should that matter to you?"

"He summoned me," she lied. "I am really his apprentice. I wanted to ask him some things."

Seus did not look pleased.

"Understand this... We are one. You apprentice to him, you serve me as well. Ethan will not wake until I decide to sleep. I hold the blood in my head, I am in command."

"Amyar is responsible for your memory, isn't he? What if there is something that requires his attention. What do you do then?"

"There is little that is more important than my work, when I am awake. He steals enough of my time when he is dominant."

"Are you never awake at the same time?"

"Yes, and then we fight, unless Ethan is there as well."

"Ethan is the leader among you," she said, beginning to understand.

"You shouldn't wish for him. The longer he stays conscious, the closer the Apocalypse comes."

Seus turned back to the shards, exposing the back of his head. The fabric had slid down again to cover the troubled face.

"When does Ethan awaken again?"

The triple head whirled, Seus stared her down with eyes like chips of blue stone. "Why are you so keen to awaken the others!" he snarled. "Learn from me, and learn well. My touch does the most to bring the correction this world needs. Ethan spends all his life in slumber. Leave him be!"

He seemed almost afraid of his sibling, far more so than he was of Amyar.

"Everything must change!" he declared.

"If everything needs to change, who changes you?"

"I… I don't need to change!" he cried out. "I…" But he didn't continue. He gripped her close, inspecting her with his icy glare. "I know this face! Brother Ethan was lying, thinking to fool me with the tale of an apprentice. I know you! You are the L-l-lifesinger. *Ulaäan ma maar!* I face you tomorrow!" he looked out the window. "I face you today!"

Then, in the distance, a faint singing voice came on the wind, faint but persuasive. Tabitha knew at once who it was. Ethea.

"She sings!" exclaimed Seus. "It has begun!"

He left her then and strode across to the distant windows. "Wake up, my brothers, wake up!" he crowed.

He took the mallet and shattered an orb overhead. Something almost liquid dropped to the floor, something which altered the light, a translucent space. He stepped into that space and was gone.

Tabitha raced across the room. She looked out and saw the scene at the sacrifice, far, far below. Little figures clustered like insects upon a sticky treasure; they filled the land around the great figure of the Wicker Man. The colossus stood facing her like a fighter waiting for a bell. The fires had been stoked and their flames danced like occult beacons in the rising, swirling smoke. Birds shot by, kites and gulls, eagles and doves, hawks, finches, vultures and geese, thrown forward on the raging wind. It seemed as if all the birds in the world had come to circle around the Goddess in her pool, a mad spiral of witnesses. As Tabitha sent her senses ahead, the sounds came to her: a raging chant, off-key, rough and guttural, and the clashing of metal, and a stomp, stomp, stomp that pulsed through the ground. Horns blared like the screams of an angry animal. And, through it all, priests chanted in some ancient language, creating a thread of arcane guidance.

Ethea!

She ran to the bench, where the shards of mirror-glass lay. Which one was Twardy Zarost? She couldn't see him in any of them, only swirling Chaos. She gathered all four of them then she stepped into the space Ametheus had used.

It didn't work. She remained in the chamber. She would have to make her own way down to the pool. In the distance, she could hear the voice of Ethea, lilting in a mournful melody.

Oh no, oh no, oh no! She was going to sing the Destroyer into being.

And, something terrible had happened to Garyll.

Tabitha ran from the chamber, out the arched door, across the tilted slab, into the sinuous passage leading down, down, into Chaos and the end of the world. She desperately wished Garyll was there. She needed his conviction—she needed his strength. She wished for Ashley. She wished for Twardy Zarost—anyone who could help her.

But she was alone against her fears.

41. CONVERGING ON CHAOS

"Life is a race against time, with a trend:
Time cheats more as you approach the end."—Zarost

A crack shot through his world and Zarost turned not an instant too soon. The air split beside his face and again at his back, leaving him standing in a narrow strip. On either hand there was now darkness, a void which he could not cross with his awareness, an end. He was in a collapsing world.

He was crippled with uncertainty. The whole scene might exist only because the Sorcerer had enchanted him and he could not tell illusion from reality. Then again, he could be wrong and this could be real.

Zarost faced the narrow flames. A sharp retort sounded behind him. The sand and sky fell away.

He could not reach infinity, he could not transfer away because he could not become big enough; he could not stretch far enough. His body was trapped in a shrinking space; his world was too small.

What if he made *himself* incredibly small, he wondered? He might reach a limit of physical impossibility, when the cells of his body could no longer become denser, but if he drew his *attention* down into the tiniest point, and left his body unchanged, would his body become the relative infinity? It would be the opposite of Transference, a reflection of one of the great paradoxes of magic.

A reflected paradox. Would that be a truth, or an absurdity?

He would call it Inference, he decided—if it worked.

The crack which split his failing world ran straight for his forehead. He dropped, watching his toes, which was all that he could see. By the choke of a mustard smoke, this was becoming a bad joke! He remained crouched, because he could not stand. He breathed out and closed his eyes. He thought of his heart beating within him. He became the heart, then the blood within his heart, then a warm ring-like red cell floating in an endless warm fluid. Deeper, deeper, and smaller he took his awareness. Zarost sensed nothing except tumbling cycles of energy bound in strange patterns. On the fringe of his mind, his body seemed to rush outward as he rushed in.

Deeper, deeper still. A shivering shimmer of hazy light, one curled streak. A point.

His destination would be unknown. He hoped that something, somehow, would provide the bridge to anchor him in place and time. It was a little hope. Then again, he'd never been one to scorn little hopes.

He disappeared into his own singularity.

ᘓᘔᘓᘔᘓᘔ

They began at the great range of mountains. They sped through a gap and there Sassraline fell like a diving hawk, into the heart of a citadel, a place perched over twin falls at the limit of the upper lands. The buildings spread out as hey sped, down at the shingled roofs.

Ashley's plan was simple. He was sure he'd be able to identify Tabitha from the air if he was close enough, using the advantages of his mind, because the people he had encountered were odd; their thoughts, cultures and memories so very strange. He was sure he would recognise the worldview of an Eyrian within the strangeness. They would stand out like beacons of normality in the chaos. He sent his awareness outward and rushed like a wave through the many minds.

He struck gold in the citadel. He found memories of Garyll Glavenor, Gabrielle and Prince Bevn in the minds of others, bright images framed with the blinding fear of the wildfire strikes that followed. They had been there, in the citadel the inhabitants called Slipper, but despite the vivid *psychima* which made Ashley speed north-west, he soon lost the trail. Some faint memories that might have been left by Gabrielle and Prince Bevn lingered in the lowlands. Garyll Glavenor had not been seen again. He couldn't find memories of Tabitha Serannon at all.

Sassraline flew on, ranging over the hills and marshes in lazy loops and, as she flew, he sat still and quiet, trying to extend his awareness further and further through the minds he encountered, straining for omniscience. He wished he could sit close to Sassraline's neck to avoid the icy blast, but she clutched him like prey with her mighty talons. She flew fast, too fast, covering great distances, and the farther they went, the more Ashley worried that they'd passed Tabitha and the others. They couldn't have come so far, so fast. The daylight died in the west, and Sassraline began to tire, but he pushed her on into the night. He would not abandon his friends. The wild lowlands rolled on far beneath his feet.

As the moon burst from the crowded clouds, they passed over a pale plain where hundreds of small figures toiled westward, as if on a march to some common goal. He stayed in his fugue, searching through the fine threads of the many minds below. He urged Sassraline lower and lower. The concentration of sifting through so many minds drained his strength. Hunger raged in his belly. It had been a long time since he'd eaten.

Sassraline wheeled and dived over the crowds. Suddenly a flame issued forth from her snout, a giant tongue of yellow fire that parted the mob and set them to running. She gave another great belch of fire, this time from close enough to scorch the slow-witted tail-enders. The plainsfolk screamed and ran.

He had communicated his hunger to Sassraline, he realised. She was obeying his command.

A LITTLE HUMAN, JUST THE RIGHT SIZE FOR A SNACK.

The figures looked upward, straining to follow them in the dark night sky.

"Sassraline," Ashley called out. "Sassraline!" His little voice whipped away in the wind.

I'LL LET THOSE TASTIES RUN A BIT, TAKE THEM AT THE HILL.

The doomed figures fled. Ashley stepped into her mind. "Oh great and mighty dragon, they are honoured to witness you. Don't kill them yet, they would behold your beauty a moment longer."

He had the horrible feeling his flattery wasn't going to work. The wind battered his face as his dragon dived.

LITTLE SPEAKER! NAUGHTY HUMAN. WHERE DID YOU GO?

He projected his thoughts strongly. "Wondrous and magnificent dragon, your skin looks so perfect, brushed by the light of the stars." To the people below, she would be a dark formless immensity overhead. "Your wings are so full, the tips are so sharp. They must be entranced by every detail." She had banked, but nothing about her shape was entrancing. Sassraline was a deadly hulk, swooping lower. "Surely only one dragon can be so beautiful? Surely no other has the splendour of Sassraline?"

Sassraline croaked, a joyous sound despite its awful volume.

IT IS I!

"Leave them be! Leave the people. They are not good food."

YOU WOULD NOT EAT THEM? WHY DO YOU NOT EAT EACH OTHER?

"I eat fruit, and breads, and vegetables."

I DO NOT KNOW THESE THINGS. MEAT?

"I suppose I do eat meat, but something like sheep is better."

SHEEP? THE LITTLE MORSELS COVERED WITH THE FIREFLUFF?

Ashley supposed that was an accurate definition for a dragon. He looked to the hills and saw a few clusters of goats, huddled upon a high slope, their fleeces silver in the moonlight.

That thought became the end of many goats.

He did manage to teach Sassraline to cook one properly, by using a gentle bubbling whisper instead of a scorching blast. He had nothing else to supplement his meal, and Ashley was too hungry to care. They shared a meal of meat. He supposed if he asked Sassraline to find him vegetables, she'd come back with a chicken.

He was too tired to fly any farther that night. He lay curled up against her side, just behind the forelegs. It was the least smelly place he could find. He didn't want to admit it to Sassraline, but she really stank, especially at the front and back end. At least she was warm and, with his belly full at last, he settled down and began to fall toward a welcome sleep.

I HAVE TRIED YOUR DREAMING, BUT IT DOES NOT WORK.

Ashley spoke to her without opening his tired eyes. "When you close your eyes, what do you see?"

NOTHING. HOW CAN THERE BE ANYTHING THERE? IT IS DARK UNDER MY EYELIDS.

"Well that's what dreaming is. You have to think of something that isn't there, like a golden sunrise, or a cloud. I don't know. Make something up, like a pink butterfly flying above your head. That's the beginning of a dream."

I DON'T UNDERSTAND. THERE IS NOTHING ABOVE MY HEAD.

"Here, try this." He imagined a pink butterfly for her and extending his mind into her cavernous consciousness.

OH! "Now follow that around. Make up other things. You'll get the hang of it."

Some time later, just as he was dozing off at last, Sassraline shifted against him. STILL NOTHING.

He sighed and allowed his mind to seep into hers again. The dragon had no imagination at all.

He dreamed for her instead.

The night crept past him and his mind wandered onto the plains. He encountered the dreams of the pilgrims where they camped around flickering fires. They were unsettling dreams, dark and strange, and Ashley felt as if he'd ventured into a place he'd rather not be, like diving into a pool of black oil. Visions erupted into one mind, then another, then all of them together, so the dreams were shared and wherever he drifted, the dream was the same: insistent; demanding. He tried to claw his way back but the dream drew him in, like a hungry swamp. One shared dream ruled their minds, a composite face, like a picture he'd seen once in Stormhaven painted on many canvasses. Only once he'd seen the many canvasses together did the true picture emerge.

Warm darkness swirled around him, and he sank into a dizzying depth. He tried to flail his arms but he couldn't use them. He fell and, as darkness whipped past him, a great face formed, a dark face, with fire-dappled skin and a singular silver eye that watched him with a dreadful awareness. He fell toward it, but it was so vast he came no closer to the scorched skin. The world tipped and the face rose over him, yet it still felt as if he was falling, falling. Gravity made no sense. Time slipped away, and he ached, oh how he ached, all over, inside and out.

The face filled his vision. One dark eye watched him. The other socket was terribly hollow.

He knew mortal fear. He wanted to refuse, but his own lips betrayed him in the dream, beginning a mantra shared by so many minds. "The world is a vapour, an illusion in my mind, we shall be wrenched from our folly to join the emptiness behind. We shall be broken by your will, life will burst and bend, for this world never was. What has begun shall end. What has begun, shall end."

Who was this great and dreadful being? But he knew, as the plainspeople knew. The watcher was a primitive force; he had been there since before Ashley had been born, he'd be there after. He was the ender of things, the ruin of the universe, the Destroyer. Apocalypse. *How long have you been standing there in the corner of my mind, waiting for this moment when I recognise you?*

The voice, in a sonorous awesome volume of an ancient language, shook him through and through.

"*Prøssŋ çæss ÿ.*"

The words whipped into his mind like arrows; the meaning of the words infused the sounds and resonated in his bones. *Pilgrim, I see you.* Ashley trembled before the timeless face. He could feel the fragility of his own existence; he knew how impermanent he was. A tide of worthlessness flooded over him, as if he was drowning. He understood that everything would be ended, that everything *had* been ended in the moment it had begun. He was alive only within the illusion. He wasn't truly alive at all. Life as he knew it was a brief stutter of energy, just one blink of a firefly in the vastness. The reality was the emptiness that surrounded life; life itself was an aberration. But, if he passed into the Apocalypse, *when* he crossed the threshold, he would become something everlasting.

"I don't want to be here," he said.

"*Barenðingåda.*" *I understand.* That great voice was like an audible form of rock and fire and thunder blended together; it swept him away. "*Karãkel ÿ.*" *You will be counted.*

"Why me?" Ashley asked, knowing his question was echoed across the plain.

The Destroyer watched him through slit lids, silver patterns quivering in his great black eye. *You will be made a God.*

A rush of visions swept across his mind, prophesies or fantasies he couldn't tell, things brought to the surface from the minds of many pilgrims—shattered trees, broken bridges, falling walls, dances with death where attackers were clubbed down, people obliterated, civilisations collapsed, houses on fire, hills on fire, skies that rained rocks, earth torn open to the lava beneath, a fist that could smash everything that stood in its way. He felt the perverse surge of pleasure that came with the annihilation. It was a very human trait, he understood, that capacity for destruction. What would the pleasure be like when whole worlds were demolished? The howling appeal of ruin spanning the universe, the inevitable end of all things: the scale of the Destroyer's lust was so immense it was overwhelming.

The time for faith has come.

It was an unavoidable element of being human—to be able to nurture, one had to be able to neglect, it was the flip side of the capability. If one could give life, one could take it away. He could be a destroyer, just like everyone else. Denied, repressed, ignored, and now, revealed.

You will be mine. Let none stand in your way.

"No!" Ashley cried. "I will not be a wrecker, I will never be yours!"

But the Destroyer just boomed with laughter, and he was swept forward on a great avalanche. He felt what it was to be destroyed, to be truly ended, with no memory and no significance, to have no time and no place, to be erased. He felt the utter dismay of death in emptiness. Non-existence was an unspeakable horror.

If he was shown this for long enough, he knew eventually he would choose any other way, even the altered life the dark God hinted at. That was the dream of the people, the pilgrims. He knew now why they walked west. They walked toward the promise. They understood ruin. They understood rage. Many of them hadn't even needed the dream in the first place. They walked toward the moment of transcendence when they would embrace the Apocalypse.

Ashley tumbled out of the dream to lie gasping on the ground.

He was alive. He existed. He was Ashley.

The ground vibrated gently in a rhythmical manner. A wall of green scales rose around him. The green was dull, but when he rubbed across it with his leather sleeve it glistened.

Sassraline nudged him with her snout.

I DON'T THINK I LIKE DREAMING.

The dawn was coming. The light ran first through the cracks in the sky, exploring the empty veins between the altered panels of various hues. Already broken, he realised. This world was falling apart, and there was worse than Chaos waiting for them all at the end of it. He tried to ignore the pit of panic the dream had left within his guts, and set his mind to the task of finding Tabitha.

With no warning at all, Sassraline snatched him up. He had long ago forgotten to continue the mental dialogue of praise that kept her tame. Before he could grasp at her mind to prevent her eating him, she had flipped him onto a cluster of spines high on her neck. The spines were uncomfortable, but dull-edged enough that they wouldn't cut him. He was to ride on top.

They took to the wing. Sassraline wanted to cool off and Ashley couldn't agree more. He hadn't designed his leathers to be opened, and down in these lowlands, even so early in the day, he was sweltering.

The dawn seeped into the sky like a swirl of blood above the great canvas of the lowlands. The dark countryside slid by beneath his feet, fast and fluid. They sped over the rumpled ground. In places, ruins made great patterns. From the air it looked as if some grand designer had been scribing plans across the landscapes of Oldenworld. However, when they came close to the designs, he could see the roads, pipes and networks were broken. Abandoned. Plants were reclaiming what industry had built. As they went farther west the vegetation became more rampant, the ground wetter, the air warmer. They passed none of those coppery lampposts anymore, and Sassraline became grumpy because there was nothing else tasty to snack on that Ashley would allow, while he rode. She also didn't like the growing heat.

The ground below them festered. Figures moved across it, that constant staggering flow of humanity and inhumanity, things that looked fearfully over their hunched shoulders then scattered when they saw him. They drew their way forward with their tall sticks and fluttering red pennants. The great pilgrimage was afoot, and Ashley followed the many minds, searching for someone unique.

He knew Tabitha was heading for the Sorcerer's Pillar, and every mind shared that singular goal. The great call that had been made to the populace was to come to Turmodin, and although every creature had a personal compass pointing like a needle at the accursed source of their various distresses, they walked toward it now with a perverse faith. The great god had promised he would end the Sorcerer; he would end everything. They had faith, and faith, Ashley discovered, didn't need logic, it didn't need reason. It needed belief.

The pilgrims would be mighty and their rage would clean all Oldenworld with fire and wrath. There would be an end to suffering, and a beginning to the punishment of others. What was coming was not just the chance to worship. It was the chance to become a god.

Ashley could understand the madness of it. He flew and his eyes stung.

When a god spoke to one personally, one believed, but just because He existed, didn't make what He aspired to do right. The people had abandoned reason, because they had faith instead. The problem with gods, Ashley decided, was that people wanted to bow down to them. Because they had so much more power than people, people assumed they were right and people wrong.

What if the god was wrong?

The day wore on, becoming hot and clammy, the air growing moist and insubstantial under Sassraline's tiring wings, yet still he found no trace of Tabitha, and as he searched on and on he realised he was following the flow of pilgrims himself. He was carried on the same irresistible current drawing them all toward Turmodin.

His legs were beginning to hurt. Sassraline's heat was becoming unbearable. His hands had blistered and flaked. He didn't think he could spend much more time on her back. Another cluster of pilgrims trudged blindly ahead, and as he swooped down over them, he encountered at last the memory of an unmistakable voice, the trace of a song so sweet it washed all doubt and suffering from his mind. They had heard the voice of the singer! They had heard Tabitha.

He guided Sassraline toward the source of the song, going back on the concentric imprints in the mental landscape. A song sung and heard across the world. She had sung the Lifesong, and the memory of it was beautiful. How had she reached the Pillar before him? Tabitha! There was so much about her that was a mystery. They sped toward Turmodin.

As they neared the coast and the Sorcerer's great crusted column rushed at them from the horizon, Ashley thought he recognised something in the thoughts below, an Eyrian mind, an aberration in the *psychima*. They swept down, only to find a singular creature floating to the surface. Strange. It rolled onto its back as they passed, ready to fight; when they had passed it continued swimming downstream, its jagged tail driving it fast and hard. Ashley and Sassraline shot low over the greasy river and carried on, heading for the Pillar and some giant structure on the plains before it—the terminus of the pilgrimage. Bright lightning flashed past them, a ragged whip of warning. They had encounterd Chaos.

ଓଌଠଔଠ

The monster floated face-down in the river, drowning in his memories, memories that rose on the hot currents, borne up by the gases of this lowland swamp until they burst in his snout like bitter reprimands. He gnashed his teeth against the anger. He was not a man. He was not fit to be a man anymore.

He remembered a man. A man had believed in justice.

The water billowed against his face.

He remembered a woman. He remembered reaching for her, across a divide. And, somehow, in the reaching, he had fallen in the space between, into Darkness, and he had never come back. Anger had taken root in his heart; it festered there and wanted to spread. Rage at the way he had been used. Killing the Darkmaster had not eased the rage, because the rage was at him. He slashed at the water with his clawed hands—so strong, so deadly. He clashed his jaws, made for violence. He flexed his arms, now so immensely strong. He had been changed. On the outside, it was so, but he knew the truth. He hadn't been changed at all. He had *become* a monster. That was why he had taken this form in the silver dust. That was why he still lived.

Rage: he was defined by it. He needed something to fight. He would find vengeance for what had been done to him; vengeance upon the thieving boy who had ruined his life; vengeance upon the Sorcerer who had polluted Oldenworld with his malice. Revenge. He could almost taste their blood. He roared into the water. But he knew such revenge would never lead to peace. It would lead to more chaos. He rose for air. Had the Sorcerer won so easily? Was he serving the ends of another master?

His old intelligence, above, battled with his new brutality, below.

The sky was veined by the red dawn. A great green creature winged over the water toward him, and he rolled onto his back to be ready to fight when it tried to scoop him from the river. It croaked and passed overhead. Then it was gone, heading downstream.

He turned his face back to his memories. The one that hurt the most blinded his eyes. Tabitha. He had lost her, lost her forever. Her memory had come on fast that morning, swooping on his mind like that winged creature, as if she were watching him from the sky. She could never love what he had become. If she had loved him before, it was because she did not know the truth. He was a monster.

She had a way of melting his anger, dissolving it with her love. She knew that, she had kept him so close ever since the massacre of Stormhaven, as if her presence alone could heal him. For a while he had believed it was possible. When they had made love he had become part of her heart. It only made the pain more terrible. He would go under with this memory; he would drown in this agony. The only response to such pain he could think of, was to fight.

A silver-strike impacted the riverbank. He had seen many on his long way down the river, he knew now what to expect. The willow trees jerked and grew suddenly, flinging new limbs to the air. One tree toppled as its roots lifted from the earth, and it entered the water and swam away. The water seething around it was grey and lumpy, and within its flow the monster noted a few creatures which had probably once been fish.

He had been changed, just as they had been. It was time to set aside his regrets. What was done was done, but there could still be justice. Justice was greater than he was; justice was the single thing that had defined him. If he followed that principle, maybe he could remember what it was to be a man.

His tail drove him downstream. Little time remained. The sorcerer Ametheus would pay.

He was not a monster, he decided. He was a weapon. He was justice.

42. CLOSING MOMENTS

"Every word must be spoken before it is heard;
Every song must be sung before it's a bird."—Zarost

There was a gap in time, but since he had no time to measure it against, it was gone in a flash of endless waiting. Twardy Zarost heard the sound of tearing fabric, felt the snatch of gravity, tumbled down someone's legs and tangled in their feet. He heard a shriek and someone falling. Warmth, light and the sounds of Chaos.

He jerked around. A fire, there had been a fire, and the wizards of the Gyre had been trapped by Ametheus. He had tried to escape, he had become so small, but... There was Tabitha Serannon, her eyes as wide as a startled calf. He struggled to his feet against a swaying, tipping world. Turmodin! He had experimented with Inference. He would have never discovered the spell had he not been so close to death, and now he was in the heart of Chaos. And there was Tabitha.

How had she got there? He had thought she had been lost, in the destruction of the Gyre temple.

Why had he ended up *here*, of all places?

Turmodin. Things were going to move very quickly. He would have to keep his wits about him.

Then he saw the blood on Tabitha's hand and the mirror shards, and he understood. She had provided the linking point into that strange separated world the Sorcerer had trapped him in. He had used Inference, but she had provided him with a lifeline. She had saved him without realising what she was doing. A lingering scent of smoke hung in the air. Did it come from his own hair? The world stood poised around him, as if time had been frozen, but from Tabitha's hand three more shards of mirror glass tumbled.

"A ta ta!" Zarost exclaimed, dancing forward to catch them before they broke on the floor. "Be careful with those!" The shards. He could save the other wizards—only three left.

A mournful melody rippled through the sounds.

"Ethea is singing, Twardy! It is happening, now! We must go!"

"Well then I am not a moment too soon. I too have something interesting for you, a docket—in my pocket." He pulled the translation out. The one Tattler Jhinny had spent so long over.

"What is it?"

"Words from the Book of Is, the words to release the Goddess—the end of the Ceremony of Invocation that was used upon her."

Tabitha snatched it from his hand and scanned it. He could see the new patterns upon her right eye, a strange complexity of silver and gold that flickered as she absorbed the knowledge.

"Your eye. Is it...working?"

"I don't know. I see...something...something beyond the page."

The page burst into flame. Tabitha squealed.

"I thought..." Tabitha put her hand to her mouth. "I just *thought*... There was a face behind it, watching me. A face in black fire."

"Then he has been drawn close already, too close," said Zarost. "He will try to prevent you."

"Who?" asked Tabitha, beginning to run.

"The Destroyer. Apocalypse. He is coming. Can you remember the words?"

Tabitha looked surprised at herself for a moment. "Yes."

"Good. Let us go! You won't get there fast enough by running." He cupped his mouth with his hands. "*Ziggeroṣṣ*!" he barked. The sound rushed ahead of them down the tubular corridor. The hooks bit and they were pulled at the speed of sound. He'd always liked the power words, the ancient language the philosophers of Kaskanzr had stolen from the Gods. He had the feeling he was going to need many more of them in the moments to come. All of them, perhaps.

CB§DCR80

Bevn could not believe his eyes. They had emerged from the Discontinuity into a scene from a fantasy. Worshippers crowded onto every undulation; he could not see the ground. The landscape was made of heads, and they moved like wheat in the wind as they chanted and swayed, their many open mouths releasing sounds like blighted seeds in the wind. Somehow, among all these people, great fires burned, throwing bitter smoke into the whipping wind, swirling into the dreadful sky. A great tree blocked the sky; behind it a tower tilted into the scudding clouds, held at a sickening angle by its weird gravity. It was hot and wet, and the air had a tainted cinnamon scent.

The Sorcerer was there, unmistakable in his split robe and bronze helmet. He was much more impressive up close; power emanated from him in shuddering waves of disturbance. He stood on a boulder, overlooking a great face—some being trapped in a pool in a way that left her face inches clear of the water. She sang a mournful song, but even though the words had some strange power, Bevn could feel in his blood, he could tell it was a pitiful attempt, as if she lacked conviction.

"The Goddess Ethea," Saladon explained in a hushed voice. "She will bring life to the Wicker Man." He pointed to the tree.

Bevn looked again. It wasn't a tree, it was a man-made structure, a giant statue, and it had people inside it. They writhed and wailed, level upon level, body upon body, and at the very top those who populated the great head swayed their fluttering hands, reaching for the sky while at the colossus's feet worshippers laid great piles of wood.

"It is progressing as it should," Saladon declared. "He will soon get what he wants, the end of all things."

"And what do you get out of it?" asked Gabrielle.

"That is none of your business," replied the Warlock.

"It is my every business! I am here because of you. You will pay your debts!"

Her raised voice drew the attention of the Sorcerer. He paused in what he was doing to the Goddess and regarded them with his watery gaze.

"You are merely a contingency plan, you and the prince," Saladon replied. "And you were promised gold. Gold you shall have. Enough to entomb you."

"Wizard!" shouted the Sorcerer, over the heads of the worshippers. "I thought you had abandoned me! Come help compel this stupid Goddess to sing properly. She resists to the very last moment of her life."

"Very well." Saladon gathered his axe and shouldered through the crowds as if they were made of straw. "And so the end-game begins," he muttered under his breath.

Bevn scampered in Saladon's wake.

As they neared the head of the Goddess and the Sorcerer on his rock, Gabrielle spoke up. "I still don't understand why you are doing this. Why allow him to bring the end of the world? What is your payoff?"

Saladon gave her a hard look. "He gets his God and the end of this world, and I get the beginning of another."

"No, you will get a dead world," said Ametheus, looking down on them.

Saladon spun. "That is not the deal! I shall have the Goddess. We agreed!"

"I decide the terms! Why should I be bound by what I say? These are just words, passed in the wind. Nothing in this world has any permanence. Those who try to make it so force their way against nature."

"But the Apocalypse will end this world! What does it matter to you, what happens elsewhere?"

"Why would I allow you to take the songbird? So you may use her magic to create something else? I am not stupid, wizard. I will keep this precious thing, and you will be gone!"

"Amyar! You made a vow. We swore on the name of Nå. You remember."

"Amyar is not here. I am Seus and I say I will never make a deal with a wizard!"

"Ethan!" the Warlock exclaimed, as if trying to appeal to another person. "This is not our agreement!"

"Agreement? Wh-why should I be bound by a w-w-word spoken? A s-sound formed by the lips is as insign-n-nificant as the wind! I-I act as I-I am inspired. You will n-not limit me."

"But the Destroyer cannot be contained!"

"Contain! Contain! Contain! You w-w-wizards always want c-c-containment! Don't you understand? Chaos is f-freedom. Your Order f-fails because it throttles f-f-freedom."

"But you can't let him destroy her as well! The whole plan was to get rid of the other wizards, to be rid of Order, not to be rid of life altogether!"

The Sorcerer's head shook as if he was fighting to keep it straight. "You are in no position to tell me what I can and cannot do. You joined me because you would die if you fought me, yet still you cling to your belief in Order and control! Spit on you! What I do is my own affair."

"We were to work together!"

"Togetherness? That is the way of your Gyre. I do not work as a team! If your actions move the world toward Chaos, then you move with the flow of these times. If you stand in the way of Chaos you will be swept aside."

Bevn had seen this kind of argument before, in the court, at home in Stormhaven.. The Warlock was being stupid. Bevn knew that when a petitioner dug his heels in during negotiation, one had to offer something more, even if one took it away again later another way.

"I can offer you this woman." He pointed at Gabrielle. "I am her king, so she is my subject."

Gabrielle reddened quickly.

"She will deny it, but she is mine," Bevn said quickly. "I'll give her to you."

Gabrielle caught Bevn by the throat, but before she could protest his pronouncement, Ametheus spoke. "Thank you for the gift, youngster, but it is not very valuable." Ametheus seemed amused. "If I cared for a woman with her looks, I could change one of my servants to appear so. I could change you into a creature like her!"

Gabrielle's grip tightened. "Creature? How dare you, you freak! You sit there on your soft arse and destroy the world, and you call me a creature? You wreck everything, you ruin life, you are a low-bred bastard. You are not worthy of me."

Oh shit, Bevn thought. Nobody challenged Ametheus, not openly, not here. No one who did would live.

Ametheus thrashed. His head swung from side to side, twisting, revealing other faces. Bevn looked on in amazement. He had three heads, all…connected!

"You swollen-breasted slut!" the smooth-faced one screamed.

"Gabrielle, shut up!" Saladon shouted. "Are you so stupid? You have pushed him too far, you've awakened all of them in the same moment…"

"I shall break you in half!" shouted the scar-faced one.

"…and throw you in the s-s-sacrifice!" exclaimed the single-eyed second.

"…and let the one half of you watch while I s-screw the other!" screamed the scar-faced third.

Bevn was bug-eyed, half at the words he was hearing, half at the terror of dying under Gabrielle's tightening grip. He couldn't breathe! He kicked frantically against Gabrielle's shins. She ignored him; her eyes were locked on Ametheus.

"I wouldn't touch you with a barge-pole," Gabrielle declared, "even if you offered me all your power!"

Bevn made a strange mewing sound.

Ametheus turned and the smooth-faced one said, "What makes you think I won't disperse you into dust, right now?"

"Because that would be too predicable. I've heard you thrive on chaos."

"You presume to anticipate my actions, wench?" His gaze became more intense. "You are a waste of my time. You shall taste the bitter end of your forked tongue." The air tightened and Gabrielle's hair blew forward over Bevn's face.

"No, wait, Seus!" exclaimed the Warlock. "I will compensate you. I wish to keep her."

"Wizard, you are in my realm and not in yours. I fear this awful woman is not yours to give or keep. You are all my prisoners, for as long as I wish to hold you here. This is Turmodin!"

A spot of light burst into Bevn's vision, as if a rainbow comet fired toward them from the tower. It wasn't a hallucination. The Sorcerer noticed it too and turned his oddly shaped head. The light was carrying something, two figures, a woman and a man, moving as if running, but impossibly fast. Light streaked around them in ribbons. With a sudden shock Bevn recognised who the woman was—the singer from Eyri. She was weaving spells in the air, singing, but nothing could be heard above the crowd's clamour. The Sorcerer turned, Gabrielle's grip slackened, and Bevn fell to his knees, losing the newcomers from view. He gasped, drawing hot air into his lungs as the light swelled above him and the sounds were suddenly stripped away from startled lips. The lash of a storm parted the crowds.

Tabitha Serannon's voice swept over them like a gale, a gale of music, unlike any Bevn had heard before. It resonated in his bones; it made him feel as if he was being dissolved in sound. It brought tears to his eyes, and an aching to his heart. He hated that she had so much power over him.

Tabitha, the singer. She had changed the atmosphere in an instant. She had replaced the Sorcerer's frenzy with her own vision of peace and harmony, if only for a few moments. The Sorcerer seemed perplexed, turning his heads backward and forward, shouting arguments at himself, trying to see with his different eyes.

"Saladon…" Gabrielle began nervously. "That's the singer from Eyri!"

"Do you think I wouldn't have planned for this?" he asked tersely. "I plan for everything. What I didn't plan on was the Riddler being here. With him here, the brothers might actually survive their stupid plan. He must be removed."

Bevn took notice of the man who danced beside Tabitha, the one the Warlock had called the Riddler. He had a beard and he wore a strange hat and moved his hands as if counteracting unseen elements. Then he called to Tabitha and they spoke together, a chant, words formed of strange syllables, words that left hooks and writhing tails in his mind.

"No!" shouted the Warlock. "No. Stop those words! Be silent!"

He raised his hands as if to cast a spell but then, as if realising where he was, he dropped his hands again. The air crackled with the potency of the Sorcerer's Chaos. There was no tolerance for spell-casting in this place, yet somehow the singer and the Riddler were able to work their magic. Bevn didn't understand it. Saladon strode toward Tabitha, but the man in the hat blocked the Warlock's advance and her voice carried over their heads. The Warlock swirled against his adversary, catching him up in a complex body-lock. The Sorcerer recovered from his stasis; he dived forward and wrenched Tabitha from her feet with a grip on her throat.

But it was too late. The words had been spoken.

The Goddess cried out from the pool and her voice rose in pitch until it felt as if his eardrums would burst. With a jolt, her body became essence. The green flash blinded Bevn and there was a sudden *gap* in his life, like a narrow but infinitely deep chasm he had passed over. The birds that had been swirling closer and closer turned as one, and they flew out, away, all over Oldenworld.

"Fuck!" shouted the Warlock.

The great green face dissolved in the water and the pool steamed with dissipating energy. The sounds rushed back at them, as if Tabitha's song had pushed the Sorcerer's world away and it now slopped back like a filthy wave. The debris clanked in the air, the sacrifices screamed, the sea roared and the worshippers wailed with new despair.

The Warlock struggled with the Riddler, but because he wanted to retain control over the man he had caught, he was limited in what else he could do. His adversary moved and twisted like a ferret, complicating every hold until the Warlock had to devise another body-lock.

"Seus!" the Warlock shouted. "Keep hold of the singer. She will do just as well, if not better, for your purposes."

"Why would she ever do what you want?" asked the Riddler.

"Because of me," said someone behind them.

"Ahh, Mystery, you have arrived," said the Warlock. "Late, of course, but just in time."

Bevn turned to see a wizard, beautiful and pale, clothed in flowing gowns, crowned with a golden circlet, that unmistakable jagged outline of Eyri. The Kingsrim! She radiated power.

She turned her sanguine gaze upon the big wizard. "Warlock," she said. "How could I avoid it? I got your note. I see the way the threads clustered her. This is the only path to follow. Yours is the only path to follow to find peace."

"Mystery, no!" exclaimed the Riddler. "He has played you for a fool!"

The Warlock spoke over his head. "You understand what I must do, then?"

"I do. I would see it end differently, but I'll walk your way for a while."

"Then you know what must be done here."

"Yes. She must sing him to life."

"Why would I do that?" Tabitha cried out from where the Sorcerer held her against a boulder.

"Because I have your ruling crown," the Mystery answered, "and I can compel you."

"No!" exclaimed Tabitha. Bevn knew she would refuse, whatever the Mystery thought to do.

"Raise your arms," commanded the Mystery.

Tabitha's arms lifted to the sky. She forced them down again, but they didn't stay down.

"You see, because you have power, you are more sensitive to it than most," explained the Mystery. "The bond of this crown is in your blood, it goes beyond what you can consciously control. You are an Eyrian, and this compels you to obey the commands of the ruling bloodline of Eyri."

"But Miss Twit, how can you wear it?" exclaimed the Riddler. "It is not meant for us!"

"I carry the bloodline now," she answered him coolly.

Bevn knew, because the Warlock had explained it to him. "You are the hell-hag!" he exclaimed. "You took my seed! But...you can't be!"

"Yes, Bevn Mellar, I carry your child and I will make sure it inherits none of your limited intelligence."

The Riddler's eyebrows disappeared under his hat.

"But why didn't you appear as you are now?" wailed Bevn. "I would have enjoyed... I would have... You could have just asked."

"Why should you have enjoyed it? I didn't." She regarded him regally. "Now be silent."

And he was, because he was an Eyrian. He couldn't move his lips. She was utterly compelling. He realised he hadn't begun to use the full powers of that crown. The wizard tapped into all of the Kingsrim. Bevn wanted that kind of power. He wanted his crown back. If he had it, he could compel the Mystery too.

The Mystery turned away from him and faced the Sorcerer and Tabitha. "I will make her sing, and you will keep your mayhem at bay."

The Warlock had originally planned for Bevn to be the one who would compel Tabitha Serannon to do his bidding. It was supposed to be *his* power, and the slag had stolen it.

"I am the king!" Bevn lunged at the Mystery. The others would be so impressed with his bravery. He dived through the air and stretched out his hand.

☙❧☙❧

Tabitha saw the prince leap, and she prepared herself for the moment when the Mystery would be distracted. The Kingsrim was affecting her so badly. It was like having a clamp on her mind. The Mystery could play her like a puppet and she was terrified about what she might be forced to do. She would have only an instant; she could try to fight the Mystery or escape using her song. She tried to anticipate what would happen if she chose to flee. Her right eye engaged and the world flared and shimmered, as if the figures burned in clear essence. They were all as insubstantial as wisps of smoke, when compared to the dark wind that was coming, the foe lurking beneath the surface of reality. His presence rose and rose, she could feel him in her blood. She could see his power. All these figures would be swept away in the Apocalypse, but she could be free.

She escaped using the song, dissolving her body into clear essence, travelling on the music in the way she had moved from the Sanctuary—gone—away through the vastness. The people screamed as the fires flared and Ametheus led the chant, and the Destroyer's influence whipped them into a frenzy of devotion. They died on the pyre, between the red flames from below and the silver fire from above. The Sorcerer's foul magic changed them into a single body, yet his art could not gift the life he wanted to bring. The Destroyer raged against his failure and he punished the Sorcerer for it. In his madness,

Ametheus continued collecting people, and Oldenworld was covered in the smoking statues of sacrifices, a forest of coalesced corpses, until every corner of Oldenworld was burnt, wasted, destroyed. The world was spared from the Destroyer in the flesh, yet the apocalypse had come to pass nonetheless. She saw it and knew it to be true.

She snapped back to the present, where any choice she made would affect the future in a different way. Tabitha couldn't flee—that much was clear. She had to try something else.

She sang the stanza of destruction, stole the air from the fires and began to dismantle the sacrifice, freeing the people, but the Mystery recovered her command and compelled her to change her tune, to fan the flames, to ensnare the people once again, to create the Destroyer. The fires burst, Chaos streaked in from the sky and wrapped the Wicker Man in silver, and she screamed life into the effigy. The Destroyer arose, his body a flickering mass of smoke, blackened flesh and fire. The singular eye spiralled at her, and His dreadful voice rose in her mind and, as He came to being, the world became fragile, and his first breath shattered the wooden bonds of the statue. His second breath blew flame across all the worshippers, yea it did so, and in his third he breathed in as if gathering the power of all of the world. Then He grasped the Sorcerer and He drew him into his body. And so Tabitha saw what the Mystery was planning.

The Destroyer would destroy Ametheus first. Ametheus was an aspect of the Destroyer; Ethan bore the eye of the Apocalypse. The Destroyer would take it back; the son and the father would become one. In that moment, the Warlock spoke the words of banishment, and the Destroyer's great body fell, as his spirit was compelled to return to the prime dimension, according to the law of the ancient invocation Ametheus had begun. So the Gyre would be rid of its enemy; the source of all Chaos would be ended.

It was a diabolical plan, but Tabitha was gripped by the realisation that it could work. She watched the shimmering forms of the future play out before her altered eye. The Chaos had allowed her to extend her sight beyond the moment. Order allowed her to understand what she was seeing.

She was almost paralysed by what she saw. In the last instant, before the Destroyer was compelled to disperse on the winds, He exploded in silver fire, a flash of such awesome power it incinerated the universe. The Warlock and The Mystery had forgotten to take account of the Destroyer's nature. Even as he died, the Destroyer would kill, and the closing of the invocation would be the last word in the world. Chaos would endure, everywhere. The Warlock would die, the Mystery, everything would end. It all happened in a split second before the Destroyer was gone. It was pure Chaos, and then... Nothing. She couldn't see beyond her own end.

She rewound the future, dragging her eye to the left and watching the world reverse, to the point where Ametheus was still separate from his father. Tabitha paused, considering the options. There was another way. If the Sorcerer fought for his own life, the Warlock's plan might work. Ametheus had to fight for just long enough to distract the Destroyer. *Oh! Ethan, this is all so unfair, but you and your brothers have brought it upon all of us.* She could see a better future as she scrolled slowly forward in time along the thread where Ametheus fought his father, one with eventual renewal, one with song—one with life.

If the Sorcerer could fight. She had to be out of the Mystery's control, she was leading the future on the wrong path. Tabitha needed the Kingsrim. Time was pressing against her, pulling, demanding. She couldn't hold onto the foresight for much longer. The moment she stepped out of the future, the present would dictate reality, unless she could choose her action. She searched among the possibilities for the way. If she cried out to the Mystery, Bevn wouldn't grasp the crown. He would knock it from her head instead and it would fall, and bounce.

☙❧☙❧

Bevn got his hand to the crown. Something strange happened to the girl, Tabitha. For the briefest instant, he saw five of her, then one version of her shone bright and the others faded. She screamed, the Mystery jerked her head aside, his hand knocked the Kingsrim off the Mystery's head, and he couldn't catch it in time. It fell and bounced away, toward Tabitha and the Sorcerer who held her.

He landed in front of the Warlock, which was a very bad place to land. Despite the bearded man whom the Warlock wrestled with, he was able to sweep Bevn from his feet and stomp a boot down on his chest, cracking ribs and pinning him to the ground.

"We need that!" the Warlock shouted to the Sorcerer over his shoulder. "Take it up!"

The world tensed with a sound like a tightening cable.

The Warlock looked down. "I have had enough of you! It is time for you to die."

"You crack that whip and you'll lose your grip," quipped the bearded Riddler.

The Mystery put her hand on the Warlock's arm. "He must go, but why don't you simply send him home? They won't see him as a hero. He is the thief who has cost Eyri everything. His father can punish him, like a bad boy."

Was she trying to save him, or doom him? It would be a miserable fate to be returned to Eyri without the crown, without magic, without anything.

"Hmh!" The Warlock nodded. "You see the future in that, no doubt." He released the Riddler, who danced away. He leant over Bevn, as if inspecting a grounded animal after a hunt, considering how best to execute it. "I doubt he'll survive the transition anyway. His mind is too feeble for great ideas."

"Goodbye, dear boy," the Mystery said, a faint smile on her lips. She flicked him with a green spark.

"But I've come all this way!" he howled. "It isn't fair!"

"I don't have to play fair anymore!" shouted Saladon, and slapped his hands against Bevn's head. "Infinity."

CRSoCRSO

Zarost could see Tabitha had miscalculated. She was playing the future threads! By the light of the sun and moon, she was an adept! But the Sorcerer had got his hand on the Kingsrim, instead of her. That was the consequence of using chaos—random motion, and a loss of control. The Sorcerer's grip had loosened on Tabitha as he turned the crown over and over. A sound like a tightening cable filled the air.

The Mystery asked for the crown, but Ametheus ignored her. He was fascinated by it.

Tabitha multiplied as she tried to see into the future again.

"Tabitha!" Zarost cried out. "Tabitha! I won't mess with your game, but I can make it simpler. The Warlock doesn't understand. If you don't succeed, we are in a pickle indeed. He hasn't considered the hidden factor."

"And what is that, Riddler?" Saladon turned to face Twardy Zarost again, his hands held low.

"The best outcome often rides upon the back of the worst; triumph is often the closest thing to failure."

"Riddler! I have planned this through to the seventeenth degree of separation. It is a true plan. It leads to Order."

"At what expense? I am prepared to risk my life to hear the Lifesong succeed."

"No, Riddler! Don't waste yourself so! I can use you. Join me. Come, Riddler, you can see we are doomed here against the might of the Sorcerer, with four of the Gyre dead. He must be supported in his gambit. There is more you do not see."

"How many more will you kill to reach your goal?"

Zarost leapt forward, under the Warlock's defences, and he touched the black wizard; his Deathduel spell threaded into him like a deadly rose thorn. It was a contact spell. He hoped it would not call the wildfire. The Warlock grabbed Zarost by the shirt front, though it was unnecessary with the strength of the prevailing spell. He could predict what Saladon would do next. He would pull them both out of Turmodin, to a place where his magic was more powerful, more controllable—deadly precise. "I accept!" boomed the Warlock.

Zarost didn't bother to fight. He wasn't that stupid. He would lose in combat against the Warlock. Anyone would, on their own. It was more important what could be done here, while the Warlock was engaged elsewhere.

"You must work with the Mystery, Tabitha!" he called past the Warlock. "You must find another end."

"You will not subvert the future! You transfer with my leader, or I'll sunder you across infinity!" the Warlock warned. "A moment, Mystery! Let me be rid of this pest." They spread their awareness outward through the worlds and stars, and into the beyond. With the word, they were dispersed, and they ceased to be in Turmodin. Stars and blackness, but no cold. It was a race for time now, for seconds. The longer he could delay the Warlock, the longer Tabitha would have, to succeed.

The Warlock led, dragging Zarost with his compelling grip through the vastness of the eternal cosmos. Zarost resigned himself to the journey, knowing the Warlock would choose a place of calm where his martial power would be at its peak, somewhere dry and deserted, where no traces of the Sorcerer's influence could interfere. He would not strip Zarost to pieces in infinity as he had threatened. That was not dramatic enough for the Warlock's sensibilities. The Warlock would wait until they had transferred somewhere like the Great Deserts of the south before he did that. He braced himself. He prayed Tabitha triumphed at Turmodin. If she didn't succeed, they were all dead.

There! He had played his own Chaos card.

The desert sands stretched to the horizon. The dry, hot wind blew against his face. Never a footprint here; never a soul to interrupt his peace. He liked the desert. It made him feel big. He turned to face the Warlock and felt small again.

"What are those mirrors for?" demanded the Warlock, towering over him.

"You don't recognise these? You helped put them there." Zarost pierced his hands with the shards. They bit, and the blood created the bridge for the trapped wizards.

"No!" the Warlock cried out. "No you cannot bring them out here, fool. It will tip the scales the wrong way!"

The Warlock swung at him, but it was too late. The Cosmologer and the Mentalist tumbled to the ground.

"Ah, for pity's sake!" exclaimed the Warlock, leaping away. He understood the danger at once, and he would need to restrategise carefully. Two wizards would be balanced against him; three together might overwhelm him. Because of the blood, they were united in this battle, against him. He was going to have to do some quick talking. That was to the Riddler's advantage, because no one could talk quicker than the Riddler.

"Thanks Riddler, but by the blazes you could have pulled us sooner!" said the Mentalist. "A second later and I'd have been dust!"

"Sorry, sorry, to bring you out before was a bit of a worry. I was so close to the Pillar you would have been flux-hole filler."

"What's *he* doing here?"

Zarost didn't answer. He glanced at the Cosmologer instead. She was in a bad way, a mess of blood, her clothing ripped to tatters and tears streaked her soot-smeared face. However, when she took in her surroundings, and the essence winding through the air, she was instantly furious.

"You have brought us out into a death duel!" she screeched at Zarost. "A death duel! With him!"

"Good grief, Riddler!" exclaimed the Mentalist, his hair writhing out around him. "Good grief!"

"This was not my idea, Renetta," said the Warlock, already looking for allies among his adversaries. *Renetta?* That was a name he'd never heard used for the Cosmologer.

"Ask who betrayed you to the shattered world in the first place," said Zarost. "It was not I, Cosmologer, it was he!"

She turned slowly, very slowly, toward the Warlock, her face becoming an unreadable mask, but that displayed her emotion more than anything. When the Cosmologer had gone beyond screeching senility, when the Cosmologer had gone calm, there would be hell to pay.

The Warlock began his fast-talking. "Everything I've done is to gain the Sorcerer's trust, and I have it! He sees the future. He would not have believed me if I could not have made the events that have passed real for him to see. Release me from this diversion, Riddler, or I will have to kill you all to end it. Ametheus *must* call the Destroyer into being, because it will be the end of him! Don't you see? With his magic he is the biggest threat to the Destroyer. He will be the first to be destroyed."

"He is calling the Destroyer?" asked the Mentalist, incredulous.

"You have helped the Sorcerer to bring about the Apocalypse?" asked the Cosmologer, with an acid tone.

"We haven't beaten Ametheus because he could never be beaten, because half of him was a God," replied the Warlock. "With Apocalypse manifest, Ametheus will be ended and then I can banish the God. I have the words. They are fundamentals. They cannot be ignored once spoken."

"No, Warlock, you are mistaken. Those words would not work. He would have killed you before you completed them."

The Warlock ignored him. "I have devised the ultimate spell! He would not have lived here longer than a few heartbeats! You have already jeopardised so much, Riddler, I had the plan to end the Sorcerer *and* send the Apocalypse to the end of Time. Think of it! We would have seen Order established forever."

"Why did you hide the words of release from the rest of us then?" demanded the Mentalist. "Why not tell the Gyre long ago?"

"*Ach!* None of you fools had enough courage to take this risk. I had to hide the words of release to prevent someone releasing the Goddess Ethea. She was always a stepping-stone, to progress the plan to where we are now, or where we were until *you* interfered. The Destroyer must come through, or there will be no end to Ametheus."

Zarost took a moment. Could it be true? No, the Warlock was playing a desperate gambit, hoping to confuse him. He wouldn't have been able to dodge the Destroyer; his plan would have failed.

"Why would we want Order unending?" asked Zarost. "It is as bad as the Chaos."

"What?" cried the Cosmologer.

"But Riddler! You have fought for Order for so long. Are you a traitor to our cause?"

A rich accusation, coming from the Warlock, but maybe the Warlock had been preparing Ametheus for failure, all this time. He was making him doubt his own doubt.

"My oath to the Gyre was the same as yours, to fight for Order. While Chaos is so unbalanced and so strong, I am compelled to fight for Order. When the balance comes, the need to fight the Chaos will diminish, and so, I will leave the Gyre."

The Mentalist looked more than concerned. "Riddler! You cannot play both sides of this axis."

"Why ever not? It is what we must do with the first and second axis to master them. Why not the third? The Gyre wants everything to be Order. Ametheus wants Chaos complete. There is no resolution to that divide, only conflict between opposing poles, Chaos against Order, as it has been for hundreds of years, thousands. Thus the third axis of magic remains unbalanced, mastered by neither of the poles. We must grasp it in its centre, take command of all the axes."

"No, Riddler," boomed the Warlock. "Order must triumph here, or we are doomed."

"We are doomed if we reach for Order unending. That is how we came to this state of affairs!"

"You!" exclaimed the Cosmologer. "Don't you dare blame this all on wizardry, Riddler. We did not cause the Chaos!"

"And I have a plan which ends the Chaos," asserted the Warlock.

"You might be able to strategise more moves than I can, Warlock, but I see the final plays of this game."

"You and your prophecy! It is as worthless as an old hag foretelling the future in floating leaves."

"Nonetheless, I see this future and you do not," replied Zarost. "I see a world governed by the Lifesong."

"*Ugh!* I am not going to argue with you academics. The end is upon us just as much here as if we were standing in Turmodin. Do you understand who will be walking in the world in a moment? The Apocalypse will end everything. I must return to complete my plan, or it will all be for *nit!*"

"Have you forgotten that a Death-duel ties you to us? You cannot leave us to protect your interests. Just like your strategy in Slipper, not so? You should be careful what tricks you use, because they can always be played the other way around."

"Riddler! Release us! This is madness."

"No, I think he did something wise, for once." The Cosmologer raised her hands slowly. The ground buckled as gravity gathered.

"You should have thought first about gaining my trust, instead of the Sorcerer's," said the Mentalist. "I do not believe you either." There was a jolt as the Mentalist gathered the currents of thought.

The Warlock drew his battleaxe into his hands and made a slow rising circle with the tip.

"Well then I shall end it fast, and be back in time to change the play," he announced.

"And I shall play fast, in time to change the end," said the Riddler.

They squared off: the Mentalist, the Cosmologer, the Riddler and the Warlock, but where the others saw four sides, Zarost saw five. There was an *in*side he could use in this battle. The Warlock didn't know about inference. None of them did. The Death-duel tied them together with its barbed coils. Transference would drag all of them together, they would not escape from each other until the maker revoked its pact, or resolved, leaving one fewer wizard to complicate his plan, possibly two. But inference was a peculiar delight: Twardy Zarost was the only one who could step out of the standoff.

Zarost clapped to a strange rhythm and sang a guttural shamanic invocation. He sang gibberish. Let the Warlock wonder. The Warlock swung his axe in a blazing arc, aiming for Zarost.

"Gib," said Zarost, ending his invocation, and he was gone. Let them infer what they could.

And, if anyone had been counting, they would know he had an extra wizard in his pocket.

ᎶᏏᎾᏟᏏᎾ

Tabitha pitied him, the man trapped in his madness, the boy tormented by his brothers, by his nature, but she had seen the future, and she knew the Destroyer would kill him and that it was the only way to end the ruin Ametheus brought upon the world. She would speak the words, and he and his father would be ended. So she knew she must sing.

"Oh Ethan, you didn't want this, I know!"

First, Tabitha needed silence. Silence to replace the babble, calm where there was discord, so she could sing her song and have it heard without disruption. She needed a foundation of stillness to work from in this strange place where visions of reality had such power, where the world was responsive to her thoughts. She knew she couldn't find that peace outside of herself, with so many threats competing for her attention: she had to find it within.

It was almost like music, the barks and broken cries, the grinding groans and ratchet cracks, each sound yielding a slightly different tone, each clapping and slapping a different rhythm so the combined volume cycled with a lilting effect, layers and layers of instrumental tapestries, the concert of a broken orchestra. As she focused on the sounds alone, she felt the beat more acutely, a stuttering pressure upon her skin. The rumble in the earth far below became stamping on the floor. She perceived the sound as if it were formed of waves, rushing through the air and wood, converging in a wild place deep within her. She descended into that inner space, a fundamental place of seeing, secret and yet linked to everything. The wall and its rough red plaster grew dim in her eyes.

She saw the sharp peaks and deep troughs of the sound's interference, as if she was caught upon a raft in a storm with the great swells all around her. Moving with the sounds, she allowed her voice to wander, up and down, faster and faster, matching the movement of the peaked sea dancing in that place of convergence. She understood its nature; she could feel its urgent demand. Then she reversed her movement, sinking as the sea rose, upward as it sank, her voice gathering in volume and command, until the sounds of Turmodin towered over her like a great wave, and she had sunk deep beneath it. Then the sound fell toward her, and she rose to meet it, both sound and song searching toward the stasis, the final note that would cut through that violent sea, equalising the phases, half-way between peak and trough, balancing the brutal disturbance at its midpoint.

"You can't do it without Saladon here!" shouted Gabrielle, rushing for her with a sudden drawn blade. "Don't be a stupid bitch. Don't do it!"

But the Mystery flew across Gabrielle's path, caught her blade hand, and redirected her charge. She moved like a dancer, touching Gabrielle with gentle nudges, turning her knees, throwing her strikes backward, driving her away. Maybe she was fearful to use her magic so close to Ametheus, but she had a way of foretelling where Gabrielle would move, moving an instant before her. She would buy Tabitha the time she needed.

Tabitha concentrated on the sounds. She wasn't trying to change the world without, for that was governed by the Sorcerer's vision. She was trying to change the world within: her world, her vision. Tabitha reached the final note. There was a strange dual tone then her voice and the rough sounds of Turmodin became one.

Tabitha held onto her note, the only note in a new and perfect silence around it.

The cacophony was gone. She allowed her song to drop into the stillness.

The lyre came to life in her hands. Her fingers plucked the notes instinctively as she opened herself to the source of the Lifesong. The air shimmered as her connection with the clear essence expanded. Then the flames shimmered too, and Ametheus, and all the others, those poor doomed figures on the sacrifice, as if they were temporary figures made from clear essence as well, as if their forms were only a pattern and colouring of the underlying clear essence. Her song would give them all release. Their suffering would end. The world became her dream.

The vision shimmered around her, waiting for her command, she kept her mind as still as a pool, willing no change at all. Her music spread like a rising tide, the threads of Chaos were dissolved in her resonant harmony.

Ametheus watched her out of his single eye, entranced. His brothers faced away toward the shimmering form of the Wicker Man, to watch what would come, but Ethan watched her, solitary and sad. The dancing of his eye had slowed; it was steady.

"You knew this moment would come," she said. "You knew he would come. You knew he would kill you."

He said nothing, turning the crown over and over in his hands.

"Will you fight for me?" she asked. "Will you fight for life?"

He stepped forward and placed the crown on her head.

Tears ran down his pasty cheeks. "I think I know why the birds sing," he whispered.

She sang and allowed the dark God to come up through her mind to inhabit the life she had created for him.

43. ANOTHER VIEW

"The greater the number of ripples in motion
The harder to judge the waves in the ocean."—Zarost

The sky turned around it, detritus spiralled in the air; even the clouds were whipped around in a sickening circle. The pilgrims were thick on the ground, chanting, stomping, beating metal, excited and desperate to impress. They were a pushing, shoving, fighting, biting and rutting frenzy of devotion.

Then Ashley and Sassraline came past the structure, and he beheld the horror of it, the great figure of a man, blocked out with a colossal wooden frame, a wicker structure crammed with living people, figures that writhed, moaned and cried within, figures that clambered on the outside and lashed more sacrifices onto those beneath. It was horrific; it looked as if some bodies had even been sawn short to fit into the corners. Smoke billowed from the lower levels, flame licking at the flesh, and screams filled the air. In their minds he could see what would come. The Destroyer would be made from their many bodies. He would step into their flesh and stride out of the fires from the Wicker Man to break the world. His presence rose through them, a living nightmare, a fatal possession.

And there, below the threatening God-to-be, stood Tabitha, beside the Sorcerer Ametheus. Her thoughts were hidden from him, but she was singing. He suspected she was being used in the ceremony, used for her magic. The people screamed; she had the power to end their suffering, by granting life to the one they would become. If she tried anything else, she would doom the people to death in flames. She would have to witness their massed death. She was crying, but she couldn't look away from the rising flames. She was in torment.

In that moment, he knew his target. As he knew it, so did his dragon.

"Sing," he shouted down to Tabitha. "Tabitha! Sing!"

Ashley and his dragon rose into the roaring sky.

Let the God come. There was one man who would not worship Him.

CRSOCRSO

Ethan saw his father's face. It was forming before him, in the pool of blood, amid the other dark forms swimming and swirling there, waiting to come through. He remembered the dream and, as he did so, he touched Amyar and Seus, and it became real. Finally, he would be able to rest, for they would all be ended. The wizards would be gone.

The beautiful girl sang the song and the crowds chanted as the priests had taught them to, and the fires burst. Seus jerked wildfire down and Amyar forced their body around so that he could watch the face taking form in the shimmering flesh of the Wicker Man, in the head of many heads, as the change happened in the essence, in the ichor, the blood of the Gods.

Then it was done. The Apocalypse had come, smoking, flaming. Living.

Ethan remembered he was going to do something special, because of the girl, because of beauty, because she had shown him something, but then his father clenched his fist and Ethan was possessed so harshly he lost all idea of what he had been trying to achieve. He only knew that the One before him could stop his heart in an instant. His father. He fell to his knees. Like an egg crushed with a sudden slap, his mind burst. He felt himself leaking out all over the place. The single eye was watching him, watching him, watching him; the single eye was watching, over the space between.

"*Bahnk benistu km tóm*," his father said.

The world lurched underfoot and disintegrated into a thousand flakes, as if everything Ethan had seen had been only the surface of a painting on a thin sheet of stone, and that stone had been shattered. In one piece he recognised Tabitha's surprised face, in another a worshipper. The air became tumbling shards. He saw his own body represented on many different pieces. It was the mirror-shard spell, the one his father had shown Seus, but this time it was cast on the whole world. The Destroyer had touched him with a spell Ethan couldn't begin to understand.

Ethan didn't feel fear. He had been afraid of the wizards. His father went beyond a threat to be faced or fled—he was a fundamental presence throughout everything. Ethan's existence was at the whim of his father before him. He would be dead before he began to run, snuffed out by a wish. There was no fear, only acceptance.

Everything snapped back into place. Ethan was whole again, the rock was beneath his feet, and his father was watching, watching,

watching, his father was watching, over the space between. A great beast was diving down from the sky, from his blind side. Sparkling and green. Ethan didn't think his father had seen the threat.

"Very good," said the Destroyer. "You will not fight me. Come to me."

Ethan hesitated. If he could resist his father, the girl might have a chance. Tabitha.

"*Bahnk benistu kalemgårda,*" his father commanded, spreading his colossal hands. The world was stripped to pieces, a thousand strings, as if everything Ethan saw had been made of threads writhing away from their places. He had no defence against this assault. His father was too powerful, his magic too fundamental. He didn't know how to fight. His brothers were too strong; they hauled him toward the union with his father. When that happened, his father would be unstoppable, his power absolute. The singer would die! The song would die! He wished it could be otherwise.

Then there was an animal roar. The world snapped back to a steady state and he saw that the great beast had fallen on his father. It beat its wings against his shoulders; it struck at him with a predator's jaws— a dragon from the high Winterblades. Someone rode the beast, a man in leathers, high on its head. The dragon vomited flame in his father's face, and his father roared in anger. It would not beat fire with fire.

He saw another beast attacking—it leapt for him. It had come through the worshippers, from the side. It was green-scaled, muscled, and its one arm ended in a stump, but the other hand was viciously taloned and its jaws were full of pointed teeth. It would slice through flesh faster than any blade. It leapt for him and he had an instant to reach for Seus or Amyar for defence.

He knew what he should do. If he didn't tell his brothers, if he kept his thoughts private from them and gave them no warning, he would die, and his father would be denied his power. His father would not be complete. Maybe that would be enough to give Tabitha a chance. Maybe it would be enough to give the song a chance. He stood immobile, paralysed by the horror of his seditious thoughts.

He understood it, at last. The understanding was a bright heat, like the sun rising inside his chest. He had never felt anything like it before. It made him happy. It made him want to cry.

"I know why the birds sing!" he exclaimed. He did know, at last.

The green monster fell upon him and tore out his throat.

His brothers summoned the wildfire hard, in a defence that was too late. The sky tightened.

"No, Ethan, no!" Tabitha shouted, running. "Turn the wildfire aside, you must both live!"

But the wildfire came at him from all directions, drawn fast in threads of silver light.

Ethan turned his head to her, forcing his brothers to look away.

"You cared!" he tried to say in surprise, but his voice didn't work.

And the wretched light struck him and lit him like the sun.

He was Chaos, and he burned bright, and so did the monster who had fallen upon him.

ᏪᏰᎧᏟᏣᏰᎧ

Within, his mind was still, poised and deadly. Everything had become lines and targets to Garyll, distances, speeds and openings. There was no fear. There was no anger. Only a weapon, the blade exposed, and the weapon was Garyll Glavenor. He blurred and struck.

Then his flesh burned with silver fire—the Chaos seethed within him. Visions tore across his mind and, as they did, his fury burst with blinding force and a husk blew away from his soul, a shroud of self-loathing. Garyll Glavenor filled his body. He knew himself. He was justice.

"I have paid enough!" he shouted.

The Sorcerer was dead at his feet. He had paid for his crimes against the world.

He looked up to see Tabitha, the most delicate singer on the most awful battlefield. She was wearing the Kingsrim, and it made her look intense yet beautiful. He wanted to worship her. She stared at him, silent and speechless, her fingers poised on her lyre.

Behind her, the great figure of the dark God fought with the dragon, but the dragon was losing; its fire belched forth in short gasps and its wings dragged on the ground. It lunged at the God but He caught its neck with one hand and the tail with the other, and He folded it in half. There was a wrenching snapping sound, and a high squeal, and the dragon dropped to the ground, dead. A small figure fell from the dragon's head, no doubt a worshipper who had been hooked up in the violence of the struggle.

The Destroyer turned his eye on them, and the world began to fall apart again.

ᏪᏰᎧᏟᏣᏰᎧ

Tabitha caught herself. She had recognised the monster who had fallen upon Ametheus, and the knowledge had petrified her. Then the wildfire bloomed upon him, and she reached out to the Chaos, and a great ringing assaulted her ears. An even greater heat consumed her and she sang one note alone yet it was not enough, and just as her heart drove her voice to break, Garyll appeared before her: in the midst of the blinding colour, as if stepping from a dream—defined by his belief, redeemed by her love. She had risked death in the wildfire without thinking, and she realised in that moment she would do anything to save Garyll, regardless of what he had done, regardless of the consequences. She understood at last what he had done for her in Eyri. He had sacrificed himself, his principles, everything, to save her. That was the essence of love.

She wanted to run to him and hold him, to know that he was real, but at his feet lay Ametheus, dead. He had given her the chance—they both had—to banish the Destroyer. She could do it now. The words shimmered in her memory, dark symbols on a burning parchment, but around that image her thoughts were in chaos, she could not breathe or think or speak. Her heart was in turmoil. Now that Garyll was here, she was terrified she would lose him.

Tabitha slowly drew breath. She had promised to fight for life.

"*Jégeswo şuĥnustód ĥést y niĥhil,*" she tried.

The Destroyer shuddered as the banishment touched his soul, but he remained standing, incarnate. Her voice was too faint; she did not have the command she needed. Yet, Garyll had come. Some things she had wished for *had* come true.

Before Garyll could reach her, a bearded young man staggered from the crowd, a man clad in rough leathers, with wild blond hair and a green disc glinting on his neck. He grasped at Garyll's arms and, as Garyll held him up, they shared a moment. They turned as one to face Tabitha, and a presence touched her—a familiar mind. There was sudden understanding and he took the words from her like a pip from a fruit.

"*Jégeswo şuĥnustód ĥést y niĥhil,*" he repeated.

Ashley! He had grown wild, and he looked tired enough to fall without Garyll's support. How had he come to be here? Another friend who had appeared, to answer her need. He turned and threw his arms out to the crowds and Tabitha felt a mental surge.

"*Jégeswo!*" roared the crowd. "*Niĥhil!*"

He had come to save her.

They chanted the banishment together—Tabitha, Garyll, Ashley and a growing number of the crowd—and this time, Tabitha felt the hooks bite. The Destroyer pressed his giant fists to his head and crumpled to his knees. A war broke out among the worshippers, between those who chanted the banishment and those who tried to silence the revolution, but the worshippers closest to Tabitha held the others at bay, for they were affected most by her presence, and Tabitha raised her voice, and Ashley pushed the words out farther, and they chanted together, their voices carried across the plains. The Destroyer swelled again as the last word didn't bite; there was something wrong with the banishment, right at the end. It failed to compel Him.

"Repeat the last word!" shouted Tabitha. "We must repeat the last word!"

Ashley nodded. "*Niħhil.*" Chanted the crowd. "*Niħhil.*"

Banishment, and a terrible resistance. In the final moment of doom, the Apocalypse rose against them. He roared and the horrid sound spread, pulsing Chaos through discordant veins.

ᴄꙅᴇᴏᴄꙅᴇᴏ

Twardy Zarost found himself on the boulder. Travelling by inference was a delight. When he *inferred* himself into a place, it wasn't like travelling at all—it was more like finding the version of reality in which he was already in the place he sought. There was no pop of appearance, the jolt that startled inhabitants. He simply was there, as if he had always been there: Turmodin, or what was left of it.

Zarost marvelled at the mayhem. It was incredibly over-magicked, but then they had all been drawn to the heart of Chaos, and things had been bound to get overwrought. There had been a wildfire strike, that much was plain to see. The Mystery had abandoned them, wisely leaving the future to chance. She must have transferred away. The Shadowcaster had fled as well. Under Tabitha's lead, the crowds were chanting, and Zarost recognised the final words of the banishment. It was almost as he would have said it, but there was something wrong, the last word didn't have the right hooks in, and the Destroyer was a prime God—the banishment would need not only the hooks, but breath control as well. Language became more advanced the further back one went; mankind had inherited language from the Gods in the first place then slowly pulled it to pieces with years of innovation.

He could not have devised a better challenge to elevate Tabitha's gift. He would not have risked a God so soon, he would never have done what had been done to Ethea to get there, but the Warlock's excesses were a boon. It was the perfect pinnacle of riddling: if one needed a champion, present the candidate with a deadly challenge, and if they failed, they weren't the champion. If they had the gift, they would be forged in the crucible of dire circumstance to exercise the talents which made them the champion. Depending on how one set up the conflict, one achieved a different result. This would be spectacular.

The Destroyer towered over them all, defying the ancient lore, a lore that had failed because it was being used incorrectly. Well, that was simple then; they faced the end of the world.

He pulled the Lorewarden from his pocket.

Only a second remained to save everything. It all relied on the Lorewarden's memory.

It was a quiz night and the Lorewarden was the star. Twardy Zarost pricked his finger on the shard.

The Lorewarden tumbled out. He blinked in the wild light, his eyes bulging as he took in the form of the Destroyer, towering over them all, gathering the end of the world.

"Quiz: what is the last word in the banishment of The Book of Is?" asked Twardy Zarost.

The Destroyer's hands closed around them, dragging the end of the world from the sides, crushing, breaking, tearing through earth, air, flesh and life.

The Lorewarden blinked. "*N|ihhil,*" he replied.

"*N|ihhil,*" repeated Zarost, emphasising the correct accents and breath control. Useless, he knew, unless she was the One, unless she truly had the power of ultimate command. He had gambled his life on this moment. He had gambled all of their lives.

"*N|ihhil*" repeated Tabitha, copying her Riddler.

"*N|ihhil,*" repeated the young man in leathers whom Zarost couldn't place. Then, to Zarost's great delight, the young man distributed his mind and touched thousands, a grand and dazzling network of thought. It was Logán, the Lightgifter from Eyri, the young man who had poked into Zarost's mind one day long ago. Lightgifter no more! He was a wizard, one entirely of his own making. Nothing could have impressed Zarost more.

"*N|ihhil,*" roared the crowd.

Zarost felt the severing of the great soul. *Aha! Aha!*

With an endless hollow moan, the spirit of the Destroyer abandoned the plane of mankind. His great body fell to the ground, an empty sack, heavy as a mountain. Everyone was thrown down as the ground quaked and cracked. It was ended.

Zarost lay where he had fallen on his face.

Hell's bells, but that had all happened quickly! He savoured the taste of dirt and rock-dust. It meant they were all alive. When he had rigged the game with his acts of prophecy, he had never anticipated how dangerous it would become for him, but he should have known. It was never possible to foresee oneself until one was living in the moment foreseen. Success and failure were always separated by an instant, and the greater the success he reached for, the greater the potential failure. In the distance he watched the Pillar fall. They had been separated from disaster by a sliver of a second. The knife-edge of knowledge had saved them. Sometimes an accurate fact really was the last word in a fight.

"Did I win a prize?" the Lorewarden asked, lying beside Zarost. His eyes wobbled like eggs on stalks. He was still in shock. He *had* won a prize, worth more than anything in the world.

Now Zarost could begin his ultimate plan. He had formed the right players in the crucible of manipulated fate. He had traded some pieces from his Gyre, it was true, but he had gained so much. He had the one card in his hand that trumped all the others.

"Yes," Zarost replied. "Yes indeed. Listen."

44. SORCERER'S SONG

"A treasured life; a small death.
Life spent; a coming alive."—Zarost

The song rose on the winds.

At last she understood. Life was the ruling magic; it was the Lifesong that brought all the colours to the world. Reality was made of essence and formed by visions. The Lifesong guided the visions and so had an influence over everything. The Lifesong was like a fluid beneath a sponge; it soaked reality with vitality. The song was in everything, in substance and in the spaces in between. The world was the way it was because others had imagined parts of it before her, others like Ametheus, and the wizards before him. If the song was sung properly, it could inspire others to see the world in the way she saw it, and that vision would become reality. She had to take ownership of the vision of the world. She had to see it healed. She had to sing her song, to tell the story as she would have it come to pass.

There was so much beauty to be expressed. It seemed to her that Life was a never-ending dance, and the more freedom there was to dance, the more beauty there was in the world. Tabitha gathered every scrap of essence to herself, felt it activate like a shimmering sea. She would strive to spread the Lifesong through everything, through the earth, through the air. She opened to the power and let it flow. The greater wisdom came upon her, she heard her voice alter and deepen in power. Ancient memories filled her mind, flashes of colour, of conflict, of the forming symphony of the elements, and under it all, a sense of time, aeons and aeons of time, as the stars danced in the darkness, as the patterns of the universe grew into order then were spun away in chaos, as a music breathed through it all, bringing life for a moment, then taking it away again.

Ethea was with her. She sang the new melodies that filled her, tunes that drew her on and away into a rich tapestry of music that filled her soul and let her soul fill the universe. She plucked a carrier note, spread her attention wide, and released the song all around her in a sonic wave, to travel as far as she could reach. She tried to touch everything, and to see everything in a natural state—uncontrolled, untainted, renewed. So the spell resonated through the earth and air, extending her power farther and wider than she had ever attempted before.

The black corpse of the Destroyer rippled as the ruined bodies were changed, writhing, growing, rising under her guidance to form a living monument to those who had died. It became a great tree, a sweeping tower of majestic curves, limbs that spread out to the sky, growing and growing until it was the greatest tree in all Oldenworld, the greatest tree that would ever be.

At the edge of her sonic wave, the light changed, and colours danced like an exploded rainbow. The ground rippled with verdant vegetation, a sudden growth that rushed across the scorched earth and under the feet of the thousands of witnesses, leaving insects flittering in the air and small birds darting among them. New trees stood in quiet huddled copses, throwing long shadows over their toes. Tabitha's music resounded from every leaf, bird and butterfly in that landscape. She was filled with the melodies; she could feel everything as clusters of notes, streams of harmony, woven together.

Still, there was more to do, for the devastation upon Oldenworld was far-reaching. Ametheus might be ended, but Tabitha knew his wildfire was not rendered harmless. It lay like poison upon the land and across the sky, and the power within it was dormant until it found life. Anyone who was touched by that silver fire would become blighted. She sent her music running away on the threads of wildfire, seeking out Chaos and calming the essence.

The words formed on her lips. Tabitha played the lyre with abandon; her spirit was swept up in the intensity of creation. Although the music was something that had existed long before she had been born, something that would live long after her death, it bound everything into one theme, unifying them all.

She held the final note, which completed the aria. It was not a note she could hold on her lyre. As she sang it, she could sense the air growing thick around her, the rock solidifying underfoot and the clouds growing heavy above. The note reverberated through her and all the world, in a similar way to the Shiver, that high piercing note she had used to split the Shield of Eyri. This note was its opposite, the sound upon which all things could be drawn together—the binder: the unifier of Life and Death, Dark and Light, Chaos and Order. Everything was touched by the sound. All the axes could find a meeting in this centre.

Tabitha reached out with her hands and her awareness. The spirit of Ethea infused her for a glorious timeless moment. She felt connected to everything that lived, everything created, all the elements of earth, every place of fire, all the liquid seas and streams of water, all the air far above the mountains and beyond the high clouds, beyond the stars, beyond infinity. She was the centre of all reality for a moment, she touched it all and knew it all, through her note of integration— one sound which balanced everything.

There was no reference to lay her knowledge of immensity upon. She was at the beginning, middle and end of reality all at once. The long line of Time was turned upon its end, and Tabitha saw the whole of her life, and beyond. She was so young she had just been conceived, yet she was older than she could imagine, wise and full of knowing. In this strange place within the song's climactic release, her life and death touched. She knew her highest moments of joy and her deepest sorrows together. Her triumphs and failures unified: her wrongs and rights, the good and evil, the Dark and Light welded into instantaneous coexistence. Energy and Matter were fused. Chaos and Order were one.

When her vision deepened, she could see the full extent of her being, a presence beyond one lifetime, beyond a thousand. She was overwhelmed. She saw the goddess Ethea.

She was the Goddess Ethea.

The world exploded with life.

Then the song was sung and she cried from the beauty of what she had seen. She returned to herself and, with her tears, came the rains.

ॐ ॐ

The dreamer who dreams has awoken,
the fearless have passed beyond fears,
the one who seeks wings, shall forever be free;
their song echoes through all the years.
Without you I am but a shadow,
yet your love fills me with light,
for I live in your grace and your beauty
and your vision inspires my sight.
Our dance is the centre of circles,
as the Lifesong weaves us tight.

SPREAD THE WORD!

Visit www.greghamerton.com to submit your short review of Second Sight and stand a chance to win a free copy of any future releases.

Send an email to greg@greghamerton.com and you'll get a personal notification from the author when further fantasy novels are released, as well as news and special offers.

Or post a comment on your favourite reading site. Every note helps to spread the Lifesong. I'd like to hear from you.

Regards,
Greg Hamerton